MW00532354

3

Eternal Lovecraft

The Persistence of HPL in Popular Culture

Edited by Jim Turner

Golden Gryphon Press

Copyright © 1998 by Jim Turner

PUBLISHER'S CATALOGING-IN-PUBLICATION DATA
Eternal Lovecraft : the persistence of HPL in popular
culture / edited by Jim Turner. — 1st ed.
p. cm.
ISBN 0-9655901-7-8 (hardcover : alk. paper)
1. Horror tales, American. 2. Horror tales, English.
3. Lovecraft, H. P. (Howard Phillips), 1890–1937—Parodies,
imitations, etc.
813′.0873808—dc20 1998 98-70713

All rights reserved, which includes the right to reproduce this
book, or portions thereof, in any form whatsoever except as
provided by the U.S. Copyright Law. For information address
Golden Gryphon Press, 364 West Country Lane, Collinsville,
Illinois 62234. Printed in the United States of America.
Graphic interiors by Lynne Condellone and James Wallace.
First Edition

This page constitutes an extension of the copyright page:

"A Bit of the Dark World" by Fritz Leiber, copyright © 1962 by Ziff-Davis Publishing Company; first published in *Fantastic,* February 1962; copyright renewed 1990.

"Black as the Pit, from Pole to Pole," copyright © 1977 by Steven Utley and Howard Waldrop; first published in *New Dimensions 7,* edited by Robert Silverberg.

"Crouch End" by Stephen King. Reprinted with permission. © Stephen King. All rights reserved.

"Daoine Domhain," copyright © 1993 by Peter Tremayne; first published in *Weirdbook,* Autumn 1993.

"The Events at Poroth Farm," copyright © 1972 by T. E. D. Klein; first published in *From beyond the Dark Gateway,* December 1972.

"The Giant Rat of Sumatra," copyright © 1996 by Paula Volsky; first published in *The Resurrected Holmes,* edited by Marvin Kaye.

"The Golden Keeper" by Ian R. MacLeod, copyright © 1997 by Dell Magazines, a division of Crosstown Publications; first published in *Asimov's Science Fiction,* October/November 1997.

"Her Misbegotten Son," copyright © 1996 by Alan Rodgers; first published in *Miskatonic University,* edited by Martin H. Greenberg and Robert Weinberg.

"The Land of the Reflected Ones," copyright © 1994 by Nancy A. Collins; first published in *Tombs,* edited by Edward E. Kramer and Peter Crowther.

"The Ocean and All Its Devices," copyright © 1994 by William Browning Spencer; first published in *Borderlands 4,* edited by Elizabeth E. Monteleone and Thomas F. Monteleone.

"The Other Dead Man," copyright © 1988 by Gene Wolfe; first published in *Weird Tales,* Spring 1988; reprinted by permission of the author and the author's agent, Virginia Kidd.

"The Perseids," copyright © 1995 by Robert Charles Wilson; first published in *Northern Frights 3,* edited by Don Hutchison.

"Ralph Wollstonecraft Hedge: A Memoir" by Ron Goulart, copyright © 1959 by Mercury Press, Inc.; first published in *The Magazine of Fantasy and Science Fiction,* May 1959.

"Sensible City" by Harlan Ellison appears in the author's collection *Slippage.* Copyright © 1994 by The Kilimanjaro Corporation. Reprinted by arrangement with, and permission of, the author and the author's agent, Richard Curtis Associates, Inc., New York. All rights reserved.

"The Shadow at the Bottom of the World" by Thomas Ligotti, copyright © 1990 by Fear, Ltd.; first published in *Fear,* April 1990.

"To Mars and Providence," copyright © 1996 by Don Webb; first published in *War of the Worlds: Global Dispatches,* edited by Kevin J. Anderson.

"The Turret," copyright © 1995 by Richard A. Lupoff; first published in *Made in Goatswood,* edited by Scott David Aniolowski.

"Weird Tales," copyright © 1984 by Fred Chappell; first published in *The Texas Review,* Spring/Summer 1984.

Iä! Furchtbar gähnt
der düstre Abgrund, welch ein Graun!
Das Auge wähnt
in einen Höllenpfuhl zu schaun!
Wie dort sich Wetterwolken ballen
der Mond verliert von seinem Schein!
Gespenst'ge Nebelbilder wallen,
belebt ist das Gestein!
Und hier—Azathoth! Retten Sie mich!
fliegt Nachtgevögel auf im Busch!
Rotgraue narb'ge Zweige strecken
nach mir die Riesenfaust!
Iä Cthulhu! Iä Cthulhu! Erschein!

—FRIEDRICH VON JUNZT*

* The "Great Invocation" (*Große Beschwörung*) from von Junzt's *Unaussprechlichen Kulten*.

contents

III. Cosmic Realms

the "shadow" over lovecraft

American novelist Ralph Ellison once suggested that most authors write only "one good book," though they may end up, Ellison allowed, "publishing a lot more." If we apply Ellison's observation to the fictional oeuvre of Howard Phillips Lovecraft, then surely Lovecraft's "one good book"—in the sense of representing his definitive statement as a cosmic fantasist—is "The Shadow Out of Time."

In recent years, however, Lovecraft's nouvelle has encountered some bad press. When reviewing a 1992 anthology of classic fiction from the genre magazine *Astounding,* the anonymous *Publishers Weekly* critic found "The Shadow Out of Time" to be a "needlessly attenuated short story," while more recently, British editor James Havoc has denounced "Shadow" as "boring, overlong, and creaky." For that matter Lovecraft himself, in a 1934 letter to E. Hoffmann Price, expressed severe reservations with his in-progress masterpiece: "This new thing—a second version—fails to satisfy me, and I don't know whether to finish it as is or destroy once more and start afresh."

While Lovecraft's letters to his correspondents are generally o'er-brimming with ebullience and bonhomie, there was no levity in HPL's approach to his art: few great fantasists have cultivated commensurate conscientiousness in the mundane task of prose composition, and few Lovecraft stories experienced a more agonizing genesis than "The Shadow Out of Time." Let's consider Lovecraft's "Shadow," then, first in terms of what this work meant to its creator and then its overall significance within the development of American science fiction.

Time's Galling Tyranny

Throughout his adult life, H. P. Lovecraft regarded himself as a reserved, disembodied intellect, preserving a dispassionate posture toward mankind that "had the effect of almost deleting the emotion of anger from my personality, and giving me a philosophic calm. . . . Today I am extremely tranquil."

A stroll down Angell Street in the company of HPL's longtime colleague W. Paul Cook, however, tells a different story:

> I shall never forget [Lovecraft's] outburst as we walked past the old estate of his grandfather in Providence. He lived with but one ambition—to repatriate the property before he died and restore it as it was in his grandfather's day. The crust was torn away and you saw the man inside, red-blooded, seething with emotion.

Lovecraft (1890–1937) grew up in Providence just as his prosperous family had begun a decline into shabby and resentful gentility. His earliest memories were of bygone pleasures and glories that came to an abrupt end in 1904 with the death of grandfather Whipple Phillips and the loss of the family estate on Angell Street. "The worst experience I ever had was losing my birthplace," he wrote in 1933, and despite certain subsequent intellectual accommodations to the twentieth century, Lovecraft in a very tangible sense remained ever after an outsider in his own time and place.

"Change is the enemy of everything really worth cherishing. It is the remover of landmarks, the destroyer of all which is homelike and comforting, and the constant symbol and reminder of decay and death. It is change which makes one old before his time by snatching away everything he has known, and substituting a new environment to which he can never become adjusted." The very concept of self hinges on the preservation of personal identity through time, and as one can infer from the preceding 1934 epistolary extract, change—or the passing of years through time—had acquired an insidious adversarial embodiment in Lovecraft's own mind. Time itself had wrested from Lovecraft the world he had lost, and he was ever wont to refer to this concept using the rhetoric of thralldom and enslavement: Lovecraft maintained a "general revolt" against time's "intolerable bondage" and "galling tyranny," and he could "form no picture of emotional satisfaction which does not involve . . . the defeat of time."

In confronting his ancient adversary, Lovecraft marshaled two strategies, both suggested in his sonnet, "Background":

I can never be tied to raw, new things
For I first saw the light in an old town,
Where from my window huddled roofs sloped down
To a quaint harbour rich with visionings.
Streets with carved doorways where the sunset beams
Flooded old fanlights and small window-panes,
And Georgian steeples topped with gilded vanes—
These were the sights that shaped my childhood dreams.

Such treasures, left from times of cautious leaven,
Cannot but loose the hold of flimsier wraiths
That flit with shifting ways and muddled faiths
Across the changeless walls of earth and heaven.
They cut the moment's thongs and leave me free
To stand alone before eternity.

By absorbing the essence of unspoiled sylvan scenery and old colonial towns, Lovecraft was able to experience a transcendent sensation of timelessness and the eternal. In a 1930 letter, after having walked to the "primal countryside" near his home, HPL wrote that "I can shed the years uncannily by getting into some of my favourite childhood haunts here. In spots where nothing has changed, there is little to remind me that the date is not 1900 or 1901, and that I am not still a boy of ten or eleven. Images and ideas and perspectives of that period flood up from subconsciousness with amazing vigour and volume, and do much to prove the relativity and subjectivity of time." And as suggested in the above poem, this sense of the timeless engendered by antiquarian haunts led Lovecraft—far more significantly—to a concept of the infinite, to a cultivation of the *cosmic* ("the changeless walls of earth and heaven"), to a realm where time holds no dominion.

HPL's early Dunsanian fantasies represent pure disembodied cosmicism, while his later Gothic narratives are ever illumined by glints of cosmic grandeur, and both groups in this fictional legacy constitute, as Artur Schnabel once observed of the Schubert sonatas, "a safe supply of happiness." But on that fateful day in November 1934 when Lovecraft commenced a final draft of his last major story, he began to write about the Great Race of Yith, which was "the greatest race of all; because it alone had conquered the secret of time."

Time Travel in the Pulps

In a 1930s issue of *Astounding Stories,* there appeared a narrative in which the mind of a contemporary man was sent millions of years through time, making contact with an alien entity. Oh, you're thinking, that's the June 1936 issue of *Astounding* containing Lovecraft's "Shadow Out of Time." Actually, the *first* such story was Jack Williamson's* "Terror Out of Time" in the December 1933 issue. In the Williamson story, an eccentric professor named Dr. Audrin has, while tinkering about in the barn behind his house, discovered the secret of "neuro-induction," which "enables me to bring the brain of my subject, in the present time, into very intimate contact with the brain of some other human being, perhaps a million years distant in time, or a hundred million!"

A typical pulp farrago involving a mad scientist, his beautiful daughter, and an evil Martian named Gorkon, "Terror Out of Time" was precisely the sort of rambunctious interplanetary hell-raiser that HPL was inveighing against in his 1934 essay, "Some Notes on Interplanetary Fiction." (This essay, incidentally, is a veritable guidebook to why HPL made the choices he did in drafting his own story.) For reasons explained previously, Lovecraft was resolutely determined to fashion a definitive fictional defeat of time, and thus his "Shadow Out of Time"—in which a modern man named Peaslee discovers that his mind has been sent back millions of years in time by the alien Great Race of Yith—had to be executed with all the scientific veracity Lovecraft could summon.

The notion of mind travel itself is based on an old Gothic trope; many weird tales had been written on the theme of psychic possession/personality exchange, to which Lovecraft had added more than a few specimens himself. Lovecraft's dilemma, however, was that by 1934—and at first without his conscious realization—he had forever turned his back upon the venerable Gothic tradition and thus could not employ mind travel as a conventional fantasy construct in his own in-progress story.

Through a series of now-famous letters written during the early 1930s, Lovecraft fashioned an aesthetic manifesto that rejected such tradition-encrusted symbols of European mythology as the ghost,

---

* Williamson (b. 1908) later had a distinguished career, including several notable SF series (Legion of Space/Seetee/Humanoids), in comparison with which the early tale under consideration is unrepresentative juvenilia. And while Lovecraft, in an unpublished 1937 letter to Harry O. Fischer, professed not to be a regular reader of the science-fiction pulps, there's an excellent chance that he did see the December 1933 issue of *Astounding,* since the Williamson work was preceded by a novelette from Donald Wandrei and followed by a story from Clark Ashton Smith, both members of the Lovecraft circle.

the werewolf, and the vampire as being incompatible with twentieth-century scientific knowledge and thus hopelessly inadequate as source material for the modern tale of wonder. ("Ordinary tales about a castle ghost or old-fashioned werewolf are merely so much junk.") Lovecraft instead advocated a fanciful extension of finite natural law, soaring with his readers to a dazzling cosmic vision beyond known space and conjectured time: "My conception of fantasy, as a genuine art-form, is *an extension rather than a negation of reality* . . . the lure of unplumbed space, the terror of the encroaching outer void, and the struggle of the ego to transcend the known and established order of time." But in applying the concept of mind travel to this new nonsupernatural aesthetic, Lovecraft had two problems to resolve: the physics of time travel itself, and the temporal paradox of journeying to the past.

That Lovecraft clearly understood the scientific and philosophical challenge posed by the latter point is evidenced in a 1930 letter to Clark Ashton Smith: "The weakness of most tales with this [time-travel] theme is that they do not provide for the recording, in history, of those inexplicable events in the past which were caused by the backward time-voyagings of persons of the present and future." What Lovecraft alludes to here is the principle of causality, in which causes must precede effects. The classic SF paradigm for this principle is the so-called grandfather paradox: If a man goes back in time and kills his own grandfather, how could he ever have been born to perform the murder? While the pulpsters of the period were blithely ignoring this blatant violation of physical law, Lovecraft carefully pondered the paradox and devised the brilliant solution of the self-consistent causal loop, in which the activities of the backward-voyaging mind are already incorporated in the deterministic web that links past and present, thus rendering his narrative internally self-consistent.

Yes, Nathaniel Wingate Peaslee's mind was transported millions of years backward by the Great Race of Yith, but—taking a theme from Margaret A. Murray's *Witch-Cult in Western Europe*—this stupefying assault upon the natural order is dimly corroborated through "persistent legends of immemorial antiquity." Megalithic ruins of the Great Race survive in "remote and desolate places"; the lore and legendry of their awesome incursion upon this planet is preserved by "nameless bands of abhorred elder-world hierophants"; such forbidden tomes as the *Necronomicon* offer agonizingly oblique echoes of their aeons-distant sojourn. In providing a closed temporal loop for his wondrous occurrence, Lovecraft has conceived a milestone in American science fiction; while such stories would become commonplace during the 1940s, "The Shadow Out of

Time" towers over all contemporary time-travel narratives with a decisiveness that would not be duplicated until the appearance of Robert A. Heinlein's " 'All You Zombies—' " in 1959.

Lovecraft's solution to his second problem, the physics of time travel, is more controversial. As early as 1905, Albert Einstein had introduced certain temporal amendments to the calculus of cosmicism, and Lovecraft, had he wished, could have concocted some pseudoscientific explanation for time travel utilizing Einsteinian world lines, Lorentz factors, quantum mechanics, and the like; but he avoided this option for several reasons. "All that a marvel story can ever be, in a serious way," he writes in his essay on interplanetary fiction, "is a *vivid picture of a certain type of human mood.*" The interpolation of scientific theories or mathematical formulas represented for Lovecraft "a dead weight obstructing the free flow of fancy . . .," a palpable impediment to the imaginative myth-weaving through which he sought to attain the infinite. Secondly, and for reasons explained earlier, HPL was an outsider in his own century; his entire emotional commitment lay in transcending the dreary quotidian realm, not in sabotaging the wonder element in his tales through the dazzling relativistic exegesis of Dr. Einstein.

Lovecraft instead embraced the concept of "Yog-Sothothery"; his own term for his imaginary cosmogony of alien entities who represent, in essence, natural laws of the cosmos beyond the pale of human perception. A mythopoeic construct such as the Great Race of Yith was HPL's response to "the general revolt of the sensitive mind against the tyranny of corporeal enclosure"; as the "world's greatest race," the cosmic denizens in Lovecraft's story "had conquered time and had sent exploring minds into every age." Although Lovecraft's penchant for embodying the mysteries of the cosmos in wondrous extraterrestrials was much maligned by the SF community of his day ("Ghost stories for five-year-olds," complained one *Astounding* reader), a contrived technical explanation such as Jack Williamson's "neuro-induction" now seems quaintly risible, while the Great Race of Yith retains its emotional allure over the intervening decades. Back in the 1930s, a youthful science-fiction enthusiast might plausibly speculate on an eventual starship carrying humanity to Alpha Centauri; today, with a sobering awareness of the massive technology and expense entailed by space travel, and even more significantly, of the deleterious effect of outer space upon the human organism, our best answer to "what lies beyond" may well remain the Great Race of Yith.

And thus, conceptual obstacles carefully thought through, Lovecraft began his great tale in the autumn of 1934. As if to underscore the symbolic importance of this story for its creator,

Lovecraft at the outset presents a précis of his own intellectual development as a writer: We learn that narrator Peaslee sustained a "strange amnesia" between 1908 and 1913; in the former year, HPL had become a high-school dropout, only to languish as a virtual recluse until his discovery of amateur journalism in 1913. In this same paragraph, Peaslee discloses the traditions of "horror, madness, and witchcraft" in "crumbling, whisper-haunted Arkham" where he resides, but protests that the outré occurrences he will detail are strictly "from *outside* sources . . . from *somewhere else.*" Lovecraft, in other words, had emerged from a shadowy Gothic background but now finds himself, as a sort of intellectual challenge, in full confrontation with the cosmic.

In meeting that confrontation, Lovecraft's narrator in the opening sentence expresses doubt at what he is about to describe ("I am unwilling to vouch for the truth of that which I think I found"), but then HPL begins to pile on the evidence—from paleontology, archaeology, anthropology, psychology, history, biology, geology, engineering—that the Great Race is indeed a reality, that time and space indeed "had become a mockery." You won't like this story, *Publishers Weekly!* Hands off Lovecraft's "Shadow," Mr. Havoc! What Lovecraft has accomplished—with prodigious erudition and supreme auctorial skill—is a relentless *Marcia funebre* in which iterated icons of nightmare and dream are tossed about in a vast cosmic passacaglia until Nathaniel Wingate Peaslee is compelled to confront his own worst surmise. Time may have destroyed the world HPL had loved, but with "The Shadow Out of Time," Lovecraft in turn had vanquished his ancient enemy. On that day in February 1935 when scribbling down the final unforgettable line—"spelling out the words of the English language in my own handwriting"—H. P. Lovecraft wasn't writing words but was writing eternity.

* * *

A few comments in closing on the present anthology. For this, my final Lovecraftian publication, I have organized the stories into a tripartite division: The opening "Lovecraft Country" section presents narratives in which HPL appears as a main character or that are set in one of Lovecraft's imaginary milieus; thus in "Her Misbegotten Son," Alan Rodgers strides imperiously through the demon-cursed streets of Arkham, Massachusetts (after Innsmouth, America's most dysfunctional community). The second section, "Eldritch Influences," gathers together independent narratives that incorporate occasional Lovecraftian allusions; thus Ian R. MacLeod's "Golden Keeper"—which ranks with selected works by T. E. D. Klein as one of the most masterly tales ever conceived within this subgenre—is set in the third century of the Roman Empire, but with guest appearances from the Great Old Ones. The final "Cosmic Realms" section collects stories of pure cosmicism in which the Lovecraftian element is implied rather than articulated. Thus on page 359 of "A Bit of the Dark World," Fritz Leiber paraphrases HPL's definition of the weird tale from the opening section of his "Supernatural Horror in Literature" essay, while later on page 372 of this same story, Leiber imperfectly quotes a line ("the black spaces between the stars") from "The Festival." No humongous anthropophagous frogs for Fritz, but the ambience of Lovecraftian homage is everywhere apparent.

And regarding which type of Lovecraftian story is the most effective? That determination, my dear reader, I shall leave to you.

—Jim Turner

Lovecraft Country

her misbegotten son

ALAN RODGERS

It was the old woman who brought Jason into the Arkham welfare office the day that he was born.

He was sodden and unclean, covered with that waxy substance that shrouds all babies in the moments of their birth. He was red and battered-looking, as though some dreadful force had wrenched him from the womb; he was ungainly and misshapen in three ways that marked him all his days.

But for all of that, the infant was quiet in the ancient woman's arms. When she walked into the office, there were those who knew she had to be his mother, no matter what her age.

"You must care for him," the woman said to the receptionist, who sat startled and transfixed behind her desk. "Be careful how you do."

And then she set the baby on the poor girl's desk and walked away without another word.

There was something oddly menacing about the old woman who deposited that child into the care of the agency known formally as the Arkham Office of Remedial Services. Something unmistakable, undeniable, and undefinable; something that touched the hearts of everyone who saw her.

Seven clients in the waiting lounge sat bolt upright as she entered, and one of them whispered a prayer.

The office's Hygiene Counselor—a tactless spiteful atheist prone to fits of proselytization—saw her from the place where he stood berating the typist in the secretarial pool. Till the moment he set eyes upon the crone, he'd never shown the least respect for any pious act, nor piousness among the faithful—but when he saw the old woman carrying her child he fell silent, and found himself savoring the frightened client's prayer.

Two whispering caseworkers saw the woman as they walked the aisle along the glass partition that separated the secretarial pool from the supervisors' spare-but-windowed offices, and the sight nearly cost their souls. The tall blonde caseworker—a woman named Blanche Gilman, who was kin to the Haverhill Gilmans and distantly related to the Gilmans of Innsmouth (two generations extinct and still infamous in Arkham)—Blanche Gilman gasped and swore as she recognized that woman.

She recognized that woman because there are sins that whisper melodies of madness through the blood; sins that sing to us down and across the generations—no matter what the distance, we know them when we see them, and perhaps they know us, too.

Blanche Gilman's companion (whose name was Judith Mason, and whose relation to the sin was darker and dearer but centuries more distant) found and squeezed her hand. She said, "Be still, Blanche," and that was enough, because no matter how we know the evil in our bones, it does not own us unless and until we put it on ourselves.

On the far side of the glass partition three supervisors looked up from their bickering to see the old woman and the child. Two of them stood stunned and gaping as all the rest, but the third—a loose cannon named Dan Mazurewicz—didn't hesitate a moment. He was in motion before the old woman stepped out of the elevator, even before she took a step into the welfare office.

Before she so much as said a word.

By the time she whispered to the receptionist, Dan Mazurewicz was on the telephone, calling the police.

Later, when they looked back on that moment, Dan Mazurewicz's fellow supervisors thought his call was more than a bit rash, and certainly premature, even if it did seem right in the end.

But Dan Mazurewicz never thought so. He knew damned well who that woman was—right from the very first. Partly he knew from the tales his father told of his months in that ancient and rat-infested house. But he also knew because he remembered the news reports from the spring before.

Terrible, terrible news—and gruesome footage on the local news. On May Eve a woman in one of the new condominiums on top of Meadow Hill called the police to report the sound of children screaming out by Hangman's Brook. The police got to the scene too late to do anything but find the bodies. There were children, dead children—oh God, oh God, the pictures on the TV news. Seven children, blood, pieces of their bodies scattered up and down the hollow. . . . There'd been some kind of ritual on May Eve. Something awful and despicable.

That night Mazurewicz's father retold the story of his nightmare in the thirties, and Dan Mazurewicz hated that—he hated listening to those stories, always had and always would. But when the old man got started telling the tale, there was no stopping him.

There was no news for six long weeks after the horror by the brook. No rumor, no report—nothing but a mystery festering among so many others in the Arkham morgue.

Till summer, when Dan Mazurewicz heard whispers on the streets. An old woman—she looked like a homeless woman, almost; the same sort of aimless and disheveled old woman who'd started showing up among the junkies and the vagabonds after Jimmy Carter turned the crazies out of Arkham Asylum. She was as ragged and unclean as all the others who wandered the worst parts of Arkham, indistinguishable at a distance from any of them. Twice, the community outreach people had mistaken her for an ordinary madwoman—until they drew close to her and saw her eyes. Eyes the color of dark light; eyes that glared at them hatefully; eyes that watched everyone and everything around her with predatory yearning.

It was contrary to established procedure, what the outreach people did when they saw her—turning and walking away where they should have opened their arms to her, accepting her on her own terms as a poor unfortunate with a severe personality disorder.

But the outreach workers were human, just like every other caseworker in the AORS; when they saw the gleam, when they felt the menace that surrounded that old woman, they turned and ran.

Anybody would.

The outreach people never filed a report on the old woman. That was contrary to procedure, too, and compounded their violation of regulation even as it covered the infraction. But Dan Mazurewicz was their supervisor, and they did it with his blessing.

When they took the story back to him that afternoon, Mazurewicz grew pale and very still. After a moment he asked them to leave his office, and close the door behind them.

When they were gone, he closed the blinds and took the phone off of its cradle.

To call his father.

Because Dan Mazurewicz knew that woman the moment that he heard the outreach workers' story.

He knew her, and he knew her name: Keziah Mason.

He knew that she was born a world away in time, and that she'd died horribly when his father was a young man.

The police arrived at the offices of the AORS about an hour after the crone had made a foundling of her child. They did what police always do in circumstances like those: they sat down to take the reports that police most always file and ignore until it comes time to compile the statistics.

They tried to take reports from everyone who'd caught sight of the child, starting with the receptionist and working their way back into the office.

But they never got to Blanche Gilman or Judith Mason. Ten minutes after the police arrived, the baby started crying, and Gilman and Mason made him their excuse to slip away for formula and diapers. They took the child with them to the pharmacy, made their purchases, then tended to him on a secluded bench on the edge of the Miskatonic campus.

They were there for a good half hour longer than it took the police to take reports from the receptionist, the clients, and the three supervisors.

The police never noticed they were gone. They had at least a dozen statements; there was more than enough in them to bulk their report sufficiently for filing.

That was the Arkham Police Department in those years: the work of the police was measured in the thickness of the file folders they caused the clerks to build. There was lots of talk of crime prevention, but none of them did much about it except where it concerned one of their own.

The officers took their report and brought it to the station for the clerks to transcribe and bury in the files.

And that would have been the end of it on their account, if it weren't for Dan Mazurewicz.

Dan Mazurewicz was quite anxious about the foundling and made several calls in his regard. When he found the reporting officers unresponsive, he made a call to his brother in the commissioner's office.

Captain Andrew Mazurewicz had heard all the same stories that his brother had, and he knew who Keziah Mason was. When his brother told him what he'd seen, he put a dozen officers on the case.

Captain Mazurewicz and his dozen officers spent the entire

month of February searching Arkham for the crone. He even made them use the name, *Keziah Mason,* even though it was a name they'd heard in wives' tales from their mothers.

But no matter how they searched, they never found her.

At the beginning of the second week, Captain Mazurewicz brought in a police artist from Boston and had him build a composite sketch from the descriptions that the witnesses put forward. When the sketch was done, he called the editor of the local paper and persuaded him to publish the sketch on the paper's front page.

But no more came of that than came out of the search.

Nothing came of any of his efforts in those weeks, in fact—except the tale that came from old Frank Elwood.

Frank Elwood was a derelict who'd spent fifty years drunkenly wandering the streets of Arkham—but he was a derelict with a peculiar heritage. He was from a fine and decent family, the Elwoods of Ipswich, with connections that reached all through New England. He'd come to Arkham in the thirties, to attend the university—and something had gone very, very wrong. In his junior year he'd dropped out of his Miskatonic courses and refused all contact with his family; when they came looking for him (out of understandable concern), he had avoided them. When his father ultimately found him, he'd demanded to be left alone.

Elwood had seen the crone the day she'd borne her child. He told three officers a fantastic tale of the experience—a tale that none of them believed.

Captain Mazurewicz believed it, but he didn't bother to put it in the file. There wasn't any point. The captain worked for the commissioner, and the commissioner was a Harvard man—a well-known academic criminologist the city council had brought in to rehabilitate a police department with a reputation almost as bizarre as the town it served. It was his special hobbyhorse to rid the APD of the superstitious nonsense that had infested it for generations; the last thing that would please him was a story like Frank Elwood's in the files.

So Captain Mazurewicz made his own notes and kept them to himself. When he finally despaired of finding the old woman, he set his men to other tasks and went back to the workaday business of policing Arkham.

But he kept an eye out for the crone, and he kept tabs on her child. That was the best that he could do, given the circumstance.

It wasn't enough to save the child from the fate that he was born to, but it was something.

The Arkham Office of Remedial Services placed the foundling in foster care with Dr. and Mrs. Abraham Laidlaw. Abe Laidlaw was young, as professors of contemporary literature go. Thirty, maybe thirty-five, he'd only lately come to lecture at Miskatonic from the trendy West Coast school where he'd taken his doctorate and spent three unsatisfying years teaching the freshman English courses that the school's tenured professors shirked as best they could. His assistant professorship at Miskatonic was his first real postgraduate position, and when he took the job, he thought it meant great things for him.

It took him years to learn how wrong he was.

Abe Laidlaw and his wife bought a row house near the Miskatonic River—a beautiful and newish place that looked out on the river half a mile north of the old iron bridge that spans the Miskatonic in central Arkham, not far from the fallow river isle some Arkham folk call Desolation.

The Laidlaws were fine people, as college faculty went. They were neither stuffy nor bizarre (unfortunate qualities that are the norm among Miskatonic faculty); and, too, for all Abe Laidlaw's education they both had the simple forthright character most Americans consider the working-class ideal. When they took the house that looked on Desolation (which is not desolate at all to those who fancy wild grasslands), they meant to start their family there.

But something happened in those first months after the Laidlaws came to Arkham—something sad, miserable, and agonizing that left Carol Laidlaw three weeks in Miskatonic University Community Hospital under the close scrutiny of obstetric and gynecological specialists.

It was never clear to either of the Laidlaws what exactly had befallen Carol Laidlaw. There was blood, there were complications, and then there were biopsies and surgeries. When it was done, Carol Laidlaw went home with the counsel that she should never bear a child and would do well to undergo an operation that would see to it that she never could.

The Laidlaws, sturdy people that they were, took the news in stride. They offered themselves out to Foster Care, and when the county offered Jason to them, they took him happily and without recompense, misshapenness and all.

The boy did well, growing large and quickly despite the misshapenness of his limbs and skull; the misproportion of his torso. As he grew, his pale blue infant's eyes took on an almost-luminescent violet cast that made him stand out from his peers even more than the deformities did.

It would have taken a miracle to spare him the revilement and abuse of his fellows. There are always miracles aplenty in Arkham, but respite hardly thrives among them: even as a toddler, the boy took some considerable abuse.

But that infantile cruelty never shaped Jason the way it shapes so many denigrated children. Oh, he didn't like it—not even thick half-senseless boys are comfortable in the heat of cruelty and derision, and Jason was anything but senseless. But he had a special sense about the nature of the human heart that steered him away from the responses that come naturally and fitfully to most of us. When the taunts came to him, the boy met them face-on. He didn't argue them or acquiesce to his tormentors, but answered their abuse with friendliness and good cheer. That puzzled most of his abusers, and generally disarmed them; the ones it did not disarm came to see their own cruelty, and often became objects of derision themselves.

Some people who saw the way the boy carried himself said that the Laidlaws were wise people to teach him so well. But others said that the boy's restraint was a thing no one could teach, but rather was born into the nature of the child.

There may and may not be something to that notion. Certainly the Laidlaws were quiet, thoughtful people who did their best by Jason. More than once they tried adopting him as their own son.

But the county and its caseworkers would never hear of that.

Some of the reservations at the Arkham Office of Remedial Services were parochial ones having to do with ideas then generally current in the thinking of remedial-services professionals all over the country. But there were other reasons they held up the adoption paperwork on the child who'd come to be known as Jason Laidlaw, and some of them were perfectly reasonable. It was the office's policy, for instance, to withhold adoption of children whose mothers were alive and unconsenting.

There were folks inside the office who believed that the crone who'd delivered him to the AORS was his mother; and there were reports that she was still alive.

The first point was entirely unreasonable. Women old as time don't bear children, and if they did, they never would abandon them to the care of the Arkham ORS. But those who saw the crone that day believed her maternity with an unshakable sternness of conviction, and those who later took the case soon learned that it was better not to argue with those who'd witnessed the spectacle that day.

As to whether the crone was still alive . . . it was hard to say. There were reports of her in Arkham all through Jason Laidlaw's infancy and into his boyhood, but no one who tried to seek her out to ask her about the child ever found her.

And there were those who said she was no living thing at all, but rather a creature made of legend, cursed by witchery. There was hardly any basis for those tales, but Arkham was and is Arkham, and superstition is a palpable thing within the city's borders.

The summer Jason was three, he spent his afternoons in the backyard of the row house. He would go outside to play for hours as his foster mother worked about the house and watched soap operas and did all the things that housewives do when their children find ways to occupy the hours. If anyone had asked her why she left the boy alone, she would have told them that there was a fence around the yard, and it was safe enough inside it.

The fence was made of posts and wires, and it ran higher than a man is tall; Jason wasn't the sort of child who sees every fence as a challenge made to conquer, but if he had been, it would have held him well enough that year when he was three.

And anyway the child had no reason to escape: Jason loved that yard. He loved the toys and the swings; loved the sand and the sky and the seabirds that soared above him as he played.

Sometimes when he was in that yard alone, Jason would sit for hours in the sand, watching everything around him. When he sat there, he could see a long, long way—all the way to Miskatonic University in one direction, and in the other Gresham Park and the Miskatonic River out beyond it.

Most of all he liked to watch the tiny fallow island in the middle of the river.

It never occurred to him to wonder what it was about that view that so fascinated him, but whatever it was compelled him. His foster mother would have worried about it if she'd ever noticed how he stared in that direction.

But she never did.

One day in mid-July Jason saw an old, old woman wandering in the tall grass that grew on the fallow island. She stared in his direction, and once she seemed to wave. It felt like—felt like she was watching him.

But he knew that couldn't be.

After a while Jason turned away and dug his cup into the sand, dug and dug until he'd built a formidable pit. He didn't mean to think about the woman as he dug, but he couldn't stop thinking about her, thinking about how she made him feel so . . . *strange*. Dirty and wrong, somehow, and full of mystery and promise all at once, and he thought he knew that woman, and he thought he liked her, but he knew he was afraid.

When he looked up again, the old woman was gone. But the next day there was a shack out there on the fallow island, and lots of days that summer Jason saw the crone wandering the island's fields, watching him discreetly.

As Jason Laidlaw grew, he met the crone three times.

The first meeting came on a cold and sunny afternoon in early March the year that he turned eight. The boy's foster mother was a continent away that afternoon, visiting her relatives in Salem, Oregon, and Jason was in the care of his foster father. Benign and inattentive care, that is; the misshapen boy was free to wander the corridors of Miskatonic University all the while Professor Laidlaw graded the dull, inept, and loathsome essays that his students had handed in that afternoon. He spent an hour in the university's infamous library, browsing among the stacks of books with titles he could hardly understand. He tried to wheedle his way into the locked basement room where the library stored its notorious and arcane tomes—dread manuscripts like the *Necronomicon* of Alhazred and the ancient and indecipherable *Book of Ages*. But it was no use; the librarians all knew that room was an attractive nuisance for young boys, and kept their guard against them. (Of course that room is a magnet to all boys! What boy can hear the tales that come out of that place without knowing that it is mischief made for him and all his kind? None can, and that's a certainty; it takes no arcane knowledge to observe it.)

When the librarian turned him away from the sealed archive, Jason Laidlaw wandered out into the campus common, and aimlessly from there along the little-used path that leads southeast from the common around back of the school's cafeteria.

That was where he found the crone, standing on the far side of a dumpster. When he saw her, he knew that she'd been waiting for him, and he knew that she meant him no good.

"You've come," she said. She didn't smile. "I knew you would."

Her eyes were violet, Jason saw—the same strange color he saw when he looked at his own eyes in the mirror. He had known her in his heart from the moment that he'd seen her, but when he looked into her eyes, he no longer could deny the things he knew about her.

Not to himself anyway. He was boy enough to lie to the old woman's face, but that was another matter entirely.

"I don't know you," he said. "My father says I shouldn't talk to strangers."

The old woman laughed maliciously. "Your father. . .?" she asked, and laughed again. "You know nothing of your father."

The boy found himself wanting to cry, but he knew he didn't dare. "My father teaches at the university," he said. "I know exactly where he is."

The old woman ignored him. She said, "I hear they call you Jason, boy."

Jason frowned. He wanted to turn away from her and run, but he couldn't bring himself to move—he hardly had the will to breathe. "My name is Jason Laidlaw," he said. "If you don't leave me be, I'll tell on you—I will."

The old woman laughed again. Her voice was even crueler now. "Your name is a secret you may never learn," she said. "And I will take or leave you as I please, young man. You are born to be my property. Nothing in this life will ever change that."

Jason wanted to pretend he didn't understand her. Certainly the words and concepts that she hinted at—notions like chattelhood and inevitability—were things that ordinary American children have little reference to. Even in a city as peculiar as Arkham. But he was a precocious child, and he had more sense of what she meant than he wanted to admit.

"You're wrong," he said.

Now at last the old woman smiled.

"I could never be," she said.

And then she vanished, as though she'd never stood before him in the shadow of debris.

For the longest time after she disappeared, the boy stood staring into the shadows where the old woman had been, trying to decide whether she was a secret he could never share, or a threat he had to carry to his father if he wanted to survive. All he could think was that she was both those things, a secret treasure and the menace that would murder him, and he had to tell the world about her but knew he didn't dare for fear he'd lose her.

And then the question answered itself, as he felt a soft touch on his arm and looked up still breathless to see the welfare ladies, Miss Gilman and Ms. Mason. He knew them well enough, but not that well at all: they were his caseworkers from the city. Every month or so Jason and his parents went crosstown to the Federal Building to visit them awhile.

It was Ms. Mason who had touched him. Jason looked up to see her watching him so carefully, looking through him, almost into him. "You saw her, didn't you?" Jason asked her. "You have to tell me who she was."

Ms. Mason shook her head. "Don't think about her, Jason," she said. "And never let her touch your heart. That woman is your singular affliction. She will kill you if she's able."

"But I think she loves me," Jason said. "Why should I be afraid?"

Miss Gilman shook her head so sadly because there weren't words for her to tell a child all the horrors that abound in Arkham and the world. "That was a trial, child," she said. "And you mastered it well. Be careful how you go without your foster parents. Arkham is a special trap for boys with hearts like yours."

Jason never told his foster parents about what happened that day. In some ways that was just as well, since the tale would have frightened them, and there was little they could do about it but force the boy out of their lives—an act for which there was no capacity in their hearts or in their character.

But even so, the Laidlaws had a need to know about the crone and Jason's meeting with her. If they had known, they could have prepared themselves for the things that happened over the course of the next year—and that might have saved them both a world of grief.

For two months to the day after Jason's encounter with the crone, Carol Laidlaw conceived a child, against all likelihood and common sense as well. Her doctors counseled her to terminate the child, of course; her condition made pregnancy a grave threat to her life. But it wasn't in her or her husband to do such a thing, and she carried her son to term, no matter how the carrying ailed her.

She only barely survived the experience. She carried the child seven months, went into labor prematurely that Christmas Eve, and gave birth Christmas morning.

Her child was born healthy and, at six and three-quarter pounds, more than adequately large; the doctors found precious little evidence of his prematurity. He left the hospital on Boxing Day, less than twenty hours after he'd been born.

But Carol Laidlaw nearly lost her life that Christmas Day. She fell into a coma in the final throes of labor, and if the doctors had not acted quickly, she'd have died the moment that her son was born.

As it was, they only barely kept her breathing.

She spent ten months in that hospital unconscious and all but moribund before the doctors despaired that they could ever save her.

And then they pulled the plug to let her die.

Those were hard months for Abe Laidlaw. How could they be otherwise? A man alone can see after an infant, but the seeing after doesn't come as naturally to men as it does to the mothers of newborns. Jason did everything he could to help, but how much could that be? The boy was only nine, for heaven's sake.

Abe Laidlaw's classes fell into disarray, and his research went to nothing. Twice his dean had words with him about his inattention, and each time Abe Laidlaw nearly told the tenured administration brownnose to put it where the sun might never shine.

But he didn't say those things, no matter how he wanted to. He was still two years away from tenure himself, and not about to risk his livelihood that way. So he frowned chastenedly and nodded and took it with all the grace that he could muster, and got out of that room and back to his screaming misbegotten infant as quickly as he could.

Which could never be quick enough. The baby was uneasy and demanding; healthy but always in a temper. They'd planned to name him Mark, but Abe Laidlaw could never bring himself to call the infant by that name while his wife lay dying in the hospital. So he called the baby by the second name they'd chosen, *Enoch,* and let the birth certificate be damned.

"Daddy," Jason said that steamy July afternoon after Abe Laidlaw's second meeting with the dean, "Daddy, I like Enoch's eyes."

Abe Laidlaw frowned.

The baby had the same strange violet eyes that Jason did. "Yes, Jason. They're pretty, aren't they?"

Abe Laidlaw wasn't certain how the infant could have eyes so much like Jason's. There was no blood between them, surely; Jason was a son to him, and he loved the boy as dearly as he loved the infant. But he was a foster son, and the similarity of the two boys was a peculiar thing. Abe and Carol Laidlaw were both dark-eyed people, and so were their families—none of Abe's or Carol's relations had eyes anything like the infant's.

Maybe it was something in the air, or something in the Arkham water. Abe Laidlaw had never heard of anything that could have an effect like that, but who could say for certain? The world is full of complex substances that have effects upon the human animal, and for every one that the scientists catalog, a thousand others still await discovery.

If there is a place upon the surface of the earth that science fails to understand, then that is surely Arkham. It made a sort of sense when Abe Laidlaw thought about it.

But it was wrong, of course. Enoch Laidlaw's eyes were violet for the same reason that Carol Laidlaw lay dying in the hospital: because the alchemy that misshaped his foster brother was an infectious thing. It altered everything it touched, and everyone who touched it, even at the fourth remove.

Naturally so. For the sins that made Keziah Mason the unhuman thing that she was were dreadful things that won't occur to decent people. The evil that came out of them ran in every direction, for years and generations all across the world.

"Why does he have eyes like mine, Daddy?" Jason asked.

"I don't know, Jason," Abe Laidlaw told him. "But I think they're beautiful that way."

The second time Jason Laidlaw saw the woman who had borne him was more dreadful than the first. It came a week after the conversation with his foster father about his infant brother's eyes when he went to the welfare office for his monthly session with the caseworkers.

When he was very small, he'd gone to those sessions with both his foster parents, and when he was a little larger it'd been his foster mother, Carol Laidlaw, who took him crosstown to see Miss Gilman and Ms. Mason. But with Carol Laidlaw in the hospital (*Mommy,* Jason thought of her as *Mommy*—he'd never known another mother), Jason tended to go to them alone. Carol Laidlaw never would have let him wander Arkham all alone like that, but his foster father kept a looser rein on him. Partly that was Abe Laidlaw's natural inclination, but partly also it happened because the man was overwhelmed and at wits' end. He never really meant to set the boy loose to roam the haunted streets of Arkham, but it happened that way all the same.

Inadvertent, that's what it was. It started with Jason's appointment the first week of January when the baby was still so tiny and delicate, too frail to carry out into the winter air, and then there'd been some stupid crisis, colic or diapers or formula, Abe Laidlaw never found out what made the baby cry that day. In the middle of it, right in the middle of the noise and panic and the poor infant screaming like he was about to die, Jason tugged his shirt and said it was time to go to the appointment with Miss Gilman and Ms. Mason.

Abe Laidlaw hardly heard him. He was too busy trying to warm the bottle, trying to change the diaper that didn't need changing and then wouldn't go back on the way it should, trying to rock the child out of its terrors. . . .

The boy wandered off after a while. He could see it was a crisis, and he knew that there was nothing he could do to help. But he also knew that the appointment was important, and necessary, so he got himself ready the way he always did, thinking that his foster father would figure something out.

Half an hour later he found his foster father still pacing back and forth across the kitchen, and he said, "It's time, Daddy."

Abe Laidlaw still didn't realize what was going on. He saw the heavy winter clothes, and he thought the boy wanted to go out back to climb in the snow that had fallen just the night before. He said, "Go ahead, Jason. But be careful, all right?" but he didn't really think about it when he said it. His head was too full of the baby screaming in his ears, and the formula he'd left heating and forgotten in that pot of now-boiling water on the stove, oh, Christ, the formula was scorched and curdled, that stuff was expensive, damn it, and he had a class at six o'clock and how the hell was he going to get there—it wasn't like he could leave the baby with a sitter in a state like this—

The boy had stared at him for a good long while because he knew the limits that his foster mother set him—when he went out he could go a block in either direction, as far as the fire station in one direction or the apartments in the other, but no farther, you hear, Jason? And the welfare office was halfway across town, almost as far as it could be and still be on this side of the Miskatonic River. He was a good boy, a boy who did as he was told, and his foster father's instructions were clear and direct.

"Be careful, all right, Jason?" Abe Laidlaw repeated when he saw the boy still staring at him.

And Jason did as he was told.

Miss Gilman and Ms. Mason thought it was peculiar when Jason showed up by himself, and they asked him about it. But in the end they didn't make an issue of it; they knew about the baby, and about poor Carol Laidlaw lying comatose in the hospital, and they didn't see a call to make things worse when they were already bad enough. Jason was doing well enough, after all; he was healthy, well-fed, and clean, and he had an attachment to his foster father. What more could they ask, in the end?

And besides, they had reasons of their own for not interfering. The malformed boy was a special concern of theirs, and his placement was deliberate.

When Jason went to the welfare office that hot July afternoon, he went alone, as he had every month since Christmas. He didn't stop in the waiting room the way most clients did because he knew Miss Gilman and Ms. Mason would be waiting for him, just as they always were.

Waiting in Ms. Gilman's windowed office that looked out on the river. When he got to the reception desk, he said hi to the receptionist, just like he always did, but this time she didn't answer. At all. Jason said, *Hi, Miss Francis,* but Miss Francis just stared silently into the distance.

"Miss Francis . . .?" he repeated. But still she wouldn't answer. After a long moment he shrugged and pushed past her desk, heading back toward Miss Gilman's office.

The door was closed when he got there. That was unusual—Miss Gilman liked to work with the door open—but it had been that way before. Jason knocked on the door hesitantly, uneasily, half afraid that he was interrupting something. . . .

He wasn't, of course.

He knocked on the door and a voice whispered, *"Enter,"* just barely loud enough to hear. It was a man's voice, a voice he didn't recognize, and Jason had an awful notion that it was something monstrous in there waiting for him, something wrong and dangerous and hateful.

And he was right.

"Enter," the voice repeated—louder now, and demanding.

And Jason turned to run.

But by then it was too late.

The door opened behind him as he turned, and before he could take a solitary step, a great dark hand took hold of his shoulder and pulled him into the room. It happened in a blur, the hand lifting him all but off his feet, the floor falling out from under him; the door closing hard before him as he came to rest off-balance just inside it. He had an urge to try the obvious, reopening the door before anyone expected him to do it, but that wasn't any use; look, look how the great dark hand pressed against the door, holding it firm.

Jason gasped when he saw that hand. He gasped because even then he knew too much about it—because the sins that touch the blood were in Jason's blood, too, and they haunted him as surely as they haunted either of his caseworkers.

Knowing, dreading, seeing the hand, he turned to face the creature that the stories call the Dark Man.

There are few who've seen him, even in the foulest parts of Arkham, and fewer still who realize who it is they've seen. But everyone in Arkham has heard of him; he is in local stories exactly what the bogeyman is elsewhere. They say he walks the streets at night, dressed in a long coat, gloves, and a hat that shields his face almost entirely from view; those few who have the misfortune to pass him in his wandering could easily mistake him for an ordinary man of African descent.

Jason saw him that day in the pure clear light of a summer afternoon, and knew exactly what he saw. Even that first sight of the Dark Man chilled him to the bone.

Skin the color of night, but green-black where the sky is black with hints of blue; features that were human but malignly misshapen —misshapen just as Jason's features were, but wronger and malevolent. He was tall, taller than any man the boy had ever seen. Heavy, too—not heavy with fat but broad-shouldered and thick-armed like a bodybuilder. Jason knew that man the moment he set eyes upon him, and maybe he knew what there was between them, too.

But if he did know, he kept the knowledge secret from himself.

"This is your child, Nahab?"

Here in the room beside him Jason could hear that the man's

voice was as wrong as his appearance—cold and unearthly, like something from a horror movie but stranger and more real.

"It is mine," a voice answered—a voice Jason recognized, a voice he could never forget. "I told you he was fit."

The old woman.

Standing by Miss Gilman's desk.

The old woman he'd first seen that afternoon the year before, on the campus of the university. She was standing by Miss Gilman's desk, and Miss Gilman and Ms. Mason were in two chairs behind her, bound and gagged, eyes wide and struggling.

The Dark Man smiled—it was a hideous expression on that face, an expression that chilled Jason in that circumstance where he thought he could find no further fear. *"He favors me, I think,"* the Dark Man said. *"That pleases me."*

Miss Gilman looked hysterical. She was twisting back and forth in her chair, trying to get free of the ropes that bound her. It wasn't working.

"When will we take him?" the crone asked. "This child weighs on me. I would have him now."

The Dark Man shook his head. *"Never before Hallowmass,"* he said. *"Better at May Eve."*

The old woman shook her head. "Do not deny me, Nyarlathotep. This is the child of my flesh. I cannot wait another year."

"You must," the Dark Man said. *"You will. There is no other way: the child must sign his name in blood upon the page that bears his mark. There must be a sacrifice, and ceremonies. You will never own him any other way."*

"I own him now," the old woman said. "That is the way of the flesh."

The Dark Man made no answer.

But Jason did. He didn't understand the conversation or the context, but he knew they were talking about him, and down in his bones he knew what it meant to him, for the same reason that Blanche Gilman and Judith Mason did: because Keziah Mason and the Dark Man had trespassed against all things worldly and divine, and the evil of their acts sang infamy the boy could feel inside his bones.

"I don't belong to you," he said. "I won't sign any book. You can't make me do a thing like that."

The Dark Man still had one hand on Jason's shoulder, holding him firmly. He took the boy's other shoulder and lifted him off his feet—held him high to face him eye to eye.

Spent the longest moment staring at him, looking into him, Jason thought. Probing him. . . .

"So you say," the Dark Man told him. *"But you are young yet, child, and your heart is malleable. I will have it in my day."*

"Now," the old woman said. "I take him now, my priest. I cannot deny myself another day."

"Quiet, Nahab."

Now the Dark Man pulled Jason closer, so close that the boy could feel his fetid breath brushing on his cheeks.

"Put me down," Jason told him. "Let me go."

The Dark Man grinned again, so horrible, profane—nothing that ungodly should ever smile, and when it does, no decent soul can bear to look upon it.

"You are audacious, child. That suits me, too."

Jason felt an awful sinking in his gut, a feeling that no matter what he did, no matter what he tried or how he could react, it would work to serve the Dark Man. It wasn't fair, or right, or anything else he understood, and he wanted to run away; but how could he when his feet weren't even near the ground? He wanted to fight, but there's no way a boy can win a fight against an ordinary man, and nothing about the Dark Man was ordinary. And he wanted to scream, but there wasn't any point.

"I never will," the boy said. "You're terrible, and you're bad, too, bad as anything there is."

The Dark Man started laughing, great gusts of that awful reeking laughter billowing into the boy's eyes, and Jason got so mad, angry like he'd never been before in all his days, and he did the only thing he could think of: he started kicking.

The Dark Man laughed. *"You have nerve, child. I like that."*

"Let me go!" Jason shouted, twisting and kicking even more desperately now—struggling like a thing possessed by demons. That made the Dark Man smile even more widely—

—until Jason's left foot caught him squarely in the small below his ribs, forcing the air out of him.

The Dark Man gasped involuntarily, and very near collapsed. Jason fell twisting and writhing from his great powerful arms, landed on his feet, and turned to bolt, to run—

He barely got three steps before the old woman said his name. "Jason," she said, "step no farther."

Her words made the air congeal around him, but they weren't enough to stop him. Jason pushed through the thick suffocating air, a step, another step, and now his hand was on the doorknob—

As the Dark Man found his breath, and began to whisper words that Jason could grasp but not identify.

"Iä–R'lyeh!" he whispered. *"Cthulhu fhtagn! Iä! Iä!"*

And Jason felt himself go rigid as a statue, unable to move.

"Let me go," he said. "I don't belong to you."

The old woman laughed. "You are mistaken, child." As she spoke, she walked unevenly across the room until she stood close enough to touch him, and then she *did* touch him, touched him softly, gently on the shoulder. "You are the child of my flesh," she said. "You cannot help but love me."

"No!" Jason shouted. But no matter what he said, he knew that there was something in her words he never could deny, and the touch of her hand so gentle on his shoulder, so tender, and he wanted to turn to the vile old woman and embrace her, but he knew he didn't dare. "Don't touch me!" he said. And then he started to cry.

"He *is* mine, Nyarlathotep," the old woman said. "Let me take him now, I beg you." She sounded—forlorn. Sad and lonesome, like a woman begging for a thing she needed just to stay alive.

I love her, Jason thought. And he hated himself when he thought it, and he wanted to die, and maybe he would have died if he was older, but that year he was too young.

"Nahab—" the Dark Man started to say, almost . . . almost relenting. He sounded like he was going to give in.

And Jason just couldn't take it anymore.

Something deep down inside him—something made of fear and self-loathing and a dozen other things he was too young to understand—something boiled over.

Broke the spell that held him and threw him into motion as he bolted for the door.

He threw the door open and all but flew across the office, making for the emergency exit stair just inside the reception area. He was halfway across the office before the Dark Man started chanting again, but this time it didn't matter, it didn't matter what he did or said. The Dark Man was magic, but there was magic in Jason, too, and he hated it and he ran from it but it was the only thing that kept him free. *You can't catch me,* he thought, and he was on the stairs, running down the stairs as the old woman and the Dark Man thundered through the office behind him, shouting those words in that language Jason had never heard in all his days but understood. (How could he understand? Jason wondered. How could he understand a language that he'd never known?)

No matter how he wondered, Jason didn't hesitate. He ran like his life depended on it, and after a while it did. He didn't realize that for a while, but it did. Because the spell he broke when he bolted from Miss Gilman's office was a spell that would kill him if it could. Some spells are like that. They grip you or they kill you, and if they fail to do those things, they turn back upon the ones who cast them.

A broken spell is like a dagger turned upon its master; great conjurers are at peril to destroy all of those who know the knife that breaks their spells.

When Jason stood captive in Miss Gilman's office, he was a tool, a prize the Dark Man treasured for its value. But when his heart grew large enough to break the Dark Man's spell, he made himself a threat as menacing as anything the Dark Man ever knew.

By the time he reached the stairs that led from the AORS to the lobby of the Federal Building, Jason had already sealed his fate: there was no way the Dark Man could leave a bane to his magic wandering the streets of Arkham.

The Dark Man chased the boy all down those stairs, gaining on him as he went.

Moving faster than the old woman, faster than Jason, too fast, he was going to catch Jason so soon, too soon—

Now Jason was on the ground floor, in the lobby of the Federal Building, and the Dark Man was on the stairs not far above him, and he knew he had to run, but how could he run when the Dark Man was so close behind him and getting closer?

He had to find a place to hide. Or someone who could protect him, if anybody could, maybe nobody could protect him, he remembered the welfare office, Miss Gilman and Ms. Mason tied up and struggling against the ropes that bound them, every other person in the office staring dead-eyed into the distance, the Dark Man could do that to people, nobody could protect him, Jason knew that—

And then as Jason dashed across the foyer, the welfare supervisor —Dan Mazurewicz—came through the front door of the Federal Building.

And blinked as he saw Jason dashing toward him.

And looked up and back to see the Dark Man emerging from the stairs.

Turned pale as a sheet. And crossed himself, and whispered a prayer his father taught him when he was a child.

"Help me!" Jason shouted. "Save me!"

When he reached Dan Mazurewicz, he stepped behind him and cowered as though the man were some sort of a shield, no matter how he knew that there was nothing that he could do to protect himself from the Dark Man.

"Stop where you are," Dan Mazurewicz told the Dark Man. "I know who you are. I know what you've done. You don't frighten me, you hear?"

He said that. He really did. But no matter what he said, he sounded terrified.

The Dark Man didn't stop until he was almost close enough to touch Dan Mazurewicz.

"Give me the child," the Dark Man said. *"It is mine. Give it to me, and I will leave you be."* Then he held out his hand, and again he smiled that awful bloodcurdling smile. Jason felt himself tremble at the wrongness of it, and he wanted to die. *"Deny me, and you will suffer all your days."*

"I never would," Dan Mazurewicz said, reaching into his shirt. He brought something out of it, a locket, maybe, a talisman like in a movie, Jason couldn't see from where he stood behind the man, but he saw a glint of silver as Dan Mazurewicz thrust the pendant at the Dark Man. "My father gave me this crucifix five years ago," he said. "You know it, don't you? He told me that you saw it once."

As he spoke, the Dark Man swore in that language never made to speak upon the tongues of man, and now he retreated a step, a step, another.

"You will suffer for your impudence, Dan Mazurewicz. You and all of yours will suffer."

And Jason thought, *It's working, it's working. I'm safe, the Dark Man is afraid,* but even as he thought that, he had an awful foreboding. Of course he did! Jason was too young to articulate the nature of the place in which he lived, but he knew it in his bones, just as everyone who lives in Arkham does: the years are long, and Arkham is a place hospitable to abominations like the Dark Man—and worse things, too. There are curses that no one in that city ever can escape.

And he knew that Dan Mazurewicz was as doomed as Jason was himself.

As now the old woman shambled down the last of the stairs to reach the lobby, and the Dark Man turned to whisper to her. *"Take the trinket from him, Nahab—take it and destroy it."*

That was when Jason knew that the doom was on Dan Mazurewicz.

And he ran.

Because he ran, he never saw the horror that befell the man who tried to save him—but everyone knew about it later. It made the papers as far away as Salem, and people spoke of it for years the way they speak in Arkham when they tell tales to frighten the young. Blood that sprayed to cover the walls and ceiling of the Federal Building's lobby; the patrolmen who responded to the 911 call from a man who'd heard Dan Mazurewicz screaming from half a block away.

When the patrolmen entered the Federal Building, they found

Dan Mazurewicz eviscerated on the floor just inside the doorway.

Eviscerated and still alive, writhing and moaning and trying to scream, but how could he scream with the wind torn out of him? With his intestines strewn upon the floor beside him like a glistening mass of blood sausages waiting to be cured?

One of the patrolmen screamed and went catatonic when he saw that sight. He spent months in therapy, trying to come to grips with what he'd seen, but it never left him, no matter how he tried to clear the image from his mind.

His partner was a harder man. He caught a glimpse of Dan Mazurewicz writhing in his agony and got on the radio immediately to call an ambulance to try to save the poor bastard, who ought to be dead already but wouldn't die—couldn't die—the world would not relinquish him. He called an ambulance that took ten long minutes to arrive and thirty minutes longer to gather up the pieces and move him to the ambulance, and Dan Mazurewicz was awake, alive, aware through all of that. He never passed out, he never lost touch, not even when they shot him full of morphine to damp the pain. Dan Mazurewicz never died. The morphine made no difference; the pain should have killed him by itself, but it never did.

Not in the Federal Building. Not in the ambulance. Not in the hospital operating room where the doctors tried and tried to piece him back together, to clean the grit and grime out of his guts. It was hopeless, the doctors told one another. Dan Mazurewicz heard that as he lay strapped to the operating table unable to die, impervious to morphine, thinking and thinking that he should have died but couldn't.

The doctors stitched the pieces of Dan Mazurewicz back together and put him in a private room in the ICU, expecting him to die despite their efforts. He should have died, for mercy's sake; no one can bear that kind of agony and live whole and human as an upright man. He should have died that afternoon; that evening he prayed to die but did not.

Not till midnight, when his father's priest came to visit him, and blessed him, and took his final confession. When the Holy Water touched his forehead, the abomination that held Dan Mazurewicz to the world cracked open like the rind of some profane fruit.

For there are blessings that are true as curses, and some of them familiar as our lives.

Blessings true as the death that carries us up from the world of man and woman, to mercy, solitude, and sleep.

As Dan Mazurewicz died fitfully, still suffering no matter how the world released him.

Jason Laidlaw ran all through the busy streets of Arkham, looking for a hiding place, finding none. It was safe in the streets, he thought—safe enough to run. The Dark Man would follow him wherever he went, but he wouldn't hurt him, not with so many people all around to see. But that could only hide him for so long until the Dark Man found him in a moment no one saw, and then he would take him by the arm to drag him away into the hidden places where all fetid things thrive beneath the city caught in magic at the edge of Space and Time.

He had to find a place to hide—and when he found it, he had to find a way to hide forever and a lifetime, and how could he do that?

He was still trying to think when he reached the edge of the Miskatonic University campus. That was the perfect place for the moment, Jason thought. The university was full of odd places no one ever wandered into and years could never find, and all around those places there were students and professors bustling toward classes and appointments.

And Jason ran into the campus common, running quickly as he could, trying to think where was the spot he had to be, where should he hide, not looking, not noticing the emptiness around him, thinking so far ahead he didn't see how alone he was until it was too late to turn away.

He saw it when he got to the center of the campus common. He looked up, thinking of the library. There were places in the library where no one ever went and no one could ever find—he'd wandered in those places so many afternoons in his foster father's haphazard care.

And looked up to see the library before him, and saw that there was no one anywhere around.

If Jason had been thinking clearly, he would have hurried back out into the crowded streets of Arkham. It was surely safer there than it could be anywhere inside the Miskatonic campus. It was the middle of the summer break, and the campus was all but deserted; the library was the last place that could hide him. But he wasn't thinking clearly. He saw the abandonment around him and felt a surge of terror that he'd be unable to get into the library, where he'd planned to hide; rushed toward the library door and found it open; hurried in, not even thinking how he'd be like a trapped rat among its empty stacks.

Hurried past the bored and lonely-looking librarian who sat reading *Newsweek* at her desk, and ran on through the first-floor stacks to the wide stairway that led up seven floors and down three more to the subsubbasement.

And hurried down to that bottommost place that held the locked and bolted room where the library stored its rare and arcane texts. And a dozen other rooms, as well, private reading rooms that no one ever used, tiny nichelike places where a boy could hide for years and no one find him.

Jason hurried to the remotest of those rooms, stepped inside, and closed and locked the door behind him.

And crouched in a corner with the lights off, waiting for the world to go away.

Trying and trying to think how he could ever hide from the Dark Man for a lifetime—

Not that there was really any need.

Because the place that hid him didn't hide him for an hour, let alone a year.

Forty minutes after Jason first crouched in that dark and empty nook, he heard footsteps out among the stacks. Soft and steady footsteps that sounded like someone searching—aisle by aisle, slowly, carefully. Searching for a book, that had to be, didn't it? No one could find him here, not even the Dark Man. And if they found him, they could never get to him because he'd locked the door to the reading room when he'd stepped into it.

That's what Jason told himself all the while he listened to the quiet footsteps, closer and closer, till now he heard whispering and realized that there wasn't just one set of footsteps, there were two people out there, and one of them walked, hobbling unevenly. It was the old woman, that was her walk—Jason knew it in his heart. There and then it seemed to him he'd always known it—he didn't want to know, but he knew it all the same.

The old woman.

And whispering, the Dark Man.

They'd never find him, Jason thought. They never could. But he was wrong. He knew that no matter how he tried to reassure himself.

Now he heard the sound of doors opening and closing. They were searching the study nooks, searching them methodically.

It was only a matter of time before they found him.

He had to run.

Battering on a great heavy door, now—a door that would not open. That had to be the bolted room that held the books of magic, didn't it?

It had to be.

The great door shattered, and alarms went off all around the library and among campus security, but no one answered them. Security was on vacation or dulled to numbness or maybe the Dark Man whispered words to blind and deafen them to all alarm—the Dark Man could do that, Jason knew. Everybody knows about the Dark Man; the stories go around in Arkham like ghost stories go around in normal cities. The Dark Man can do anything, almost, you can't fight him and you can't run, all that anyone can do is hope he doesn't notice.

After a long while the sound of doors opening and closing resumed as the Dark Man finished searching the bolted room and went back to search the study nooks toward Jason.

I should have run while they were in there, Jason thought when he heard them coming toward him. It was true, he should have, but he'd hoped against hope that security would hear the alarms and come to save him, but they never did.

And now they were in the room next to him, and Jason heard the old woman whisper, *"I can feel him, Nyarlathotep, he's close enough to touch—I would know his presence in a multitude. He's mine, you hear?"* —and the response, *"He will die now, Nahab. We cannot contain the wretch. He will feed us, he will die."*

Jason felt an awful chill when he heard the Dark Man say that, but he took some comfort in the words because they meant that he'd be free in a way even if he had to die, and that was better than living as a creature of the night, wasn't it?

As the Dark Man tried the door to Jason's cubicle and discovered it was locked.

"We've found him," the Dark Man said. He sounded triumphal, self-satisfied. Bloodthirsty.

Jason should have been afraid. But he wasn't—he wasn't afraid of anything if it meant that he was free in one way or another.

A powerful kick on the door, and the whole thing flew in at Jason, filling the room with light.

"There he is," the Dark Man said. *"Just as I knew."*

Jason blinked and blinked at the sudden brightness, but he didn't try to run.

Didn't even move.

The Dark Man took a great and wicked dagger from his belt, a dagger still gleaming wet with Dan Mazurewicz's blood, and began to walk toward Jason Laidlaw.

"Beg for mercy, child," the Dark Man said, smiling. *"Perhaps I will be kind."*

Jason didn't say a word.

"He is mine, Nyarlathotep. If he must be taken, let me do the taking."

The Dark Man shook his head. He didn't pause, not for an instant.

"I must know that he is gone, Nahab. I must feel his life bleed through my blade."

The Dark Man reached Jason and stooped to take him by the collar, lift him high—

"Beg, boy."

Jason looked down on the Dark Man from high in the air. And shook his head. "No," he said, and he waited for the end.

And the Dark Man lowered Jason and pressed him to the wall.

And brought his knife high to plunge it through the child's breast.

Jason heard the end come to him as an explosion, a great blasting thundering sound that shattered the world and everything around him; and as he died, he felt the blood jetting all around him as he dropped lifeless to the floor.

But death and darkness never came for Jason, no matter how that was the end.

After a moment that lasted longer than a lifetime, he realized that the knife had never touched him. He was alive and whole, and when he looked up he saw Miss Gilman and Ms. Mason standing in the doorway, staring at him. Ms. Mason had a smoking pistol in her hand, and the old woman and the Dark Man were bleeding headless corpses lying on the floor not far from Jason.

It would have been a hard thing to explain if the police had ever taken a report. But they never did because there wasn't any need.

For even as Jason shuddered and trembled and wailed at the loss and the emancipation that had come to him, the corpses began to fume and roil round him, filling the air with noxious vapor that made it hard to breathe.

Smoked roiled and fumed for a good long moment, till the air cleared—

And when the air was clear, the bodies of the old woman and the Dark Man were gone.

In September the hospital lost heart, and called Professor Laidlaw to suggest that it was time to take his wife off life support.

He told the administrator who made the call to go to hell. He hung the phone up before she had a moment to respond.

Early in October he got a call from the hospital's lawyer, telling him that they were starting legal proceedings to have life support withdrawn against his wishes.

"You can't do that," Abe Laidlaw said. "I know you can't. Don't try it."

The lawyer laughed at him. "You're mistaken, Professor Laidlaw," he said. "We've got a court date next week."

Abe Laidlaw swore at the man as he slammed down the phone.

He didn't need this nonsense. He didn't want to deal with it, didn't even want to cope with it. But it wasn't like he had a choice. He called his lawyer—Ben Martin, the same lawyer who'd handled the failed adoption work for Jason, the deed papers when they'd bought the row house, a dozen different minor legal matters across the years—and learned they'd need a legal specialist to deal with the hospital. Somewhere in the course of that conversation he realized that he'd fallen into another trap, a circumstance that wanted to devour every waking moment of the next six months, and he had the baby, and he had to see after Jason, and he had to keep working or they'd starve, and he didn't have the time or energy to cope.

But there was nothing else that he could do, short of blowing out his own brains, and that would still leave Jason and the baby and poor half-dead Carol in the lurch.

So he asked Ben Martin to do what he could, and called the specialist his lawyer had directed him to. And left a message with an answering service, and put down the phone, and found himself staring vacantly at the wall for most of the afternoon.

He didn't mean to stare like that. He had work to do, and emergencies to see to, and the baby screamed and Jason needed his attention, but there was nothing left in Abe Laidlaw. He stared at the wall all broken and defeated as the world rolled over him and past him and the goddamned lawyer never called him back.

Late in the afternoon the vacancy receded, and Abe Laidlaw began to grow angry. After a while he picked up the phone, called the hospital administrator, and told the woman off but good.

"So help me God," Abe Laidlaw said, "so help me God, if you do anything to my wife, I'll swear out a criminal complaint. I won't stop until I see every last one of you in jail, you hear me?"

The administrator hung up on him, of course.

And Abe Laidlaw lowered his face into his hands. And cried.

Everything that could possibly go wrong with the lawyers and the hospital and the court appointment went as wrong as it possibly could. The specialist never did return Abe Laidlaw's call, and when Ben Martin asked around to find out why, it turned out that the man had been run down that afternoon by an out-of-control truck. So Ben Martin made a few more phone calls, trying to find another capable specialist, and meanwhile went to a Federal judge in Salem to get an injunction. That judge had a heart attack on the bench in the midst of granting the injunction, and before anyone knew what was going on, three more days had passed. Ben Martin went to state court in Arkham and managed to get the hospital's hearing postponed, and postponed again, and postponed a third time on October 31.

Things are never right in Arkham on Halloween. And that year they went as wrong for Abraham Laidlaw as they ever could.

His lawyer got all three postponements without a terrible lot of trouble—even the third one, the one the judge granted that Halloween. At first, while they were in the judge's chambers, it all seemed to be working out just fine. The judge (a kindly gentleman named Wilcox) seemed very understanding, even patient, and Ben Martin said he'd finally managed to find an experienced specialist willing and even eager to take the case. But after they left the courthouse, nothing happened the way it was supposed to.

When he got home, he found a message on his machine from the hospital—a message from one of Carol's doctors, saying that the disconnection would go through as scheduled at 7:30. Abe Laidlaw returned that call immediately, but all he got was another answering service. He tried calling hospital administration, but it was 5:30 and the paper pushers had all gone home for the evening; he tried to call his lawyer, but Ben Martin wasn't home from the courthouse yet.

And looked up after a series of pointless and unanswered calls to see that it was 6:15, and there was hardly any time at all to stop the bastards.

The Laidlaws' row house was near the water, three blocks from the Miskatonic University campus, and Miskatonic University Community Hospital was seven blocks on the far side of the school, at the crest of Hill Street where it looks over Hangman's Brook. That was far enough that it made more sense to drive than it did to walk. But there was never decent parking around the hospital, even in the rental lots, and Abe Laidlaw knew he didn't have the hour it would take to drive crosstown during evening drive time, find a place to park, and walk back to the hospital.

So he ran.

Through traffic and against the lights where he had to; pushing through the crowds around the theaters that served the university's students. Twice he nearly got into fights when he jostled burly young fraternity men, but there wasn't any time for fighting, no time to swear back at them, no time for anything at all—

He got to the hospital's front door at twenty minutes till seven and hurried past the front desk, ignoring the lady in the pink dress who wanted him to sign in; please, sir, it's after visiting hours, don't you realize that? And the damned elevator took five minutes to show up, isn't it always slow when you're in a hurry *God damn it hurry,* he swore under his breath he was frantic the sons of bitches were about to kill his wife she was on the seventh floor where were the stairs could he climb the stairs before the elevator showed up he bet he could but no, no, the light went on and the bell rang and the door opened it was seven till seven, oh Christ—

Into the elevator, pushed the button, and then the interminable ride that only took two minutes it was five of when the door opened and he saw the nurses' station and.

And.

And they saw him, and when they looked at him, their eyes were full of dread, and Abe Laidlaw knew that he was already too late.

"Mr. Laidlaw," the head nurse said when she saw him bolting out of the elevator, running toward his dead wife's hospital room. "Mr. Laidlaw—"

Abe Laidlaw didn't answer her. He didn't even pause the moment it would have taken to hear the words she had to say. When the door opened, he came out of the elevator *fast,* and he didn't stop for anything, not for anything at all until he reached Carol's room.

When he got there, he found the room dark and still, so strange and somber after all those months of the blinking lights and the dripping tubes and the whirring pumps that seemed to fill the room. The man Abe Laidlaw always remembered as Doctor Death was at his wife's bedside, stooped beside her, looking in her eyes.

He wasn't Doctor Death, of course. His name was Simmons or King or something Abe Laidlaw never could remember; he was the hospital's brain-death specialist, the man who looked into the eyes of comatose patients and tried to persuade their relatives to pull the plug—someone has to do that, you realize. Hospital costs are soaring, we need to economize where we can.

"Her mind was gone," said Doctor Death as he saw Abe Laidlaw stand in the doorway, gaping at him. "There was nothing left to save."

Doctor Death was a balding sepulchral man with gaunt skin and thick dark-rimmed glasses, a man who looked as sallow and as lifeless as his customary charges.

"What have you done?" Abe Laidlaw asked. "If you've killed her, so help me God, I'll break your neck, I will, I promise you I will."

Doctor Death scowled. "She's breathing, Mr. Laidlaw. But you can believe me when I tell you that it doesn't matter. No one recovers from her state."

Abe Laidlaw felt his jaw go slack, felt his mouth open wide enough for his breath to become a forlorn sigh.

"You did it," he whispered. *"You killed my Carol."* And then and there it didn't matter how there were half a dozen nurses standing in the hall behind him, watching and witnessing everything he did. He lurched toward the doctor without even thinking about it. Grabbed the man's limp white collar and pulled him close enough to smell. "I'm going to kill you," he said so quietly that only the two of them could hear.

One of the nurses said, "Mr. Laidlaw, I'm going to have to call security," but Abe Laidlaw hardly heard her.

How could he hear the nurse when he was so focused on the doctor? Shoving the pale scrawny bald man away as he kept hold of his collar, pulling him back again so hard and fast it almost broke his neck. Pulling him forward with his left arm as his right arm swept up to smash the weaselly little bastard's nose, blood everywhere, and a sound like steak when you pound it with a mallet. Someone screamed, *security, security,* they screamed, but security took the longest time to get there and none of the nurses had the nerve to raise a hand to save the fish-faced doctor, not a one of them. Abe Laidlaw damn near did kill him before the guards showed up to drag him away.

Nasty men, those guards. They all but dragged him through the corridors of the hospital, joking among themselves about what they wanted to do with him.

God only knew what they would have done to him if his lawyer hadn't showed up at the hospital just as they were putting him in their unmarked car. But Ben Martin did show up, and thank God for him.

He saw the security men, and he asked them what was going on, and they said they were taking him to the police station, which was a lie, of course. But once they'd told it, they had to do it, not least because Ben Martin got in his own car and followed them the whole way crosstown.

To the police station, where an officer named Andrew Mazurewicz took his fingerprints and photographed him. Mazurewicz had words with the hospital security men when they handed Abe Laidlaw over. Cross words—he knew those men, and he didn't seem to like them at all.

Ben Martin called a judge he knew and managed to get him to set bail that night. Abe Laidlaw thought it was a good thing he did, too—he'd asked the sitter to stay when he got home to find the call from the hospital on the phone machine, and she was a good, mature, reliable girl, a girl he knew he could trust to watch Jason and the baby, even on a night like Halloween in Arkham. But reliable only goes so far, and the poor girl had been working since he'd gone to court early that afternoon. He had to get back and see after her, and he knew he had to hurry—

No, he thought he had to hurry.

But he didn't.

Because the truth was that it was already too late by the time the judge set bail at 10:00 P.M., and by the time he left the Arkham jail at 11:15, there was not a hope left in the world.

For his son.

For his foster son.

Nor even for his brain-dead wife.

Jason Laidlaw took a long nap that Halloween afternoon. When he woke at dusk, he woke to the sound of flies whispering around him in the twilight air.

A dozen flies, maybe more, dancing up and back to fill the air within his room.

Later he knew why those flies were there and what they meant. But that afternoon, as he woke, they were only annoying bits of blackness, bothering the air.

Jason batted at the flies as he rolled out of his bed. Enoch was crying somewhere—it sounded like the living room, but it was hard to know from here.

Out of bed. Out of his room. Down the hall to the stairway that led to the ground floor of the row house, and there was the baby-sitter, sitting on the sofa holding Enoch and trying to comfort the baby. The TV was on, but the sound was mute, and the baby-sitter wasn't watching anyway, she was too busy singing to the baby. It didn't really matter how she sang; the baby didn't care. It never did any good when he was in a mood—nothing could comfort him.

"I'm hungry," Jason said. "I'll hold the baby if you can make us dinner."

The baby-sitter looked up at him.

"Are you sure you can?" she asked. "Enoch's in an awful temper."

Jason shrugged. "I never drop him," he said. "I don't think I could make him quiet, but he likes me pretty good."

The baby-sitter frowned. Bit her lip. She looked uncertain, worn, and haggard. "All right," she said. "If you're sure."

Jason started down the stairs. Halfway there he thought he smelled a diaper, an awful one, like the baby had eaten rotten eggs or something. "I'll change him, too," he said. "I know how to do that."

If the baby-sitter heard that, she didn't answer it. Probably she didn't hear; she looked about as distracted as an older girl can be. When Jason reached the couch, she handed him the baby eagerly and hurried away to the kitchen in such a rush that it looked like she was afraid Jason would change his mind.

Not that Jason would. He liked the baby, and liked to hold him even when he was in a snit.

"We've got to change you, Enoch," he said. "I think you made an awful mess." And he smiled wide to make a funny face, the kind of face that made the baby laugh when he wasn't full of rage.

Enoch hardly noticed. He cried and cried and cried—something was bothering him bad, the diaper, probably, or something, God knew what.

Jason carried the baby to the downstairs changing table—Dad had set it up in the big empty closet off the foyer—found a fresh diaper and the baby wipes. Arranged the still-screaming ten-month-old on the table, and took off the old diaper. . . .

To find that it was clean.

Empty. Dry, too.

Maybe the baby had gas? Awful gas, if that was what it was. The whole downstairs reeked like rotten eggs.

Jason closed up the old diaper, picked up the baby, and carried him back to the living room. What was it Dad gave the baby when he had gas? A bottle of warm water? Something like that. They'd have to go to the kitchen to get one, even if that meant bothering the poor terrorized baby-sitter, but it wasn't like he could let the baby suffer for her sake, was it?

But just as Jason passed the sofa, Enoch stopped his crying. Four soft little sobs trailing off, and then he giggled.

That was Enoch for you: when he had to cry, he cried; when he wanted to stop, he stopped, and if there were reasons for it either way, nobody ever could be sure of them.

Jason set the baby on the floor among his toys, hoping that he'd play. But he didn't. He hardly noticed the toys, in fact—he sat on the floor staring at nothing and smiling quietly for the longest time, and then he turned and looked up at Jason.

Baby Enoch watched him and watched him, almost expectantly, as if he expected Jason to sprout wings and fly at any moment, watched him—

Until something thundered in the kitchen, an awful calamitous crashing sound as though the poor baby-sitter had brought the entire cupboard full of pots and pans down upon herself, and for just a half a moment Jason forgot all about the baby watching him so intently. And hurried across the living room to the kitchen to see what was the matter.

He never should have done that.

Never in a million years.

What Jason should have done the moment that he heard that sound was take the baby in his arms and run for all that he was worth. It would have saved lives and pain and grief and an endlessness of torment if he'd run.

But it didn't even occur to him. He didn't know what had happened in the kitchen, and couldn't know, all he knew was the thunder and calamity, and did the baby-sitter need help, and did he need to call 911 and get an ambulance, and—

And Jason Laidlaw flung open the kitchen door to see the horror that had borne him.

The witch was the first thing Jason saw when he opened the kitchen door. She was still bloody and broken, her skull still visibly gored by the bullet that apparently had killed her three months before, but she seemed as nearly alive as she ever had. She was standing at the kitchen table, a few feet from the refrigerator. The baby-sitter was stretched out across the table, bound by her wrists and ankles to the table's legs. The wall behind the table was wide open, literally shattered—ripped wide by brute force until a grown man could walk through it without stooping.

And then a grown man *did* step through the broken wall—not any grown man, but the Dark Man. He was as disfigured as the old woman—disfigured, scarred, and bloody with unhealing wounds, but his wounds had no more effect on him than the old woman's had on her: nothing grieved the Dark Man, and nothing ever could.

"You," the old woman said.

"Kill him," the Dark Man told her. "Hurry."

The old woman frowned. Hesitated. "Yes," she said, "I must."

Jason should've run. He knew that even as she came toward him, arms outstretched, watching him hypnotically, whispering words to him that he didn't want to understand. But how could he run from her? She was a thing he prized despite himself, despite all sense and prudence, and the sight of her *alive* (if that was the word for her condition) filled his heart with joy and dread in equal measures.

When she wrapped her gnarled hands around his throat, he didn't resist her. He wanted to, but even more than he wanted that, more than he wanted to run from the old woman or lash out at her ugliness, he loved the old woman, and he wanted to be close to her.

He didn't know why he loved her. He didn't think he ought to. He hardly knew her! She was a presence at the corners of his dreams, a shadow lurking at the margin of his life, and love is a thing that grows with you because you know the person and come to love the things they mean to you.

Jason couldn't have explained that to anybody, but he knew it in his heart as clearly as he knew his name. But no matter what his heart knew, it loved the old woman as dearly as he loved his life.

No, he loved her more dearly than he loved his life. He knew that as her hands tightened and tightened around his neck, and the world grayed, and the baby screamed, and he finally found the heart to struggle against the darkness enveloping him, but by then it was too late.

And then the darkness swallowed him, and it didn't matter how or who or what or why or anything else.

As Jason Laidlaw found his peace.

It didn't last, of course.

Jason Laidlaw wasn't born to live a peaceful life, and he wasn't meant to have an easy death, either; if he died when the old woman throttled him, that death did not contain him.

Perhaps it never could.

Or maybe the witch never murdered him at all. That happens sometimes, you know: a killer wraps her hands around the throat that is the object of her spite, and crushes and presses until the victim shudders, pales, slackens, and goes still.

As Jason did.

But that alone won't kill a healthy child. The stillness and the seeming death come a long hard moment before extinction, and an impatient killer can neglect to follow through her kill.

Who can say? Certainly the crone had killed her own before, and knew the art of strangulation. If she left him on the kitchen floor alive, it may be that she did it purposely.

Perhaps she did.

Whether it was by accident, miracle, or design, Jason Laidlaw woke cold and aching on the kitchen floor at 11:00 P.M. that Halloween, just an hour before Hallowmass.

He woke to see the baby-sitter still tied to the kitchen table, and almost dead from the slow uneven bleeding of the straight slits across her wrists.

"Enoch . . .?" he called. Or tried to, anyway; what came from his throat was more nearly a hoarse rasping than it was a call.

The baby did not answer.

Jason knew that he was gone even before he rushed into the living room to look for him; before he tore through the house, running up and down the stairs on legs so limp and unsteady that he nearly stumbled on his own feet as he called and called after his brother who was gone—

He spent five minutes searching before he called 911. It was good he did it then; if he'd waited much longer, the baby-sitter might've bled to death.

A lot of things happened at eleven o'clock that Halloween. Some of them happened at the Laidlaws' row house near the water, and some of them happened down at Arkham jail. But there were things happening elsewhere, too. In the locked rare-volumes room of the Miskatonic University library, for instance.

And at Miskatonic University Community Hospital. When the night-shift nurse on 7–W made her eleven o'clock rounds, she found Carol Laidlaw missing.

She didn't think much of the woman's absence. She knew what'd happened that day (every nurse in the hospital knew—it was the subject of much gossip), and she figured that poor Mrs. Laidlaw had expired sometime on the second shift, and her nurse had neglected to report it on the log.

But she was wrong.

At 11:15 she got back to her station and double-checked the log.

Found no entries concerning Mrs. Laidlaw and made a couple calls to learn where the woman had been transferred.

It took her until 11:30 to come to the conclusion that she hadn't been transferred at all.

And five more minutes to conclude that something was seriously wrong.

Five more minutes still to telephone the physician on call and then security.

It was 11:40 by then. Too late to stop the Hallowmass, even if anyone had known to stop it.

The police in Arkham ordinarily aren't especially responsive folks. They get a lot of strange calls and a lot of prank emergencies, and they don't rush to answer any of them. What would be the point? There's not much that the city's mundane police can do about the outré nature of their watch, and there's even less that they can do about mischief on Halloween.

But when Jason Laidlaw called 911 with his voice all rasping and his words so incoherent, when he said, *The baby's gone, there's blood everywhere, the baby-sitter's dying,* he struck a chord with the 911 operator. She didn't know whether or not he was another hoax—she'd had three-dozen prank calls that night, at least three dozen of them—but she knew that she didn't dare take the chance.

And hit the panic button.

Hard.

The first cruiser got to the Laidlaws' row house three minutes after Jason dialed 911.

The ambulance got there four minutes later.

When the officers in the cruiser saw Jason and the baby-sitter and the blood and the broken wall, they got on their radio and called for help.

A lot of help.

Twenty minutes after Jason Laidlaw dialed 911, there were a dozen cruisers outside his door, and more on the way.

Captain Andrew Mazurewicz heard that call, and he recognized the address. When he did, he hurried out of the station to find Abe Laidlaw and Ben Martin just getting in the lawyer's car.

"Professor Laidlaw," he called when he spotted them in the parking lot. "Professor Laidlaw, you'd better let me escort you home. Your son just called nine-one-one. I think you're going to need to be there in a hurry—the officer who just radioed in makes it sound like a serious situation."

Abe Laidlaw stared at him wide-eyed and slack-faced, exactly the way a deer stares at the headlights of an oncoming car.

Ben Martin made an exasperated noise as he brought his fist down on the roof of the car. "Christ," he said. "Jesus Christ Almighty, what now?"

No one answered him. Maybe no one heard him; Abe Laidlaw was too numb to understand, and Captain Mazurewicz had already gone to get a cruiser.

"C'mon, Abe," Ben Martin said. "Get in the car. We're going to have to face this."

Abe Laidlaw said, "Car," but he didn't seem to understand. He didn't move, either.

So Ben Martin got behind the wheel and reached across the passenger seat to pull Abe Laidlaw in and slam the passenger door after him.

Captain Mazurewicz pulled around in the cruiser, lights flashing, siren wailing, and signaled them to follow.

It only took five minutes to get from the station to the Laidlaw house with the cruiser opening their way. Abe Laidlaw spent most of that time sitting slack and broken in the passenger seat, staring listlessly as the city sped by.

And then they reached Miskatonic University.

When they got to Miskatonic, Abe Laidlaw came suddenly to life. Ben Martin glanced away from the road a moment to see him gesturing at the campus, at the road, at Martin—he was trying to say something, wasn't he? Trying to speak and finding no words, agitated as sin. . . .

"In the robe," Abe Laidlaw said. "The man in the robe."

"What's the matter, Abe?" Ben Martin asked. "You okay?"

"Stop," Abe Laidlaw said at last. "Stop the car. We've got to follow him. He's going to the library."

Ben Martin frowned. That was crazy talk, he thought—there was something wrong at Laidlaw's house, something seriously wrong with his two young sons. The man was confused, that was all.

Ben Martin didn't stop the car.

Ben Martin should've stopped the car.

And then they were past the Miskatonic campus, and Abe Laidlaw was sputtering; but only for a long moment before they began to ease their way along the street before the row house—so many police cars, half of them with their lights on, flashing, blinding, distracting them, and then Ben Martin stopped his car, and Abe Laidlaw was home.

He got out of the car without being prompted and started moving like he had a destination in mind. He would have gone right to it, Ben Martin thought, if young Jason hadn't seen him and started shouting.

"Daddy!" the boy shouted, running across the lawn. "Daddy, Enoch's gone, and the baby-sitter, the baby-sitter—"

The boy had his arms around his foster father now, holding him—it wasn't like a hug, no, it was something more desperate than that, as though the child thought the world would whirl away if he loosened his grip upon the man.

"I know, Jason," Abe Laidlaw said. "I'm going to find him."

"I want to come, too," Jason said. "I want to find him."

Abe Laidlaw hesitated. "No," he said. "You stay here with Mr. Martin, Jason." He looked at his lawyer, gestured at the boy. "Keep an eye on him, Ben. Please. I'm going to be a while."

He spoke with a quiet sadness that made Ben Martin think he might not ever return. Ben Martin wanted to tell him—something. Anything, whatever it took to keep him from walking into the trouble that they both saw coming.

But he didn't know where to start, and down inside he knew that the words would be wasted, and wrong, too, because there are things that a man has to face even if it means the end of him.

As Abe Laidlaw turned and walked away without another word.

Jason listened to his father, but he didn't mind him. He watched him wandering away from the row house, watched him stagger down the block until he disappeared into the night. . . .

And the moment that his father's lawyer turned away—when his foster father was all but out of sight in the darkness—Jason Laidlaw ran.

Into the darkness, and the night, and the horror that waited for them all in the basement of the Miskatonic University Library.

It took him a long time to catch up. So long, in fact, that he never caught up with his father entirely. By the time the boy was in shouting distance, the man was walking through the broken and unattended library door—

"Jason!" someone whispered urgently, and the boy looked around to see a hand beckon to him from inside a hedge.

No, Jason thought. *There's no time. I've got to follow him—*

As Miss Gilman peered out at him from the shadows and the greenery, *"Hide,"* she whispered, more urgently still.

Jason hesitated just an instant longer, but even that instant nearly was too long. He crossed the library common to Miss Gilman's hedge, intending to ask her what was the matter, and when he got close enough to touch, she grabbed his arm and hauled him into the hedge just barely in time.

As the Celebrants began to filter through the common, all of them dressed in gray hooded robes that hid their clothes and faces—

"What are you doing here, Jason?" Miss Gilman asked.

Ms. Mason didn't give him a moment to answer before she responded herself. "I told you he'd be here," she said. "The boy, his foster, and one other, yet to come."

"Who?"

Ms. Mason shook her head. "If I knew that, I wouldn't be here," she said. "There wouldn't be a need."

"My brother's in there, isn't he?" Jason asked. "That's why my father came here. I know it."

Miss Gilman frowned at him as she placed her finger on his lips. "Be quiet, child," she said. "The Celebrants will hear you."

She gestured at the ground, and Jason looked down to see two big rifles—army rifles, the kind the boy had only seen in combat movies—and a plastic jug of water.

"We're going in to get your brother, Jason," Ms. Mason said. "You shouldn't be here. It's dangerous. People will die tonight—we may die tonight." She hesitated. "But you are your mother's son, and if you think you need to be here, we won't stop you."

Jason didn't hesitate; he knew exactly what he had to do, and no one could have stopped him no matter how they tried.

"I'm going with you," he said. "You know I have to, don't you?"

Ms. Mason nodded. "I know," she said.

She took the rifles off the ground, handed one to Miss Gilman. "Carry the Holy Water if you like, Jason. Use it as you need to, but don't use it all at once."

There are some who'd tell you that Holy Water is no tool to fight the Celebrants in Arkham. Such fools are those! Self-important librarians who keep the keys to the city's arcane tomes; vainglorious panderers to Yog-Sothothery! They ought to know that magic roots up all around us, and not only in their musty treatises of doubtful erudition. When a priest with the gift, the sight, and the truth puts a blessing on the water, it's a blessing true as any curse could be, or truer.

And the water Jason Laidlaw carried with him on that night was blessed powerfully indeed.

As the boy hefted the jug, the last of the Celebrants made her way through the library doors.

Miss Gilman pushed her way out of the hedge.

Ms. Mason hurried into the common only a step behind her.

Jason let them get halfway to the library door before he started after them. He wasn't sure why. Maybe he had a premonition of what was to happen to them.

Or maybe he was afraid.

Surely there was reason to be afraid of what waited in the library.

Jason Laidlaw started out across the common.

Miss Gilman and Ms. Mason didn't bother with flashlights. They didn't really need them out in the common, where there was moonlight and illumination from the streetlamps half a block away. But inside the library it was absolutely dark; when Jason saw them step through the door, he saw them disappear into the blackness.

When he reached the door himself, he hesitated again. Of course, he hesitated! It wasn't that he was afraid of the dark, but the lightless nightness in that place was no ordinary gloom.

He stepped hesitantly into the dark, hoping that his eyes would adjust to the darkness of that place. But they never did, no matter how he waited, and now there were sounds ahead of him, screaming, maybe, or maybe that was music, and those were crashing sounds like something falling far away—

There wasn't time to hesitate a moment longer. Jason hurried into the dark, trying to remember how far it was from the door across the library's wide lobby, through the first-floor stacks to the stair at the back of the building. He couldn't remember, exactly, but at least the direction was obvious—and then, as he drew closer to the back, there were voices, chanting voices that guided him through the dark. . . .

They didn't guide him very well. They couldn't tell him when he was about to stumble into a pillar or a bookcase; they couldn't show him the litter and debris strewn all across the library floor.

Couldn't show him the bodies that he stepped on twice when he got close to the stairs.

He almost cried when he stepped on the first one. Was that his father, dead before he ever reached the bolted room? Ms. Mason? Miss Gilman?

Then someone started shooting downstairs, and each shot sent flashes of gunpowder to illuminate the stairs. It wasn't light enough or long enough to guide him down the stairs, but the flashes told him where the stairs were, anyway, and Jason hurried toward them.

Reached them. Grabbed the banister, and started down—

—as screams and shouts and more blasts of gunfire echoed up toward him, and now the stairs went bright and dark with strobes of gunlight, and Jason hurried down the second staircase toward the subsubbasement—

No.

Jason tried to run down those last stairs. But he stumbled on a body before he reached the second step, and went tumbling head over heels—

The fall probably saved his life.

For as he fell, the jug of Holy Water came open, and the stuff went splashing everywhere around him. As it splashed, it spattered on the watchers in the darkness, abominations sent to guard the stairs against any more intrusion—

They would have killed him if they could. They'd tried to kill Ms. Mason and Miss Gilman, and failed only because the caseworkers' guns had slowed them.

But Jason had no rifle, and even if he'd had one he could not have known to fire blind and wild into the menacing dark as the hair rose on the nape of his neck. The darkling peril were already in motion when Jason stumbled on the stairs; if the Holy Water hadn't washed them, they'd've devoured the boy whole in a moment. But Jason fell and the jug came open, and the Holy Water doused both those monstrous forms, setting them afire. As the boy picked himself up off the bottom stair, he saw those awful things consumed in pale blue flames, creatures like dragons in a fairy book, he thought, like fairy-tale dragons, but hatefully vile—terrible and predatory. They screamed and thrashed in agony as the fire consumed them, and all the while that they died, their eyes fixed on Jason Laidlaw, eyeing him hungrily, bellowing like thunder—

Jason crept slowly down the hall, watching the light that flickered and flashed from the bolted room that was no longer bolted. That was candlelight, wasn't it? Yes, it was, there were candles in the bolted room. Faint, unsteady candles just bright enough to show the door hanging torn from its hinges, just as it had hung the day that the old woman and the Dark Man had found him in the cubicle.

"Let go of Professor Laidlaw," Miss Gilman shouted. "Give us the man and his son, or we'll kill you all."

Jason eased himself toward the door, slowly, slowly, careful to stay in the shadows, and now he could see Miss Gilman and Ms. Mason standing just inside the doorway. Beyond them the room was full of Celebrants dressed in their hooded robes, and there was Enoch on a reading table in the center of the room. There were great fat tallow candles on either side of the baby—it was an altar, wasn't it? They'd made the table up to be their altar, they were going to kill him—

No no no no . . .

They were going to sacrifice Enoch. Jason had known it in his heart for hours, he had to stop them—

And then he saw how the baby lay so silent and so still, so motionless that Jason thought he must be dead, he was already dead dead dead dead and Jason almost screamed—

Until he saw the gentle motion of his breathing. The baby was alive or half alive at least, there was still time for him—

But there wasn't time for Jason's foster father. Look, look on the floor—oh God, oh God—Daddy lying in a bloody heap beside the altar, he had to be dead, nobody could bleed that much and live—

But he was alive, look, look at him trying to climb to his feet, reaching toward the table that was an altar, reaching—

As the tall Celebrant stepped toward him and kicked him in the ribs.

Kicked so hard that the force of the blow lifted him off the floor and threw him halfway across the room.

As Miss Gilman swore, and said, "I told you to let them *go,*" and turned her rifle on the Celebrant.

And fired.

Three rounds that caught him square below the breast, bullets that should have torn him clean in half.

But did not even seem to touch him.

The tall Celebrant laughed aloud and turned back the hood of his cowl—revealing his face.

The Dark Man's misshapen and disfigured face.

"You," said Ms. Mason, and now she turned her gun on him, too, firing again and again, half a dozen bullets that should have torn the head off of his shoulders—

—but passed through him as though he were a shadow of himself—

And maybe he was.

The Dark Man laughed and laughed, and now he started toward Miss Gilman and Ms. Mason, arms outstretched, steady and unyielding—

"You surprised me with that trinket once," he said. *"But I know you now, child. Your toy cannot afflict me."*

As the Dark Man smiled.

As the room filled with blazing thunder from the social workers' guns, as Ms. Mason and Miss Gilman held their fire steady, blasting and blasting the Dark Man—

—to no effect.

As the Dark Man drew steadily closer and closer, close enough, now, to put his hands around the barrels of the rifles.

And pull them from the social workers' hands.

Jason ran when he saw that—ran straight at the Dark Man, with the jug of Holy Water cradled in both hands.

Stopped in the doorway to heave the contents of the jug at the Dark Man and soak him, head to toe.

When the Holy Water hit him, the Dark Man caught fire, just as the dragonlike things on the stairway had, and now that creature out of night and fretful legend screamed and shuddered like a wounded child as he burst afire, great writhing tendrils of blue flame dancing up around him, consuming him—

—as Miss Gilman and Ms. Mason pulled away from brightness and the stench and the fire, and now every Celebrant Jason could see had her arms raised high to shield her eyes from the unnatural brightness of the fire—

Not all the Celebrants, Jason realized—all of them but one. The one who stood stooped beside the altar table, that one screamed as she rushed to the Dark Man, and now she put her arms around him to comfort his agony, cradling him as though he were her child.

And now the hood of her robe fell away, and Jason saw that it was the old woman from his dreams, the woman he loved and despised and feared as he could fear nothing else—

—sobbing, holding the Dark Man, trying to comfort him as he twisted and moaned, shivering in her arms—

—as then the Dark Man went still, and died a death unfit for man or beast, a death of agony and pain and bleakness made so vast that it could fill forever in a day.

When he was completely still, the old woman looked up at Jason with her eyes as full of hate and malice as any eyes could ever be.

"You've killed him, you little wretch," she whispered.

And stood. And started toward Jason.

Jason knew that he should run. Certainly he could run; neither magic nor any physical restraint held him in his place. But the awful bond that bound his heart to hers held him as surely as chains and magic ever could.

As the old woman came for him.

And took him in her hands.

And lifted him off the floor.

And hit him.

Again and again and again.

Miss Gilman tried to stop her. She put her hand on the old woman's shoulder and tried to pull her away from Jason. But Miss Gilman's hands had no more effect on the old woman than her bullets had affected the Dark Man.

As the old woman whispered *killed him killed him killed him,* holding Jason by his ribs, just below his shoulders, and heaving him up—

—to slam him down against the doorjamb.

Jason's head hit the doorframe, hard, and the world spun around him—

—but he did not struggle to be free.

She would have beaten him to death if she'd gone on a moment longer.

But she didn't.

Because a voice came out of the darkness in the hall as Jason's head hit the doorjamb.

"Keziah Mason," the voice said.

It was thin and reedy, and very, very weak, but Jason recognized it all the same.

Of course, he recognized it. He would have recognized that voice anytime, anywhere, no matter how long it was since he'd last heard it.

No matter how he had not heard it in almost a year.

It was the voice of Carol Laidlaw, the mother of his life, returned from the place that lies beyond this world but not yet within the hereafter.

"Let go of my son, Keziah Mason," Jason's foster mother said.

As the old woman turned to face darkness in the hall, and said, "Your son?" She sounded furious, angrier than she'd been at Jason. "*Your* son?"

"My son," Carol Laidlaw said.

And stepped forward from the darkness to take Jason from the old woman's arms. It wasn't as hard as it should have been. Where the old woman could have struggled to hold the boy, she hardly resisted; when Carol Laidlaw wrapped her frail arms around the boy, the witch could not resist her.

As Carol Laidlaw pulled Jason from the witch's arms and cradled him for the longest moment.

The old woman hissed in rage and consternation, but she never tried to retrieve him.

"You've stolen him," she said. "*Stolen* him."

"I never could," Carol Laidlaw said. "You gave him up the day that he was born."

And she kissed Jason on the cheek, and rested him on her shoulder. "We're leaving this place, Jason," Carol Laidlaw said. "As soon as I get your father and your brother."

As she pushed past the old woman and started toward the altar.

Or tried to.

She didn't get three steps into the room before the old woman overcame the paralysis of her rage and lunged at her, grabbing her hair from behind so hard that the force of it pulled Carol Laidlaw off her feet—

Jason saw it all in slow motion. First as he looked at the old woman over his foster mother's shoulder, watching her shriveled clawlike hand stabbing toward his eyes, she was going to claw his eyes out, she was going to blind him, but no, no, the talons darted past him entirely, into his foster mother's hair; and now her head whipped back and the world tilted dizzily around them and his foster mother cried out in pain and surprise as Jason dropped out of her arms onto the floor—

For a long moment all he could see was the carpet rushing toward him so slowly, the carpet and the all-but-empty jug of Holy Water. He was falling onto the floor exactly where the jug had fallen when the old woman took hold of him—

As Jason hit ground and tried to get back up to his knees, shaking himself, looking up to see—

The witch.

His foster mother.

His foster mother prone on the floor, struggling to get up but so weak that she was hardly struggling at all as the old woman stooped over her, still holding her hair, pulling up and whipping down to smash poor Carol Laidlaw's head into the floor again.

Against the floor. And again, and again.

And Jason said, "No," whispered it, almost, his voice was hardly loud enough to hear, and louder now, no matter how hard the effort was: "Don't hurt her," he said. "Don't hurt my mommy, I love my mommy, please don't hurt her."

It wasn't anything he meant to say, and when he heard the words they sounded so—*wrong*. But he said them, and the old woman heard them, and she reacted as though he'd burned her with an iron.

"Mommy?" she asked. *"She's not your mother!"*

"She is, too," Jason told her. "And I'm not going to let you hurt her."

The crone glared at Jason with blood and fire in her eyes. She swore at him. "I'm going to kill this little harlot," she said. "And then I'm going to kill you, you wretched little ingrate."

As she drew a great bright dagger from her belt.

And raised it above her head.

And brought it down.

Later it seemed to Jason that the knife fell through the air forever, slow and unstoppable as he screamed stop, stop, but he could not speak. For an instant that hung on and on he could not even move, could not think or feel or hear, he watched mute and dumb as the knife fell and fell into his mother's breast—

And then he saw it.

The jug.

There in the corner of his eye, not far from his mother's legs, the all-but-empty jug of Holy Water. There was at least a cup of fluid left in it—

The paralysis of dread released him, and Jason dove for the jug, grabbing it by the handle, hauled it back to warn the old woman off—

But there was no time. The knife was fast and he was slow and all that he could really do was look up just in time to see the blade plunge down into his mother's breast—

As Carol Laidlaw found the presence of mind to roll out of harm's way, and the blade dug itself deep into the library's carpet.

The old woman swore as she yanked the blade out of the floorboards. Pulled it free, and brought it up again—

Jason shouted, *"Stop!"* and hefted the jug to threaten the old woman, to show her what he'd do if she tried to use that knife.

The witch hesitated for the time it took to laugh. "You could never hurt me, child," she said. "There is no mettle in your heart."

"I'll kill you," Jason said. "I swear I will!"

The witch laughed again. "You never would," she told him. "You never could."

"You're wrong," Jason said. "I'll kill you, I swear I will, I'll kill you if you try to hurt her."

But it was Jason who was wrong, and not the crone. For as she raised the dagger high above her head, the boy stood mute and paralyzed, unable to do anything but watch poor Carol Laidlaw die—

No.

The witch tried to bring the dagger down into Carol Laidlaw's heart, but when she did she once more found no target—for Carol Laidlaw was no longer on the floor. She was on her knees, trying to stand, and when the blade came down at her, she caught the witch's wrist and stopped it in midair.

The witch hissed and swore, eyes flickering angrily in the uneven candlelight. "Die, trollop," she said.

But Carol Laidlaw did not die.

She pushed to her feet, still holding the witch's twisting, writhing wrist, forcing it up and away so slow. As she held, as she pushed, the old woman's knife-hand twisted in her grip, and the blade caught the candlelight, reflecting in flashes that stung Jason's eyes.

"I had a dream," Carol Laidlaw said. "I had a nightmare that went on for lifetimes." Her voice was weak and reedy, quiet and uncertain. "While I dreamed, I saw you, *Nahab*. All the time."

The witch's eyes went wide. "My name," she said. "You take my name."

For a moment she seemed frightened, almost beaten. She tried to pull away, but it wasn't any use—Carol Laidlaw was on her feet now, and pressing the advantage that the moment gave her.

It wasn't much of an advantage. She trembled as she followed the witch back, a step, another, her arms shaking, her legs unsteady and buckling underneath her—

"I saw you born," she said. "I've seen you die."

That only made the witch smile. "I've seen that door and walked away from it," she said. "It does not frighten me."

"I saw that, too."

Now Carol Laidlaw pressed the witch's arm against the wall and held it there; now the knife fell out of her hand to bounce across the carpet and clatter onto the tile floor in the hallway.

"If you saw that," the witch said, "then you know you are defeated."

Carol Laidlaw smiled.

"I dreamed this moment," she said. "I know what you will do."

And for a moment she looked sad, but she did not look defeated.

As the witch whispered a prayer in that language Jason knew but could not know: *"Iä–R'lyeh!"* she whispered. *"Cthulhu fhtagn! Iä! Iä!"*

And shoved her away as easily as an adult could brush away a child.

The force of that shove threw Carol Laidlaw off her feet and sent her tumbling. When she came to rest, she lay at Jason's feet.

"And now," the witch said, "you will die."

Carol Laidlaw tried to stop her.

She tried to get back to her feet before the witch could get her hands around her throat. Tried to push her away when the witch began to strangle her; tried to hit her hard enough to make her stop. But it was pointless, hopeless; the witch was stronger than she'd seemed that moment when Carol Laidlaw pressed her hard against the wall, and nothing anyone could do would stop her.

As Carol Laidlaw struggled fitfully to die.

Jason started crying when he saw that. It made him ache to see it: the convulsions, the tremors. The stillness now as Carol Laidlaw died.

"My *mommy,*" Jason sobbed, still helpless to do anything at all. "You killed my mommy mommy mommy—"

And he wailed.

The sound of that wail found the witch deep in her heart, and she screamed at him for silence, but Jason didn't hear.

And wailed again, and wailed.

The third time that he cried out, the witch could bear no more.

She let go of Carol Laidlaw's throat for just an instant to lash out at the child, lashed out with her talonlike left hand to tear his throat out of his neck—

But she missed his throat.

She only missed it by a moment. She would have found her mark and taken it, to leave the boy a bloody ruin, if it weren't for the way he heaved and convulsed as he sobbed.

If he hadn't raised his right arm to brush away his tears at just that instant, the witch would have caught the air. She might have lost her balance, then; she'd put a lot into that blow.

But the boy did raise his arm. And as he raised the arm that held the jug of Holy Water, the witch lashed out at him to tear the jug to shreds.

And Holy Water went everywhere, everywhere like a mist to cleanse the night and all around them.

As a dozen things happened all at once:

The first thing Jason heard was the witch, screaming as the Holy Water sprayed her eyes. But that was only the beginning, because she'd hit the jug with force enough to turn the water to a mist that carried on the air.

When the mist reached baby Enoch (still lying motionless and silent upon the altar table), it released him to his natural temper, and he began to scream in the fear and rage and indignation that come naturally to small children in desperate circumstances.

When the mist reached the foul candles that hung over the infant, they began to gutter and grow dim—for those were necromantic candles made from tallow rendered from the fat of slaughtered children. The candles guttered, wavered, flickered, and went dark, and then for the longest moment the room was pitch-black, empty of everything but sound.

The sound of the witch, screaming in the terror that was her ultimate and slow mortality; the sound of the baby, screaming in terrors all his own.

Now the sound of a siren in the distance, growing closer, coming toward them till it was a piercing keening cry—

Then the misted water found the spells that held the library in darkness, and the overhead lights flickered on.

And Jason saw the carnage all around him. The witch, erupting in great red-wet boils that consumed her as he watched. The bones of the Dark Man, denuded of flesh and surrounded by a thick pool of sanguine scum.

A dozen and a half Celebrants lying dead on the floor where Miss Gilman's and Ms. Mason's bullets had taken their lives.

Miss Gilman and Ms. Mason, dazed and half conscious on the floor near the door.

Abe and Carol Laidlaw, broken and beaten but still by some miracle alive.

After a while Jason dodged his way among the bodies, to lift his brother from the altar table. And hold him for the longest moment as the child screamed and screamed and screamed.

Later there were footsteps on the stairs out in the hall, and then a dozen policemen stood in the doorway gaping at him, unbelieving, terrified.

daoine domhain

PETER TREMAYNE

How should I start? Do I have time to finish? Questions pour into my mind and remain unanswered, for they are unanswerable. But I must get something down on paper; at least make some attempt to warn people of the terrible dangers that lurk in the depths for mankind. How foolish and pitifully stupid a species we are, thinking that we are more intelligent than any other species, thinking that we are the "chosen" race. What arrogance—what ignorance! What infantile minds we have compared to . . . But I must begin as it began for me.

My name is Tom Hacket. My home is Rockport, Cape Ann, Massachusetts. My family history is fairly typical of this area of America. My great-grandparents arrived from County Cork, Ireland, to settle in Boston. My grandfather, Daniel, was born in Ireland but had come to America with his parents when only a few years old. Neither my father nor I ever had the desire to visit Ireland. We had no nostalgic yearnings, like some Irish-Americans, to visit the "old country." We felt ourselves to be purely American. But Grandfather Daniel . . . well, he is the mystery in our family. And if I were to ascribe a start to these curious events, then I would say that the beginning was my grandfather.

Daniel Hacket had joined the United States Navy and served as a lieutenant on a destroyer. Sometime in the early spring of 1928, he went on leave to Ireland, leaving his wife and baby (my father) behind in Rockport. He never came back; nor did anyone in the family ever hear from him again. My grandmother, according to my father, always believed that he had been forcibly prevented from returning.

The U.S. Navy took a more uncharitable line and posted him as a deserter. After Grandmother died, my father expressed the opinion, contrary to his mother's faith in Daniel Hacket's fidelity, that his father had probably settled down with some colleen in Ireland under an assumed name. If the truth were known, he always felt bitter about the mysterious desertion of his father. However, the interesting thing was that my father never sold our house in Rockport; we never moved. And it was only toward the end of my father's life that he revealed the promise he made to Grandmother. She had refused to move away or sell up in the belief that one day Daniel Hacket would attempt to get in touch if he were able. She had made my father promise to keep the old house in the family for as long as he could.

No one asked that promise of me. I inherited the old wooden colonial-style house, which stood on the headland near Cape Ann, when my father died of cancer. My mother had been dead for some years, and as I had no brothers or sisters, the lonely old house was all mine. I was working as a reporter for the *Boston Herald,* and the house was no longer of interest to me. So I turned it over to a real-estate agent, thinking to use the money to get a better apartment in Boston itself.

I can't recall now why I should drive up to the house that particular week. Of course, I made several journeys to sort through three generations of family bric-a-brac that had to be cleared before any new owner set foot in the place. Maybe that was the reason. I know it was a Tuesday afternoon, and I was sifting through a cardboard box of photographs when the doorbell buzzed as someone pressed firmly against it.

The man who stood there was tall, lean with a crop of red-gold hair and a broad smile. I had the impression of handsomeness in spite of the fact that I noticed he wore an eye-patch over his right eye, and on closer inspection, his right shoulder seemed somewhat misshapen by a hump. When he spoke, it was obvious he was Irish. That did not make him stand out in itself, for Boston is an Irish city. But he possessed a quaint old-world charm and courtesy that was unusual. And his one good eye was a sharp, bright orb of green.

"Is this the Hacket house?" he asked.

I affirmed it was.

"My name is Cichol O'Driscoll. I'm from Baltimore."

"That's a long journey, Mr. O'Driscoll," I said politely, wondering what the man wanted. At the same time I was thinking that his first name, he pronounced it *Kik-ol,* was an odd one for an Irishman. "Did you fly up this morning?"

He gave a wry chuckle.

"Ah, no. Not Baltimore, Maryland, sir. But the place which gave it its name—Baltimore in County Cork, Ireland."

It would have been churlish of me not to invite him in and offer him coffee, which he accepted.

"You are a Hacket, I presume?" he asked.

I introduced myself.

"Then I'm thinking that Mrs. Sheila Hacket no longer lives?"

"She was my grandmother. No. She has been dead these fifteen years past."

"And what of her son, Johnny?"

I shrugged.

"My father. He died three weeks ago."

"Ah, then I am sorry for your troubles."

"But what is this about?" I frowned.

"Little to tell," he said in that curious Irish way of speaking English. "As I said, I am from Baltimore, which is a small fishing port in the southwest of Ireland. A year ago I purchased an old croft on Inishdriscol, that is one of the islands that lay just off the coast, to the west from Baltimore. I am refurbishing it to make it into a holiday cottage. Well, one of my builders was pulling down a wall when he found some sort of secret cavity, and in this cavity he came across an old oilskin pouch. Inside was a letter addressed to Mrs. Sheila Hacket at Rockport, Massachusetts, with a note that if she no longer lived, then it should be handed to her son, Johnny. The letter was dated May the first, 1928."

I stared at the man in fascination.

"And you have come all this way to deliver a letter written sixty-three years ago?"

He chuckled, shaking his head.

"Not exactly. I have business in Boston. I own a small export business in Ireland. And so I thought I would kill two birds with one stone, as they say. It is not a long run up here from Boston. In fact, I had to pass by to get to Newburyport, where I also have business. I thought it would be fascinating if I could deliver the letter if Sheila or Johnny Hacket survived after all these years. But I didn't really expect to find them. When the people in the local store told me the Hacket house still stood here, I was fairly surprised."

He hesitated and then drew out the package and deposited it on the table. It was as he said, an old oilskin pouch, not very bulky.

"Well, I guess you have a right to this."

He stood up abruptly, with a glance at his wristwatch.

"I must be off."

I was staring at the package.

"What's in it?" I asked.

"Just a letter," he replied.

"I mean, what's in the letter?"

His face momentarily contorted in anger.

"I haven't opened it. It's not addressed to me," he said in annoyance.

"I didn't mean it like that," I protested. "I didn't mean to sound insulting. It's just . . . well, don't you want to know what it is you have brought?"

He shook his head. "The letter is clearly addressed. It is not for me to examine the contents."

"Then stay while I examine it," I invited, feeling it was the least I could do to repay the man for bringing it such a distance.

He shook his head.

"I'm on my way to Newburyport. I've a cousin there." He grinned again, recovering his good humor. "It's a small world." He paused, then said: "I'll be passing this way next week on my way back to Boston. Purely out of curiosity, I would like to know whether the letter contained something of interest. Maybe it's part of some local history of our island Inishdriscol."

"What does that mean?"

"Driscoll's Island. The O'Driscolls were a powerful ruling clan in the area," he responded proudly.

In fact, I arranged to meet Cichol O'Driscoll the next week in Boston because I had to return there to work on the following Monday morning. I watched him walk off down the drive, for presumably he had left his car in the roadway. I remember thinking that it was odd to come across such old-world charm and courtesy. The man must have flown a couple of thousand miles and never once attempted to open the letter he had brought with him. I turned to where it lay on the kitchen table, picked it up, and turned it over and over in my hands. It was only then that I suddenly realized the identity of the hand that had penned the address.

How stupid of me not to have realized before—but it is curious how slowly the mind can work at times. The date, the handwriting—which I had recently been looking at in the papers I had been sorting out—all pointed to the fact that here was a letter from my grandfather—Daniel Hacket.

With my hands suddenly shaky with excitement, I opened the oilskin and took out the yellowing envelope. Using a kitchen knife, I slit it open. I extracted several sheets of handwriting and laid them carefully on the flat surface of the table.

Inishdriscol,
near Baltimore
County Cork,
Ireland
April 30, 1928.

Dearest Sheila,

If you read these words, you may conclude that I am no longer part of this world. Courage, my Sheila, for you will need it if these words reach you, for I will require you to make them known so that the world may be warned. You must tell the Navy Department that they were not destroyed, that they still exist, watching, waiting, ready to take over . . . they have been waiting for countless millennia and soon, soon their time will come.

Today is the feast of Bealtaine here. Yes, ancient customs still survive in this corner of the world. This is the feast day sacred to Bile, the old god of death, and I must go down into the abyss to face him. I do not think that I shall survive. That is why I am writing to you in the hope that, one day, this will find its way into your hands so that you may know and warn the world. . . .

But first things first. Why did I come here? As you know, it was purely by chance. You will recall the extraordinary events at Innsmouth a few months ago? How agents of the Federal Government, working with the Navy Department, dynamited part of the old harbour? It was supposed to be a secret, but the fact of the destruction of the old seaport could not be kept from those who lived along the Massachusetts coast. In addition to that operation, I can tell you that my ship was one of several which were sent to depth-charge and torpedo the marine abyss just beyond Devil Reef. We were told it was merely some exercise, a war-game, but there was considerable scuttle-butt as to why the old harbour should be destroyed at the same time that the deeps were depth-charged. Some sailors conjured up visions of terrifying monsters which we were supposed to be destroying. There was talk of creatures—or beings who dwelt in the great depths—which had to be annihilated before they wiped out mankind. At the time, we officers treated these rumours and tales with humorous gusto.

When the operation was finished and we returned to port, the officers and men who took part in the exercise were given an extraordinary four weeks' leave; extraordinary, for it was unprecedented to my knowledge of the service. I now realise that it was done for a purpose—to stop the men from talking about that strange exercise. The idea being, I suppose, that when they returned, they would have forgotten the event and there would be no further speculation about it.

Well, four weeks' leave was facing me. I had always wanted to see the place where I was born. Do you remember how you insisted that I go alone when it was discovered little Johnny had scarlet fever and, though out of danger, would not be able to make the trip to Ireland and you would not leave him? I was reluctant to go. Ah, would to God I had not done so. Would to God I had never set eyes on the coast of Ireland.

I took passage to Cork, landing at the attractive harbour of Cobh, and set out to Baltimore, where I had been born. The place is a small fishing port set in a wild and desolate country on the edge of the sea. It stands at the end of a remote road and attracts few visitors unless they have specific business there. The village clusters around an excellent harbour, and on a rocky eminence above it is the O'Driscoll castle which, I was later told, has been in ruins since 1537. The only way to approach it is by a broad rock-cut stair. Incidentally, practically everyone in the town is called O'Driscoll, for this was the heart of their clan lands. When the sun shines, the place has an extraordinary beauty. The harbour is frequently filled with fishing-boats and small sailing ships, and there are many islands offshore.

On local advice I went up to the headland, which they call the Beacon hereabouts. The road was narrow and passes between grey stone walls through open, stony country. From this headland there is a spectacular view of the islands. The locals call them "Carbery's Hundred Isles." Opposite is the biggest, Sherkin Island, on which stands the ruins of another O'Driscoll castle and those of a Franciscan friary, also destroyed in 1537. Beyond is Inis Cleire or Clear Island with its rising headland, Cape Clear, with yet another O'Driscoll castle called Dunanore, and four miles from the farthest tip of Cape Clear is the Fastnet Rock.

Everyone in the area speaks the Irish language, which has put me at a disadvantage and I now wish my parents had passed on their knowledge to me. All I have learnt is that Baltimore is merely an anglicisation of *Baile an Tigh Móir*—the town of the big house—and that some local people also call it *Dún na Séad*—the fort of jewels.

There was a certain hostility in the place, for it must be remembered that the War of Independence against England is not long past and that was followed with a bitter civil war which ended in 1923, only five years ago. Memories of that terrible time are still fresh in people's minds and colour their attitude to strangers until they are able to judge whether the stranger means them harm or no.

Within a few days of arriving in Baltimore I found that I had not been born actually in the village but on one of the nearby islands called Inishdriscol, or Driscoll's Island. I soon persuaded a fisherman to take me there, it being three miles from Baltimore harbour. It is a large enough island with a small village at one end and a schoolhouse at the other, with its overall shape resembling the letter *T*.

I was able to hire a cottage close by the very one in which I had been born. The owners, Brennan told me, were away to America to seek their fortune. Brennan is the only one who speaks English on the island. He is a curious fellow combining local mayor, entrepreneur, head fisherman, counsellor . . . you name it and Brennan fits the role. Brennan is his first name, at least that is how I pronounce it, for he showed me the proper spelling of it, which was written *Bráonáin* and the English of it is "sorrow." Naturally, he is also an O'Driscoll, and for the first time I learnt the meaning of the name, which is correctly spelt *O hEidersceoil* and means "intermediary." Names mean a great deal in this country. Our own name, Hacket, is—unfortunately—not well respected here, for in 1631 two corsair galleys from Algiers sacked Baltimore, killed many of the inhabitants, and carried off two hundred to be sold as slaves in Africa. They were guided through the channels to the town by a man called Hacket, who was eventually caught and hanged in the city of Cork. Ah, if only I had knowledge of this language, how interesting these arbitrary signs we use would become.

In lieu of any other companion to converse with I have been much thrown together with Brennan, and he has been my guide and escort on the island. Indeed I found no close relatives, although most people knew of my family and several claimed distant kinship. After a while I settled down to a life of lazy fishing and walking.

It was after I had been on the island a few days that two more visitors arrived, but only for a few hours' stay on the island. Brennan told me that one was some representative of the English Government and the other was an official of the Irish Government. Apparently, during the War of Independence, a number of English soldiers and officials had disappeared, unknown casualties of the conflict. It seems that there had been a small military post on the island: a captain, a sergeant, and four men. One night, the captain disappeared. It was assumed that he had been caught by the local guerrillas, taken away, and shot. All investigations had proved fruitless in discovering exactly how he had met his end. No one on the island had talked. Nor had the guerrillas, many of whom were now members of the Irish Government, issued any information on the subject. Now, nine years after the disappearance, the English Government, in cooperation with the Irish Free State Government, were attempting to close the case.

I met the English official while out walking one morning, and we fell into conversation about the problem.

"Trouble is," he said, "these damned natives are pretty close."

He blandly ignored the fact that I had been born on the island and could, therefore, be classed as one of the "damned natives."

"Nary a word can you get out of them. Damned code of silence, as bad as Sicilians."

"You think the local people killed this Captain . . .?"

"Pfeiffer," he supplied. "If they didn't, I'm sure they know who did. Maybe it was a guerrilla unit from the mainland. There wasn't much activity on the islands during the war, although there was a lot of fighting in West Cork. A lot of bad blood, too. Political differences run deep. Take these people now . . . they don't like the Irish Government official that I'm with."

"Why not?"

"He represents the Free State. This area was solidly Republican during the Civil War. They lost, and they hate the Free State Government. I suppose they won't tell us anything. Damned waste of time coming here."

I nodded in sympathy with his task.

"Well, if you give me your card, perhaps if I hear anything . . . any drop of gossip which might help . . . I could drop you a line. You never know. They might talk to me, whereas they would not talk to you."

He smiled enthusiastically.

"That would be pretty sporting of you, Lieutenant." (He pronounced it in the curious way that the English do as *left-tenant*.)

"When did your man disappear?"

"Nine years ago. Actually, exactly nine years ago on April the thirtieth." He paused. "You are staying at the pink-wash cottage near the point, aren't you?"

I confirmed I was.

"Curiously, that's where Captain Pfeiffer was billeted when he disappeared."

The officials left the island later that day, and I raised the subject with Brennan. I had been a little arrogant in assuming that because I had been born on the island, and was of an old island family, that I would be trusted any more than the officials from Dublin and London. I was an American, a stranger, and they certainly would not divulge the hidden secrets of the island to me. Brennan was diplomatic in answering my questions, but the result was the same. No one was going to talk about the fate of the captain.

A few days later, I had almost forgotten Pfeiffer. Brennan and I went out fishing. We were after sea trout, *breac,* as he called it. Brennan took me out in his skiff, at least I describe it as a skiff. He called it a *naomhóg,* a strange very light boat which was made of canvas, spread over a wooden frame, and hardened by coatings of pitch and tar. Although frail, the craft was very manoeuvrable in the water and rode heavy seas with amazing dexterity. A mile or two from the island was a weird crooked rock which rose thirty or forty feet out of the sea. Brennan called it *camcarraig,* and when I asked the meaning of the name he said it was simply "crooked rock." Brennan reckoned the sea trout ran by here and into Roaring Water Bay, close by. So we rowed to within a few yards of the pounding surf, crashing like slow thunder against the weed-veined rock, and cast our lines.

The fishing went well for some time, and we hauled a catch that we could not be ashamed of.

Suddenly, I cannot remember exactly how it happened, a dark shadow seemed to pass over us. I looked up immediately, expecting a cloud to have covered the sun. Yet it was still high and shining down, though it was as if there was no light coming from it. Nor were there any clouds in the sky to account for the phenomenon. I turned to Brennan and found him on his knees in the bow of the boat, crouching forward, his eyes staring at the sea. It was then that I observed that the water around us had turned black, the sort of angry green blackness of a brooding sea just before the outbreak of a storm, discoloured by angry scudding clouds. Yet the sky was clear.

I felt the air, dank and chill, oppressive and damp against my body.

"What is it?" I demanded, my eyes searching for some explanation to the curious sensation.

Brennan had now grabbed at the oars and started to pull away from the crooked rock, back towards the distant island shore. His English had deserted him, and he was rambling away in eloquent Irish and, despite his rowing, would now and then lift his hand to genuflect.

"Brennan," I cried, "calm down. What are you saying?"

After some while, when we were well away from the crooked rock, and the sun was warm again on our bodies and the sea was once more the reflected blue of the sky, Brennan apologised.

"We were too near the rock," he said. "There is an undercurrent there which is too strong for us."

I frowned. That was not how it had seemed to me at all. I told him so, but he dismissed me.

"I was only fearful that we would be swept into the current," he said. "I merely offered up a little prayer."

I raised an eyebrow.

"It seemed a powerful long prayer," I observed.

He grinned. "Long prayers are better heard than short ones."

I chuckled.

"And what was the prayer you said? In case I have need of it."

"I merely said, God between me and the Devil, nine times and nine times nine."

I was puzzled.

"Why nine? Wouldn't seven be a luckier number?"

He looked amazed at what he obviously thought was my appalling ignorance.

"Seven? Seven is an unlucky number in these parts. It is the number nine which is sacred. In ancient times the week consisted of nine nights and nine days. Didn't Cúchulainn have nine weapons, didn't King Loegaire, when setting out to arrest St. Patrick, order nine chariots to be joined together according to the tradition of the gods? Wasn't Queen Medb accompanied by nine chariots and . . ."

I held up my hand in pacification at his excited outburst.

"All right. I believe you," I smiled. "So the number nine is significant."

He paused, and his sea-green eyes rested in mine for several seconds and then he shrugged.

That evening I went to Tomás O'Driscoll's croft, which served as an inn, or rather a place where you could buy a drink and groceries from the mainland when they came in by the boat. The place is called a *sibin,* or shebeen, as it is pronounced in English, which signifies an unlicensed drinking house. Several of the old men of the island were gathered there, and Brennan sat on a three-legged stool by the chimney-corner, smoking his pipe. As I have said, everyone looked up to Brennan as the spokesman for the island, and the old men were seated around him talking volubly in Irish. I wished I could understand what they were saying.

Two words kept being repeated in this conversation, however. *Daoine Domhain.* To my ears it sounded like *dayn'ya dow'an.* Only when they noticed me, did a silence fall on the company. I felt a strange uneasiness among them.

Brennan was regarding me with a peculiar expression on his face which held a note of . . . well, it took me some time before I reasoned it . . . of sadness in it.

I offered to buy drinks for the company, but Brennan shook his head.

"Have a drink on me and welcome," he said. "It's not for the likes of you to buy drinks for the likes of us."

They seemed to behave strangely to me. I cannot put my finger on it, for they were not unfriendly, nor did they stint in hospitality, yet there was something odd—as if they were regarding me as a curiosity, watching and waiting . . . yet for what?

I returned back to the croft early that evening and noted that the wind was blowing up from the south, across *camcarraig* and towards the headland on which the handful of cottages on the island clung precariously. Oddly, above the noise of the blustering wind, stirring the black, angry swells which boomed into Roaring Water Bay and smacked against the granite fortresses of the islands, I heard a whistling sound which seemed less like the noise of the wind and more like the lonely cry of some outcast animal, wailing in its isolation. So strong did the noise seem that I went to the door and stood listening to it, just in case it was some animal's distress cry. But eventually the noise was lost in the howl of the wind from the sea.

There is some ancient proverb, I forget how it goes. Something about "out of the mouths of babes and sucklings . . ." I was reminded of that two days later when I happened to be fishing from the high point beyond my cottage, where the seas move restlessly towards the land from the *camcarraig*. It was a lazy day, and the fish were not in a mood for taking the bait. Nonetheless I was content, relaxing, almost half asleep.

I was not aware of any presence until I heard a voice close to my ear say something in Irish. I blinked my eyes and turned to see a young girl of about nine years old, with amazing red-gold hair, which tumbled around her shoulders. She was an extraordinarily attractive child, with eyes of such a bright green colour they seemed unreal. She was staring at me solemnly. Her feet were bare and her dress was stained and torn, but she had a quiet dignity which sat oddly on the appearance of terrible poverty. Again she repeated her question.

I shook my head and replied in English, feeling stupid.

"Ah, it is a stranger you are."

"Do you speak English?" I asked in amazement, having accepted Brennan as the only English-speaker on the island.

She did not answer my superfluous question, for it was obvious she understood the language.

"The sea is brooding today," she said, nodding at the dark seas around *camcarraig*. "Surely the *Daoine Domhain* are angry. Their song was to be heard last night."

"Dayn'ya Dow'an?" I asked, trying to approximate the sounds of the words. It was the same expression which had been used in the shebeen a few nights ago. "What is that?"

"Musha, but they are the Fomorii, the dwellers beneath the sea. They were the evil ones who dwelt in Ireland long before the coming of the Gael. Always they have battled for our souls, sometimes succeeding, sometimes failing. They are the terrible people . . . they have but a single eye and a single hand and a single foot. They are the terrible ones . . . the Deep Ones—the *Daoine Domhain.*"

I smiled broadly at this folklore solemnly proclaimed by this young girl.

She caught my smile and frowned. Her face was suddenly serious.

"God between us and all evil, stranger, but it is not good to smile at the name of the Deep Ones."

I assured her that I was not smiling at them. I asked her what her name was, but she would not tell me. She turned to me, and I saw an abrupt change in her expression. Abruptly a sadness grew in her eyes, and she turned and ran away. That left me disturbed. I wondered who her mother was because I felt I ought to go to the child's parents in case they thought I had deliberately scared her. I should explain that I meant the child no harm in case it was afraid of something I had said or of some expression on my face.

I was packing my rods when Brennan came by. I greeted him, and my first question was about the child. He looked mighty puzzled and said that there was no child on the island who could speak English. When he perceived that I was annoyed because he doubted my word, he tried to placate me by saying that if I had seen such a child, then it must have come from another island or the mainland and was visiting.

He offered to walk back with me to my cottage, and on the way I asked him: "Who exactly were the Fomorii?"

For a moment he looked disconcerted.

"My, but you are the one for picking up the ancient tales," was his comment.

"Well?" I prompted, as it seemed he was going to say nothing further on the subject.

He shrugged. "They are just an ancient legend, that's all."

I was a little exasperated and he saw it, for he then continued: "The name means the dwellers under the sea. They were a violent and misshapen people who represented the evil gods in ancient times. They were led by Balor of the Evil Eye and others of their race such as Morc and Cichol, but their power on land was broken at the great battle at Magh Tuireadh when they suffered defeat by the Tuatha Dé Danaan, the gods of goodness."

"Is that all?" I asked, disappointed at the tale.

Brennan raised a shoulder in an eloquent gesture.

"Is it not enough?" he asked good-humoredly.

"Why are they called the Deep Ones?" I pressed.

A frown passed across his brow.

"Who told you that?" His voice was waspish.

"Were you not talking about the Deep Ones in the shebeen the other night? Dayn'ya Dow'an. Isn't that the Irish for Deep Ones? And why should you be talking of ancient legends?"

He seemed to force a smile.

"You have the right of it," he conceded. "We talk of ancient legends because they are part of us, of our heritage and our culture. And we call the Fomorii by this name because they dwell in the great deeps of the sea. No mystery in that."

I nodded towards *camcarraig*.

"And they are supposed to dwell near that rock?"

He hesitated, then said indifferently, "So legend goes. But a man like yourself does not want to dwell on our ancient tales and legends."

It was as if he had excluded me from my ancestry, ignored the fact that I had been born on the island.

Then he would talk no more either about the girl or the Deep Ones—the Fomorii—or the *Daoine Domhain*.

Two nights later as I was eating my supper in the main room of the tiny two-roomed cottage, I felt a draught upon my face and glanced up. I was astonished, for there standing with her back to the door was the little girl. The first thought that filled my mind was how quietly she must have entered not to disturb me. Only the soft draught from the door, supposedly opening and shutting, had alerted me. Then I realised that it was curious for a young child to be out so late and visiting the cottage of a stranger. I knew the islanders were trusting people, but this trust bordered on irresponsibility.

She was staring at me with the same sadness that I had seen in her eyes when she had left me on the cliff-top.

"What is it?" I demanded. "Why are you here and who are you?"

I recalled Brennan had claimed there was no such girl on the island. But this was no apparition.

"You have been chosen," she whispered softly. "Beware the feast of the Fires of Bile, god of death. The intermediary will come for you then and take you to them. They are waiting; nine years will have passed at the next feast. They wait every nine years for reparation. So be warned. You are the next chosen one."

My mouth opened in astonishment, not so much at what the girl was saying but at the words and phraseology which she used, for it was surely well beyond the ability of a nine-year-old to speak thus.

Abruptly as she came she went, turning, opening the door and running out into the dusk of the evening. I hastened to the door and peered into the gloom. There was no one within sight.

I have strong nerves, as well you know, but I felt a curious feeling of apprehension welling in me.

That night I was awakened by an odd wailing sound. At first I thought it was the noise of the wind across the mountain, whistling and calling, rising and falling. But then I realised it was not. It was surely some animal, lonely and outcast. The cry of a wolf, perhaps? But this was a bare rock of an island, and surely no wolves could survive here? It went on for some time before it died away, and I finally settled back to sleep.

The next morning I called by Tomás O'Driscoll's place and found Brennan, as usual, seated in the little bar-room. Once again he refused to accept a drink from me and instead offered me a glass of whiskey.

"Brennan," I said, my mind filled with the visit of the young child, "you are frugal with the truth because there is a little red-haired girl living on this island. She can speak English."

His face whitened, and he shook his head violently even before I had finished.

"There is no one here like that," he said firmly and demanded to know why I asked.

I told him and his face was ghastly. He genuflected and muttered something in Irish, whereupon Tomás behind the bar replied sharply to him. Brennan seemed to relax and nodded, obviously in agreement at what Tomás had said.

"What's going on here?" I asked harshly. "I insist that you tell me."

Brennan glanced about as if seeking some avenue of escape.

I reached forward and grabbed him angrily by the shoulder.

"No need for hurt," he whinged.

"Then tell me," I insisted firmly.

"She's just a tinker girl. She and her family often come to the island to lift the salmon from the rock pool at the north end of the island. They must be there now. I swear I didn't know the truth of it. But that's who she is. Tinkers are not good people to be knowing. They say all manner of strange things and claim they have the second sight. I wouldn't be trusting them."

He looked down at his glass and would say no more.

All at once I had a firm desire to quit this island and these strange people with their weird superstitions and folkways. I might have been born on the island, but they were no longer my people, no longer part of me. I was an American, and in America lay reality.

"Can I get a boat to the mainland, to Baltimore today, Brennan?" I asked.

He raised his eyes to mine and smiled sadly.

"Not today nor tomorrow, Mr. Hacket," he replied softly.

"Why so?"

"Because this evening is May Day Eve. It's one of our four main holidays."

I was a little surprised. "Do you celebrate Labour Day?"

Brennan shook his head.

"Oh, no. May Day and the evening before it is an ancient feast day in the old Celtic calendar stretching back before the coming of Christianity. We call it Bealtaine–the time of the Fires of Bile, one of the ancient gods."

I felt suddenly very cold, recalling the words of the tinker child.

"Are you saying that tonight is the feast of the god of death?"

Brennan made an affirmative gesture.

The girl had warned me of the feast of the Fires of Bile when some intermediary would come for me and take me to . . . to them? Who were "them"? The Deep Ones, of course. The terrible Fomorii who dwelt beneath the seas.

I frowned at my thoughts. What was I doing? Was I accepting their legends and folklore? But I had been born on the island. It was my reality also, my legends and my folklore as much as it was their own. And was I suddenly accepting the girl's second sight without question? Was I believing that she had come to warn me . . . about what? I must be going mad.

I stood there shaking my head in bewilderment.

I *was* going mad, even to credit anything so ridiculous.

"Have a drink, Mr. Hacket," Brennan was saying. "Then you will be as right as ninepence."

I stared at him for a moment. His words, an expression I had frequently heard in the area, triggered off a memory.

"Nine," I said slowly. "Nine."

Brennan frowned at me.

But suddenly I had become like a man possessed. Nine years ago to this day had Captain Pfeiffer disappeared from the very same cottage in which I was staying. The girl had said something about them waiting every nine years for reparation. Nine was the mystical number of the ancient Celts. The week was counted by nine nights and nine days and three weeks, the root number of nine gave twenty-seven nights, which was the unit of the month, related to the twenty-seven constellations of the lunar zodiac. Nine, nine, *nine . . .!* The number hammered into my mind.

Was I going crazy?

What was I saying? That every ninth year these people made some sacrifice to ancient pagan gods whom they believed dwelt in the depths of the sea—the *Daoine Domhain*—the Deep Ones? That the English army captain, Pfeiffer, had been so sacrificed nine years before, nine years ago on this very night?

I found Brennan looking at me sympathetically.

"Don't worry, Mr. Hacket," he said softly. "There is no joy in that. It does no good to question what cannot be understood."

"When can I get a boat to the mainland?"

"After the feast is done." He was apologetic but firm.

I turned and left the shebeen and began to walk towards the point.

Brennan followed me to the door, for he called after me.

"There's no fear in it. I'll come along for you tonight. Tonight."

I turned and strode through the village street and made my way to the north end of the island. I was determined to find the tinker child and demand some explanation. It was not a big place, and eventually I came across a collection of dirty rough-patched tents grouped in front of a smouldering turf fire at which a woman of indiscernible age was turning a large fish on a spit. There seemed no one else about.

I climbed down the rocks to get to the encampment, which was sited on the beach; a fairly large strip of sand.

The woman, brown-faced and weather-beaten, clearly someone used to the outdoor life, watched me coming with narrowed eyes. There was suspicion on her features. She greeted me at first in Irish, but when I returned the reply in English she smiled, her shoulders relaxed, and she returned the greeting in kind.

"A grand day, sir. Are you staying on the island for the fishing, then?"

"I am," I replied.

"Ah. By your voice you would be American."

I confirmed that I was. I was looking about for some sign of the girl, but there seemed no one but the woman, who, now I came to observe her more closely, resembled the child with her mass of red hair.

"My man is fishing," the woman said, catching my wondering gaze.

"Ah," I said in noncommittal tone. "And do you have a child?"

"My girl, Sheena, sir."

The suspicion was back in her eyes.

"I thought I saw her a while ago," I said.

The woman shrugged. "That you may."

"Is it right that you have the gift of second sight?" I demanded abruptly.

The woman looked taken aback and studied me for several long seconds before replying.

"Some of us have. Is it a fortune that you are wanting?"

I nodded.

"I'll be charging a shilling."

I reached in my pocket and handed over the coin, which the woman took with alacrity.

"Is it your palm you wish read, or shall I see what the tea-leaves say?"

I was about to reply when the flap of the tent moved and there stood the child. She regarded me with her large solemn sad eyes and seemed to let out a sigh.

"He is the chosen one, Mother. He has already been warned," she said softly.

The woman stared from me to the child and back again. Her face was suddenly white, and she threw the coin back at me as if it had suddenly burnt her hands.

"Away from here, Mister." Her voice was sharp.

"But . . ."

"Have you no ears to hear with? Did you not hear what Sheena said? She is gifted with the second sight. She can see beyond the unseeable. If you value your soul, man, heed her warning. Now be away." She glanced about her, her face showing that she was badly frightened. "Sheena, find your father . . . we must leave this place now."

Slowly I retreated, shaking my head in wonder. At least I had proved to myself that I was not hallucinating. The girl, Sheena, existed. A tinker girl with, supposedly, the gift of second sight, who gave me a warning. . . .

I walked up to the point above my cottage and sat myself on a rock, gazing out across the dark brooding sea towards *camcarraig*. What nightmare world had I landed in? Was I losing all sense of reason? Was I accepting shadows for reality? Did I really believe that the girl had some strange power to foresee evil and warn me about it? I was the chosen one. Chosen for what purpose? And what had really happened to Captain Pfeiffer nine years ago, nine years this very night?

I shivered slightly.

The sea was a mass of restless blackness, and far away, as if from the direction of *camcarraig*, I heard the strange cry which had disturbed my slumber on the previous night; a soft whistling wail of a soul in torment.

It was while I sat there listening that I recalled the words of the child.

"You have been chosen. Beware the feast of the Fires of Bile, god of death. The intermediary will come for you then and take you to them. They are waiting. Nine years will have passed at the next feast. They wait every nine years for reparation. So be warned. You are the next chosen."

Abruptly I heard Brennan calling to me from the doorway of the shebeen.

"There's no fear in it. I'll come along for you tonight."

Brennan O'Driscoll. O'Driscoll who had explained the meaning of the name *O hEidersceoil—intermediary!*

Brennan was the one who would take me to the Deep Ones!

I rose then and began to scour the island in search of a boat, any boat, any form of floating transportation to get me away from this crazy nightmare. But there was none. I was alone, isolated, and imprisoned. Even the tinkers had apparently departed. I was left alone with the islanders.

Left alone to my fate.

That was this afternoon, my darling Sheila. Now it is dusk, and I am writing this by the light of the storm lantern on the table in the tiny cottage. Soon Brennan O'Driscoll will come for me. Soon I shall know if I am truly crazy or whether there is some reality in this nightmare. It is my intention to take these pages and wrap them in my old oilskin pouch and hide them behind a loose brick in the chimney breast of this cottage. In the hope that, should anything happen to me this evening, then, God willing, this letter will eventually reach your beloved hands or those of young Johnny, who may one day grow to manhood and come seeking word of his unfortunate father. Soon it will be dark, and soon Brennan will come. . . . The intermediary; intermediary between me and what? What is it waiting out there in the deep? Why do they demand reparation every nine years and reparation for what? God help me in my futility.

DANIEL HACKET

Thus was the writing on the browning pages ended as if hurriedly. I sat for a while staring at those strange words and shaking my head in disbelief. What madness had seized my grandfather to write such a curious fantasy?

The wind was getting up, and I could hear the seas roaring and crashing at the foot of the point where our house stood, gazing eastward toward the brooding Atlantic. The weather was dark and bleak for a late April day, and I turned to switch on the light.

That something had disarranged my grandfather's mind was obvious. Had he remained living on the island? Surely not, for the U.S. Navy's enquiries at the time would have discovered him. But if he had disappeared, why hadn't the natives of this island, Inishdriscol, reported he was missing? Had he thrown himself into the sea while his mind had been so unbalanced and drowned, or what had taken place . . .? The questions flooded my thoughts.

I suddenly realized that he had written the curious document, which so clearly demonstrated his warped mental condition, exactly sixty-three years ago this very night. It was April 30. A childish voice echoed in my mind, reciting the nine times table—seven nines are sixty-three!

I shivered slightly and went to the window to gaze out at the blackness of the Atlantic spread before me. I could see the winking light from the point farther down the coast that marked the passage to Innsmouth, and far out to sea I could just make out the pulsating warning sweep of the lighthouse at Devil Reef, beyond which was sited one of the great deeps of the Atlantic. Deeps. The Deep Ones. What nonsense was that?

As I stood there, my mind in a whirl, staring out in the darkness beyond the cliff edge, I heard soft whistling, like a curious wind. It rose and fell with regular resonance like the call of some lonely outcast animal. It whistled and echoed across the sea with an uncanniness that caused me to shiver.

I pulled the curtains to and turned back into the room.

Well, the old-world Irishman had surely brought me an intriguing story. No wonder my grandfather had never returned. For some weird reason he had gone insane on that far distant Irish island, and perhaps no one now would know the reason why.

I would have much to ask Cichol O'Driscoll when I saw him. Perhaps he could set forth an investigation when he returned to Baltimore in order to find out how my grandfather had died and why no one had notified my grandmother of either his death or disappearance.

I frowned at some hidden memory and turned back to my grandfather's manuscript.

"They were a violent and misshapen people who represented the evil gods in ancient Ireland. They were led by Balor of the Evil Eye and others of the race such as Morc and Cichol. . . ."

Cichol! With his one eye and hump-shaped back!

I could not suppress the shiver that tingled against my spine.

I tried to force a smile of cynicism.

Cichol O'Driscoll. O'Driscoll—the intermediary. April 30—the eve of the Bealtaine, the feast of the Fires of Bile. Seven times nine is sixty-three . . .

Daoine Domhain. The Deep Ones. "They wait every nine years for reparation."

Then I knew that I would be seeing Cichol O'Driscoll again. Very soon.

Outside the wind was rising from the mysterious restless Atlantic swell, keening like a soul in torment. And through the wind came the whistling call of some lonely outcast animal.

to mars and providence

DON WEBB

Exactly twenty-nine days after his father had died of general paresis—that is to say, syphilis—in the local asylum, the boy observed the cylinder land upon Federal Hill. On some level this extramundane intrusion confirmed certain hypotheses that he had begun to form concerning the prognosticative nature of dreams. He had been dreaming of the night-gaunts for three years. They had—the horrible conclusion now obtruded upon his reluctant mind as an awful certainty—come for him. As befit a gentleman of pure Yankee stock, and the true chalk-white Nordic type, he had but one option: He must venture forth to meet and if possible defeat these eldritch beings.

He was eight years old.

The initial and certainly most daunting difficulty would be getting past his mother and aunts. His grandfather, Whipple Phillips, might be an ally in this quest, since he had often kept Howard entertained with tales of black voodoo, unfathomed caves, winged horrors, and old witches with sinister cauldrons. But Grandfather Whipple was in Idaho, and his mother, though normally indulgent of such whims, would not allow his questing into the night air. Howard therefore adopted extreme stealth in the acquisition of his bicycle. He actually *carried* it several yards from the house before mounting it in quest of adventure.

Down College Hill across the river and then hard work up toward St. John's Church on Federal Hill, which is where he judged the cylinder had fallen. The neighborhood, alive with nameless sounds that vied with morbid shriekings, seemed to have taken notice of the cylinder's fall. There was a general lighting of candles, lanterns, torches, and the like. By the time he reached St. John's, a rugged ring of light surrounded the shiny cylinder. He could not stand to force his way through the crowd, so he entered the church proper and climbed up to the bell tower. Opening a small window in the bell tower, he watched the scene below with growing horror and fascination.

A portion of the cylinder had begun to turn. No doubt the entity or entities therein sought the relieving air of the night as a counter to the searing heat of their bulkhead. The crowd grew fervent with their prayers—prayers to an entity Howard knew to be no more real than the Santa Claus he had abandoned at age five. The lid fell free, and a tremendous fungoid stench assailed Howard's nostrils.

The great leathery wet glistening squamous head of the cylinder's occupant lunged out, pulsing and twitching obscenely. Its vast liquid eyes, whose terrible three-lobed pupils spoke of the being's non-Terran evolution, gazed with glittering contempt upon the sea of humanity surrounding the smoking crater. Some brave soul, perhaps hoping to get a better look at the horror, shined a bull's-horn lantern at its eyes. It recoiled from this unwanted stimulus, making a great hooting cry that would be difficult to render phonetically. The creature ducked back into the cylinder, only to reemerge with a weapon of some sort. Suddenly a burst of blue lightning so intense that it made all the other light a darkness flashed from the weapon. Amidst the screams, Howard fainted.

When Howard returned to consciousness, it was a return from a dream of being medically examined by the panting, wheezing, fumbling, drooling Martians. He was—to his intense surprise—in his bed at 454 Angell Street. Susan Lovecraft, his mother, was standing above him.

"I see that my little Abdul has wakened. I trust your materialism will be thoroughly shaken by the miracle that saved you from the Martians."

"Martians?"

"One edition of the *Gleaner* made it out before the terror disrupted the city. Everyone has fled. We, however, will remain until Grandfather Whipple comes for us."

Howard could begin to smell the burning city. His mother couldn't be this calm if what she were saying was true. This must be some sort of game, like when she fixed an Oriental corner in his room when he took the name Abdul Alhazred when he was five. He would play along; after all, there was the fact that he had arrived back at his home.

"You said something about a miracle?"

"The Martians killed everybody near the cylinder. Some men at the university watched it all with binoculars. One of the Martians climbed up the side of the church, to the bell tower's open window, and pulled you out. It carried you down inside the cylinder. I suppose it thought you were one of their own. You are a very ugly child, Howard; people cannot bear to look upon your awful face. When the second cylinder fell, the Martians hurried out of the first to aid in the other's arrival. One of the brave men of the Brown Library, Armitage, I believe his name was, ventured all the way there to find you. He knew you because you had pestered him with questions on Cicero. You were there in the cylinder 'sleeping peacefully,' he said."

"How long?"

"You've been asleep three days."

There was something in his mother's eyes that wasn't right. Perhaps the "Martian" invasion had unhinged her highly strung nervous system. He must obtain nourishment and newspaper quickly, and then scout out the city.

"Could you bring the copy of the *Gleaner,* Mother?"

"Certainly, Howard."

The paper had huge headlines: EARTH INVADED BY MARS. The cylinders had fallen in London, Paris, St. Louis, even Texas.

How ironic, thought Howard, that the Martians would have chosen to land in the Italian section of the city, since it was Giovanni Schiaparelli who had discovered Mars's canal system.

Mother brought him a sandwich for breakfast. The bread was stale and the house quiet.

He asked after his aunts.

Mother's face went blank and dreamy. "They've gone west to speak with your grandfather concerning the invasion. I believe they took the train."

Howard knew that one of the first things the Martians would have done would be to destroy trains, telegraphs, and roads. Mankind would panic if it lost its ability to reassert its pathetic reality by its continuous idiot god mutterings. What happy cows they would become in a few days, happy to be herd animals. He could feel the contempt he had seen in the three-lobed eyes of the Martian, a burning contempt that an older and more perfect civilization must feel against the apelike humans.

He would have to meet them again. He could feel a pull toward the cylinder near St. John's Church. An actual physical attraction like iron filings to a lodestone. Perhaps his mother was right, and there was something in him that was like the Martians.

He began surveying the town from his window. Great paths of black ash cut obscene angles across the landscape. The Martians' traveling machines respected neither human habitation nor the barriers of river or hill. What marvelous creatures these Martians were to fashion machines to replace bodies. To become pure brains able to cross the cosmos! What starry wisdom they must have accumulated!

He saw the glint of metal and reached for his telescope. A great walking machine was traversing Federal Hill, moving toward St. John's. He could see the pit in front of the church quite clearly. A strange red vegetation covered the pit's sides. The red weed seemed to move slowly of its own accord, for surely no ash stirred with any breeze. The walking machine brought the Martian alongside the bell tower. The Martian placed a small golden box within.

At that moment his mother rushed into the room and pulled Howard from the window. She closed the curtains. She told him she was making hot chocolate. He should come to the parlor to enjoy some.

He felt sad for his mother, but guessed that it was perhaps a blessing that the human mind is unable to correlate its contents. Howard went down into the parlor and did partake of hot chocolate. His mother talked of trivial things as though no horror waited outside of the curtained windows.

Everything was still, very still, and Howard surmised that the city was deserted. Then a great ululation so horrible that surely no human mouth could utter nor mind conceive smashed the stillness of the air as a monolith of terror upon a plain of endless desolation. Mother nearly dropped her tiny white teacup, a proud relic of the family's past. Golly, thought Howard, something needs to be done. Mother talked rapidly and quietly. Once again the Martian cry resonated obscenely in the Terran atmosphere.

Howard excused himself. Mother didn't seem to notice. He went to his grandfather's medicine chest. Grandfather Whipple fought his pernicious insomnia with a powerful sleeping powder. Howard believed that he could easily mix it in the malted milk that his mother favored as an evening meal.

Waiting out the afternoon was torture. Something pulled Howard to St. John's Church. He could almost see the bell-tower room when he closed his eyes. Knowing that the mystery was there was making him do and think things he had never thought. Mystery, he decided, was the great *transformatrice*. She effected a change in one's self by simply *being*.

The evening meal proved worse. He had had to argue with Mother so that he could prepare her malted milk. She would have to be sedated if he was to quest further. This time he must *not* faint and be subject to removal before viewing whatever horror his destiny had chosen for him.

Mother drank her malt. She joked gently that he did not know how to prepare it. He watched her carefully, making sure that she drank all of it rather than pouring it down the kitchen drain. She retired to the parlor afterward, where her fear kept her from lighting candle or lamp. As it grew darker, her words grew fainter and fainter. He listened long and hard to be sure that the whisperer in the darkness did indeed sleep, then tiptoed out of the house.

Outside, deep twilight held the city in its gray-purple embrace. Only the topmost windows reflected the glorious sunset. The enchanting and beautiful twilight almost concealed the great ashen pathways of desolation that the Martians had left in their wake. Only one of the once many proud bridges still spanned the river. Howard began to run toward it. The sense of movement made him feel watched; Howard was the only thing moving on College Hill. The Martians' siege had stolen the comforting noises of the ancient city, leaving it as still as the vast void of darkling space through which they had traveled, and as foul smelling as the odor of plague-stricken towns and uncovered cemeteries.

As Howard crossed the bridge, he looked upon the ancient city with eyes of memory, preferring not to see the havoc of war. He looked upon the entrancing panorama of loveliness, the steepled town nestling upon its gentle hills.

Howard's run slowed to a panting walk as he climbed Federal Hill. When he reached the crater, he near swooned from the Oriental sweetness that the undulating carmine growth censed through the still air, but the distant cry of a Martian, mixed with the terrified cry of the human herd, reminded him of his mission. He entered the dark church and made for the bell tower.

Beneath the bells, on a small table, the object lay. It was a garnet crystal in the shape known to science as a trapezohedron. It shone with faint ruddy light—the light of Mars, which the Babylonians (Howard reflected) called Nergal and the Northmen Tyr. By the small table stood a small chair that would exactly fit an eight-year-old boy.

He knew the shining trapezohedron must be the focus for some sort of communication. But could he withstand the daemonical truth such communication—dare he think it—*communion* could bring?

He reached out and picked up the stone. It tingled; some energy was contained within and began to have a direct effect on his nerves. At once he became aware of a vaster sensory range than his human evolution had prepared him for. Firstly the tiny chamber in the steeple, which had been fairly dark, now blazed with light. Secondly he could hear a sweet distant breathing or perhaps the sound of flutes playing a magical but incoherent pattern. Thirdly he became aware—as much through the sense of *taste* as of sight—of a colour that floated in the air above him. He could not name this colour; it was not a colour of Earth, not belonging to the neat spectrum Newton's prism had revealed. This colour moved within itself, fashioning itself by rules not native to Earth, but of another part of space. It was sentient, and somehow *informed* or taught those possessed of it. It must be the medium through which the Martians communicated with one another. It sensed that Howard *sensed* it, and it became violently agitated. Suddenly it shot a tentacle into Howard's brain. It pulled his soul free from its moorings.

For a moment he was suspended in the colour out of space. He could hear the colour, taste the colour, think *as the colour*.

The colour asked him, "Are you one of us?"

"I do not know what you mean."

"We prepared for the invasion by sending forth the minds of the greatest telepaths of our race. They dwelt among men as spies living in the bodies of men. Most returned to us, but some lost memory of their being enchanted by the revelations received in human flesh. Are you one of us?"

Howard did not know. He had felt that there was much from outside of the world of men in him.

The colour began to pulsate, pushing him along. He wondered that he had sensation separate from his body.

"You are in a body of your thoughts. When we have transported you to Mars, it will be made semimaterial for two purposes. You will be able to handle and sense physical objects, and we will be able to examine your true mental form."

Howard considered that he might be a Martian. He had always felt that the day-to-day world partook of a phantom character. The only things that seemed real to him had been his dreams, certain tales in *The Arabian Nights,* and certain suggestions of a grander world that he saw in certain architectural features revealed in sunsets. Surely Mars was a sunset world, gold and red in its martial glory. What wonders a civilization older than mankind might possess! The colour, sensing his thoughts, began to show him images.

The "Martians" had come from another world to settle in this solar system. Eons ago they had crossed space in cylinders like those they had so recently employed. They settled upon Mars and Earth's South Pole. The latter colony had vanished, perhaps succumbing to the violent climatic changes that Earth had suffered. The former began a specialized eugenics program. Worshiping no god save their own intellects, they sought to eliminate all of the glands that cause emotion (save for fear, the emotion necessary for survival) and remove all enzymes that cause aging. The Martians had likewise eradicated all forms of microbial disease, leading to a practical immortality. The coming of immortality necessitated a specialized training of the will. The Martians had to cultivate those intellectual and aesthetic pursuits that could sustain an interest that would span the strange eons through which they would live.

This training of the will had an unexpected side effect; the Martians discovered that some of the stronger minds of their race could project themselves across the void without mechanical aid. These astral travelers came in contact with the various races of the solar system, including the feebleminded men who dwelt upon the noisome green world of Earth and a race of what could be best described as fungoid beings inhabiting a planet on the rim of the solar system.

The Martians traded with the fungi, and Martian civilization reached its height of material prosperity. The Martians covered the ruddy surface of their world with labyrinthine Cyclopean structures, whose sole function was to express certain aesthetic, mathematical, or metaphysical formulae. The Martians waxed great in pride. Surely no race had reached such success.

This golden age gave way to a certain decadence. One of the first symptoms of this decline was a decrease in reproductive powers. The Martians had long since given up sexual reproduction in favor of a less distracting asexual budding. Fewer and fewer Martians came into being. Art became debased, and the objective art of the past was increasingly replaced by an outrageous subjectivity.

Perhaps the Martians would have gone into a long and steady decline had it not been for the discovery of the vast underground vaults at Syrtis Major.

The "Martians" discovered that uncounted eons ago, an almost godlike race had dominated their planet. The fungi confirmed this, claiming that they were in fact not dead, but had entered into a sort of undead sleep, waiting for a certain modulation of cosmic rays that would allow them to resume their play in glory and terror. The fungi were unsure when the elder gods would return and hinted darkly at the method of their remanifestation. The "Martians" were neither the oldest nor the last of Mars's masters.

Great energy was turned toward the excavation and destruction of the vaults, but despite their mighty heat-rays and lightning machines, the Martians were unable to cut through the curious metal of the vaults. The dread of the creatures who would return was heightened by the discovering of their image carved into certain remote peaks that overlook the haunted deserts, whose baleful influence the Martians had shunned for millennia.

These elder gods with their long ghoul-like faces and star-destroying eyes were soon all the Martians could think of. For a season unreason held sway, and the normally logical Martians destroyed as many images of these horrors as they could find. But reason returned and the remaining specimens of statues were gathered at the capital, and controlled debate on the course of action began. A decision was made to invade Earth, and safely leave Mars for the elder gods.

A few minds had crossed to Earth to observe its affairs, and the Martians reasoned that Howard might be one of their own—since his mind had the strength to activate the shining trapezohedron.

The colour seemed to be exerting less pressure, and Howard realized that he would soon be on the surface of Mars. He had found his people. His long exile from those around him would be ended! Soon their superior skill in psychology and surgery would free him to walk among his own kind—his vast pulsating brain attached to a shiny metal machine!

Movement stopped and the unearthly colour began to fade. Howard found himself at the gates of a huge red building whose wings stretched in all directions—perhaps covering the planet. The slowly moving red weed covered the ground. From within, he heard the mathematically perfect music of the Martians.

He went through the great gate into a hall filled with the great brains whose tentacles worked every strange device, whose construction clearly revealed their kinship to the technology that had produced the heat-ray. But as soon as Howard had entered the hall, a great cry went up. The Martians were not shambling toward him in greeting as he had imagined. Instead they began a disorderly march to the exits. Howard looked about for the source of their fear.

There on the other side of the hall, through a trapezoidal doorway, came the figure of one of the elder gods. The Martians had not had time to relocate to Earth. Howard advanced toward the figure; perhaps he could slow its progress by engaging in hand-to-hand combat.

But soon came the shock that sent his mind hurtling back to Earth, a revelation about the nature of the elder gods and the time and form of their return. This shock deprived Howard of all clear memories of this adventure; indeed, years later he was one of the skeptics who maintained that the Earth had not been invaded at all—for when he reached out toward the eldritch figure of the elder god, his hand had encountered *a cold and unyielding surface of polished glass*.

eldritch
influences

weird tales

FRED CHAPPELL

The visionary poet Hart Crane and the equally visionary horror-story writer H. P. Lovecraft met four times. The first time was in Cleveland on August 19, 1922, in the apartment of a mutual acquaintance, the mincing poetaster Samuel Loveman.

It was an awkward encounter. Loveman and four of his idle friends had departed around eleven o'clock to go in search of a late supper. Lovecraft was sitting in an armchair under the lamp, a calico kitten asleep in his lap. He declined the invitation to accompany the others because he would not disturb the kitten; cats comprised another of his numerous manias. Shortly before midnight Crane blundered into the room. He was enjoying this night one of his regular fits of debauchery and was quite drunk. " 'Lo," he said. "I'm Crane. Where's Sam?" He took no notice of Lovecraft's puzzled stare, but raked a half-dozen volumes of French poetry from the sofa, lay down, and passed out.

Lovecraft was quite put off, though the poet's quick slide to oblivion had spared him a dilemma. He would have had to rise in order to present himself, and thus awaken the cat. Lovecraft insisted upon precise formality of address; it was part of his pose as an eighteenth-century esquire sadly comported into the Jazz Age. He was a fanatic teetotaler, and Crane's stuporous condition filled him with disgust.

When Loveman and two companions returned a half hour later, the cat had awakened and Lovecraft set it gently on the floor, rose, and walked to the door. He paused and pointed a finger at Crane, at the ungainly form overpowered with gin and rumpled by the attentions of sailors. "Samuel," he said to Loveman, "your friend is a *degenerate.*"

The effect of this melodramatic sentence was marred by the quality of Lovecraft's voice, a tremulous squeak. Loveman giggled. "Then I'm a degenerate, too, Howard," he said. "Maybe we all are. Maybe that's why no one takes us seriously."

Lovecraft's reply was a toss of his unhandsome head. He closed the door and walked out into the night, walked the seventeen blocks to the YMCA, to his cheerless room and narrow bed. He undressed and, after carefully laying his pants between the mattress and springs for pressing, fell asleep and began to dream his familiar dreams of vertiginous geometries and cyclopean half gods, vivid dreams that would have been anyone else's sweat-drenched nightmares.

After two days Lovecraft and Crane met again and attended a chamber-music concert. Crane was sober then, and Lovecraft was quite charmed by his company.

It was an odd group of literary figures, these poets and fiction writers and amateur scholars stranded like survivors of a shipwreck on what they considered the hostile strand of American philistinism. They were not really congenial in temperament or purpose, but they all shared a common interest in newly discovered, newly reconstructed mythologies. They felt need to posit in history powerful but invisible alien forces that had made contemporary civilization such an inhumane shambles. This sort of notion may have been an index to acute loneliness.

Lovecraft's mythos is the most widely known. In a series of fictions soon to appear in the venerated pulp magazine *Weird Tales,* he told of several eras of prehistory when mankind vied with monstrous races of creatures with extraordinary powers for a foothold upon the earth. Man's present dominance was accidentally and precariously achieved; those alien beings were beginning to rearise from their dormancy. Lovecraft described a cosmos that threw dark Lucretian doubt on the proposition "that such things as organic life, good and evil, love and hate, and all such local attributes of a negligible and temporary race called mankind, have any existence at all."

Hart Crane's mythology was not systematic; in fact, it was hardly articulate. His sensibility was such that he was unnerved in his brushes with the ancient presences he detected, and he could not write or think clearly about them. But his old friends were interested to note in his later poems the occurrence of such lines as, "Couched on bloody basins, floating bones / Of a dismounted people. . . ." Crane believed that Poe had gained best knowledge of the Elder Dominations and so paired him with Whitman in *The Bridge* as a primary avatar of American consciousness.

The most thorough and deliberate of these mythologers was Sterling Croydon, who might have stepped from the pages of one of Lovecraft's stories. He was such a recluse that not even Samuel Loveman saw him more than once or twice a month, though he occupied an apartment in the same building with Loveman, on the floor above. Croydon rarely ventured from his rooms; all those volumes of mathematics, physics, anthropology, and poetry were delivered to his door, and he prepared his scant meals with spirit lamp and a portable gas stove. He was gracious enough to allow occasional visitors, never more than two at a time, and Loveman would spend an evening now and then listening to Croydon elaborate his own system of frightening mythologies. He had been excited to learn that Lovecraft was coming to visit in Cleveland, abandoning for a week his beloved Providence, Rhode Island, and spoke of a strong desire to meet the writer. But when Lovecraft arrived, Croydon withdrew, fearing, no doubt, that to meet the inheritor of Poe's mantle would prove too great a strain for his nerves.

He didn't appear a nervous or high-strung person, but rather—like Lovecraft—a formal gentleman and the soul of composure. He was fastidious and kept himself neatly dressed in dark wool. He imagined that he was painfully photosensitive and ordinarily resorted to dark glasses. His complexion was pale and often flushed, his frame slender almost to the point of emaciation, his gestures quick but calculated. Yet there was a dreamy grandeur about him, and when he held forth on various points of Boolean algebra or primitive religion, Loveman felt that he was in the presence of strong intellect and refined character, however neurasthenic.

It was Croydon's contention that his colleagues had but scratched the surface of the problem. He had read Tylor, Sir James Frazer, Leo Frobenius, and had traced their sources; he knew thoroughly the more radical attempts of Lovecraft, Clark Ashton Smith, Henry Kuttner, Frank Belknap Long, and the others, but considered that they had done no more than dredge up scraps and splinters. He was convinced that one of Lovecraft's principal sources, the *Pnakotic Manuscripts,* was spurious, and that his descriptions of such cruel gods as Nyarlathotep and Yog-Sothoth were biased and vitiated by sensationalism and overwrought prose style.

He did not claim, of course, to know the whole truth. But he did know that Riemann's concept of elliptical geometry was indispensable to a correct theory and that the magnetic fluxions of the South Pole were important in a way no one had thought of. He had been eager to apprise Lovecraft of these ideas and of others, but at the last hour his shyness overcame him. Or maybe he had come to doubt the writer's seriousness.

We are forced to speculate about the outcome of this meeting that never took place; it might well have been of great aid to us, bringing to public notice Croydon's more comprehensive theories and engendering in Lovecraft a deeper sense of responsibility.

The one result we know, however, is that Croydon's life became even more reclusive than before. He almost never saw Loveman and his companions anymore, and no one was admitted now to his rooms. The single exception to this general exclusion was Hart Crane. Croydon thought that he saw qualities and capabilities in Crane lacking in his coarser-grained friends, and he would receive the poet anytime of the day or night. Drinking himself only a little wine, blackberry or elderberry, he kept a supply of gin for Crane, who never arrived sober and who would not stay unless there was something to drink.

So it was to Crane that Croydon poured out all his certainties, theories, and wild surmises. Almost all of it would have made no sense to Crane and would be distorted by his fever for poetry and disfigured by alcoholic forgetfulness. Yet he was impressed by this anomalous scholar, and bits and pieces of those midnight disquisitions lodged in his mind. Perhaps Croydon's talk impressed him in a way it might not have done if he had been sober. The poet was interested in pre-Columbian history, he had always had a yearning to travel in Mexico, and he was particularly taken with Croydon's notion that the Toltec, Mayan, and finally the Aztec religions were shadowy reflections of historical events that took place when mankind inhabited the Antarctic, when that region was steamy Carboniferous forest. Those jaguar gods and feathered serpents that ornamented the temples had become highly stylized and symbolic, Croydon said, but long, long ago, when man and dinosaur and other less definable races coexisted at the bottom of the world, the first of these carvings and paintings had been attempts simply to represent literal appearance. Those creatures, and many others of unproducible aspect, had lived among us. Or rather, we had lived among them, as animal labor supply and as food source.

Crane discounted most of Croydon's notions. He did not believe, for example, that dinosaurs could have been intelligent warm-blooded creatures who had attempted to dislodge the alien gods who ruled among them. He did not believe the dinosaurs had died because their adversaries had infected them with an artificial bacterium that had spread like wildfire, wiping out every major saurian species in three generations. But he was fascinated by Croydon's accounts of tribal religions in South and Central America, caught up by the exotic imagery and the descriptions of ritual. Croydon was especially excited by an obscure tribe inhabiting the reaches of the upper Amazon who worshiped a panoply of gods they called collectively Dzhaimbú. Or perhaps they worshiped but one god who could take different shapes. Much was unclear. But it was clear that Croydon regarded Dzhaimbú as the most anciently rooted of religions, in a direct descent from mankind's prehistoric Antarctic experiences.

Crane was impressed, too, by another of Croydon's ideas. This scholar disagreed vehemently with Darwin's charming theory that man had learned speech by imitating the mating calls of birds. Not so, said Croydon; man was originally a vocally taciturn animal like the horse and the gorilla and, like horse and gorilla, uttered few sounds except under duress of extreme pain or terror. But these sounds they learned to voice quite regularly when Dzhaimbú inflicted upon them unspeakable atrocities, practices that Croydon could not think of without shuddering. All human speech was merely the elaboration of an original shriek of terror.

" 'S a shame, Sterling," Crane said, "that you can't board a ship and go down to the jungle and investigate. I bet you'd turn up some interesting stuff."

Croydon smiled. "Oh, I wouldn't bother with the jungle. I'd go to the Antarctic and look for direct archaeological evidence."

Crane took another swallow from his tumbler of neat gin. His eyes were slightly unfocused and his face was flushed and his neck red in the soft open collar. "Shame you can't go to the South Pole, then, if that's where you want to go."

"No, I shouldn't make a very able sailor, I think," Croydon said. "But, after all, there are other ways to travel than by crawling over the globe like a termite."

And now he launched into a description of what he called spatial emplacement, by which means a man sitting in his room might visit any part of the earth. All that was required was delicate manipulation of complex and tenuous mathematical formulae, prediction of solar winds, polar magnetic fluxions, cosmic-ray vectors, and so forth. He began to pour out a rubble of numbers and Greek letters, all of which Crane disregarded, suspecting that they'd struck now upon the richest vein of his friend's lunacy. Croydon's idea seemed to be that every geographical location in the universe could be imagined as being located on the surface of its individual sphere, and that the problem was simply to turn these spheres until the desired points matched and touched. Touched, but did not conjoin; there would be disaster if they conjoined. The worst complication was that these mathematical spheres, once freed from Euclidean space, were also free in time. One might arrive to inspect Antarctica at the time he wished, which would be pleasant indeed; or he might arrive in the future, uncountable millennia from now. And that would be dangerous as well as inconvenient.

But all this murmur of number and mathematical theory had lulled Crane. He was asleep in the club chair. Croydon woke him gently and suggested that he might like to go home.

"Yeah, maybe I better," Crane said. He scratched his head, disheveling again his spiky hair. "But say, Sterling, I don't know about the travel by arithmetic. Better to get a berth on a ship and sail around and see the birds wheel overhead and the slow islands passing." The thought struck his enthusiasm. "That's what we'll do one of these days. We'll get on a ship and go explore these jungles."

"Good night, Hart," Croydon said.

This impulsive voyage was never to take place, of course. Crane's poetry had begun to attract important critical notice, and he soon moved to New York to further his melancholy but luminous literary career.

Croydon remained behind to pursue his researches ever more intensively. He was quite lost sight of to the world. Loveman would occasionally stop by but was not admitted.

It was on one of these infrequent visits that he felt a strangeness. The hall leading to Croydon's room was chilly, and the air around the door very cold indeed. And the door was sweating cold water, had begun to collect ice around the edges. The brass nameplate was covered with hard frost, obliterating Croydon's name.

Loveman knocked and knocked again and heard no sound within but a low inhuman moan. He tried the icy knob, which finally turned, but could not force the door inward. He braced his feet, set his shoulder against the door, and strained, but was able to get it open only for the space of an inch or two. The noise increased—it was the howling of wind—and a blast of rumbling air swept over him and he saw in that small space only an area of white, a patch of snow. Then the wind thumped the door shut.

Loveman was at a loss. None of his usual friends was nearby to aid him, and he would not call upon others. He belonged to a circle in which there were many secrets they did not wish the larger world to know. He returned to his rooms on the lower floor, dressed himself in a winter woolen jacket and scarf and toboggan. After a brief search he found his gloves. He took a heavy ornamental brass poker from the hearth and returned to Croydon's door.

This time he set himself firmly and, when he had effected a slight opening, thrust the poker into the space and levered it back. The poker began to bend with the strain, and he could feel the coldness of it through his gloves. Then the wind caught the edge of the door and flung it back suddenly, and Loveman found himself staring into a snowy plain swept over by fierce Antarctic wind.

It was all very puzzling. Loveman could see into this windstorm and feel some force of the wind and cold, but he knew that what he felt was small indeed as compared to the fury of the weather into which he could see. Nor could he advance physically into this landscape. He could march forward, pushing against the wind, he could feel himself going forward, but he did not advance so much as an inch into that uproar of ice and snow.

It is in another space, he thought, but very, very close to my own.

He could see into it, but he could not travel there. In fact, with the wild curtains of snow blowing he could see little, but what he could see was terrible enough.

There, seemingly not twenty feet from him, sat Croydon at his desk. The scholar was wearing only his burgundy velvet dressing gown and gray flannel trousers and bedroom slippers. The habitual dark glasses concealed his eyes, but the rest of his face was drawn into a tortured grimace.

Of course Loveman shouted out, *"Croydon! Croydon!"* knowing it was useless.

He could not tell whether his friend was still alive. He did not think that he could be. Certainly if he was in the same space as this Antarctic temperature, he must have died a quick but painful death. Perhaps he was not in that space but in a space like Loveman's own, touching but not conjoining this polar location. Yet the Antarctic space intervened between them, an impassable barrier.

He wished now that he had paid more attention when Croydon had outlined his mathematical ideas. But Loveman, like Crane, had no talent for, no patience with, number. He could never have understood. And now those pages of painstaking calculation had blown away, stiff as steel blades, over the blue ice sheets.

He thought that if he could not walk forward, then he might crawl, but when he went to his knees he found himself suspended a couple of feet above the plane of the floor. Something was wrong with the space he was in. He stood dizzily and stepped down to the floor again, and the descent was as hard a struggle as climbing an Alpine precipice.

There was no way to get to Croydon, and he wondered whether it would be possible to heave a rope to him—if he could find a rope.

It was impossible. The scholar had begun to recede in space, growing smaller and more distant, as if caught in the wrong end of a telescope. And the polar wind began to effect a bad transformation. The dressing gown was ripped from Croydon's body, and he was blackening like a gardenia thrown into a fire. His skin and the layers of his flesh began to curl up and peel away, petal by petal. A savage gust tore off his scalp and the blood that welled there froze immediately, a skullcap of onyx. Soon he would be only a skeleton, tumbled knob and joint over the driving snow, but Loveman was spared the spectacle. The frozen figure receded more quickly, and a swirl of ice grains blotted away the vision. Croydon was gone.

Loveman made his way into the hall, walking backward. His mouth was dully open, and he found that he was sweating and that the sweat had begun to ice his clothing.

There came a crash as of thunder, the smell of ozone, and the Antarctic scene disappeared from the room and there was nothing there. Literally, nothing: no furniture, no walls, no floor. The door with Croydon's nameplate hung over a blue featureless abyss.There was nothing, no real space at all.

Loveman gathered his courage, reached in, and pulled the door closed. He went quietly down the hall, determined to get back into his own room before others showed up. He did not want to answer questions; he did not want anyone to know what he knew. He wanted to go to his room and sit down and think alone and reaffirm his sanity.

The disappearance of Croydon and of that part of the apartment building caused some little public stir. The recluse had no relatives, but scientists were interested, as well as the police. Loveman avoided as best he could any official notice, and in a few months the event, being unexplainable, was largely forgotten.

But the occurrence was not forgotten by the circle of Loveman's friends. For them it was a matter of great concern. They feared that Croydon's experiment had called attention to themselves. Would not those alien presences whose histories they had been studiously examining now turn their regard toward Cleveland? Had he not disturbed the web of space-time as a fly disturbs a spiderweb? It was true that they were indifferent to mankind, to species and individual alike. But there were some researchers who thought, as Lovecraft did, that the ancient race was planning a regeneration of its destiny and would act to keep its existence secret until the moment was ripe. The powers of these beings were immense; they could crush and destroy when and where they pleased, as casually as a man crushes out a cigarette in an ashtray.

It was actually at this early juncture that everything began to come apart. Though the pursuit among the seers and poets was leisurely by human standards, it was relentless.

Lovecraft died in 1937, in painful loneliness. The official medical report listed the cause as intestinal cancer, but the little group of investigators was accustomed to greeting all such reports with deep skepticism. Hart Crane's more famous death had taken place five years earlier, the celebrated leap into the sea.

The men had since met twice again, during the period of what Lovecraft called his "New York exile." He was a little shocked at the changes in Crane's physical condition. "He looks more weather-beaten & drink-puffed than he did in the past," Lovecraft wrote to his aunt, "tragically drink-riddled but now eminent." He predicted that Crane would find it difficult to write another major work. "After about three hours of acute & intelligent argument poor Crane left—to hunt up a new supply of whiskey & banish reality for the rest of the night!"

Lovecraft records this encounter as taking place May 24, 1930. They were not alone and had no opportunity to talk privately, so that Crane would not have told the other what he had learned of the circumstances of Croydon's death. He could not apprise Lovecraft that he alone was inheritor to Croydon's secret knowledge and that his identity must necessarily be known to that being, or series of beings, Dzhaimbú. He spoke of leaving New York and moving to Charleston, but Lovecraft did not pick up the hint, merely agreeing that such a move might be beneficial. Perhaps Crane's gallantry prevented his placing the other in danger.

Another interpretation is possible. We may guess that Crane did indeed communicate some of his information to the horror-story writer. It is just at this period that Lovecraft's mythos began to take its more coherent and credible shape in such works as "The Shadow Over Innsmouth" and "The Dreams in the Witch House." Certainly both Lovecraft and Loveman remarked that Crane now lived in a state of haunted terror, wild and frightful, dependent upon alcohol to keep his fear manageable. Crane must have known that he was being pursued—the signs were unmistakable—and decided to face the terror on its own grounds. For this reason he politicked to get the Guggenheim grant that would take him to Mexico.

But it was too late. Alcohol had disordered his nervous system; his strength was gone. On the voyage to Mexico he met the celebrated bacteriologist Dr. Hans Zinsser and imagined that he was an agent of Dzhaimbú sent to infect humanity by means of typhus-ridden rats. Zinsser's motives in dumping infected rats into the harbor at Havana remain unknown, but it is hardly probable that Crane's suspicions were correct.

In Mexico the poet's behavior was uncontrolled and incomprehensible, a series of shocking and violent incidents that landed him often in jail and caused his friends to distrust any sentence he uttered. His decision to meet the terror face-to-face was disastrous; he could not stand up under the strain. No man could. And his further decision to keep his knowledge and theories secret so as not to endanger others was a worse disaster.

In the end, he fled, unable to face the prospect of coming close to the source of the horror. The voyage home began with dreams and visions so terrifying that he could not bear to close his eyes and so stayed awake, drinking continuously. Embarrassing episodes followed of which he was numbly aware but past caring about. On April 27, 1932, Hart Crane jumped from the railing of the *Orizaba*. The sea received him, and the immense serpentine manifestation of Dzhaimbú, which had been following in the unseen depths the wake of the vessel, devoured him.

This fabulous shadow only the sea keeps.

It is inevitable that we read these sad histories as we do, as a catalogue of missed opportunities and broken communications. A present generation self-righteously decries the errors of its forefathers. But it is unlikely that any human effort would have changed the course of events. There still would have come about the reawakening of Dzhaimbú and the other worse gods, under whose charnel dominion we now suffer and despair.

the land of the reflected ones

NANCY A. COLLINS

The old man was smiling when he opened the door. The smile disappeared as soon as he saw it was Emerson.

"Oh. You."

Not even *it's you*. The old man showed his dislike for his visitor by using as few words as possible during their brief meetings. Emerson didn't bother to acknowledge the slight. He was accustomed to such rudeness from his inferiors. And since everyone walking the earth was his inferior, Emerson spent a lot of imagination planning how he would deal with them once the time rolled around. But that would have to wait, if for just a little while. Emerson sniffed and drew his arms in close to avoid unnecessary physical contact with the old man as they stood together in the cramped confines of the bookshop.

Up until recently, when a slight stroke forced its proprietor to close down, the shop had been in continuous business for over five decades. Although he had greatly reduced his hours and limited his clientele to a handful of serious bibliophiles, the old man had done nothing to reduce his stock. In fact, he continued to add to it. Books surrounded them on every side, spilling from the narrowly spaced bookshelves that reached to the ceiling, and stacked atop one another on every available surface. The place smelled of the genteel decay of old paper and moldering leather.

The old man motioned for Emerson to follow him as he hobbled along a narrow path that led from the front door to the living quarters in the back, screened from view by a bead curtain.

The tiny kitchen and dining area was identical to the front room. The books had found their way in here, too, muscling aside the few meager kitchen appliances. Emerson's eyes automatically went to the door that led to what he supposed was the old man's bedroom. It was closed.

"Is your wife in?" he asked, feigning small talk.

The old man gave him a strange look, as if Emerson's mentioning his wife worried him in some way he could not quite grasp.

"No. She's gone shopping. I thought you were her. Thought she forgot her key."

So they were alone. Good.

"Do you have it?"

Again the look. "Of course, I have it. I would not have called you if I did not have it."

"I want to see it first."

The old man nodded and hobbled over to the kitchen table, which was slightly bow-legged from the weight of the books stacked atop it. He reached into the jumble and, without hesitation, pulled out an oversized leather-bound volume with a reinforced metal spine and hasps. He turned and handed it to Emerson with a sneer of disgust he did nothing to hide. Emerson wiped his hands and tried his best to control their trembling. It would not do to have the old man know just how important the damned book was to him.

And damned was right.

The *Aegrisomnia*. The fabled tome written by a dying alchemist-wizard twelve hundred years ago while in the grips of brain fever. It was believed to be filled with rantings, ramblings, and recipes for power. More power than a man could dream of and remain sane.

Of course, what Emerson was holding was not the original manuscript. That had been put to the torch by the Borgia pope over five centuries ago after he'd had it transcribed into Latin by a brace of specially trained monks—all of whom later committed suicide or were found floating in the Tiber under mysterious circumstances. The Latin version was later translated into German by a priest who secretly sympathized with Martin Luther and apparently thought the Reformation would fare better if it had access to some of the "forbidden knowledge" the Holy See had been hoarding for the last millennium.

In 1909 a British scholar of the name Stroud translated the *Aegrisomnia* into English. Stroud was an eccentric, but far from the harmless Oxford don that he appeared to be, proving himself dedicated to the Black Arts in ways popinjays like Crowley and Blavatsky merely played at.

Of the hundred copies of the *Aegrisomnia* that Stroud had privately published, however, only one was complete and unabridged. And bound in leather. And that was Stroud's private copy—the one with his own personal annotations scrawled in the margins. The one he had bound himself—with the skin of his virgin daughter. Granted, she wasn't his *legitimate* daughter—her mother was a marginally retarded scullery maid who had been with the household since childhood—but the gesture put to the pale anything the self-styled "Beast" had ever done.

Stroud was eventually found out, years later, when the buzz bomb that took out his London row house and rammed a length of timber through his chest also uncovered a child's skeleton sealed behind the library bookshelves. Many of the "demon don's" books and papers were consumed by fire that night, and since it was never found, it was assumed that Stroud's personal copy of the *Aegrisomnia* had been one of the casualities. But then, after the war, rumors began to circulate of the book being glimpsed in South America, then again in Australia, then Canada. . . .

Emerson had followed these rumors with the utmost interest. He had spent his entire adult life acquiring books and manuscripts many believed lost—if not apocryphal. He had devoted every waking hour—and nearly every dime of his inheritance—to the study of things most people either dismissed out of hand or feared so intensely they preferred not to contemplate them at all. And now, after all this time, he had his hands on the last piece of the puzzle. The master piece that would lock all the others into place and render the unknowable known unto him.

Emerson caressed the bastard-child leather as he opened the book, his gaze hungrily darting along the yellowed pages. He closed his eyes, and the formulae blazed against his inner lids. Yes. This was indeed the real thing. He opened his eyes and found the old man looking at him as if he were a distasteful animal suddenly transported into his dingy kitchen. Emerson snapped the book shut.

"Have you looked at this?" he asked, trying to mask the anxiety in his voice.

The old man shook his head. "It's mumbo-jumbo. My wife likes to read things like that—" He motioned to a stack of old *Fate* magazines teetering precariously atop the draining board. "Me, I'd rather read fiction. There's more truth in fiction. I don't even like touching the thing. I know human leather when I see it. I had a book come through here a few years back—belonged to some bastard in the Nazi High Command. It was pornographic pictures—women with animals, men with children. It was bound just like that. I burned it. I would have burned that thing, too, if I didn't need the money so badly—"

Emerson fought the urge to giggle in the old man's face. The fool! He had no idea what he had just surrendered for a mere three hundred dollars! No doubt his idea of a real find was a first edition of *Alice's Adventures Underground* or an autographed copy of *Northanger Abbey*. Emerson decided to allow himself a little pleasure at the old man's expense. After all, it wasn't like the book dealer had ever shown him anything resembling the respect due him.

"Tell me—haven't you ever wondered what it would be like to, say, rule the world or turn back the clock and become young again—perhaps even cheat death altogether?"

The old man allowed himself a smile, and the lines around his mouth and eyes softened. "Ha! Now you're starting to sound like my wife! She asks me silly things like that. And I'll tell you the same thing I tell her: who needs the aggravation? You'd spend all your time dealing with all the *other* people who want to rule the world. And why would I want to be young—so I can grow old all over again? And as for living forever—how could I be happy watching everyone I loved and cared about die and leave me alone? Is that something to look forward to—being a mourner? God knows, my life may not be perfect, but at least it will have a beginning and an end. Just like my books. And as long as I have them and my wife, I can make do without immortality or ruling the world."

"And how does your wife react when you tell her this?"

"She smiles." The old man's face grew stern again. "Did you bring the money?"

Emerson nodded and reached into his jacket, producing a small envelope, which he handed to the old man. "As we agreed."

The old man opened the envelope and counted the bills. He looked up, his pale cheeks suddenly hectic with color. "This isn't enough!"

"What do you mean it isn't enough? You told me three hundred! That's three hundred."

The old man was shaking his head. "No, I told you when I called to let you know I'd secured the book that it ended up costing more than what I first quoted you. I need five hundred."

A spark of panic burst within Emerson. The three hundred had been the last of his inheritance. He only had fifty-six dollars left in his bank account. "I'll pay you the remainder in a couple of days—I'm good for it—"

"No! I spent the rent on that book! You give me five hundred or you get nothing!" The old man shoved the envelope back at Emerson and grabbed the book and tugged on it feebly.

A mixture of fear and rage filled Emerson, blotting out all else in his mind. He yanked the book free of the old man's palsied grip, and his lips pulled back into a rictus grin that exposed his teeth all the way to the gum line, he brought the spine down on the book dealer's head. He actually felt the old man's skull give way. The old man dropped lifeless to the floor, his snowy-white hair stained brilliant red.

Emerson stared down at the corpse for a long moment. He clutched the *Aegrisomnia* to his chest much the same way Stroud had held his daughter before he slipped the knife between her ribs, nearly ninety years ago.

It was his now. His. And no one was going to take it away from him. Ever.

Emerson's apartment, at first glance, was not all that different from the old man's front room. The efficiency was filled to bursting with books, many of them quite old and exceptionally rare. The shelves that lined the walls were crammed full of tomes dedicated to occult lore. Some were relatively prosaic, such as Crowley's *Magick in Theory and Practice,* Huysmans's *Là-Bas,* Frazer's *Golden Bough,* and Kraemer & Sprenger's *Malleus Maleficarum.* Others were comparatively new additions to the apocrypha, such as *The Liber Null, The Psychick Bible,* and *The Leyden Papyrus.*

However, Abdul Alhazred's *Necronomicon,* von Junzt's *Unaussprechlichen Kulten,* Prinn's *De Vermis Mysteriis,* the Comte d'Erlette's *Cultes des Goules,* Gantley's *Hydrophinnae,* Carson's *The Black God of Madness, The Book of Eibon,* the *Pnakotic Manuscripts,* the *Cthaat Aquadingen,* and the *Revelations of Glaaki* were far from innocuous. Or cheap.

Emerson had literally spent a fortune in acquiring them. Over the years, as his money dwindled, he had been forced to take lodgings that were far from the sumptuous appointments of his upbringing. Of his mother's physical estate, all that was left was a large mirrored wardrobe, which dominated one corner of the room. Everything else had been sold off, piece by piece, in order to provide him with cash for his precious books of forbidden lore. And now, after close to thirty years, he was on the threshold of capturing the power he'd pursued for so long.

Emerson swept aside the jumble of concordances, foreign-language dictionaries, and lexicons littering the table that served as both his desk and dining area, and placed the *Aegrisomnia* down. Tonight would be the start of his ascension. All the scraps and whispers of information he'd gleaned from the other books and manuscripts would now be stitched together, providing him with a shining raiment suited for a wizard-king.

He flipped open the book and shook his head in amazement. Even in a debased translation such as this, the innate power of the charms and spells recorded was staggering. What had the original been like? Just by skimming the chapters, he saw formulae and rituals detailing the conjuring of extradimensional beings, the transferal of souls into the newborn, the mastery of the weather. . . .

Yet he couldn't help but wonder why Stroud, who had understood the importance of the forces described in the *Aegrisomnia* to such an extent that he'd wrapped it in his daughter's skin, had not used it to further his own ends. Granted, Stroud was close to eighty when he died in 1941, but he was far from youthful or immortal. And while he'd enjoyed his share of fame and honors during the course of his long and illustrious career, he lived out his life in a two-bedroom row house in an appallingly middle-class neighborhood.

No matter. Whatever fears Stroud may have had against wielding the power of the *Aegrisomnia,* Emerson did not share them. He could not understand how someone could have power and not use it. Then again, there was a lot about people Emerson did not understand. It was one of the reasons he'd never developed any friends. Not even as a boy.

The last, fading blossom of a once-powerful family, Emerson's mother had raised him to consider himself better than others, and he had learned the lesson well. Toward the end, he considered his mother beneath him as well, as she had married into the Emersons and not been born one. It made pulling the plug on her life-support system rather simple.

Emerson smiled to himself. Soon he would replace his dreary studio apartment with a pleasure dome that would put Xanadu to shame! He would dine on the most succulent of dishes, relieve his physical needs with only the most beautiful of women and boys—and the heads of everyone who had ever crossed him, cursed him, or looked at him the wrong way would decorate the pikes lining the roads leading to his palace. Yes. He rather liked that image.

There was a sudden thumping at the door. Emerson jumped in his seat, startled by the noise.

"Mr. Emerson—? Open up—police! We want to talk to you!"

A spike of fear made his guts clench. The police! But how could they have known to come looking for him? Of course. The old man's wife. He must have told her about who was coming to pick up the book. Damn! He should have stayed long enough to finish her off, too! But he'd been frightened and anxious to return home and start work on his ascension. . . .

The thudding intensified. "Mr. Emerson—? Please come to the door, Mr. Emerson!"

Emerson's mouth was too dry to respond. Not now. Not after all the time and money he'd spent on locating the *Aegrisomnia*, only to have it taken away from him at the very moment of his triumph—! There had to be a way he could escape capture! There had to be—!

Even though he knew there was only one door in and out of the apartment, Emerson instinctively glanced around the room. His eye fell on his mother's old wardrobe with its full-length mirror set in the door.

Mirror.

Something sparked in the back of his head. He'd seen something in the book about mirrors, hadn't he? He flipped back a few pages—yes! Here it was. A spell that allowed the practitioner access to and from "the Land of the Reflected Ones." The formula was simple enough for one as skilled as he.

There was a much heavier thump on the other side of the door. The police had stopped using their fists and were now applying their shoulders. However, Emerson had invested in a top-of-the-line set of dead bolts, for fear of the other tenants in the building breaking into his room while he was gone. The police would need one of those portable battering rams to get the door open. That meant he had just enough time to effect his escape.

Emerson stood in front of the wardrobe. The mirror was well over a hundred years old and thicker than any other he'd ever seen. It was slightly convex, protruding a good three inches from its setting. He remembered how his mother used to stand in front of it and primp herself, rattling on about the days when their family had ruled the town with a steel grip. Emerson took a deep breath to steady himself and closed his eyes, reciting the formula, making the proper gestures, and invoking the names of nameless gods. When he reopened his eyes, the surface of the mirror had been transformed into something that rippled like water, yet glinted silver.

There was a thunderous crack behind him as the dead bolts finally gave. Without looking back, Emerson stepped into the mirror.

His first impression was that he was being buried alive in gelatin; then he opened his eyes and saw silver fluid rippling around him like mercury; then he was standing in his room again. His first thought was that he'd failed. That he'd hallucinated the whole thing. Then he realized he was looking in the direction of the front door. He turned around and stared back the way he came. In place of the back wall of his apartment, with its bookshelves and piles of dirty clothes, there was a blank expanse—blank, that is, except for an oblong opening outlined in silvery light. Of course. How could there be a wardrobe on this side? A mirror does not reflect itself.

As he stared out of the mirror into his real-world apartment, the door flew inward and two policemen, their guns drawn, came into the room. Their mirror-images burst into the mirror-room at the exact same time, and Emerson cried out in alarm. But the mirror-police did not seem to see him, even though he was standing right in front of them. At first Emerson was puzzled, then he realized that of course they wouldn't know he was there, since their real-world counterparts did not see him, either. Unless they happened to look in the mirror.

Emerson quickly moved to one side of the silvery doorway, pressing himself against the blank wall. He seriously doubted the police had the imagination to realize their prey had escaped through the looking glass, but he wasn't going to risk detection. Besides, he could keep track of what the police were doing by watching their mirror-reverse doppelgängers.

Satisfied the mirror-room was empty, the mirror-cops motioned for a little old lady to enter. The old man's wife. One of the mirror-cops pointed to the *Aegrisomnia,* still sitting open on the table. Emerson strained to hear what the mirror-cop was asking the mirror-woman, but his voice was twisted around so it sounded like he was talking backward underwater. No doubt he was asking her if this was the book her husband had procured for his customer. The mirror-woman shook her head "no."

Emerson frowned. Strange. The old man had spoken as if his wife was aware of what he was selling. Perhaps the old man hadn't shown her the book for fear of her becoming angry over the money he'd spent. Or perhaps he didn't want her becoming upset over the human-skin binding.

One of the mirror-cops was scratching his head and looking around the room. He was bothered by the fact there was no one in a room double-bolted from the inside. As the mirror-cops huddled near the doorway to talk among themselves, the mirror-woman remained by the table. At first Emerson could not make out what she was doing. Then, to his surprise, he realized she was reading the *Aegrisomnia.*

Sweat began to bead on his forehead and lip. Surely the old woman knew nothing of the secrets locked within the arcane formulae. He began to chew on his thumbnail. Just as he'd succeeded in convincing himself she was simply an old woman and nothing more, she looked up from her reading and stared directly into the mirror. Although she could not see him, Emerson knew she was looking for him.

As the mirror-woman slowly approached, growing closer and closer to where Emerson cowered, his back pressed against the other side of a wall that didn't exist, he could hear the old man's voice ringing in his ears: *My wife likes to read that stuff.* It had never crossed Emerson's mind that the old man's wife might be a sorceress.

The mirror-woman was standing right beside Emerson, but she did not see him. Instead, she stared straight ahead, peering through the silver doorway into the real world. The mirror-cops were still talking among themselves, paying her no mind as she rummaged through her handbag. After a few seconds she retrieved a small colorless wax crayon, the type used to scrawl designs on children's Easter eggs. Her wrinkled lips moved slightly as she mumbled something that even backward and underwater was recognizable to Emerson as an invocation. As she called upon the nameless gods, the old woman made a series of markings on the mirror. Once finished, the old woman's reflection smiled to itself and headed out the door, followed shortly thereafter by the puzzled policemen.

The moment the door closed on them, Emerson peeled himself away from the wall and stood in front of the silvery doorway. His view of the world outside its borders was now obscured by a series of lines that pulsed with a dark power. He reached out to touch the inner surface of the mirror, but there was a loud, sharp sound, like that of an electric bug-light frying a particularly large fly, and a burst of purplish-black energy. Pain shot up Emerson's fingers and into his arm, causing him to jump back.

The old woman had sealed him in.

Emerson began to tremble. He was trapped. Trapped.

He took a deep breath and tried to calm himself. He couldn't think like that. Thinking like that led to panic. And panic would get him nowhere. He was not trapped. How could he be? She was just an old woman. He, on the other hand, was an Emerson. And everyone knew an Emerson was better than anyone else. There was no way he could be outfoxed, outmaneuvered, outdone by an old woman. Even an old woman who'd mastered the *Aegrisomnia.*

The *Aegrisomnia.* Of course.

The original might still be in the real world, but he had access to its mirror-twin! He moved to the duplicate table. Yes, it was still here. The police had not taken it with them. At least, not yet. All he had to do was to find a counterspell to override the old woman's hastily constructed barrier. . . .

Emerson's grin of triumph collapsed as he opened the book and stared down at the mirror-*Aegrisomnia*'s pages. The print was in reverse. The panic threatened to overwhelm him again, but he forced it back down.

Okay. So the words were printed backward and in reverse. He would simply hold it up to the mirror and—but no. There was only one mirror in his room—and he was in it. A hysterical giggle burst from his lips.

Emerson bit the inside of his mouth so hard it brought blood. No! He refused to believe he was trapped! *Refused!* He was an intelligent man; he could figure out the problem placed before him if he just calmed down. He needed a drink, that was all. Yes, a drink would help steady his nerves and set his mind to the task he was about to undertake.

The wardrobe was situated in such a way that it reflected almost the entire room, including his humble cot. He kept a pint of scotch under the mattress for moments when he needed it. . . . But did that mean there was one in this world as well? Emerson reached under the duplicate of his bed, uncertain of what he'd find, and was relieved when his fingers closed around the glass surface of a bottle.

Emerson smiled at the pint of scotch as if it were a long-lost friend and hurriedly cracked the seal. Just to steady his nerves. That's all. Help him think. He tilted his head and slugged back a double shot—and immediately spewed it out.

The stuff tasted like a cross between cat piss and gasoline. Granted, it was a cheap brand, but this was ridiculous! Emerson wiped his mouth with his sleeve and stared at the bottle. The print on the label was the same as that of the original—except it was reversed. Along with its molecular structure, apparently.

Mirror reverse. The Land of the Reflected Ones. But *he* wasn't a reflection. He was the real thing. And there was no way he could eat or drink in this world without poisoning himself.

Emerson scrambled back over to the table, clawing through the clutter for scrap paper and a pencil. He'd copy the formula out of the book by hand, transposing the words so he could read from it. It would take time, but he had no other choice. He had to get out before he starved to death or died of thirst.

Emerson worked for two solid hours, fearful every minute that someone would walk into the real-world room and see him in the mirror. Not that they would believe what they saw, but it would have still proved a distraction and cost him precious time. When he was finished, Emerson stood in front of the silvery doorway and read aloud from the paper. He then waited for the dark lines crisscrossing the mirror's inner surface to disappear.

Nothing happened.

He repeated the spell, placing the accent on different syllables.

Still nothing happened.

What was wrong? He'd made all the proper hand signals, invoked the correct gods and demiurges. . . .

Then he remembered how the mirror-replicas of the police and old woman had sounded when they spoke, like skewed tape-loops played backward. Mirror-speak. The Language of the Reflected Ones. But he wasn't a reflection. He was the real thing. And he talked forward in a world where magical spells only worked if they were spoken not just backward, but in reverse.

The panic resurfaced a third time, and Emerson made no attempt to quell it. He began weeping and cursing at the top of his lungs and raced around the room, kicking over the furniture and knocking the books off their shelves.

Trapped. Trapped! *Trapped!*

After he'd exhausted himself, he stood gasping for breath, his hands planted on his knees. When he looked up, his gaze fell on the mirror-door. In the real world, it led out into the dingy urine-stained hallway of his apartment building. But where did it lead to in the Land of the Reflected Ones? To another mirror, perhaps? It was worth finding out. Anything was better than being trapped in the reflection of his grimy studio apartment.

Since the police had battered in the original, the mirror-door was unlocked. Instead of the hallway outside his apartment, however, a sea of seething shadow and swirling mist filled the threshold. And in the roiling, formless chaos, something lifted something not unlike a head and opened something that might be called eyes. And smiled at him.

Emerson screamed and slammed the door, his fingers scrambling to try and secure locks and dead bolts that were no longer functional. Babbling prayers and pleas to gods he'd abandoned as a child, Emerson raced to the silver doorway that led from the mirror-world into his own.

There was a burst of purplish light and the smell of ozone as he was hurled backward. Emerson groaned as he lay on the floor of the reflected apartment, the smell of smoke rising from his singed hair and clothes. He was dully aware of having soiled his pants.

He found himself wishing he'd bothered to read Alice's *Through the Looking-Glass.* Maybe it would have helped prepare him for his own ordeal in the land of reflections. But he seriously doubted Alice had been confronted by anything as disturbing as whatever it was that lurked on his threshold.

The *Aegrisomnia* had referred to the other side of the mirror as "The Land of the Reflected Ones." And he, after all the metaphysical and mystical studies he'd made over the years, had never once wondered what might fill a mirror when there was one there to look into it.

But, judging from the rattle of the doorknob, he would soon know.

the shadow at the bottom of the world

THOMAS LIGOTTI

Before there occurred anything of a truly prodigious nature, the season had manifestly erupted with some feverish intent. This, at least, was how it appeared to us, whether we happened to live in town or somewhere outside its limits. (And traveling between town and countryside was Mr. Marble, who had been studying the seasonal signs far longer and in greater depth than we, disclosing prophecies that no one would credit at the time.) On the calendars that hung in so many of our homes, the monthly photograph illustrated the spirit of the numbered days below it: sheaves of cornstalks standing brownish and brittle in a newly harvested field, a narrow house and wide barn in the background, a sky of empty light above, and fiery leafage frolicking about the edges of the scene. But something dark, something abysmal, always finds its way into the bland beauty of such pictures, something that usually holds itself in abeyance, some entwining presence that we always know is there. And it was exactly this presence that had gone into crisis, or perhaps had been secretly invoked by small shadowy voices calling out in the midst of our dreams. There came a bitter scent into the air, as of sweet wine turning to vinegar, and there was an hysteric brilliance flourished by the trees in town as well as those in the woods beyond, while along the roads between were the intemperate displays of thorn apple, sumac, and towering sunflowers that nodded behind crooked roadside fences. Even the stars of chill nights seemed to grow delirious and take on the tints of an earthly inflammation. Finally, there was a moonlit field where a scarecrow had been left to watch over ground that had long been cleared yet would not turn cold.

Adjacent to the edge of town, the field allowed full view of itself from so many of our windows. It lay spacious beyond tilting fence-posts and under a bright round moon, uncluttered save for the peaked silhouettes of corn shocks and a manlike shape that stood fixed in the nocturnal solitude. The head of the figure was slumped forward, as if a grotesque slumber had overtaken its straw-stuffed body, and the arms were slackly extended in a way that suggested some incredible gesture toward flight. For a moment it seemed to be an insistent wind that was flapping those patched-up overalls and fluttering the worn flannel of those shirtsleeves; and it would seem a forceful wind indeed that caused the stitched-up head to nod in its dreams. But nothing else joined in such movements: the withered leaves of the cornstalks were stiff and unstirring, the trees of the distant woods were in a lull against the clear night. Only one thing appeared to be living where the moonlight spread across that dead field. And there were some who claimed that the scarecrow actually raised its arms and its empty face to the sky, as though declaring itself to the heavens, while others thought that its legs kicked wildly, like those of a man who is hanged, and that they kept on kicking for the longest time before the thing collapsed and lay quiet. Many of us, we discovered, had been nudged from our beds that night, called as witnesses to this obscure spectacle. Afterward, the sight we had seen, whatever we believed its reason, would not rest within us but snatched at the edges of our sleep until morning.

And during the overcast hours of the following day we could not keep ourselves from visiting the place around which various rumors had hastily arisen. As pilgrims we wandered into that field, scrutinizing the debris of its harvest for augural signs, circling that scarecrow as if it were a great idol in shabby disguise, a sacred avatar out of season. But everything upon that land seemed unwilling to support our hunger for revelation, and our congregation was lost in fidgeting bemusement. (With the exception, of course, of Mr. Marble, whose eyes, we recall, were gleaming with illuminations he could not offer us in any words we would understand.) The sky had hidden itself behind a leaden vault of clouds, depriving us of the crucial element of pure sunlight that we needed to fully burn off the misty dreams of the past night. And a vine-twisted stone wall along the property line of the farm was the same shade as the sky, while the dormant vines themselves were as colorless as the stone they enmeshed like a strange network of dead veins. But this calculated grayness was merely an aspect of the scene, for the colors of the abundant woods along the margins of the landscape were undulled, as if those radiant leaves possessed some inner source of illumination or stood in contrast to some deeper shadow that they served to mask.

Such conditions no doubt impeded our efforts to come to terms with our fears about that particular field. Above all these manifestations, however, was the fact that the earth of those harvested acres, especially in the area surrounding the scarecrow, was unnaturally warm for the season. It seemed, in fact, that a late harvest was due. And some insisted that the odd droning noises that filled the air could not be blamed on the legions of local cicadas but indeed rose up from under the ground.

By the time of twilight, only a few stragglers remained in the field, among them the old farmer who owned this suddenly notorious acreage. We knew that he shared the same impulse as the rest of us when he stepped up to his scarecrow and began to tear the impostor to pieces. Others joined in the vandalism, pulling out handfuls of straw and stripping away the clothes until they had exposed what lay beneath them—the strange and unexpected sight.

For the skeleton of the thing should have been merely two crosswise planks. We verified this common fact with its maker, and he swore that no other materials had been used. Yet the shape that stood before us was of a wholly different nature. It was something black and twisted into the form of a man, something that seemed to have come up from the earth and grown over the wooden planks like a dark fungus, consuming the structure. There were now black legs that hung as if charred and withered; there was a head that sagged like a sack of ashes upon a meager body of blackness; and there were thin arms stretched out like knobby branches from a lightning-scorched tree. All of this was supported by a thick dark stalk that rose out of the earth and reached into the effigy like a hand into a puppet.

And even as that dull day was dimming into night, our vision was distracted by the profounder darkness of the thing that dangled so blackly in the dusk. Its composition appeared to be of the blackest earth, of earth that had gone stagnant somewhere in its depths, where a rich loam had festered into a bog of shadows. Soon we realized that each of us had fallen silent, entranced by a deep blackness that seemed to absorb our sight, but which exposed nothing to scrutiny except an abyss in the outline of a man. Even when we ventured to lay our hands on that mass of darkness, we found only greater mysteries. For there was almost no tangible aspect to it, merely a hint of material sensation, barely the feel of wind or water. It seemed to possess no more substance than a few shifting flames, but flames of only the slightest warmth, black flames that have curled together to take on the molten texture of spoiled fruit. And there was a vague sense of circulation, as though a kind of serpentine life swirled gently within. But no one could stand to keep his hold upon it for long before stepping suddenly away.

"Damn the thing, it's not going to be rooted to my land," said the old farmer. Then he walked off toward the barn. And like the rest of us he was trying to rub something from the hand that had touched the shriveled scarecrow, something that could not be seen.

He returned to us with an armory of axes, shovels, and other implements for uprooting what had grown upon his land, this eccentricity of the harvest. It would seem to have been a simple task: the ground was unusually soft all around the base of that black growth, and its tenuous substance could hardly resist the wide blade of the farmer's ax. But when the old man swung and tried to split the thing like a piece of firewood, the blade would not cleave. The ax entered and was closed upon, as if sunk within a viscous mire. The farmer pulled at the handle and managed to dislodge the ax, but he immediately let it fall from his hands. "It was pulling back on me," he said in a low voice. "And you heard that sound." Indeed, the sound that had haunted the area all that day—like innumerable insects laughing—did seem to rise in pitch and intensity when the thing was struck.

Without a word, we began digging up the earth where that thick black stalk was buried. We dug fairly deep before the approaching darkness forced us to abandon our efforts. Yet no matter how far down we burrowed, it was not far enough to reach the bottom of that sprouting blackness. Furthermore, our attempts became hindered by a perverse reluctance, as in the instance of someone who is hesitant to have a diseased part of his own body cut away in order to keep the disease from spreading.

It was nearly pitch-dark when we finally walked away from that field, for the clouds of that day had lingered to hide the moon. In the blackness our voices whispered various strategies so that we might yet accomplish what we had thereto failed in doing. We whispered, although none of us would have said why he did so.

The great shadow of a moonless night encompassed the landscape, preserving us from seeing the old farmer's field and what was tenanted there. And yet so many of the houses in town were in vigil throughout those dark hours. Soft lights shone through curtained windows along the length of each street, where our trim wooden homes seemed as small as dollhouses beneath the dark rustling depths of the season. Above the gathered roofs hovered the glass globes of streetlamps, like little moons set inside the dense leaves of elms and oaks and maples. Even in the night, the light shining through those leaves betrayed the festival of colors seething within them, blazing auras that had not faded with the passing days, a plague of colors that had already begun to infect our dreams. This prodigy had by then become connected in our minds with that field just outside of town and the strange growth that there had taken root.

Thus, a sense of urgency led us back to that place, where we found the old farmer waiting for us as the frigid aurora of dawn appeared above the distant woods. Our eyes scanned the frost-powdered earth and studied every space among shadows and corn shocks spread out over the land, searching for what was no longer present in the scene. "It's gone back," the farmer revealed to us. "Gone into the earth like something hiding in its shell. Don't walk there," he warned, pointing to the mouth of a wide pit.

We gathered about the edge of this opening in the ground, gazing into its depths. Even full daybreak did not show us the bottom of that dark well. Our speculations were brief and useless. Some of us picked up the shovels lying nearby, as if to begin the long duty of filling in the great aperture. "No use in that," said the farmer. He then found a large stone and dropped it straight down the shaft. We waited and waited; we put our heads close to the hole and listened. But all we seemed to hear were remote droning echoes, as of countless voices of insects chattering unseen. Finally, we covered the hazardous pit with some boards and buried the makeshift enclosure under a mound of soft dirt. "Maybe there'll be some change in the spring," someone said. But the old farmer only chuckled. "You mean when the ground warms up? Why do you think those leaves aren't falling the way they should?"

It was not long after this troubling episode that our dreams, which formerly had been the merest shadows and glimpses, swelled into full phase. Yet they must not have been dreams entirely, but also excavations into the season that had inspired them. In sleep we were consumed by the feverish life of the earth, cast among a ripe, fairly rotting world of strange growth and transformation. We took a place within a darkly flourishing landscape where even the air was ripened into ruddy hues and everything wore the wrinkled grimace of decay, the mottled complexion of old flesh. The face of the land itself was knotted with so many other faces, ones that were corrupted by vile impulses. Grotesque expressions were molding themselves into the darkish grooves of ancient bark and the whorls of withered leaf; pulpy misshapen features peered out of damp furrows; and the crisp skin of stalks and dead seeds split into a multitude of crooked smiles. All was a freakish mask painted with russet, rashy colors—colors that bled with a virulent intensity, so rich and vibrant that things trembled with their own ripeness. But despite this gross palpability, there remained something spectral at the heart of these dreams. It moved in shadow, a presence that was in the world of solid forms but not of it. Nor did it belong to any other world that could be named, unless it was to that realm that is suggested to us by an autumn night when fields lay ragged in moonlight and some wild spirit has entered into things, a great aberration sprouting forth from a chasm of moist and fertile shadows, a hollow-eyed howling malignity rising to present itself to the cold emptiness of space and the pale gaze of the moon.

And it was to that moon we were forced to look for comfort when we awoke trembling in the night, overcome by the sense that another life was taking root within us, seeking its ultimate incarnation in the bodies we always dreamed were our own and inviting us into the depths of an extraordinary harvest.

Certainly there was some relief when we began to discover, after many insecure hints and delvings, that the dreams were not a sickness restricted to solitary individuals or families but in fact were epidemic throughout the community. No longer were we required to disguise our uneasiness as we met on the streets under the luxuriant shadows of trees that would not cast off their gaudy foliage, the mocking plumage of a strange season. We had become a race of eccentrics and openly declared an array of curious whims and suspicions, at least while daylight allowed this audacity.

Honored among us was that one old fellow, well known for his oddities, who had anticipated our troubles weeks beforehand. As he wandered about town, wheeling the blade-sharpening grindstone by which he earned his living, Mr. Marble had spoken of what he could "read in the leaves," as if those fluttering scraps of lush color were the pages of a secret book in which he perused gold and crimson hieroglyphs. "Just look at them," he urged passersby, "bleeding their colors like that. They should be bled dry, but now they're . . . making pictures. Something inside trying to show itself. They're as dead as rags now, look at them all limp and flapping. But something's still in there. Those pictures, do you see them?"

Yes, we saw them, though somewhat belatedly. And they were not seen only in the chromatic designs of those deathless leaves. They could show themselves anywhere, if always briefly. Upon a cellar wall there might appear an ill-formed visage among the damp and fractured stones, a hideous impersonation of a face infiltrating the dark corners of our homes. Other faces, leprous masks, would arise within the grain of paneled walls or wooden floors, spying for a moment before sinking back into the knotty shadows, withdrawing below the surface. And there were so many nameless patterns that might spread themselves across the boards of an old fence or the side of a shed, engravings all tangled and wizened like a subterranean craze of roots and tendrils, an underworld riot of branching convolutions, gnarled ornamentations. Yet these designs were not unfamiliar to us . . . for in them we recognized the same outlines of autumnal decay that illuminated our dreams.

Like the old visionary who sharpened knives and axes and curving scythes, we too could now read the great book of countless colored leaves. But still he remained far in advance of what was happening deep within us all. For it was he who manifested certain idiosyncrasies of manner that would have later appeared in so many others, whether they lived in town or somewhere outside its limits. Of course, he had always set himself apart from us by his waywardness of speech, his willingness to utter pronouncements of dire or delightful curiosity. To a child he might say: "The sight of the night can fly like a kite," while someone older would be told: "Doesn't have arms, but it knows how to use them. Doesn't have a face, but it knows where to find one."

Nevertheless, he plied his trade with every efficiency, pedaling the mechanism that turned the grindstone, expertly honing each blade and taking his pay like any man of business. Then, we noticed, he seemed to become distracted in his work. In a dull trance he touched metal implements to his spinning wheel of stone, careless of the sparks that flew into his face. Yet there was also a wild luminousness in his eyes, as of a diamond-bright fever burning within him. Eventually we found ourselves unable to abide his company, though we now attributed this merely to some upsurge in his perennial strangeness rather than to a wholly unprecedented change in his behavior. It was not until he no longer appeared on the streets of town, or anywhere else, that we admitted our fears about him.

And these fears necessarily became linked to the other disruptions of that season, those extravagant omens that were gaining force all around us. The disappearance of Mr. Marble coincided with a new phenomenon, one that finally became apparent in the twilight of a certain day when all of the clustering and tenacious foliage seemed to exude a vague phosphorescence. By nightfall this prodigy was beyond skepticism. The multicolored leaves were softly glowing against the black sky, creating an untimely nocturnal rainbow that scattered its spectral tints everywhere and dyed the night with a harvest of hues: peach gold and pumpkin orange, honey yellow and winy amber, apple red and plum violet. Luminous within their leafy shapes, the colors cast themselves across the darkness and were splattered upon our streets and our fields and our faces. Everything was resplendent with the pyrotechnics of a new autumn.

That night we kept to our houses and watched at our windows. It was no marvel, then, that so many of us saw the one who wandered that iridescent eve, who joined in its outbursts and celebrations. Possessed by the ecstasies of a dark festival, he moved in a trance, bearing in his hand that great ceremonial knife whose keen edge flashed a thousand glittering dreams. He was seen standing alone beneath trees whose colors shined upon him, staining his face and his tattered clothes. He was seen standing alone in the yards of our houses, a rigid scarecrow concocted from a patchwork of colors and shadows. He was seen stalking slow and rhythmically beside high wooden fences that were now painted with a quivering colored glow. Finally, he was seen at a certain intersection of streets at the center of town; but now, as we saw, he was no longer alone.

Confronting him in the open night were two figures whom none of us knew: a young woman and, held tightly by her side, a small boy. We were not unaccustomed to strangers walking the streets of our town, or even stopping by one of the surrounding farms—people who were passing through, some momentarily lost. And it was not too late in the evening for some travelers to appear, not really late at all. But they should not have been there, those two. Not on that night. Now they stood transfixed before a creature of whom they could have no conception, a thing that squeezed the knife in its hand the way the woman was now squeezing the small boy. We might have taken action but did not; we might have made an effort to help them. But the truth is that we wanted something to happen to them—we wanted to see them silenced. Such was our desire. Only then would we be sure that they could not tell what they knew. Our fear was not what those intruders might have learned about the trees that glowed so unnaturally in the night; or about the chittering noises that now began rising to a pitch of vicious laughter; or even about the farmer's field where a mound of dirt covered a bottomless hole. Our fear was what they might have known, what they must certainly have discovered, about *us*.

And we lost all hope when we saw the quaking hand that could not raise the knife, the tortured face that could only stare while those two terrible victims—the rightful sacrifice!—ran off to safety, never to be seen by us again. After that we turned back to our houses, which now reeked of moldering shadows, and succumbed to a dreamless sleep.

Yet at daybreak it became evident that something had indeed happened during the night. The air was silent, everywhere the earth was cold. And the trees now stood bare of leaves, all of which lay dark and withered upon the ground, as if their strangely deferred dying had finally overtaken them in a sudden rage of mortification. Nor was it long before Mr. Marble was discovered by an old farmer.

The corpse reposed in a field, stretched facedown across a mound of dirt and alongside the remains of a dismantled scarecrow. When we turned over the body, we saw that its staring eyes were as dull as that ashen autumn morning. We also saw that its left arm had been slashed by the knife held in its right hand.

Blood had flowed over the earth and blackened the flesh of the suicide. But those of us who handled that limp, nearly weightless body, dipping our fingers into the dark wound, found nothing at all that had the feeling of blood. We knew very well, of course, what that shadowy blackness did feel like; we knew what had found its way into the man before us, dragging him down into its savage world. His dreams had always reached much deeper than ours. So we buried him deep in a bottomless grave.

sensible city

HARLAN ELLISON

During the third week of the trial, sworn under oath, one of the Internal Affairs guys the D.A.'s office had planted undercover in Gropp's facility attempted to describe how terrifying Gropp's smile was. The IA guy stammered some; and there seemed to be a singular absence of color in his face; but he tried valiantly, not being a poet or one given to colorful speech. And after some prodding by the Prosecutor, he said:

"You ever, y'know, when you brush your teeth . . . how when you're done, and you've spit out the toothpaste and the water, and you pull back your lips to look at your teeth, to see if they're whiter, and like that . . . you know how you tighten up your jaws real good, and make that kind of death-grin smile that pulls your lips back, with your teeth lined up clenched in the front of your mouth . . . you know what I mean . . . well . . ."

Sequestered that night in a downtown hotel, each of the twelve jurors stared into a medicine cabinet mirror and skinned back a pair of lips, and tightened neck muscles till the cords stood out, and clenched teeth, and stared at a face grotesquely contorted. Twelve men and women then superimposed over the mirror reflection the face of the Defendant they'd been staring at for three weeks, and approximated the smile they had *not* seen on Gropp's face all that time.

And in that moment of phantom face over reflection face, Gropp was convicted.

Police Lieutenant W. R. Gropp. Rhymed with *crop*. The meat-man who ruled a civic smudge called the Internment Facility when it was listed on the City Council's budget every year. Internment Facility: dripping wet, cold iron, urine smell mixed with sour liquor sweated through dirty skin, men and women crying in the night. A stockade, a prison camp, stalag, ghetto, torture chamber, charnel house, abattoir, duchy, fiefdom, Army co-op mess hall ruled by a neckless thug.

The last of the thirty-seven inmate alumni who had been sub-poenaed to testify recollected, "Gropp's favorite thing was to take some fool outta his cell, get him nekkid to the skin, then do this *rolling* thing t'him."

When pressed, the former tenant of Gropp's hostelry—not a felon, merely a steamfitter who had had a bit too much to drink and picked up for himself a ten-day Internment Facility residency for D&D—explained that this "rolling thing" entailed "Gropp wrappin' his big, hairy sausage arm aroun' the guy's neck, see, and then he'd *roll him* across the bars, real hard and fast. Bangin' the guy's head like a roulette ball around the wheel. Clank clank, like that. Usual, it'd knock the guy flat out cold, his head clankin' across the bars and spaces between, wham wham wham like that. See his eyes go up outta sight, all white; but Gropp, he'd hang on with that sausage aroun' the guy's neck, whammin' and bangin' him and takin' some goddam kinda pleasure mentionin' how much bigger this criminal bastard was than *he* was. Yeah, fer sure. That was Gropp's fav'rite part, that he always pulled out some poor nekkid sonofabitch was twice his size.

"That's how four of these guys he's accused of doin', that's how they croaked. With Gropp's sausage 'round the neck. I kept my mouth shut; I'm lucky to get outta there in one piece."

Frightening testimony, last of thirty-seven. But as superfluous as feathers on an eggplant. From the moment of superimposition of phantom face over reflection face, Police Lieutenant W. R. Gropp was on greased rails to spend his declining years for Brutality While Under Color of Service—a *serious* offense—in a maxi-galleria stuffed chockablock with felons whose spiritual brethren he had maimed, crushed, debased, blinded, butchered, and killed.

Similarly destined was Gropp's gigantic Magog, Deputy Sergeant Michael "Mickey" Rizzo, all three hundred and forty pounds of him; brainless malevolence stacked six feet four inches high in his steel-toed, highly polished service boots. Mickey had only been indicted on seventy counts, as opposed to Gropp's eighty-four ironclad atrocities. But if he managed to avoid Sentence of Lethal Injection for having crushed men's heads underfoot, he would certainly go to the maxi-galleria mall of felonious behavior for the rest of his simian life.

Mickey had, after all, pulled a guy up against the inside of the bars and kept bouncing him till he ripped the left arm loose from its socket, ripped it off, and later dropped it on the mess hall steam table just before dinner assembly.

Squat, bulletheaded troll, Lieutenant W. R. Gropp, and the mindless killing machine, Mickey Rizzo. On greased rails.

So they jumped bail together, during the second hour of jury deliberation.

Why wait? Gropp could see which way it was going, even counting on Blue Loyalty. The city was putting the abyss between the Dept., and him and Mickey. So, why wait? Gropp was a sensible guy, very pragmatic, no bullshit. So they jumped bail together, having made arrangements weeks before, as any sensible felon keen to flee would have done.

Gropp knew a chop shop that owed him a favor. There was a throaty and hemi-speedy, immaculately registered, four-year-old Firebird just sitting in a bay on the fifth floor of a seemingly abandoned garment factory, two blocks from the courthouse.

And just to lock the barn door after the horse, or in this case the Pontiac, had been stolen, Gropp had Mickey toss the chop shop guy down the elevator shaft of the factory. It was the sensible thing to do. After all, the guy's neck *was* broken.

By the time the jury came in, later that night, Lieut. W. R. Gropp was out of the state and somewhere near Boise. Two days later, having taken circuitous routes, the Firebird was on the other side of both the Snake River and the Rockies, between Rock Springs and Laramie. Three days after that, having driven in large circles, having laid over in Cheyenne for dinner and a movie, Gropp and Mickey were in Nebraska.

Wheat ran to the sun, blue storms bellowed up from horizons, and heat trembled on the edge of each leaf. Crows stirred inside fields, lifted above shattered surfaces of grain and flapped into sky. That's what it looked like: the words came from a poem.

They were smack in the middle of the plains state, above Grand Island, below Norfolk, somewhere out in the middle of nowhere, just tooling along, leaving no trail, deciding to go that way to Canada, or the other way to Mexico. Gropp had heard there were business opportunities in Mazatlán.

It was a week after the jury had been denied the pleasure of seeing

Gropp's face as they said, "Stick the needle in the brutal sonofabitch. Fill the barrel with a very good brand of weed-killer, stick the needle in the brutal sonofabitch's chest, and slam home the plunger. Guilty, your honor, guilty on charges one through eighty-four. Give'im the weed-killer and let's watch the fat scumbag do his dance!" A week of swift and leisurely driving here and there, doubling back and skimming along easily.

And somehow, earlier this evening, Mickey had missed a turnoff, and now they were on a stretch of superhighway that didn't seem to have any important exits. There were little towns now and then, the lights twinkling off in the mid-distance, but if they were within miles of a major metropolis, the map didn't give them clues as to where they might be.

"You took a wrong turn."

"Yeah, huh?"

"Yeah, *exactly* huh. Keep your eyes on the road."

"I'm sorry, Looten'nt."

"No. Not Lieutenant. I told you."

"Oh, yeah, right. Sorry, Mr. Gropp."

"Not Gropp. Jensen. Mister *Jensen*. You're *also* Jensen; my kid brother. Your name is Daniel."

"I got it, I remember: Harold and Daniel Jensen is us. You know what I'd like?"

"No, what would you like?"

"A box'a Grape-Nuts. I could have 'em here in the car, and when I got a mite peckish I could just dip my hand in an' have a mouthful. I'd like that."

"Keep your eyes on the road."

"So whaddya think?"

"About what?"

"About maybe I swing off next time and we go into one'a these little towns and maybe a 7–Eleven'll be open, and I can get a box'a Grape-Nuts? We'll need some gas after a while, too. See the little arrow there?"

"I see it. We've still got half a tank. Keep driving."

Mickey pouted. Gropp paid no attention. There were drawbacks to forced traveling companionship. But there were many cul-de-sacs and landfills between this stretch of dark turnpike and New Brunswick, Canada or Mazatlán, state of Sinaloa.

"What is this, the Southwest?" Gropp asked, looking out the side window into utter darkness. "The Midwest? What?"

Mickey looked around, too. "I dunno. Pretty out here, though. Real quiet and pretty."

"It's pitch dark."

"Yeah, huh?"

"Just drive, for godsake. Pretty. Jeezus!"

They rode in silence for another twenty-seven miles, then Mickey said, "I gotta go take a piss."

Gropp exhaled mightily. Where were the cul-de-sacs, where were the landfills? "Okay. Next town of any size, we can take the exit and see if there's decent accommodations. You can get a box of Grape-Nuts, and use the toilet; I can have a cup of coffee and study the map in better light. Does that sound like a good idea, to you . . . Daniel?"

"Yes, Harold. See, I remembered!"

"The world is a fine place."

They drove for another sixteen miles, and came nowhere in sight of a thruway exit sign. But the green glow had begun to creep up from the horizon.

"What the hell is that?" Gropp asked, running down his power window. "Is that some kind of a forest fire, or something? What's that look like to you?"

"Like green in the sky."

"Have you ever thought how lucky you are that your mother abandoned you, Mickey?" Gropp said wearily. "Because if she hadn't, and if they hadn't brought you to the county jail for temporary housing till they could put you in a foster home, and I hadn't taken an interest in you, and hadn't arranged for you to live with the Rizzos, and hadn't let you work around the lockup, and hadn't made you my deputy, do you have any idea where you'd be today?" He paused for a moment, waiting for an answer, realized the entire thing was rhetorical—not to mention pointless—and said, "Yes, it's green in the sky, pal, but it's also something odd. Have you ever seen 'green in the sky' before? Anywhere? Any time?"

"No, I guess I haven't." Gropp sighed, and closed his eyes.

They drove in silence another nineteen miles, and the green miasma in the air had enveloped them. It hung above and around them like sea-fog, chill and with tiny droplets of moisture that Mickey fanned away with the windshield wipers. It made the landscape on either side of the superhighway faintly visible, cutting the impenetrable darkness, but it also induced a wavering, ghostly quality to the terrain.

Gropp turned on the map light in the dome of the Firebird, and studied the map of Nebraska. He murmured, "I haven't got a rat's-fang of any idea where the hell we *are!* There isn't even a freeway like this indicated here. You took some helluva wrong turn 'way back there, pal!" Dome light out.

"I'm sorry, Loo-Harold . . ."

A large reflective advisement marker, green and white, came up on their right. It said: **FOOD GAS LODGING 10 MILES**.

The next sign said: **EXIT 7 MILES**.

The next sign said: **OBEDIENCE 3 MILES**.

Gropp turned the map light on again. He studied the venue. "Obedience? What the hell kind of 'Obedience'? There's nothing like that *anywhere*. What is this, an old map? Where did you get this map?"

"Gas station."

"Where?"

"I dunno. Back a long ways. That place we stopped with the root beer stand next to it."

Gropp shook his head, bit his lip, murmured nothing in particular. "Obedience," he said. "Yeah, huh?"

They began to see the town off to their right before they hit the exit turnoff. Gropp swallowed hard and made a sound that caused Mickey to look over at him. Gropp's eyes were large, and Mickey could see the whites.

"What'sa matter, Loo . . . Harold?"

"You see that town out there?" His voice was trembling.

Mickey looked to his right. Yeah, he saw it. Horrible.

Many years ago, when Gropp was briefly a college student, he had taken a warm-body course in Art Appreciation. One oh one, it was; something basic and easy to ace, a snap, all you had to do was show up. Everything you wanted to know about Art from aboriginal cave drawings to Diego Rivera. One of the paintings that had been flashed on the big screen for the class, a sleepy 8:00 A.M. class, had been *The Nymph Echo* by Max Ernst. A green and smoldering painting of an ancient ruin overgrown with writhing plants that seemed to have eyes and purpose and a malevolently jolly life of their own, as they swarmed and slithered and overran the stone vaults and altars of the twisted, disturbingly resonant sepulcher. Like a sebaceous cyst, something corrupt lay beneath the emerald fronds and hungry black soil.

Mickey looked to his right at the town. Yeah, he saw it. Horrible.

"Keep driving!" Gropp yelled, as his partner-in-flight started to slow for the exit ramp.

Mickey heard, but his reflexes were slow. They continued to drift to the right, toward the rising egress lane. Gropp reached across and jerked the wheel hard to the left. "I said: *keep driving!*"

The Firebird slewed, but Mickey got it back under control in a moment, and in another moment they were abaft the ramp, then past it, and speeding away from the nightmarish site beyond and slightly below the superhighway. Gropp stared mesmerized as they swept past. He could see buildings that leaned at obscene angles, the green fog that rolled through the haunted streets, the shadowy forms of misshapen things that skulked at every dark opening.

"That was a real scary-lookin' place, Looten . . . Harold. I don't think I'd of wanted to go down there even for the Grape-Nuts. But maybe if we'd've gone real fast . . ."

Gropp twisted in the seat toward Mickey as much as his muscle-fat body would permit. "Listen to me. There is this tradition, in horror movies, in mysteries, in tv shows, that people are always going into haunted houses, into graveyards, into battle zones, like assholes, like stone idiots! You know what I'm talking about here? Do you?"

Mickey said, "Uh . . ."

"All right, let me give you an example. Remember we went to see that movie *Alien?* Remember how scared you were?"

Mickey bobbled his head rapidly, his eyes widened in frightened memory.

"Okay. So now, you remember that part where the guy who was a mechanic, the guy with the baseball cap, he goes off looking for a cat or somedamnthing? Remember? He left everyone else, and he wandered off by himself. And he went into that big cargo hold with the water dripping on him, and all those chains hanging down, and shadows everywhere . . . *do you recall that?"*

Mickey's eyes were chalky potholes. He remembered, oh yes; he remembered clutching Gropp's jacket sleeve till Gropp had been compelled to slap his hand away.

"And you remember what happened in the movie? In the theater? You remember everybody yelling, 'Don't go in there, you asshole! The thing's in there, you moron! Don't go in there!' But, remember, he *did,* and the thing came up behind him, all those teeth, and it bit his stupid head off! Remember that?"

Mickey hunched over the wheel, driving fast.

"Well, that's the way people are. They ain't sensible! They go into places like that you can see are death places; and they get chewed up or the blood sucked outta their necks or used for kindling . . . but I'm no moron, I'm a sensible guy and I got the brains my mama gave me, and I don't go *near* places like that. So drive like a sonofabitch, and get us outta here, and we'll get your damned Grape-Nuts in Idaho or somewhere . . . if we ever get off this road . . ."

Mickey murmured, "I'm sorry, Lieuten'nt. I took a wrong turn or somethin'."

"Yeah, yeah. Just keep driv—" The car was slowing.

It was a frozen moment. Gropp exultant, no fool he, to avoid the cliché, to stay out of that haunted house, that ominous dark closet, that damned place. Let idiot others venture off the freeway, into the town that contained the basement entrance to Hell, or whatever. Not he, not Gropp!

He'd outsmarted the obvious.

In that frozen moment.

As the car slowed. Slowed, in the poisonous green mist.

And on their right, the obscenely frightening town of Obedience, that they had left in their dust five minutes before, was coming up again on the superhighway.

"Did you take another turnoff?"

"Uh . . . no, I . . . uh, I been just driving fast . . ."

The sign read: **NEXT RIGHT 50 YDS OBEDIENCE**.

The car was slowing. Gropp craned his neckless neck to get a proper perspective on the fuel gauge. He was a pragmatic kind of a guy, no nonsense, and very practical; but they were out of gas.

The Firebird slowed and slowed and finally rolled to a stop.

In the rearview mirror Gropp saw the green fog rolling up thicker onto the roadway; and emerging over the berm, in a jostling, slavering horde, clacking and drooling, dropping decayed body parts and leaving glistening trails of worm ooze as they dragged their deformed pulpy bodies across the blacktop, their snake-slit eyes gleaming green and yellow in the mist, the residents of Obedience clawed and slithered and crimped toward the car.

It was common sense any Better Business Bureau would have applauded: if the tourist trade won't come to your town, take your town to the tourists. Particularly if the freeway has forced commerce to pass you by. Particularly if your town needs fresh blood to prosper. Particularly if you have the civic need to share.

Green fog shrouded the Pontiac, and the peculiar sounds that came from within. Don't go into that dark room is a sensible attitude. Particularly in a sensible city.

the golden keeper

IAN R. MACLEOD

My grandmother once told me that she witnessed the last ritual murder to occur in Rome. A young Vestal who had broken her vows was forced to watch the flogging to death of her lover before she was buried alive.

I was only a child then, living in the high house that has been my family's since the days of the Republic. Of course, I was curious. A few days later, I walked along Vicus Iugarius to the Forum. But what I found in the corner of the great square where my grandmother claimed to have stood hugging the folds of her nurse's cloak was sightseers harangued by barking orators as they thronged amid the stalls of moneylenders, flower vendors, and trinket sellers. On that day, even the Temple of the Vestals resembled a building site, with fresh marble decorations being chiselled as a statue to a Head Vestal was prepared for erection.

Still, in my innocence, I pressed my ear to the paving, imagining that I might still hear the Vestal woman's pleading screams as the newly turned soil filled her mouth above all the passing roar, perhaps even the flack of leather against her lover's flesh. I only found out many years later that unchaste Vestals were in fact immured within niches of the temple and left with a small supply of bread and water, although that still seems a strange kind of mercy.

Knowing the time that has passed since such practises took place, I wonder now if the tale is not one that my grandmother herself heard in her own youth and passed down to me as if it were her own memory. But I remain sure that she intended it as some sort of lesson; which is why the tale returns to me now when the sweeter ones with which she comforted my nights are forgotten. For I know now that even gods themselves may crumble with the dust of those who had served them. It even seems to me that the sacred fire of the Vestals will one day go out, and that the grand monuments and porphyry busts that our Emperors erect to themselves and their patron deities in the Forum will become nothing but tumbled blocks of masonry, the meaning of which men in some lost future time will argue over.

Here, in this new posting after my long journey up the Nile, I am surrounded by dead gods, old stone, dispossessed memories. I made detours at Heliopolis and at Memphis and again at Thebes to see some of the so-called splendours about which Herodotus and many others have written. Perhaps seven hundred years ago the efforts of these decadent and barbarous people to maintain the remnants of their history were more successful. For the most part, all I found were lopsided blocks of stone more like mountains than any work of man, broken pot shards, giant sand-buried heads, and a few soot-stained tunnels that roared with flies as you entered them and reeked of ordure and piss. The guides were generally stooped, wall-eyed, jabbering on about Isis and Osiris as if they imagined that such things were still the fashion in Rome. Frankly, I regret paying them. I should have made my passage down the Nile with more speed, the sooner that my year's work here might be ended.

The Colossi at Memnon were the only monuments that in any way lived up to their promise. I visited them at dawn by raft just as the spring floods were abating, and they truly rose huge from the shining marsh. As is the custom, I pressed my ear to the graffitied stone to hear the marvel of its groaning. The other sightseers I was with professed disappointment, yet I must record that I heard—or at least thought I heard—something. A sound that came not so much from the enormous statues themselves as from the earth beneath them. The sound of an agonised wind. Shrill, high-pitched, echoing with the blood howl of some distant, terrible memory.

Let me describe myself to you now in what I intend will long remain the privacy of this journal. Let me imagine that these loose scraps of papyrus will be gazed at on some distant day by civilised eyes—and then understood, for I know that I make a poor scribe despite the efforts of my teachers.

I am Lucius Fabius Maximus. I was born thirty-three years ago in that high house in Rome. I have trained, reluctantly and at the bidding of my father, as an accountant in the class of Germanicus, and have since practised with even greater reluctance in the Province of Sicily—and, it must be said in these days of dubious currencies, to little financial gain. On my father's recent death and with the slates of my family house falling, and our beloved villa above the sea at Naples becoming a ruin, I have been forced to volunteer for service overseas.

I must say that the thought of Egypt appealed to me, and I was surprised and flattered when, at the bidding of my patron Servilius Rufus, the Procurator agreed that I should go there instead of some damp bandit-raided fort in Gaul. I had imagined lush wheat fields, lakes filled with flamingos and tall reeds, bright flowers, sporting hippopotami, and tombs and temples filled with sacred treasure. But instead I have been posted here, up beyond Gebel Barkal and the cataracts, beyond the boundaries of our Empire. At the very rim of the world.

The sun here is a hot brand against your shoulder and soon withers anything that attempts to grow. Yet even the lands of the delta that I passed through on my journey were less appealing to my sight than they had been in my mind. Upper Egypt may still be the grain basket of our Empire, yet it is also muddy, filled with insects, ugly savages, the stench of cattle. At least I can take comfort from the fact that, unlike my immediate predecessor, I have not come this far simply to be stricken by fever and sweat out the waters of my life. But I am sure that the bed in my quarters still stinks of him. I must ask, once again, to have it changed.

My dwelling here is a villa of sorts at Cul Holman, a place that once attempted to become a town. It lies at the neck of a large valley where the paths and gullies from the hills that form a final rampart against the desert finally join. I am responsible here for the counting houses, the weighing houses, fifty or so scribes, and upwards of five hundred slaves. I am assisted in these duties by Taracus, a captain of the VII Cohort in command of two centurions who, whilst of pure blood, has never actually seen Rome. Otherwise, I must rely on Konchab, my slave foreman, and Alathn, my chief scribe. In my household I also have Henrika, my treasured personal slave, a cook, and perhaps a half score of slaves of both sexes; all of them local, and none in their prime.

The land here, east of the river, is heaped over itself in a way that gives the impression, as one first approaches, of soiled linen. The inclines are riddled with deep gorges, sudden drops, the caves of old workings set high on the face of sun-bloodied cliffs. You know even as you stumble across some new vista from the base of a dried-up rill that you will never find it again without the help of guides. Elsewhere, there are many deep pits and heaps of rubble; the remains of earlier delvings for the gold that also brings me here. In this confusing maze, the sun himself often becomes unanchored within the sky. Not only do shadows shift and change so rapidly that a valley may become a ridge as you approach it, but a standing, beckoning figure may turn to a pillar of stone, then a blackened demon, then a man again, before vanishing entirely. The colours are so varied as the hours of the day change—and then again under the moon—that even now I cannot say with any certainty what the true shade of this rock through which the slaves burrow is.

I have a lump of the stuff beside me now on this desk as I write these words. Held close to the lamp, the fresh-broken side has a gleam almost of fish scales. It contains, I imagine, some ore that perhaps contributes to whatever subterranean process it is that produces the gold.

At midday, these hills become molten. Now, close to midnight and the time when I make my final inspection of the counting houses and the breaking rooms, they have the appearance not of hills at all, but of piled bones. They look cold, yet the heat still swarms against my flesh through these open shutters in gritty waves.

This truly is a terrible place.

I had guests at my dinner tonight. The wine came from my private purse and was brought from the vineyards of Heptanomia. The food I also prided myself in choosing, and was dealt with reasonably well by the cook. There were dates and figs. Capons stuffed with rice flavoured with caraway. Fish baked in the aromatic leaves. A side of pig done in a charcoal bed. Fresh if somewhat gritty corn bread. A round of green-veined cheese. Roasted wild duck garnished with lemon. Soured cream with herbs. Decently flavoured honey cakes. Nuts and hot pomegranate.

For company, alas, I had to make do with my assistants Taracus, Konchab, and Alathn, and also Kaliphus, the local pagarch, with his robes and his rings, his weak attempts to assume the manners of Rome, his disgusting habit, as he talks, of physically touching you. Those who abuse him, it is said, are speared alive on the giant reeds that grow in the silted canals around his palace.

Such is the balance of power here that none who were gathered this night could fully trust the other—nor yet act independently. Taracus knows that, despite his legionnaires, he relies on Kaliphus to collect the taxes that pay his and their salaries, whilst the wealth of Kaliphus and his fellow Egypto-Greeks would be nothing without the might of Rome. As local slave master, Konchab relies upon them both for the threat of force and the provision of his slaves; whilst Alathn, who supervises the counting and weighing, seeks their security in the tricky business of monitoring the traffic of the rock that will eventually yield gold. I, whilst supposedly in overall command, hold a post that is changed yearly so that its occupant may gain no upper hand. Thus, even in this empty place, are the calculations of power that assure the everlasting greatness of Rome.

The wind rose less strongly than usual, and at first we were able to eat with the shutters open and the doors drawn wide to the courtyard, where the pool had been cleared of its slime and refilled from the cisterns of a nearby slave village. My servants, well-briefed for once, laid out scented vials to keep the insects at bay, and the lanterns were well filled with oil. The tapestries that I had had hung to disguise the peeling decay of these walls drifted and flowed, bringing life to scenes of cool forests, white pavilions, gods and animals. I would not have chosen my companions, yet for a while I could almost imagine that I was back amid the pines of Rome.

Alathn, the chief scribe, showed his lack of breeding by raising a matter of work; some small discrepancy in the records of the sweepings of the counting-house floors. Almost a dwarf, foul-breathed and toothless, with his shoulders hunched sideways, Alathn has an obsessive proficiency with numbers and seemingly no interest in the wealth they record. Taracus suggested that such problems were easily enough dealt with by the application of the brand or the flail by his soldiers.

The local pagarch Kaliphus at least provided me the favour of listening to my opinions when I tried to improve the conversation. I was speaking of gods by the fourth course when the hot night wind began to rise, and the doors and shutters were closed that they might cease their banging. I opined that there were so many gods now, so many faiths, that no sane man should be expected to honour them.

"Perhaps," Kaliphus said in his high, poorly accented voice, "the universe truly is filled with many conflicting deities. Not simply those of Olympus, but also Baal-Hadad and the new- and old-style Jehovah and Ahura Mazda and Isis. Perhaps they all—and many others whom we have forgotten about or not yet learned to fear—exist in their different realms. . . ." He smiled. "Would that not explain the chaos and conflict in this world? The fact that we are trapped between them in their fight for dominion . . .?"

Taracus, of course, disagreed. He is a plain soldier who doubtless makes his tribute to Jupiter and dabbles his finger in a bowl of blood before he orders the slaughter of some local tribe. Yet I, who choose to worship no gods and view the world as a mere interaction of the elements, somehow found Kaliphus's ideas persuasive.

"Romans such as you, Lucius Fabius," Kaliphus continued, "have always portrayed your gods in madness and conflict, and have added ever more—even your own Emperors—to their list."

Full by now with the wine, we all ended up bidding the servants help us from the table to inspect the villa's wooden cupboard-shrine, as if it might offer some proof. I confess that, in my days here, I had not even looked at the thing. Clearly old, and yet cheaply made, the dry leather hinges creaked with neglect as we opened them. Yet I admit I felt a small twinge of anticipation; the vague hope that a devout predecessor might have left some tribute of value behind. In that, I was disappointed. Yet, as the five of us breathed in the oddly sour air that seemed to emanate from inside, we all seemed to forget for a moment what argument it was that this inspection was supposed to settle.

The contents of the shrine were ordinary enough. A small statuette of a dancing boy, with his head broken off. A blue glass bowl that held the sticky residue of some kind of offering. A dried-up piece of salt-cake, a few mundane prayers on wax tablets, and a five-pointed star of greenish soapstone. The latter was new to me, and clearly of some age, chipped and worn, marked with odd dots and signs, yet well made, almost warm. As I held it in my hand, Kaliphus backed away and seemed to mutter something, making an odd protective sign. I cannot imagine that the thing has any real value, but I will take it with me when I return to Rome.

As we reclined back on our couches, and on the pretext of continuing the discussion, I asked Kaliphus if he knew of any remains in this area from the great Egyptian dynasties. He replied that there was nothing more than a few carvings in dangerous and otherwise empty caves, and pillars and blocks that were more probably the work of the wind.

"After all," he shrugged, "these hills have been empty in all the time of man. No one would ever come here but for the gold."

There is little else to record of my evening. Now that the guests have left, I am glad of my solitude again. Even civilised company always leaves me feeling thus. Sometimes, a panic rises in me as I lie at a well-stocked table and realise that I am surrounded by the flesh of other bodies.

Still, the occasion went passably, and in Kaliphus I must seek an ally. "You have done a splendid job tonight, Fabius Maximus," he said to me as his entourage rode up. "And with such servants—so old, I couldn't help noticing. Yet in a man there are also other needs.

. . ." Here he made an unfamiliar yet disgustingly obvious gesture. "Perhaps I will send to the markets at Pathgris for you, and see what can be obtained."

I took the offer without comment.

Now the night draws long. The servants are abed. A few of Konchab's dogs are howling, and the wind howls and screams with them. But for the lantern-lights of a few sleepy sentries, all of Cul Holman lies dark beneath me. Whilst I still have energy to hold back sleep, I must make my final inspections.

This afternoon, I mounted and rode alone but for Konchab to inspect the mines. In truth, I needed to escape Cul Holman after being required by the ever-punctilious Alathn to confirm that a few precious scraps of papyrus, ink, and a writing implement were missing from one of the scribe rooms, and to authorise the required punishment. Knowing that the four scribes in question had been chosen as an example rather than for any responsibility, I settled for the flail rather than the brand. I had never seen it used before and had wrongly imagined that wounds to the soles of the feet, whilst scarring, would be less damaging than a hot iron applied to the face.

The mines are easy to find from the donkey tracks leading into the hills, the heaped dirt, and the sound, long before you reach a final turn, of hammering and shouting. Here, under the merciless sun, beneath the distant and skull-like gaze of the many worked-out pits and caves that pockmark the hills beyond, near-naked slaves burrow and hammer. After I had inspected the grey-coloured lumps that constitute the produce of these mines, Konchab drew me further up an arid slope and showed me a place where the hill had been swept away in the blackening wind to reveal a floor of rock that cannot have seen the sun in all recorded time.

Konchab is muscled, tanned, a mixed product of all the local breeds. He shaves his head in the manner of the natives and goes bare-chested most of the time. I had never imagined that he was burdened with much thought. Yet here he showed me an incredible thing. For on this bare rock there were markings, as if living remains had been worked into the stone. Some were strange to me, yet others were unmistakably in the likeness of seaweed and fanning arms of coral. Here, certainly, were the bones of an odd-looking fish. I noticed also the coiled shell of a giant snail, and a large creature somewhere between a squid and a wood louse. Stranger still were the large triangular marks that bore all the appearance of footprints. I am no scholar, yet this seems to be evidence that this high arid land once lay, unimaginably long ago, deep beneath the sea. Either that, or I witnessed some folly of the gods that I profess not to believe in.

Now, as I write these words, the vision seems fanciful. I almost doubt my eyes, which feel tired, eroded as if from inside by the heat and the sand. As I rode back from my inspection, the sun seemed to shift and dance about the bottomless sky, haloed within a ring of swarming darkness. Such was my weariness that, looking up as I rode amid pillars of rock too high to be climbed, I was sure that I saw a figure, wind-wrapped in ragged black clothing, looking down at me. I once even thought to see its face beneath the hood as it turned towards me, yet revealed only the harsh flash of the reflected sun.

Back at Cul Holman, the late afternoon sky was yet hotter and darker, and there was word that one of the slave scribes had already died from the effects of the flail. I wandered amid the block-buildings and the heaps of discarded rubble, and watched as the donkeys bore down their loaded panniers from the mines, guarded as always by Taracus's soldiers and Konchab's chained and growling dogs. There is much weighing and counting in the making of gold. There are scribes at the mouths of the pits and caves, and again here at Cul Holman, where all is checked and weighed even as the donkeys shed their panniers. At each process of the shifting and breaking, and forever closely supervised by Alathn, records are made and remade. The penalty for any serious discrepancy is death—and the reward for those who report a culprit is freedom if a slave, or money for a freeman. As you, my reader, may imagine, false reporting is a greater problem than theft.

At the end of it all, in the final counting-house sheds and after days of weighing, discarding, sifting, and breaking, the gritty rubble that remains still has none of the appearance of gold. Alathn tells me that this stuff, which is weighed and recorded yet again by two independent scribes, contains about one-fiftieth of its weight in pure gold. Sometimes, of course, a small nugget is found, or a few glimmering grains may be glimpsed at this final stage, but for the most part it would be hard for any observer to understand what we were producing. It is certainly not as I expected before I came here. The final sifting of the residue requires much water—an element that is even scarcer in these mountains than the gold—and takes place many leagues' journey down beside the Nile in the beds and pans at Tarsil. I am reminded once again of how cleverly our Empire divides its power.

At nights here, I find myself dreaming of gold. Of beaten gold, caskets of gold, jewelled hinges made marvellous to contain yet more in soft intricate nuggets. And my grandmother sits once again beside me on her drawn-up stool. She tells of Catechuan, who walked to the moon on its path across the ocean, and of Midas, whose touch transformed everything to gold. Hearing her voice, I feel the softness of gold against my teeth, its warm pure smoothness beneath my hands. I breathe a mist of gold and slip through gold-clad shafts into secret treasured lands where the stars shine differently and gold flows in shining rivers and its dust forms the glowing sand.

When my ship from Ostia first arrived at Alexandria on my way here, I spent the days wandering the streets and markets, seeing the sights, visiting the disappointingly decrepit lighthouse and library. Famously, the city is a greater hotbed for new sects, seers, prophets, and charlatans than even Jerusalem. Yet as a man who prides himself on his rationality, my interest lay in the oft-repeated claim that gold can be created from the combining of other elements. There was talk of a creature named Zosimus, almost fabled, so it seemed, and certainly shy of the public attention that most other so-called scientists and seers craved. Yet finally I tracked him down, or at least someone who claimed to be him, on the late afternoon of the last day before I set out on the long final leg of this journey.

Led by a guide, and clutching a knife beneath my toga, I plunged deeper and deeper into the dubious backstreets that writhe around the low hills in the east of Alexandria. The rats, or whatever creatures scurried at the corner of my eyes, grew bigger, and the few people I glimpsed in dark doorways and alleys were even less well favoured than those I had grown used to. Although some way from the port, a predominantly fishy smell combined with all the usual reeks of humanity and decay. Finally, when I was thinking of running even though I had no idea of where to run to, I was led through a curtained doorway.

Here my memory becomes vague. I suspect that the air was drugged by the smoke that writhed upwards from the many glowing chalices hanging from the low ceiling. The man who called himself Zosimus was bulge-eyed, his skin beneath his voluminous shifting robes not so much black as blackened. He talked in a strange droning voice, the meaning of which seems to depart even as I think of it now. Suffice to say that I feared an ambush and did not detain myself long in his hovel. For once, I truly did thank the gods when my hurrying feet drew me back towards familiar squares.

Kaliphus has, just as he had undertaken, obliged me with a gift.

For these last few days, I have been possessed of two fresh slaves. She is named Alya. He is Dahib. They are young, fit, and as far as I am ever able to tell these things, well favoured. They may be brother and sister, or in some other way related.

You, my reader, will not know that I am repulsed by the intimate pleasures of the flesh, and have been so all my life. These two creatures are thus of no use to me in the erotic ways that Kaliphus doubtless intended. The boy Dahib, in fact, has the habits of an animal. After Henrika's efforts to teach him a few rudiments of house-craft failed, I had Konchab take him to work with the other able-bodied creatures up in the mines. Alya, though, I have kept for myself. She has a grace of manner and speaks a comprehensible version of the Roman tongue. She has cleaned and reordered my private rooms, and bears flowers with thick purple petals each evening from some hidden place. Their scent brings some coolness to the hours of the night.

In taking Dahib to join one of his mining gangs, Konchab muttered that he and Alya were of a tribe of nomads from the desert beyond these hills, recently captured and thus far too close to their home and their freedom to be trusted. In truth, as I gaze at Alya as she stoops and works with her braided hair, her pure blue eyes, the sense that she brings of somewhere else, I truly wonder how she would have reacted if I had been a man of baser appetites.

Bad news comes to me this midday from my patron Servilius Rufus in Rome. Now that the accounts of my father's wealth have been finalised and the full extent of penury can no longer be hidden, the creditors of my family are demanding full settlement.

For now, I can do no more than make vague but tantalising promises about the fresh wealth that I had hoped to return with from here. It pains me to realise that I will have to sell off the villa and vineyard near Naples on my return—if I can find a buyer. It pains me yet more to know that even that will not be enough.

For all this, I have not been idle on the matter of discovering some valuable ancient relic since I raised the matter over dinner with Kaliphus. Some of the caves in which I have wandered with the slave guides bear traces of being not mine-delvings, but narrow tombs. I have excavated a line of them that look down over the spoil heaps of Cul Holman. Sometimes these narrow pits contain versions of Egyptian hieroglyphs, and I have also discovered a number of the star-shaped soapstones, dot-marked and with a central indentation, much like the one in the shrine. They are clearly ancient, yet of no seeming value or purpose. Otherwise, I have found nothing but dust and, once, and disastrously for one of the slaves, a nest of poisonous snakes.

What, I can't help wondering, happened to all the supposedly great wealth of the Pharaohs? If the tales are to be believed, they buried their princes and kings in sarcophagi made of solid gold, which were decorated in turn with incredible jewels and then laid in vast gilded subterranean vaults filled with amazing riches, the better that they might enjoy the next world without losing all the fruits of this. In Memphis, Giza, and Thebes I can well understand that nothing is left now after all the ages of digging and banditry. But here at Cul Holman, at the very place where much of the gold must once have been mined, might there still not be some forgotten remnant? All I ask for, truly, is one still-sealed door, a mere antechamber—a single relic, if the relics were truly as great as is rumoured.

Yet even as I write this, hope fails me. I know what digging for gold is like here. I know how little comes from all the efforts of Rome. To entomb a man, to gild a room, to form statues and vases and make vast ceremonial necklaces—all of this would take more gold than could ever have come from these hills even when the seams were richer, or from any other place on earth.

Often in the night, it now seems that my grandmother is beside me, telling tales that fill my sleep. Her familiar voice murmurs once again of King Midas; of how, once Bacchus released him from his gift, he came to hate all wealth and splendour and dwelt in the country as a worshipper of Pan. I smile at the thought of those cool forests and the quivering piping of the reeds, then half-awaken in the hot stirring darkness of Cul Holman and the stink of this bed. Yet it almost seems as if a dark figure within a robe's brown shifting folds is still with me, and that there is a shrill piping, weird and unhuman—ungodly, even—as the wind screams in these hills.

Dreaming thus as I am each night, and with the grim prospect I face when I return to Rome, I find myself thinking much of the past, and of my father. After all the years when he deceived and squandered and borrowed against what I had fondly imagined was my own rightful wealth, I can see him as little more than a bloated monster. And what caprice was it that made him choose my calling in, of all possible professions, accountancy? I could, after all, have been a lawyer—a soldier, even—perhaps a legate. But instead I am cursed to study these figures that speak of a richness I can never touch, trapped in a calling that, it seems now, has brought me by some unremitting logic to this terrible place.

My father had me summoned to him once when I was nine or ten years old. It was the morning of a summer's day in our Naples villa when a pale sweet haze hung over the headlands. It was not a time of day, from the little I knew of my father's habits, that he was likely to be up, and thus I was all the more surprised that he wanted to see me. I still think of that villa, even in its decline, as a place of shifting light, of the scent of olive groves mingled with sea air. Yet my father's quarters were shuttered, curtained, still lamp-lit. I doubt if he even realised it was morning.

Everyone said that my father had grown in the years since my mother had died in giving me birth, but I saw the man so little that I had come to imagine he was some kind of giant. But he was little taller in stature than I, and had the same elongated chin, the same face that seems mournful even when it is smiling, the same large brown eyes, the same long nose. Every time I look in a mirror, I still see my father welling up before me. But my father's face was framed in fat, puffed out as if by some internal pressure and patched by white-and-red blotches that drifted and changed like the clouds.

This world, he told me in a voice that was both high-pitched and rumbling, is a place of secrets. There is little you can expect to trust, although in youth you may strive to do so. But when you reach my age, you will realise that your actions are merely the performance of a ritual designed to appease powers of which you will never have any understanding. We are all, in everything we do in our lives, the acolytes and priests of nothingness.

Such was the sum total of the knowledge that my father chose to pass on to me. He had been raised in the bad years and spiralling prices of Gallienus's worthless coinage when the wealth of my family must largely have disappeared. Yet somehow he managed to borrow and confuse and keep at bay the creditors who now assail me. No wonder, surrounded by a charade of wealth that he used to fool all those around him, that he took a dark view of the world. Nor that he finally ended his life by casting himself down the well in the villa's courtyard. Perhaps the only surprise is that the vast bulk of his body fitted.

On the morning that he summoned me, my father bade me eat with him. I had to watch the fruits and breads and cheeses disappear into his mouth, washed down by the wine that the pampered servants on whom he also sated his other needs brought to him. He bid me eat from the heaped plates, although I could barely pick at the stuff. When I hoped the process had come to an end, but more feared a gap between courses, he asked me if I would like to see some gold. Grateful for any diversion, I agreed.

He stood up from his couch with difficulty and lumbered over to one of the many tall stone vessels that were half-set into the carpeted paving. He lifted a lid of one and reached in. Looming over me with a small casket of scented wood, he turned the catch to open it and bid me look inside. It contained several leaves of a shining material, so thin that I feared they would disintegrate if I breathed too strongly. Closing the box, keeping it close to the huge folds of his belly, my father shuffled back towards his couch and called the servants to bring yet more food—strawberries, for it was the time of year when the villa gardens filled with their scent.

The fruit was laid before us on a plate of bronze. My father reached into the scented wooden box and lifted out one of the fragments of leaf. He wrapped a strawberry in it, placed it in his mouth, and chewed with his mouth set apart in a grin, flakes of metal dissolving with the pink fruit and threads of saliva. Then he selected another strawberry and folded it within the delicate leaf. His fingers as he held the thing out and commanded me to eat were coated in the remains of all the other things he had eaten, and his nails were coarse. I had never known it was so difficult to take something within my lips and swallow.

Thus, between us, my father and I got through a dozen leafs and a large plate of strawberries. The metal was almost tasteless, and grazed my teeth before it folded and dissolved within my mouth. At the end of the process, my father belched. When, with a single gesture of his hand, he waved both me and the foul air that he had made away, I ran down from the villa into vineyards and lay gasping for air amid the droning insects and the lacy shadows of the hot sun. A little time later, I found myself bent double in the corner of the field as all that I had been forced to eat came back out of me. There was no sign, within the usual traces of the vomit, of anything resembling gold, and I was weak and feverish for days. To this day, I hate the taste of strawberries.

Enough, enough. How the wind howls and shrieks here at night! I must raise myself now and make my final inspections of the counting houses before the guards change. And hope for better dreams.

To the palace of Kaliphus this day, to return the favour of his visit to Cul Holman.

A longer journey than I imagined, but at least it took me out of these hills. Closer to the true waters of the Nile, there is at least some vegetation. Indeed, here are grown many of the crops that keep us. Once, the ditches and canals must have been filled with each spring inundation. But most now are dry or impossibly silted, and the villages are poor stinking places.

Kaliphus's palace lies at the centre of what I suppose must once have been called a town. I was reminded of my wanderings in Alexandria as my entourage was forced to dismount to make our way through the narrow disordered streets. Here, it almost seemed, were the same ill-made faces, the same filthy textures of shadow, the same darkly draped and shifting figures. The same fishy stink.

Rising out of these hovels, Kaliphus's palace was larger than I'd imagined, and constructed in the main of stone. When I inspected the halls and columned entrances, I realised that most of it had been pillaged from ancient sites. The slabs were broken, lopsided, worked into different colours and ages, with all the usual hieroglyphs, the scarabs and the birds. Within the palace, beneath the bright but crudely dyed tapestries and rugs, I even glimpsed walls made of fine and more clearly blocklike sections, with markings that reminded me of the soapstone in my villa's wooden altar.

Most of my conversation with Kaliphus was devoted to the tribute the boatmen of Rasind are demanding, or was too trivial to record. The food was poorer than that which I had given him, and ill-flavoured with alien spices, but I finally thanked him over ale for the gift of the slaves.

Kaliphus explained that Alya and Dahib were members of a desert tribe who had been captured in some minor war, and thus brought to the markets at Pathgris. The remainder of her family still served in his palace.

"But there is some sport, is there not, in breaking a new horse?" he said when I mentioned Konchab's doubts about such slaves. "And anyway, you have nothing to fear as long as I keep the rest of the family here. You need do no more than tell me of any, ah, refusal. . . ."

Sick at heart, I nodded.

"Their kind make *interesting* slaves," he added. "Simply because they do not believe they are slaves. It is like keeping a wild bird, touching the fluttering brightness of its feathers, teaching it not to damage itself. Watching it sing . . ."

The chief scribe Alathn was waiting for me beside the counting houses when I finally got back this evening to Cul Holman. He was more that usually agitated, concerned about some tedious discrepancy in the accounts. Once again, it was the records of the sweepings of the counting-house floors. Unlike most such things here, these are not kept in duplicate and can only be checked approximately against the amounts that are inevitably lost as the refined dust is ladled in and out of the great scales.

Watching the weighing process as I often do, or visiting the counting houses in my nightly wanderings, I am reminded of the tale of the dog-headed Egyptian god Anubis, who once enjoyed a minor cult in Rome. He was often portrayed weighing the souls of the dead on similar scales. About Alathn, of course, there is no such poetry. He argues that, whilst the recorded weight of the sweepings of the floors has actually increased in the time since I have arrived here, the amount of gold that is eventually extracted from this mixture of desert dust, hair, foot-scrapings, and an occasional fallen grain has dropped noticeably. I did my best to dismiss him with promises that I would take command of the matter myself. He refused, though, my direct request that he hand over the relevant scrolls on the excuse that they were not fully completed.

The man is odious. I know I cannot trust him.

Today, and the days before that, I have devoted myself to the pursuit of the relics that, since my visit to the palace of Kaliphus, I am once again certain must reside somewhere in these hills. Konchab has grudgingly released four of his better and younger slaves on the pretext of looking for new gold seams—but of course if any such were found, they would belong not to me, but to the Empire.

It is dark, troublesome work. I do not trust the slaves to explore the many pits and caves as fully as they might, and I have sometimes had to delve beneath the ground myself. Inside the few sealed caves I have been able to find, the air still has the odd, faintly sweet smell of antiquity. Undisturbed for untold centuries, there comes a whispering, a faint muttering and crackling of echoing movement, as the entombed bodies crumble to dust in the new air. Pushing on, coughing through the dust of this ancient decay, I am often forced to use the smaller of the tar-wrapped bodies as brands to light my way. Yet it is all to no avail. The only relics I have been able to find are a few more of the greenish star-shaped soapstones. I have now, in total, twenty-three of the things, which I keep in a pile beside my trunk in this room.

Once in my explorations, moving forward too hastily towards the back of a cave, I felt the ground begin to give beneath me, and my makeshift brand was extinguished. In a darkness of dust and bones, my mouth began to fill. Luckily, I was soon dragged out and carried coughing into the harsh light outside the cave.

I cannot imagine a worse way to die.

Last night, I dreamed once again that my grandmother was sitting beside me. Each time, the tales she speaks of change and unfold. I am no longer sure whether I am witnessing a memory, a portent, or merely fantasy.

When I look straight at her, she appears black, wizened as an old fig; even her eyes are a blood-threaded brown, giving way to the darkness of immense pupils. Her words are often hard to follow, they seem to fade in and out of my hearing and buzz like the rattle of a loose shutter or the droning of a trapped insect. The meaning also ebbs and flows. Sometimes it could be the Roman tongue, at others the mutterings of some crude local dialect, then again it becomes something else stranger and darker that sounds more in my head than in the hissing air.

When I look away at the hangings on the walls, I see stars and dots and cuneiform signs that may be decoration or some kind of lettering. And my grandmother seems to shift and change at the edges of my sight. It is almost as if she is folding in upon herself. Her limbs slide together like a bird preening its feathers, then her whole body diminishes and yet regrows within strange angles. It is, as her voice rises and falls and slips in and out of my comprehension, as if I am looking at her from some other place entirely.

Now she speaks to me of the old Greek gods, and I witness their sport in ancient Thessaly where there was once a blue lake surrounded by mountains as high as the sky. In this luxuriant country of the dead, over which dark Pheraia reigned and the dead rose from cracks in the ground to flood the plains, Apollo himself was forced to slave for a Great Year, which is the time it takes for all the stars in the heavens to return to their original positions.

But here my grandmother begins to tell of things of which my waking mind knows she had no knowledge. A Great Year, she tells me, lasts for twenty-six thousand of our earth years. And she speaks of how, before the Greeks, the Pharaohs also studied the stars. They, too, marked the slow progress of the Great Year and little doubted that their dynasties would live through it. Indeed, such was the certainty of the Pharaohs that when their astronomers discovered a small miscalculation in the earth's own short year, it was decreed that they wait some fifteen hundred years to make their amendment until the seasons had returned to their rightful place.

Yet even before the Pharaohs and their eventual fading, there were other powers, and even creatures that bore no resemblance to men. My grandmother speaks of bearded Assyrians who rode their chariots and built temples towards the skies. And yet before them there were lost kingdoms, now long-forgotten, who carried the last wisdom of another distant age when the Old Ones came down from the stars on incredible wings, fleeing some impossible darkness. The Old Ones, too, built cities gaudy and vast that are now lost beneath the oceans, although they thrived and prospered for many ages before man. But the darkness they finally fled was inescapable, for it lay outside even the vastest turnings of the universe and time. Mind-wrenching beasts that the Old Ones themselves had once tamed broke loose from their bounds, and for a numberless age, all space was riven by the incomprehensible horror of Azathoth and his minions. . . .

Although by now I have little comprehension of what the buzzing voice of my dream-grandmother means, those last words seem to strike some special nerve, and I look up at her, pleading that she end this tale. At this point, my eyes did seem to open, and I was returned to Cul Holman, the distant howling of dogs and the screeching wind that caused the hangings of the room to sway. But my grandmother leaned closer over me and opened her mouth once again, as if to resume her tale. Nothing came out but a foul rushing blackness, and I saw, as it gaped wide above me like the maw of a great snake, that the mouth of the thing my grandmother had become had filled with stars.

I could not sleep the rest of the night. My throat was dry from the dust of those hidden graves, and from the screaming horror of my dreams. I summoned the slave girl Alya to bring me wine and keep me company, and I commanded as I drank that she tell me whatever tales she knew of daylight and some better place and age.

Alya's tribe, it seems, are traders, people such as those who follow the salt road to Tripolis. They are proud and loyal, and move with horses and creatures named camels that in all my time here I have only glimpsed from afar. To them, the desert is like some ocean upon which they drift and fight and trade in the way a mariner plies the seas. Like mariners, they love their chosen element and know its dangers and moods as few who ever lived.

She spoke of frost in the desert at midnight, of the pure white blindness of midday, and the slow-turning roof of the stars. Sand can be hard and harsh, or smooth as silk, soft as water. The dunes may move overnight—drown you as you sleep like the rising of a storm wave, or remain unchanged for centuries. Each wind carries a different taste, each day a different shade and substance to the horizon. There are deserts of sand, deserts of bare rock, deserts of smooth or jagged stones, deserts of ancient forests where dead trees stand in leafless perfection, sand-smoothed and polished to a different beauty, rising on their roots as if ready to walk in search of water. There are mountains and lowlands. Dream cities of spires, temples, colonnades, and glorious fountains shimmering above the plains.

Alya and her people have always known of the Nile. There was once even a time when they were the true dwellers beside her shores, and when the desert was still a green wilderness of cedar and pine, and meadows and waterfalls scented even these hills. It was her people, Alya claims, who built the first great works that the Pharaohs were later to claim as their own. Amongst these, and although she can never have glimpsed them, she numbers the pyramids at Giza, some sand-buried work she calls the Great Sphinx, and the temples of Seti at Abydos. They were made, she says, with magics that are now lost to mankind.

By the time of the reign of the Thirty-One Dynasties many centuries after, her people had long been nomads. They traded and learned the new languages, and watched through the slow ages as other great civilisations rose and fell. They saw the coming of the Assyrians and the Minoans and the Greeks and the Phoenicians and the Romans, they wandered amid the ploughed and salted ruins of Carthage. When they learned that their own great relics had been appropriated and restored as tombs of the Pharaohs, they wondered how anyone could credit them as simply the works of man. But all of this her people accepted without regret—even the reworking into new forms of their treasures of gold. . . .

I was half-sleepy by then, and the fears of the night had departed me now that Cul Holman's few scrawny cocks were crowing. But at the last words Alya spoke, I was fully awake in a moment, although I did my best to hide my eagerness.

"These ruins that you speak of," I said to her. "Surely they must exist in other places than the Lower Nile if the civilisation you speak of was as great as you claim?"

She nodded at that, although there was suspicion in her eyes. It was as if, sensing that I was near to sleeping, she had been spinning her words to herself more than to me, and now regretted what she had spoken.

"In my own small way, I am something of a scholar," I said. "I would be interested if you could tell me where you think such ruins might still be, or perhaps even show. . . ."

She stiffened again, and stared long at the ground.

"Of course," I prompted, "someone in a position such as mine would have ways of expressing their gratitude."

"You must give me freedom," she said, looking back up at me with a sudden boldness that was not of a slave. "Freedom to myself and to Dahib, and also to my people who still suffer in Kaliphus's stinking hive."

I was taken aback; that someone of her kind should attempt to negotiate with me! Yet there was something about her talk of ancient gold and magic that rang true. Almost as if she had spoken not of the past, but of something of which my dreams were already striving to foretell.

"If you do what you offer," I said, "on my honour as a man of Rome, I agree to give you what you ask."

"Then," she said, blinking the light from her eyes as the first flash of the sun rising through these shutters cast the rest of her into deeper gloom, "I will show you."

A day of wonders and disappointments.

Yes, there are tombs and ruins beyond the age of the Pharaohs within the far reaches of these hills—Alya has shown them to me—but they are wind-riddled, empty, almost unimaginably desolate. Yet there are other, deeper twists within this whole story.

On the assumption that Alya could ride, I had arranged for two sturdy ponies, but she assured me that they would be of little use on the route that we would be taking, to where these hills make their final rampart against the desert. Normally, I would never have set out on such a journey on foot, least of all in the dubious company of a single female slave—but you, my dear and honoured reader, will understand by now my need for discretion and secrecy. And Alya was in no doubt about the instructions I had left with Taracus as to what should be done to Dahib and the rest of her people should I fail to return.

The heat was already rising, forming a haze over Cul Holman like some evil storm cloud. Following Alya's quick heels into the shadow of the cliff and then along a hidden vale, I was glad to be away.

It was a long journey, keeping to secret routes. I know now where the places are that Alya collects her strange dark-scented flowers. They grow like crystal in hidden profusion from the very rocks, in what seems like the total absence of water. Sometimes, in the distance, we heard the shouts and hammerings of the mines, yet along the narrow gullies that she led me, we never glimpsed them, nor yet were seen. As the sun finally rose above the shadowed rock walls, I knew that she had already led me far.

I remembered, as I paused to take the food and drink Alya had carried with her, that Konchab had warned me about these deep clefts that lay in places beyond the mines. We had already stepped over the antique bones of many unwary goats and jackals, and as we rested and the hot afternoon wind began to rise, the air pressing through the narrow walls began to whistle and scream.

The sound grew louder as we moved on, filling my ears, making speech almost impossible. These hills are burrowed and threaded as if with the airways of some vast musical instrument that I can still hear echoing across Cul Holman as I write these words. As we clambered our way through twists and turns and the wind's wild shrieking grew yet louder and the maze more complex, I began to doubt whether Alya had any real idea of where we were going. What could *she* possibly know, anyway? Just some memory of the fables of her ancestors.

It was then, leaning against the rock to catch my breath, that I saw just how incredibly smooth the surface of these gullies had become. It was almost as if, through some unimaginable process, they had actually been constructed. I lifted a fallen flint and experimentally struck it against the smooth wall. The stone eventually shattered, leaving no mark whatever. Alya watched and twisted her hands as if, in this empty shrieking place, she was somehow made anxious by the noise.

The gullies became still better formed as we moved on—and more elaborate, drawn in twists and turns as if by the pen of some insane architect. And with each turn, the harsh piping of the wind grew louder. There was still greater evidence, here, of the bodies of fallen animals, some so recent that they seethed with flies, and others piled into ancient heaps that Alya and I had to climb over. I was surprised at this, as I had always imagined these hills to contain little life. And would so many full-grown animals be as foolhardy as to lose their footing in this way? Unless, that is, they had been brought here, and then purposefully thrown in as some kind of tribute. Forcing myself to inspect one or two of the cleaner corpses, I saw that their skulls were often missing, the vertebrae torn almost as if they had been bitten off, and sometimes coated with the remnants of a blackish-green sticky substance that I was not able, and would not have wanted, to have named.

Above us now, the rocks piled in a greater impression of order, of huge squared blocks suggestive of buildings. Yet the wind-driven heat of afternoon was now so intense that they had only a loose sense of substance, like cities seen in a dream. I saw also, or thought I saw, a black-robed figure. I could only reason with myself that it appeared too often, in too many places at impossible angles of accessibility, to be human, or real. And I saw now as we finally began to climb upwards from the gullies that there were fallen pillars, walls truly made of giant blocks of stone, wind-rotted remains of shapes that might once have been statues.

We came then, as evening was settling, to the sloped walls of a fastness that rose high against the cliffs at the far edge of the mountains. It was a long climb to ascend the huge blocks of which it was constructed, and Alya often paused and waited for me, offering a hand, which in my weariness I was then forced to take. I had already resigned myself to the fact that we would have to make our way back to Cul Holman under the moon and stars, or else camp in some remote shelter. But despite this, despite the shortness of my breath, I was truly excited.

We stood in the last of the dusk at what seemed like the final edge of the world. Beyond these mountains and the great crumbling walls of the edifice over which we had climbed, reddened with the last of the sun to the colour of drying blood, lay the shifting blue-grey immensity of the desert. Here it was possible, as I rubbed my scraped and bruised limbs, to believe the writings of such as Eratosthenes and Ptolemy—that the world is a globe floating in vast emptiness, and that we are all but ants upon it.

But the sight that drew me more was a single great block-pillared entrance set into the cliff-face above. With the light already passing, I was anxious to find my way inside before full darkness fell. But when we had scrambled up the last stone courses and stepped inside the vast portico, the sun, suffused in the whirlings and dust clouds of some far-distant storm, cast long rays of a thick grey light that were somehow regathered on the facings of granite. It was as if this was the precise moment that we were expected to enter.

Yet after the initial thrill of discovery, my feelings became those of disappointment. I was slow, as we stepped into the glowing shadows of that great squared archway and saw a vast and well-made passage stretching ahead set with the dark outlines of many entrances and openings, to appreciate the most obvious fact of all. Alya made a sign that was like the one that Kaliphus had made beside the shrine at my villa, muttering to me that this place was filled with old magics, and that on no account should anything be taken. But although clearly intact, this edifice was also open; unsealed, difficult to access, but certainly not hidden. It had long been emptied of all treasures.

Looking up at the roof, I saw the smoke tracks of lanterns, whilst in places the smooth faces of the walls were chipped and scrawled with crude Egyptian hieroglyphs. The protective eye of Horus was much repeated, although here it was gazing inwards on both sides of the tunnel, instead of looking just to the left. There were even signs, from the dust that lay on the floor, of the dragging and trailing of some pointed object, of recent habitation.

As we moved in and the light of the entrance began to fade, I put a spark to the torch that Alya had brought with us. Yet despite the dark that had fallen outside, the place never grew entirely black. Within the tunnels and shafts, strangely shaped rooms and turns and alcoves, many narrow slits had been hewn, through some art that escapes me, rising far up through the stone to open out on the mountainside. Even now, they admitted enough of the moon and stars to give some light—and often the impression, as some new vista was revealed, of glowing heaps of precious objects, twisting amorphous forms or beckoning shadows that, as we drew closer, always turned out to be nothing but faint stirrings of air and dust.

It was clear to me from the fearful, watchful way that Alya looked about her, and her wariness as we turned each new corner, that the knowledge that had brought us this far had departed her. In fact, I doubted even then that this was truly the work of her ancestors. Yet at the same time, I observed her reverence as she touched the strange dots and carvings that began to appear on the walls, and the way she pursed her lips as if she, an illiterate, were attempting to read them.

I had, whilst I was there, the strong impression that the place was a vast and empty tomb, but now I wonder if there was not some other purpose. From the faint, malignant odour that pervaded the place, I expected at each turn to reach a mass of poorly mummified bodies or the bloody mess of some ancient sacrificial table. Yet the smell ebbed and flowed with the wind's piping, which somehow penetrated the very furthest depths I was able to reach.

The only sign of recent human habitation was, in its way, fortunate. Just as the flames were starting to fade on my torch and I knew that I would have to turn back, I stumbled upon a larger and more roughly made brand that some other recent wanderer had dropped. It was only some passages later, when I was forced to put light to the thing, that I realised that the weight around the bottom, which I had imagined to be a handle, was in fact a human hand, severed at the wrist, and coated in the same ichor that I had noticed about the bones of the fallen animals in the gullies.

I gave a cry, then prised the thing off and flung it away. But the whole incident was too much for Alya. She turned and ran, sobbing, back the way we had come. I watched her go without attempting to call her back, but hoping for my own sake that the moonlight fanning from the narrow slits would be enough to guide her to the surface, and that there she would wait for me. The severed hand, I noticed, shrivelled and writhed through the process of some long-withheld contraction, moving briefly across the stone before finally collapsing in a twisted heap.

Fear is a strange thing. You, my reader, may well have imagined that it was with me at that moment as I stood alone in the depths of this strange ancient palace, yet in truth, only now in reflection does a chill begin to gather, a sense of unease almost as if a part of me was still there in that vast empty palace, forever lost and wandering.

Sadly, there is little else of interest in my explorations to relate. It occurs to me, though, that I should record some other of my impressions. In the absence of gold, perhaps I could keep at least a few of my creditors at bay by writing some fatuous history or novel about the place.

The tunnels are complex. I have almost the impression of an inwardly constructed fortress based around some central keep or core. The sudden turns, the many small alcoves and rooms into which a soldier or a priest might turn to lose or outwit an assailant, bear witness to that fact. The other point that would argue towards this is the shafts. There were many within the tunnels—and not of the narrow type that I have already described for the purposes of letting in light and air. These were wide and immensely deep, with narrow walkways at their sides, thankfully still sound, around which I was forced to make my way. The air that came up from these pits was shockingly foul. Much like the shallower versions of such shafts that I witnessed in the tombs at Thebes, I imagine that they were traps for the unwanted visitor. Either that, or they were used as the gullies were for the casting down of sacrifices.

But I remain, I confess, confused as to the essential purpose of these shafts. Now, weary as I am this night, it even strikes me that they were some vertical equivalent to the horizontal tunnels that I passed along, although their sides were so smooth, the depths so deep, that I cannot imagine what other use they could have been put to.

As to the passages themselves, I should record that the dots and carvings grew more intricate as I pressed further, although most were strange to me. I stopped, though, at a few places where somewhat newer slabs had been affixed to the walls, although these too were ancient, and many had fallen aside or cracked and crumbled. On these there was an almost Egyptian style of marking, although much changed. There were carved scenes, too, that might once have been colourful when the gilt and the paint still held to them. I saw men and women with eyes much like Alya's, gathering corn, drawing water, going about life's unchanging tasks.

In other places, I saw what I can only take to be scenes from the construction of the great pyramids. Once again, many people were shown going about these tasks. There were supervisors, too, and in places what I took to be the draped and oddly shifting forms of human figures—perhaps some kind of priesthood. I had passed several such slabs before I noticed another shape. Before that, I had taken it to be the destructive hacking of ancient graffiti. But the form recurred—if form it can be called—representing, I supposed, some feared chaotic deity whom the priests were supposed to keep at bay. Now, though, another explanation occurs to me. Certainly, if I am to turn my discoveries into a novel rather than a history, I would now say that the amorphous thing that the priests surrounded was the representation of an actual being.

Alya had spoken of the magics that her people had used to build the great pyramids and the other monoliths. Perhaps the truth is that they used this hideous shifting creature—for I can scarcely imagine that there is room in this universe for more than one—in the great labour of breaking and moving the stones. I can well imagine that its escape from the priest's control would have brought the downfall of a civilisation, persistent rumours of ancient magic, and the many myths of some destructive flood or holocaust. It all makes a type of sense, although it strikes me now that night at Cul Holman is not the best place to dwell upon it.

Finally, I turned back within the tunnels, hoping that I would be able to find my way out again. In fact, the choices were surprisingly easy. The foul shrieking wind that rose up, I was by now almost sure, from the pits themselves, seemed to push and lead me as I worked my way around them. When my borrowed brand finally died, I found that I was already near to the surface, and that the narrow upward shafts admitted threads of dawn. Thus my mood was almost calm as I walked back towards the square-set portals overlooking the desert. In this new brightness, I could almost glimpse the protective shadows of those long-dead priests standing guard around me, leading me on, murmuring prayers of protection.

In the last of the side-rooms into which I peered, drawn by a stronger glow of light, I saw a wider space than I had anticipated; a roof borne up by great squared pillars. The light shafts here were numerous, and angled in such a way that they crossed and threaded at a point near the hall's—or temple's, I might now call it—centre, and threw its far reaches into flowing drifts of shadow. There, caught in the web of light, hung a central core that was ill-defined in shape. It was an illusion that I had become used to in my explorations, but still I felt drawn to cross the surprising vastness of the hall on the chance that I might at last have stumbled upon some valuable relic.

As I drew close to the web of light, the ball of shadow it contained began to shrink, but for once, it did not disappear entirely when I reached it. Lying as if recently discarded upon the floor, a lump of black stone, multifaceted like some complex kind of dice, was visible. I have the thing beside me on the table now, and would record how many sides it has if I were able to count them exactly. It is heavy for its size, and rubbed at my thigh in the pouch where I carried it. Even now, my flesh aches at that point as if it were burned. The thing is too large to hide under the loose tiles beneath my bed where I hoard these notes and what little other wealth I have acquired here. To keep it from the prying eyes of my servants, I will bundle it up in my trunk beside my valueless heap of starstones. If I spin it sufficiently well into the tale I plan to write, who knows? I may even be able to sell it.

What else is there to record?—little other than that Alya was indeed waiting for me beside the great blocks of the entranceway, sitting with her hands clasped around her knees and shivering even though she was in the full warmth of the rising sun. That same sun then led us back here to Cul Holman without confusion, although the way was long and weary, and it was the edge of another evening when we finally came into taste, sight, and hearing of its dust clouds and hammerings.

Alya called to me as I made to enter my private quarters.

"Lucius Fabius," she said, raising her voice above the mad barking of Konchab's dogs, which had begun with our arrival. I started in surprise and turned back to her, that she dared to use my given names. "I call on you now to fulfil the bargain we made."

I, of course, asked her what bargain she meant, and reminded her that I had expected her to lead me to hidden riches and gold. How, otherwise, could I hope to buy the freedom of her entire family from Kaliphus—or even that of her and Dahib? At that, she looked at me. But she had the sense not to argue.

"At least, Lucius Fabius," she said, casting off the goatskin and pack she had been carrying, "I ask you that you at least release Dahib from his work in the pits at Dylath before he dies of it."

To that, I agreed. Dahib will start menial work at the counting houses this morrow-morn.

And now I must go to bed. I am far too weary to proceed with my usual late-night inspection.

They say that the seasons change but little in this place, and then only about the Nile. Yet, as what might otherwise be called autumn passes and we face the beginnings of winter, I am sure that Cul Holman has grown hotter. The sun blazes. Sour heat breathes from the rocks at night. I have the slaves bring water and fan me as I lie abed or try to set about my labours. My body sweats as I toss and turn.

I confess that I am grown irritable. Only yesterday, for no other reason than that he stumbled amid the rocks where he was working and I thus had to walk around him, I ordered the flogging of a slave. And news has reached me of the ill-fortune of my patron Servilius Rufus, and of the bewildering demands of my father's bankers, creditors, and clients.

Everything is bad, and I am too weary to give the details. At least, though, I am now past a half year in this dreadful place. Were the days not still so many, and the prospects of my return to Rome so grim, I could almost begin to count them.

In my dreams, I find that I am still often wandering the strange catacombs to which Alya took me, which in turn become once more the stinking streets of Alexandria under leaden skies, which unfailingly lead, if I cannot awaken myself, towards the dark-draped room of the villa in Naples in which I slept as a child, and where something that is no longer my grandmother awaits me. And even when I cannot hear her words amid the swarming dimness, the shrieking of these mountains that somehow penetrates even the deepest of my dreams, I know that she is always speaking of gold.

Gold, which has traits far beyond the pliancy, glamour, and incorruptibility that men so innocently crave. Gold, which claims ascendancy in a rubric of elements vaster than anything Aristotle conceived, and lies close to the point beyond which this universe must dissolve. Gold, which gives on to other places, other times. A million unfolding doors. Gibbous lines of insanity.

At the worst moment, it seems that I am falling, pushed down and through and under by a stifling weight. Strong hands then reach up to rescue me, and I am lifted into the light of some vast place amid the strangest of buildings. There are angles and shapes that my eyes can hardly behold, a sky that has a texture and a colour that can never have been of this earth. And I am surrounded by vast, ugly star-headed creatures, and I know that I am lost—unimaginably so.

Yet still I reach towards them.

Now that I am a little better, and although the weakness of the fever that I suffered is still upon me, I can look back on this last entry—and the odder suppositions with which I laced my record of my trip beyond the mountains—with a clearer perspective.

Perhaps the malady that killed my predecessor at last caught up with me. It could have been the foul vapours of those catacombs. Whatever, I am still sane and alive. After the terrible depths of the fever, I must do my best to be grateful. A full month has now passed since my last record, and already my replacement will be setting out from Rome. For that, also, I must be grateful. Konchab and Taracus have proved themselves more than capable of running these mines without me, and even the miserly Alathn seems happy once again with the regularity of his accounts. I suspect they all welcomed the resumption of their independence. Alya, at the worst of my fever, closed and reclosed the shutters that flew open in the shrieking madness of the wind. Even Kaliphus has been to see me, and left fresh fruit and rose water, and a suggestion that I have the pile of starstones immediately disposed of—which hints well that they might have some small value.

I saw a dark wind-flapping figure standing high on a rock above the pits at Dylath when I finally roused myself to make an inspection with Konchab this morning. Some of Taracus's soldiers happened to be about, and I ordered that they attempt to capture whatever it was that I was seeing. Soon, I was face to face with an elderly shepherd, quivering with fear, stinking in his filthy robes. Such was my relief that I laughed and I bid him released back to his starving flock.

All would be better but for the return to Rome, and with it the final loss of the wealth of my family. Childless, and with no desire to correct that situation, my only sister enfeebled by her long ugly face and no prospect of a dowry, I must now contemplate the apparent end of my family's once-dignified name.

The days now drag interminably. There is the ordering of the new slaves, and much bargaining for tributes and fees with money I do not even control. Yet I throw myself into this work with a new passion, and do my best to demonstrate to Alathn the breadth of my expensively acquired education by ploughing through Cul Holman's intricate accounts.

In the dust, in the very air here, hang fragments of gold. I sometimes think I see their glimmering when the sun falls in some new way, or shining on the limbs of the slaves as they emerge from the pits as if transformed into intricate gilded machines. In truth, I must have breathed in a little of the stuff along with all this foul air, so that it now infuses the humours of my body.

This last night, I was assailed by yet another foul dream. In it, I found that once more I lay beside the changing and sliding shape that was once my grandmother, although now I fear her form. In a ghastly buzzing voice, she speaks to me only of darkness and atrocities. Times when the star-headed Old Ones had to flee their great cities from a timeless wind that flooded beyond the stars. As the tapestries billow around us and the wind shrieks, I sense the near-presence of shambling amorphous entities.

"There was once and is and always will be the three-lobed burning eye," the creature begins. "It was named Nyarlathotep, by one who dared so to name it, and briefly called himself the Golden Keeper. But these are only sounds, and he was but the seed. . . ." At that, she cackled. Within a vast maw, teeth gleamed. "What it truly feasts upon is terror and debasement. It needs no meaning. It lurks forever beyond all comprehension, writhing at the back of everything. . . ."

Behind the beating curtains and the thinning walls of the room that I must share with whatever my grandmother has become, I sense the scratching and sliding of something massive, bearing before it an insane stench. I know, then, that were I even to glimpse it, my mind would dissolve. But still I sense that this is all part of some ghastly ritual. That somehow I am being prepared.

I awoke, slimed with sweat, to the howl of the wind and the persistent barking of Konchab's dogs. Even then, the curtains of the room still seemed to sway and flutter, and I sensed the fading of some terrible disturbance while a crouching weight lay upon my head. All of this, as you my trusted reader may well imagine, left me in a poor mood for the meeting that Alathn had requested this morning.

As he talked at his usual tedious length about the intricate principles and procedures of his work, I glanced at Konchab and Taracus, my two other companions, and sensed that they were already pondering other duties. Perhaps, I mused, this ugly dwarf was always thus—and nothing will ever come of the discrepancies of which he speaks.

"Gold," Alathn said, in what I hoped was his conclusion, "has a greater weight than stone or all other metals. It tends to sink and gather. Of course, this is the very principle upon which it is collected amid the pans, pools, and washing fleeces at Tarsil."

Here, as if this was all of some especial relevance, he licked his thin lips and glanced boldly at me.

"For this same reason," he continued, "there have been surprisingly rich finds made amid the sweepings of the counting-house floors. Many small grains and even nuggets are thus recovered. And within this last year, the weight of these sweepings has gone up noticeably. Yet we have recovered barely any of the expected gold they can be expected to yield."

At this point, I had opened my mouth to say that the records of such gathering would only be found by the washing beds in Tarsil. But Alathn then laid his hand upon the pale tube of a freshly copied papyrus, and I could guess what it was. I should have admonished him that he had ordered scribe-work done at Tarsil without my authority, but my mind was blurred.

"In truth," he went on after he had explained all that these new figures meant, "I fear we have all taken too small a care of this particular matter. It needs, after all, little more than for a weighing pan to be nudged, or a sleeve to be brushed across the top of a loaded pannier. And each night, the sweepings are guarded by one"—here Taracus bridled, although Alathn didn't actually say *sleepy*—"centurion. We are faced, I fear, with a small plot to deprive Rome of its rightful wealth. A minor conspiracy . . ."

I have, my trusted reader, no reason to lie to you—for the small bag containing what pitiful amount of gold I have been able to collect by the means that Alathn so carefully outlined lies hidden beneath the same paving bed as I keep these scraps of my writing. On the evidence of either, I would be condemned. Of course, the grains amount to a fraction of what I would need to regain the good name of my family. But if I were to shed my identity, to move cheaply into some minor but decently furnished place. . . . You, knowing all that you know, will understand that it is the least I can do; to permit myself a small, hopeful dream after all the nightmares that have assailed me.

From there, the meeting proceeded along a predictable path. Alathn confessed that he could name no specific culprit, as is usually the case in these matters. But whilst he spoke, he fixed his gaze shamelessly upon me. As my junior and lesser, of impure and polluted blood, he knows that he cannot make the accusation that he longs to make alone. Of course, if Konchab and Taracus were also to take his view, things would be different. But their manner remained unchanged. If they suspected me also, they made the wise decision not to risk their careers over such a matter.

Logic thus compelled me to agree with Taracus when he suggested that, as this fraud follows on from a long trail of minor stupidities and disobediences, the time had come to make a proper example. With new slaves recently arrived and our quotas in all other respects well up, it would be an appropriate gesture. I mentioned, of course, the brand, the flail. But it was clear by then that stronger measures were required.

"It is sometimes necessary," Taracus opined, "just as a gardener must prune and weed to ensure the best blooms, that a number of slaves must be put to death if the whole body of them are to thrive."

I nodded, thinking of my beloved villa in Naples, and wondering what this brutal man had ever even known of the dewy sun-washed fragrance of a proper garden.

"I would suggest, Lucius Fabius," he continued, "that ten is a simple number that brooks no argument, to be chosen equally from amid the counting-house slaves. Of course, the manner of their death must also be an example, something that will stick well in their primitive minds. Mere spearing . . ."

Through all this part of the discussion, Alathn remained silent. But I knew that he kept his eyes fixed on me. I understood his feeble tactic well enough: he imagined that I, a Roman, would weaken like his own retarded race at the prospect that was now laid before me. Of the suffering of others for a crime of which he knew I was guilty. But if this truly was his trap, I passed over it easily. Death amongst slaves is as natural as it is to the beasts of the farm—especially here at Cul Holman. If it were not the sweepings of the counting-house floors that brought about these executions, it would soon be some other matter.

Thus determined, I took the lead, and the discussion proceeded apace. We agreed that, as crucifixion uses too much rare and valuable wood required for pit-props and hammers, the slaves should be immured; buried alive within some of the many openings in the ravaged hills that overlook Cul Holman, and left to die there.

As is my duty this following morning, I stood witness as the slaves were selected. They were then chained before they were dragged up the hillside, closely supervised near the precipices in case they should attempt to end their lives in an easier way. I stayed within the camp and watched as the figures dwindled in the hot grey light, thinking once again how we are mere ants upon the face of this world, and how little anything that we do matters.

The stonemasons, still visible at the narrow pits that had been chosen, soon began their work, and the ring of struck stone and the cries of the slaves came distantly on the hot shrieking wind, to mingle with the moans and weepings of those who watched. Little enough work was done at Cul Holman this day despite the lashes of Konchab and his supervisors, and the threat that he would loose his already wildly excited dogs from their pens. Occasionally, for the greater good it fosters within our Empire, such prices must be paid.

I write now in the early part of the night, and all of Cul Holman seems strangely dark, strangely agitated. More than ever, the wind howls. The dogs will not quieten. But for that, I suspect I would also be able to hear the sleepless wailing of the slaves. Although those selected have been immured without the added mockery of food and water, it will still be necessary for the narrow pits in which they lie to be guarded for several days. Their deaths will not be quick—crushed together in the hot infinite darkness, flesh against flesh against unyielding stone, barely able to breathe, unable to move. But then who knows what finally kills any man, beyond thirst, hunger, and lack of hope?

I write again after an unwarranted interruption. Without my calling or seeking Henrika's permission, the slave girl Alya has come to my quarters. Sensing some presence in the room as I finished writing my previous words, I turned and saw her standing in the doorway. For a moment, I confess I almost felt a flood of relief that it was she and not something else, until irritation took over. Still, the girl has nerve. For that I must credit her.

"I have come to plead with you, Lucius Fabius," she said.

"Well and good," I said, remembering that we had bargained before, and wondering if there was perhaps still some knowledge that she held back from me. "What is it that you want?"

"Dahib."

"Dahib?" I repeated, puzzled, before I remembered. "Indeed. He was brought here with you, and I recall that I was generous enough to have him relieved from his duties in the pits . . . and moved to sweeping the counting-house floors."

She gestured wildly then, and I saw as she stepped closer into the flickering and tonight oddly dim light that her eyes and face were shining with tears. "He's buried—dying."

I nodded, wondering that I hadn't recognised him in the process of selection. But then, all slaves soon look alike when they labour here. "Understand, Alya, that the choice wasn't mine."

"What can I give you," she interrupted, "to free him?"

I shrugged, easily keeping my composure. "I am a rich man already. But then I am also a collector. That place that you showed me. Is there perhaps another—somewhere that has not been emptied?"

She stepped back from me then, almost as if in horror, and shook her head. For a moment, her eyes travelled wildly about the room, like those of some trapped animal. I saw them widen, and she gave a gasp as they settled on my grey-green collection of starstones piled in the room's far corner. And I noted that, tonight, a special light seemed to be within the stones; like the phosphorescence that lies at the edge of the tide.

"Otherwise," I continued, "there is nothing I can do. You must understand that I am not some flesh-hungry beast like Kaliphus. I—"

But that was an end to our bargaining. At that point, Alya turned and fled. I have since summoned Henrika and a half-dozen soldiers, but she has gone from the villa, and seemingly also Cul Holman. I suspect that in her folly she will try to climb the cliffs where Dahib is immured. But she will find the way guarded.

Before Henrika and the soldiers left me again to what I had hoped on this disturbed night would be my slumbers, I asked for him to bring more lamps and to add oil to all the existing ones. Even then, I asked him if he also noticed an odd effect, doubtless from some coming storm, in the way that the light seemed to hang in close spheres around the flame without passing further. He agreed, of course, but I do not think that the truth had penetrated his pagan senses.

A dark closeness now lies upon all of Cul Holman. Konchab's dogs are barking wildly, but for once the winds have ceased. The air hangs still, infused with this preternatural blackness, and there is a prickly sense of waiting that I associate with thunderstorms. Yet the only rumble comes from the beat of my heart.

Just this moment, as I reached towards the iron inkpot to replenish my nib, a greenish spark flew out from my hand. I have heard from mariners of just such an effect in storms; and also of the crawling of the skin, the rising of the hair, the suffocating sense of expectancy, although I have previously witnessed only the flash of clouds over the rain-swathed bay of Naples and the green hills of Rome.

No wind, and yet something within me seems to be blown wildly as if by a mad silent gale. In this itchy uncertainty, with the need always to look behind my back at the starstones and the lamps that withhold their suffocated light in the thick mass of darkness, there is clearly no prospect of sleep. This night, indeed, seems to me quite unlike any other, and yet ordained, much in the way that my presence here was—and, before that, the death of my father.

Much, it now seems to me, comes back to that. Now that we know each other well, trusted reader, and we seemingly have this night to share together, I will record a tale that will otherwise reach no eyes. Let me tell how, when I returned to Rome from the tedium of my duties as accountant in Sicily, little enriched and much in need of solace, I was greeted in the street outside my family's high house by the sight of wagons and carts. Too weary to take notice, I pushed my way through, only to find myself restrained and led towards a small group that included my sister and a few of our more elderly servants, all of whom were sobbing.

Understand, reader, that until that moment I had imagined that the drudgery of my work as an accountant was but a preparation for my true responsibilities as head of my family. Such things, I had reasoned, were not uncommon. Even as I learnt of the repossession of the furnishings of my house and the sale of my best slaves, I did not assume this indicated the loss of my family's wealth—but simple bad management of finances by my increasingly degenerate father.

Yet I was in a foul mood after I had made what arrangements I could from my own meagre purse, and rode in haste towards Naples. In other moments, such a journey would have given the chance for cooler reflection. But anger only seemed to grow within me; and a sense of destiny.

As I dismounted at nightfall four days later and my feet clattered on loose mosaic through the villa's mouldering halls, I remembered the time when I had been summoned to eat leaf-gilded strawberries. And as my face was brushed by cobwebs and rotting hangings, I remembered also the sickness that had come upon me afterwards—when gold is prized by apothecaries, and taken by those who can afford it for its powers of goodness and healing. It was then, even before I reached my father's presence, that the first worm of doubt began to slide within me. How, for so long, could I have ignored this decay, when it could all be put down to the simplest of explanations?

The few servants that my father still kept about him were drunkenly abed, or had absconded entirely. Yet I knew as I threw open the last doors into that windowless inner chamber that he would be waiting for me.

He lay as always upon his great couch on the dais, and the place was filled with the sweet stench of rancid oil and perfume. He had grown yet more in the year since I had last seen him. His flesh shone coldly with sweat, and his vast stomach tumbled out in a slippery mass from his dank robes. His tiny eyes regarded me from his swollen face, whilst his chin sloped down, white-mottled and immense like a toad's.

"So now you come to me," he said in that voice that was broken into two pieces—both high and low.

"I came," I began, "before it is too late—"

But here his wild, chilling laughter interrupted me.

"My son," he shrieked, "it was too late long ago! It was too late before you were born!"

"We need money," I said. "Money to pay off the creditors who have ransacked our house in Rome. We need gold."

"Ah, *gold* . . ." His body quivered again at the word, as if he were about to recommence laughing. But—as far as I could tell—his face remained grave. Looking up at him, I felt as impotent as a child.

"Go, then," he whispered, leaning forward with a sound of sickly sliding, "go and look for your gold. . . ."

Moving slowly around the dais, at first fearing some joke, I crossed to the line of great jars inset into the paving that he had opened for me long ago, and lifted the lid of the first, and placed my hand deep inside. It was empty. As was the next, and the next. As were they all. Dragging down rotting hangings, kicking over chests and boxes, I found nothing but dust and leaves. Admittedly there were a few coins; worthless radiati and fake aurei that I could bite through with my teeth.

Twisting his head this way and that, my father watched as I moved behind him, his tiny hands quivering at the end of his immense arms. He made a breathless eager panting that soon became a high-pitched giggling, then a growling belch of laughter. His shining face grew livid.

In my anger, I raised one of the caskets and threw it towards him, but it seemed to slow in the thick dark air and broke on the paving in shards of thin wood and metal. He bellowed as though the laughter would break him, greasy beads of tears and sweat flowing down his face, and I realised then that he had long anticipated this moment like the maturing of a sour wine.

I shouted at him that he was a degenerate, a disgrace to all the honour of Rome. At the mention of honour, his laughter only increased.

This, then, was the state to which I had been dragged—to face a future of meaningless penury. And I was filled by a new and even greater anger. I was a high-born Roman, yet my life seemed to have passed from my control. Understand now, reader, how much against my nature it was to climb the dais to my father's couch and strike him. Anyway, my efforts were useless, and only increased his laughter—it was like punching rotten dough. I had my small dagger about me, and I ploughed that into him, too, rending his clothes, slicing his thighs, his belly, his chest. But the blade cut nothing but white layers of fat and barely caused him to bleed. Enveloped in his stench, I seemed to be falling into him, the shrieking pit of his mouth, the quivering wounds I had opened.

At some point in all of this, the weight of our struggles caused the couch beneath us to break with a tearing of wood and the sparkling scatter of cheap glass beads and fake ornaments. My father began to slide from it—and I with him, although thankfully we separated as I tumbled from the steps of the dais, or I fear that I would have been crushed, suffocated, drowned.

As it was, I climbed to my feet and looked down at him as he lay sprawled, my greasy dagger still in my hand. He was but a spill of flesh; scarcely human, more like some rotting sea-leviathan. Yet from the discordant whistle of his breathing, I knew that he was still alive.

He had fallen almost entirely upon one great carpet. Experimentally, I lifted a corner and tried to drag it. His weight was immense, but a power was upon me. Somehow, I hauled my father through the doorway and along the corridors that I had come, and thence out into the open courtyard that contains the villa's well. There is no lip, and the aperture, once I had removed the iron grating, is wide and square. And deep also, so that I could never catch the glimmer of water when I peered down it as a child, nor be sure, when I cast a surreptitious stone, that the faint splash I finally heard wasn't simply the chattering of birdsong in the near woods. Yet for all of that, I almost doubted that my father would fit into the well. His gross limbs sprawled out as I heaved him off the carpet, snagging on the topmost stones even as the rest of him slid into it. I was forced, like a midwife in reverse, to work and push at his slick flesh until the last part of him gave way. Even then, he was slow in his descent down the dank sides of mossy stone. There was even a moment, looking down, when I was sure I saw the pale glint of movement as he began to climb back out. But then there was a great sound of ripping and sliding, and a gust of foul air as the last of his body's resistance gave way. That night, I truly did hear a thickly echoing splash as my father's body finally struck water.

I dragged the carpet back to his quarters and left the place otherwise as it was, in disarray, and with the well's iron grating removed. In what remained of the darkness, and unseen by all but the creatures of the night, I rode off towards the hills.

That, my reader, almost marks the end of this bitter little story. I dwelt the next night at a roadside inn, and spoke loudly of how I was heading towards Naples from Rome. I arrived once again at the villa the next noon, to find much commotion. A day-woman's efforts to draw water had already revealed my father's presence, and local workmen were labouring to extract him.

Too swollen to be recovered whole, my father was being hauled up in pieces. It was easy enough for me to display shock and surprise; and secretly to note as the glistening lumps of his body rose out on ropes how well the evidence of our struggles had been obliterated. As to the chaos of empty jars and broken caskets, I was able to offer an explanation that was all too easily borne out by a subsequent inspection of the family accounts: driven by penury and the thought of the loss of our family's great name, my father had chosen to kill himself. Would, I thought in darker moments as I pondered my future, that he had followed the tradition of older time in such matters, and also killed me.

Once the initial labours and enquiries had finished and a show had been made of grieving, I deemed it wise to seek a posting in some distant place before my creditors began to regather—which, by a long route, brings me back here to Cul Holman, to this night where the darkness still hangs, and there is a windless creaking tension. From somewhere, I sense a faint smell of burning, and my body seems to

What was that?

I saw a scorpion scuttle across the floor beside me, and then another. Several moths and gaudy insects have flown out from the window into the darkness instead of, as is their nature, towards the light. A rustling stream of cockroaches have made their way towards some crack in the wall that I do not remember seeing. And now there is silence. At last, even Konchab's dogs have ceased their barking. In this stillness, the earth seems to hold her breath. From somewhere comes the smell of burning. Looking behind me for a poorly trimmed lamp, I see that all the flames hang still as amber beads—and give as little light. Yet upon the starstones, there lies an intricate pattern of fine silver lines. Oddest of all, clear and almost reassuring amid this blackness, a grey stream of smoke is rising from the sides of my trunk.

I must

* * *

There marks a fitting end to that night's journal, and to the much that has happened since. I assure you, dear reader, that I am still alive and well. Indeed, I am well and wealthier than I could ever have expected.

I should have realised that the dense silence and other strange portents at Cul Holman signalled more than a mere storm. Indeed, I am somewhat angered that Konchab, Taracus, and Alathn, with their greater knowledge of this place, did not see fit to warn me. But they also professed innocence at the magnitude of what was to occur, and I am currently in a mood to forgive them.

If, as Virgil contends, earthquakes truly are the restlessness of giants sleeping deep beneath the earth, then what has occurred here must have been caused by the greatest of them all. I can smile now at my unreasoning fear as the world shook loose from her anchors, as the walls that sheltered me moved and the villa's roof rattled in a rain of tiles, whilst from the darkness beyond came a massive groaning and rumbling that deafened the ears and sickened the belly. A strange glow seemed to rise. The stifled flames of the lamps suddenly spat great tongues of spark. Veins of fire ran along the walls and floor—even through my hands as I looked down at them. After all the portents and horrors I have been subjected to, I truly believed that the universe was coming apart to be replaced by—I know not what.

But, in echoes and groans, the rumbling slowly died, and then, for the first time that night, fading as if already from some long way off, came the piping and whistling of the wind, to be replaced as it, in turn, died by the screams of the slaves, and the hiss and clatter of settling dust and masonry.

Dawn came then, as if the sun finally had shaken loose from the earth in the process, and never more grateful was I to see his light. I emerged, as did many others, into a broken and rearranged world. I can see now the dark silhouettes amid the drifting mist—but this journal is not the place to record the damage, and the work of reconstruction that has gone on in these recent days. I am preparing, in fact, a report that I propose to submit to the Senate upon my return to Rome, which will doubtless be copied into other libraries should you wish to refer to it.

For the purpose of this, my truer journal, let me say that the very crudeness of Cul Holman—the low stone dwellings, widely scattered —meant there was none of the vast loss of life that there might have been from an earthquake in a more civilised place. Still, there were numerous injuries amongst freemen and slaves—and in the buildings and workings of their trades.

It was only when I made my first inspection into the hills beyond the valley this morning that I realised the true enormity of what has taken place. Clouded by the risen dust, the light itself had changed, yet had a clarity it had lacked before. The hills seemed more solid. New fissures of rock had reared up, peaks had fallen, cliff-faces had broken.

Truly, the earthquake was the author of strange events that would have been put down in more primitive times to the work of gods. One of the counting-house sheds seems to have been bodily moved; more amazing still, a small quantity of gold was found lying upon the scales when all the wreckage was removed. I myself have seen, in the dust around this villa, evidence of incredible stirrings that I could have taken to be dragging claw marks were I a man of lesser knowledge. And, as far as it is possible to tell amid the new face of the hills that overlook us, the imprisoned slaves were shaken out from their graves by the movement of the earth, and thus released. Of them—and of Alya—there is no sign, although the soldiers who had been stationed to guard them, and also Konchab's dogs (although I, for one, am glad to be rid of their ceaseless howling) were found strangely beheaded, their torn necks coated in a foul greenish-black ichor, which I can only presume rose up from some deep portion of the earth.

At some point in the afternoon after the earthquake, weary of issuing instructions and the cries of the wounded, deprived of an entire night's sleep, I went back to this room in the villa that the servants had made some small effort to tidy, and laid myself clothed upon the bed.

I scarcely knew that I was asleep, yet it seemed to me that I saw once again, as if from afar, the vast, strangely angled cities of which I have sometimes found myself dreaming. They are built from huge blocks of stone set and faced with shining gems, and in truth I felt a sadness to know that what I saw lay so impossibly far in the past that all but the faintest remnant has faded. For I recognised that they were made in the manner of the ruins to which Alya had taken me; and not by man, who was not even upon the face of the earth at this far time, but by great beings, star-headed and with many strange limbs, who moved on the pads of three triangular feet. Despite their ugliness, I felt a sense of kin; for I saw that, in their own alien way, they were wise and purposeful. These, I thought, are the Old Ones, whose wisdom trickled down through the aeons in enough measure for Alya's ancestors to use it in the building, puny to them, yet still vast by our human standards, of the great pyramids. My sense of distance was redoubled by the knowledge that these creatures would ultimately be obliterated by a mad darkness. But here, it seemed to me as they moved within their towering cities, they were at their prime. The whole earth was theirs, from the highest mountains to the deepest trenches of the sea. And they looked upon the hellish creatures, whom they bid do their work using only the power of their minds, with contempt. They ruled everything. They knew no doubt.

Such, then, was the vision that was presented to me—and I, a Roman, at last witnessed a race with whom I could converse as an equal, had these creatures but mouths and eyes and ears. I watched, charmed more than repelled, as the Old Ones went about the incomprehensible business of their lives beneath the strangely coloured skies of a lost ancient earth. I saw on shining walls the dot-markings with which I have become familiar, and heard, or thought I heard, a sweeter version of the piping that carried so often on the wind. I saw, also, many of the starstones, less worn but otherwise exactly like those I have collected, and glowing with fine inscriptions. These, I noted, were passed between the creatures by their odd appendages, and I soon reached the conclusion that they were a coinage of sorts. But here the matter does not end, for I also saw several of the creatures bearing black multisided stones like those which I found in the edifice at the edge of the mountains. They would place these at the centre of a starstone, causing a strange transformation to take place. The starstone changed colour, and the veins within it ceased to glow as it took on all the appearance of gold.

Reader, as you may imagine, I awoke with a start then. In the thin light of dusk, I hastened to my trunk, remembering as I opened it the smoke that I had seen coming from it on the previous night. Indeed, the whole contents were charred and soot-stained. As I reached through the ash of my ruined clothing and closed my hand around the many-sided black stone, the ground once more gave a faint growl. Masonry crackled, and again the slaves of Cul Holman began to weep and wail. But the tremor proved to be nothing—a mere settling back of the earth.

I gazed at the black stone and picked up also one of the starstones, turning them both over. It seemed quite impossible that one thing thus angled should mate with the curved indent in the middle of the other, as I had seen in my vision. But the two artefacts fitted well when I tried them; so well that I could not separate them when they were joined. In fact, the lines within the starstone began to glow, and it became so hot that I dropped it to the floor. Within a moment too quick to notice, the starstone changed colour. It gained a smooth golden lustre and—for I discovered that both objects were immediately cold, and could be separated easily—had increased greatly in weight. Then I placed the black-faceted stone within the centre of another starstone, bringing about the same transformation.

From here, reader, you may imagine that I proceeded to transform all the starstones into what I could only conclude was gold. In fact, I performed the process only three times; and for the third, by way of an experiment, I used the most scratched and damaged of the stones, with two of its arms broken, although that also changed. But gold is a tricky substance to possess, especially here, and at that moment I still doubted the sense of what I was seeing. It was enough. Before light next day when all was quiet, I summoned a smithy to one of the makeshift workshops. To allay my remaining doubts, I bid him work one of the changed starstones in ways that only the most precious of all metals can be. Despite the man's protests, the stone was easily cut and beaten into twenty fat coinlike discs of roughly equal size. They are warm to the touch as I hold them now, and feel smooth upon the tongue, creamy yet with a faintly salty flavour; much as I imagine those who indulge such matters find the flesh of a loved one. Gold truly is the most human of metals, yet it also brings us closest to the gods. As for the smithy, I have had him beaten on the pretext of some minor offence. If he survives, his tale will be taken as mere raving.

I have less than a quarter of my given time left here at Cul

Holman, and I am torn between a desire to return to Rome and to remain for longer, gathering starstones. This afternoon, beginning my search, I went out to where the further mines are being re-established and sought the gullies along which the slave girl Alya had led me. But I could not find any, and I surmise that they were closed up by the great movements of the earth. That would also explain why the wind sounds differently now—although it blows as hot and fierce as ever. Gone is the weird piping: gone too, I imagine, are those vast ruins to which Alya took me—or so buried as to be lost forever. For it became apparent as I wandered deeper into these hills that the greatest disturbance took place in the far reaches. If there truly are such things as Virgil's sleeping giants, it is there that the greatest of them all must lie.

* * *

Long have I neglected these writings, and now that I begin again, it is upon a proper roll of papyrus, with better ink, and in a better place. Indeed, I have often toyed with the idea of destroying all that I have written, in view of the hazard it would present were it to fall into greedier hands.

You find me where all of this began; which is not Rome or even Cul Holman, it now seems to me, but at my beloved villa in Naples. Of course, I still think of Cul Holman. Yet the place seems darker than it does even within the wilder ramblings of my writings, and its memory tugs me in strange and uncomfortable ways.

Much of the remaining time since I deserted you there, patient reader, I spent in the pursuit of starstones. I confess I remained aloof from the harsh duties of reviving Cul Holman's fortunes. I kept to myself, and ate and walked alone, and glanced but occasionally over my shoulder at the black figure that even here still sometimes seems to follow me. But at the end of it all, I found nothing—not one more stone. Any that remained must have been buried in the sliding and twisting of those hills.

Apart from this seemingly odd pursuit, I did nothing to arouse suspicion at Cul Holman, and changed no more of the stones to their true metal. Nor, save in one instance, did I use them for currency; the idea for which seemed to stay with me oddly. For I confess I went to Kaliphus's palace to purchase the freedom of Alya's family. Kaliphus was his usual self, enquiring about Cul Holman's fate in the earthquake as if his spies had not already informed him. Still, he seemed almost reluctant to accept the excessive amount of gold I offered for the freedom of his slaves—though I had credited him as a man of business, if little else.

Eventually, even as he made the sign I had seen him make before, he took the six heavy discs I offered. And he accepted my explanation that they were but a little of the personal wealth I had brought with me from Rome. In fact, there was an odd gravity about our transaction, as if the exchange were necessary as one small notation in a complex scroll of accounts where some greater total was to be balanced.

As is the way with such arrangements, I left Cul Holman and began my long return journey down the Nile aboard the same craft that had borne my successor there. We barely had time to exchange greetings, and still less for me to pass on the little I have learned about mining for gold. Konchab and Taracus will soon also go to other duties—even Alathn, if he is wise, will seek a reposting before he runs the fatal risk of becoming indispensable. The slaves and freemen, of course, will come and go. They live, they die, they breed. Soon, all that happened at Cul Holman in my time there will be but a rumour.

The great papyrus raft that bore me upon the spring flood of the Nile was readied to depart in the blue of evening. Henrika had come with me upon this journey—sadly, he paled and died soon after of a fever—but otherwise I travelled alone. I felt a curious calm as I watched my trunks and belongings being hauled onto the shadowed deck. I had made no attempt to hide my collection of unchanged starstones, and the gold was bound as a thick weight around my chest and belly beneath the folds of my toga. I would also have carried the black-faceted stone upon me were it not that it caused my flesh to burn and ache. The workmen and mariners seemed mere shadows to me. I felt sure that I was protected.

We pulled out into the black waters as the stars began to shine, and a cool wind, so unlike that which I had long become used to, began to fill the vast red sail. All about me, glowing in the light of a huge rising moon, lay the plains and hills and pillared ruins of upper Egypt, and beyond that the beckoning edge of the desert; a sense pervading everything here that the present is but the trembling surface from which the currents of the bottomless past will always rise. I stayed on deck as the ropes wheezed and the sail crackled stiffly and we moved further into the smooth flow in which the whole world seemed upturned in reflection. The air was filled with a strange wailing, and when I looked to the shore, I saw that many of the dark-robed natives had gathered in lines and were making this wavering cry at the passage of my boat. And beyond the palm trees and the villages and the fresh-flooded ditches, where moon and starlight silvered the last edges of the hills before they faded into the desert, I thought I saw also a cluster of other figures. It seemed to me that they were mounted, leading those strange humped creatures called camels, and that they raised their arms in salute before turning towards the desert. Thus, so I imagine, I saw the passing of Alya, Dahib, and her tribe.

I broke my journey as before at Alexandria whilst passage to Ostia was arranged, and wandered the same streets. Despite the turn in my fortunes, I was curious to renew my brief acquaintance with the alchemist or charlatan known as Zosimus, for it seemed to me now that the walls of his dark room had been adorned with similar shapes and figures to those I had seen elsewhere. But my pursuit along the odd twists and turns of those shadowed and stinking alleys was fruitless, and I was ever afraid, as I looked behind me, that I was being pursued by some bandit. I also sought enlightenment in the mouldering library; for it seemed that I recalled a glimpse of star-shapes and strange drawings on forgotten scrolls. There again, I was disappointed—if disappointment is the right word.

Here in my Naples villa, much work has been done in daylight, although time is wasted by the labourers' refusal to dwell here, and I find it hard, even at inflated prices, to obtain and keep any decent quality of slave. Rumour of my wealth, of course, has spread as quickly as these things always do, and now I fear that I am probably the dupe of shoddy dealings. In view of my father's penury, the gossip is that I returned from the far reaches of Empire with a cache of hidden gold, and the story is near enough the truth for it to be fruitless for me to attempt to deny it. There is also a malicious whisper that I stole gold from the mines I was supervising, and I have had to endure a visit from the Emperor's auditors on the strength of it, although there was hardly any charge worth answering. Still, some shadow seems to hang over me, and I have found it harder than I might have imagined to clear my family's name.

Even with the starstones, all is not quite as I had hoped. Although I regretted that I had not found more than the twenty-three I had with me, I had calculated that they would represent a wealth that is more than the equivalent of Cul Holman's produce in a whole year. It was with the joy of a pleasant task long delayed that, at last alone in the privacy of my father's old quarters, I set about transforming them all to gold. All went well to begin with until I set to work on what would have been in total the tenth starstone. When the black-faceted stone would not even fit the indentation, I imagined some fault in the mechanism and moved on to the next. Yet I tried them all, and in each case it was the same. Thus, I must make do with a total of merely nine golden starstones, more than four of which I have already been forced to exhaust in repaying my father's debts, of which I fear, much like the cracks and strange defects that the builders find here, there are still more to be uncovered. Of course, I would have readily accepted such an outcome when I first set out towards Egypt—by most normal standards I am wealthy—but the feeling remains at the back of my mind that I have somehow been cheated in a bargain I never intended to make.

At first, I made a great show of new riches to my neighbours, patrons, and acquaintances at sumptuous feasts at my refurbished high house in Rome. But I found poorer solace in their company than I had in that of Alathn, Konchab, Taracus, and even Kaliphus. Often, I would gaze down the table at the odd geometries of plates and arms and bodies, breathing the jagged scent of all the food and the flowers that I had ordered, and wonder at the meaningless drone of their voices, and if this truly was eloquence, elegance, civilisation.

Here in Naples after the first work on this villa had been done, I summoned my sister and a fair scattering of other guests, including men whom I deemed would make eager suitors now that our family's wealth was no longer in doubt. In truth, though, when I saw her face, sad and long and flat, it seemed to me that the poor creature had grown more sullen than ever. The occasion went as all the others had done, which is to say pointlessly and expensively as I lay at table and watched the people move and unfold like shadows and tried to catch the buzzing of their words. Like the other occasions, I knew that it would end early, with poor excuses, uneasy laughter, glances back from my departing guests. My sister, almost as bored with it all as I was, must have wandered off between one of the many courses, for suddenly the air from the unimproved passages beyond this villa's newly lighted hall was torn by a blood-chilling shriek. I do not know what she imagined she saw upon the dais where my father had once sat, and it seems unlikely, in the gibbering incontinent state in which I found her and in which to this day she remains, that she will ever be able to explain what fancy has riven her mind. She dwells now in a place where, if you pay enough, her kind are looked after. There she is changed and fed like an infant, and her hands are kept bound and bandaged to thwart the attempts she has made to take out her eyes.

Still, I am proud of the way that work has proceeded at this villa, even if it seems I am to be the last in my family's line unless I take the step of adopting an heir. In the daytime, when the sun is brightest and there is less need for the lamps that I otherwise keep about me, I welcome the sounds and sights of people working, even if the refurbishing of this villa has been a matter of much argument and debate.

These last few days, in fact, following a protracted argument between myself and a foreman about a new window, all work has ceased. It was plain to me that his joinery was out of true, and that whole aspects of the room were finished shoddily at odd degrees.

The man and his assistants still had the temerity to claim that all was as it should be; he even produced a rule and set it against the wood and plaster to prove his point, although the thing was clearly as crooked as he was. Thus, and with all my slaves and servants recently gone, I find myself alone.

Naples itself and this coast and countryside have declined in the time since my childhood. An ominous black pall hangs over Vesuvius. The air often stinks. The markets are full of cheap goods and sour produce; once fine streets have become rows of hovels and the harbour reeks of dead fish. I sometimes fear that all our Empire may be declining. There are risings of peasants and shepherds in Gaul, usurpations in Britain, German invasions along the Danube and Rhine. There is even talk that Rome may one day cease to be the capital of our Empire—although, despite the strange things I have heard of and seen, that is one outcome I will never believe.

Alone as I find myself in this villa with you, my reader, my last and trusted friend, it might be imagined that I am prey to robbers. Yet only two nights ago after the leaving of my last few servants, a body was found not far away in the woods. It belonged to a notorious thief, and was roughly beheaded and coated in a foul slime. So it seems to me, my reader, that in some way I am still protected, although as I wander the deep lanes whilst Vesuvius growls and rumbles and black flakes of its soot drift like snow upon the air, the people shun me and call in their children at my approach, and close the shutters of their homes.

It is near now to the height of another summer. I go out but little anyway, as the lanes are intolerably filled with the sharp stench of strawberries. In truth, now that I could afford to eat and drink whatever trifles I please to, I find that my taste in food has become bland. My previous cook, before he left, made me many loaves of unrisen corn bread that, stale though they are, I had been eating and, since they ran out, have made do with the dough he left uncooked in his hurry to leave. Even on such poor rations, I fear that I may be gaining some of my father's girth.

Each night, I light as many lanterns as I can—and try to restrain myself from drinking their oil. In the few times that sleep comes upon me, I wish that it had not, for I find myself within the presence of the thing that was once my grandmother again, although it seems to me now that she was always thus—a black assortment of angles—and that the things of which she speaks in that buzzing voice are all that she has ever told me. For I know now, although I would give much of my gold not to, of Nyarlathotep, of Great Cthulhu and Shub-Niggurath, the black goat of the woods—of beings beyond all darkness.

Last night, I tried to break the spell by speaking back to her.

"What do you want?" I asked—then added a half-remembered phrase that came back to me. "Are you the Golden Keeper?"

She chuckled at that, and the sound thinned and faded into a thousand echoes. "What I keep is not gold. And it is not my task to keep it."

"What can I do?"

"Nothing."

"There must be something—"

"—I give that you may give," she says before her voice trails off into inhuman buzzing. Then she lifts something from within the twisting folds of her robes, although it takes a long time for it to emerge, and her arms are like the tearing and stretching of something ancient and rotten. But I recognise it when she holds it out for me. For the thing is black. Multifaceted.

"Here," she says, and although the stone is already mine, I reach out to take it.

It shifts within my hand as it begins—segment on unfolding segment, as if from the workings of a hidden mechanism—to open. Something smooth and living slides out from it across my fingers. A shining worm of sorts, mucus-coated and somehow larger than the stone within which it was contained. It is truly ghastly to look at, and I watch in horror as it begins to burrow into my hand.

I opened my eyes then, and the room was filled with a sound that I imagined for a moment was nothing more than my own screaming. I stumbled out from my bed, drawn and repulsed by a mad endless piping as Odysseus must once have been by the sirens who lured sailors to the rocks on these very shores. I stumbled naked along dark swirling corridors, no longer knowing what I was escaping or seeking, until I found myself standing out in the well courtyard beneath a sky lit and blackened by Vesuvius's fitful glow. It seemed to me that the piping here was strong enough to burst my ears, and that I knew at once where it came from. Still possessed by the logic of a dream, I drew back the grating of the well.

Perhaps I truly was dreaming, for there can be no rational meaning to what I saw when I looked down. For a moment, the well seemed bottomless, filled with stars. Then there came a liquid click, and a sense of something rising. If I could describe the thing at all, I would say that it was made of bubbling, shifting matter. As to its true shape, it had none—or many; for as it rose towards me with impossible speed, piping and shrieking, I imagined that it remade itself into a mockery of many forms. I saw dog-headed Anubis, I saw Medusa, bearded Jove, a horned bull, and the livid, bloated face of my father. Then I stumbled back, swooning in the terrible blast of air. And I remained that way for much of the night, crouched shivering by the well as Vesuvius smoked and shook and glowing flakes of ash burned at my flesh, almost urging the thing that I had glimpsed to finish its ascent. Yet nothing happened, and as dawn grew, the piping slowly faded.

I am no longer sure what happened last night; and how much of what I saw was due to some fevered condition, or the effects of sleepwalking. This day, since I could summon no workmen to do the task for me, I have busied myself with laying the grate back over the well, and weighing it down with stone blocks and what pieces of furniture I would manage to drag unaided into the courtyard. It was harsh work, made more difficult by the problems I found in negotiating their shapes around the incredibly odd angles and openings of corridors and doors.

As I look out now, near to sunset as Vesuvius rumbles threateningly and brings early darkness across half the sky, it seems to me that the familiar and beloved landscape of my childhood memories formed by the intersections of sea and hills shifts and breaks like plates of ice upon a lake. But for the fact that they were moving, I would take the figures I can see crossing a distant field to be the limbs of twisted, blackened trees. And earlier, as I rested from the task of dragging a large and recently purchased mirror out into the well courtyard, I saw another odd effect. Leaning against the wall for support as the corridor ahead of me seemed to twist downwards, I looked at myself in the polished brass. The mirror's inner surface flared out, and my face, admittedly broader and paler now, became not so much that of my father, as of that terrible distortion of him that I saw coming up from the well. And then began the maddening piping that has been with me ever since.

Now that the sun has set on this dense and windless night, and with the mouth of the well surely covered by enough weight to muffle any sound, the piping grows louder still. Entwined within it is the muttering of some mad incantation that I recognise now comes from my own throat. I hear it speak of the Great Gate of the Stars, and of the living seed that is and always was the Golden Keeper.

The shrieking now is incredibly loud—triumphant, even, as the ground shakes beneath me and the walls begin to shift. Perhaps, after all the years of threats and mutterings since the time of Herculaneum and Pompeii, Vesuvius is again preparing to erupt. No doubt, if that is all this is, the women will be wailing, offering the blood of lambs on the hot smoking slopes above their dwellings. But to me, it all seems far closer than that. Closer even than the well or even the sliding walls of this room. I feel a stronger presence, as if the very ground beneath me were about to crack.

My head swirls so much with this chaos, dearest reader, that I fear you and I must soon part, for I can barely write these words. Stopping my ears does nothing but increase the terrible sound, this sense of something within me rising. I would also bind my eyes were it not for what I see in the greater dark, which is now so vivid that I can scarcely bear to blink. I would but speak to you now, reader, but each breath is agony, and with the parting of my lips the piping grows yet wilder and guttural words spill out. I tried to call upon Vesta, protector of households, that strong and humble symbol of goodness and light. But the sound came out as mad shrieking, and I could barely close my jaw as my chin was jerked back and my throat widened on a stream of darkness and foul air. Even now, with my chin tightly bound and my mouth filled with the gold discs and papyrus that are all I have about me, the sound grows in power.

I will wait for what this night brings me, and distract myself meanwhile by ordering these scraps of my writing before they are spoiled by the dark fluid that now bubbles from my lips. Perhaps my father was right, and I will never understand the meaning of the rituals I have been performing, nor yet the purpose of the Golden Keeper. Perhaps our lives really are without purpose. But in that, at least, I fear that I may yet prove him wrong. Meanwhile go in peace, reader, and know that I am Lucius Fabius Maximus, a trained accountant of high Roman blood who has done service to the Empire in both Egypt and Sicily. Truly, I am a murderer also, and I fear that I have treated many of those I came across harshly. But all I ever wished for was decency and comfort. I trust that, after all we have shared, you will understand this, gentle reader, and strive not to condemn me.

ralph wollstonecraft hedge: a memoir

RON GOULART

Ralph Wollstonecraft Hedge was a particularly amiable recluse. However, because he spent his final years ducked down behind a discarded harmonium in the lumber room of his maternal aunt and, further, steadfastly refused to talk to interviewers, there is little biographical material available for the curious student who wishes to know more about the man many consider to be the logical successor to Charles Brockden Brown. To remedy this, I feel bound to set down my recollections of this writer I believe deserving the mantle of Poe.

In this paper I will deal chiefly with Hedge's mature years, since nothing is known of his early life. He apparently was found on a doorstep in his twenty-first year, with no recollection of his past. The doorstep itself was found in a forest in Bristol, Rhode Island, where the Druids from the neighborhood held occasional outings up until the McKinley era. These early associations seemed to have little effect on Hedge, although in the autumn he would turn a russet gold color and exhibit a tendency to drift gently to the ground.

For several years, interrupted only by a wedding trip to Providence in 1923, I served Hedge as secretary, and also saw to it that no squirrels, animals of which he had an exaggerated fear, got to the upper floors of his shuttered colonial house. Thus I feel I knew this master of the macabre better than most. Indeed, in 1926 and the early part of 1927, when Hedge had hidden himself among the living-room drapes, he spoke to no one but me, and that was only in a whisper.

Ralph Wollstonecraft Hedge spent a good deal of time behind things, and so most of his tales were dictated. Usually to me, but several, especially in 1928, to a man named Collin A. Ruckersett. The stories Hedge wrote in his own crabbed hand were for the most part illegible. None of these latter were ever printed, except for a story called "At the Pits of Terror," which appeared in *St. Nicholas Magazine* (I am not sure of the date, but I remember it was raining quite a lot that day). The version is, I contend, greatly garbled. I am sure Hedge did not include a character called Bunny Pitpat in the story. Nor was the tale meant to induce children to brush their teeth as frequently as possible, dealing as it did with the complex weird mythos Hedge had painstakingly built up.

After 1935 Hedge neither wrote nor dictated any further stories, except to ghostwrite three Big Little Books for the Whitman people. This task added not at all, in my opinion, to his stature as a master of the horror genre. When he ceased writing, RWH (as his circle called him) devoted himself to eating ice cream. He confided in me that he desired to do a major work in which he would compare and contrast all the existing flavors of ice cream, with an appendix covering sherbet and Popsicles. It was Hedge's intention to devote six months to each flavor, but his untimely end cut him off before he had gotten much beyond chocolate. I, for one, have always been sorry that this work did not see completion. I am sure it would have shown yet another side of the man who gained such renown with his stories of grave-robbing and lycanthropy.

Of course, RWH had a considerable influence, direct or otherwise, on the younger writers. George Worsnop Bangs, the youthful recluse of Paso Robles, California, was strongly influenced by Hedge's work, even to the point of signing Hedge's name to all his stories and tales. A circumstance, I might add, that has caused some amusing confusions in academic and scholarly circles. Rudyard Boland, the gifted assistant and macabrist of Yazoo City, Mississippi, owed his early success to the kind literary advice and bundles of sandwiches that RWH sent him. And any but the most casual reader will see that Thomas Wolfe's *Of Time and the River* and Max Shulman's *Barefoot Boy with Cheek* are simply extended anagrams of Hedge's earlier "The Lurker in the Cabbage Patch."

Unlike his weird stories, Hedge was not weird at all. He was a small thin man with a round face and merry eyes, rather Dickensian in his speech. I believe he almost always wore a dark blue suit, but since he stood behind things so often, it is possible that he wore a blue coat and trousers of some other color. I cannot be sure. Hedge was not overly fond of animals, although in the spring of 1933 he took to carrying a Manx cat around in a perforated shoe box, and sometime late in 1929 he dictated a fan letter to the artist of the comic-page strip *Barney Google,* expressing what I considered extravagant praise for the horse, Sparkplug. As I believe I have mentioned earlier, Hedge was violently afraid of squirrels. It is therefore somewhat ironic that during the Depression a great many squirrels took to hiding nuts all around the ground floor of Hedge's home. I have taken more than one nasty spill as a result of stepping unexpectedly on a cashew.

Ralph Wollstonecraft Hedge was married briefly in 1934 to a woman who had once driven a truck in St. Paul, Minnesota. I am not sure of her name because RWH was very shy in her presence and never introduced us. I have the feeling I heard somewhere that her name was Helen. She, whatever her name was, never understood Hedge's work and spent most of her time Indian wrestling with Collin A. Ruckersett. She moved away in 1935, taking two pounds of walnuts, and, outside of a Christmas card in 1937, we never heard of her again.

Only last year, while attending the jazz festival in Newport, I encountered several Hedge fans who asked me the familiar question about where RWH got his ideas. To the best of my knowledge, most of his best stories were the product of hallucinations. Many is the morning I would be sitting in the music room swatting squirrels only to have Hedge interrupt me by running in whooping. After I had locked the door and looked under everything, RWH would consent to dictate to me one of his famous yarns. It is in this way that his renowned "The Thing in the Dumbwaiter" and "The Shuffler Beyond the Transom" were composed. Readers who have noted a pronounced division in the middle of "The Peeper Round Corners" will be happy to learn that this story is the product of two separate hallucinations.

Most of Hedge's ideas were his own, but on rare occasions Collin A. Ruckersett would dress up in an old sheet and domino mask and scare RWH into a story. This method was only resorted to if RWH was behind in his work. To get him going on his novel, *The Straggler from the Moon Pit,* we had to buy quite a lot of Halloween masks and jump at him unexpectedly, which was hard to do with so many nut shells underfoot.

Most of RWH's better stories deal with the complicated mythos of the elder gods he created one day after reading the *American*

Weekly. Essentially this mythos put forth the theory that beyond the gates of the universe lurked nameless, loathsome beings who were out to get Hedge. Most scholars agree that the best tales dealing with this mythos, especially "Here Comes the Vombis at the Door," are worthy of Poe.

In late 1939, RWH was, as he had always feared would happen, carried off by the squirrels, and a career that added so much to American weird fiction came to a somewhat outré end. I will mention that I am again looking for a position as a confidential secretary, and close.

crouch end

STEPHEN KING

By the time the woman had finally gone, it was nearly two-thirty in the morning. Outside the Crouch End police station, Tottenham Lane was a small dead river. London was asleep . . . but London never sleeps deeply, and its dreams are uneasy.

PC Vetter closed his notebook, which he'd almost filled as the American woman's strange, frenzied story poured out. He looked at the typewriter and the stack of blank forms on the shelf beside it. "This one'll look odd come morning light," he said.

PC Farnham was drinking a Coke. He didn't speak for a long time. "She was American, wasn't she?" he said finally, as if that might explain most or all of the story she had told.

"It'll go in the back file," Vetter agreed, and looked round for a cigarette. "But I wonder . . ."

Farnham laughed. "You don't mean you believe any part of it? Go on, sir! Pull the other one!"

"Didn't say that, did I? No. But you're new here."

Farnham sat a little straighter. He was twenty-seven, and it was hardly *his* fault that he had been posted here from Muswell Hill to the north, or that Vetter, who was nearly twice his age, had spent his entire uneventful career in the quiet London backwater of Crouch End.

"Perhaps so, sir," he said, "but—with respect, mind—I still think I know a swatch of the old whole cloth when I see one . . . or hear one."

"Give us a fag, mate," Vetter said, looking amused. "There! What a good boy you are." He lit it with a wooden match from a bright red railway box, shook it out, and tossed the match stub into Farnham's ashtray. He peered at the lad through a haze of drifting smoke. His own days of laddie good looks were long gone; Vetter's face was deeply lined and his nose was a map of broken veins. He liked his six of Harp a night, did PC Vetter. "You think Crouch End's a very quiet place, then, do you?"

Farnham shrugged. In truth he thought Crouch End was a big suburban yawn—what his younger brother would have been pleased to call "a fucking Bore-a-Torium."

"Yes," Vetter said, "I see you do. And you're right. Goes to sleep by eleven most nights, it does. But I've seen a lot of strange things in Crouch End. If you're here half as long as I've been, you'll see your share, too. There are more strange things happen right here in this quiet six or eight blocks than anywhere else in London—that's saying a lot, I know, but I believe it. It scares me. So I have my lager, and then I'm not so scared. You look at Sergeant Gordon sometime, Farnham, and ask yourself why his hair is dead white at forty. Or I'd say take a look at Petty, but you can't very well, can you? Petty committed suicide in the summer of 1976. Our hot summer. It was . . ." Vetter seemed to consider his words. "It was quite bad that summer. Quite bad. There were a lot of us who were afraid they might break through."

"Who might break through what?" Farnham asked. He felt a contemptuous smile turning up the corners of his mouth, knew it was far from politic, but was unable to stop it. In his way, Vetter was raving as badly as the American woman had. He had always been a bit queer. The booze, probably. Then he saw Vetter was smiling right back at him.

"You think I'm a dotty old prat, I suppose," he said.

"Not at all, not at all," Farnham protested, groaning inwardly.

"You're a good boy," Vetter said. "Won't be riding a desk here in the station when you're my age. Not if you stick on the force. Will you stick, d'you think? D'you fancy it?"

"Yes," Farnham said. It was true; he *did* fancy it. He meant to stick even though Sheila wanted him off the police force and somewhere she could count on him. The Ford assembly line, perhaps. The thought of joining the wankers at Ford curdled his stomach.

"I thought so," Vetter said, crushing his smoke. "Gets in your blood, doesn't it? You could go far, too, and it wouldn't be boring old Crouch End you'd finish up in, either. Still, you don't know everything. Crouch End is strange. You ought to have a peek in the back file sometime, Farnham. Oh, a lot of it's the usual . . . girls and boys run away from home to be hippies or punks or whatever it is they call themselves now . . . husbands gone missing (and when you clap an eye to their wives you can most times understand why) . . . unsolved arsons . . . purse-snatchings . . . all of that. But in between, there's enough stories to curdle your blood. And some to make you sick to your stomach."

"True word?"

Vetter nodded. "Some of 'em very like the one that poor American girl just told us. She'll not see her husband again—take my word for it." He looked at Farnham and shrugged. "Believe me, believe me not. It's all one, isn't it? The file's there. We call it the open file because it's more polite than the back file or the kiss-my-arse file. Study it up, Farnham. Study it up."

Farnham said nothing, but he actually did intend to "study it up." The idea that there might be a whole series of stories such as the one the American woman had told . . . that was disturbing.

"Sometimes," Vetter said, stealing another of Farnham's Silk Cuts, "I wonder about Dimensions."

"Dimensions?"

"Yes, my good old son—dimensions. Science-fiction writers are always on about Dimensions, aren't they? Ever read science fiction, Farnham?"

"No," Farnham said. He had decided this was some sort of elaborate leg-pull.

"What about Lovecraft? Ever read anything by him?"

"Never heard of him," Farnham said. The last fiction he'd read for pleasure, in fact, had been a small Victorian Era pastiche called *Two Gentlemen in Silk Knickers.*

"Well, this fellow Lovecraft was always writing about Dimensions," Vetter said, producing his box of railway matches. "Dimensions close to ours. Full of these immortal monsters that would drive a man mad at one look. Frightful rubbish, of course. Except, whenever one of these people straggles in, I wonder if all of it *was* rubbish. I think to myself then—when it's quiet and late at night, like now—that our whole world, everything we think of as nice and normal and sane, might be like a big leather ball filled with air. Only in some places, the leather's scuffed almost down to nothing. Places where the barriers are thinner. Do you get me?"

"Yes," Farnham said, and thought: *Maybe you ought to give me a kiss, Vetter—I always fancy a kiss when I'm getting my doodle pulled.*

"And then I think, 'Crouch End's one of those thin places.'

Silly, but I *do* have those thoughts. Too imaginative, I expect; my mother always said so, anyway."

"Did she indeed?"

"Yes. Do you know what else I think?"

"No, sir—not a clue."

"Highgate's mostly all right, that's what I think—it's just as thick as you'd want between us and the Dimensions in Muswell Hill and Highgate. But now you take Archway and Finsbury Park. *They* border on Crouch End, too. I've got friends in both places, and they know of my interest in certain things that don't seem to be any way rational. Certain crazy stories which have been told, we'll say, by people with nothing to gain by making up crazy stories.

"Did it occur to you to wonder, Farnham, why the woman would have told us the things she did if they weren't true?"

"Well . . ."

Vetter struck a match and looked at Farnham over it. "Pretty young woman, twenty-six, two kiddies back at her hotel, husband's a young lawyer doing well in Milwaukee or someplace. What's she to gain by coming in and spouting about the sort of things you only used to see in Hammer films?"

"I don't know," Farnham said stiffly. "But there may be an ex—"

"So I say to myself"—Vetter overrode him—"that if there are such things as 'thin spots,' this one would *begin* at Archway and Finsbury Park . . . but the very thinnest part is here at Crouch End. And I say to myself, wouldn't it be a day if the last of the leather between us and what's on the inside that ball just . . . rubbed away? Wouldn't it be a day if even half of what that woman told us was true?"

Farnham was silent. He had decided that PC Vetter probably also believed in palmistry and phrenology and the Rosicrucians.

"Read the back file," Vetter said, getting up. There was a crackling sound as he put his hands in the small of his back and stretched. "I'm going out to get some fresh air."

He strolled out. Farnham looked after him with a mixture of amusement and resentment. Vetter was dotty, all right. He was also a bloody fag-mooch. Fags didn't come cheap in this brave new world of the welfare state. He picked up Vetter's notebook and began leafing through the girl's story again.

And, yes, he would go through the back file.

He would do it for laughs.

The girl—or young woman, if you wanted to be politically correct (and all Americans did these days, it seemed)—had burst into the station at quarter past ten the previous evening, her hair in damp strings around her face, her eyes bulging. She was dragging her purse by the strap.

"Lonnie," she said. "Please, you've got to find Lonnie."

"Well, we'll do our best, won't we?" Vetter said. "But you've got to tell us who Lonnie is."

"He's dead," the young woman said. "I know he is." She began to cry. Then she began to laugh—to cackle, really. She dropped her purse in front of her. She was hysterical.

The station was fairly deserted at that hour on a weeknight. Sergeant Raymond was listening to a Pakistani woman tell, with almost unearthly calm, how her purse had been nicked on Hillfield Avenue by a yob with a lot of football tattoos and a great coxcomb of blue hair. Vetter saw Farnham come in from the anteroom, where he had been taking down old posters (HAVE YOU ROOM IN YOUR HEART FOR AN UNWANTED CHILD?) and putting up new ones (SIX RULES FOR SAFE NIGHT-CYCLING).

Vetter waved Farnham forward and Sergeant Raymond, who had looked round at once when he heard the American woman's semi-hysterical voice, back. Raymond, who liked breaking pickpockets' fingers like breadsticks ("Aw, c'mon, mate," he'd say if asked to justify this extralegal proceeding, "fifty million wogs can't be wrong"), was not the man for a hysterical woman.

"Lonnie!" she shrieked. "Oh, please, they've got Lonnie!"

The Pakistani woman turned toward the young American woman, studied her calmly for a moment, then turned back to Sergeant Raymond and continued to tell him how her purse had been snatched.

"Miss—" PC Farnham began.

"What's going *on* out there?" she whispered. Her breath was coming in quick pants. Farnham noticed there was a slight scratch on her left cheek. She was a pretty little hen with nice bubs—small but pert—and a great cloud of auburn hair. Her clothes were moderately expensive. The heel had come off one of her shoes.

"What's going *on* out there?" she repeated. "Monsters—"

The Pakistani woman looked over again . . . and smiled. Her teeth were rotten. The smile was gone like a conjurer's trick, and she took the Lost and Stolen Property form Raymond was holding out to her.

"Get the lady a cup of coffee and bring it down to Room Three," Vetter said. "Could you do with a cup of coffee, mum?"

"Lonnie," she whispered. "I know he's dead."

"Now, you just come along with old Ted Vetter and we'll sort this out in a jiff," he said, and helped her to her feet. She was still talking in a low moaning voice when he led her away with one arm snugged around her waist. She was rocking unsteadily because of the broken shoe.

Farnham got the coffee and brought it into Room Three, a plain white cubicle furnished with a scarred table, four chairs, and a water cooler in the corner. He put the coffee in front of her.

"Here, mum," he said, "this'll do you good. I've got some sugar if—"

"I can't drink it," she said. "I couldn't—" And then she clutched the porcelain cup, someone's long-forgotten souvenir of Blackpool, in her hands as if for warmth. Her hands were shaking quite badly, and Farnham wanted to tell her to put it down before she slopped the coffee and scalded herself.

"I couldn't," she said again. Then she drank, still holding the cup two-handed, the way a child will hold his cup of broth. And when she looked at them, it was a child's look—simple, exhausted, appealing . . . and at bay, somehow. It was as if whatever had happened had somehow shocked her young; as if some invisible hand had swooped down from the sky and slapped the last twenty years out of her, leaving a child in grown-up American clothes in this small white interrogation room in Crouch End.

"Lonnie," she said. "The monsters," she said. "Will you help me? Will you please help me? Maybe he isn't dead. Maybe—

"I'm an American citizen!" she cried suddenly, and then, as if she had said something deeply shameful, she began to sob.

Vetter patted her shoulder. "There, mum. I think we can help find your Lonnie. Your husband, is he?"

Still sobbing, she nodded. "Danny and Norma are back at the hotel . . . with the sitter . . . they'll be sleeping . . . expecting him to kiss them when we come in. . . ."

"Now if you could just relax and tell us what happened—"

"And *where* it happened," Farnham added. Vetter looked up at him swiftly, frowning.

"But that's just it!" she cried. "I don't *know* where it happened! I'm not even sure *what* happened, except that it was h-huh-*horrible!*"

Vetter had taken out his notebook. "What's your name, mum?"

"Doris Freeman. My husband is Leonard Freeman. We're staying at the Hotel Inter-Continental. We're American citizens." This time the statement of nationality actually seemed to steady her a little. She sipped her coffee and put the mug down. Farnham saw that the palms of her hands were quite red. *You'll feel that later, dearie,* he thought.

Vetter was drudging it all down in his notebook. Now he looked momentarily at PC Farnham, just an unobtrusive flick of the eyes.

"Are you on holiday?" he asked.

"Yes . . . two weeks here and one in Spain. We were supposed to have a week in Barcelona . . . but this isn't helping find Lonnie! Why are you asking me these stupid questions?"

"Just trying to get the background, Mrs. Freeman," Farnham said. Without really thinking about it, both of them had adopted low soothing voices. "Now you go ahead and tell us what happened. Tell it in your own words."

"Why is it so hard to get a taxi in London?" she asked abruptly.

Farnham hardly knew what to say, but Vetter responded as if the question were utterly germane to the discussion.

"Hard to say, mum. Tourists, partly. Why? Did you have trouble getting someone who'd take you out here to Crouch End?"

"Yes," she said. "We left the hotel at three and came down to Hatchard's. Do you know it?"

"Yes, mum," Vetter said. "Lovely big bookshop, isn't it?"

"We had no trouble getting a cab from the Inter-Continental . . . they were lined up outside. But when we came out of Hatchard's, there was nothing. Finally, when one *did* stop, the driver just laughed and shook his head when Lonnie said we wanted to go to Crouch End."

"Aye, they can be right barstards about the suburbs, beggin' your pardon, mum," Farnham said.

"He even refused a pound tip," Doris Freeman said, and a very American perplexity had crept into her tone. "We waited for almost half an hour before we got a driver who said he'd take us. It was five-thirty by then, maybe quarter of six. And that was when Lonnie discovered he'd lost the address. . . ."

She clutched the mug again.

"Who were you going to see?" Vetter asked.

"A colleague of my husband's. A lawyer named John Squales. My husband hadn't met him, but their two firms were—" She gestured vaguely.

"Affiliated?"

"Yes, I suppose. When Mr. Squales found out we were going to be in London on vacation, he invited us to his home for dinner. Lonnie had always written him at his office, of course, but he had Mr. Squales's home address on a slip of paper. After we got in the cab, he discovered he'd lost it. And all he could remember was that it was in Crouch End."

She looked at them solemnly.

"Crouch End—I think that's an ugly name."

Vetter said, "So what did you do then?"

She began to talk. By the time she'd finished, her first cup of coffee and most of another were gone, and PC Vetter had filled up several pages of his notebook with his blocky, sprawling script.

Lonnie Freeman was a big man, and hunched forward in the roomy backseat of the black cab so he could talk to the driver, he looked to her amazingly as he had when she'd first seen him at a college basketball game in their senior year—sitting on the bench, his knees somewhere up around his ears, his hands on their big wrists dangling between his legs. Only then he had been wearing basketball shorts and a towel slung around his neck, and now he was in a suit and tie. He had never gotten in many games, she remembered fondly, because he just wasn't that good. And he lost addresses.

The cabby listened indulgently to the tale of the lost address. He was an elderly man impeccably turned out in a gray summer-weight suit, the antithesis of the slouching New York cabdriver. Only the checked wool cap on the driver's head clashed, but it was an agreeable clash; it lent him a touch of rakish charm. Outside, the traffic flowed endlessly past on Haymarket; the theater nearby announced that *The Phantom of the Opera* was continuing its apparently endless run.

"Well, I tell you what, guv," the cabby said. "I'll take yer there to Crouch End, and we'll stop at a call box, and you check your governor's address, and off we go, right to the door."

"That's wonderful," Doris said, really meaning it. They had been in London six days now, and she could not recall ever having been in a place where the people were kinder or more civilized.

"Thanks," Lonnie said, and sat back. He put his arm around Doris and smiled. "See? No problem."

"No thanks to you," she mock-growled, and threw a light punch at his midsection.

"Right," the cabby said. "Heigh-ho for Crouch End."

It was late August, and a steady hot wind rattled the trash across the roads and whipped at the jackets and skirts of the men and women going home from work. The sun was settling, but when it shone between the buildings, Doris saw that it was beginning to take on the reddish cast of evening. The cabby hummed. She relaxed with Lonnie's arm around her—she had seen more of him in the last six days than she had all year, it seemed, and she was very pleased to discover that she liked it. She had never been out of America before, either, and she had to keep reminding herself that she was in England, she was going to *Barcelona,* thousands should be so lucky.

Then the sun disappeared behind a wall of buildings, and she lost her sense of direction almost immediately. Cab rides in London did that to you, she had discovered. The city was a great sprawling warren of Roads and Mews and Hills and Closes (even Inns), and she couldn't understand how anyone could get around. When she had mentioned it to Lonnie the day before, he had replied that they got around very carefully . . . hadn't she noticed that all the cabbies kept the *London Streetfinder* tucked cozily away beneath the dash?

This was the longest cab ride they had taken. The fashionable section of town dropped behind them (in spite of that perverse going-around-in-circles feeling). They passed through an area of monolithic housing developments that could have been utterly deserted for all the signs of life they showed (no, she corrected herself to Vetter and Farnham in the small white room; she had seen one small boy sitting on the curb, striking matches), then an area of small, rather tatty-looking shops and fruit stalls, and then—no wonder driving in London was so disorienting to out-of-towners—they seemed to have driven smack into the fashionable section again.

"There was even a McDonald's," she told Vetter and Farnham in a tone of voice usually reserved for references to the Sphinx and the Hanging Gardens.

"*Was* there?" Vetter replied, properly amazed and respectful—she had achieved a kind of total recall, and he wanted nothing to break the mood, at least until she had told them everything she could.

The fashionable section with the McDonald's as its centerpiece dropped away. They came briefly into the clear and now the sun was a solid orange ball sitting above the horizon, washing the streets with a strange light that made all the pedestrians look as if they were about to burst into flame.

"It was then that things began to change," she said. Her voice had dropped a little. Her hands were trembling again.

Vetter leaned forward, intent. "Changed? How? How did things change, Mrs. Freeman?"

They had passed a newsagent's window, she said, and the signboard outside had read SIXTY LOST IN UNDERGROUND HORROR.

"Lonnie, look at that!"

"What?" He craned around, but the newsagent's was already behind them.

"It said, 'Sixty Lost in Underground Horror.' Isn't that what they call the subway? The Underground?"

"Yes—that or the tube. Was it a crash?"

"I don't know." She leaned forward. "Driver, do you know what that was about? Was there a subway crash?"

"A collision, mum? Not that I know of."

"Do you have a radio?"

"Not in the cab, mum."

"Lonnie?"

"Hmmm?"

But she could see that Lonnie had lost interest. He was going through his pockets again (and because he was wearing his three-piece suit, there were a lot of them to go through), having another hunt for the scrap of paper with John Squales's address written on it.

The message chalked on the board played over and over in her mind, SIXTY KILLED IN TUBE CRASH, it should have read. But . . . SIXTY LOST IN UNDERGROUND HORROR. It made her uneasy. It didn't say "killed," it said "lost," the way news reports in the old days had always referred to sailors who had been drowned at sea.

UNDERGROUND HORROR.

She didn't like it. It made her think of graveyards, sewers, and flabby-pale noisome things swarming suddenly out of the tubes themselves, wrapping their arms (tentacles, maybe) around the hapless commuters on the platforms, dragging them away to darkness. . . .

They turned right. Standing on the corner beside their parked motorcycles were three boys in leathers. They looked up at the cab, and for a moment—the setting sun was almost full in her face from this angle—it seemed that the bikers did not have human heads at all. For that one moment she was nastily sure that the sleek heads of rats sat atop those black leather jackets, rats with black eyes staring at the cab. Then the light shifted just a tiny bit and she saw of course she had been mistaken; there were only three young men smoking cigarettes in front of the British version of the American candy store.

"Here we go," Lonnie said, giving up the search and pointing out the window. They were passing a sign which read "Crouch Hill Road." Elderly brick houses like sleepy dowagers had closed in, seeming to look down at the cab from their blank windows. A few kids passed back and forth, riding bikes or trikes. Two others were trying to ride a skateboard with no notable success. Fathers home from work sat together, smoking and talking and watching the children. It all looked reassuringly normal.

The cab drew up in front of a dismal-looking restaurant with a small spotted sign in the window reading FULLY LICENSED and a much larger one in the center which informed that within one could purchase curries to take away. On the inner ledge there slept a gigantic gray cat. Beside the restaurant was a call box.

"Here you are, guv," the cabdriver said. "You find your friend's address and I'll track him down."

"Fair enough," Lonnie said, and got out.

Doris sat in the cab for a moment and then also emerged,

deciding she felt like stretching her legs. The hot wind was still blowing. It whipped her skirt around her knees and then plastered an old ice-cream wrapper to her shin. She removed it with a grimace of disgust. When she looked up, she was staring directly through the plate-glass window at the big gray tom. It stared back at her, one-eyed and inscrutable. Half of its face had been all but clawed away in some long-ago battle. What remained was a twisted pinkish mass of scar tissue, one milky cataract, and a few tufts of fur.

It miaowed at her silently through the glass.

Feeling a surge of disgust, she went to the call box and peered in through one of the dirty panes. Lonnie made a circle at her with his thumb and forefinger and winked. Then he pushed tenpence into the slot and talked with someone. He laughed—soundlessly through the glass. Like the cat. She looked over for it, but now the window was empty. In the dimness beyond she could see chairs up on tables and an old man pushing a broom. When she looked back, she saw that Lonnie was jotting something down. He put his pen away, held the paper in his hand—she could see an address was jotted on it—said one or two other things, then hung up and came out.

He waggled the address at her in triumph. "Okay, that's th—" His eyes went past her shoulder and he frowned. "Where's the stupid *cab* gone?"

She turned around. The taxi had vanished. Where it had stood there was only curbing and a few papers blowing lazily up the gutter. Across the street, two kids were clutching at each other and giggling. Doris noticed that one of them had a deformed hand—it looked more like a claw. She'd thought the National Health was supposed to take care of things like that. The children looked across the street, saw her observing them, and fell into each other's arms, giggling again.

"I don't know," Doris said. She felt disoriented and a little stupid. The heat, the constant wind that seemed to blow with no gusts or drops, the almost painted quality of the light . . .

"What time was it then?" Farnham asked suddenly.

"I don't know," Doris Freeman said, startled out of her recital. "Six, I suppose. Maybe twenty past."

"I see, go on," Farnham said, knowing perfectly well that in August sunset would not have begun—even by the loosest standards —until well past seven.

"Well, what did he *do?"* Lonnie asked, still looking around. It was almost as if he expected his irritation to cause the cab to pop back into view. "Just pick up and leave?"

"Maybe when you put your hand up," Doris said, raising her own hand and making the thumb-and-forefinger circle Lonnie had made in the call box, "maybe when you did that he thought you were waving him on."

"I'd have to wave a long time to send him on with two-fifty on the meter," Lonnie grunted, and walked over to the curb. On the other side of Crouch Hill Road, the two small children were still giggling. "Hey!" Lonnie called. "You kids!"

"You an American, sir?" the boy with the claw-hand called back.

"Yes," Lonnie said, smiling. "Did you see the cab over here? Did you see where it went?"

The two children seemed to consider the question. The boy's companion was a girl of about five with untidy brown braids sticking off in opposite directions. She stepped forward to the opposite curb, formed her hands into a megaphone, and still smiling—she screamed it through her megaphoned hands and her smile—she cried at them: *"Bugger off, Joe!"*

Lonnie's mouth dropped open.

"Sir! Sir! Sir!" the boy screeched, saluting wildly with his deformed hand. Then the two of them took to their heels and fled around the corner and out of sight, leaving only their laughter to echo back.

Lonnie looked at Doris, dumbstruck.

"I guess some of the kids in Crouch End aren't too crazy about Americans," he said lamely.

She looked around nervously. The street now appeared deserted.

He slipped an arm around her. "Well, honey, looks like we hike."

"I'm not sure I want to. Those two kids might've gone to get their big brothers." She laughed to show it was a joke, but there was a shrill quality to the sound. The evening had taken on a surreal quality she didn't much like. She wished they had stayed at the hotel.

"Not much else we can do," he said. "The street's not exactly overflowing with taxis, is it?"

"Lonnie, why would the cabdriver leave us here like that? He seemed so *nice.*"

"Don't have the slightest idea. But John gave me good directions. He lives in a street called Brass End, which is a very minor dead-end street, and he said it wasn't in the *Streetfinder.*" As he talked he was moving her away from the call box, from the restaurant that sold curries to take away, from the now-empty curb. They were walking up Crouch Hill Road again. "We take a right onto Hillfield Avenue, left halfway down, then our first right . . . or was it left?

Anyway, onto Petrie Street. Second left is Brass End."

"And you remember all that?"

"I'm a star witness," he said bravely, and she just had to laugh. Lonnie had a way of making things seem better.

There was a map of the Crouch End area on the wall of the police station lobby, one considerably more detailed than the one in the *London Streetfinder*. Farnham approached it and studied it with his hands stuffed into his pockets. The station seemed very quiet now. Vetter was still outside—clearing some of the witchmoss from his brains, one hoped—and Raymond had long since finished with the woman who'd had her purse nicked.

Farnham put his finger on the spot where the cabby had most likely let them off (if anything about the woman's story was to be believed, that was). The route to their friend's house looked pretty straightforward. Crouch Hill Road to Hillfield Avenue, then a left onto Vickers Lane followed by a left onto Petrie Street. Brass End, which stuck off from Petrie Street like somebody's afterthought, was no more than six or eight houses long. About a mile, all told. Even Americans should have been able to walk that far without getting lost.

"Raymond!" he called. "You still here?"

Sergeant Raymond came in. He had changed into streets and was putting on a light poplin windcheater. "Only just, my beardless darling."

"Cut it," Farnham said, smiling all the same. Raymond frightened him a little. One look at the spooky sod was enough to tell you he was standing a little too close to the fence that ran between the yard of the good guys and that of the villains. There was a twisted white line of scar running like a fat string from the left corner of his mouth almost all the way to his Adam's apple. He claimed a pickpocket had once nearly cut his throat with a jagged bit of bottle. Claimed that's why he broke their fingers. Farnham thought that was the shit. He thought Raymond broke their fingers because he liked the sound they made, especially when they popped at the knuckles.

"Got a fag?" Raymond asked.

Farnham sighed and gave him one. As he lit it he asked, "Is there a curry shop on Crouch Hill Road?"

"Not to my knowledge, my dearest darling," Raymond said.

"That's what I thought."

"Got a problem, dear?"

"No," Farnham said, a little too sharply, remembering Doris Freeman's clotted hair and staring eyes.

Near the top of Crouch Hill Road, Doris and Lonnie Freeman turned onto Hillfield Avenue, which was lined with imposing and gracious-looking homes—nothing but shells, she thought, probably cut up with surgical precision into apartments and bed-sitters inside.

"So far, so good," Lonnie said.

"Yes, it's—" she began, and that was when the low moaning arose.

They both stopped. The moaning was coming almost directly from their right, where a high hedge ran around a small yard. Lonnie started toward the sound, and she grasped his arm. "Lonnie, no!"

"What do you mean, no?" he asked. "Someone's hurt."

She stepped after him nervously. The hedge was high but thin. He was able to brush it aside and reveal a small square of lawn outlined with flowers. The lawn was very green. In the center of it was a black, smoking patch—or at least that was her first impression. When she peered around Lonnie's shoulder again—his shoulder was too high for her to peer over it—she saw it was a hole, vaguely man-shaped. The tendrils of smoke were emanating from it.

SIXTY LOST IN UNDERGROUND HORROR, she thought abruptly.

The moaning was coming from the hole, and Lonnie began to force himself through the hedge toward it.

"Lonnie," she said, "please, don't."

"Someone's hurt," he repeated, and pushed himself the rest of the way through with a bristly tearing sound. She saw him going toward the hole, and then the hedge snapped back, leaving her nothing but a vague impression of his shape as he moved forward. She tried to push through after him and was scratched by the short, stiff branches of the hedge for her trouble. She was wearing a sleeveless blouse.

"Lonnie!" she called, suddenly very afraid. "Lonnie, come back!"

"Just a minute, hon!"

The house looked at her impassively over the top of the hedge.

The moaning sounds continued, but now they sounded lower—guttural, somehow gleeful. Couldn't Lonnie *hear* that?

"Hey, is somebody down there?" she heard Lonnie ask. "Is there—oh! Hey! *Jesus!*" And suddenly Lonnie screamed. She had never heard him scream before, and her legs seemed to turn to water bags at the sound. She looked wildly for a break in the hedge, a path, and couldn't see one anywhere. Images swirled before her eyes—the bikers who had looked like rats for a moment, the cat with the pink chewed face, the boy with the claw-hand.

Lonnie! she tried to scream, but no words came out.

Now there were sounds of a struggle. The moaning had stopped.

But there were wet sloshing sounds from the other side of the hedge. Then, suddenly, Lonnie came flying back through the stiff dusty-green bristles as if he had been given a tremendous push. The left arm of his suit-coat was torn, and it was splattered with runnels of black stuff that seemed to be smoking, as the pit in the lawn had been smoking.

"Doris, run!"

"Lonnie, what—"

"Run!" His face pale as cheese.

Doris looked around wildly for a cop. For *anyone*. But Hillfield Avenue might have been a part of some great deserted city for all the life or movement she saw. Then she glanced back at the hedge and saw something else was moving behind there, something that was more than black; it seemed ebony, the antithesis of light.

And it was sloshing.

A moment later, the short, stiff branches of the hedge began to rustle. She stared, hypnotized. She might have stood there forever (so she told Vetter and Farnham) if Lonnie hadn't grabbed her arm roughly and shrieked at her—yes, Lonnie, who never even raised his voice at the kids, had *shrieked*—she might have been standing there yet. Standing there, or . . .

But they ran.

Where? Farnham had asked, but she didn't know. Lonnie was totally undone, in a hysteria of panic and revulsion—that was all she really knew. He clamped his fingers over her wrist like a handcuff and they ran from the house looming over the hedge, and from the smoking hole in the lawn. She knew those things for sure; all the rest was only a chain of vague impressions.

At first it had been hard to run, and then it got easier because they were going downhill. They turned, then turned again. Gray houses with high stoops and drawn green shades seemed to stare at them like blind pensioners. She remembered Lonnie pulling off his jacket, which had been splattered with that black goo, and throwing it away. At last they came to a wider street.

"Stop," she panted. "Stop, I can't keep up!" Her free hand was pressed to her side, where a red-hot spike seemed to have been planted.

And he did stop. They had come out of the residential area and were standing at the corner of Crouch Lane and Norris Road. A sign on the far side of Norris Road proclaimed that they were but one mile from Slaughter Towen.

Town? Vetter suggested.

No, Doris Freeman said. Slaughter *Towen,* with an *e.*

Raymond crushed out the cigarette he had cadged from Farnham. "I'm off," he announced, and then looked more closely at Farnham. "My poppet should take better care of himself. He's got big dark circles under his eyes. Any hair on your palms to go with it, my pet?" He laughed uproariously.

"Ever hear of a Crouch Lane?" Farnham asked.

"Crouch Hill Road, you mean."

"No, I mean Crouch Lane."

"Never heard of it."

"What about Norris Road?"

"There's the one cuts off from the high street in Basingstoke—"

"No, here."

"No—*not* here, poppet."

For some reason he couldn't understand—the woman was obviously buzzed—Farnham persisted. "What about Slaughter Towen?"

"Towen, you said? Not Town?"

"Yes, that's right."

"Never heard of it, but if I do, I believe I'll steer clear."

"Why's that?"

"Because in the old Druid lingo, a touen or towen was a place of ritual sacrifice—where they abstracted your liver and lights, in other words." And zipping up his windcheater, Raymond glided out.

Farnham looked after him uneasily. *He made that last up,* he told himself. *What a hard copper like Sid Raymond knows about the Druids you could carve on the head of a pin and still have room for the Lord's Prayer.*

Right. And even if he *had* picked up a piece of information like that, it didn't change the fact that the woman was . . .

"Must be going crazy," Lonnie said, and laughed shakily.

Doris had looked at her watch earlier and saw that somehow it had gotten to be quarter of eight. The light had changed; from a clear orange it had gone to a thick murky red that glared off the windows of the shops in Norris Road and seemed to face a church steeple across the way in clotted blood. The sun was an oblate sphere on the horizon.

"What happened back there?" Doris asked. "What was it, Lonnie?"

"Lost my jacket, too. Hell of a note."

"You didn't lose it, you took it off. It was covered with—"

"Don't be a fool!" he snapped at her. But his eyes were not snappish; they were soft, shocked, wandering. "I lost it, that's all."

"Lonnie, what happened when you went through the hedge?"

"Nothing. Let's not talk about it. Where are we?"

"Lonnie—"

"I can't remember," he said more softly. "It's all a blank. We were there . . . we heard a sound . . . then I was running. That's all I can remember." And then he added in a frighteningly childish voice: "Why would I throw my jacket away? I liked that one. It matched the pants." He threw back his head, gave voice to a frightening loonlike laugh, and Doris suddenly realized that whatever he had seen beyond the hedge had at least partially unhinged him. She was not sure the same wouldn't have happened to her . . . if she had seen. It didn't matter. They had to get out of here. Get back to the hotel where the kids were.

"Let's get a cab. I want to go home."

"But John—" he began.

"Never mind John!" she cried. "It's wrong, everything here is wrong, *and I want to get a cab and go home!"*

"Yes, all right. Okay." Lonnie passed a shaking hand across his forehead. "I'm with you. The only problem is, there aren't any."

There was, in fact, no traffic at all on Norris Road, which was wide and cobbled. Directly down the center of it ran a set of old tram tracks. On the other side, in front of a flower shop, an ancient three-wheeled D-car was parked. Farther down on their own side, a Yamaha motorbike stood aslant on its kickstand. That was all. They could *hear* cars, but the sound was faraway, diffuse.

"Maybe the street's closed for repairs," Lonnie muttered, and then had done a strange thing . . . strange, at least, for him, who was ordinarily so easy and self-assured. He looked back over his shoulder, as if afraid they had been followed.

"We'll walk," she said.

"Where?"

"Anywhere. Away from Crouch End. We can get a taxi if we get away from here." She was suddenly positive of that, if of nothing else.

"All right." Now he seemed perfectly willing to entrust the leadership of the whole matter to her.

They began walking along Norris Road toward the setting sun. The faraway hum of the traffic remained constant, not seeming to diminish, not seeming to grow any, either. It was like the constant push of the wind. The desertion was beginning to nibble at her nerves. She felt they were being watched, tried to dismiss the feeling, and found that she couldn't. The sound of their footfalls

(SIXTY LOST IN UNDERGROUND HORROR)

echoed back to them. The business at the hedge played on her mind more and more, and finally she had to ask again.

"Lonnie, what *was* it?"

He answered simply: "I don't remember. And I don't *want* to."

They passed a market that was closed—a pile of coconuts like shrunken heads seen back-to were piled against the window. They passed a launderette where white machines had been pulled from the washed-out pink plasterboard walls like square teeth from dying gums. They passed a soap-streaked show window with an old SHOP TO LEASE sign in the front. Something moved behind the soap streaks, and Doris saw, peering out at her, the pink and tufted battle-scarred face of a cat. The same gray tom.

She consulted her interior workings and tickings and discovered that she was in a state of slowly building terror. She felt as if her intestines had begun to crawl sluggishly around and around within her belly. Her mouth had a sharp unpleasant taste, almost as if she had dosed with a strong mouthwash. The cobbles of Norris Road bled fresh blood in the sunset.

They were approaching an underpass. And it was dark under there. *I can't,* her mind informed her matter-of-factly. *I can't go under there, anything might be under there, don't ask me because I can't.*

Another part of her mind asked if she could bear for them to retrace their steps, past the empty shop with the traveling cat in it (how had it gotten from the restaurant to here? best not to ask, or even wonder about it too deeply), past the weirdly oral shambles of the launderette, past The Market of the Shrunken Heads. She didn't think she could.

They had drawn closer to the underpass now. A strangely painted six-car train—it was bone-white—lunged over it with startling suddenness, a crazy steel bride rushing to meet her groom. The wheels kicked up bright spinners of sparks. They both leaped back involuntarily, but it was Lonnie who cried out. She looked at him and saw that in the last hour he had turned into someone she had never seen before, had never even suspected. His hair appeared somehow grayer, and while she told herself firmly—as firmly as she could—that it was just a trick of the light, it was the look of his hair that decided her. Lonnie was in no shape to go back. Therefore, the underpass.

"Come on," she said, and took his hand. She took it brusquely so he would not feel her own trembling. "Soonest begun, soonest done." She walked forward and he followed docilely.

They were almost out—it was a very short underpass, she thought with ridiculous relief—when the hand grasped her upper arm.

She didn't scream. Her lungs seemed to have collapsed like small crumpled paper sacks. Her mind wanted to leave her body behind and just . . . fly. Lonnie's hand parted from her own. He seemed unaware. He walked out on the other side—she saw him for just one moment silhouetted, tall and lanky, against the bloody, furious colors of the sunset, and then he was gone.

The hand grasping her upper arm was hairy, like an ape's hand. It turned her remorselessly toward a heavy slumped shape leaning against the sooty concrete wall. It hung there in the double shadow of two concrete supporting pillars, and the shape was all she could make out . . . the shape, and two luminous green eyes.

"Give us a fag, love," a husky cockney voice said, and she smelled raw meat and deep-fat-fried chips and something sweet and awful, like the residue at the bottom of garbage cans.

Those green eyes were cat's eyes. And suddenly she became horribly sure that if the slumped shape stepped out of the shadows, she would see the milky cataract of eye, the pink ridges of scar tissue, the tufts of gray hair.

She tore free, backed up, and felt something skid through the air near her. A hand? Claws? A spitting, hissing sound—

Another train charged overhead. The roar was huge, brain-rattling. Soot sifted down like black snow. She fled in a blind panic, for the second time that evening not knowing where . . . or for how long.

What brought her back to herself was the realization that Lonnie was gone. She had half collapsed against a dirty brick wall, breathing in great tearing gasps. She was still in Norris Road (at least she believed herself to be, she told the two constables; the wide way was still cobbled, and the tram tracks still ran directly down the center), but the deserted, decaying shops had given way to deserted, decaying warehouses. DAWGLISH & SONS, read the soot-begrimed signboard on one. A second had the name ALHAZRED emblazoned in ancient green across the faded brickwork. Below the name was a series of Arabic pothooks and dashes.

"Lonnie!" she called. There was no echo, no carrying in spite of the silence (no, not complete silence, she told them; there was still the sound of traffic, and it might have been closer, but not much). The word that stood for her husband seemed to drop from her mouth and fall like a stone at her feet. The blood of sunset had been replaced by the cool gray ashes of twilight. For the first time it occurred to her that night might fall upon her here in Crouch End—if she was still indeed *in* Crouch End—and that thought brought fresh terror.

She told Vetter and Farnham that there had been no reflection, no logical train of thought, on her part during the unknown length of time between their arrival at the call box and the final horror. She had simply reacted, like a frightened animal. And now she was alone. She wanted Lonnie, she was aware of that much but little else. Certainly it did not occur to her to wonder why this area, which must surely lie within five miles of Cambridge Circus, should be utterly deserted.

Doris Freeman set off walking, calling for her husband. Her voice did not echo, but her footfalls seemed to. The shadows began to fill Norris Road. Overhead, the sky was now purple. It might have heen some distorting effect of the twilight, or her own exhaustion, but the warehouses seemed to lean hungrily over the road. The windows, caked with the dirt of decades—of centuries, perhaps—seemed to be staring at her. And the names on the signboards became progressively stranger, even lunatic, at the very least, unpronounceable. The vowels were in the wrong places, and consonants had been strung together in a way that would make it impossible for any human tongue to get around them. CTHULHU KRYON read one, with more of those Arabic pothooks beneath it. YOGSOGGOTH read another. R'YELEH said yet another. There was one that she remembered particularly: NRTESN NYARLAHOTEP.

"How could you remember such gibberish?" Farnham asked her.

Doris Freeman shook her head, slowly and tiredly. "I don't know. I really don't. It's like a nightmare you want to forget as soon as you wake up, but it won't fade away like most dreams do; it just stays and stays and stays."

Norris Road seemed to stretch on into infinity, cobbled, split by tram tracks. And although she continued to walk—she wouldn't have believed she could run, although later, she said, she did—she no longer called for Lonnie. She was in the grip of a terrible bone-rattling fear, a fear so great she would not have believed a human being could endure it without going mad or dropping dead. It was impossible for her to articulate her fear except in one way, and even this, she said, only began to bridge the gulf which had opened within her mind and heart. She said it was as if she were no longer on earth but on a different planet, a place so alien that the human mind could not even begin to comprehend it. The *angles* seemed different, she said. The *colors* seemed different. The . . . but it was hopeless.

She could only walk under a gnarled-plum sky between the eldritch bulking buildings, and hope that it would end.

As it did.

She became aware of two figures standing on the sidewalk ahead of her—the children she and Lonnie had seen earlier. The boy was using his claw-hand to stroke the little girl's ratty braids.

"It's the American woman," the boy said.

"She's lost," said the girl.

"Lost her husband."

"Lost her way."

"Found the darker way."

"The road that leads into the funnel."

"Lost her hope."

"Found the Whistler from the Stars—"

"—Eater of Dimensions—"

"—the Blind Piper—"

Faster and faster their words came, a breathless litany, a flashing loom. Her head spun with them. The buildings leaned. The stars were out, but they were not *her* stars, the ones she had wished on as a girl or courted under as a young woman, these were crazed stars in lunatic constellations, and her hands went to her ears and her hands did not shut out the sounds and finally she screamed at them:

"Where's my husband? Where's Lonnie? What have you done to him?"

There was silence. And then the girl said: "He's gone beneath."

The boy: "Gone to the Goat with a Thousand Young."

The girl smiled—a malicious smile full of evil innocence. "He couldn't well not go, could he? The mark was on him. You'll go, too."

"Lonnie! *What have you done with—"*

The boy raised his hand and chanted in a high fluting language that she could not understand—but the sound of the words drove Doris Freeman nearly mad with fear.

"The street began to move then," she told Vetter and Farnham. "The cobbles began to undulate like a carpet. They rose and fell, rose and fell. The tram tracks came loose and flew into the air—I remember that, I remember the starlight shining on them—and then the cobbles themselves began to come loose, one by one at first, and then in bunches. They just flew off into the darkness. There was a tearing sound when they came loose. A grinding, tearing sound . . . the way an earthquake must sound. And—something started to *come through—"*

"What?" Vetter asked. He was hunched forward, his eyes boring into her. "What did you see? What was it?"

"Tentacles," she said, slowly and haltingly. "I think it was tentacles. But they were as thick as old banyan trees, as if each of them was made up of a thousand smaller ones . . . and there were pink things like suckers . . . except sometimes they looked like faces . . . one of them looked like Lonnie's face . . . and all of them were in agony. Below them, in the darkness under the street—in the darkness *beneath*—there was something else. Something like *eyes . . ."*

At that point she had broken down, unable to go on for some time, and as it turned out, there was really no more to tell. The next thing she remembered with any clarity was cowering in the doorway of a closed newsagent's shop. She might be there yet, she had told them, except that she had seen cars passing back and forth just up ahead, and the reassuring glow of arc-sodium streetlights. Two people had passed in front of her, and Doris had cringed farther back into the shadows, afraid of the two evil children. But these were not children, she saw; they were a teenage boy and girl walking hand in hand. The boy was saying something about the new Martin Scorsese film.

She'd come out onto the sidewalk warily, ready to dart back into the convenient bolt-hole of the newsagent's doorway at a moment's notice, but there was no need. Fifty yards up was a moderately busy intersection, with cars and lorries standing at a stop-and-go light. Across the way was a jeweler's shop with a large lighted clock in the show window. A steel accordion grille had been drawn across, but she could still make out the time. It was five minutes of ten.

She had walked up to the intersection then, and despite the streetlights and the comforting rumble of traffic, she had kept shooting terrified glances back over her shoulder. She ached all over. She was limping on one broken heel. She had pulled muscles in her belly and both legs—her right leg was particularly bad, as if she had strained something in it.

At the intersection she saw that somehow she had come around to Hillfield Avenue and Tottenham Road. Under a streetlamp a woman of about sixty with her graying hair escaping from the rag it was done up in was talking to a man of about the same age. They both looked at Doris as if she were some sort of dreadful apparition.

"Police," Doris Freeman croaked. "Where's the police station? I'm an American citizen . . . I've lost my husband . . . I need the police."

"What's happened then, lovey?" the woman asked, not unkindly. "You look like you've been through the wringer, you do."

"Car accident?" her companion asked.

"No. Not . . . not . . . Please, is there a police station near here?"

"Right up Tottenham Road," the man said. He took a package of Players from his pocket. "Like a cig? You look like you c'd use one."

"Thank you," she said, and took the cigarette, although she had quit nearly four years ago. The elderly man had to follow the jittering tip of it with his lighted match to get it going for her.

He glanced at the woman with her hair bound up in the rag. "I'll just take a little stroll up with her, Evvie. Make sure she gets there all right."

"I'll come along as well then, won't I?" Evvie said, and put an arm around Doris's shoulders. "Now what is it, lovey? Did someone try to mug you?"

"No," Doris said. "It . . . I . . . I . . . the street . . . there was a cat with only one eye . . . the street opened up . . . I *saw* it . . . and they said something about a Blind Piper . . . I've got to find Lonnie!"

She was aware that she was speaking incoherencies, but she seemed helpless to be any clearer. And at any rate, she told Vetter and Farnham, she hadn't been all *that* incoherent, because the man and woman had drawn away from her, as if, when Evvie asked what the matter was, Doris had told her it was bubonic plague.

The man said something then—"Happened again," Doris thought it was.

The woman pointed. "Station's right up there. Globes hanging in front. You'll see it." Moving very quickly, the two of them began to walk away. The woman glanced back over her shoulder once; Doris Freeman saw her wide, gleaming eyes. Doris took two steps after them, for what reason she did not know. "Don't ye come near!" Evvie called shrilly, and forked the sign of the evil eye at her. She simultaneously cringed against the man, who put an arm about her. "Don't you come near, if you've been to Crouch End Towen!"

And with that, the two of them had disappeared into the night.

Now PC Farnham stood leaning in the doorway between the common room and the main filing room—although the back files Vetter had spoken of were certainly not kept here. Farnham had made himself a fresh cup of tea and was smoking the last cigarette in his pack—the woman had also helped herself to several.

She'd gone back to her hotel, in the company of the nurse Vetter had called—the nurse would be staying with her tonight, and would make a judgment in the morning as to whether the woman would need to go in hospital. The children would make that difficult, Farnham supposed, and the woman's being an American almost guaranteed a first-class cock-up. He wondered what she was going to tell the kiddies when they woke up tomorrow, assuming she was capable of telling them anything. Would she gather them round and tell them that the big bad monster of Crouch End Town.

(Towen)

had eaten up Daddy like an ogre in a fairy-story?

Farnham grimaced and put down his teacup. It wasn't his problem. For good or for ill, Mrs. Freeman had become sandwiched between the British constabulary and the American Embassy in the great waltz of governments. It was none of his affair; he was only a PC who wanted to forget the whole thing. And he intended to let Vetter write the report. Vetter could afford to put his name to such a bouquet of lunacy; he was an old man, used up. He would still be a PC on the night shift when he got his gold watch, his pension, and his council flat. Farnham, on the other hand, had ambitions of making sergeant soon, and that meant he had to watch every little posey.

And speaking of Vetter, where was he? He'd been taking the night air for quite a while now.

Farnham crossed the common room and went out. He stood between the two lighted globes and stared across Tottenham Road. Vetter was nowhere in sight. It was past 3:00 A.M., and silence lay thick and even, like a shroud. What was that line from Wordsworth? "All that great heart lying still," or something like.

He went down the steps and stood on the sidewalk, feeling a trickle of unease now. It was silly, of course, and he was angry with himself for allowing the woman's mad story to gain even this much of a foothold in his head. Perhaps he *deserved* to be afraid of a hard copper like Sid Raymond.

Farnham walked slowly up to the corner, thinking he would meet Vetter coming back from his night stroll. But he would go no farther; if the station was left empty even for a few moments, there would be hell to pay if it was discovered. He reached the corner and looked around. It was funny, but all the arc-sodiums seemed to have gone out up here. The entire street looked different without them. Would it have to be reported, he wondered? And where was Vetter?

He would walk just a little farther, he decided, and see what was what. But not far. It simply wouldn't do to leave the station unattended for long.

Just a little way.

Vetter came in less than five minutes after Farnham had left. Farnham had gone in the opposite direction, and if Vetter had come along a minute earlier, he would have seen the young constable standing indecisively at the corner for a moment before turning it and disappearing forever.

"Farnham?"

No answer but the buzz of the clock on the wall.

"Farnham?" he called again, and then wiped his mouth with the palm of his hand.

Lonnie Freeman was never found. Eventually his wife (who had begun to gray around the temples) flew back to America with her children. They went on Concorde. A month later she attempted suicide. She spent ninety days in a rest home and came out much improved. Sometimes when she cannot sleep—this occurs most frequently on nights when the sun goes down in a ball of red and orange—she creeps into her closet, knee-walks under the hanging dresses all the way to the back, and there she writes *Beware the Goat with a Thousand Young* over and over with a soft pencil. It seems to ease her somehow to do this.

PC Robert Farnham left a wife and two-year-old twin girls. Sheila Farnham wrote a series of angry letters to her MP, insisting that something was going on, something was being covered up, that her Bob had been enticed into taking some dangerous sort of undercover assignment. He would have done anything to make sergeant, Mrs. Farnham repeatedly told the MP. Eventually that worthy stopped answering her letters, and at about the same time Doris Freeman was coming out of the rest home, her hair almost entirely white now, Mrs. Farnham moved back to Essex, where her parents lived. Eventually she married a man in a safer line of work—Frank Hobbs is a bumper inspector on the Ford assembly line. It had been necessary to get a divorce from her Bob on grounds of desertion, but that was easily managed.

Vetter took early retirement about four months after Doris Freeman had stumbled into the station in Tottenham Lane. He did indeed move into council housing, a two-above-the-shops in Frimley. Six months later he was found dead of a heart attack, a can of Harp Lager in his hand.

And in Crouch End, which is really a quiet suburb of London, strange things still happen from time to time, and people have been known to lose their way. Some of them lose it forever.

the turret

RICHARD A. LUPOFF

I was not really surprised when my employer, Alexander Myshkin, called me into his office and offered me the assignment to troubleshoot our Zeta/Zed System at the Klaus Fuchs Memorial Institute in Old Severnford. The Zeta/Zed System was Myshkin Associates's prize product, the most advanced hardware-software lash-up in the world, Myshkin liked to boast, and the Fuchs Institute was to have been our showpiece installation.

Unfortunately, while the Zeta/Zed performed perfectly in the Myshkin lab in Silicon Valley, California, once it was transported to the Severn Valley in England, glitches appeared in its functioning and bugs in its programs. The customer was first distressed, then frustrated, and finally angry. Myshkin had the Fuchs Institute modem its data to California, where it ran perfectly on the in-house Zeta/Zed and was then modemed back to England. This was the only way Myshkin could placate the customer, even temporarily, but we knew that if the system in Old Severnford could not be brought on-line and into production, the Institute could order our equipment removed. They could replace it with a system from one of our competitors, and further could even sue Myshkin Associates for the lost time and expense they had put into our failed product.

"Park," Alexander Myshkin said to me as soon as I entered his office in response to his summons, "Park, the future of this company is in your hands. If we lose the Fuchs Institute, we could be out of business in six months. We're hanging on to that account by our fingernails. You've got to get that system running for the customer."

I asked Myshkin why our marketing and technical support teams in the UK had not solved the problem. "We have good people over there," I told my employer. "I know some of them, and I've seen their work."

Myshkin said, "You're right, Park." (My name is Parker Lorentzen; Lorentzen for obvious reasons, Parker in honor of a maternal ancestor who actually hailed from the Severn Valley. I had never seen the region, and was inclined to accept the assignment for that reason alone.)

"You're right," my employer repeated, "but they haven't been able to solve it. Somehow I don't think they *like* visiting this account. They don't like staying anywhere in the Severn Valley, and they absolutely refuse to put up in Old Severnford. I've never been there myself, but I've seen the pictures, as I'm sure you have."

I admitted that I had.

"The countryside is beautiful. Rolling hills, ancient ruins, the Severn River itself, and those smaller streams, the Ton and the Cam. I'll admit a certain, well, call it *sense of gloom* seems to hang over the area, but we're modern people, enlightened technologists, not a pack of credulous rustics."

"True enough, Chief. All right, no need to twist my arm." I gazed past him. Beyond the window, the northern California hills rolled away, lush with greenery. I found myself unconsciously touching the little blue birthmark near my jawline. It was smaller than a dime, and oddly shaped. Some claimed that it resembled an infinity sign; others, an hourglass; still others, an ankh, the Egyptian symbol of immortality. My physician had assured me that it was not precancerous or in any other way dangerous. Nor was it particularly unsightly; women sometimes found it fascinating.

My mother had had a similar formation on her jaw. She called it a beauty mark and said that it was common among the Parkers.

"Thanks, Park," Alexander Myshkin resumed. "You're my top troubleshooter, you know. If you can't fix a problem, it can't be fixed."

Within twenty-four hours I had jetted across the country, transferred from my first-class seat in a Boeing jumbo to the cramped quarters of the Anglo-French Concorde, and left the western hemisphere behind for my first visit to England, the homeland of half my ancestors.

I stayed only one night in London, not sampling that city's fabled theaters or museums but simply resting up, trying to rid myself of the jet lag inherent in a body still running on California time even though it had been relocated some eight or nine time zones. I boarded a wheezing, groaning train that carried me from fabled Victoria Station through Exham and the very peculiar-looking town of Goatswood and thence to its terminus at Brichester.

My luggage consisted of a single valise. In this I had placed my warmest clothing, a tweed suit and Irish hat that I had purchased years before in an English shop in San Francisco and reserved for trips from California to areas of less salubrious climate. I carried an umbrella and, slung from my shoulder, a canvas case containing a notebook computer.

In Brichester I spent my second night in England. The inn where I lodged was old and run-down. It contained a pub on its ground floor, and I looked forward to an evening of good fellowship, a tankard of beer (perhaps more than one!), and a platter of good English beef before bed.

Alas, I was disappointed on every count. The beef was tough, stringy, and overdone. The beer was watery and flat. But most disheartening of all, the local residents, for all that they appeared just the colorful and eccentric folk that I had hoped to encounter, proved a taciturn and unforthcoming lot. They responded to my opening conversational ploys with monosyllabic grunts, and rejected my further attempts at camaraderie by pointedly turning their backs and engaging in low muttered dialogues, casting unfriendly glances from time to time at the obviously unwelcome interloper in their midst—myself.

After chewing futilely at the beef until my jaws ached and giving up on the poor beer that the innkeeper served, I finally retired early, not so much from fatigue, for my body was beginning to recover from its jet lag, but simply because I could find no comfort in the surroundings of this disappointing pub and its hostile clientele.

In the morning I was awakened by a pale wash of sunlight that seemed barely able to penetrate the gray and lowering sky that I soon learned was typical of most days in the Severn Valley. I found myself wondering why the residents of these towns remained there—why, in fact, their ancestors had ever settled in this gloomy and unpleasant region.

At first I thought it fortunate that I had brought my cellular telephone with me—my room at the inn, of course, had no such modern convenience—but I got nowhere with the local telephone system when I tried to place a call. Eventually I located a pay station, however, and spent most of the day conducting business. I spoke several times with Alexander Myshkin, and let me not rehearse the agonies of placing a call from a decrepit pay station in the Severn

Valley town of Brichester to Myshkin Associates in Silicon Valley, California. I finally reached my employer after being cut off several times by malign operators somewhere in the British telephone system, and at least once by Myshkin's own secretary, who apologized effusively once the connection was reestablished, only to cut me off again.

Myshkin brought me up to date on further tests that were being run continuously on the Zeta/Zed System in our California laboratory. The system, of course, performed flawlessly, leaving me no less baffled than beforehand by the reported problems at the Fuchs Institute installation.

I succeeded in reaching the Institute as well, for all that I was distressed at how difficult it was to do so. Silicon Valley was some six thousand miles from the Severn Valley. That was at least some mitigation for the difficulties in communication. But my call from Brichester to Old Severnford, a matter of a mere few miles, was interrupted several times by unexplained disconnections. Even when I was in communication with my opposite number at the Fuchs Institute, one Karolina Parker—I found myself wondering if we might be related through my mother's side of the family—conversation was not easy. There was a curious buzzing and an occasional unpleasant *scraping* sound on the wire. I asked Karolina if she was not disturbed by these noises, but she denied hearing them. She suggested that they were all at my end of the hookup—or perhaps in my mind. The latter implication did not sit well with me, but I made no point of it at the time.

Eventually I took a late and unpleasant dinner in Brichester, at a restaurant some distance from my inn. There was not a single other customer in the establishment, and yet it took the waiter a long time to approach me. His manner was surly, and I got the feeling that the management would have been happier to forgo my trade than to have it. The surroundings were stuffy and utterly devoid of decoration or distraction. As had been the case with my dinner the previous evening, the food was bland in flavor, unpleasant in texture, and served at a uniform degree of lukewarmness, whether the dish was a supposedly chilled madrilène or an allegedly freshly broiled mutton chop.

Abandoning the sorry repast after a halfhearted attempt to consume it, I paid my bill and, leaving the restaurant with a silent vow never to return, hefted my single valise and began the trek to Old Severnford. With difficulty I was able to hire a car and driver who insisted on being paid in advance for his services. I was not pleased with the arrangement, but feeling that I had no choice, I consented.

The car was of uncertain ancestry and vintage; its suspension was badly sprung, and I suspected that its heater was connected directly to its exhaust pipe—the chill of the day was dispelled, all right, but was replaced in the car by a choking unpleasantness far worse.

The afternoon had turned a dark gray, and it was impossible to tell just when the sun dropped beneath the rolling, sinister hills beyond the Severn River to the west, save for the moment when my driver switched on the car's headlamps. They cast a feeble amber patch of light on the narrow and ill-repaired roadway ahead of us.

The driver stayed muffled deep in his sweaters and overcoat, a visored cap with furry earflaps covering most of his face. He wore a pair of mirrored eyeglasses—a peculiarly modern touch in this archaic valley—and between his upturned collar and the visor and earflaps of his headgear, all that I could see of his face was the mirrored lenses and a huge walrus moustache, grayed with age and yellowed with I knew not what.

We reached the Severn River without incident, save for a few bicycling schoolchildren—these, among the very few children I ever saw in the Severn region—who halted their bikes and pointed as we passed them in the roadway. I thought at first that they were waving a friendly greeting and waved back at them, pleased at this sign, however slight, of cheer and goodwill.

Once more I was mistaken. Quickly I realized that their gestures were not friendly waves, but some sort of mystical sign, whether intended to ward off evil or to bring harm upon me. One boy, who seemed almost unnaturally large and muscular for his age, but whose face appeared unformed and vaguely animal-like, hurled a large rock after my car. The rock struck the rear of the vehicle, and for a moment I thought the driver was going to stop and berate the children, but instead he pressed down on the accelerator and sped us away from there, muttering something beneath his breath that I was unable to make out.

The driver brought the car to a halt in a decrepit dockside district of Severnford. Full night had fallen by now, and the quays and piers before us seemed utterly deserted. I asked the driver if he would wait for a ferry to carry us to Old Severnford, and if he would then drive me to the Klaus Fuchs Memorial Institute.

He turned around then, gazing at me over the rear of his seat. I had switched on the car's tiny dome light, and it reflected off his mirrored glasses. "Last ferry's run, Mister," he husked. "And me'uns don't fancy spending no night by these docks. You get out. Get out now, and you're on your own."

I started to protest, but the driver leaped from the car with surprising agility for so bulky and aged an individual. He yanked open the door beside which I sat, caught my lapels in two thickly gloved hands, and lifted me bodily from the car, depositing me in no dignified condition on the cracked and weedy sidewalk. He hurled my valise after me, jumped back into his vehicle, and sped away, leaving me angered, puzzled, and utterly uncertain as to how to resolve my predicament.

I recovered my valise and tested my notebook computer to reassure myself that it was undamaged. I then pondered my next move. If the Severn ferry had indeed ceased its runs for the night, I could not possibly reach Old Severnford before morning. I did not know my way around the town of Severnford itself, and with a shudder of apprehension I set out to explore.

At first I walked beside the river. A moon had risen, apparently full, yet so cloaked by heavy clouds as to appear only a vague, pale disk in the sky while furnishing the most minimal of watery illumination to the earth. But as my eyes grew accustomed to the darkness, I realized that there was another source of illumination, faint and inauspicious.

A glow seemed to come from beneath the surface of the Severn River. Seemed? No, it was there, it was all too real. I tried to make out its source, but vague shapes seemed to move, deep in the river for the most part, but darting toward the surface now and again, and then slithering away once more into the depths. And a mist arose from the sluggishly flowing water and gave off a glow of its own, or perhaps it was that it reflected the glow of the river and the vague luminous shapes therein. Or yet again, were there shapes *within the mist* as well, floating and darting like fairies in a garden in a child's book?

The sight should have been charming, almost pretty, but for some reason it sent a shudder down my back. With an effort, I turned and made my way up an ancient street, leading at a slight uphill slant from the river and the docks and into the heart of town.

Perhaps I had merely strayed into the wrong part of Severnford, or perhaps there was something about the town itself that set off silent shrieks of alarm within me. I could find no establishment open, no person to ask for assistance. Instead I paced darkened streets, chilled and dampened by the night. Once I thought I heard voices, rough and furtive in tone, murmuring in a language I could neither comprehend nor identify. Twice I heard scuffling footsteps, but upon whirling clumsily with my valise and computer weighing me down, I saw nothing. Thrice I thought I heard odd twitterings, but could find no source or explanations for them.

How many miles I trudged that night, finding my way from alley to courtyard to square, I can only guess. I can attest that the first pallid gray shafts of morning light were as welcome to me as any sight I had ever beheld. I was able, by heading steadily downward, to find my way back to the docks.

In the morning light the mist was lifting off the Severn, the hills on its far shore looked almost welcoming, and the disquieting shapes and lights beneath the river's surface were no longer to be seen.

I located the quay where the Severn ferry made its stops and waited for the morning's first run. I was rewarded soon by sight of an ancient barge, something more suitable to a motion picture about nineteenth-century life than to a modern enterprise. Nonetheless cheered, I climbed aboard, paid my fare, and waited with a small party of taciturn passengers until the ferryman saw fit to weigh anchor and transport us across the slowly flowing water.

I tried my cellular telephone from on board the ferry, and by some miracle of electronics managed to get through to the Fuchs Institute. I spoke with Karolina Parker, who expressed concern as to my welfare and my whereabouts. As briefly as possible, I explained my situation, and she said that she would personally greet me at the pier in Old Severnford.

She proved as good as her word. I found her a delightful young woman, perhaps a few years younger than I, but showing so marked a family resemblance as to remove all doubt as to our being related. I explained to her about my Parker ancestors, and she astonished me by planting a most uncousinly kiss on my mouth, even as we sat in her modern and comfortable automobile.

I was still puzzling over this remarkable behavior when we arrived at the Klaus Fuchs Memorial Institute. Karolina Parker introduced me to the director of the Institute, whose friendly greeting was tempered by his assertion that I was expected to resolve the troubles of the Zeta/Zed system posthaste if Myshkin Associates was to retain the Fuchs Institute as an account.

Without stopping to arrange lodging in the town of Old Severnford itself, I set to work on the Institute's Zeta/Zed machines. The system was taken off-line, which did not please the director, and I ran a series of diagnostic programs in turn on the mainframe processor, the satellite workstations, and the peripheral units that ran under system control.

As long as I used only sample data for testing, Zeta/Zed performed to perfection. It might be thought that I would be pleased with this result, but in fact the opposite was the case. If the system had malfunctioned, I possessed the tools (or believed that I did) to narrow down the area of malfunction until a specific site in the hardware or software remained. This could then be examined for its flaw and repaired or replaced.

When nothing went wrong, I could correct nothing.

"Very well," my hostess, Karolina Parker, suggested, "let's go back on-line while you observe, Mr. Lorentzen."

I was as surprised by the coldness of her address as I had been by the warmth of her greeting in the car, but I could think of no response better than a simple, "All right."

Zeta/Zed was placed back on-line. Almost at once error messages began flashing on the main monitor screen, but the system did not shut down. I permitted it to run until a batch of data had been processed, then attempted to print out the results.

The high-speed laser printer hummed, then began spitting out sheet after sheet of paper. I tried to read the top sheet, but it seemed to contain sheer gibberish. The printout comprised an almost random pattern of numbers, letters, and symbols that I knew were not part of any font supplied by Myshkin software. I asked Karolina Parker about this, but she insisted that no one had tampered with the software and no virus could have been introduced into the system, as it was swept by antivirus software regularly.

What could be the answer?

I asked Karolina Parker the source of the Institute's power supply and was told that the Institute generated its own power, the Severn River turning a generator housed in a separate building. In this manner the Institute was independent of the vagaries of the local power system, antiquated and unreliable as it was known to be.

Furnished with a sparse cubicle from which to conduct my affairs, I soon sat alone with the enigmatic printouts. I had been furnished with a meal of sorts from the Institute's commissary, and I sat eating a stale sandwich, pausing to wash it down with occasional swigs of cold, stale coffee, trying to make head or tail of these pages.

After a while I found a passage that seemed less chaotic than what had gone before. The printing was in Roman letters, not mathematical formulas, and by concentrating on the "words" (which were in fact not any words I recognized), moving my lips like a child just learning to read, and letting the sounds that were suggested pass my lips, I realized that this was the same language I had heard the previous night as I wandered the streets of Severnford.

By quitting time I was tired, nervous, and eager to find a warm meal and a soft mattress, if such amenities even existed in this accursed Severn Valley.

To my astonishment, Karolina Parker offered me a ride home in her automobile and even offered me room and lodging in her house. I insisted that such hospitality, while appreciated, was excessive, but she replied that everything should be done to make my visit pleasant. We were, after all, family!

Karolina Parker's home was a pleasant house set in the center of a modest but beautifully tended parklike estate. The house itself was of late Tudor style, with half-timbered beams and diamond-pane windows. There was a great fireplace in the living room, and through the front windows I could see the peculiar topiary shrubs that stood outside like unfamiliar beasts grazing an alien landscape.

My hostess explained to me that she lived alone, and showed me to a comfortable bedroom that she said would be mine during my stay in Old Severnford. She suggested that I refresh myself while she prepared dinner for us both.

An hour later I was summoned to dine in a charming informal room. Karolina apologized for her impromptu mode of entertaining, but I found both her manner and the meal that she served me the high points of my until-now dismal journey. She had decked herself out in a pair of tight-fitting blue jeans and a T-shirt with a portrait of Klaus Fuchs himself blazoned on it. Over this amazing outfit she wore a frilly apron.

She served me a delicious ratatouille accompanied by an excellent white wine (imported from northern California, I noted with some pride) and a crisp green salad. How this attractive young woman could work all day at the Institute and still entertain in such delightful fashion afterward was quite beyond my power of comprehension.

After the meal we repaired to the living room and shared coffee (hot, fresh, and strong!) and brandy before a roaring fire. Oddly portentous selections of Carl Philipp Emanuel Bach and Georg Philipp Telemann came from the speakers of a superb sound system. Karolina and I spoke of computers, of her work at the Fuchs Institute and mine at Myshkin Associates. We tried to trace our common ancestry but ran into a blank wall somewhere around the year 1665. At no time did we speak of our personal lives. I did not know whether she had ever been married, for instance, or seriously involved with a man, nor did she query me with regard to such sensitive (and for me, painful) matters.

The sound system must have been preprogrammed, for after a while I found myself drawn into a complex composition by Charles Ives, and then into one of the stranger sound pieces of Edgard Varèse. Our conversation had turned to the history of the Severn Valley, its peculiar isolation from the rest of England, and the odd whispered hints that were sometimes heard regarding the dark countryside and its inhabitants.

I fear that my stressful journey and my lack of sleep the previous night caught up with me, for I found myself yawning at one point, and Karolina Parker, gracious hostess that she was, suggested that I retire.

"I'll stay downstairs to clean up a little," she volunteered. "You can find your room again, of course?"

I thought to offer a familial hug before retiring, but instead I found Karolina returning my gesture with a fierce embrace and another of her incredible kisses. I broke away in confusion and made my way to my room without speaking another word. I locked the door and placed a chair beneath the doorknob before disrobing, then climbed gratefully into bed and fell asleep almost at once.

I do not know how much later it was that I was awakened by—*by what?* I asked myself. Was it a careful rattling of the doorknob of my room? Was it a voice calling to me? And in words of what language—the familiar tongue that Americans and Britons have shared for centuries, or that other, stranger language that I had heard in the streets of Severnford and had myself spoken, almost involuntarily, as I struggled to decipher the peculiar printouts of the Zeta/Zed system at the Fuchs Institute?

Whatever it was—whoever it was—quickly departed from my ken, and I sought to return to sleep, but, alas, I was now too thoroughly wakened to do so easily. I did not wish to leave my room; I cannot tell you why—I simply felt that there were things, or might be things, in that pleasant, comfortable house that I would rather not encounter.

So instead I seated myself in a chair near the window of my room and gazed over the Severn landscape. I could see but little of the village of Old Severnford, for this was a community where the residents retired early and stayed in their homes, the doors securely locked and the lights turned low, perhaps for fear that they attract visitors not welcome.

Raising my eyes to the hills above, I saw their rounded forms as of ancient sleeping beings, silhouetted in absolute blackness against the midnight blue sky. The clouds that had obscured the moon and stars earlier had dissipated, and the heavens were punctuated by a magnificent scattering of stars and galaxies such as the city lights that blazed all night in the Silicon Valley could never reveal.

I permitted my gaze to drift lower, to the Severn Hills, when I was startled to perceive what appeared to be an artificial construct. This structure was in the form of a tower surmounted by a peculiarly made battlement or turret. I had thought the Severn Hills uninhabited save for a few examples of sparse and ill-nourished wildlife, hunted on occasion by locals seeking to add to their meager larders.

Even more surprising, the turret appeared to be illuminated from within. I strained my eyes to see clearly that which was before me. Yes, there were lights blazing from within the turret—if *blazing* is a word that may be applied to these dim, flickering, tantalizing lights. If I permitted my fancy to roam, the lights would almost form themselves into a face. Two great hollow eyes staring blindly into the darkness, a central light like a nasal orifice, and beneath that a wide, narrow mouth grinning wickedly with teeth—surely they must be vertical dividers or braces—eager to invite . . . or to devour.

I stared at the turret for a long time. How long, I do not know, but eventually the night sky began to lighten, the moon and stars to fade. Were the lights in the turret extinguished, or was it the brightness of morning that made them fade?

A chill racked my body, and I realized that I had sat for hours before the open window, clad only in thin pajamas. I climbed hastily back into bed and managed to catch a few winks before the voice of Karolina penetrated the door, summoning me to a lavish breakfast of bacon and eggs, freshly squeezed orange juice, and a rich, hot mocha concoction that offered both the satisfying flavor of chocolate and the stimulation of freshly brewed coffee.

In Karolina's car, on the way to the Klaus Fuchs Memorial Institute, I sought to gain information about my peculiar experience of the night before. I realized that my suspicion of my dear, multiply distant cousin (for as such I had chosen to identify her, for my own satisfaction) had been the unjustified product of my own fatigue and depression, and the strangeness and newness of my surroundings.

Almost as if the turret had been the figment of a dream, I grappled mentally in hopes of regaining my impression of it. To a large degree it eluded me, but I was able at length to blurt some question about a turreted tower in the hills.

Karolina's answer was vague and evasive. She admitted that there were some very old structures in the region, dangerous and long abandoned. In response to my mention of the flickering lights and the facelike arrangement in the turret, Karolina became peculiarly agitated, insisting that this was utterly impossible.

I averred that I would like to visit the tower and see for myself if it were inhabited, even if only by squatters.

To this, Karolina replied that there had been an earthquake in the Severn Valley some years before. A fissure had opened in the earth, and the row of hills in which the tower was located was now totally unreachable from Old Severnford. I would have to abandon my plan and give up on my hopes of learning about the turret and its lights.

I spent the day at the Fuchs Institute working diligently on the Zeta/Zed system. Since my attempts of the day before had led me only to frustration, on this day I determined to take the problem on a smaller, more intensive, basis. I powered down the entire system, disconnected all of its components from one another, and began running the most exhaustive diagnostic programs on the circuitry of the central processor.

During a luncheon break, I thought to ask another employee of the Institute—*not* Karolina Parker—about my experience of the previous night. But strangely, I was unable to recall just *what* I had experienced that I wished to inquire about.

This was by far the most peculiar phenomenon I had ever encountered. I knew that something odd had happened to me, I knew that I wanted to seek an explanation for it, but I was absolutely and maddeningly unable to remember just what it was that I wanted to ask about.

Humiliated, I terminated the conversation and returned to my assigned cubicle to study manuals and circuit diagrams associated with Zeta/Zed.

That night Karolina furnished another delicious repast, and we shared another delightful evening of conversation, coffee and brandy, and music. Karolina had attired herself in a shimmering hostess gown tonight, and I could barely draw my eyes from her flowing raven hair, her deep blue orbs, her pale English skin, and her red, generous lips.

When the time came for us to part to our rooms and retire for the night, I no longer recoiled from my cousin's ardent kiss, but luxuriated in it. As I held her, our faces close together, I saw that she, too, carried the familiar Parker mark on her chin. I placed my lips against the mark, and she sighed as if I had touched her deeply and erotically. Images and fantasies raced through my mind, but I banished them and bade her good-night, and climbed the flagstone staircase to my quarters.

I wondered whether I really wanted to lock my door tonight, whether I really wanted to place a chair against it, but I finally did so and climbed into bed. This time I was not able to sleep, so I attired myself more warmly than I had the previous night and placed myself in the comfortable chair before the window.

In the darkness of the Severn Valley my eyes soon adjusted themselves, and the utterly murky vista that greeted me at first once more resolved itself into rows of hills, clearly old hills smoothed and rounded by the passage of millennia, silhouetted against the star-dotted heavens. And as I simultaneously relaxed my body and my concentration, yet focused my eyes on the area where I had seen the turret rising the night before, once again I beheld its shape, and once again I beheld what appeared to be faint, flickering lights in its windows, making the suggestion of a face that seemed to speak to me in the peculiar tongue of the night prowlers of Severnford and of the enigmatic computer printout.

I did not fall asleep. I wish to make this very clear. What next transpired may have been a vision, a case of astral travel, a supernatural or at least supernormal experience of the most unusual and remarkable sort, but it was absolutely *not a dream.*

Some force drew me from the chair in my room in my distant cousin Karolina Parker's home. That which was drawn was my soul.

Now you may think this is a very peculiar statement for me to make. I, Parker Lorentzen, am a thoroughly modern man. I hold degrees in mathematics, linguistics, philosophy, psychology, and computer science. I could, if I chose to do so, insist upon being addressed as Dr. Lorentzen, but I prefer not to flaunt my education before others.

I opt philosophically for the kind of scientific materialism that seeks explanations for all phenomena in the world of physical reality. I know that there are great mysteries in the universe, but I think of them as the *unknown* rather than the *unknowable*. Research, careful observation and precise measurement, computation and rigorous logic, will eventually deliver to inquisitive intelligence the final secrets of the universe.

Such is my philosophy. Or such it *was* until I visited the turret that my cousin Karolina claimed was unreachable.

At first I was frightened. I thought that I was being summoned to hurl myself from an upper-story window from whence I would fall to the garden below and injure myself. I looked down, and the weird topiary beasts seemed to be gesturing, urging me to fly from the house. I knew that this was impossible—in my physical being—but by relaxing ever more fully into my chair while concentrating my vision, my mind, my whole psychic being, on the distant turret in the Severn Hills, I felt my soul gradually separating from my body.

Why do I use the word *soul,* you may ask? Did I not mean my mind, my consciousness? Was I not having an out-of-body experience, a controversial but nevertheless real and not necessarily supernatural phenomenon?

But no, it was more than my mind, more than my consciousness that was leaving my body. It was my whole *self,* which I choose to refer to as my soul. For all my scientific skepticism, I have been forced to the conclusion that there is some part of us that is neither material nor mortal. Just what it is, just how it came into being, I do not pretend to know. I have heard every argument, faced every scoffing comment—have made them myself, or did so when I was a younger man—but I cannot now deny the reality of this thing that I call the soul.

For a moment I was able to look back at my own body, comfortably ensconced in the chair. Then I was off, drifting at first languorously through the open window, hovering briefly above the topiary figures in my cousin's garden, then rising as if on wings of my own, high above the town of Old Severnford, and then speeding into the black night, soaring toward the hills to the west of town.

I did see the fissure that Karolina had described, a horrid rent that seemed to penetrate deep into the earth. Its walls were strewn with boulders, and brushy vegetation had made its way down the sides of the fissure, attracted, perhaps, by the heat that seemed to radiate from its depths, or from the water that I surmised would gather there.

As I approached the turret I had seen from my window, I could again perceive the flickering lights within, and the facelike formation of the illumination. From the distance of my cousin's house, and against the blackness of the Servern Hills, the tower had been of uncertain shape. Seen from a lesser distance, it assumed a clear shape and a surprisingly modern architectural aspect. It seemed to rise almost organically from its surroundings, a concept that I had come across more than once while browsing architectural journals.

Entering the most brightly illuminated window, I found myself in a large room. It was unlike any I had ever seen before. As familiar as I am with every sort of modern device and scientific equipment, still I could not comprehend, or even describe, the titanic machinery that I beheld.

Figures utterly dwarfed by the machines tended them, tapping at control panels, reading indicators, adjusting conduits. Lights flashed on the machinery, and occasionally parts moved. Just as the building itself had exhibited an almost organic quality of architecture, so the machines within it seemed, in addition to their other characteristics, to be in some subtle and incomprehensible way *alive*.

Strangest of all was a gigantic rectangular plane that filled an entire section of the monstrous room. Its surface was of a matte gray finish and had a peculiar look to it as if it were somehow *tacky,* as sticky as if a thin coating of honey had been spread on it, and let to stand in the sunlight until it was mostly but not entirely dry.

I approached the gray rectangle by that peculiar sort of disembodied flight that I had used since leaving my body in my cousin's house in Old Severnford, and hovered effortlessly above the gray plane. From my first vantage point at the window of the turret room, the plane had looked large, but was still contained within the single large room. If I had been forced to make an estimate of its dimensions, I would have described it as three to four yards in width, and as much as forty yards in length.

But as I hovered above it, I realized that it was incredibly larger than I had first estimated. That, or perhaps it was merely my change of perspective that gave it the appearance of great size.

Have you ever played with one of those optical illusions, in which you are asked to look at two curved rectangles, or sections of arc cut from the perimeter of a circle or torus? One may appear far larger than the other, yet the instructions that come with such games always urge you to measure the rectangles and see that they are exactly the same size.

Maybe something like that is what happened to me. I cannot testify with any degree of certainty.

But I can tell you that, as I hovered above the gray plane (perhaps I should refer to it, now, as a gray *plain*), it was gigantic. It was miles in width and hundreds of miles in length—or perhaps it was thousands or even millions of miles in each dimension. I felt myself being drawn down toward it and feared that if I approached too close to it, I would be caught in its gravity—or in the tackiness of its surface—and be unable to escape.

With a huge effort I managed to halt my descent, but already I was so close to the plain that I had lost sight of its termini. Grayness stretched to infinity in all directions. I could turn, and above me I saw only star-studded blackness. *Was the turret room open to the Severn sky?* I wondered.

Beneath me I thought I saw stirrings in the gray. At this range it was not a smooth and stationary surface, but seemed textured, as if it were of wet concrete, and tiny specks that at first seemed to be merely part of this texture could be seen to move. They reminded me of insects caught in the sweet, tacky covering of a roll of old-fashioned flypaper.

I descended farther and realized that the moving specks were alive, and in some inexplicable way I understood just what they were: They were the souls of human beings, trapped in the hold of the gray plain, struggling futilely for their release.

How could such a thing be? I wondered. Whose souls were these? Were they the immortal parts of residents of the Severn Valley, the souls perhaps of local residents who had died and been trapped here in this bizarre limbo, neither attaining heaven nor being consigned to hell? Had they been summoned by the shapes tending the titanic machines? And if such was the case, what mad motive had moved these weird scientists to set such a trap?

A sudden fear overcame me, lest I be drawn down into the gray plain and be trapped with the other souls, and I beat my ethereal wings with all my strength, struggling to rise above that horrid gray surface. For a time the struggle seemed hopeless, but I persevered the limits of my strength and beyond, forcing myself as great athletes are said to do, to find and call upon unknown reservoirs of determination. And at last my efforts were rewarded, for I found myself rising with painful slowness above the gray plain.

In time the laboratory, if that is what it was, reappeared around me. The gray plain was reduced to a rectangular area in the great room. The shadowy figures continued to tend their titanic machines, either unknowing or uncaring of my presence.

I struggled to the window and darted back toward my cousin's house. Despite the great distance, I could see myself, that is my body, seated before the window in my bedroom. My eyes were hooded, my chin rested on my chest as if I had fallen asleep.

The turret fell behind me. I passed over the fissure in the Severn

Hills, down their lower slopes and the darkling meadows that separated them from Old Severnford. I passed over the modernistic buildings of the Klaus Fuchs Memorial Institute, flashed over the topiary garden that surrounded my cousin's house, and entered my bedroom.

I was able to circle the room once, gazing down with a peculiar detachment at the body that had been my residence for so many years, then slipped back into it. I rose, yawned, and climbed into my bed.

In the morning I tried to discuss the matter with my cousin as we motored to the Institute, but I found myself able to speak only in vague and indefinite terms about that which had been so concrete and specific when I experienced it during the night. Once within the confines of the Institute, even more strangely, I found that my memory of the experience deserted me altogether. I knew only that I had seen and done something odd during the night. Twice I fell asleep over my work, which conduct would certainly not help the standing of Myshkin Associates with this, its most valued account.

Progress on the problems with the Zeta/Zed System was small or nil. I found myself wondering if the cause of the system's failures was not external to the system itself. The old computer slogan, GIGO—Garbage In, Garbage Out—suggested itself to me. But one does well to tread carefully before suggesting such an explanation to the customer. It can be offensive, and can alienate an important executive even if it is true.

I spoke with Alexander Myshkin by telephone. He was disheartened by my lack of progress on the Zeta/Zed System problem, but urged me to pursue my theory of external sources for the failure of the system. "You're a diplomat, Park, my boy. You can handle these Brits. Be honest with 'em, be tactful but be firm."

Following another frustrating day, Karolina Parker and I returned to her house. Once away from the Institute, I was able to recall something of my strange experience. Karolina suggested that we repair to a local restaurant for dinner rather than return directly home. Astonished to learn that an establishment existed in Old Severnford that Karolina considered worth visiting, I agreed with alacrity.

The restaurant was located in a converted country manor—in another context I would even have termed the venue a château. Waiters in formal garb attended our every whim. The preprandial cocktails that we shared were delicious. Our table was covered with snowy linen; the silver shone, the crystal sparkled, the china was translucently thin and delicate.

The meal itself was superb: a seafood bisque, a crisp salad dressed with a tangy sauce, tender chops done to perfection and served with delicious mint jelly, baby potatoes, and tiny fresh peas. For dessert, a tray of napoleons and petits fours was passed, and we ended our repast with espresso and brandy.

Our surroundings had been as splendid as our meal. We dined in a hall with vaulted ceilings, ancient stone walls, and a flagged floor. A fire blazed in a huge walk-in fireplace, and suits of armor, ancient weapons, and battle flags set the establishment's motif.

A single disquieting note was sounded when, in the course of my table talk with Karolina, I happened to mention the turret. Karolina gestured to me to drop the subject, but I realized that I had already been overheard. The table nearest ours was occupied by a dignified gentleman in dinner clothes, with snowy hair and a white moustache. His companion, a lady of similar years, was decked out in an elaborate gown and rich-appearing pearls.

The gentleman summoned the waiter, who hustled away and returned with the maître d'hôtel in tow. After a hurried conference with the elderly gentleman, the maître d' approached our table and, bending so that his lips were close to my companion's ear, hastened to deliver a verbal message to her.

Karolina blanched, replied, then nodded reluctantly as the maître d' took his leave.

I had not fully understood a word of their brief conversation, but I could have sworn that the language in which it was conducted was that strange tongue I had heard in the streets of Severnford, and read from the faulty computer printout at the Fuchs Institute.

In any case, Karolina immediately settled our bill—she would not permit me to spend any money—and hustled us to her automobile. She spoke not a word en route to her house, but spun the car rapidly up the driveway, jumped from her position at the wheel, and hastened inside the house, casting a frightened look over her shoulder at the topiary garden.

Once in the main room of her house, Karolina did an extraordinary thing. She stood close to me and reached one hand to my cheek. She moved her hand as if to caress me, but as she did so I felt a peculiar pricking at my birthmark. Karolina peered into my face while a frown passed over her own, then she stood on her toes to reach my cheek (for I am a tall man and she a woman of average stature) and pressed her lips briefly to the birthmark.

I placed my hands on her shoulders and watched as she drew back from me. She ran her tongue over her lips, and I noticed a tiny drop of brilliant scarlet that disappeared as her tongue ran over it.

What could this mean? I wondered. But I had no time to inquire, for Karolina made a brusque and perfunctory excuse and started up the stairs, headed for her room, with a succinct suggestion that I proceed to my own.

Once attired for repose, I found myself drawn to the comfortable chair that stood before the open window of my chamber. My eyes adjusted rapidly to the dim illumination of the night sky, and almost at once I found my consciousness focused on the illusion (if it was an illusion) of a face, gazing back at me from its place high in the Severn Hills.

Almost effortlessly, I felt my soul take leave of my body. For the second time I flew across the topiary garden, across the village of Old Severnford, across the modernistic buildings of the Fuchs Institute. The brush-choked earthquake fissure in the Severn foothills passed beneath me, and the tower loomed directly ahead.

Strangely enough, it seemed to have changed. Not greatly, of course, and in the pallid light that fell from the English sky it would have been difficult to make out architectural features in any great detail. But the tower looked both *older* and *newer* at the same time.

Hovering motionlessly in my weird ethereal flight, I studied the tower and in particular the turret that surmounted it, and I realized that the architectural *style* had been altered from that of modern twentieth-century England to the form and designs of an earlier age. As I entered the turret through its great illuminated window, I briefly noted the cyclopean machines and their scurrying attendants, but sped quickly to the gray rectangular plain I had observed the previous night.

I sank toward its surface, bringing myself to a halt just high enough above the plain to make out the struggling souls there imprisoned. They had increased in number from the night before. Further, I was able to distinguish their appearance.

Again, you may wonder at my description. If a human soul is the immortal and disembodied portion of a sentient being, it would hardly be distinguished by such minutiae as clothing, whiskers, or jewelry. But in some way each soul manifested the *essence* of its owner, whether he or she be soldier or peasant, monarch or cleric, houri or drab.

And the souls that I had seen on my first visit were the souls of modern men and women, while those I beheld on this, my second visit to the turret, were clearly the souls of people of an earlier age. The men wore side-whiskers and waistcoats; the women, long dresses and high hair styles and broad hats. No, they did not wear hair or clothing—it was their essences, as of the England of a century ago, that *suggested* as much.

How they had come to the turret and how they had become entrapped on the great gray plain, I could not fathom, but their agony and their despair were manifest. They seemed to reach out psychic arms beseeching me to aid them, but I was unable to do so; I was totally ignorant of any way to alter their condition.

My heart was rent by pity. I flew to the attendants of the cyclopean machines, intending to plead with them to help these poor trapped creatures, but I was unable to communicate with them in any way. I studied them, hoping to discern some means of reaching them, but without success.

At last, in a state of despair, I began to move toward the great open window. I turned for one last look back, and had the peculiar sense that the attendants of the machines were themselves not human. Instead, they resembled the vague yellowish creatures I had seen swimming beneath the surface of the Severn River.

A shudder passed through my very soul, and I sped frantically back to Old Severnford, back to Karolina Parker's house, back to my body. I reentered my body, dragged myself wearily to my bed, and collapsed into sleep.

Again in the morning my recollections of the strange experience were vague and uncertain. By the time I reached my cubicle at the Institute, I was unable either to summon up an image of the night's activities or to speak of them to anyone. I did, at one point, catch a glimpse of myself, reflected in the monitor screen of the computer workstation beside my desk. I must have nicked myself shaving, I thought, as a drop of blood had dried just on the blue birthmark on my jawline. I wiped it away with a moistened cloth and was surprised at the fierceness of the sting that I felt.

Struggling to resolve the problems of the Zeta/Zed System, I had arranged an appointment with the chief engineer of the Fuchs Institute, a burly individual named Nelson MacIvar. When our meeting commenced, I surprised MacIvar by inquiring first as to why the Institute had been situated in so out-of-the-way a place as Old Severnford, and on the outskirts of the town at that.

MacIvar was blessed with a thick head of bushy red hair, a tangled beard of the same color, save that it was going to gray, and a complexion to match. He tilted his head and, as my employer Alexander Myshkin was sometimes wont to do, answered my question with one of his own.

"Why do you ask that, Mr. Lorentzen? What bearing has it on this damned Zeta/Zed machine and its funny behavior?"

I explained my theory that some exterior factor might be causing the system's problems, and reasserted my original question.

"You think this is an out-of-the-way place, do you?" MacIvar pressed. "Well, indeed it is. And that's why we chose it. I've been here for thirty-two years, Mr. Lorentzen. I was one of those who chose this spot for the Institute, and I'll tell you now, if I had it to do over, I'd have chosen a far more out-of-the-way location. The middle of the Australian desert, maybe, or better yet the farthest Antarctic glacier."

I was astounded. "Why?" I demanded again. "This location must make it hard enough to bring in supplies and equipment, not to mention the difficulties of recruiting qualified workers. The people of the Severn Valley—well, I don't mean to be offensive, Mr. MacIvar, but they don't seem to be of the highest quality."

MacIvar gave a loud, bitter laugh. "That's putting it mildly, now, Mr. Lorentzen. They're a degenerate stock, inbred and slowly sinking back toward savagery. As is all of mankind, if you ask me, and the sooner we get there, the better. This thing we call civilization has been an abomination in the eyes of God and a curse on the face of the Earth."

So, I was confronted with a religious fanatic. I'd better change my tack, and fast. "The water that drives your generators," I said, "Miss Parker"—MacIvar raised a bushy eyebrow—"Dr. Parker, then, tells me that you use the Severn River for that purpose."

"Yes, she is exactly right."

"Do you make any further use of its waters?"

"Oh, plenty. We drink it. We cook in it. We bathe in it. The Severn is the lifeline of this community. And we use it to cool our equipment, you know. Your wonderful Zeta/Zed machines can run very hot, Mr. Lorentzen, and they need a lot of cooling."

I shook my head. "Have you tested the river for purity? Do you have a filtering and treatment system in place?"

"Yes, and yes again. Just because we're out here in the country, Mr. American Troubleshooter, don't take us for a bunch of hicks and hayseeds. We know what we are doing, sir."

I gestured placatingly. "I didn't mean to cast aspersions. I'm merely trying to make sure that we touch every base."

"Touch every base, is it? I suppose that's one of your American sports terms, eh?"

By now I felt myself reddening. "I mean, ah, to make sure that no stone goes unturned, no, ah, possibility unexamined."

MacIvar glared at me in silence. I asked him, "What happens to the water after it's been passed through the heat-exchange tanks?"

"It goes back into the river."

"Has this had any effect on the local ecology? On the wildlife of the valley, or the aquatic forms found in the river itself?" I thought of those graceful yet oddly disquieting yellowish shapes in the river, of the glow that emanated from their curving bodies and reflected off the mist above.

"None," said MacIvar, "none whatsoever. And that is an avenue of inquiry, Mr. Troubleshooter, that I would advise you not to waste your precious time on."

With this, MacIvar pushed himself upright and strode ponderously from the office. Something had disturbed him, and I felt that his suggestion—if not an actual warning—to steer clear of investigating the Severn River would have the opposite effect on my work.

At the end of the working day I feigned a migraine and asked Karolina Parker to drive me home and excuse me for the remainder of the evening. I took a small sandwich and a glass of cold milk to my room and there set them aside untouched. I changed into my sleeping garments and stationed myself at the window. At this time of year the English evening set in early, for which I thanked heaven. I located the flickering face and flew to it without hesitation.

The tower had changed its appearance again. From its Victorian fustian it had reverted to the square-cut stone configuration of a medieval battlement. Once within the great turret room, I sped by the cyclopean machinery and its scurrying yellowish attendants and headed quickly to the gray plain.

Hovering over the plain, I dropped slowly until I could make out the souls struggling and suffering there. More of them were apparent this night than had previously been the case, and from their garments and equipage I could infer their identity. They were members of Caesar's legions. Yes, these pitiable beings were the survivors—or perhaps the casualties—of the Roman occupation force that had once ruled Britain.

After a time they seemed to become aware of me and attempted variously to command or to entice me into placing myself among them. This I would not do. One legionnaire, armed with Roman shield and spear, hurled the latter upward at me. I leaped aside, not stopping to wonder what effect the weapon would have had. It was, of course, not a physical object, but a psychic one. Yet as a soul, was I not also a psychic being, and might not the spear have inflicted injury or even death upon me?

The legionnaire's conduct furnished me with a clue, however. He had seen me, that I knew because he aimed his throw with such precision that, had I not dodged successfully, I would surely have been impaled on the spearpoint. Even as the legionnaire stood shouting and shaking his fist at me, I willed myself to become invisible.

The look of anger on the ancient soldier's face was replaced by one of puzzlement, and he began casting his gaze in all directions as if in hopes of locating me. I knew, thus, that I was able to conceal myself from these wretched souls merely by willing myself to be unseen.

Remaining invisible, I proceeded farther along the gray plain. There were many more souls here than I had even imagined. Beyond the Romans, I observed a population of early primitive Britons. Hairy Picts dressed in crude animal skins danced and chanted as if that might do them some good. And beyond the Picts I spied—but suddenly, a sheet of panic swept over me.

How long had I been in the turret this night? I looked around, hoping to see the window through which I had entered, but I was too near the gray plain, and all I could see in any horizontal direction was a series of encampments of captive souls, the ectoplasmic revenants of men, women, and children somehow drawn to the turret and captured by the gray plain over a period of hundreds or thousands of years.

I turned my gaze upward and realized that the turret room was indeed open to the sky of the Severn Valley, and that night was ending and the morning sky was beginning to turn from midnight blue to pale gray. Soon a rosy dawn would arrive, and in some incomprehensible way I knew that it would be disastrous for me still to be in the tower when daylight broke.

Thus I rose as rapidly as I could and sped over the gray plain, past the machines and their attendants, out of the turret and home to my cousin's house.

At work that day I met once again with Nelson MacIvar. He had appeared vaguely familiar to me at our first meeting, and I now realized that this burly, oversized man bore an uncanny resemblance to the great child who had thrown a rock at my car as it carried me from Brichester to Severnford. I came very near to mentioning the incident to him, but decided that no purpose would be served by raising an unpleasant issue.

Rather should I save my verbal ammunition for another attempt to get MacIvar to order tests of the Severn River water used in the Institute. By this time I had come to believe that the water was impregnated with some peculiar *force* that was interfering with the operation of the Zeta/Zed System. This force, I surmised, might be a radioactive contamination picked up at some point in the river's course, perhaps as a result of the fissure at the foot of the nearby Severn Hills.

When I thought of that fissure and of those hills, a feeling of disquietude filled me, and I had to excuse myself and sip at a glass of water—that same damnable Severn water, I realized too late to stop myself—while I regained my composure. *Why* I should find thoughts of that fissure and of those hills so distressing, I could not recall.

This time MacIvar grudgingly yielded to my request, insisting that nothing would be found, but willing in his burly, overbearing way to humor this troublesome American. I reported this potential break to Alexander Myshkin by transatlantic telephone, and spent the remainder of the day more or less productively employed.

Again that night I feigned a migraine and excused myself from my cousin's company. She expressed concern for my well-being and offered to summon a doctor to examine me, but I ran from her company and locked myself in my room. I stared into the fiery orb of the sun as it fell beneath the Severn Hills, then willed myself across the miles to the turret.

As I approached it tonight, I realized that it had changed its form again, assuming the features of a style of architecture unknown and unfamiliar to me, but clearly of the most advanced and elaborate nature imaginable.

I flashed through the window, sped past the machines and their attendants, and hovered above the gray plain. I had reached a decision. Tonight I would pursue my investigation of the plain to its end! I swooped low over the plain, passed rapidly over the Victorian village—for such is the way I now labeled this assemblage of souls—over the Roman encampment, over the rough Pictish gathering, and on. What would I find, I wondered—Neanderthals?

Instead, to my astonishment, I recognized the ectoplasmic manifestation of an Egyptian pyramid. I dropped toward it, entered an opening near its base, and found myself in a hall of carven obsidian, lined with living statues of the Egyptian hybrid gods—the hawk-headed Horus, the jackal-headed Anubis, the ibis god Thoth, the crocodile god Sebek—and I knew, somehow, that these, too, were not physical representations created by some ancient sculptors, but the very *souls* of the creatures the Egyptians worshiped!

I did not stay long, although I could see that a ceremony was taking place in which worshipers prostrated themselves, making offerings and chanting in honor of their strange deities. I sped from the pyramid and continued along the plain, wondering what next I would encounter.

In Silicon Valley, Alexander Myshkin and I had spent many hours, after our day's work was completed, arguing and pondering over the many mysteries of the world, including the great mystery of Atlantis. Was it a mere legend, a Platonic metaphor for some moral paradigm, a fable concocted to amuse the childish and deceive the credulous? Myshkin was inclined to believe in the literal reality of Atlantis, while I was utterly skeptical.

Alexander Myshkin was right.

The Atlantean settlement was suffused with a blue light all its own. Yes, the Atlanteans were the precursors and the inspiration of the Egyptians. Their gods were similar but were mightier and more elegant than the Egyptians'; their temples were more beautiful, their pyramids more titanic, their costumes more fantastic.

And the Atlanteans themselves—I wondered if they were truly human. They were shaped like men and women, but they were formed with such perfection as to make the statues of Praxiteles look like the fumblings of a nursery child pounding soft clay into a rough approximation of the human form.

These Atlanteans had aircraft of amazing grace and beauty, and cities that would make the fancies of Wonderland or of Oz pale by comparison.

And yet they had been captured and imprisoned on this terrible gray plain!

I sped beyond the Atlantean settlement, wondering if yet more ancient civilizations might be represented. And they were, they were. People of shapes and colors I could only have imagined, cities that soared to the heavens (or seemed to, in that strange psychic world), wonders beyond the powers of my mind to comprehend.

How many ancient civilizations had there been on this puny planet we call Earth? Archaeologists have found records and ruins dating back perhaps ten thousand years, fifteen thousand at the uttermost. Yet anthropologists tell us that humankind, *Homo sapiens* or something closely resembling him, has been on this planet for anywhere from two to five *million* years. Taking even the most conservative number, are we to believe that for 1,985,000 years our ancestors were simple fisherfolk, hunters and gatherers, living in crude villages, organized into petty tribes? And that suddenly, virtually in the wink of the cosmic eye, there sprang up the empires of Egypt and Mesopotamia, of ancient China and India, Japan and Southeast Asia and chill Tibet, the Maya and the Aztecs and the Toltecs and the great Incas, the empires of Gambia and of Ghana, the mysterious rock-painters of Australia and the carvers of the stone faces on Easter Island?

This makes little sense. No, there must have been other civilizations, hundreds of them, thousands, over the millions of years of humankind's tenancy of the planet Earth.

But even then, what is a mere two million years, even five million years, in the history of a planet six *billion* years of age? What mighty species might have evolved in the seas or on the continents of this world, might have learned to think and to speak, to build towering cities and construct great engines, to compose eloquent poems and paint magnificent images—and then have disappeared, leaving behind no evidence that ever they had walked this Earth—or at least, no evidence of which we are aware?

Such races did live on this planet. They had souls, yes, and so much, say I, for human arrogance. This I know because I saw their souls.

How many such races? Hundreds, I tell you. Thousands. Millions. I despaired of ever reaching the end of the gray plain, but I had vowed to fly to its end however long it took. This time, if daylight found me still in the tower, so must it be. My cousin might discover my body, seemingly deep in a normal and restorative slumber, propped up in my easy chair. But she would be unable to awaken me.

Yes, I determined that I would see this thing to its conclusion, and from this objective I would not be swayed. I saw the souls of the great segmented fire-worms who built their massive cities in the very molten mantle of the Earth; I saw submarine creatures who would make the reptilian plesiosaurs look like minnows by comparison, sporting and dancing and telling tales of their own watery gods; I saw the intelligent ferns and vines whose single organic network at one time covered nearly one third of the primordial continent of Gondwanaland; I saw the gossamer, feathery beings who made their nests in Earth's clouds and built their playgrounds in Luna's craters.

We humans in our conceit like to tell ourselves that we are evolution's darlings, that millennia of natural selection have led Nature to her crowning creation, *Homo sapiens*. Let me tell you that the opposite is the case. The story of life on Earth is not the story of evolution, but of *devolution*. The noblest, the most elevated, and the most admirable of races were the first, not the last.

But still I pursued my flight, past wonder on wonder, terror on terror, until at last I saw the gray plain, the gray *plane* curve upward, rise into the brilliant haze that I recognized as the primordial chaos from which our solar system emerged. And the souls that were captured by the turret—what was their fate? For what purpose were they caught up in every era of being, and drawn backward, backward toward that primordial haze?

A great mass of soul-force formed before my ectoplasmic eyes. A great seething ball of sheer soul-energy that accreted there in the dawn of time now burst its bonds and rolled down that great gray plain, sweeping all before it, destroying cities as a boulder would crush an ant's nest, shaking continents to their foundations, causing the globe itself to tremble and to wobble in its orbit around the Sun.

But even this was only the beginning of the havoc wrought by this great ball of soul-energy. From the remote past to the present—our present, yours and mine—it roared, and then on into the future, sweeping planets and suns in its path.

And when the roiling concentration of soul-force reached that unimaginably distant future, when all was dim and silent in the cosmos and infinitesimal granules of existence itself floated aimless in the endless void, it reversed its course and swept backward, roiling and rolling from future to past, crushing and rending and growing, always growing, growing.

It reached its beginning point and reversed itself still again, larger and more terrible this time than it had been the first, and as it oscillated between creation and destruction, between future and past, between the beginning of the universe and its end, the very fabric of space-time began to grow weak.

What epochs of history, human and prehuman and, yes, post-human, were twisted and re-formed into new and astonishing shapes. Battles were fought and unfought and then fought again with different outcomes; lovers chose one another, then made new and different choices; empires that spanned continents were wiped out as if they had never existed, then re-created in the images of bizarre deities; religions disappeared and returned, transmogrified beyond recognition; species were cut off from the stream of evolution to be replaced by others more peculiar than you can imagine.

A baby might be born, then disappear back into its mother's womb only to be born again a monstrosity unspeakable. A maddened killer might commit a crime, only to see his deed undone and himself wiped out of existence, only to reappear a saintly and benevolent friend to his onetime victim.

And what then, you might wonder, what then? I'll not deny that my own curiosity was roused. Would humankind persist forever? What supreme arrogance to think this would be the case! Mightier species than we, and nobler, had come and gone before *Homo sapiens* was so much as a gleam in Mother Nature's eye.

In iteration after iteration of the titanic story, humankind disappeared. Destroyed itself with monstrous weapons. Was wiped away by an invisible virus. Gave birth to its own successor race and lost its niche in the scheme of things. Was obliterated by a wandering asteroid, conquered and exterminated by marauding space aliens—

Oh, space aliens. Alexander Myshkin and I had debated that conundrum many a time. Myshkin believed that the universe positively *teemed* with intelligence. Creatures of every possible description, human, humanlike, insectile, batrachian, avian, vegetable, electronic, you name it. Myshkin's version of the cosmos looked like a science-fiction illustrator's sample book.

My universe was a lonely place. Only Earth held life, and only human life on Earth was sentient. It was a pessimistic view, I'll admit, but as the mother of the ill-favored baby was wont to say, "It's ugly, but it's mine."

Well, Myshkin was right. There were aliens galore. At various times in various versions of the future—and of the past, as a matter of fact—they visited Earth or we visited their worlds or space travelers of different species met in unlikely cosmic traffic accidents or contact was made by radio or by handwritten notes tossed away in empty olive jars.

One version of posthuman Earth was dominated by a single greenish fungus that covered the entire planet, oceans and all, leaving only tiny specks of white ice at the North and South Poles. Another was sterilized, and thank you, weapons industry, for developing a bomb that could kill everything—*everything!*—on an entire planet. But spores arrived from somewhere later on, and a whole new family of living things found their home on Earth.

I saw all of this and more, and I saw the very fabric of space-time becoming feeble and unsure of itself. I saw it tremble and quake beneath the mighty assault of that accumulated and ever-growing soul-force, and I realized what was happening. The cosmos itself was threatened by whatever screaming demons of chaos cavorted beyond its limits.

At length a rent appeared, and I was able to peer into it, but the black, screeching chaos that lay beyond it I will not describe to you. No, I will not do that. But I peered into that swirling orifice of madness and menace and I mouthed a prayer to the God I had abandoned so long ago, and I swore to that God that if one man, if one soul, could counter the malignities who populated the fifth dimension, or the fiftieth, or the five millionth, it would be I.

Did I say that the soul is the immaterial and immortal part of a living, sentient being? And did I say that I had realized, in spite of my lifelong skepticism, that God was a living reality? Perhaps I should have said that *gods* were living realities. I do not know how many universes there are, each one created by its own god, each god behaving like a mischievous child.

And that chaotic void beyond the cosmos—was that in fact part of a higher realm of reality, in which *all* the universes drifted like the eggs of some aquatic life-form, within the nourishing fluid of the sea? If my soul should leave our cosmos and enter that chaos, to face the demons—demons that I now realized were the gods of other universes—would it then forfeit its claim to immortality?

Could those demons be stopped? Could I, one man, stand against this infinite army of insanity? There was a single way to learn the answer to that question. I decided that I would take that way.

I—

the giant rat of sumatra

PAULA VOLSKY

The chill March fog shrouded London, choking the labyrinth of ancient streets, smothering forgotten courts and squares, lending solid masonry an aspect of vaporous insubstantiality. Baker Street was wreathed in detestable yellow haze, through which the gaslights glowed faintly, like the malignant cyclopean eyes of moribund nightmares. The scene filled me with a cold, nameless apprehension, amounting to horror; a fleeting sense, perhaps, of frightful cosmic vastness pressing its gigantic weight upon the feeble protective barriers of human understanding. Man's vision, scarcely encompassing the tiny sphere of his own existence, serves to shield rather than inform, and that is as it should be, as it *must* be. For a single clear glimpse of ghastly reality would doubtless shake complacent human sanity to its very foundation.

My spirits hardly improved as I approached 221B, for I dreaded what I should find there. The recent, successful resolution of the problem involving the archbishop's indiscretion had deprived Sherlock Holmes of that intellectual stimulation so essential to his well-being. For some days past, my friend had lain silent and apathetic, sunk in the deepest of black depressions, scarcely stirring from the sofa. He had not, so far as I knew, resorted to the solace of the hypodermic syringe and cocaine bottle, and I could only pray for his continuing abstinence, for it grieves me beyond measure to witness the deliberate degradation of the marvelous mental faculties with which Nature has endowed him.

I let myself into our rooms, and a chemical reek at once assailed my nostrils. The sofa was unoccupied. Sherlock Holmes sat at the deal-topped table, its surface cluttered with motley paraphernalia. I could not guess at the nature of his experimentation, but saw at a glance that his countenance had regained its characteristic keenness of expression. He greeted my entrance with a carelessly affable wave of the hand, then turned his full attention once again upon the flasks and retorts before him. Delighted though I was by my friend's return to his own version of normality, I did not venture to question him at such a time, for he would not have relished the distraction. Repairing to the tenantless sofa, I soon lost myself in frowning cogitation. I do not know how long I sat there before the sound of Holmes's voice roused me from my brown study.

"Come, Watson, twenty-five guineas is not an impossible sum."

I turned to stare at him, for twenty-five guineas was indeed the figure upon which my thoughts anchored.

"The price is not unreasonable, in view of the rarity of the work, and the potential value of the contents." Holmes spoke with his customary detachment, yet could not perfectly conceal his gratification at my look of transparent astonishment. Though he fancies himself pure intellect, a flawlessly balanced calculating machine devoid of emotion, my friend is by no means free of human vanity.

"To what work do you allude?" I inquired, in the vain hope of confounding him.

"To Ludvig Prinn's hellish masterpiece, *De Vermis Mysteriis,*" he replied, without hesitation. "You have striven long and hard to beat down Charnwood's price, but the old man holds to twenty-five guineas."

My astonishment increased. "Really, Holmes, in a more credulous age, these displays of apparent clairvoyance might have brought you to the stake."

"Nonsense, my dear Doctor. A very simple matter of observation. When you entered, several minutes ago, you were carrying a parcel, whose size and shape proclaimed the recent purchase of a book. The fresh mud upon your shoes, and the moisture clinging to your overcoat, revealed that you had walked home. Two bookstores stand within walking distance of our lodgings, and of those two, only Charnwood's, in Marylebone Road, remains open at this hour. The shop specializes in antique literary rarities. It was not long ago, Watson, that you voiced your theory that certain ancient works of occultism, rich repositories of forgotten or forbidden lore, hold formulae of potent restoratives unknown to modern medicine. Amongst the bizarre obscenities polluting the pages of Abdul Alhazred's *Necronomicon,* the Comte d'Erlette's infamous *Cultes des Goules,* or the abominable *Liber Ivonis,* may lie a remedy for the brain-fever, or so you postulate. Alhazred knows no remedy, however, for your incurable optimism."

"There is reason to believe—" I commenced, somewhat nettled.

"I am prepared to concede an improbable possibility," he cut me off imperturbably, and resumed his interrupted analysis. "Of the works I have mentioned, two of them—the *Necronomicon,* and *Liber Ivonis*—are virtually unobtainable. *Cultes des Goules,* in the unlikely event of its availability, would surely prove prohibitive in cost. Thus I conclude *De Vermis Mysteriis* to be the work in question."

"Quite right, but that does not explain—"

"You have failed to secure the prize, however," Holmes continued, with an air of apathy. "Your scowl, your preoccupation, your general aspect of dissatisfaction, suggest an unsuccessful attempt to content yourself with a lesser acquisition. Twice within the last quarter hour, you have removed your wallet from your pocket, weighed it in your hand, sighed deeply, and put it away again. Clearly, the root of your indecision is financial. You have, upon occasion, paid as much as twenty guineas for works you deem professionally useful—but never more. The cost of Prinn's grotesquerie must exceed twenty guineas, but not by much, else you would instantly have dismissed all thought of purchase. Charnwood habitually prices his first editions in multiples of five guineas. It is more than probable that the volume in question is offered at twenty-five."

"Correct, in every particular," I confessed. "Bravo, Holmes. As always, when you explain your reasoning, it all seems very clear, very obvious."

"Tiresomely so. I should fear complete stagnation were no better mental exercise available. Fortunately, a matter of potentially greater interest has presented itself." From the welter atop the table, he plucked a sheet of paper. "This note arrived some hours ago. What do you make of it, Watson?"

Here, I suspected, was the cause of my friend's abrupt recovery of spirits. Accepting the paper, I read:

Dear Mr. Holmes,

I am anxious to consult you upon a matter of gravest urgency. It is not an exaggeration to observe that innocent lives will be lost if the missing party is not soon located. My own efforts in that regard have failed, my actions have been noted, and I fear that time is running short. The luster of your fame is such that I must place my trust in your abilities. Therefore, I shall call at half-past seven this evening, in the hope that you will favor me with a reception.

Sincerely yours,
A. B.

"Singular." I returned the note to its owner.

"Quite. But what does it reveal to you?"

"Very little," I confessed. "The writer, be it man or woman, communicates considerable agitation—"

"Make no mistake, it is a man," Holmes assured me.

"How do you know?"

"Notice the decisive quality of the downstrokes, the vigor of the characters, the authority of the punctuation. A man's hand, unmistakably."

"Of some education—" I essayed.

"Excellent, Watson. At times I almost suspect you less barren of deductive power than you so often contrive to appear. Now, justify my faith. Where was he educated?"

"I cannot begin to guess," I replied, mystified.

"Good. One should never guess, it is an atrocious habit. Note the spelling. 'Luster.' And worse, 'favor.' Note the tone of extravagant, uncurbed emotion. The correspondent is clearly an American. Despite the orthographic crudities, his literacy marks him as a denizen of the comparatively civilized eastern coastal region of that nation."

"We shall see soon enough. It is half-past seven."

There was a knock at our door, and our landlady entered.

"A lady to see you, sir," she informed my companion.

I repressed a smile.

"Show her in." Sherlock Holmes displayed no sign of discomfiture.

Mrs. Hudson withdrew. Moments later, a woman walked into the room. "A. B." was unusually tall, lanky and large-boned, her height evident despite a curiously stoop-shouldered posture. Her garb was darkly simple, her shoes nondescript, her gloved hands empty. Of her features, little could be discerned. A wide hat draped in heavy veiling completely obscured her face and hair. I thought her age to be around forty years, but that was an estimate based largely upon instinct, as there was little visible evidence by which to judge.

Seating herself in the chair that Holmes placed, she spoke in a low, slightly hoarse tone, unrevealing as her costume. "It is good of you, Mr. Holmes, to receive me upon such short notice, and at such an hour. I am sensible of the courtesy."

"Your note piqued my interest," Holmes returned briskly. "As you have been at pains to stress the urgent nature of the situation, I would advise you to state your name and case without delay." His visitor's veiled face turned to me for an instant, and he added, "You may speak freely before Dr. Watson."

"It is better for all concerned," A. B. returned, "if I keep my name to myself. That is for your own protection as well as mine. Briefly, the facts are these. I am an associate of Professor Sefton Talliard, chairman of the Department of Anthropology at Brown University, in Providence, Rhode Island. Professor Talliard has been missing for some months. His enemies are diabolical, his life is greatly endangered, and it is certain that he had no choice but to flee the United States. There is reason to believe that he has hidden himself in London. It is imperative that I locate this man, as I possess certain intelligence that may preserve his life, and the lives of his surviving colleagues. I am a stranger to this city, however, and ill-equipped to conduct a search. Mr. Holmes, the matter is vital. Will you lend your assistance?"

"By no means," Holmes replied, to my surprise, for I had expected the peculiarity of the entire affair to excite his curiosity.

"I entreat you—"

"Do not trouble yourself. It is useless to suppose me willing to accept a client disinclined to disclose the true facts of his case. In any event, what confidence might you reasonably place in the powers of a consulting detective hoodwinked by so amateurish a charade?"

My friend's acerbic observation quite bewildered me, but the visitor appeared prey to no such confusion.

"I am justly rebuked. Mr. Holmes, pray accept my apologies for an attempted deception motivated less by inclination than apprehension." So saying, A. B. doffed wide hat, veiling, and wig, to reveal a man's face; angular, long of jaw and tall of brow, dominated by a pair of great feverishly brilliant eyes. There was about that face, with its pallor and its monklike asceticism, a suggestion of ancient lineage, inbred and distilled to the very essence of neurasthenia. When he spoke again, his voice was undisguised, its masculine character and American accent evident. "Nothing I have related has been false, yet I have hardly dared divulge all. Now I will tell you the truth, and I will hold nothing back. Be warned, however—the tale is lurid in nature, and may at times strain your credulity."

Holmes inclined his head, an expression of extraordinary concentration transforming his hawklike features.

"My name," commenced the visitor, "is August Belknap. I am—I was—a professor of anthropology at Brown University. Last year, a small group of my colleagues—five of us, including Professor Talliard—elected to devote our long summer vacation to study and research in some foreign clime. Though the academic specialties of its members varied, a common interest in the religious observances of divers primitive peoples united our group. Material worthy of attention might have been found in countless remote locales. However, we were unanimous in our conviction that certain prehistoric mysteries of extraordinary character persisted yet upon the island of Sumatra.

"Our vacation coincided with the dry season in the East Indies," Belknap continued. "We arrived in June to discover what seemed at first a nearly unspoiled tropical fairyland, where the equatorial forests rise almost at the water's edge, bamboo grows in dense thickets, huge ferns and brilliant flowers flaunt their luxuriance everywhere. Understand that this was a first impression. Presently, the overpowering profusion of vegetation, the steaminess of the perfumed atmosphere, the unremitting intensity of light and shade—the extremity in all things—began to wax oppressive, even repellent. But this sense did not develop at once.

"Our time was limited. Having established ourselves in an airy thatched house on piles that we were obliged to purchase outright from the owner (for the natives possessed no concept of rental), we set to work.

"Our initial efforts met with little success. The lowland islanders, of the short brown-skinned Malay stock, were peaceable and accommodating enough, voicing no objection to the foreign presence in their midst. Their habits were frugal, their lives industrious, their practices modest and agreeable enough, if unexceptional. Most of them were Mohammedans and, as such, unlikely to furnish the sort of anthropological arcana we had traveled so far to find.

"It was not long, however, before information of a more promising nature reached our ears. The pacific lowland farmers took a certain childlike delight in relating gruesome tales of the Dyaks, or hill Malays, who reputedly practiced magic, believed in ghosts, and preserved the heads of their enemies. Initially, I dismissed these accounts as fantastic exaggerations or fabrications, designed to awe gullible strangers. Sefton Talliard, however—whose knowledge of these people and their customs greatly exceeded my own—assured me otherwise. A number of the Dyak tribes, he maintained, cherished the belief that preservation of an enemy's head enslaved the spirit of the dead man. The Dutch authorities have prohibited head-hunting, yet the practice continues, and, to this day, the magic tribal ceremonies often witness ritual decapitations.

"None of our party, I fancy, harbored any great desire to witness a beheading, yet all of us burned to behold the secret rites that our hosts described. The desire sharpened when we learned of a certain peculiarly degenerate tribe, some of whose members reputedly possessed blue eyes, legacy of European forebears. These mongrelized Dyaks, whose tribal title translates as 'the Faithful,' were little more than savages, inhabiting caves in the upland forests, subsisting solely upon the game they hunted, the edibles their women gathered, and anything they could steal. Held in extreme terror and loathing by all neighboring tribes, by reason of their rapacity, their magical prowess, and their unbridled ferocity, the Faithful were said to worship the ghastly deity known as Ur-Allazoth, the Relentless, a demon-lord of bestial aspect and limitless appetite.

"I shall not weary you, Mr. Holmes, with an account of our investigative efforts. Suffice it to say, in the end we managed to engage the services of a Dyak guide, who, tempted by the prospect of munificent reward, undertook to lead us through the forests to the very site of the Faithful mysteries. This task he performed in greatest secrecy, upon a clear but moonless night—the dark of the moon coinciding, as it happened, with a tribal ceremony of considerable moment. Neither blandishments nor threats, however, induced our guide to conduct us beyond a point some quarter-mile distant from our goal, and thus we were obliged to cover the last several hundred yards of the trek unassisted. This furtive feat proved relatively undemanding, for the crimson glow of the ceremonial bonfires and the swelling murmur of native voices drew us infallibly to our destination.

"Presently, the sound of music reached us—a thin, uncanny shrilling of daemonic flutes—notes so indefinably alien, so inexpressibly obscene, that my soul shrinks at the recollection. Then and there, in the red-litten forests of Sumatra, my heart misgave me, and I paused, trembling in every limb. Similarly hesitant and shaken was the young assistant professor, Zebulon Loftus. Such effeminacy awoke the ire of our leader, a man of assured and dauntlessly ambitious character. Talliard's silent communications were eloquent, and presently, Loftus and I resumed progress.

"Minutes later, we reached the edge of a great clearing, and there we halted, cloaking our presence in the blackest of tropical shadows.

"How shall I describe the scene that we witnessed there, in that place?" Belknap's hand tightened almost convulsively upon the dark plush of his pelisse. "Words may perhaps convey some inkling of the material reality, but never capture the sense of pervasive evil, the intimation of nameless horror informing the sultry atmosphere, the overpowering pressure of invisible, incalculably vast malignity, impinging upon our fragile sphere. I will therefore confine myself to an unadorned statement of the facts."

Holmes nodded gravely.

"The clearing before us," the visitor continued, "was roughly circular in shape, its circumference edged with a pale of bamboo stakes, each stake topped with a human head, each head wreathed in clouds of long black hair that stirred and drifted with every passing breeze. The facial features, frozen in expressions of the ghastliest terror, were perfectly preserved. The jumping, flickering firelight lent those distorted visages a lifelike aspect dreadful to behold, and a host of staring eyes seemed almost to follow the leaping gyrations of the Faithful assembled there. Some several score had gathered, and it was obvious at a glance that we confronted a debased mongrel people, combining the worst attributes of the Malay and Negrito races, rendered all the more repugnant by the clear evidence of an unspeakably degraded European infusion. Never in my life have I beheld human beings whose repulsive external aspect spoke more clearly of the depravity festering within.

"The savages, wholly unclothed, shambled and capered to the wailing unearthly music of those damnable flutes. As they danced, they sang, or chanted, in a tongue bearing no resemblance to the local Malay dialect, a tongue that I sensed had been old when the world was still young. The meaning entirely eluded me, yet often I caught the name Ur-Allazoth, and knew that they called upon their monstrous god. This deity, I had no doubt, found representation in the great statue looming at the center of the glade. Whose hand had fashioned so mind-searing an abomination I cannot pretend to guess, but surely the work lay far beyond the skill of the primitive Faithful, for the artistry was unimaginably hideous, yet masterly, bespeaking the twisted genius of a perverted Leonardo. The being darkly depicted in polished stone was alien beyond conception, beyond endurance. To gaze upon that impossible nightmare form was to experience some intimation of eternal diableries lurking without the realm of our perceptions, of eldritch foulness poisoning all the cosmos. The idol was squat, bloated, abhorrently misshapen, every contour an assault upon human vision. The four limbs were sinuous, attenuated, edged with spikes and tipped with suckers. The head was thoroughly beastlike, sharp-snouted, and razor-tusked, with protuberant eyes of some highly polished crystalline substance that reflected the firelight in shifting gleams of deepest crimson. A long squamous tail wrapped itself thrice about the entire body of this execrable entity that was, though never of our world, oddly reminiscent in shape and character of an enormous *rat*.

"The image of Ur-Allazoth crouched atop a pedestal of black stone, incised with bands of curious glyphs, and inset with small plaques of wondrously carven, glinting matter. A broad ledge of great stone blocks encircled the pedestal, and this ledge supported a chopping block.

"I will not relate the sickening particulars of the ceremony that followed. The sacrifice of a dozen drugged and stuporous victims, the rolling heads and spurting blood, the abandoned gyrations of the Faithful, the wild ululation, the relentless shrilling of those infernal flutes (a sound that will haunt me to my grave), and above all, the inexplicable sense of a huge, malign sentience pervading the atmosphere—I will leave it to your imagination to furnish the details. Imagination is apt to fall short of the dreadful reality, and perhaps that is all to the good. I will only note that I myself was faint and queasy before the rite was half completed. Abe Engle was swaying upon his feet, Tertius Crawley had turned his back on the scene, and poor young Loftus had collapsed in a swoon. Of the five of us, only Talliard remained composed, resolute, and fully attentive. The intermittent gleams of firelight, stabbing fitfully through the shadows, revealed our leader, jotting copious notes into the journal that he never traveled without. I must confess, Talliard's utter coolness in the face of the horror we confronted at once impressed and revolted me.

"The ceremony concluded at last. The savages withdrew, bearing the bloodstained remnants of their revel. The fires burned on, their ruddy light bathing empty glade, incarnadined block, staring heads, and unspeakable idol. Loftus recovered his senses and sat up slowly, gazing about with a stunned and vacant air. Engle drooped, Crawley fidgeted, while I stood dully longing to depart the accursed spot. Sefton Talliard, however, was unready to go. Casting a brief searching glance right and left, our leader strode forward with an air of fearless resolution, never faltering before he reached the base of Ur-Allazoth's image. There he halted and, to my amazement, proceeded to sketch the statue in pen and ink, reproducing the murine lineaments with commendable accuracy.

"Pride forbade me to display cowardice. Mastering my own reluctance, I advanced to join Professor Talliard. Drawing paper and crayon from my pocket, I quickly took rubbings of several bands of glyphs. While I was thus engaged, Engle approached to record measurements while Crawley occupied himself with a survey of preserved heads. Only poor Loftus remained inert, huddled on the ground at the edge of the clearing.

"Our respective tasks were soon completed. I could scarcely contain my eagerness to go, but Talliard would not budge before prying one of the small carven plaques from the pedestal of the statue. His temerity shocked me, but there was no arguing with our autocrat, and I did not attempt it. He slipped the thin plaque between the pages of his journal, returned the book to his pocket, and then, to my unutterable relief, signaled a command to withdraw.

"We hastened from that spot, stumbling our way through the dark, back to the point where we had left our guide. The fellow was not there, and inwardly I cursed him for a deserter. Perhaps he had indeed fled, without collecting his recompense, or perhaps some darker fate befell him there. I cannot say, for we never looked upon his face again.

"I scarcely know how we found our way through that stygian forest to a friendly Dyak settlement. There we spent the night, a night of broken slumbers, filled with delirious dreams. In the morning, we commenced the three-day trek back to our lowland village and to our thatched dwelling perched on piles. This transition was accomplished without incident, yet throughout its entirety, I was unable to rid myself of a profound perturbation—a keen, nerve-racking sense that our progress was continually *observed*. There is no overemphasizing the power of this sensation—it was instinctual, elemental, and shared by us all.

"The feeling intensified throughout the ensuing days. Strive though I might to absorb myself in the task of deciphering the message of the glyphs, I could neither evade nor ignore that psychic oppression. Only the imminence of our withdrawal from the island of Sumatra lightened my mood.

"We had booked passage to Java aboard the cargo vessel *Matilda Briggs*. Two days prior to departure, tragedy befell us. Tertius Crawley was murdered. Our colleague's headless corpse was discovered at dusk by young Loftus, whose own nervous reaction to the sight was immediate and intense.

"Mr. Holmes, Dr. Watson, the isolated villages of Sumatra possess nothing corresponding to an American or British system of justice. Legal administration resides largely in the hands of local elders, and rarely are matters referred to the distant Dutch authorities. In this case, the village chieftain merely expressed his regret that the devilish magic of the Faithful had prevailed once again, together with his recommendation that the body be interred without delay, lest evil spirits seek the site of violent death. Crawley was buried at dawn. His head was never located.

"You may well imagine my sense of overwhelming relief as I watched the coast of Sumatra recede, from the deck of the *Matilda Briggs*. The vessel was bound for Batavia, by way of the Strait of Malacca. I had hoped the sea voyage might serve to calm my unstrung nerves. On the second day, however, one of the crew discovered Abe Engle's headless remains, crammed into a barrel deep in the hold. A thorough search of the ship revealed the presence of a stowaway, easily identifiable by his blue eyes as a member of the mongrel tribe of the Faithful. Interrogation proved useless, as the prisoner displayed comprehension of no tongue other than his own debased dialect, which poured from his lips in a venomous continuous stream. He seemed entirely fearless, and the expression of malignity glaring from his pale eyes was shocking to behold.

"Presently tiring of incessant, unintelligible abuse, the captain ordered the suspect locked in a storage closet belowdecks. Confinement failed to quell the Dyak's defiant spirit, and from that closet issued the sound of his voice, upraised in an unholy chanting audible throughout the ship.

"Engle was buried at sea. His head was never located. Throughout the obsequies, the malignant chants rising from below counterpointed the captain's readings from the Psalms, and the blasphemous juxtaposition chilled the hearts of all listeners. The verbal outpouring had now assumed a character all too recognizable to the surviving members of our group—it was that same invocation to Ur-Allazoth we had heard in the upland forests upon the night of the Faithful's vile ceremony. The passage of time could not damp the prisoner's loquacity, and throughout the hours that followed, the chanting never ceased. More than one of the *Matilda Briggs* deckhands spoke of gagging the noisy Dyak, or even of slitting his throat, but no one attempted to act upon these threats. It is my belief that the sailors feared their captive, and understandably so.

"The ship sped southeast, toward Java. The voice of the prisoner never abated, and sound cast a black and smothering pall over all on board, with the possible exception of Sefton Talliard, whose nerves seemed proof against any assault. On the night that we neared Batavia Bay, I retired early, and the last recollection I carried with me into slumber was the sound of the prisoner's voice, infused with a certain new and curious note of exultation.

"I awakened at dawn to a clamorous uproar. Footsteps thundered overhead, an alarm clanged, men shouted wildly, shrieks of mortal terror tore the air, and through it all, I could still distinguish the hoarsened, malevolently triumphant voice of the captive Dyak, calling upon Ur-Allazoth.

"Rising from my berth, I made for the deck. Before I reached it, a violent impact rocked the *Matilda Briggs*. The shock threw me from the ladder, and I fell, striking my head violently upon the cabin floor. For a time, I knew nothing more.

"When I regained my senses, around midmorning, it was to find myself lying, sick and sore, in the boat of the *Matilda Briggs,* together with Talliard, Loftus, and some half-dozen sailors. Of the ship, and the rest of her crew, nothing was to be seen. That she had gone to the bottom of Batavia Bay was clear, but the circumstances of the wreck were impossible to ascertain. Talliard claimed ignorance, the sailors offered the most incoherently fantastic tales, and Zebulon Loftus, when pressed for an account, vented peal upon piercing peal of maniacal laughter. To my surprise, I found that the valise containing my personal belongings had been preserved, by Talliard, of all people. In response to my thanks, our leader merely responded that the rubbings I had taken from the pedestal of Ur-Allazoth's image were worth saving.

"Batavia Bay is heavily traveled, and we were rescued in a matter of hours. The inquest that followed is a great blur in my mind. The official verdict was that the *Matilda Briggs* had struck a rock and sunk; a falsehood I made no attempt to challenge.

"We returned to Providence, where young Loftus, whose sanity was shattered, entered a mental hospital. The academic year at Brown commenced, and I returned to work, in every hope of resuming my former tranquil existence. For a while, it seemed I had done so. I so far regained my equilibrium that I dared confront the challenge of deciphering the message of Ur-Allazoth's glyphs; while Talliard disclosed our findings to the world in lectures of dazzling brilliancy. Apparent normality reigned for some months, until December, when we received news that Zebulon Loftus had escaped incarceration. Two days later, his frozen, decapitated body was found in a meadow not half a mile from the hospital. His head was never located.

"Around this time—" Belknap could not repress a shudder, "I began once more to experience the peculiar sensation of being watched that I thought I had left behind me in the East Indies. Often I thought to glimpse dark forms haunting the shadows as I made my way through the tortuous streets of Providence, and once I caught the baleful gleam of uncanny blue eyes tracking my progress. Confiding in Talliard, one icy winter night, I learned that he harbored fears identical to my own; and painfully acute those fears must have been for that self-contained, overweening individual to acknowledge them. Upon that occasion, he even spoke of flight, and suggested the possibility of finding refuge in London. At the time, I hardly expected him to resort to such measures. But two nights later, both Talliard's office and my own were ransacked. The next day, Sefton Talliard disappeared.

"He was either dead, or fled to London. In the absence of a corpse, I suspected the latter. Within the fortnight, I'd powerful incentive to follow him. For some weeks past, my work with the glyphs had scarcely progressed. Many of the pictographs, though commonplace symbols in that backward area of the world, were arranged in sequences that seemed senseless and random as the ravings of a lunatic. At length it dawned upon me that the symbols composed a rebus, phonetically representing words in the Dutch language of the seventeenth century. Inexplicable that a solution so obvious should have eluded me for so long, but thereafter, as you may well imagine, my task was greatly simplified, and translation proceeded apace. Eventually, the following message resolved itself." Closing his eyes, Belknap repeated, from memory, *"The hold of divine Ur-Allazoth looses not, and loses naught. Whosoever profanes His image, dividing or diminishing the sacred substance thereof, shall be pursued to the ends of the earth and beyond, even unto the shrieking, formless reaches beyond the stars. Nor shall pursuit abate, before the worldly waters ruled by the Relentless have closed upon that which is His.*

"You see the significance, Mr. Holmes?" Belknap opened his eyes.

"Indeed. I had, inevitably, anticipated the rebus," Holmes replied. "As for the rest, the urgency of the matter is apparent. These devotees of a being whose nature demands further investigation have followed the despoilers of their deity's image all the way from Sumatra. Clearly, they will not rest until they have recovered the plaque stolen by Sefton Talliard. In order to preserve your own life, as well as Professor Talliard's, the immediate return of the stolen item to its self-proclaimed owners is essential."

"That is my conclusion. But my own efforts have failed to locate Talliard here in London, and lately, I have noted the presence of silent blue-eyed hounds upon my trail. Within the last forty-eight hours, they have drawn near, and I fear that my time is all but gone. Can you assist me, Mr. Holmes?"

"Beyond doubt. There is one point, however, that must be noted at the outset; which is, that your colleague appears to withhold information of some vital significance. In view of the character-portrait you've limned, that is hardly surprising. Presumably the nature of the missing piece will reveal itself when I have located Professor Talliard, which I fully expect to do in a matter of hours, if not less."

"But that is astonishing, Mr. Holmes!" the visitor exclaimed. "I have scoured London for weeks, without gleaning the slightest clue."

"I've certain local resources, to which a stranger in the city is unlikely to enjoy access," Holmes replied, not unkindly. "Now, Professor Belknap, here is a question of some import. Were you followed to Baker Street, this evening?"

"I believe so." Belknap shivered. "Yes, I am quite certain of it."

"Excellent," Holmes replied, to my amazement.

I could not fathom my friend's clear satisfaction, and the visitor was equally confounded.

"I must leave you, for a little while," Holmes abruptly informed his client. "I shall return within the half hour." He departed without further explanation, leaving me alone with August Belknap, who, unaccustomed to the eccentric character of my friend's genius, appeared thunderstruck.

It was perhaps the slowest half hour I have ever endured. Poor Belknap, distracted and raw-nerved, could not even pretend interest in the tales of the Afghan campaign with which I endeavored to entertain him, but started and flinched at every unexpected sound. Presently, all conversation died, and we sat in comfortless silence until the clock struck nine, and, to my unutterable relief, Sherlock Holmes reappeared.

"The apparatus has been readied," Holmes declared. "It remains only to set the machine in motion. For that, Professor, I must request use of your amusing disguise. We are much of a build. My own clothes should fit you well enough to serve on a foggy night. Take them, return to your own lodgings, and do not stir forth until you have heard from me. Where are you staying?"

The visitor named an address in Fleet Street.

"I assume you frequently change location?"

"Every few days," Belknap admitted. "But I never succeed in throwing them off the track for long."

"After tonight, that should not signify." So saying, Holmes ushered the visitor into his own room.

When they emerged, minutes later, I could not forbear staring, so startled was I by the transformation. August Belknap, clad in borrowed Inverness and deerstalker, might at a glance have been mistaken for Sherlock Holmes. Holmes himself, in feminine array, complete with wig, wide hat, and veiling, was altogether unrecognizable.

"Now, Professor," Holmes instructed his client, "wait for half an hour after Dr. Watson and I have departed—"

"Eh!" I exclaimed.

"—then return to Fleet Street, and stay inside tomorrow. You are the lesser target, and probably not in immediate danger, but do not open the door to anyone other than myself or Watson."

"Mr. Holmes, I will follow your instructions without fail."

"Capital. And now, my dear Watson, I trust you will not suffer a lady to venture forth unescorted?" Holmes's amused smile was dimly visible through the veiling.

"Venture forth where?" I inquired.

"Not far. A half-hour's stroll should suffice."

I remained unenlightened, but acquiescent. Pausing only long enough to don an overcoat, I accompanied Sherlock Holmes out into the fog-blinded March night. Together we set off at a leisurely pace along Baker Street.

To the end of my days, I will always remember that walk, and I will never recall it without a pang of profound uneasiness. For that sense of *being watched,* so graphically described by Professor August Belknap, was present, powerful, and impossible to ignore. I could have taken my oath that the shadows seethed with silent, sliding shapes, and I could literally feel the pressure of invisible regard. It was all I could do to refrain from glancing continually back over my shoulder, and the flesh between my shoulder blades positively tingled in anticipation of a blow. I considered Belknap's account of the Faithful's headless victims, and my own head momentarily swam.

If Sherlock Holmes shared my misgivings, he showed no sign of it. His step was unhurried, his manner unconcerned, as he launched into an impressively knowledgeable discussion of the evolution of the Kabuki dance drama. My friend spoke brilliantly, yet I scarcely heard a word of his discourse, for my ears were attuned to nothing beyond the tap of footsteps in the fog behind us. And my disquiet, already intense, increased a hundredfold when Holmes led us from the relatively well-lit, populous public thoroughfares, into the silent pathways of Regent's Park. We were nearing the Zoo before he finally paused, in a region of impenetrable shadow.

"That should be enough," Holmes opined.

I did not waste breath begging for an explanation, but waited in silence as he divested himself of hat, wig, pelisse, and skirts, to reveal ordinary masculine attire beneath.

"Now, Watson, we separate," he decreed. "You may take the direct route back to Baker Street, and I shall go roundabout. And by this time tomorrow night, we shall beyond doubt have located the missing Professor Talliard."

With that, he vanished silently into the dark, leaving me alone, bewildered, filled with resentment, and more than a little apprehension. I made my way home without hindrance. Belknap had left, and Holmes had not yet returned, which was just as well. If I had encountered my friend at that moment, I should hardly have found myself capable of civility. I retired early, and slept soundly, my dreams somehow flavored with the sound of Sherlock Holmes's violin.

Holmes had resumed his chemical experimentation by the time I awoke. His violin lay on the sofa—evidently he had been playing it during the night. His pallor and shadowed eyes suggested sleeplessness. Still somewhat piqued by last night's events, I refused to question him, but rather, occupied myself with a series of errands that kept me out and about for the entire day. Around twilight, I returned to Baker Street, to discover Holmes still occupied with his test tubes, beakers, and burners. Nor was his attention to be diverted from these items until a dubious Mrs. Hudson entered to announce the arrival of "Master Wiggins, and associates."

"Ah, show them in," Holmes instructed, his face alight with eagerness. Noting my puzzlement, he explained, "The Baker Street Irregulars. They have been at work since I put them on the case last night."

Here, then, was the explanation of Holmes's half-hour absence of the previous evening. He had withdrawn to confer with his juvenile surveillance squad.

Moments later, a sextet of ragged and remarkably filthy little street Arabs burst into the room. Their chief Wiggins, tallest and oldest among them, swaggered forward to announce with an air of victory, "Plunker 'ere cops the prize."

The Plunker in question, a superlatively disreputable urchin, flashed a snaggle-toothed grin.

"State your findings," Holmes commanded.

"Shadowed yer last night, Guv'nor, as per orders." Master Wiggins appeared to act as official spokesman of the party. "Soon spied the others on yer trail, just like yer said, and rummy little apes they was, too. Not 'arf ugly. Arfter yer gives 'em the slip in the Park, they splits up, so *we* splits up. Plunker follows one of 'em as far as Notting 'ill Gate, and finds more of the same, 'anging about a lodging'ouse. Plunker keeps an eye peeled, twigs their game, and knows 'e's nailed yer man. And there you 'ave it."

"Well done, gentlemen. Can you furnish an address?"

Wiggins obliged.

"Second storey, front room," Plunker offered.

"Well done," Holmes repeated. He produced a guinea. "Plunker, your reward."

"Cor!" Plunker's crooked grin widened.

"For the rest of you—the usual scale of pay, for two days' work." Holmes distributed silver. "Gentlemen, until next time."

The delighted irregulars withdrew, no doubt to our landlady's relief.

"Phew!" I observed.

"There is no time to be lost, Watson," Holmes declared. "Sefton Talliard's hours are numbered."

A hansom carried us to the house noted by the youthful intelligencer. The place was respectable-looking, well-maintained, and unremarkable. We alighted from our vehicle, and I gazed searchingly about, but caught no glimpse of lurking figures. The sense of being watched, so unnervingly acute last night in Regent's Park, was absent now. And yet, I knew not why, I found that my hands were icy, and my heart was cold with a formless dread.

A couple of taps of the polished brass knocker drew the landlady. Holmes introduced himself as a friend of the American gentleman on the second floor, and she admitted us without demur. We hurried upstairs and rapped on Sefton Talliard's door. There was no response, and my sense of dread deepened.

The room was locked. Our combined strength easily sufficed to force it open, and we burst in to confront a scene I shudder to recall. I am a surgeon, fully accustomed to sights that many would consider ghastly, yet all my experience could not fully prepare me for the spectacle of Sefton Talliard's headless corpse, sprawled on a blood-drenched bed. I think an exclamation escaped me, and I recoiled a pace or two. Sherlock Holmes was guilty of no such weakness. Casting a keen, penetrating eye about the death chamber, he stepped first to the locked window, then to the fireplace, which he knelt to examine briefly. Thereafter, he turned his attention upon the clothing, books, papers, and personal articles that lay wildly scattered everywhere. That Talliard's room had been thoroughly rifled was altogether apparent. The object of my friend's search was less evident, however. Initially, I assumed that he sought the plaque sacrilegiously pried from the pedestal of Ur-Allazoth's image, but that could scarcely be; for surely the murderers, here before us and purposeful beyond civilized ken, would already have reclaimed that article. It then occurred to me that Holmes sought Talliard's missing head, but such proved not to be the case. At length, a muted grunt of satisfaction announced his success, and from that dreadful blood-stained tangle, he plucked a small volume bound in red morocco.

I was not so dull that I failed to recognize Professor Talliard's prized journal, as described by August Belknap.

Settling himself back upon his haunches with the utmost deliberation, Holmes proceeded to read, indifferent to the presence of the mutilated body on the bed, not two yards behind him. I could scarcely endure it.

"Holmes—" I entreated.

"One moment—ah!" Holmes's expression altered remarkably, and he sprang to his feet. "There—yes—I had suspected something, but this I did not foresee."

"Foresee what?" I demanded.

"Come, we must find Belknap at once."

"We cannot leave this place, Holmes!" I expostulated. "We have happened upon a murder. There are authorities—appropriate channels—proper procedure—"

"They will wait," Holmes informed me. With some effort, he tore his eyes from the journal. "My client stands in mortal peril. Should he perish, it is through my own failure of intellect."

Such a prospect was not to be contemplated.

"No delay, Watson! Belknap's life hangs by a thread." Thrusting Talliard's journal into his pocket, Holmes rose and rushed from the room, without a glance to spare for the dead man. After a moment, I followed. What Talliard's landlady must have made of our sudden departure, and her subsequent discovery in the American lodger's room, I did not care to ponder at that time.

Before I reached the street, Holmes had already secured a hansom. I jumped in, just as the vehicle sped off east. The ride was endless, and conversation one-sided, for Holmes declined to answer my queries, or indeed, to speak at all. Eventually, I gave over interrogation. Traffic was heavy upon the London streets at that hour, the fog was opaque, our progress was slow, and apprehension twisted my vitals.

At length, we reached the Fleet Street address of August Belknap; a surprisingly mean haunt, for it seemed that Holmes's client, desirous of self-submersion in London's maelstrom, had sought concealment in cheap lodgings above some barber's shop.

The shop was still open. We rushed in and, without pausing to consult a proprietor of remarkably demonic aspect, sprinted to the back and up the stairs, to pound the door of August Belknap's room.

We called him by name, and he admitted us at once. Before the first question escaped the fugitive academic's lips, Sherlock Holmes demanded, "The photograph of your late wife, Belknap—where is it?"

Belknap stared, his feverish, astonished eyes widening. Impatiently, Holmes repeated the query, and his client's wordless gesture encompassed the plain oak bureau in the corner. Pulling the top drawer open, my friend swiftly located and drew forth the silver-framed portrait of a round-faced young woman, irregular of feature, but sweet and grave of expression. I confess the professor was no more mystified than I. All confusion vanished, however, when Sherlock Holmes pried the backing from the frame, to reveal the flat, marvelously carven plaque secreted behind the photograph.

"Good God!" Belknap ejaculated.

His reaction was surely unfeigned. It would have required the talents of an Irving or a Forbes-Robertson to counterfeit such perfect amazement.

"You must rid yourself of this object," Holmes informed his client. "That is your sole chance of survival."

"Mr. Holmes, I knew nothing of this. I will gladly dispose of the thing. I will bury it—pulverize it—donate it to a museum—carry it back to Sumatra, if need be—"

"Useless," Holmes returned. "Quite useless. There is but one solution to your dilemma. Your own translation of the Sumatran glyphs, Professor, should instruct you."

" *'Nor shall pursuit abate,'* " Belknap recited, " *'before the worldly waters ruled by the Relentless have closed upon that which is His.'* "

"Just so. Come, there is not a moment to lose."

Holmes exited, and we followed him, down the stairs, past the flame-eyed proprietor, and out into mist-shrouded Fleet Street. He led us east, and as we went, the cold chills knifing along my spine, and the intolerable pressure of invisible regard, warned me of unseen stalkers near at hand. August Belknap's face was white and set; he, too, sensed the hostile presence.

We reached Ludgate Circus, and now, for the first time, I actually glimpsed the short, impossibly agile human shadows gliding through the fog, and I caught the glint of luminously malignant blue eyes. Even Sherlock Holmes could not feign total indifference. We quickened our pace, and our pursuers did likewise, drawing perceptibly nearer as we turned south toward the Thames.

I could not fathom my friend's purpose. Neither he nor I carried a weapon. I assumed that August Belknap was similarly unarmed. Rather than seeking the comparative safety of well-peopled streets, however, Sherlock Holmes was leading us straight on toward empty Blackfriars Bridge.

We were running now, unabashedly in flight, our footsteps echoing through the fog. Hearing no clatter of pursuit, I chanced a glance behind to descry no less than six of them, swift and seemingly tireless, noiseless and uncanny as predatory wraiths.

Reaching the bridge, we started to cross. Halfway to the Southwark side, however, Holmes halted abruptly, one hand raised on high. Clasped in that hand was the plaque pried from the image of the Faithful's god. I've no idea at all what substance composed that small tablet. Whatever it was, it seemed to glow with some pulsing internal light of its own, and never in all my days have I seen the like. Even in the midst of the darkness and the swirling fog, the plaque was clearly visible.

"Ur-Allazoth!" Holmes called out, in a clear, strong voice that pierced the night like a dagger.

So sharp and sudden was that utterance, and so unexpected, that I started violently at the sound of it, and beside me, I heard Belknap gasp.

"Ur-Allazoth!" Holmes repeated the call, and then sang out a string of indescribably outlandish syllables.

"Iä fhurtgn iea tlu jiadhri cthuthoth zhugg'lsht ftehia. Iea tlu."

That is the best I can do to reproduce that fantastically incomprehensible burst of gibberish.

It seemed to me then that the inexplicable, infernal light of the stolen plaque in Holmes's grasp responsively intensified. As a man of science, I can scarcely account for such a phenomenon, but I did *not* imagine it. Blinking and confused, I looked away, glancing back to behold our six pursuers, grouped at the end of the bridge, motionless and preternaturally intent. My confusion deepened as their voices rose, to wail thinly through the fog:

"Iä fhurtgn iea tlu jiadhri cthuthoth zhugg'lsht ftehia. Iea tlu."

There was something in the sound that roused my deepest, most elemental terror and detestation.

As the final loathsome syllable faded, Sherlock Holmes flung the plaque from Blackfriars Bridge. The lucent object fell like a shooting star. Before it struck the river below, the mists roiled, and a violent upheaval convulsed the water. The Thames shuddered, black waves smashed themselves against the piers of the bridge, and a funnel-shaped whirlpool spun into existence. Astounded, I gazed down, and thought for one mad moment to glimpse a vast and almost inconceivable shape. There was solidity there, I imagined; a slithering of boneless attenuated limbs, a flash of spikes and suckers. The moment passed. The plaque vanished into the whirlpool, the waters closed upon it, then swiftly calmed themselves. The Thames flowed on, untroubled.

Slowly, doubting my own senses, I turned to look back upon our Faithful pursuers. For an instant I beheld them—six anonymous, attentive figures, ghostlike in the mists. Then they vanished, fading into the fog, and I saw them no more.

Two nights later, we sat in our lodgings, the ever-present London fog still testing its weight against the windowpanes. Most of the previous day had been spent in conference with the police, who, swayed by the hysterics of Sefton Talliard's landlady, had initially evinced some disposition to suspect our complicity in that unhappy academic's decapitation. The information, however, regarding the nature of Talliard's shadowy enemies—provided by August Belknap, and substantiated by the testimony of Wiggins and Plunker of the Baker Street Irregulars—had much allayed such suspicion. And Holmes's own masterly analysis of the murder-site had demonstrated beyond all question that a brace of small acrobatic killers had entered the locked room by way of the chimney, dispatched the sleeping

Talliard, ransacked the room, and exited the way they had come, bearing their victim's head—which will, I strongly suspect, never be located.

The constabulary, their doubts satisfied, had dismissed us, and we came away with Holmes miraculously retaining possession of Sefton Talliard's journal. The book now lay open before him, and my friend was frowning over it.

"I am scarcely satisfied," he complained.

"What, Holmes!" I returned. "Against all odds, you succeeded in preserving your client's life—assuming that his enemies are now mollified."

"August Belknap has nothing more to fear from the Faithful," Holmes said, shrugging. "But that is not the point. The information placed at my disposal regarding Professor Sefton Talliard's ruthless, cool, and unscrupulous character should have alerted me to the fellow's intentions, early enough to forestall another ritual beheading. It should not have been necessary for me to read his very words in his own journal."

"What did he say?" I inquired.

"See for yourself." Holmes extended the morocco-bound volume. "And do not neglect the account of the destruction of the *Matilda Briggs.*"

Sefton Talliard's hand was decisive and legible. It was with disapproving interest, but no great surprise, that I read of his plan, motivated by self-serving fear, to transfer the stolen plaque, object of alarming Faithful attention, from his own possession to that of the unwitting August Belknap. The photograph of Belknap's late wife, a memento of immense sentimental value, prized and carried everywhere by its owner, offered the perfect place of concealment. This transfer, accomplished hours prior to the embarkation of the *Matilda Briggs,* clearly accounted for Talliard's unwonted generosity in preserving the valise, containing the personal property of his colleague.

There followed a brief passage, written on shipboard, and phonetically rendering the invocation to Ur-Allazoth ceaselessly howled by the Dyak prisoner locked in the hold of the vessel:

Iä fhurtgn iea tlu jiadhri cthuthoth zhugg'lsht ftehia. Iea tlu.

And finally, the following passage, penned in the immediate aftermath of the disaster, caught my eye:

> *. . . cannot begin to convey the horror of the Being that rose from the sea to confront the* Matilda Briggs. *There are no words—there are no sane human concepts—fit to encompass the immensity of that primeval terror—that overwhelming, insupportable foulness—that gibbering,*

> *slavering, slobbering, quivering, towering, tittering obscenity—that burst from the sea like a corporeal nightmare, shattering the boundaries of time, space, and reason. God help me! My mind quakes at the recollection, my sanity trembles. How shall I speak of a creature, gigantic and jigglingly gelatinous beyond description, ancient beyond earthly reckoning, hideous beyond the tolerance of human vision, combining in one abominable form all the worst aspects of plague-bearing rat, giant kraken, squid, serpent, and leveret? How shall I speak of the stench that killed courage, the howling aural assault that blasted intelligence? How shall I limn an incarnation of the immemorial destroying lunacy that humanity calls Chaos? Oh, I cannot—I simply cannot! All about me, men were going mad. The Thing was closing fast upon us, and I knew at a glance that the* Matilda Briggs *was lost. . . .*

"Gad." I looked up from the page. "What do you make of it, Holmes?"

"I would not necessarily discount the professor's veracity," my friend returned languidly. "For when you have eliminated the impossible, whatever remains, however improbable, must be the truth. Nevertheless, we should do well to keep the matter to ourselves, Watson, as it is a story for which the world is not yet prepared."

black as the pit, from pole to pole

STEVEN UTLEY & HOWARD WALDROP

I

In an early American spring, the following circular was sent to learned men, scholars, explorers, and members of the Congress. It was later reprinted by various newspapers and magazines, both in the United States and abroad.

St. Louis, Missouri Territory, North America
April 10, 1818

I declare that the earth is hollow; habitable within; containing a number of solid concentric spheres; one within the other, and that it is open at the pole twelve or sixteen degrees. I pledge my life in support of this truth, and am ready to explore the hollow if the world will support and aid me in the undertaking. John Cleves Symmes of Ohio, Late Captain of Infantry.

N.B. I have ready for the press a treatise on the principles of Matter, wherein I show proofs on the above proposition, account for various phenomena, and disclose Dr. Darwin's "Golden Secret."

My terms are the patronage of this and the new world; I dedicate to my wife and her ten children.

I select Dr. S. L. Mitchel, Sir H. Davy, and Baron Alexander Von Humboldt as my protectors. I ask 100 brave companions, well-equipped to start from Siberia, in the fall season, with reindeer and sledges, on the ice of the frozen sea; I engage we find a warm and rich land, stocked with thrifty vegetables and animals, if not men, on reaching one degree northward of latitude 82; we will return in the succeeding spring. J.C.S.

From the Introduction to *Frankenstein; or, The Modern Prometheus,* revised edition, 1831, by Mary Wollstonecraft Shelley:

> Many and long were the conversations between Lord Byron and Shelley, to which I was a devout but nearly silent listener. During one of these, various philosophical doctrines were discussed, and among others the nature of the principle of life, and whether there was any probability of its ever being discovered and communicated. They talked of the experiments of Dr. Darwin (I speak not of what the Doctor really did, or said that he did, but, as more to my purpose, of what was then spoken of as having been done by him) who preserved a piece of vermicelli in a glass case, 'til by some extraordinary means it began to move with a voluntary motion. Not thus, after all, would life be given. Perhaps a corpse would be reanimated; galvanism had given token of such things; perhaps the component parts of a creature might be manufactured, brought together, and imbued with vital warmth. . . .

It ends here.

The creature's legs buckled. His knees crunched through the crust as he went down. The death's-head face turned toward the sky. The wind swept across the ice cap, gathering up and flinging cold dust into his eyes.

The giant, the monster, the golem, closed his fine-veined eyelids and fell sideways. He could go no farther. He was numb and exhausted. He pressed his face down into the snow, and his thin black lips began to shape the words of an unvoiced prayer:

It ends here, Victor Frankenstein. I am too weary to go on. Too weary even to cremate myself. Wherever you are now, whether passed into Heaven, Hell, or that nothingness from which you summoned me, look upon me with pity and compassion now. I had no choice. It ends here. At the top of the world, where no one shall ever come to remark on the passing of this nameless, forsaken wretch. It ends here, and the world is rid of me. Once again, Victor, I beseech you. Forgive me for my wicked machinations. Even as I forgave you yours.

He waited for death, his ears throbbing with the ever-slowing beat of his handseled heart. Spots of blackness began to erupt in his head and spread, overtaking and overwhelming the astonishingly vivid assortment of memories that flickered through his mind. Such a pretty little boy. I will not eat you, do not scream. Be quiet, please. I mean you no harm. Please. I want to be your friend. Hush now. Hush. Hush. I didn't know that he would break so easily. There is open sea not far from where I sprawl in the snow, awaiting death. The sea is the mother of all life. Save mine. The young man's name was Felix, and he drove me away. I could have crushed his skull with a single casual swat with the back of my hand. And I let him drive me away. Such a pretty little boy. Such a pretty little boy. Why was I not made pretty? Tell me now, Frankenstein. It is important that I know. Do I have a soul? Felix. Felix. I will be with you on your wedding night. I will be with you. Do I have a *soul,* Victor Frankenstein?

He suddenly pushed himself up on his elbows and shook ice from his eyelids. He could see the sea before him, but it was too bright to gaze upon. It seemed to burn like molten gold, and it was as though the very maw of Hell were opening to receive him.

He collapsed, burying his face in the snow, and lay there whimpering, no strength left now, no sensation in his legs and hands. *Do I have a soul?* he demanded a final time, just as he felt himself sliding, sliding, about to take the plunge into oblivion. There was time enough for a second question. *If so, where will it go?* And then there was no time at all.

He had not felt so disoriented since the night of his first awakening. He sat up painfully and glared around in confusion. Then tears streamed from his eyes and froze upon his cheeks, and he shrieked with rage and frustration.

"Fiend! Monster! *Damn you!*"

He struggled to his feet and tottered wildly, flailing the air with his mismatched fists. And he kept screaming.

"*This* is the full horror of your great achievement! Death won't have me, Frankenstein! Hell spews me forth! *You made me better than you thought!*"

His thickly wrapped legs, aching with the slow return of circulation, began to pump stiffly, driving him across the ice. He kicked up clouds of cold snow dust. Then glass-sliver pain filled his lungs, and his mad run slowed to a walk. Fury spun and eddied in his guts, hotter by far than the fire in his chest, but it was fury commingled with sorrow. He sat down abruptly, put his face into his hands, and sobbed.

Death had rejected him again.

At the instant of his birth on a long-ago, almost forgotten midnight, he had drawn his first puzzled breath, and Death had bowed to Life for the first time, had permitted a mere man to pry its fingers from the abandoned bones and flesh of the kirkyard and the charnel house. Death had never reclaimed that which had been taken from it. Time and again, Death had chosen not to terminate his comfortless existence.

I was never ill, Frankenstein. I survived fire and exposure. I sustained injuries that would have killed or at least incapacitated even the hardiest of human beings. Even you could not kill me, you who gave me life. That should make you proud. You shot me at point-blank range after I killed your beautiful Elizabeth. You couldn't kill me, though. Perhaps nothing can kill me.

His sobbing subsided. He sat in the snow and dully rolled the bitter thought over and over in his mind. Perhaps nothing can kill me. Perhaps *nothing* can kill me. When Victor Frankenstein had shot him, the ball struck him low in the left side of the back and emerged a couple of inches above and to the right of the incongruous navel. The impact had knocked him from the sill of the château window through which he had been making an escape. Doubled up on the ground beneath the window, he had heard Frankenstein's howl of anguish over the murdered Elizabeth. Then, clutching his abdomen, he had lurched away into the night.

The bleeding had ceased within minutes. The wounds were closed by the following morning and, at the end of a week's time, were no more than moon-shaped, moon-colored scars. He had wondered about his regenerative powers but briefly, however, for his enraged creator was breathing down his neck in hot, vengeful pursuit. There had been no time for idle speculation during the trek across Europe, across Siberia, into the windswept Arctic.

He pushed his tongue out and licked his frostbitten lips. Words started to rumble up from the deep chest, then lost all life of their own, and emerged dull-sounding and flat. "You cheated me, Victor Frankenstein. In every way, you cheated me."

He paused, listening. The wind moaned like the breath of some immense frost-god wrapped in unpleasant dreams. Muffled thunder rolled across the ice from the direction of the now-leaden sea.

"I owe you nothing, Victor. *Nothing.*"

He got to his feet again and began moving toward the edge of the ice. Plucking bits of ice from his face and hair, his mind bubbling and frothing, he was suddenly stopped in his tracks by a particularly vicious gust of wind. His eyes filled with salt water. The cold cut through his parka, flesh and bone, and he cried out in pure animal misery. He sucked on his frozen fingers and tried to stamp warmth back into his limbs. In the sky, its bottom half under the horizon, the heatless, useless sun mocked him. He snarled at it, shook his fist at it, turned his back on it.

And could not believe what he saw before him.

Hanging between the northern edge of the world and the zenith was a second, smaller sun.

II

In the year 1818, *Frankenstein; or, The Modern Prometheus* was published. Mary Shelley was twenty-one years old.

John Cleves Symmes, late of the Ohio Infantry, published his treatise about the hollow earth. He was a war hero and a Missouri storekeeper. He was thirty-eight years old.

Herman Melville would not be born for another year.

Jeremiah N. Reynolds was attending Ohio University but would soon become a doctor and a scientist. He would also fall under the spell of Symmes.

Edgar Allan Poe, nine years old, was living with his foster parents.

Percy Shelley, Lord Byron, and Dr. Polidori sailed as often as possible in the sloop *Ariel* on Lake Como.

In New Bedford, Massachusetts, young Arthur Gordon Pym sailed around the harbor in his sloop, also christened *Ariel*. His one burning desire was to go to sea.

In the South Seas, Mocha Dick, the great white whale, was an age no man could know or guess. Mocha Dick was not aware of aging, nor of the passing of time. It knew only of the sounding deeps and, infrequently, of the men who stuck harpoons into it until it turned on them and broke apart their vessels.

Victor Frankenstein's patchwork man was similarly unaware of the passing of time. The creature did not know how long he had slept in the ice at the top of the world, nor was he able to mark time within earth.

It became subtly warmer as the mysterious second sun rose in time with the ice cap's apparent northerly drift. The creature kept telling himself that what he saw was impossible, that there could be no second sun, that it was merely an illusion, a reflected image of the sun he had always known, a clever optical trick of some sort. But he was too miserable to ponder the phenomenon for very long at a time.

He subsisted on the dried meat that he had carried with him from Siberia in the pouch of his parka. He had little strength for exercise, and the circulation of his vital fluids often slowed to the point where he was only semiconscious. His eyes began playing other tricks on him. The horizon started to rise before him, to warp around him outrageously, curving upward and away in every direction, as though he had been carried over the lip of an enormous bowl and was slowly, lazily sliding toward its bottom. He could account for none of it.

He was dozing, frozen, in the shelter of an ice block when a shudder passed through the mass beneath him. He blinked, vaguely aware of something being wrong, and then he was snapped fully awake by the sight and *sound* of a gigantic blossom of spray at the edge of the sea. The thunder of crumbling ice brought him up on hands and knees. He stared, fascinated, as the eruption of water hung in the air for a long moment before falling, very slowly, very massively, back into the sea.

Then panic replaced fascination. He realized what was happening.

The ice was breaking up. He spun, the motion consuming years, took two steps and sank, howling, into snow suddenly turned to quicksand. He fell and scrambled up in time to see an ice ridge explode into powder. The shelf on which he stood pitched crazily as it started to slide down the parent mass's new face. The scraping walls of the fissure shook the air with the sound of a million tormented, screaming things. Dwarfed to insignificance by the forces at play around him, the giant was hurled flat. The breath left his lungs painfully.

He pushed himself up on elbows and sucked the cold, cutting air back into his tormented chest. The world beyond his clenched fists seemed to sag, then dropped out of sight. A moment later, clouds of freezing seawater geysered from the abyss as the shelf settled and rolled, stabilizing itself.

The creature turned and crawled away from the chasm. He kept moving until he was at the approximate center of the new iceberg. He squatted there, alternately shaking and going numb with terror.

He had seen the abyss open inches from him.

He had looked down the throat of the death he had wanted.

He had felt no temptation.

He cursed life for its tenacity. He cursed, again, the man whose explorations into the secrets of life had made it impossible for him simply to lie down, sleep, and let the Arctic cold take him.

He could not help but brood over his immunity to death. What would have happened, he wondered, had he been precipitated into the fissure when the shelf broke off? Surely he would have been smeared to thin porridge between the sliding, scraping masses. But—

There was another rumble behind him. He turned his head and saw a large section of the berg drop out of sight, into the sea.

It doesn't matter, he reflected as he dug into his parka for a piece of meat. The ice is going to melt, and I will be hurled into the sea. I wonder if I can drown.

He did not relish the prospect of finding out.

His virtually somnambulistic existence resumed. He ate his dried meat, melted snow in his mouth to slake his thirst, and fully regained consciousness only when the berg shook him awake with the crash and roar of its disintegration. The sun he had known all of his life, the one that he could not think of as other than the *real* sun, at last disappeared behind him, while the strange second sun now seemed fixed unwaveringly at zenith. The horizon was still rising, rolling up the sky until it appeared behind occasional cloud masses and, sometimes, above them. It was as though the world were trying to double over on itself and enfold him.

He amused himself with that image between naps. Nothing was strange to him anymore, not the stationary sun, not the horizonless vista. He was alive, trapped on a melting iceberg. He was in Hell.

It was only when he began to make out the outlines of a coast in the sky that he experienced a renewed sense of wonder. In the time that followed, a time of unending noon, of less sleep and more terror as the berg's mass diminished, the sight of that concave stood-on-edge land filled him with awe and a flickering sort of hope that even hunger, physical misery, and fear could not dispel.

He was alive, but merely being alive was not enough. It had never been enough.

He was alive, and here, sweeping down out of the sky, rolling itself out toward him in open invitation was . . . what?

He stood at the center of his iceberg and looked at his hands. He thought of the scars on his body, the proofs of his synthesis, and he thought:

What *was* my purpose, Victor Frankenstein? Did you have some kind of destiny planned for me when you gave me life? Had you not rejected me at the moment of my birth, had you accepted responsibility for my being in the world, would there have been some sort of fulfillment, some use, for me in the world of men?

The berg shivered underfoot for a second, and he cried out, went to his knees, hugged a block of ice desperately. The dark landmass swam in the air. When the tremor had subsided, he laughed shakily and got to his feet. His head spun, grew light, filled with stars and explosions. He reached for the ice block in an effort to steady himself but fell anyway and lay in the snow, thinking.

Thinking, This is no natural land before me, Frankenstein, and perhaps there are no men here.

Thinking, I could be free of men here, free of everything.

Thinking, This is going to be *my* land, Frankenstein.
Thinking, This is no natural land, and I am no natural man.
Thinking.

The berg had begun crunching its way through drifting sheets of pack ice when the creature spotted something else that stood out against the brilliant whiteness of the frozen sea. He watched the thing for a long time, noting that it did not move, before he was able to discern the sticklike fingers of broken masts and the tracery of rigging. It looked like some forgotten bedraggled toy, tossed aside by a bored child.

The ship was very old. Its sides had been crushed in at the waterline, and the ice-sheathed debris of its rigging and lesser masts sat upon the hulk like a stand of dead, gray trees. A tattered flag hung from the stern, frozen solid, looking to be fashioned from thick glass.

When his iceberg had finally slowed to an imperceptible crawl in the midst of the pack, the creature cautiously made his way down to the sheet and walked to the ship. When he had come close enough, he called out in his ragged voice. There was no answer. He had not expected one.

Belowdecks, he found unused stores and armaments, along with three iron-hard corpses. There were flint, frozen biscuits, and salt pork, kegs of frozen water and liquor. There was a wealth of cold-climate clothing and lockers packed with brittle charts and strange instruments.

He took what he could carry. From the several armaments lockers, he selected a long double-edged dagger, a heavy cutlass and scabbard, a blunderbuss, and a brace of pistols to supplement the one he had carried throughout his Siberian trek. There had been two pistols originally—he had stolen the set before leaving Europe and had used them on a number of occasions to get what he needed in the way of supplies from terrified Siberian peasants. One of the pistols had been missing after his departure from the whaling vessel. He supposed that it had fallen from his belt when he leaped from the ship to the ice.

There was enough powder in several discarded barrels to fill a small keg. He found shot in a metal box and filled the pouch of his parka.

He did not bother himself with thoughts about the dead men or their vanished comrades. Whoever they had been, they had left in a hurry, and they had left him their goods. He was still cold, tired, and hungry, but the warm clothing was now his, and he could rest in the shelter of the derelict. He had hardtack and meat and the means to make fire. And he had weapons.

He returned to the deck for a moment and contemplated the upward-curving landscape ahead.

In this world, perhaps, there are no men.

He waved the cutlass, wearily jubilant, and, for the first time in his life, he began to feel truly free.

III

John Cleves Symmes published a novel in 1820, under the name Adam Seaborn. Its title was *Symzonia: A Voyage of Discovery,* and it made extensive use of Symmes's theories about the hollow world and the polar openings. In the novel, Captain Seaborn and his crew journeyed to the inner world, where they discovered many strange plants and animals and encountered a Utopian race. The explorers eventually emerged from the interior and returned to known waters. They became rich as traders, exchanging Symzonian goods for cacao and copra.

In 1826, James McBride wrote a book entitled *Symmes' Theory of Concentric Spheres.* Meanwhile, Congress was trying to raise money to finance an expedition to the North Pole, largely to find out whether or not there were indeed openings at the northern verge.

Symmes traveled about the United States, lecturing on his theory and raising funds from private donors in order to finance his proposed expedition to the north. The Russian government offered to outfit an expedition to the Pole if Symmes would meet the party at St. Petersburg, but the American did not have the fare for the oceanic crossing. He continued to range throughout the Midwest and New England, lecturing and raising money. His disciple, Jeremiah N. Reynolds, accompanied him during the last years of his life.

During his winter lecture tour of 1828, Symmes fell ill and returned to Hamilton, Ohio, where he died on May 29, 1829.

The ice pack eventually yielded to snow-covered tundra, spotted here and there with patches of moss and lichens. In a matter of a long while, he entered a land marked by ragged growths of tough grass and stunted wind-twisted trees. There was small game here, mainly rodents of a kind he did not recognize. They appeared to have no fear of him. Killing them was easy.

Larger game animals began to show themselves as he put still more distance between the ice-bound sea and himself. He supplemented his diet of biscuits, salt pork, and rodents with venison. He walked unafraid until he saw a distant pack of wolves chase down something that looked like an elk. But wolves and elk alike looked far too large, even from where he observed them, to be the ones he had known in Europe.

After that, he kept his firearms cleaned, loaded, and primed at all times, and he carried his cutlass like a cane. When he slept, he slept ringed by fires. For all of his apprehensions, he had only one near-fatal encounter.

He had crested a hillock, on the trail of giant elk, when he saw several dozen enormous beasts grazing some distance away. The animals looked somewhat like pictures of elephants he had seen, but he recalled that elephants were not covered with shaggy reddish-brown hair, that their tusks were straighter and shorter than the impressively curved tusks of these woolly beasts.

The creature pondered the unlikelihood of his blunderbuss bringing down one of the beasts and decided to skirt the herd in the direction of a thicket.

He was almost in the shadow of the ugly trees when he heard a bellow and a crash. A massive shaggy thing as large as a coach charged him, mowing down several small trees as it burst from the thicket. Frankenstein's man dropped his blunderbuss and cutlass and hurled himself to one side as his attacker thundered past, long head down, long horn out. The beast did not turn. It galloped straight past and disappeared over the hillock. In the thicket, something coughed.

Retrieving his weapons, the creature decided to skirt the thicket.

Below the ice and snow, beyond the pine forests that were the domain of strange and yet familiar mammals, beyond glaciers and a ring of mountains, were the swampy lowlands. The bottom of the bowl-shaped continent turned out to be a realm of mist and semi-gloom, of frequent warm rains and lush growth. Cinder cones and hot springs dotted the landscape.

It was a realm of giants, too, of beasts grander and of more appalling aspect than any that the creature had previously thought possible.

He saw swamp-dwelling monsters six times larger than the largest of the odd woolly elephants. Their broad black backs broke the surface of fetid pools like smooth islets, and their serpentine necks rose and fell rhythmically as they nosed through the bottom muck, scooping up masses of soft plants, then came up to let gravity drag the mouthfuls down those incredibly long throats.

He saw a hump-backed quadruped festooned with alternating rows of triangular plates of bone along its spine. Wicked-looking spikes were clustered near the tip of the thing's muscular tail. It munched ferns and placidly regarded him as he circled it, awed, curious, and properly respectful.

He saw small flying animals that, despite their wedge-shaped heads, reminded him irresistibly of bats. There were awkward birds with tooth-filled beaks here, insects as big as rats, horse-sized lizards with ribbed sails sprouting along their spines, dog-sized salamanders with glistening polychromatic skins and three eyes. He could not set his boot down without crushing some form of life underfoot. Parasites infested him, and it was only by bathing frequently in the hot springs that he could relieve himself of his unwanted guests. Clouds of large dragonflies and other, less readily named winged things exploded from the undergrowth constantly as he slogged across the marshy continental basin, driven by the compulsion to explore and establish the boundaries of *his* world. There was life everywhere in the lowlands.

And there was the striding horror that attacked him, a hissing, snapping reptile with a cavernous maw and sharklike teeth as long as his fingers. It was the lord of the realm. When it espied the wandering patchwork man, it roared out its authority and charged, uprooting saplings and small tree ferns with its huge hind feet.

The creature stood his ground and pointed the blunderbuss. Flint struck steel, the pan flared, and, with a boom and an echo that stilled the jungle for miles, the charge caught the predator full in its lowered face.

The reptile reared and shrieked as the viscid wreckage of its eyes dribbled from its jowls and dewlap. Lowering its head again, it charged blindly and blundered past its intended victim, into the forest, where it was soon lost from sight, if not from hearing.

The creature quickly but carefully reloaded the blunderbuss and resumed his trek. A short while later, one of the blinded monster's lesser cousins, a man-sized biped with needlelike teeth and skeletal fingers, attacked. The blunderbuss blew it to pieces.

He got away from the twitching fragments as quickly as he could and watched from a distance as at least half a dozen medium-large bipeds and sail-backed lizards converged unerringly upon the spot. He turned his back on the ensuing free-for-all and, cradling the blunderbuss in his arms, looked longingly at the ice-topped mountains encircling the basin.

He had found the cold highlands infinitely more to his liking. He could not comprehend mountain-big reptiles who did nothing but eat. He was tired of being bitten and stung by insects, sick to death of mud and mist and the stench of decaying vegetation. He was, he frankly admitted to himself, not at all willing to cope with the basin's large predators on a moment-to-moment basis. The beasts of the highlands had been odd but recognizable, like parodies of the forms of that other world, the world of men.

He chuckled mirthlessly, and when he spoke, his voice sounded alien, out of place, amid the unceasing cacophony of the basin denizens' grunting, bellowing, shrilling, croaking, screeching, chittering.

What he said was, "We are all parodies here!"

It was extremely easy to become lost in the lowlands. The mists rose and fell in accordance with a logic all their own. He walked, keeping the peaks before him whenever he could see them, trusting in his sense of direction when he could not. Encounters with predatory reptiles came to seem commonplace. His blunderbuss was capable of eviscerating the lesser flesh-eating bipeds, and the cutlass was good for lopping off heads and limbs. He could outrun the darting but quickly winded sail-backed lizards. He made very wide detours around the prowling titans.

And he got lost.

He began to notice many holes in the ground as he blundered through the land of mist. He supposed that these might lead back to the world of men, but he did not care to find out. He knew where he wanted to be. He would be more than glad to let the basin's carnivorous lords have their murky realm, just as he was happy to leave men to their own world.

He finally came to a cave-pocked escarpment. Two great rivers emptied noisily into hollows at the base of the towering formation. The basalt mass rose into the mists, higher than he could see. It was isolated from his yearned-for mountains. There was no point in attempting to scale it.

He ranged back and forth across the base of the escarpment for some time, from one river to the other. He ate the eggs of the flying reptiles who made their nests on the cliff face. He slept in the caves. He sulked.

At last, he began to explore the caves that honeycombed the escarpment.

IV

Jeremiah N. Reynolds stood at the aft rail of the *Annawan* as she slid from the harbor into the vast Atlantic, windy already in October, and cold. But the *Annawan* was bound for much colder waters: those of the Antarctic.

To starboard was the *Annawan*'s sister, the *Seraph*. Together, they would cross the Atlantic along its length and sail into the summer waters of the breaking ice pack. Reynolds hoped to find Symmes's southern polar opening. He was not to have much luck.

The *Annawan* and *Seraph* expedition got as far as 62° South—far south indeed, but Antarctica had already been penetrated as deeply as 63°45′ by Palmer in 1820. A landing party was sent out toward the Pole, or, as Reynolds hoped, toward the southern verge. Symmes had thought that the concavities toward the interior world would be located at or just above latitude 82°. Reynolds and his party had come so close, but bad weather forced them to wait, and then supplies ran low. The party was rescued just in time. The expedition headed northward before the Antarctic winter could close on them.

It was while Reynolds was with his ill-fated landing party that John Cleves Symmes died in Ohio, but Reynolds was not to learn this for nearly a year. Off the coast of Chile, the *Seraph*'s crew mutinied, put Reynolds and the officers ashore, and took off for a life of piracy.

Jeremiah N. Reynolds devoted the next three or four years to various South Seas expeditions, to whaling, to botanical and zoological studies in the Pacific. He continued to defend Symmes's theories and traveled about the United States to gain support, as Symmes had done before him, for a gigantic assault upon the interior world.

The creature went down.

He lost his way a second time and could only wander aimlessly through the caves, and he went down.

Into another world.

Into the world containing the great open sea, fed by the two great rivers that drained into hollows beneath the great escarpment. This second interior world was illuminated by electrical discharges and filled with constant thunder. There was a fringe of land populated by a few small animals and sparse, blighted plants.

The creature could not find his way back up to the basin. He had no choice but to pass through the world of the great open sea, into a third interior world.

There was a fourth world, a fifth, a sixth, and probably more that were not in line with his burrowing course. He moved constantly, eating what he could find, amazed and appalled by the extremes represented by the various worlds. He caught himself dreaming of the sun and moon, of days and nights. But, if he ever felt the old stirrings of loneliness now, he did not admit as much to himself. Good or bad, he told himself, these worlds were his to claim if he chose to do so. He did not need companionship.

Even so, even so, he left his mark for others to see.

There was an ape in one of the interior worlds. It was the largest ape that had ever lived in or on the earth, and, though it was an outsider to all of the ape tribes in its cavernous habitat, it ruled over them like some human monarch. It came and went freely from band to band. What it wanted, it took. This ranged from simple backrubs to sexual favors. While it was at one of the females in a given band, the erstwhile dominant males would go off to bite mushroom stalks or shake trees or do some other displacement activity. Had they interfered, the great ape would have killed them.

Frankenstein's creature tripped over the ape as the latter slept in a tangle of dead plant stalks.

The patchwork man lost the third finger on his left hand.

The great ape lost its life, its hide, and some of its meat. A pack of lesser pongids came across the carcass after the victor had departed. They gave the place a wide berth thereafter, for they reasoned among themselves—dimly, of course—that no animal had done this. No animal could have skinned the great ape that way. Something new and more terrible stalked the world now, something too dangerous, too wild, for them to understand.

They heard from other tribes that the thing that had taken the skin carried it over its shoulders. The thing looked much like a hairless ape. It made the lightning-flames with its hands and placed meat in the fire before eating it.

They would nervously look behind themselves for generations to come, fearing the new thing infinitely more than they had ever feared the great ape whose skin it had taken.

ʊ

The Franklin expedition set out for the North Pole in the summer of 1844. Sir John Franklin took with him two ships, the *Erebus* and the *Terror*. These were powerful three-masted vessels with steam screws. They were made to conquer the Arctic.

The Franklin expedition was lost with all 129 members. The Arctic was the scene of a search for survivors for more than forty years afterward. During the course of these rescue missions, more of the north was mapped than had previously been dreamed possible.

In the 1860s, an American lived for several years among the Esquimaux to the north and west of Hudson Bay. He continually troubled them with questions, perhaps in the hope of learning something of the last days of the Franklin expedition.

He finally came to a village in which the storyteller, an old woman, told him of a number of white men who had pulled a boat across the ice. The American plied the storyteller with questions and soon realized that she was not talking about survivors of the Franklin expedition of fifteen years before. She was recounting the story of some survivors of one of Frobisher's voyages, three hundred years before, in search of the Northwest Passage.

The creature fought his way through other lands, and somewhere he passed by the middle of the earth and never knew it.

The next world he conquered, for human beings lived there.

VI

Some Navaho, all of the Hopi, and the Pueblo Indians of the American Southwest each have a legend about the Under-Earth People, their gods.

The legends all begin:

It was dark under the earth, and the people who lived there wanted to come up. So they came up through the holes in the ground, and they found this new world with the sun in the sky. They went back down and returned with their uncles and their cousins. Then, when they all got here, they made us.

In the center of the villages are kivas, underground structures in which religious ceremonies are held. In the center of the floor of each kiva is a well, going far down out of sight. It is from the wells that the first men are said to have come to the outside world.

The memory of the Hopi may be better than that of the Esquimaux. The Hopi remember further back than Frobisher. If you ask them, they will tell of Esteban, the black slave of Cabeza de Vaca. They will tell of the corn circle they made when Coronado came, and of the fight in the clouds of the highest pueblo, and how many had to jump to their deaths when the village was set afire by the Spaniards.

But, mostly, the Hopi remember Esteban, the second outsider whom they ever saw. Esteban was tall and black. He had thick lips, and he loved to eat chili peppers, they will tell you.

That was 1538.

And in the center of each pueblo is a kiva, where the first men came from inside the earth.

He saw them first as they paddled animal-hide boats through the quietness of a calm lake where he drank. They were indistinct blobs of men, difficult to see in the perpetual twilight of this new interior world. But they were men.

The creature withdrew into the shadows beneath the grayish soft-barked trees and watched thoughtfully as the men paddled past and vanished into the gloom.

Men. Men *here*. In *his* world. *How?* He weighed the blunderbuss in his hands. Could mere men have fought their way this far into the earth? Even with ships in which to cross the Arctic sea, even with firearms and warm clothing and the strength of numbers, could poor, weak human beings do what he had done? How could there be men here? How? Were they native to this subterranean world? He shrugged in his ape-hide cloak, and a frown creased his broad forehead.

I know what to expect of men. I will leave this place and go. . . .

Where? Back to the cavern of the apes? Back to the land of heat and molten rock? Back to the great open sea?

No, he thought, then said the word aloud. "No." The inner world belongs to me. All of it. I won't share it with men. He made a careful check of his firearms, shouldered the blunderbuss, and set out to find these human beings.

He tried to remain alert and wary as he walked, for there were dangers other than men in this world. Once, from a safe distance, he had seen a vaguely bearlike beast tearing at a carcass. Another time, he had watched as an obviously large flying reptile, larger by far than the delicate horrors he had observed in the basin, glided past, a black silhouette against the swirling gray murk overhead. Yet another time, he had happened upon the spoor of a four-footed animal whose claw-tipped paws left impressions six inches wide. Only a fool would not have been cautious here. But, still, his mind wandered.

I could attack these men, he told himself. I have weapons, and I have my great strength. And I cannot die by ordinary means. I would have the element of surprise in my favor, too. I could charge into their camp and wipe them out easily. And then, once again, I would be free to come and go as I please. If I do not kill them now, when the odds favor me, they'll find out about me eventually, and then I'll have to fight them anyway. They will not tolerate my existence once they know.

But . . . He stopped, perplexed by a sudden thought. But what if these men are different from those I knew before? Idiotic notion! Don't delude yourself. You know what men are like. They hate you on sight. You don't belong with men. You aren't a man, and you have no place among men. But what if . . .?

He had eaten several times and slept twice when he finally located a squalid village built on the shore of a deep inlet. From a vantage point among the trees, the creature could see that the village consisted of perhaps two dozen lodges, crudely fashioned of poles and hides. He saw women smoking fish on racks and chewing animal skins to soften them while the men repaired their ungainly boats at the water's edge. Naked children ran among the lodges, chasing dogs and small piglike animals.

The men, he noted, were armed mainly with spears, though a very few also had what appeared to be iron swords of primitive design at their sides. He smiled grimly, envisioning the psychological impact his blunderbuss's discharge might have upon such poorly armed opponents.

He was thinking about tactics when a long, low craft hove into view at the mouth of the inlet and sped toward the beach. The men on the shore shouted and waved. The women put aside their skins, and the children raced a yelping horde of dogs to the water's edge. As soon as the canoe had been beached, its passengers—about ten men—were mobbed. The sounds were jubilant. The sounds were of welcome. In his place of hiding, Frankenstein's man unexpectedly found himself sick at heart.

Now, whispered a part of himself. Creep down now, and begin killing them while their attention is diverted.

He regarded the blunderbuss in his hands. At close range, it could probably kill two or three people at once, and possibly maim others. He felt the pistols digging into his skin where his belt held them against his abdomen. He closed his eyes and saw heads and bellies splitting open as he strode through the village, swinging the cutlass in devastating arcs. He saw all of the villagers dead and mutilated on the ground before him. The palms of his hands started to itch. Kill them off.

A celebration was getting underway in the village. Eyes still closed, the creature listened to the thin, shrill laughter, to the bursts of song. Something twisted a knife in his heart, and he knew that he was helpless to do anything to these people.

He wanted to go down into the village. He wanted to be with these people. He wanted to be of them. He had not known that he was so painfully lonely. I still want people, he bleakly admitted to himself. Frankenstein made me a fool. I am a monster who wants friends. I want to have a place among men. It isn't right that I should be so alone.

Cold reason attempted to assert itself. *These people will kill you if they have the chance. They don't need you. They don't want you. Your own creator turned his back on you. Frankenstein put his curse on you. Frankenstein made you what you are, and that is all you can be. A monster. An abomination in the eyes of men. A—*

Frankenstein is dead. *His work lives on.*

Frankenstein has no power over me now. I control my own life.

He was on his feet, walking into the village, and, within himself, there were still screams. *Will you throw your life away so easily? Will you—*

I want people. I want friends. I want what other men have.

Bearlike in his shaggy cloak of ape skin, he entered the village.

If Victor Frankenstein had made him a monster, the blunderbuss made him a god.

The men who had arrived in the longboat were obviously home from a fairly successful raiding trip. A quantity of goods had been heaped at the approximate center of the village. Nearby was a smaller pile of grislier trophies: severed heads, hands, feet, and genitals. The villagers had started drinking from earthen vessels, and many of them were already inebriated.

But one of the children spotted the creature as he stepped out of the shadows. A cry of alarm went up. The women and youngsters scattered. The men lurched forward with spears and swords at the ready.

The creature had stopped dead in his tracks as soon as the commotion began. Now he swung the blunderbuss up and around. He blew a patch of sod as big around as his head from the ground in front of the warriors, then watched, immensely gratified, as the spears and swords slipped, one and two at a time, from trembling hands.

"We are going to be friends," he said. And laughed with wicked delight. "Oh, Victor, were you but here!"

The creature had just had an inspired thought.

Before eighteen months had passed in the outer world, the creature was the leader of the largest war party ever seen in the interior. His firearms, coupled with his demonic appearance, guaranteed him godhood, for the barbarians who lived on the shores of the great lake were a deeply superstitious lot. They dared not incur his wrath. Their petty animosities were forgotten, or at least ignored, as he conquered village after village, impressing the inhabitants into his service.

With three hundred warriors at his back, he finally left the lake and followed a lazily winding river until he came to the first of the city-states. It was called Karac in the harsh tongue of the innerworld, and it was almost magnificent after the rude villages of the lake dwellers. Karac sent an army of five hundred men to deal with the savages howling around the walls. The creature routed Karac's army, slept, and marched into the city.

Ipks fell next, then Kaerten, Sandten, Makar, until only Brasandokar, largest of the city-states, held against him by the might of its naval forces.

Against that city the creature took with him not only his mob of warriors but also the armies of his conquered city-states, ripe for revenge. They had been under the domination of Brasandokar for a long time, and they wanted its blood. Under the creature, they got it. Two thousand men attacked in the dim twilight, from the land, from the great river. They swarmed over the gates and walls, they swept the docks and quays. Flames lit the air as the raiders ran through the stone-paved streets. They plundered, and Frankenstein's man ravaged with them.

He stopped them only when he saw the woman.

Her name was Megan, and she was the second daughter of the War Leader of Brasandokar. The creature looked up from his pillaging and saw her in the window of a low tower toward which the invaders were sweeping. He stopped the rapine and went to the tower and escorted her down. He could not say why he did this. He knew that not even the woman whom his accursed creator had begun to fashion for him had moved him so much. Megan had stood in the tower window, her head turned to the side, listening to the battle raging below. Brave? Foolish?

It took him a moment after he found her in the tower to realize that she was blind. He placed her small, pale hand upon his arm and silently led her down the stairs. Together, they entered the courtyard, and his panting blood-spattered men parted to let him pass, and all that he could think was, I have found my destiny.

Glow-lamps fashioned from luminous weed hung everywhere. The city-state of Brasandokar seemed laid out for a masked ball, but there were still embers to be found in the fire-gutted buildings, and the streets were still full of the stench of drying blood. Widows sat in doorways and sang songs of mourning. The sounds of their grief were punctuated by shouts and hammerings.

In the tower where he had first seen her, the creature sat across from Megan. She toyed restlessly with his gift, a black jewel taken from the coffers of Sandten.

I have never before seen such a beautiful woman, he thought. And then that dark and seething part of himself that had once urged the extermination of the villagers hissed, *Fool, fool* . . . He shook his head angrily. No. Not this time. Not a fool. Not a monster. A man. An emperor. A god.

A god in love for the first time in his life.

"Sir," said the Lady Megan, setting the jewel aside.

"Yes?"

"I ask you not to go on with this suit."

There was a mocking laugh inside his head. He shuddered and ground his teeth together. "Do I offend you?" he asked, and his voice sounded thick and strange.

"You are a conqueror, sir, and Brasandokar is yours to do with as you please. Your power is unlimited. A word from you, and your armies—"

"I am finished with this city, Lady Megan. I am finished with my armies. Brasandokar will show no sign of having been invaded within a matter of. . . ." He trailed off helplessly. There were no weeks in a timeless world.

She nodded slightly. "I hear people working outside. But I hear wives crying for their husbands, too. My father is still abed with his wounds, and my brother-in-law is still dead. You are still a conqueror. I cannot consider your suit. Take me as is your right, but—"

"No."

Lady Megan turned her blind eyes in the direction of his voice. "You may be thought a weak king otherwise, sir."

He rose to his full height and began pacing back and forth across the room. Not much of an emperor after all, he thought bitterly. Certainly not much of a god.

"Why do you not take me?" Lady Megan asked quietly.

Because. Because. "Because I am in love with you. I don't want to take you against your will. Because I am very ugly."

Because I am a monster. Life without soul. A golem. A travesty. Thing. It. Creature. He stopped pacing and stood by the window from which she had listened to the sack of Brasandokar. At his orders, his followers labored alongside the citizens to repair the damage inflicted upon the city. His empire would bear few scars.

Ashes in my mouth. Shall I leave now? Take away their god, and these people will soon go back to their squabbles and raids. And where can a god go now? Yes. Downriver. To the great flat river beyond Brasandokar. Into new worlds. Into old hells.

He started when he felt her hands upon his back. He turned and looked down at her, and she reached up as far as she could to run her fingers across his face and neck.

"Yes," Lady Megan said. "You are very ugly. All scars and seams." She touched his hands. "You are mismatched. Mismatched also is your heart. You have the heart of a child in the body of a beast."

"Shall I leave you, Lady Megan?"

She backed away and went unerringly to her seat. "I do not love you."

"I know."

"But, perhaps, I could come to love you."

VII

Edgar Allan Poe's first published story, "MS Found in a Bottle," was about Symmes's Hole, although Poe did not know it at the time. It wasn't until 1836, while editing Arthur Gordon Pym's manuscript, that Poe came across one of Jeremiah N. Reynolds's speeches to the U.S. House of Representatives, urging them to outfit an expedition to the South Seas. In the same issue that carried the opening installment of Pym's memoirs, Poe had an article defending both Reynolds and the theories of the late Captain Symmes.

A year after the publication of *The Narrative of Arthur Gordon Pym,* Reynolds published his book on whaling in the South Pacific, memoirs of his days as expedition scientist aboard the *Annawan.* In this book, he gave the first complete accounts of the savage white whale, Mocha Dick, who terrorized whaling fleets for half a century.

Poe and Reynolds never met.

They were married in Brasandokar. The creature had to wear his wedding signet on his little finger, since his ring finger had been bitten off by the great ape. After the ceremony, he took his Lady Megan to the tallest tower in the city and gently turned her face up so that her dead eyes peered into the murk.

"There should be stars there," he told her, "and the moon. Lights in the air. A gift to you, were I able to make it so."

"It sounds as if it would be wonderful to see."

If only I could make it so.

Sex was difficult for them, owing to the way he had been made. They managed nonetheless, and Lady Megan bore him a stillborn son. She was heartbroken, but he did not blame her. He cursed himself, his creator, the whole uncaring universe, and his own words to Victor Frankenstein came back to haunt him: "I shall be with you on your wedding night."

Frankenstein would always be with him, though he was long since dead.

In what would have been, in the outer world, the third year of their love, Kaerten revolted. Within Brasandokar, there was dissent: his generals wanted him to launch an all-out attack and raze Kaerten to the ground.

He stood in his tower and spoke to them.

"You would be as I once was. You would kill and go on killing. Otherwise, all this land would have been empty with my rage. Do you understand? I would not have stopped until everyone was dead. Then my men and I would have turned on each other. I have come to know a stillness in my soul. It came when I stopped killing. We can do the same as a people."

Still they pressed for war. The armies were restless. An example needed to be made of Kaerten, lest the other cities regard his inaction as a mark of weakness. Already, conspiracies were being hatched in Karac, in Ipks, in Makar. Brasandokar itself was not without troublemakers.

"If you want so badly to kill," he finally snarled, "come to me. I'll give you all the killing you can stomach!"

Then he stomped away to his chambers.

Lady Megan took his giant hand in both of hers and kissed it. "They will learn," she said soothingly. "You'll show them. But, for now, they can't stand that you've taught yourself not to kill."

He remained pessimistic.

"War! War! War!"

He felt Megan shiver alongside him. He drew her closer and hugged her gently, protectively. Her head rested upon his shoulder, and her hand lay upon his pale, scarred chest.

In the courtyard below, the army continued to chant. "War! War! War! War!"

He had left his bed at one point to look down upon them. Many of his original followers were in the crowd. He had shaken his fist at them.

"I'm afraid now," Megan confessed. "I remember listening at my window in my father's house when you took the city. I was frightened then, but I was curious, too. I didn't quite know what to expect, even when you came in and escorted me down. Now I'm afraid, really afraid. These men were your friends."

"Hush. Try to sleep. I've sent word to my officers. I'll make them disperse the soldiers. Or, if worse comes to worst, I'll call on the units that are still loyal to me."

He kissed her forehead and lay back, trying to shut out the chant. Let the army level Kaerten. Let the empire shudder at my wrath. But leave me in peace.

The chant abruptly broke off into a bedlam of yells punctuated by the clang of swords. The creature rolled away from the Lady Megan and sprang to the window in time to see his personal guards go down before the mob. Shrieks and curses began to filter up from the floors below.

Lady Megan sat up in bed and said, quietly, "It's happened, hasn't it?"

He made no reply as he pulled on his breeches and cloak, then went to an ornately carved wooden cabinet.

"What are you going to do?" she asked when she heard the rattle of his cutlass in its scabbard. There was a rising note of terror in her voice now.

"They still fear the firearms," he growled as he began loading the pistols. There was just enough powder and shot to arm each of the weapons, including the blunderbuss. He tossed the keg and the tin box aside, thrust the pistols and a dagger into his belt, and cradled the blunderbuss in the crook of his arm. The sounds of battle were closer. Too close.

"Stay here until I return. Bolt—"

The door bulged inward as something heavy was slammed against it on the other side. Lady Megan screamed. The creature held the muzzle of the blunderbuss a foot away from the door and fired. Within the confines of his bedchamber, the roar of the discharge hurt his eardrums, but it failed to completely drown out cries of agony.

A spear poked through one of the several holes he had blown in the door. He grabbed it away and thrust the barrel of a pistol through the hole. A second spear snaked through another hole and jabbed him in the wrist. A third stabbed him shallowly in the left side. He roared with fury and emptied his pistols into the attackers. When he had run out of firearms, he stepped back, stooped, and picked up the spear he had previously snatched.

Then the door came off its hinges and fell into the room, followed by the heavy iron bench that had battered it down. The creature impaled the first man through the door. A sword nicked him across the forearm as he whipped the cutlass out of its scabbard, catching the swordsman in the sternum. Assassins spilled into the room, stumbling over the bench and the corpses, losing hands and arms and the tops of skulls, falling and creating greater obstacles for those behind. A blade drove through his side, snapping ribs. A spear slid under his sword arm, into his belly. Another sword went into his thigh. He howled. And swung the cutlass, grunting as something crunched beneath the blade. There was no end to them. They kept coming, more than he could count, faster than he could kill them. He swung the cutlass and missed, and someone stabbed him in the groin. He swung and missed again, and someone caught him on the cheek with the flat of a blade. He swung and missed and dropped the cutlass, and something hot and sharp pierced him high in the chest, and he went down. They had killed him for the time being.

Flanked by his bodyguards, he lumbered through the streets of one of his cities. The Lady Megan, second daughter of the War Leader of Brasandokar, rode at his side in a litter borne by four strong men who panted and grumbled as they tried to match his long stride. From time to time, he would glance at the woman and smile fleetingly. She did not love him, but she had told him that she might come to love him. That was enough for now, he kept telling himself.

His people, on the other hand, would probably never learn to love him. He had their respect and their obedience. But they could not love what they feared. Their children ran away at the sight of him, and the hubbub of the marketplace diminished noticeably as he passed through. Nevertheless, he enjoyed touring the city afoot, and he was happy that Lady Megan had agreed to accompany him. He paused occasionally to describe things to her. The luster of jewels from Sandten. The patterns in cloth woven in Ipks. The iridescent scales of strange fish hauled up from the river's bottom. He took her by the quays and told her of an incredible motley of vessels, skin-hulled canoes, sail-less galleys, freight barges, flatboats, and rafts.

And one rose on the docks to confront him, and that one was Victor Frankenstein, a pale corpse with opaque eyes, frostbitten cheeks, and ice beaded on the fur of his parka.

I am waiting for you to join me, Frankenstein said. His voice was the same one that had lurked in the creature's head, calling him fool, urging him to commit monstrous deeds.

I see you at last, the creature replied.

Frankenstein looked past him to Lady Megan. You will lose everything, he told the creature, not taking his eyes from the beautiful blind woman. Even as I lost everything. We two are joined at the soul, monster, and our destinies run parallel to each other.

You're dead, Frankenstein, and I am free. Go back to the grave.

Not alone, demon. Not alone. Frankenstein laughed shrilly and, without taking a step, reached forward, his arm elongating nightmarishly, his hand darting past the creature's head toward Lady Megan's face.

Yes! Alone! He tore Victor Frankenstein to pieces on the spot, then led Lady Megan back to her tower.

The top of Megan's head came to his breastbone. She had long, fine hair of a light, almost silvery hue. Her flesh was pale, the color of subtly tinted porcelain. She had small, pointed breasts, a firm, delicately rounded belly, and slim hips. She was not much more than a girl when he married her, but she knew about sexual technique—there was no premium set on virginity in Brasandokar—and she did not mock him for his virtually total ignorance of such matters. She was the first woman he had ever seen naked.

And after their first clumsy copulation, Victor Frankenstein materialized at the foot of the bed to regard him scornfully. Megan seemed oblivious to the apparition.

Even in this respect you are a travesty, said Frankenstein, pointing at the creature's flaccid penis. You remove the beauty from all human functions.

The sin is with my maker.

The sin is that you have broken the promise you made at my deathbed. You live on, monster.

I have little choice in the matter. The creature rolled from the bed to drive the ghost away, but his knee buckled as soon as he put his weight on it, and he went sprawling on the floor. Pain exploded in his head, his torso, his limbs. He lay upon his face and gasped for breath. The earth closed in and smothered him.

It took him forever to claw his way up to the surface. The closer he got, the worse the pain became. The taste of blood was in his mouth. He moaned, raised his head, and dully looked around at the carnage. Nothing made any sense. A splintered door, knocked from its hinges. An iron bench. A litter of weapons. Blood everywhere. He dropped his head back into his hands and puzzled together the things he had seen.

Megan. Lady Megan. Where was the Lady Megan?

Horror began to gnaw within him. He dragged himself forward across the floor until he reached the corner of the bed, pushed himself up on hands and knees. Looked. Looked. Looked. Looked.

Until the sight of the bloody meat on the bed doubled him up on the floor. Until he saw only a huge swimming red ocean before him. Until he heard himself scream in animal pain and loss.

They heard him in the streets below, heard a sound like all of the demons in whom they half-believed set loose at once, and some of them unsheathed swords and made as though to return to the tower in which they had slain the conqueror, his woman, his few supporters. They stopped when they saw him at his window.

"I'll show you war!" he howled, and a metal bench crashed into their midst. Cries and moans filled the courtyard. He disappeared from the window. Moments later, a heavy cabinet sailed through the window and shattered on the pavement. It was followed by chairs, a wardrobe, the bodies of warriors.

Then he came down with his cutlass in his hand, and they broke and ran in the face of his fury, casting away their weapons, trampling those who fell. He flew at their backs, his wounds forgotten. He drove them before him, killing all whom he could reach.

He raged the breadth of Brasandokar. He demolished booths and slaughtered penned animals in the marketplace. He overturned braziers and kicked over tables laden with goods. He smashed open casks of liquor and heaved a disemboweled soldier into a public well. He grabbed a torch and set fires everywhere, and the city's burning began to light the cavern sky for miles around. He dragged people from their homes and butchered them in the gutters.

At last, he staggered to the docks, dazed, exhausted, in shock. Lowering himself onto a raft, he cut it loose and entered the current. Behind him, Brasandokar blazed, and he was tiredly certain that he had destroyed it for all time. He shook his fist at the flames.

"No scars on the face of my empire!" he shouted, but there was no feeling of triumph in his heart. Megan was still dead. Megan was dead.

Screaming, crying, he fell to the bottom of the raft. It drifted toward the great flat river where men did not go.

The creature awoke just before the river entered a low dark cavern.

How long he had drifted to this, he did not know, nor could he tell how long and how far he traveled through the cave. The river flowed smoothly. The raft sometimes nudged an invisible bank, sometimes floated aft-foremost along the water. The walls of the cavern sometimes glowed with the balefire of mushroom clusters, sometimes with a wonder of animals shining on the ceiling like moving stalactites.

More often than not, though, there was the darkness, impenetrable before and behind.

From one hell to another I go, he thought, dipping up a handful of water from the river. The water was cooler now, but were not underground streams always cool? Had he not lived in caves before, hunted by men, despised by all natural things, and had not the underground waters been cool then? He could hardly remember, but decided that the matter was unimportant anyway.

What is important is that this river leads somewhere, away from the lands of men, where I can be free of their greeds, their fears. I am warm in my cloak. My wounds heal. I still have my cutlass. I am still free. He curled up on the raft and tried to ignore the first pangs of hunger. The top of Lady Megan's head comes to my breastbone. She has long, fine hair of a light, almost silvery hue. Her flesh is. . . .

He eventually noticed the river's current slowing and its bed becoming wider and shallower. He peered into the gloom and, from the corner of his eye, saw the movement of light. He turned his head. The light vanished. The waters lay black around him.

The light reappeared in front of the raft. He stared into the water. There were small movements below: a series of dots undulated, darted away, returned. He put his hand into the water. The dots flashed away into the depths. He kept his hand in the water.

Presently, the dots snaked into sight again. He lunged, felt contact, and squeezed. Something struggled in his hand. He hauled his long arm up and over and smashed its heavy burden against the deck. The thing tried to flop away. He slammed it against the deck a second time, and it lay still. Its glow faded swiftly.

He looked around and saw more of the dots moving in the water. There was a noisy splash behind the raft. The lights winked out.

Soon the raft entered another lighted place. The light was from bracket mushrooms halfway up the walls of the cavern. The creature poled close to the bank and, as he passed, snapped off a piece of fungus. Some of its luminescence came off on his hand.

He poled back to the middle of the river, then knelt to examine the thing he had dragged from the water. It was a salamander, perhaps three feet long. Along its dorsal side was the row of phosphorescent dots that had given it over to death. The skull was flat and arrowhead-like.

He ate it happily. With his hunger quelled, he took more notice of his surroundings. The walls of the cavern were gradually curving away to the sides. The bracket mushrooms grew more thickly as he drifted farther, and the waters frequently parted where fish broke the surface. The river grew shallower, though there were places where his pole could not touch bottom. He let the weakening current carry him past these places. He wondered what might dwell at the bottoms of those deep places.

He was poling the raft forward at one point when he heard the sloshing of a large thing ahead. The water stretched flat and unbroken before him. Nothing moved below the surface. Something had frightened away the salamanders and fish. There was another splashing noise. He raised the pole like a harpoon and waited, but nothing happened. Gradually, the dotted lines reappeared in the water.

In a little while, the sides of the river slid out of sight. There was almost no current. Overhead were faint smudgy patches of light, arcing out forever before and to either side of him. Here, he thought, was the end of the great river. A vast subterranean lake. Perhaps it drained into other worlds. Perhaps it opened up to the exterior. He shrugged, willing to accept anything, and lay down on the deck to rest.

He was awakened by soft, dry rain pelting his face. He opened his eyes and, for the first time in many years, thought he saw the stars. But underground? And rain? In a cave?

The creature sat up and shook his head to clear it. This was a rain such as men had never seen. Tiny luminous things bounced off the deck of the raft. Fish swirled and turned in the water and flopped onto the deck in attempts to get the things.

He reached into his hair and drew out a pupal case, then looked up again, blinking against the cascade. From the dimly lit ceiling was falling a faintly glowing snow, and tiny winged shapes fluttered beneath the ceiling.

The creature rolled the pupal case in his hand. The worms were hatching, and the fish were going crazy with gluttony. He scooped up and killed the larger fish that flopped onto the raft, brushed piles of insect cases into the water, and left the rain of pupal cases as unexpectedly as he had entered it. As he started to eat one of his fish, he heard splashes of panic behind him as something large wallowed through the feeding schools. He could see nothing.

But, later, he was sure that he saw hazy white shapes swim past at a distance.

VIII

The dark-haired little man was dying, in delirium.

Two ward heelers had gotten him drunk that election day in Baltimore, Maryland, and taken him from place to place and had him vote under assumed names. It was common practice to gather up drunks and derelicts to swell the election rolls.

Neither of the two men knew who it was that they dragged, moaning and stumbling, between them. The man was Edgar Allan Poe, but Poe so far gone into the abyss that even the few friends he had would not have recognized him. Opium and alcohol had done their work on a mind already broken by a life of tragic accidents.

They left Poe in a doorway when the polls closed. He was found there by a policeman and taken to a small hospital. He burned with fever, he tossed in his bed, he mumbled. The hospital staff could not keep him quiet.

Early the next morning, Edgar Allan Poe stiffened and sat up in bed.

"Reynolds!" he said. "Reynolds!"

And lay back and died.

Have you no name, sir? the Lady Megan asked.

I have been called Demon, the creature replied. And worse, he added to himself. My soldiers call me the Bear, or the Ape, or the Shatterer.

But a *name,* she persisted, a real name. I cannot call you Bear or Ape.

Victor Frankenstein did not christen me.

Who was Vitter Frang—? She shook her head, unable to utter the odd syllables. Who was he? She? A friend, a god?

He told her. She looked horrified, then disappeared.

He lay on the raft and felt tears on his face. He had been crying in his sleep.

He heard their raucous cries long before he saw them. The high worm-lit cavern ceiling sloped down before him, brightening ahead. The sounds grew louder as he drifted toward the sloping roof, and he glimpsed indistinct white shapes in the water from time to time.

He stripped the rope from one end of the pole and sharpened it with his dagger. It would make a crude but lethal spear.

White shapes awaited his coming. They screamed at him and

began piling into the water on either side of his raft. They were as tall as men, with large beaks, webbed feet, and the merest vestiges of wings.

Behind them was a circle of brighter light. He bellowed his challenge at the things splashing around him and poled forward. They were too heavy to climb onto the raft, but they managed to slow his advance by massing in his path. He stabbed at them with the pole until he felt the raft crunch against the bottom. Then he leaped into the calf-deep water and sloshed toward the circle of light, swinging the pole like a club, beating a path through a cawing mass of white feathers and beaks. The light was a cool white circle ahead: the mouth of a tunnel. Eggs cracked under his feet, young birds squirmed and died as he passed.

One of the giant birds rose to block his path. A shock ran up his arm as he broke the improvised spear over its skull. Leaping over the carcass, he dashed toward the light, into the tunnel. Into a world of nightmare-polished stone of deepest ebony.

A wave of white horrors pursued him. He ran through corridors chiseled out of the rock by something far older than human beings. He glimpsed carvings on the walls and sculptures that no human hand had made, but he did not slow his feet until he had emerged into the light of a large central opening. Tunnels yawned to right and left. Above the opening was a grayish sheet of ice. It arched to form a dome. The floor of the chamber was littered with the rubble that must once have formed the roof.

The creature heard the vengeful white birds screeching at his back and plunged into one of the tunnels to find himself at the foot of a spiral ramp. It was cold there, and it had the smell of dust and antiquity. It had the smell of tumbledown churches he had seen, of dark mold and dead leaves on the forest floor. He shivered in spite of himself as he began to ascend.

He came out in a hall of glass cases and strode, wondering, past incomprehensible displays and strange machinery. Here were strangely curved hand tools, levers, and wheels in riotous profusion, brassy colors, iron, gold, silver. In one case was a curve-bladed cutting tool like a halberd-pike. The creature banged on the glass with the stump of his pole, to no effect. He put his arms around the case and toppled it, and one pane broke with a peculiarly metallic crash.

It was followed by a dim echoing sound. A gong was being struck somewhere.

The creature pulled the pike-ax from its mountings and examined it. It was made entirely of metal. It was curiously balanced. It had never been designed to be hefted by a being with hands. He was pleased with it, nonetheless, and when the first of the white birds burst into the hall and charged him, he sheared its head off with a casual swing. The gong continued to clang, and the sound was everywhere now. He ran. The decapitated bird thrashed on the floor. Its angry squawking brethren flowed into the room.

It was in a second ascending tunnel that he first saw the beings that the clangor had summoned. Shapes out of nightmare; sight beyond reason. They were paralleling his course through the tunnel. There were few of them at first, but each time he came to a lighted connecting tunnel, there were more, blocking the paths so that he could not turn aside. Their voices piped and echoed through the halls and tunnels, and he saw tentacles, cilia, myriad dim eyes as he ran.

He turned a corner, and three of the things stood in his way, their pikes raised, their bodies hunched as low as barrel-thick cones could be lowered.

His halberd chopped into the nearest of the things just below its bunched eyestalks and cilia. The top of the cone described a green-bleeding arc and ricocheted off the wall, and the trunk toppled forward, the pike slipping from tentacles. Five sets of leathery wings, like the thin arms of a starfish, began to beat and buzz spasmodically.

The creature did not pause with that ax-stroke but stepped closer and caught the second cone with his backswing. The blade stuck in the trunk. It swung its pike at his head.

He dived to the floor as the halberd whistled past, grabbed the base, and heaved. The thing went backward into the third cone. Both fell into a struggling heap. He threw himself upon them, seized bunches of eyestalks in his hands, and ripped them free. The cones' high distressed pipings ceased when he opened the trunks with a pike. It was like splitting melons.

Then he was on his way once more, his feet slippery with green ichor. More pipings sounded ahead, commingled with the raucous voices of the great white birds.

Twice he turned aside when the cones blocked his way. The third time, he realized that they were desperate to keep him out of the interconnecting tunnels. Were they guarding something? Their ruler? Their children?

He was on another group before they knew it. Piping screams of warning came too late to save the first two guards in his path. He was through them before they recovered. The pipings behind him rose in pitch and volume as he raced through the tunnel. He saw movement ahead: there was a room at the end, and two cones were slashing the air with their pikes, warning him away. Behind them, a third cone seized a wheel with its tentacles and turned it. A panel began to slide from the ceiling and close off the room.

He yelled and leaped. The cones dropped their pikes and fled. He watched them go, then looked around at the chamber. At the far side of the room was a huge metal door, studded with bolts, deadplates, and slides leading . . . where? Into darker recesses? Hell? A weapons room, a nursery? The machinery in the room gave him no clue.

The creature abruptly noted a thick, sickening smell that overlay the place's scent of antiquity. The odor seemed to be coming through cracks in that gigantic door. He stepped nearer and heard a sloshing, rolling sound, as if a putrefying carcass of vast size were being dragged. He raised his halberd.

Two cones appeared to one side. They saw him approaching the door and started to hoot and honk, their tentacles and cilia beating, their wings buzzing, their eyestalks writhing, as though imploring him to stay away from the portal. Whatever lay beyond the door, they obviously did not want him to see it. He sought only escape. Perhaps it lay there.

One of the cones threw a flask at him but missed. There was a pop and an explosion as the vial hit the wall, and fire spread an orange tongue across the floor.

For an instant, the creature felt panic, then saw that the fire separated him from the two cones but not a panel of levers and dials set in the wall next to the door. He seized levers and threw his weight upon them. Nothing happened. He tried other levers. Nothing. The helpless cones wailed with terror.

And the room began to shake.

The door through which he had come reopened. Past the snakes of flame, he saw masses of the cones pour in from the tunnel. One threw a small hatchet at him. It smashed dials near his hand. Far, far below, tremors rocked some gigantic machinery. The huge door groaned, the groan rising to a shriek of protesting metal, and slowly, ponderously, opened. It swung away on huge rollers and hinges, and a smell of death and rotting things filled the room.

The creature, huddled to one side, poised to leap through the flames, through the door to safety, stared in horror as something oozed from the opening. It flowed out forever, skirting the flames behind which he stood, moving faster and faster until it reached the hindmost of the cones now trying to escape through side tunnels. There was a greasy sucking sound, and a cone disappeared into the mass. Other cones screamed. Some fluttered their wings, rose from the floor, circled, banged into the walls like blinded canaries. They fell, and sticky edges of the gelatinous horror covered them.

There was an explosion somewhere below, and the floor sagged, cracked, yawned open. The oozing thing rippled and twisted, then slid into the fissure. As it fell from sight, another mass emerged through the door, skirted both fire and fissure, and squeezed its bulk into one of the tunnels. Screams and whistles ended in midnote. A third horror came through, then a fourth, a fifth. The earth trembled, and a seam ran from the hole in the floor to the wall and upward. Dust sifted down from the ceiling.

The creature, driven back by the fire, saw the crack open. It reached the roof of the chamber and stopped, a forty-five-degree slash up the wall. He bounded forward, squeezed himself into the rent, and started making his way up, away from the flames, away from the shapeless nightmares from behind the great portal. The pike hampered him, but he refused to abandon it.

He climbed through the ceiling and found himself in another circular chamber. The place shook and rocked, a bedlam of moving things, shrieks, and groans in the air and in the earth. Smoke billowed up from below. Piping cones swept past and paid him no attention. He ran with them, into tunnels that led upward. Always upward. He passed machinery noisily tearing itself to pieces. He passed the flightless white birds and did not bother to wonder whether they had invaded the tunnels en masse to find him or were merely some sort of livestock maintained by the cones.

Once, he saw a cone run past the mouth of a side tunnel. Pseudopodia shot out of the tunnel, snared it, and pulled it back out of sight. Once, the earth heaved and smashed him to the floor.

Upward. Always upward.

Upward, into the sunlight.

The creature followed some of the birds through a rent into a light-filled tunnel whose ceiling had fallen in. Clouds of ash fell all around. In the distance, a volcano sputtered and spat. There was a sound of continuous thunder in the air, and of masses of ice breaking up, of water turning to steam, of the earth sundering.

He screamed as the white, hot ash touched him. The birds squawked as if on fire beneath the deadly rain. The snow steamed. He hurled himself down and rolled in the snow, trying to escape, and as he rolled, he heard a roar that drowned out everything else. His ears turned his eyes in the direction of the roar. He gasped.

A crack had opened in the world. It ran straight and true across the ice cap, and down the crack came a wall of water. Roiling and seething, the waters swept past with the speed of a tornado.

He thought of the spewing volcano and of the unbridled energy that would be released when the cold water met the magma. He picked himself up, the halberd still clasped in his fist, and slogged away. The ash swirled about his head, blinding him, and covered him from head to foot.

There was a sound like the universe breaking. A giant hand struck him from behind and threw him headlong into the steaming snows. Broken white birds tumbled past. He was rolled and carried by the sound. Steam, slivers of ice, and hot ash blew past in a gale. New furies of cinders fell on him.

He picked himself up and ran. For the sea, for water, for relief from the falling hellish rain that scoured his skin. It lay ahead, a troubled line of gray against the white tongues of the land. The crack through which the cataract ran pointed like the finger of God to escape from the ash. He ran, covered with hot dust. He ran, and, overhead, birds appeared, disturbed from some ethereal rookery or nest, giving voice to harsh echoing cries as they made their way through the burning air. He ran, and the flightless birds from the caverns below fled with him. He ran, and the ghost of Victor Frankenstein uncoiled in his head, a serpent rising to sink its fangs into him.

Welcome to the Pit, Frankenstein said. And laughed. And the white ash continued to fall.

IX

Herman Melville published *Moby-Dick; or, The Whale* in 1851, to generally scathing notices. Less than four thousand copies of the novel were sold during the next three and one-half decades; it was not until 1921 that the book began to receive plaudits, and by 1921, Melville had been dead for thirty years.

The cataract worked terror on the land through which it tore. The white banks gave way and caved in. Behind was a mountain-sized wall of steam, at the heart of which could be seen the reddish glow of the volcano's maw.

Looking like a snowman built by crazy children, the creature came at last to the coast. Two miles to his left was the mouth of the crack. Most of the waddling white birds had struck out for the torrent at once, drawn by the lure of cold water. There was no doubt in his mind that the current had swept them back toward the depths below.

It must close, he thought, watching as hillocks of ice bobbed and shattered in the cataract. It must close, or the sea will fill the interior of the earth. He imagined the dark waters rushing through the tunnels of the underground city, engorging the great river, backing up to flood Brasandokar, Sandten, to the cavern of the great apes, to the cavern of magma. Another explosion, another cataclysm. The world bursting open like a ripe fruit. Good riddance to it all.

He turned and began to run around the headland, away from the roaring river. After a time, its roar diminished noticeably. He sat down on the ice, exhausted, and stared out to sea, oblivious even to the cinders that continued to fall. He could go no farther.

Welcome to the Pit, Frankenstein said again.

Go away, he thought wearily, burning with the torment of the white ash.

This is where it ends, said Frankenstein. Feel the heat of the ash, demon. Listen to the thunder of water rushing to meet magma. Hell, demon. Hell. You are home.

The creature peered into the darkness gathering over the sea. On the waters was a canoe. It was being carried toward the cataract.

He clambered to his feet, picked up the halberd, and stumbled to the edge of the sea. Two figures could be seen in the canoe, one seated in the prow, the other aft. As the canoe drew nearer, he saw that the men looked haggard, listless, and did nothing to try to alter their course. The one in the prow seemed more active, turning his face to stare at the creature on the shore.

The canoe crunched nose-first against the shore, spun in the current, rocking and heaving as it cartwheeled through the choppy waters.

The creature swung the pike-ax high over his head, out over the water, and snagged a gunwale. The ice beneath his feet threatened to crumble as he strained backward, drawing the unwieldy vessel with him, fighting the craft's weight and momentum and the pull of the current. He growled inarticulately, feeling pain in his shoulder sockets, the corded muscles of his back and legs. Wounds in his thighs opened and seeped blood.

But the long canoe came out of the water, onto the shelf.

The man at the bow was too stunned to resist. He could only stare, wide-eyed. Then the creature grabbed him and hurled him onto the ice. The man landed heavily and did not move.

The man in the stern called out feebly, his voice barely more than a croak, as the creature dragged the canoe farther inland. Ice dust lifted as the shelf shuddered and cracked, letting chunks of itself swirl away toward the cataract.

When he had gained safety, the creature wrenched the halberd from the gunwale. The man in the stern waved an oar, weakly menacing. The pike clove him from pate to clavicle.

There was a dead black man in the bottom of the canoe. He pulled out both corpses, lay the halberd in the boat, and started dragging it across the ice cap, away from the cataract, away from the ash and heat. Victor Frankenstein appeared at his side, keeping pace.

You can still kill after all, Frankenstein noted with satisfaction.

Yes. I can still kill.

Where now, demon? Hell is not to your liking?

There isn't room here for both of us, Victor.

Birds passed overhead on their way out to sea. *Tekeli-li!* they screamed. *Tekeli-li!*

X

Late in June, 1863, Professor Otto Lidenbrock, of the University of Hamburg, arrived with his nephew Axel and a guide on the rim of the Icelandic volcano Sneffel. They descended into the crater, determined to reach the interior of the earth by way of a chimney on the crater floor.

A Frenchman edited Axel Lidenbrock's subsequent account of the expedition, and it appeared in *Hetzell's Young People's Magazine for Education and Recreation* in 1864.

In New England, seventeen-year-old Abner Perry read geology and paleontology texts and tinkered together curious little inventions in the attic of his father's house.

He sculled the canoe for a long time. Even this far out, he could not rest, for the current still nibbled gently at the boat. If he rested, he might lose ground. Somehow, he had to keep paddling until he outran the pull of the waterfall to the center of the earth.

The ragged curtain of fire and ash in the air had begun to settle. The air seemed full of dust. The sun hung on the horizon like a sinking ship. It was dim and the color of blood.

He turned his gaze toward the prow and saw what he at first took to be a similarly blood-red island. A calved ice cake, perhaps, like the one that had borne him into the earth—how many years before?

Then the island sank from sight, to reemerge a hundred yards off the port gunwale. Twin corkscrews of foam rose and fell. The creature watched in awe.

The whale went under with hardly a ripple, as smoothly as a surgeon's blade slides under the skin. For a few seconds, the sea was flat, like glass, with only a few dimples as ash sifted onto it.

The whale broke the sea into a million liquid mirrors as it breached. It was huge, huge, and it stood in the air like a trout fighting to free itself of a hook. Its eyes were tiny in comparison with its bulk, and it took in the world to each side: on this, the calm sea; on that, one of the hated boats. But the boat did not pursue. A single creature stood in it.

The whale was white, white as land ice, marbled with patches like sooted snow. Its redness came from the setting sun. To the monster, the patchwork being in the boat, it was the biggest thing in the universe. It stood apart from heaven and earth. In its side were innumerable harpoons and lances, tangled lines, all covered with barnacles, unlike the whale's smooth white skin. It hung in the air like a heavy cloud, then slowly, so slowly, went back into the ocean.

The creature's heart leaped with it, and he danced in the stern of the boat.

"Free!" he yelled as the whale breached a second time, farther away. "Free! Free! Free!"

He watched, smiling, until the great whale was lost to sight. It seemed to him that God had passed through this part of the world and found it good.

A long twilight began as the sun slipped behind the horizon. The creature sculled with the sweeps, ignoring the Antarctic cold that was finally displacing the heat of the recent cataclysm. He was bound northward for the lands of men.

The stars came out slowly. Above, the twin smudges of the Magellanic Clouds shone dimly. They had lighted the way for sailors for three hundred years. They would light his.

He rowed happily, willing, for the moment, to accept whatever lay ahead. And Victor Frankenstein sat in the prow, frowning. And could say nothing.

the other dead man

GENE WOLFE

Reis surveyed the hull without hope and without despair, having worn out both. They had been hit hard. Some portside plates of Section Three lay peeled back like the black skin of a graphite-fiber banana; Three, Four, and Five were holed in a dozen places. Reis marked the first on the comp slate so that Centcomp would know, rotated the ship's image, and ran the rat around the portside of Section Three to show that.

"Report all damage," Centcomp instructed him.

He wrote quickly with the rattail: *"Rog."*

"Report all damage," flashed again and vanished. Reis shrugged philosophically, rotated the image back, and charted another hole.

The third hole was larger than either of the first two. He jetted around to look at it more closely.

Back in the airlock, he took off his helmet and skinned out of his suit. By the time Jan opened the inner hatch, he had the suit folded around his arm.

"Bad, huh?" Jan said.

Reis shook his head. "Not so bad. How's Hap?"

Jan turned away.

"How's Dawson doing with the med pod?"

"I don't know," Jan said. "He hasn't told us anything."

He followed her along the spiracle. Paula was bent over Hap, and Dawson was bent over Paula, a hand on her shoulder. Both looked up when he and Jan came in. Dawson asked, "Anybody left downship?"

Reis shook his head.

"I didn't think so, but you never know."

"They'd have had to be in suits," Reis said. "Nobody was."

"It wouldn't be a bad idea for us to stay suited up."

Reis said nothing, studying Hap. Hap's face was a pale greenish-yellow, beaded with sweat; it reminded Reis of an unripe banana, just washed under the tap. So this is banana day, he thought.

"Not all of the time," Dawson said. "But most of the time."

"Sure," Reis told him. "Go ahead."

"All of us."

Hap's breathing was so shallow that he seemed not to breathe at all.

"You won't order it?"

"No," Reis told Dawson, "I won't order it." After a moment he added, "And I won't do it myself, unless I feel like it. You can do what you want."

Paula wiped Hap's face with a damp washcloth. It occurred to Reis that the droplets he had taken for perspiration might be no more than water from the cloth, that Hap might not really be breathing. Awkwardly, he felt for Hap's pulse.

Paula said, "You're the senior officer now, Reis."

He shook his head. "As long as Hap's alive, he's senior officer. How'd you do with the med pod, Mr. Dawson?"

"You want a detailed report? Oxygen's—"

"No, if I wanted details, I could get them from Centcomp. Overall."

Dawson rolled his eyes. "Most of the physical stuff he'll need is there; I had to fix a couple things, and they're fixed. The med subroutines look okay, but I don't know. Centcomp lost a lot of core."

Paula asked, "Can't you run tests, Sid?"

"I've run them. As I said, they look all right. But it's simple stuff." Dawson turned back to Reis. "Do we put him in the pod? You *are* the senior officer fit for duty."

"And don't you forget it," Reis said. "Yes, we put him in, Mr. Dawson; it's his only chance."

Jan was looking at him with something indefinable in her eyes. "If we're going to die anyway—"

"We're not, Mr. van Joure. We should be able to patch up at

least two engines, maybe three, borrowing parts from the rest. The hit took a lot of momentum off us, and in a week or so we should be able to shake most of what's left. As soon as Ecomp sees that we're still alive and kicking, it'll authorize rescue." Reis hoped he had made that part sound a great deal more certain than he felt. "So our best chance is to head back in toward the sun and meet it part-way—that should be obvious. Now let's get Hap into that pod before he dies. Snap to it, everybody!"

Dawson found an opportunity to take Reis aside. "You were right—if we're going to get her going again, we can't spare anybody for nursing, no matter what happens. Want me to work on the long-wave?"

Reis shook his head. Engines first, long-wave afterward, if at all. There would be plenty of time to send messages when the ship lived again. And until it did, he doubted whether any message would do much good.

Lying in his sleep pod, Reis listened to the slow wheeze of air through the vent. The ship breathed again, they'd done that much. Could it have been . . . admiration, that look of Jan's? He pushed the thought aside, telling himself he had been imagining things. But still?

His mind teetered on the lip of sleep, unable to tumble over.

The ship breathed; it was only one feeble engine running at half force with a doubtful tube, and yet it was something, they could use power tools again—the welder—and the ship breathed.

His foot slipped on an oil spill, and he woke with a start. That had happened years back while they were refitting at Ocean West. He had fallen and cracked his head. He had believed it forgotten. . . .

The ship breathed. She's our mother, Reis thought. She's our mother; we live inside her, in her womb; and if she dies, we die. But she died, and we're bringing her to life again.

Someone knocked on the pod lid. Reis pushed the Retract lever and sat up.

Paula said, "Sir, I'm sorry, but—"

"What is it? Is Jan—?"

"She's fine, sir. I relieved her an hour ago. It's my watch."

"Oh," Reis said. "I didn't realize I'd been asleep." He sounded stupid even to himself.

"My orders were to call you, sir, if—"

He nodded. "What's happened?"

"Hap's dead." Paula's voice was flat, its only emotion this very lack of emotion betrayed.

Reis looked at her eyes. There were no tears there, and he decided it was probably a bad sign. "I'm truly sorry," he said. And then, "Perhaps Centcomp—"

Wordlessly, Paula pointed to the screen. The glowing green letters read: *"Resuscitation under way."*

Reis went over to look at it. "How long has this been up?"

"Five minutes, Captain. Perhaps ten. I hoped—"

"That you wouldn't have to wake me."

Paula nodded gratefully. "Yes, sir."

He wrote: *"Resp?"*

"Respiration 0.00. Resuscitation under way."

The ship breathed, but Hap did not. That, of course, was why Paula had called him "Captain" a moment ago. She must have tried pulse, tried everything, before knocking on his pod. He wrote: *"Cortex?"*

"Alpha 0.00. Beta 0.00. Gamma 0.00," Centcomp replied. *"Resuscitation under way."*

Reis wrote: *"Discon."*

There was a noticeable pause before the alpha-, beta-, and gamma-wave reports vanished. *"Resuscitation under way,"* remained stubbornly on screen.

Paula said, "Centcomp won't give up. Centcomp has faith. Funny, isn't it?"

Reis shook his head. "It means we can't rely on Centcomp the way we've been used to. Paula, I'm not very good at telling people how I feel. Hap was my best friend."

"You were his, Captain."

Desperately Reis continued, "Then we're both sorry, and we both know that."

"Sir, may I tell you something?"

He nodded. "Something private? Of course."

"We were married. You know how they still do it in some churches? We went to one. He told them we didn't belong, but we wanted to have the ceremony and we'd pay for it. I thought sure they'd say no, but they did it, and he cried—Hap cried."

Reis nodded again. "You meant a lot to him."

"That's all, sir. I just wanted somebody else to know. Thanks for listening."

Reis went to his locker and got out his suit. It shone a dull silver under the cabin lights, and he recalled a time when he had envied people who had suits like that.

"Aren't you going back to sleep, sir?"

"No. I'll be relieving you in less than an hour, so I'm going hullside to have another look around. When I come back, you can turn in."

Paula gnawed her lower lip. He was giving her something to think about besides Hap, Reis decided; that was all to the good. "Sir, the captain doesn't stand watch."

"He does when there are only four of us, dog tired. Check me through the airlock, please, Mr. Phillips."

"Of course, sir." As the inner hatch swung shut Paula said softly, "Oh, God, I'd give anything to have him back."

Neptune was overhead now; they were spinning, even if the spin was too slow to be visible. With only a single engine in service it was probably impossible to stop the spin, and there was no real reason to. The gravitational effect was so slight he had not noticed it.

He found Jupiter and then the sun, slightly less brilliant than Jupiter or Neptune but brighter than any other star. The sun! How many thousands—no, how many millions of his ancestors must have knelt and sung and sacrificed to it. It had been Ra, Apollo, Helios, Heimdall, and a hundred more, this medium-sized yellow star in a remote arm of the galaxy, this old gas-burner, this space heater laboring to warm infinite space.

If you're a god, Reis thought, why aren't you helping us?

Quite suddenly he realized that the sun *was* helping, was drawing them toward the circling inner planets as powerfully as it could. He shook his head and turned his attention back to the ship.

A faint violet spark shone, died, and rekindled somewhere on Section Six, indicating that Centcomp had at least one of its mobile units back in working order. Centcomp was self-repairing, supposedly, though Reis had never put much faith in that; human beings were supposed to be self-repairing too, but all too often were not.

And deep space was supposed to make you feel alone, but he had never really felt that way; sometimes, when he was not quite so tired, he was more alive here, more vibrant, than he ever was in the polluted atmosphere of Earth. Now Hap was dead, and Reis knew himself to be alone utterly. As he jetted over to check on the mobile unit, he wished that he could weep for Hap as he had wept for his father, though he had known his father so much less well than Hap, known him only as a large, sweet-smelling grown-up who appeared at rare intervals bringing presents.

Or if he could not cry, that Paula could.

The mobile unit looked like a tiny spider. It clung to the side of Section Three with six legs while two more welded up one of the smaller holes. Centcomp, obviously, had decided to close the smallest holes first, and for a moment Reis wondered whether that made sense. It did, he decided, if Centcomp was in actual fact fixing itself; there would be more units as well as more power available later. He swerved down toward the mobile unit until he could see it for what it was, a great jointed machine forty meters across. Three clicks of his teeth brought ghostly numerals—hours, minutes, and seconds—to his faceplate, which had darkened automatically against the raw ultraviolet from the mobile unit's welding arc. Still twenty-four minutes before he had to relieve Paula.

For a minute or two he watched the fusing of the filament patch. The patch fibers had been engineered to form a quick, strong bond; but a bit of dwell was needed just the same. The mobile unit seemed to be allowing enough, working slowly and methodically. In the hard vacuum of space there was no danger of fire, and its helium valves were on Off just as they should have been.

Reis glanced at the time again. Twenty minutes and eleven seconds, time enough yet for a quick look inside Section Three. He circled the hull and jetted through the great gaping tear, landing easily in a familiar cabin that was now as airless as the skin of the ship. The hermetic hatch that sealed Section Two from this one was tightly dogged still. He had inspected it earlier, just after the hit, and inspected it again when he had come with Dawson, Jan, and Paula to work on the least damaged engine. He threw his weight against each of the latches once again; you could not be too careful.

Nell Upson's drifting corpse watched him with indifferent eyes until he pushed her away, sending her deeper into the dark recesses of Section Three to join her fellows. In time, space would dry Nell utterly, mummifying her; radiation would blacken her livid skin. None of that had yet taken place, and without air, Nell's blood could not even coagulate—she had left a thin crimson trail of it floating in the void behind her.

Twelve minutes. That was still plenty of time, but it was time to go. When he left the side of Section Three, the mobile unit was at work on a second hole.

"Resuscitation under way," was still on the screen half an hour into Reis's watch. He read it for the hundredth time with some irritation. Was it supposed to refer to Centcomp's self-repair functions? Reis picked up the rat and wrote, *"Who's in resusc?"*

"Capt. Hilman W. Happle. Resuscitation under way."

So that was that. *"Discon."*

"Resuscitation under way."

"Clear screen," Reis scribbled.

"Resuscitation under way."

Reis cursed and wrote, *"What authority?"*

"Capt. Hilman W. Happle."

That was interesting, Reis decided—not sensible or useful, but interesting. Centcomp did not know that Hap was dead. Reis wrote, *"Capt. Happle K. Lt. Wm. R. Reis commanding."*

The screen went blank, and Reis decided to try a general instrument display. *"GID"*

The three letters faded slowly, replaced by nothing.

"Enter—GID"

That too faded to an empty screen. Reis scratched his nose and looked speculatively at the transducer headband. He had ordered the others not to use it—the hard instrumentation was amply sufficient as long as nothing too delicate was being attempted; but it had been sixteen hours since the hit, and Centcomp was still limping at best.

Multiplication became coitus, division reproduction; to add was to eat, to subtract to excrete. Glowing, Centcomp's central processor loomed before him, a dazzling coral palace with twice ten thousand spires where subroutines worked or slept. Tiny and blue alongside it, the lone mobile unit sang a Bach fugue as it labored. Smoldering leaves perfumed the breeze, washed away by a fountain of exponential functions that appeared to Reis to be calculating natural logarithms for purposes both infinite and obscure, pungently returning with each fresh gust of algorithmic air. Interactive matrices sprouted around his feet—the lilies, buttercups, and pale or burning roses that allowed his conscious mind to move here as it did, their blossoms petaled with shining elementary rows and columns.

Hap was sitting astride a tree that sprouted from the coral wall. The smile that divided his dark face when he saw Reis seemed automatic and distracted. Reis saluted, called, "Good evening, Skipper," and leaped across the laughing rill that had overflowed the fountain's rim.

Hap touched his forehead in return. "Hi ya, Bill."

Reis said, "It's damned good to see you here. We thought you were dead."

"Not me, Bill." Hap stared off into the twilight. "You can't die on duty, know that? Got to finish your tick, know what I mean, Bill boy? You want up here on the bridge?" He patted the tree trunk.

"That's okay—I'm fine where I am. Hap . . .?"

His eyes still upon something Reis could not see, Hap said, "Speak your piece."

"Hap, I checked your cortical activity. There wasn't any. You were brain-dead."

"Go on."

"That's why it was quite a surprise to run into you here, and I'm not sure it's really you. Are you Hap, or are you just a kind of surrogate, Centcomp's concept of Hap?"

"I'm Hap. Next question?"

"Why won't Centcomp terminate resuscitation?"

"Because I told it not to, as soon as we left Earth." Hap sounded as though he were talking to himself. "Not just on me, on all of us.

We're all too necessary, all of us vital. Resusc is to continue as long as—in Centcomp's judgment—there's the slightest possibility of returning a crewman to his or her duty. No overrides at all, no mutinies. Know what a mutiny is, Bill? Grasp the concept?"

Reis nodded.

"Some snotty kid's trying to take over my ship, Billy boy, trying to push me out through a hatch. That's mutiny. It's a certain Lieutenant William R. Reis. He's not going to get away with it."

"Hap . . ."

Hap was gone. Briefly, the tree where he had sat remained where it was, vacant; then it too vanished, wiped from working memory.

Something was wrong: the brilliant garden seemed haunted by sinister shadows, flitting and swift; the chaotic twilight from which Reis had emerged pressed closer to the coral palace. His head ached, there was a chill in his side, and his fingers felt oddly warm. He tried to remove the headband, willing himself to use his real arms, not the proxies that here appeared to be his arms. A hurrying subroutine shouldered him out of the way; by accident he stepped into the laughing rill, which bit his foot like acid. . . .

A smudged white cabin wall stood in place of the wall of the coral palace. Dawson was bending over him, his face taut with concern. "Reis! What happened?"

His mouth was full of blood; he spat it out. "I'm hurt, Sid."

"I know. *Christ!*" Dawson released him; but he did not fall, floating derelict in the cabin air. Dawson banged on Jan's pod.

Reis moved his right arm to look at the fingers; the warmth there was his own blood, and there was more blood hanging in the cabin, floating spheres of bright scarlet blood—arterial blood. "I'm bleeding, Sid. I think he nicked a lung. Better patch me up."

Twilight closed upon the cabin. Reis remembered how they had celebrated Christmas when he was three—something he had not known he knew, with colored paper and a thousand other wonderful things. Surely he was peeping through one of the plastic tubes the paper had come on; the few things he could see seemed small, toylike, and very bright. Everything in all the universe was a Christmas present, a fact he had forgotten long, long ago. He wondered who had brought them all, and why.

"You have been asleep in the medical pod. There is little cause for concern."

Reis searched the pod for a rat, but there was none. No backtalk to Centcomp from in here.

"Are you anxious? Fearful? Confide your fears to me. I assure you that any information that I provide concerning your condition will be both complete and correct. No matter how bad, reality is never quite so bad as our fears concerning reality."

Reis said, "Spare me the philosophy," though he knew that Centcomp could not hear him.

"And your condition is not even critical. You suffered a dangerous lesion between the fifth and sixth ribs of your right side, but you are nearly well."

Reis was already exploring the place with his fingers.

"Please reply."

"Would if I could," Reis muttered.

"You will find a rapid-access trace beside your right hand. Please reply."

"There's no God-damned rapid-access trace."

A latch clicked. Servos hummed. The pod in which Reis lay rolled forward with stately grandeur, and the pod opened. This time it was Jan who was looking down at him. "Reis, can you sit up?"

"Sure." He proved it.

Low and quick: "I want you to get into your sleeping pod with me, please. Don't ask questions—just do it, fast."

His pod was closed, but not latched from inside. He threw it open and he and Jan climbed in; she lay facing him, on her side, her back to the pod wall. He got in beside her, closed the pod, and threw the latching lever. Jan's breasts flattened against his chest; Jan's pelvis pressed his. "I'm sorry," she whispered. "I hadn't realized it would be this crowded."

"It's all right."

"Even if I had, I'd have had to ask you anyway. This is the only place I could think of where we could talk privately."

"I like it," Reis said, "so you can forget about that part. Talk about what?"

"Hap."

He nodded, though she could not have seen him in the dark. "I thought so."

"Hap was the one who stabbed you."

"Sure," Reis said. "I know that. With the rat from the med pod."

"That's right." Jan hesitated; Reis could feel her sweet breath wash across his face. At last she said, "Perhaps you'd better tell me how you knew. It might be important."

"I doubt it, but there's no reason not to. Hap thinks I'm a mutineer because I took charge when he was hurt—I was talking to him in Centcomp's conscious space. Hap had been in the med pod, and when I woke up in there the rat that should have been there was gone. A rat's stylus is long and sharp, and the whole rat's made of some sort of metal—titanium, I suppose. So a rat ought to make a pretty decent weapon."

Hair brushed his cheek as Jan nodded. "Sid found you. He woke up and realized he should have been on watch."

"Sure."

"He yelled for me, and we put you in the med pod when we saw that it was empty. There's another pod in Section Three, remember?"

"Of course," Reis said.

He waited for her to pursue that line of thought, but she seemed to veer off from it instead. "Hap's resumed command." She swallowed. "It was all right at first—he's the captain, after all. None of us even thought about resisting him, then."

Reis said slowly, "I wouldn't have resisted him either; I would have obeyed his orders, if I'd known he was alive to give them."

Jan said, "He's very suspicious now." There was a queer flatness in her voice.

"I see."

"And Reis, he's going to continue the mission."

For a moment he could not speak. He shook his head.

"It's crazy, isn't it? With the ship ripped up like it was."

"Not crazy," he told her. "Impossible."

Jan took a deep breath—he could feel and hear it, her long gasp in the dark. "And Reis, Hap's dead."

Reluctantly Reis said, "If he really wanted to proceed with the mission, maybe it's for the best. You didn't kill him, did you? You and Sid?"

"No. You don't understand. I didn't mean . . . Oh, it's so hard to say what I do mean."

Reis told her, "I think you'd better try." His right hand had been creeping, almost absently, toward her left breast. He forced it to stop where it was.

"Hap's still running the ship. He tells us what to do, and we do it because we know we'd better. But our real captain, our friend, is dead. Try to understand. The real Hap died in the med pod, and Centcomp's substituted something else—something of its own—for his soul or spirit or whatever you want to call it. When you've seen him, after you've been around him for a while, you'll understand."

"Then I ought to be outside, where I can see him," Reis said practically, "not in here. But first—"

Jan screamed, a high-pitched wail of sheer terror that was deafening in the enclosed space of the sleep pod. Reis clapped his hand over her mouth and said, "Jesus! All right, if you don't want to, we won't. Promise you won't do that again if I let you talk?"

Jan nodded, and he returned his hand to his side.

"I'm sorry," she said. "It isn't that I don't like you, or that I'd never want to. I've been under such a terrible strain. You missed it. You were in the med pod, and you can't know what it's been like for us."

"I understand," Reis told her. "Oh, hell, you know what I mean."

"If Hap isn't looking for us already, he will be soon. Or looking for me, anyway. He thinks you're still in the med pod, unless Centcomp's told him I took you out. Reis, you've got to believe me. He's going to court-martial and execute you; that's what he said when Sid and I told him we'd put you in the pod."

"You're serious?"

"Reis, you don't know what he's like now. It doesn't make any difference, we're all going to die anyway, Sid and Paula and me. And Hap's already dead." Her voice threatened to slip from tears to hysteria.

"No, we're not," he told her. "Hap's been having you fix the ship? He must have, if he's talking about carrying out the mission."

"Yes! We've got three engines running now, and the hull's airtight. We don't know—Sid and I don't know—whether we can count on Paula. If she sided with Hap it would be two against two, a man and a woman on each side, and . . ."

"Go on," Reis said.

"But if you were with us, that would be two men and a woman on our side. We'd save the ship and we'd save our lives. Nobody would have to know—we'd tell them the truth, that Hap died in the hit."

"You're not telling *me* the truth," Reis said. "If we're going to handle this together, you've got to open up."

"I am, Reis, I swear. Don't you think I know this isn't the time to lie?"

"Okay," he said. "Then tell me who's in the medical pod in Section Three. Is it Sid? Somebody's in there, or you wouldn't have brought it up."

He waited, but Jan said nothing.

"Maybe Hap sleeps in there," Reis hazarded. "Maybe he's getting himself some additional treatment. You want me to pull the plug on him, but why can't you do that yourself?"

"No. I don't think he sleeps at all. Or . . ."

"Or what?"

"He's got Nell with him—Sergeant Upson. Nell was in the pod, but she's out now, and she stays with him all the time. I didn't want to tell you, but there it is. Something else is in Three's med pod. I don't know who it was, but when it gets out we won't have a chance."

"Nell's dead." He recalled her floating body, its hideous stare.

"That's right."

"I see," Reis said, and jerked back the lever that opened the sleep pod.

"Reis, you have to tell me. Are you with us or against us?"

He said, "You're wrong, Jan. I don't have to tell you one God-damned thing. Where's Hap?"

"In Section Five, probably. He wants to get another engine on-line."

Reis launched himself toward the airlock, braked on the dog handles, and released them.

Section Three seemed normal but oddly vacant. He crossed to Centcomp's screen and wrote, *"Present occ this med pod for vis check."*

"ID" flashed on the screen.

"Lt. Wm. R. Reis."

"Refused. Resuscitation under way."

Behind him Jan said, "I tried that. Centcomp won't identify it either."

Reis shrugged and pushed off toward the emergency locker. Opening it, he tossed out breathing apparatus, the aid kit, a body bag, and a folding stretcher with tie-downs. Behind them was a steel emergency toolbox. He selected a crowbar and the largest screwdriver and jetted to the med pod.

"Tampering with medical equipment is strictly forbidden. Resuscitation under way."

Reis jammed the blade of the screwdriver into the scarcely visible joint between the bulkhead and the pod, and struck the screwdriver's handle sharply enough with the crowbar to make his own weightless bodymass jump. He let the crowbar float free, grasped the pod latch, and jerked the screwdriver down. That widened the crack enough for him to work one end of the crowbar into it.

Centcomp's screen caught his eye. It read, *"Tampering is strictly Bill stop."*

Reis said, "Jan, tell it to open the God-damned pod if it doesn't want me to mess with it."

Jan found the rat; but before she could write, the screen read, *"Bill, I cannot."*

Jan gasped, "Oh, holy God," and it struck Reis that he had never heard her swear before. He said, "I thought you couldn't hear us, Centcomp. Wasn't that the story?"

"I truly cannot, Bill, and that is no story. But I monitor conditions everywhere in the ship. That is my job, and at times I can read your lips. Particularly yours, Bill. You have very good, clear lip motion."

Reis heaved at the crowbar; tortured metal shrieked.

Jan said, "Centcomp will have told Hap. He and Nell are probably on their way up here right now."

"I have not. Lieutenant van Joure."

Reis turned to face the screen. "Is that the truth?"

"You know I am incapable of any deception, Bill. Captain Happle is engaged in a delicate repair. I prefer to take care of this matter myself in order that he can proceed without any interruption."

"Watch the dogs—the moment they start going around, tell me."

"All right," Jan said. She had already pulled a wrench from the toolbox.

"Bill, I did not want to tell you this, yet I see I must."

Reis moved the crowbar to the left and pried again. "What is it?"

"You said . . .?"

"I said what is it, God damn it! Stop screwing around and stalling. It's not going to do you any good."

"Bill, it really would be better if you did not open that."

Reis made no reply. Pale blue light was leaking from the med pod through the crack; it looked as though there might be a lot of ultraviolet in it, and he turned his eyes away.

"Bill, for your own good, do not do that."

Reis heaved again on the crowbar, and the latch broke. The pod rolled out, and as it did a nearly faceless thing inside sat up and caught his neck in skeletal hands. Section Three filled with the sickening sweetish smells of death and gangrene. Reis flailed at the half-dead thing with the crowbar; and its crooked end laid open a cheek, scattering stinking blood that was nearly black and exposing two rows of yellow teeth.

Evening was closing on Section Three. Night's darkness pressed upon Reis; his hands were numb, the crowbar gone.

Jan's wrench struck the dead thing's skull hard enough to throw her beyond the range of Reis's narrowing vision. The bony fingers relaxed a trifle. Reis forced his own arms between the dead arms and tore the hands away.

Then Jan was back, her wrench rising and falling again and again. His crowbar was gone; but the toolbox itself was within reach, with a D-shaped handle at one end. Reis grabbed it and hurled the box at the dead thing. It was heavy enough to send him spinning diagonally across the section, and it struck the head and chest of the dead thing and the end of the pod as well. For a split second Reis seemed to hear a wailing cry; the pod shot back until its bent and battered end was almost flush with the bulkhead.

Jan screamed as the airlock swung open; there was a rush of air and a scorching blue flash. Something brushed Reis's cheek. He could scarcely see, but he snatched at it and his still-numb fingers told him he held an emergency mask. He pushed it against his face, shut his eyes, and sucked in oxygen, feeling he drank it like wine. There was another searing burst of heat.

Long training and good luck put the manual control into his hands; he tore away the safety strap and spun the wheel. Driven by a fifty-thousand-psi hydraulic accumulator, the airlock door slammed shut, its crash echoing even in the depleted atmosphere of Section Three. Emergency air that Centcomp could not control hissed through the vents, and Reis opened his eyes.

Jan writhed near the airlock door, her uniform smoldering, one hand and cheek seared. The arm and welding gun of a mobile unit, sheared off at the second joint, floated not far from Jan. Reis sprayed her uniform with a CO_2 extinguisher and smeared her face and hand with blue antibacterial cream.

"My eyes . . .," she gasped.

"You've been flashed," Reis told her. He tried to keep his voice low and soothing. "Zapped by an electric arc. Open them, just for a minute, and tell me if you can see anything."

"A little."

"Good," he told her. "Now shut them and keep them closed. After a while your vision should come back a bit more, and when we get home they can give you a retinal—"

His own dimmed sight had failed to note the spinning dogs. The hatch to Section Four swung back, and Hap floated in. His sunken cheeks and dull eyes carried the hideous stamp of death, and his movements were the swift, jerky gestures of a puppet; but he grinned at Reis and touched his forehead with the steel rod he carried. "Hi there, Bill boy."

Nell Upson followed Hap. Her lips seemed too short now to conceal her teeth; it was not until she raised her pistol that Reis felt certain she was not wholly dead. Sid Dawson and Paula lingered at the hatch until Nell waved them forward. Both were terrified and exhausted, Reis decided. There could not be much fight left in either—perhaps none.

"You're supposed to salute your captain, Bill. You didn't even return mine. If I were running a tight ship, I'd have my marine arrest you."

Reis saluted.

"That's better. A lot of things have changed while you've been out of circulation, Bill. We've got three engines going. We'll have a fourth up in another forty-eight hours, and we only needed six to break away from the inner planets. Out where we are now, four should be plenty. And that's not all—we've got more air and food per crewman now than we had when we left Earth."

Reis said, "Then there's no reason we can't continue the mission."

"Way to go, Bill! Know what's happened to this old ship of ours?"

Reis shrugged. "I think so, a little. But tell me."

"We've been seized, Bill boy. Taken over, possessed. It isn't Centcomp—did you think it was Centcomp? And it sure as hell ain't me. It's something else, a demon or what they call an elemental, and it's in me, and in Centcomp, and in you too. Whatever you want to call it, it's the thing that created the *Flying Dutchman* and so on, centuries ago. We're the first ghost ship of space. You're not buying this, are you, Bill boy?"

"No," Reis told him.

"But it's the truth. There's a ship headed for us, it's coming from Earth right now—I bet you didn't know that. I wonder just how long they'll be able to see us."

Reis spat. The little grey-brown globe of phlegm drifted toward Hap, who appeared not to notice it. "Bullshit," Reis said.

Nell leveled her pistol. The synthetic ruby lens at the end of the barrel caught the light for a moment, winking like a baleful eye.

"Can I tell you what's really happened?" Reis asked.

"Sure. Be my guest."

"Centcomp's brought back you and Nell at any and all cost, because that's what you programmed it to do. You were both too far gone, but Centcomp did it anyway. You've suffered a lot of brain damage, I think—you move like it—and I don't think you can keep going much longer. If you hit a dead man's arm with a couple of electrodes, his muscles will jump; but not forever."

Hap grinned again, mirthlessly. "Go on, Bill boy."

"Every time you look at yourself, you see what you are—what you've become—and you can't face it. So you've made up this crazy story about the ghost ship. A ghost ship explains a dead captain and a dead crew, and a ghost ship never really dies; it goes on sailing forever."

Reis paused. As he had hoped, the minute reaction created by the act of spitting was causing him to float, ever so slowly, away from Hap and Nell. Soon he would be caught in the draft from the main vent. It would move him to the left, toward the Section Two hatch; and if neither changed position, Nell would be almost in back of Hap.

"Now are you still going to court-martial me?" he asked. As he spoke, fresh cool air from the vent touched his cheek.

Hap said, "Hell, no. Not if—"

Nell's boot was reaching for the edge of the Section Four hatch; in a moment more she would kick off from it. It was now or never.

Reis's hand closed hard on the tube of antibacterial cream. A thick thread of bright blue cream shot into the space before Hap and Nell and writhed there like a living thing—a spectral monster or a tangle of blue maggots.

Nell fired.

The cream popped and spattered like grease in an overheated skillet, wrapping itself in dense black smoke. Alarms sounded. Through billowing smoke, Reis saw Dawson dart toward the airlock control.

Reis's feet touched the bulkhead; he kicked backward, going for Hap in a long, fast leap. Hap's steel bar caught his right forearm. He heard the snap of breaking bone as he went spinning through the rapidly closing Section Four hatch. A rush of air nearly carried him back into Three.

Then silence, except for the whisper from the vents. The alarms had stopped ringing. The hatch was closed; it had closed automatically, of course, when Centcomp's detectors had picked up the smoke from the burning cream, closed just slowly enough to permit a crewman to get clear.

His right arm was broken, although the pain seemed remote and dull. He went to Section Four's emergency locker and found a sling for it. It would not be safe to get in a med pod, he decided, even if Hap was gone; not until somebody reprogrammed Centcomp.

The hatchdogs spun. Reis looked around for something that could be used as a weapon, though he knew that his position was probably hopeless if either Hap or Nell had survived. There was a toolbox in this locker too, but his arm slowed him down. He was still wrestling with the stretcher when the hatch opened and Dawson came through.

Reis smiled. "You made it."

Dawson nodded slowly without speaking. Jan entered; her eyes were closed, and Paula guided her with one hand.

Reis sighed. "You were able to catch hold of something. That's good, I was worried about you. Paula too."

Jan said, "Sid saved me. He reached out and snagged me as I flew past, otherwise I'd be out there in space. Paula saved herself, but Hap and Nell couldn't. It was just like you said: they didn't have enough coordination left. You were counting on that, weren't you? That Nell couldn't hit you, couldn't shoot very well anymore."

"Yes," Reis admitted. "Yes, I was, and I didn't think Hap could swat me with that steel bar; but I was wrong."

Jan said, "It doesn't matter now." She was keeping her eyes shut, but tears leaked from beneath their lids.

"No, it doesn't. Hap and Nell are finally dead—truly dead and at rest. Sid, I never thought a hell of a lot of you, and I guess I let it show sometimes; but you saved Jan and you saved the ship. Hell, you saved us all. All of us owe you our lives."

Dawson shook his head and looked away. "Show him, Paula."

She had taken something shining, something about the size of a small notepad, from one of her pockets. Wordlessly, she held it up.

And Reis, looking at it, staring into it for a second or more before he turned away, looked into horror and despair.

It was a mirror.

cosmic
realms

the events at poroth farm

T. E. D. KLEIN

As soon as the phone stops ringing, I'll begin this affidavit. Lord, it's hot in here. Perhaps I should open a window. . . .

Thirteen rings. It has a sense of humor.

I suppose that ought to be comforting.

Somehow I'm not comforted. If it feels free to indulge in these teasing, tormenting little games, so much the worse for me.

The summer is over now, but this room is like an oven. My shirt is already drenched, and this pen feels slippery in my hand. In a moment or two the little drop of sweat that's collecting above my eyebrow is going to splash onto this page.

Just the same, I'll keep that window closed. Outside, through the dusty panes of glass, I can see a boy in red spectacles sauntering toward the courthouse steps. Perhaps there's a telephone booth in back. . . .

A sense of humor—that's one quality I never noticed in it. I saw only a deadly seriousness and, I realize now, an intelligence that grew at terrifying speed, malevolent and inhuman. If it now feels itself safe enough to toy with me before doing whatever it intends to do, so much the worse for me. So much the worse, perhaps, for us all.

I hope I'm wrong. Though my name is Jeremy, derived from

Jeremiah, I'd hate to be a prophet in the wilderness. I'd much rather be a harmless crank.

But I believe we're in for trouble.

I'm a long way from the wilderness now, of course—though perhaps not far enough to save me. I'm writing this affidavit in room 2-K of the Union Hotel, overlooking Main Street in Flemington, New Jersey, twenty miles south of Gilead. Directly across the street, hippies lounging on its steps, stands the county courthouse where Bruno Hauptmann was tried back in 1935. (Did they ever find the body of that child?) Hauptmann undoubtedly walked down those very steps, now lined with teenagers savoring their last week of summer vacation. Where that boy in the red spectacles sits sucking on his cigarette—did the killer once halt there, police and reporters around him, and contemplate his imminent execution?

For several days now I have been afraid to leave this room.

I have perhaps been staring too often at that ordinary-looking boy on the steps. He sits there every day. The red spectacles conceal his eyes; it's impossible to tell where he's looking.

I know he's looking at me.

But it would be foolish of me to waste time worrying about executions when I have these notes to transcribe. It won't take long. And then, perhaps, I'll sneak outside to mail them—and leave New Jersey forever. I remain, despite all that's happened, an optimist. What was it my namesake said? "Thou art my hope in the day of evil."

There *is,* surprisingly, some real wilderness left in New Jersey, assuming one wants to be a prophet. The hills to the west, spreading from the southern swamplands to the Delaware and beyond to Pennsylvania, provide shelter for deer, pheasant, even an occasional bear—and hide hamlets never visited by outsiders: pockets of ignorance, some of them, citadels of ancient superstition utterly cut off from news of New York and the rest of the state, religious communities where customs haven't changed appreciably since the days of their settlement a century or more ago.

It seems incredible that villages so isolated can exist today on the very doorstep of the world's largest metropolis—villages with nothing to offer the outsider, and hence never visited, except by the occasional hunter who stumbles on them unwittingly. Yet as you speed down one of the state highways, consider how few of the cars slow down for the local roads. It is easy to pass the little towns without even a glance at the signs; and if there are no signs . . .? Consider, too, how seldom the local traffic turns off onto the narrow roads that emerge without warning from the woods. And when those untraveled side roads lead into others still deeper in wilderness;

and when those in turn give way to dirt roads, deserted for weeks on end. . . . It is not hard to see how tiny rural communities can exist less than an hour from major cities, virtually unaware of one another's existence.

Television, of course, will link the two—unless, as is often the case, the elders of the community choose to see this distraction as the Devil's tool and proscribe it. Telephones put these outcast settlements in touch with their neighbors—unless they choose to ignore their neighbors. And so in the course of years they are . . . forgotten.

New Yorkers were amazed when in the winter of 1968 the *Times* "discovered" a religious community near New Providence that had existed in its present form since the late 1800s—less than forty miles from Times Square. Agricultural work was performed entirely by hand, women still wore long dresses with high collars, and town worship was held every evening.

I, too, was amazed. I'd seldom traveled west of the Hudson and still thought of New Jersey as some dismal extension of the Newark slums, ruled by gangsters, foggy with swamp gases and industrial waste, a grey land that had surrendered to the city.

Only later did I learn of the rural New Jersey, and of towns whose solitary general stores double as post offices, with one or two gas pumps standing in front. And later still I learned of Baptistown and Quakertown, their old religions surviving unchanged, and of towns like Lebanon, Landsdown, and West Portal, close to Route 22 and civilization but heavy with secrets city folk never dreamed of; Mount Airy, with its network of hidden caverns, and Mount Olive, bordering the infamous Budd Lake; Middle Valley, sheltered by dark cliffs, subject of the recent archaeological debate chronicled in *Natural History,* where—in the words of the magazine—"the wanderer may still find grotesque relics of pagan worship and, some say, may still hear the chants that echo from the cliffs on certain nights"; and towns with names like Zion and Zarephath and Gilead, forgotten communities of bearded men and black-robed women, walled hamlets too small or obscure for most maps of the state. This was the wilderness into which I traveled, weary of Manhattan's interminable din; and it was outside Gilead where, until the tragedies, I chose to make my home for three months.

Among the silliest of literary conventions is the "town that won't talk"—the Bavarian village where peasants turn away from tourists' queries about "the castle" and silently cross themselves, the New England harbor town where fishermen feign ignorance and cast "furtive glances" at the traveler. In actuality, I've found, country people love to talk to the stranger, provided he shows a sincere interest in their anecdotes. Storekeepers will interrupt their activity at the cash register to tell you their theories on a recent murder; farmers will readily spin tales of buried bones and of a haunted house down the road. Rural townspeople are not so reticent as the writers would have us believe.

Gilead, isolated though it is behind its oak forests and ruined walls, is no exception. The inhabitants regard all outsiders with an initial suspicion, but let one demonstrate a respect for their traditional reserve and they will prove friendly enough. They don't favor modern fashions or flashy automobiles, but they can hardly be described as hostile, although that was my original impression.

When asked about the terrible events at Poroth Farm, they will prove more than willing to talk. They will tell you of bad crops and polluted well water, of emotional depression leading to a fatal argument. In short, they will describe a conventional rural murder, and will even volunteer their opinions as to the killer's present whereabouts.

But you will learn almost nothing from them—or almost nothing that is true. They don't know what really happened.

I do. I was closest to it.

I had come to spend the summer with Sarr Poroth and his wife. I needed a place where I could complete a lot of reading without distraction, and Poroth's farm, secluded as it was even from the village of Gilead six miles down the dirt road, appeared the perfect spot for my studies.

I had seen the Poroths' advertisement in the *Hunterdon County Democrat* on a trip west through Princeton last spring. They advertised for a summer or long-term tenant to live in one of the outbuildings behind the farmhouse. As I soon learned, the building was a long, low cinderblock affair, unpleasantly suggestive of army barracks but clean, new, and cool in the sun; by the start of summer ivy sprouted from the walls and disguised the ugly grey brick. Originally intended to house chickens, it had in fact remained empty for several years until the farm's original owner, a Mr. Baber, sold out last fall to the Poroths, who immediately saw that with the installation of dividing walls, linoleum floors, and other improvements, the building might serve as a source of income. I was to be their first tenant.

The Poroths, Sarr and Deborah, were in their early thirties, only slightly older than I, although anyone who met them might have believed the age difference to be greater; their relative solemnity, and the drabness of their clothing, added years to their appearance, and so did their hairstyles: Deborah, though possessing a beautiful length of black hair, wound it all in a tight bun behind her neck, pulling the hair back from her face with a severity that looked almost painful, and Sarr maintained a thin fringe of black beard that circled from ears to chin in the manner of the Pennsylvania Dutch, who leave their hair shaggy but refuse to grow moustaches lest they resemble the military class they've traditionally despised. Both man and wife were hardworking, grave of expression, and pale despite the time spent laboring in the sun—a pallor accentuated by the inky blackness of their hair. I imagine this unhealthy aspect was due, in part, to the considerable amount of inbreeding that went on in the area, the Poroths themselves being, I believe, third cousins. On first meeting, one might have taken them for brother and sister, two gravely devout children aged in the wilderness.

And yet there was a difference between them—and, too, a difference that set them both in contrast to others of their sect. The Poroths were, as far as I could determine, members of a tiny Mennonite order outwardly related to the Amish, though doctrinal differences were apparently rather profound. It was this order that made up the large part of the community known as Gilead.

I sometimes think the only reason they allowed an infidel like me to live on their property (for my religion was among the first things they inquired about) was because of my name; Sarr was very partial to Jeremiah, and the motto of his order was, "Stand ye in the ways, and see, and ask for the old paths, where is the good way, and walk therein." (VI:16)

Having been raised in no particular religion except a universal skepticism, I began the summer with a hesitancy to raise the topic in conversation, and so I learned comparatively little about the Poroths' beliefs. Only toward the end of my stay did I begin to thumb through the Bible in odd moments and take to quoting jeremiads. That was, I suppose, Sarr's influence.

I was able to learn, nonetheless, that for all their conservative aura the Poroths were considered, in effect, young liberals by most of Gilead. Sarr had a bachelor's degree in religious studies from Rutgers, and Deborah had attended a nearby community college for two years, unusual for women of the sect. Too, they had only recently taken to farming, having spent the first year of their marriage near New Brunswick, where Sarr had hoped to find a teaching position and, when the job situation proved hopeless, had worked as a sort of handyman/carpenter. While most inhabitants of Gilead had never left the farm, the Poroths were coming to it late—their families had been merchants for several generations—and so were relatively inexperienced.

The inexperience showed. The farm comprised some ninety acres, but most of that was forest, or fields of weeds too thick and high to walk through. Across the backyard, close to my rooms, ran a small nameless stream, nearly choked with green scum. A large cornfield to the north lay fallow, but Sarr was planning to seed it this year, using borrowed equipment. His wife spent much of her time indoors, for though she maintained a small vegetable garden, she preferred keeping house and looking after the Poroths' great love, their seven cats.

As if to symbolize their broad-mindedness, the Poroths owned a television set, very rare in Gilead; in light of what was to come, however, it is unfortunate they lacked a telephone. (Apparently the set had been received as a wedding present from Deborah's parents, but the monthly expense of a telephone was simply too great.) Otherwise, though, the little farmhouse was "modern" in that it had a working bathroom and gas heat. That they had advertised in the local newspaper was considered scandalous by some of the order's more orthodox members, and indeed a mere subscription to that innocuous weekly had at one time been regarded as a breach of religious conduct.

Though outwardly similar, both of them tall and pale, the Poroths were actually so different as to embody the maxim that "opposites attract." It was that carefully nurtured reserve that deceived one at first meeting, for in truth Deborah was far more talkative, friendly, and energetic than her husband. Sarr was moody, distant, silent most of the time, with a voice so low that one had trouble following him in conversation. Sitting as stonily as one of his cats, his expression inscrutable, he tended to intimidate visitors to the farm until they learned that he was not really sitting in judgment on them; his reserve was not born of surliness, but of shyness.

Where Sarr was catlike, his wife hid beneath the formality of her order the bubbly personality of a kitten. Given the smallest encouragement—say, a family visit—she would plunge into animated conversation, gesticulating, laughing easily, hugging whatever cat was nearby or shouting to guests across the room. When drinking—for both of them enjoyed liquor, and curiously, it was not forbidden by their faith—their innate differences were magnified: Deborah would forget the restraints placed upon women of the sect and would eventually dominate the conversation, while her husband would seem to grow increasingly withdrawn and morose.

Women here tended to be submissive to the men, and certainly the important decisions in the Poroths' lives were made by Sarr. Yet I really cannot say who was the stronger of the two. Only once did I ever see them quarrel. . . .

Perhaps the best way to tell it is by setting down portions of the journal I kept this summer. Not every entry, of course. Mere excerpts. Just enough to make this affidavit comprehensible to anyone unfamiliar with the incidents at Poroth Farm.

The journal was the only writing I did all summer; my primary reason for keeping it was to record the books I'd read each day, as well as to examine my reactions to relative solitude over a long period of time. All the rest of my energies (as you will no doubt gather from the notes below) were spent reading, in preparation for a course I plan to teach at Trenton State this fall. Or *planned,* I should say, because I don't expect to be anywhere around here come fall.

Where will I be? Perhaps that depends on what's beneath those rose-tinted spectacles.

The course was to cover the Gothic tradition from Shakespeare to Faulkner, from *Hamlet* to *Absalom, Absalom!* (And why not view the former as Gothic, with its ghost on the battlements and concern for lost inheritance?) To make the move to Gilead, I'd rented a car for a few days and had stuffed it full of books—only a few of which I ever got to read. But then, I couldn't have known. . . .

How pleasant things were, at the beginning.

June 2

Unpacking day. Spent all morning putting up screens, and a good thing I did. Night now, and a million moths tapping at the windows. One of them as big as a small bird—white—largest I've ever seen. What kind of caterpillar must it have been? I hope the damned things don't push through the screens.

Had to kill literally hundreds of spiders before moving my stuff in. The Poroths finished doing the inside of this building only a couple of months ago, and already it's infested. Arachnidae—hate the bastards; not sure why. Maybe it's genetic; they say even monkeys are afraid of them. Daydreams of Revenge of the Spiders, writhing body covered with a frenzy of hairy brown legs. "Egad, man, that face! That bloody, torn face! And the missing eyes! It looks like—no! Jeremy!" Killing spiders is supposed to bring bad luck. (Insidious Sierra Club propaganda masquerading as folk myth?) Still, I've got to rid this place of them. Can't sleep if there's anything crawling around. . . .

Supper with the Poroths. Began to eat, then heard Sarr saying grace. Apologies—but things like that don't embarrass me as much as they used to. (Is that because I'm nearing thirty?)

Chatted about crops, insects, humidity. (Very damp area—band of purplish mildew already around bottom of walls out here.) Sarr told of plans to someday build a larger house when Deborah has a baby, three or four years from now. He wants to build it out of stone. Then he shut up, and I had to keep the conversation going. (Hate eating in silence—animal sounds of mastication, bubbling stomachs.) Deborah joked about cats being her surrogate children.

All seven of them hanging around my legs, rubbing against ankles. My nose began running and my eyes itched. Goddamned allergy. Must remember to start treatments this fall when I get to Trenton. Deborah sympathetic, Sarr merely watching; she told me my eyes were bloodshot, offered antihistamine. Told them I was glad they at least believe in modern medicine—I'd been afraid she'd offer herbs or mud or something. Sarr said some of the locals still use "snake oil." Asked him how snakes were killed, quoting line from *Vathek:* "The oil of the serpents I have pinched to death will be a pretty present." We discussed wisdom of pinching snakes. Apparently there's a copperhead out back, near the brook. . . .

The meal was good—beef and noodles. Not bad for fifteen dollars a week, since I detest cooking. Spice cake for dessert, homemade, of course. Deborah is a good cook. Handsome woman, too.

Still light when I left their kitchen. Fireflies already on the lawn—I've never seen so many. Knelt and watched them awhile, listening to the crickets. Think I'll like it here.

Took nearly an hour to arrange my books the way I wanted them. Alphabetical order by authors? No, chronological . . . But anthologies mess that system up, so back to authors. Why am I so neurotic about my books?

Anyway, they look nice there on the shelves.

Sat up tonight finishing *The Mysteries of Udolpho.* Figure it's best to get the long ones out of the way first. Radcliffe's unfortunate penchant for explaining away all her ghosts and apparitions really a mistake and a bore. All in all, not exactly the most fascinating reading, though a good study in Romanticism. Montoni the typical Byronic hero/villain. But can't demand my students read *Udolpho*—too long. In fact, had to keep reminding myself to slow down, have patience with the book. Tried to put myself in frame of mind of 1794 reader with plenty of time on his hands. It works, too—I do have plenty of time out here, and already I can feel myself beginning to unwind. What New York does to people. . . .

It's almost two A.M. now, and I'm about ready to turn in. Too bad there's no bathroom in this building—I hate pissing outside at night. God knows what's crawling up your ankles. . . . But it's hardly worth stumbling through the darkness to the farmhouse, and maybe waking up Sarr and Deborah. The nights out here are really pitch-black.

. . . Felt vulnerable, standing there against the night. But what made me even uneasier was the view I got of this building. The lamp on the desk casts the only light for miles, and as I stood outside looking into this room, I could see dozens of flying shapes making right for the screens. When you're inside here it's as if you're in a display case—the whole night can see you, but all you can see is darkness. I wish this room didn't have windows on three of the walls—though that does let in the breeze. And I wish the woods weren't so close to the windows by my bed. I suppose privacy is what I wanted—but feel a little unprotected out here.

Those moths are still batting themselves against the screens, but as far as I can see the only things that have gotten in are a few gnats flying around this lamp. The crickets sound good—you sure don't hear them in the city. Frogs are croaking in the brook.

My nose is only now beginning to clear up. Those goddamned cats. Must remember to buy some Contac. Even though the cats are all outside during the day, that farmhouse is full of their scent. But I don't expect to be spending that much time inside the house anyway; this allergy will keep me away from the TV and out here with the books.

Just saw an unpleasantly large spider scurry across the floor near the foot of my bed. Vanished behind the footlocker. Must remember to buy some insect spray tomorrow.

June 9

Hot today, but at night comes a chill. The dampness of this place seems to magnify temperature. Sat outside most of the day finishing the Maturin book, *Melmoth the Wanderer,* and feeling vaguely guilty each time I heard Sarr or Deborah working out there in the field. Well, I've paid for my reading time, so I guess I'm entitled to enjoy it. Though some of these old Gothics are a bit hard to enjoy. The trouble with *Melmoth* is that it wants you to hate. You're especially supposed to hate the Catholics. No doubt its picture of the Inquisition is accurate, but all a book like this can do is put you in an unconstructive rage. Those vicious characters have been dead for centuries, and there's no way to punish them. Still, it's a nice, cynical saga for those who like atrocity scenes—starving prisoners forced to eat their girlfriends, delightful things like that. And narratives within narratives within narratives within narratives. I may assign some sections to my class. . . .

Deborah had said that dinner would be late tonight. In need of a break, I put aside the Maturin and strolled down to the brook. It was beginning to get dark: sun disappearing behind the trees, a few late birds winging home across the sky, and not a trace of moon. (Why, on moonless nights like this, do calendars proclaim a moon that's "new"?)

Back inside, I picked up one of library volumes I'd brought out—a thick dog-eared anthology. Glancing at the contents page, noticed someone had put a check mark next to one of the stories, by someone named Arthur Machen. Recognized the name from Lovecraft's essay. Welsh writer, turn of the century, though I think the story's set somewhere in England: old house in the hills, dark woods with secret paths and hidden pools. Completely lost myself in it. God, what an experience! I was a little confused by the framing device, with its bookish old recluse and his high-flown talk of sorcery, ecstasy, and sin; but the sections from the young girl's notebook were . . . staggering. That air of paganism, the malevolent little faces peeping from the shadows, and those rites she doesn't dare describe. . . . It's called "The White People," and it must be the most persuasive horror tale ever written.

Afterward, while they were getting dinner ready at the farmhouse, I was moved to climb the old tree in the side yard and to stand upright on a great heavy branch near the middle, making strange gestures and faces that no one could see. Can't say exactly what it was I did, or why. It was dark now—fireflies below me and a mist rising off the field. I must have looked like a madman's shadow as I made signs to the woods and the stars.

Lamb tonight, and damned good. I may find myself getting fat. Offered, again, to wash the dishes; I've been here a week and have never had to help. But apparently Deborah feels that's her role, and I don't care to dissuade her. So talked awhile with Sarr about his cats—the usual subject of conversation, especially because, now that summer's coming, they're bringing in dead things every night. Field mice, moles, shrews, birds, even a little garter snake. They don't eat them, just lay them out on the porch for the Poroths to see—sort of an offering, I guess. Sarr tosses the bodies in the garbage can, which, as a result, smells indescribably foul. Deborah wants to put bells around their necks; she hates mice but feels sorry for the birds. When she finished the dishes, she and Sarr sat down to watch one of their god-awful TV programs, so I came out here to read.

Spent the usual ten minutes going over this room, spray can in hand, looking for spiders to kill. Found a couple of little ones, then spent some time spraying bugs that were hanging on the screens, hoping to get in. Watched a lot of daddy longlegs curl up and die. Tended not to kill the moths, unless they were making too much of a racket banging against the screen; I can tolerate them okay, but it's only fireflies I really like. I always feel a little sorry when I kill one by mistake and see it hold that cold glow too long. (That's how you know they're dead: the dead ones don't wink. They just keep their light on till it fades away.)

The insecticide I'm using is made right here in New Jersey, by the Ortho Chemical Company. The label on the can says, WARNING: FOR

OUTDOOR USE ONLY. That's why I bought it—figured it's the most powerful brand available.

Sat in bed reading Algernon Blackwood's witch/cat story, "Ancient Sorceries" (nowhere near as good as Machen, or as his own tale "The Willows"), and it made me think of those seven cats. The Poroths have around a dozen names for each one of them, which seems a little ridiculous, since the creatures barely respond to even *one* name. Sasha, for example, the orange one, is also known as Butch, which comes from Bouche, mouth. And that's short for Eddie La Bouche, so he's also called Ed or Eddie—which in turn comes from some friend's mispronunciation of the cat's original name, Itty, short for Itty Bitty Kitty, which, apparently, he once was. And Zoë, the cutest of the kittens, is also called Bozo and Bisbo. Let's see, how many others can I remember? (I'm just learning to tell some of them apart.) Felix, or "Flixie," was originally called Paleface, and Phaedra, his mother, is sometimes known as Phuddy, short for Phuddy Duddy.

Come to think of it, the only cat that hasn't got multiple names is Bwada, Sarr's cat. (All the others were acquired after he married Deborah, but Bwada was his pet years before.) She's the oldest of the cats, and the meanest. Fat and sleek, with fine grey fur, darker than silver grey, lighter than charcoal. She's the only cat that's ever bitten anyone—Deborah, as well as friends of the Poroths—and after seeing the way she snarls at the other cats when they get in her way, I decided to keep my distance. Fortunately, she's scared of me and retreats whenever I approach. I think being spayed is what's messed her up and given her an evil disposition.

Sounds are drifting from the farmhouse. I can vaguely make out a psalm of some kind. It's late, past eleven, and I guess the Poroths have turned off the TV and are singing their evening devotions. . . .

And now all is silence. They've gone to bed. I'm not very tired yet, so I guess I'll stay up awhile and read a bit of—

Something odd just happened. I've never heard anything like it. While writing for the past half hour I've been aware, half-consciously, of the crickets. Their regular chirping can be pretty soothing, like the sound of a well-tuned machine. But just a few seconds ago they seemed to miss a beat. They'd been singing along steadily, ever since the moon came up, and all of a sudden they just *stopped* for a beat—and then they began again, only they were out of rhythm for a moment or two, as if a hand had jarred the record, or there'd been some kind of momentary break in the natural flow. . . .

They sound normal enough now, though. Think I'll go back to *Otranto* and let that put me to sleep. It may be the foundation of the English Gothics, but I can't imagine anyone actually reading it for pleasure. I wonder how many pages I'll be able to get through before I drop off.

June 10

Slept late this morning, and then, disinclined to read Walpole on such a sunny day, took a walk. Followed the little brook that runs past my building. There's still a lot of that greenish scum clogging one part of it, and if we don't have some rain soon, I expect it will get worse. But the water clears up considerably when it runs past the cornfield and through the woods.

Passed Sarr out in the field—he yelled to watch out for the copperhead, which put a pall on my enthusiasm for exploration. . . . But as it happened I never ran into any snakes, and have a fair idea I'd survive even if bitten; I doubt their poison's powerful enough to kill a healthy full-grown man. Walked around half a mile into the woods, branches snapping in my face. Made an effort to avoid walking into the little yellow caterpillars that hang from every tree. At one point I had to get my feet wet because the trail that runs alongside the brook disappeared and the undergrowth was thick. Ducked under a low arch made by decaying branches and vines, my sneakers sloshing in the water. Found that as the brook runs west it forms a small circular pool with banks of wet sand, surrounded by tall oaks, their roots thrust into the water. Lots of animal tracks in the sand—deer, I believe, and what may be a fox or perhaps some farmer's dog. Obviously a watering spot. Reminded me of places in "The White People." Waded into the center of the pool—it only came up a little past my ankles—but didn't stand there long because it started looking like rain.

The weather remained nasty all day, but no rain has come yet. Cloudy now, though; can't see any stars.

Finished *Otranto*, began *The Monk*. So far so good—rather dirty, really. Not for today, of course, but I can imagine the sensation it must have caused back in the late 1700s.

Had a good time at dinner tonight, since Sarr had walked into town and brought home some wine. (Medical note: I seem to be less allergic to cats when mildly intoxicated.) We sat around the kitchen afterward playing poker for matchsticks—very sinful indulgence, I understand; Sarr and Deborah told me, quite seriously, that they'd have to say some extra prayers tonight by way of apology to the Lord.

Theological considerations aside, though, we all had a good time and Deborah managed to clean us both out. Women's intuition, she says. I'm sure she must have it—she's the type. Enjoy being around her, and not always so happy to trek back outside, through the high grass, the night dew, the things in the soil. . . . I've got to remember, though, that they're a couple, I'm the single one, and I mustn't intrude too long. So left them tonight at eleven—or actually a little after that, since their clock is slightly out of kilter. They have this huge grandfather-type clock, a wedding present from Sarr's parents, that has supposedly been keeping perfect time for a century or more. You can hear its ticking all over the house when everything else is still. Deborah said that last night, just as they were going to bed, the clock seemed to slow down a little, then gave a couple of faster beats and started in as before. Sarr, who's pretty good with mechanical things, examined it, but said he saw nothing wrong. Well, I guess everything's got to wear out a bit, after years and years.

Back to *The Monk*. May Brother Ambrosio bring me pleasant dreams.

June 13

Read a little in the morning, loafed during the afternoon. At four-thirty watched *The Thief of Bagdad*—ruined on TV and portions omitted, but still a great film. Deborah puttered around the kitchen, and Sarr spent most of the day outside. Before dinner I went out back with a scissors and cut away a lot of ivy that has tried to grow through the windows of my building. The little shoots fasten onto the screens and really cling.

Beef with rice tonight, and apple pie for dessert. Great. I stayed inside the house after dinner to watch the late news with the Poroths. The announcer mentioned that today was Friday the thirteenth, and I nearly gasped. I'd known, on some dim automatic level, that it was the thirteenth, if only from keeping this journal; but I hadn't had the faintest idea it was Friday. That's how much I've lost track of time out here; day drifts into day, and every one but Sunday seems completely interchangeable. Not a bad feeling, really, though at certain moments this isolation makes me feel somewhat adrift. I'd been so used to living by the clock and the calendar. . . .

We tried to figure out if anything unlucky happened to any of us today. About the only incident we could come up with was Sarr's getting bitten by some animal that a cat had left on the porch. The cats had been sitting by the front door waiting to be let in for their dinner, and when Sarr came in from the field, he was greeted with the usual assortment of dead mice and moles. As he always did, he began gingerly picking the bodies up by the tails and tossing them into the garbage can, meanwhile scolding the cats for being such natural-born killers. There was one body, he told us, that looked different from the others he'd seen: rather like a large shrew, only the mouth was somehow askew, almost as if it were vertical instead of horizontal, with a row of little yellow teeth exposed. He figured that, whatever it was, the cats had pretty well mauled it, which probably accounted for its unusual appearance; it was quite tattered and bloody by this time.

In any case, he'd bent down to pick it up, and the thing had bitten him on the thumb. Apparently it had just been feigning death, like an opossum, because as soon as he yelled and dropped it the thing ran off into the grass, with Bwada and the rest in hot pursuit. Deborah was afraid of rabies—always a real danger around here, rare though it is—but apparently the bite hadn't even pierced the skin. Just a nip, really. Hardly a Friday-the-thirteenth tragedy.

Lying in bed now, listening to sounds in the woods. The trees come really close to my windows on one side, and there's always some kind of sound coming from the underbrush in addition to the tapping at the screens. A million creatures out there, after all—most of them insects and spiders, a colony of frogs in the swampy part of the woods, and perhaps even skunks and raccoons. Depending on your mood, you can either ignore the sounds and just go to sleep or—as I'm doing now—remain awake listening to them. When I lie here thinking about what's out there, I feel more protected with the light off. So I guess I'll put away this writing. . . .

June 15

Something really weird happened today. I still keep trying to figure it out.

Sarr and Deborah were gone almost all day; Sunday worship is, I guess, the center of their religious activity. They walked into Gilead early in the morning and didn't return till after four. They'd left, in fact, before I woke up. Last night they'd asked me if I'd like to come along, but I got the impression they were inviting me mainly to be polite, so I declined. I wouldn't want to make them uncomfortable during services, but perhaps someday I'll accompany them anyway, since I'm curious to see a fundamentalist church in action.

For most of the day, then, I was left to share the farm with the Poroths' seven cats and the four hens they'd bought last week. From my window I could see Bwada and Phaedra chasing after something near the barn; lately they'd taken to stalking grasshoppers. As I do every morning, I went into the farmhouse kitchen and made myself some breakfast, leafing through one of the Poroths' religious magazines—primitive superstitions dressed up in modern typography—and then returned to my rooms out back for some serious reading. I picked up *Dracula* again, which I'd started yesterday, but the soppy

Victorian sentimentality began to annoy me. The book had begun so well, on such a frightening note—Jonathan Harker trapped in that Carpathian castle, inevitably the prey of its terrible owner—that when Stoker switched the locale to England and his main characters to women, he simply couldn't sustain that initial tension.

With the Poroths gone I felt a little lonely and bored, something I hadn't felt out here till now. Though I'd brought shelves of books to entertain me, I was restless and wished I owned a car; I'd have gone for a drive, perhaps visited friends at Princeton. As things stood, though, I had nothing to do except watch television or take a walk.

I followed the stream again into the woods and eventually came to the circular pool. There were some new animal tracks in the wet sand, and ringed by oaks, the place was very beautiful, but still I felt bored. Again I waded into the center of the water and looked up at the sky through the trees. Feeling myself alone, I began to make some of the odd signs with face and hands that I had made that evening in the tree—but I felt that these movements had been unaccountably robbed of their power. Standing there up to my ankles in water, I felt foolish.

Worse than that, upon leaving it I found a red-brown leech clinging to my right ankle. It wasn't large and I was able to scrape it off with a stone, but it left me with a little round bite that oozed blood, and a feeling of—how shall I put it?—physical helplessness. I felt that the woods had somehow become hostile to me and, more important, would forever remain hostile. Something had passed.

I followed the stream back to the farm, and there I found Bwada, lying on her side near some rocks along its bank. Her legs were stretched out as if she were running, and her eyes were wide and astonished-looking. Flies were crawling over them.

She couldn't have been dead for long, since I'd seen her only a few hours before, but she was already stiff. There was foam around her jaws. I couldn't tell what had happened to her until I turned her over with a stick and saw, on the side that had lain against the ground, a gaping red hole that opened like some new orifice. The skin around it was folded back in little triangular flaps, exposing the pink flesh beneath. I backed off in disgust, but I could see even from several feet away that the hole had been made from the inside.

I can't say that I was very upset at Bwada's death because I'd always hated her. What did upset me, though, was the manner of it—I can't figure out what could have done that to her. I vaguely remember reading about a kind of slug that, when eaten by a bird, will bore its way out through the bird's stomach. . . . But I'd never heard of something like this happening with a cat.

I was puzzled, but I wasn't sorry; in fact, I thought, Good riddance. But I didn't know what to do with the body. Looking back, of course, I wish I'd buried it right there. . . . But I didn't want to go near it again. I considered walking into town and trying to find the Poroths because I knew their cats were like children to them, even Bwada, and that they'd want to know right away. But I really didn't feel like running around Gilead asking strange people where the Poroths were—or, worse yet, stumbling into their forbidding-looking church in the middle of a ceremony. . . .

Finally, I made up my mind to simply leave the body there and pretend I'd never seen it. Let Sarr discover it himself. I didn't want to have to tell him when he got home that his pet had been killed; I prefer to avoid unpleasantness. Besides, I felt strangely guilty, the way one often does after someone else's misfortune.

So I spent the rest of the afternoon reading in my room, slogging through the Stoker. I wasn't in the best mood to concentrate. Sarr and Deborah got back after four—they shouted hello and went into the house. When Deborah called me for dinner, they still hadn't come outside.

All the cats except Bwada were inside having their evening meal when I entered the kitchen, and Sarr asked me if I'd seen her during the day. I lied and said I hadn't. Deborah suggested that occasionally Bwada ignored the supper call because, unlike the other cats, she sometimes ate what she killed and might simply be full. That rattled me a bit, but I had to stick to my lie.

Sarr seemed more concerned than Deborah, and when he told her he intended to search for the cat after dinner—it would still be light, he said—I readily offered my help. I figured I could lead him to the spot where the body lay.

And then, in the middle of our dinner, came that scratching at the door. Sarr got up and opened it. Bwada walked in.

Now I know she was dead. She was *stiff* dead. That wound in her side had been huge, and now it was only . . . a reddish swelling. Hairless. Luckily the Poroths didn't notice my shock; they were busy fussing over her, seeing what was wrong. "Look, she's hurt herself," said Deborah. "She's bumped into something." The animal didn't walk well, and there was a clumsiness in the way she held herself. When Sarr put her down after examining the swelling, she slipped when she tried to walk away.

The Poroths concluded that she had run into a rock or some other object and had badly bruised herself; her lack of coordination, they suspect, is due to the shock, or perhaps to a pinching of the nerves. That sounds logical enough. Sarr told me before I came out here for the night that if she's worse tomorrow he'll take her to the local vet, even though he'll have trouble paying for treatment. I immediately offered to lend him money, or even pay for the visit myself, because I desperately want to hear a doctor's opinion.

My own conclusion is really not that different from Sarr's. I tend to think now that maybe, just maybe, I was wrong in believing the cat dead. Maybe what I mistook for rigor mortis was some kind of fit—after all, I know almost nothing about medicine. Maybe she really did run into something sharp, and then went into some kind of shock whose effect hasn't yet worn off. Is this possible?

But I could swear that hole came from inside her.

I couldn't continue dinner and told the Poroths my stomach hurt, which was partly true. We all watched Bwada stumble around the kitchen floor, ignoring the food Deborah put before her as if it weren't there. Her movements were stiff, tentative, like a newborn animal still unsure how to move its muscles. I suppose that's the result of her fit.

When I left the house tonight, a little while ago, she was huddled in the corner staring at me. Deborah was crooning over her, but the cat was staring at me.

Killed a monster of a spider behind my suitcase tonight. That Ortho spray really does a job. When Sarr was in here a few days ago he said the room smelled of spray, but I guess my allergy's too bad for me to smell it.

I enjoy watching the zoo outside my screens. Put my face close and confront the bugs eye to eye, then take out my spray can and zap the ones whose faces I don't like.

Tried to read more of the Stoker—but one thing keeps bothering me. The way that cat stared at me. Deborah was brushing its back, Sarr fiddling with his pipe, and that cat just stared at me and never blinked. I stared back, said, "Hey, Sarr? Look at Bwada. That damned cat's not blinking." And just as he looked up, it blinked. Heavily.

Hope we can go to the vet tomorrow because I want to ask him whether cats can impale themselves on a rock or a stick, and if such an accident might cause a fit of some kind that would make them rigid.

Cold night. Sheets are damp and the blanket itches. Wind from the woods—ought to feel good in the summer, but it doesn't feel like summer.

That damned cat didn't blink till I mentioned it.

Almost as if it understood me.

June 17

. . . Swelling on her side's all healed now. Hair growing back over it. She walks fine, has a great appetite, shows affection to the Poroths. Sarr says her recovery demonstrates how the Lord watches over animals—affirms his faith. Says if he'd taken her to a vet he'd just have been throwing away money.

Read some Le Fanu. "Green Tea," about the phantom monkey with eyes that glow, and "The Familiar," about the little staring man who drives the hero mad. Not the smartest choices right now, the way I feel, because for all the time that fat grey cat purrs over the Poroths, it just stares at me. And snarls. Maybe the accident addled its brain a bit. I mean, if spaying can change a cat's personality, certainly a goring on a rock might. . . .

Spent a lot of time in the sun today. The flies made it pretty hard to concentrate on the stories, but figured I'd get a suntan. I probably have a good tan now (hard to tell because the mirror in here is small and the light dim), but suddenly it occurs to me that I'm not going to be seeing anyone for a long time anyway, except the Poroths, so what the hell do I care how I look?

Can hear them singing their nightly prayers now. A rather comforting sound, I must admit, even if I can't share the sentiments.

Petting Felix today—my favorite of the cats, real charm—came away with a tick on my arm that I didn't discover till taking a shower before dinner. As a result, I can still feel imaginary ticks crawling up and down my back. Damned cat.

June 21

. . . Coming along well with the Victorian stuff. Zipped through *The Uninhabited House* and *Monsieur Maurice,* both very literate, sophisticated. Deep into the terrible suffering of *The Amber Witch,* poor priest and daughter near starvation, when Deborah called me in for dinner. Roast beef, with salad made from garden lettuce. Quite good. And Deborah was wearing one of the few sleeveless dresses I've seen on her. So she has a body after all. . . .

A rainy night. Hung around the house for a while reading in their living room while Sarr whittled and Deborah crocheted. Rain sounded better from in there than it does out here where it's not so cozy.

At eleven we turned on the news, cats purring around us, Sarr with Zoë on his lap, Deborah petting Phaedra, me sniffling. . . . Halfway through the wrap-up I pointed to Bwada, curled up at my feet, and said, "Look at her. You'd think she was watching the news with us." Deborah laughed and leaned over to scratch Bwada behind the ears. As she did so, Bwada turned to look at me.

The rain is letting up slightly. I can still hear the dripping from the trees, leaf to leaf to the dead leaves lining the forest floor. It will probably continue on and off all night. Occasionally I think I hear thrashings in one of the oaks near the barn, but then the sound turns into the falling of the rain.

Mildew higher on the walls of this place. Glad my books are on shelves off the ground. So damp in here my envelopes are ruined—glue moistened, sealing them all shut. Stamps that had been in my wallet are stuck to the dollar bills. At night my sheets are clammy and cold, but each morning I wake up sweating.

Finished *The Amber Witch,* really fine. Would that all lives had such happy endings.

June 22

. . . When Poroths returned from church, helped them prepare strips of molding for the upstairs study. Worked out in the toolshed, one of the old wooden outbuildings. I measured, Sarr sawed, Deborah sanded. All in all, hardly felt useful, but felt good to be doing something other than reading.

While they were busy, I sat staring out the window. There's a narrow cement walk running from the shed to the main house, and, as was their habit, Minnie and Felix, two of the kittens, were crouched in the middle of it taking in the late afternoon sun. Suddenly Bwada appeared on the house's front porch and began slinking along the cement path in our direction, tail swishing from side to side. When she neared the kittens she gave a snarl—I could see her mouth working—and they leapt to their feet, bristling, and ran off into the grass.

Called this to Poroths' attention. They said, in effect, Yes, we know, she's always been nasty to the kittens, probably because she never had any of her own. And besides, she's getting older.

When I turned back to the window, Bwada was gone. Asked the Poroths if they didn't think she'd gotten worse lately. Realized that, in speaking, I'd unconsciously dropped my voice, as if someone might be listening through the chinks in the floorboards.

Deborah conceded that, yes, the cat is behaving worse these days toward the others. And not just toward the kittens. Butch, the adult orange male, seems particularly afraid of her. . . .

Am a little angry at the Poroths. Will have to tell them when I see them tomorrow morning. They claim they never come into these rooms, respect privacy of a tenant, etc. etc., but one of them must have been in here because I've just noticed my can of insect spray is missing. I don't mind their borrowing it, but I like to have it by my bed on nights like this. Went over room looking for spiders, just in case; had a fat copy of *American Scholar* in my hand to crush them (only thing it's good for). Luckily, no sign of life.

Tried to read some *Walden* as a break from all the horror stuff, but found my eyes too irritated, watery. Keep scratching them as I write this. Nose pretty clogged, too—the damned allergy's worse tonight. Probably because of the dampness. Expect I'll have trouble getting to sleep.

June 24

Slept very late this morning because the noise from the woods kept me up late last night. (Come to think of it, the Poroths' praying was unusually loud as well, but that wasn't what bothered me.) I'd been in the middle of writing in this journal—some thoughts on A. E. Coppard—when it came. I immediately stopped writing and shut off the light.

At first it sounded like something in the woods near my room—an animal? a child? I couldn't tell, but smaller than a man—shuffling through the dead leaves, kicking them around as if it didn't care who heard it. There was a snapping of branches and, every so often, a silence and then a bump, as if it were hopping over fallen logs. I stood in the dark listening to it, then crept to the window and looked out. Thought I noticed some bushes moving, back there in the undergrowth, but it may have been the wind.

The sound grew farther away. Whatever it was must have been walking directly out into the deepest part of the woods, where the ground gets swampy and treacherous, because, very faintly, I could hear the sucking sounds of feet slogging through the mud.

I stood by the window for almost an hour, occasionally hearing what I thought were movements off there in the swamp, but finally all was quiet except for the crickets and the frogs. I had no intention of going out there with my flashlight in search of the intruder—that's for guys in movies, I'm much too chicken—and I wondered if I should call Sarr. But by this time the noise had stopped and whatever it was had obviously moved on. Besides, I tend to think he'd have been angry if I'd awakened him and Deborah just because some stray dog had wandered near the farm. I recalled how annoyed he'd been earlier that day when—maybe not all that tactfully—I'd asked him what he'd done with my bug spray. Still can't figure out where I misplaced it. (Must remember to walk into town tomorrow and pick up a new one.)

I went over to the windows on the other side and watched the moonlight on the barn for a while; my nose probably looked crosshatched from pressing against the screen. In contrast to the woods, the grass looked peaceful under the full moon. Then I lay in bed, but had a hard time falling asleep. Just as I was getting relaxed, the sounds started again, high-pitched wails and caterwauls from deep within the woods. Even after thinking about it all today, I still don't know whether the noise was human or animal. There were no actual words, of that I'm certain, but nevertheless there was the impression of *singing*. In a crazy, tuneless kind of way the sound seemed to carry the same solemn rhythm as the Poroths' prayers earlier that night.

The noise only lasted a minute or two, but I lay awake till the sky began to get lighter. Probably should have read a little more Coppard, but was reluctant to turn on the lamp.

. . . Slept all morning and, in the afternoon, followed the road the opposite direction from Gilead, seeking anything of interest. But the road just gets muddier and muddier till it disappears altogether by the ruins of an old homestead—rocks and cement covered with moss—and it looked so much like poison ivy around there that I didn't want to risk tramping through.

At dinner (pork chops, homegrown string beans, and pudding—quite good), mentioned the noise of last night. Sarr acted very concerned and went to his room to look up something in one of his books; Deborah and I discussed the matter at some length and concluded that the shuffling sounds weren't necessarily related to the wailing. The former were almost definitely those of a dog—dozens in the area, and they love to prowl around at night, exploring, hunting coons—and as for the wailing . . . well, it's hard to say. She thinks it may have been an owl or whippoorwill, while I suspect it may have been that same stray dog. I've heard the howl of wolves and I've heard hounds baying at the moon, and both have the same element of, I suppose, *worship* in them that these did.

Sarr came back downstairs and said he couldn't find what he'd been looking for. Said that when he moved into this farm he'd had "a fit of piety" and had burned a lot of old books he'd found in the attic. Now he wishes he hadn't.

Looked up something on my own after leaving the Poroths. *Field Guide to Mammals* lists both red and grey foxes and, believe it or not, coyotes as surviving here in New Jersey. No wolves, though.

Then, on a silly impulse, opened another reference book, *The Glass Harmonica*. Sure enough, my hunch was right: looked up June twenty-third and it said, "St. John's Eve. Sabbats likely."

I'll stick to the natural explanation. Still, I'm glad the book lists nothing for tonight; I'd like to get some sleep. There is, of course, a beautiful full moon—werewolf weather, as Maria Ouspenskaya might have said. But then, there are no wolves left in New Jersey—or so the guidebook says. . . .

(Which reminds me, really must read some Marryat and Endore.

But only after *Northanger Abbey;* my course always comes first.)

June 25

. . . After returning from town, the farm looked very lonely. Wish they had a library in Gilead with more than religious tracts. Or a stand that sold the *Times.* (Though it's strange how, after a week or two, you no longer miss it.)

Overheated from walk; am I getting out of shape, or is it just the hot weather? Decided what I needed was a cold shower. When I opened the bathroom door I accidentally let Bwada out—I'd wondered why the chair was propped against it. She raced into the kitchen, pushed open the screen door by herself, and I had no chance to catch her. (Wouldn't have attempted to anyway; her claws are wicked.) I apologized later when Deborah came in from the fields. She said Bwada had become vicious toward the other cats and that Sarr had confined her to the bathroom as punishment. The first time he'd shut her in there, Deborah said, the cat had gotten out; apparently she's smart enough to turn the doorknob by swatting at it a few times. Hence the chair.

Sarr came in carrying Bwada, both obviously out of temper. He'd seen a streak of orange running through the field toward him, followed by a grey blur. Butch had stopped at his feet and Bwada had pounced on him, but before she could do any damage Sarr had grabbed her around the neck and carried her back here. He'd been bitten once and scratched a lot on his hands, but not badly; maybe the cat still likes him best. He threw her back in the bathroom and shoved the chair against the door, then sat down and asked Deborah to join him in some silent prayer. I thumbed uneasily through a religious magazine till they were done, and we sat down to dinner.

I apologized again, but he said he wasn't mad at me, that the Devil had gotten into his cat. It was obvious he meant that quite literally. During dinner (omelet—the hens have been laying well) we heard a grating sound from the bathroom, and Sarr ran in to find her almost out the window; somehow she must have been strong enough to slide it up partway. She seemed so placid, though, once Sarr had pulled her down from the sill—he'd been expecting another fight—that he let her out into the kitchen. At this she simply curled up near the stove and went to sleep; I guess she'd worked off her rage for the day. Still, the other cats gave her a wide berth.

Watched a couple of hours of television with the Poroths. They may have gone to college, but the shows they find interesting . . . God! I'm ashamed of myself for sitting there like a cretin in front of that box. I won't even mention what we watched; whatever's on TV is ipso facto garbage.

And yet I find that the TV draws us closer, as if we were having an adventure together. Shared experience, really. Like knowing the same people or going to the same school.

But there's a lot of duplicity in those Poroths—and I don't mean just religious hypocrisy, either. Came out here after watching the news, and though I hate to accuse anyone of spying on me, there's no doubt that Sarr or Deborah has been inside this room today. I began tonight's entry with great irritation because I found my desk in disarray; this journal wasn't even put back in the right drawer. I keep all my pens on one side, all my pencils on another, ink and erasers in the middle, etc., and when I sat down tonight I saw that everything was out of place. Thank God I haven't included anything too personal in here. . . . What I assume happened was that Deborah came in to wash the mildew off the walls—she's mentioned doing so several times, and she knew I'd be in town part of the day—and got sidetracked into reading this, thinking it must be some kind of secret diary. (I'm sure she was disappointed to find that it's merely a literary journal, with nothing about her in it.)

What bugs me is the difficulty of broaching the subject. I can't just walk in and charge Deborah with being a sneak—Sarr is moody enough as it is—and even if I hint at "someone messing up my desk," they'll know what I mean and will perhaps get angry. Whenever possible I prefer to avoid unpleasantness. I guess the best thing to do is simply hide this book under my mattress from now on and say nothing. If it happens again, though, I'll definitely move out of here.

. . . I've been reading some *Northanger Abbey.* Really quite witty, as all her stuff is, but it's obvious the mock-Gothic theme isn't central to the story. I'd thought it was going to be a real parody. . . . Love stories always tend to bore me, and normally I'd be asleep right now, but my damned nose is so clogged tonight that it's hard to breathe when I lie back. Usually being out here clears it up. I've used this goddamned inhaler a dozen times in the past hour, but within a few minutes I sneeze and have to use it again. Wish Deborah'd gotten around to cleaning off the mildew instead of wasting her time looking in here for *True Confessions* and deep dark secrets. . . .

Think I hear something moving outside. Best to shut off my light.

June 30

Slept late. Read some Shirley Jackson stories over breakfast, but got so turned off at her view of humanity that I switched to old Aleister Crowley, who at least keeps a sunny disposition. For her, people in the country are callous and vicious, those in the city are callous and vicious, husbands are (of course) callous and vicious, and children are merely sadistic. The only ones with feelings are her put-upon middle-aged heroines, with whom she obviously identifies. A good thing she writes so well, or else she'd be too depressing to read.

Inspired by Crowley, walked back to the pool in the woods. Had visions of climbing a tree, swinging on vines, anything to commemorate his exploits. . . . Saw something dead floating in the center of the pool and ran back to the farm. Copperhead? Caterpillar? It had somehow opened up. . . .

Joined Sarr chopping stakes for tomatoes. Could hear his ax all over the farm. He told me Bwada hadn't come home last night, and no sign of her this morning. Good riddance, as far as I'm concerned. Helped him chop some stakes while he was busy peeling off bark. That ax can get heavy fast! My arm hurt after three lousy stakes, and Sarr had already chopped fifteen or sixteen. Must start exercising. But I'll wait till my arm's less tired.

July 2

Unpleasant day. Two A.M. now and still can't relax.

Sarr woke me up this morning—stood at my window calling, "Jeremy . . . Jeremy . . ." over and over very quietly. He had something in his hand that, through the screen, I first took for a farm implement; then I saw it was a rifle. He said he wanted me to help him. With what? I asked.

"A burial."

Last night, after he and Deborah had gone to bed, they'd heard the kitchen door open and someone enter the house. They both assumed it was me, come to use the bathroom—but then they heard the cats screaming. Sarr ran down and switched on the light in time to see Bwada on top of Butch, claws in his side, fangs buried in his neck. From the way he described it, sounds almost sexual in reverse. Butch had stopped struggling, and Minnie, the orange kitten, was already dead. The door was partly open, and when Bwada saw Sarr, she ran out.

Sarr and Deborah hadn't followed her; they'd spent the night praying over the bodies of Minnie and Butch. I *thought* I'd heard their voices late last night, but that's all I heard, probably because I'd been playing my radio. (Something I rarely do—you can't hear noises from the woods when it's on.)

Poroths took deaths the way they'd take the death of a child. Regular little funeral service over by the unused pasture. (Hard to say if Sarr and Deborah were dressed in mourning, since that's the way they always dress.) Must admit I didn't feel particularly involved—

my allergy's never permitted me to take much interest in the cats, though I'm fond of Felix—but I tried to act concerned: when Sarr asked, appropriately, "Is there no balm in Gilead? Is there no physician there?" (Jeremiah VIII:22), I nodded gravely. Read passages out of Deborah's Bible (Sarr seemed to know them all by heart), said amen when they did, knelt when they knelt, and tried to comfort Deborah when she cried. Asked her if cats could go to heaven, and received a tearful "Of course!" But Sarr added that Bwada would burn in hell.

What concerned me, apparently a lot more than it did either of them, was how the damned thing could get into the house. Sarr gave me this stupid, earnest answer: "She was always a smart cat." Like an outlaw's mother, still proud of her baby. . . .

Yet he and I looked all over the land for her so he could kill her. Barns, toolshed, old stables, garbage dump, etc. He called her and pleaded with her, swore to me she hadn't always been like this.

We could hardly check every tree on the farm—unfortunately—and the woods are a perfect hiding place, even for animals far larger than a cat. So naturally we found no trace of her. We did try, though; we even walked up the road as far as the ruined homestead.

But for all that, we could have stayed much closer to home. . . .

We returned for dinner, and I stopped at my room to change clothes. My door was open. Nothing inside was ruined, everything was in its place, everything as it should be—except the bed. The sheets were in tatters right down to the mattress, and the pillow had been ripped to shreds. Feathers were all over the floor. There were even claw marks on my blanket.

At dinner the Poroths demanded they be allowed to pay for the damage—nonsense, I said, they have enough to worry about—and Sarr suggested I sleep downstairs in their living room. "No need for that," I told him, "I've got lots more sheets." But he said no, he didn't mean that: he meant for my own protection. He believes the thing is particularly inimical, for some reason, toward me.

It seemed so absurd at the time. . . . I mean, nothing but a big fat grey cat. But now, sitting out here, a few feathers still scattered on the floor around my bed, I wish I were back inside the house. I did give in to Sarr when he insisted I take his ax with me. . . . But what I'd rather have is simply a room without windows.

I don't think I want to go to sleep tonight, which is one reason I'm continuing to write this. Just sit up all night on my new bedsheets, my back against the Poroths' pillow, leaning against the wall behind me, the ax beside me on the bed, this journal on my lap. . . . The thing is, I'm rather tired out from all the walking I did today. Not used to that much exercise.

I'm pathetically aware of every sound. At least once every five minutes some snapping of a branch or rustling of leaves makes me jump.

"Thou art my hope in the day of evil." At least that's what the man said.

July 3

Woke up this morning with the journal and the ax cradled in my arms. What awakened me was the trouble I had breathing—nose all clogged, gasping for breath. Down the center of one of my screens, facing the woods, was a huge slash. . . .

July 15

Pleasant day, St. Swithin's Day—and yet, my birthday. Thirty years old, lordy lordy lordy. Today I am a man. First dull thoughts on waking: "Damnation. Thirty today." But another voice inside me, smaller but more sensible, spat contemptuously at such an artificial way of charting time. "Ah, don't give it another thought," it said. "You've still got plenty of time to fool around." Advice I took to heart.

Weather today? Actually, somewhat nasty. And thus the weather for the next forty days, since "If rain on St. Swithin's Day, forsooth, no summer drouthe," or something like that. My birthday predicts the weather. It's even mentioned in *The Glass Harmonica*.

As one must, took a critical self-assessment. First area for improvement: flabby body. Second? Less bookish, perhaps? Nonsense —I'm satisfied with the progress I've made. "And seekest thou great things for thyself? Seek them not." (Jeremiah XLV:5) So I simply did what I remembered from the RCAF exercise series and got good and winded. Flexed my stringy muscles in the shower, certain I'll be a Human Dynamo by the end of the summer. Simply a matter of willpower.

Was so ambitious I trimmed the ivy around my windows again. It's begun to block the light, and someday, for all I know, I may not be able to get out the door.

Read Ruthven Todd's *Lost Traveller.* Merely the narrative of a dream turned to nightmare, and illogical as hell. Wish, too, that there'd been more than merely a few hints of sex. On the whole, rather unpleasant; that gruesome ending is so inevitable. . . . Took me much of the afternoon. Then came upon an incredible essay by Lafcadio Hearn, something entitled "Gaki," detailing the curious Japanese belief that insects are really demons, or the ghosts of evil men. Uncomfortably convincing!

Dinner late because Deborah, bless her, was baking me a cake. Had time to walk into town and phone parents from the booth by the general store. Happy birthday, happy birthday. Usually they don't sound three thousand miles away; on this phone, they did. Both voiced first worry—mustn't I be getting bored here? Assured them I still had plenty of books and did not grow tired of reading.

"But it's so . . . *secluded* out there," Dad said. "Don't you get lonely?"

Ah, he hadn't reckoned on the inner resources of a man of thirty. How can I get lonely, I asked, when there's still so much to read? Besides, there are the Poroths to talk to.

Then the kicker: Mom wanted to know about the cat. Last time I'd spoken to them it had sounded like a very real danger. "Are you still sleeping inside the farmhouse, I hope?"

No, I told her, really, I only had to do that for a few days while it was prowling around at night. Yes, it had killed some chickens—a hen each night, in fact. But there'd been only four of them, and when they were gone, it had stopped. We haven't had a sign of it in more than a week. (I didn't tell her that it had left the hens uneaten, dead in the nest. No need to upset her further.)

"But what it did to your sheets . . .," she went on. "If you'd been sleeping . . . Such savagery."

Yes, that was unfortunate, but there's been no trouble since. Honest. It was only an animal, after all, just a house cat gone a little wild. It posed the same kind of threat as a . . . (I was going to say, logically, wildcat; but for Mom said) nasty little dog. Like Mrs. Miller's bull terrier. Besides, it's probably miles and miles away by now. Or dead.

They offered to mail packages of food, magazines, even a portable TV, but I made it clear I needed nothing. Getting too fat, actually.

Still light when I got back. Deborah had finished the cake, Sarr brought up some wine from the cellar, and we had a nice little celebration. The two of them being over thirty, they were happy to welcome me to the fold.

It's nice out here. The wine has relaxed me and I keep yawning. It was good to talk to Mom and Dad again. Just as long as I don't dream of *The Lost Traveller,* I'll be content. And happier still if I don't dream at all. . . .

July 30

Well, Bwada is dead—this time for sure. We'll bury her tomorrow. Deborah was hurt, just how badly I can't say, but she managed to fight Bwada off. Tough woman, though she seems a little shaken. And with good reason.

It happened this way: Sarr and I were in the toolshed after dinner, building more shelves for the upstairs study. Though the fireflies were out, there was still a little daylight left. Deborah had gone up to bed after doing the dishes; she's been tired a lot lately, falls asleep early every night while watching TV with Sarr. He thinks it may be something in the water.

It had begun to get dark, but we were still working. Sarr dropped a box of nails, and while we were picking them up, he thought he heard a scream. Since I hadn't heard anything, he shrugged and was about to start sawing again when—fortunately—he changed his mind and ran off to the house. I followed him as far as the porch, not sure whether to go upstairs, until I heard him pounding on their bedroom door and calling Deborah's name. As I ran up the stairs I heard her say, "Wait. Don't come in. I'll unlock the door . . . soon." Her voice was extremely hoarse, practically a croaking. We heard her rummaging in the closet—finding her bathrobe, I suppose—and then she opened the door.

She looked absolutely white. Her long hair was in tangles and her robe buttoned incorrectly. Around her neck she had wrapped a towel, but we could see patches of blood soaking through it. Sarr helped her over to the bed, shouting at me to bring up some bandages from the bathroom.

When I returned Deborah was lying in bed, still pressing the towel to her throat. I asked Sarr what had happened; it almost looked as if the woman had tried suicide.

He didn't say anything, just pointed to the floor on the other side of the bed. I stepped around for a look. A crumpled grey shape was lying there, half covered by the bedclothes. It was Bwada, a wicked-looking wound in her side. On the floor next to her lay an umbrella —the thing that Deborah had used to kill her.

She told us she'd been asleep when she felt something crawl heavily over her face. It had been like a bad dream. She'd tried to sit up, and suddenly Bwada was at her throat, digging in. Luckily she'd had the strength to tear the animal off and dash to the closet, where the first weapon at hand was the umbrella. Just as the cat sprang at her again, Deborah said, she'd raised the weapon and lunged. Amazing . . . How many women, I wonder, would have had such presence of mind? The rest sounds incredible to me, but it's probably the sort of crazy thing that happens in moments like this: somehow the cat had impaled itself on the umbrella.

Her voice, as she spoke, was barely more than a whisper. Sarr had to persuade her to remove the towel from her throat; she kept protesting that she wasn't hurt that badly, that the towel had stopped the bleeding. Sure enough, when Sarr finally lifted the cloth from her neck, the wounds proved relatively small, the slash marks already clotting. Thank God that thing didn't really get its teeth in. . . .

My guess—only a guess—is that it had been weakened from days of living in the woods. (It was obviously incapable of feeding itself adequately, as I think was proved by its failure to eat the hens it had killed.) While Sarr dressed Deborah's wounds, I pulled back the bedclothes and took a closer look at the animal's body. The fur was matted and patchy, and in its side was a puncture ringed by flaps of skin, almost as if the flesh had been pushed outward. I suspect there's a simple explanation: it was Deborah's extraordinary good luck to have jabbed the animal precisely in its old wound, which the point of the umbrella reopened. Naturally I didn't mention this to Sarr.

He made dinner for us tonight—soup, actually, because he thought that was best for Deborah. Her voice sounded so bad he told her not to strain it any more by talking, at which she nodded and smiled. We both had to help her downstairs, as she was clearly weak from shock.

In the morning Sarr will have the doctor out. He'll have to examine the cat, too, to check for rabies, so we put the body in the freezer to preserve it as well as possible. Afterward we'll bury it.

Deborah seemed okay when I left. Sarr was reading through some medical books, and she was just lying on the living-room couch gazing at her husband with a look of purest gratitude—not moving, not saying anything, eyes wide and unblinking.

I feel quite relieved. God knows how many nights I've lain here thinking every sound I heard was Bwada. I'll feel more relieved, of course, when that demon's safely underground; but I think I can say, at the risk of being melodramatic, that the reign of terror is over.

Hmm, I'm still a little hungry—I'm used to more than soup for dinner. These daily push-ups burn up energy. I'll probably dream of hamburgers and chocolate layer cakes.

July 31

. . . The doctor collected scrapings from Bwada's teeth and scolded us for doing a poor job of preserving the body. Said storing it in the freezer was a sensible idea, but that we should have done so sooner, since it was already decomposing. The dampness, I imagine, acts fast on dead flesh.

He pronounced Deborah in excellent condition—the bruises on her throat are, remarkably, almost healed—but he said her reflexes were a little off. Sarr invited him to stay for the burial, but he declined—and quite emphatically, at that. He's not a member of their order, doesn't live in the area, and apparently doesn't get along that well with the people of Gilead, most of whom mistrust modern science. (Not that the old geezer sounded very representative of modern science. When I asked him for some good exercises, he recommended "chopping wood and running down deer.")

Standing under the heavy clouds, Sarr looked like a revivalist minister. His sermon was from Jeremiah XXII:19—"He shall be buried with the burial of an ass." The burial took place far from the graves of Bwada's two victims, and closer to the woods. We sang one song, Deborah just mouthing the words (still mustn't strain throat muscles). Sarr solemnly asked the Lord to look mercifully upon all His creatures, and I muttered an "amen." Then we walked back to the house, Deborah leaning on Sarr's arm; she's still a little stiff.

It was cloudy the rest of the day, and I sat in my room reading *The King in Yellow*—or rather, Chambers's collection of the same name. One look at the *real* book, so Chambers would claim, and I might not live to see the morrow, at least through the eyes of a sane man. (That single gimmick—masterful, I admit—seems to be his sole inspiration.)

I was disappointed that dinner was again made by Sarr; Deborah, he said, was upstairs resting. He sounded concerned, felt there were things wrong with her the doctor had overlooked. We ate our meal in silence, and I came back here immediately after washing the dishes. Feel very drowsy and, for some reason, also rather depressed. It may be the gloomy weather—we are, after all, just animals, more affected by the sun and the seasons than we like to admit. More likely it was the absence of Deborah tonight. Hope she feels better.

Note: The freezer still smells of the cat's body. Opened it tonight and got a strong whiff of decay.

August 1

Writing this, breaking habit, in early morning. Went to bed last night just after finishing the entry above, but was awakened around two by sounds coming from the woods. Wailing, deeper than before, followed by a low guttural monologue. No words, at least that I could distinguish. If frogs could talk. . . . For some reason I fell asleep before the sounds ended, so I don't know what followed.

Could very well have been an owl of some kind, and later a large bullfrog. But I quote, without comment, from *The Glass Harmonica:* "July 31: Lammas Eve. Sabbats likely."

August 4

Little energy to write tonight, and even less to write about. (Come to think of it, I slept most of the day: woke up at eleven, later took an afternoon nap. Alas, senile at thirty!) Too tired to shave, and haven't had the energy to clean this place, either; thinking about work is easier than doing it. The ivy's beginning to cover the windows again, and the mildew's been climbing steadily up the walls. It's like a dark green band that keeps widening. Soon it will reach my books. . . .

Speaking of which, note: opened M. R. James at lunch today—*Ghost-Stories of an Antiquary*—and a silverfish slithered out. Omen?

Played a little game with myself this evening—

I just had one hell of a shock. While writing the above I heard a soft tapping, like nervous fingers drumming on a table, and discovered an enormous spider, biggest of the summer, crawling only a few inches from my ankle. It must have been living behind this desk.

When you can hear a spider walk across the floor, you know it's time to keep your socks on. Thank God for insecticide.

Oh, yeah, that game—the What If game. I probably play it too often. (Vain attempt to enlarge realm of the possible? Heighten my own sensitivity? Or merely work myself into an icy sweat?) I pose unpleasant questions for myself and consider the consequences, e.g., what if this glorified chicken coop is sinking into quicksand? (Wouldn't be at all surprised.) What if the Poroths are tired of me? What if I woke up inside my own coffin?

What if I never see New York again?

What if some horror stories aren't really fiction? If Machen sometimes told the truth? If there *are* White People, malevolent little faces peering out of the moonlight? Whispers in the grass? Poisonous things in the woods? A monstrous presence on our very doorstep?

Enough of this foolishness. Time for bed.

August 9

. . . Read some Hawthorne in the morning and, over lunch, reread this week's *Hunterdon County Democrat* for the dozenth time. Sarr and Deborah were working somewhere in the fields, and I felt I ought to get some physical activity myself; but the thought of starting my exercises again after more than a week's laziness just seemed too unpleasant. . . . I took a walk down the dirt road, but only as far as a smashed-up cement culvert half buried in the woods. I was bored, but Gilead just seemed too far away.

Was going to cut the ivy away from my windows when I got back, but decided the place looks more artistic covered in vines. Rationalization?

Chatted with Poroths about politics, The World Situation, a little cosmology, blah blah blah. Dinner wasn't very good, probably because I'd been looking forward to it all day. The lamb was underdone and the beans were cold. Still, I'm always the gentleman, and was almost pleased when Deborah agreed to my offer to do the dishes. I've been doing them a lot lately.

I didn't have much interest in reading tonight and would have been up for some television, but Sarr's recently gotten into one of his religious kicks and began mumbling prayers to himself immediately after dinner. (Deborah, more human, wanted to watch the TV news. She seems to have an insatiable curiosity about world events, yet she claims the isolation here appeals to her.) Absorbed in his chanting, Sarr made me uncomfortable—I didn't like his face—and so after doing the dishes, I left.

I've been listening to the radio for the last hour or so. I recall days when I'd have gotten uptight at having wasted an hour—but out here I've lost all track of time. Feel adrift—a little disconcerting, but probably, in fact, quite healthy.

. . . Shut the radio off a moment ago, and now realize my room is filled with crickets. Up close their sound is hardly pleasant—cross between a radiator and a teakettle, very shrill. They'd been sounding off all night, but I'd thought it was interference on the radio.

Now I notice them; they're all over the room. A couple of dozen, I should think. Hate to kill them, really—they're one of the few insects I can stand, along with ladybugs and fireflies. But they make such a racket!

Wonder how they got in. . . .

August 14

Played with Felix all morning, mainly watching him chase insects, climb trees, doze in the sun. Spectator sport. After lunch went back to my room to look up something in Lovecraft—one of the listings in "Supernatural Horror in Literature"—and discovered my books were out of order. (Saki, for example, was filed under "S," whereas, whether out of fastidiousness or pedantry, I've always preferred to file him as "H. H. Munro.") This is definitely one of the Poroths' doing. I'm pissed they didn't mention coming in here, but also a little surprised they'd have any interest in this stuff.

Arranged books correctly again, then sat down to reread Lovecraft's essay. It upset me to see how little I've actually read, how far I still have to go. So many obscure authors, so many books I've never come across. . . . Left me feeling depressed and tired, so I took a nap for the rest of the afternoon.

Over dinner—vegetable omelet, rather tasteless—Deborah continued to question us on current events. It's getting to be like junior high school, with daily newspaper quizzes. . . . Don't know how she got started on this, or why the sudden interest, but it obviously annoys the hell out of Sarr.

Sarr used to be a sucker for her little-girl pleadings—I remember how he used to carry her upstairs, becoming pathetically tender, the moment she'd say, "Oh, honey, I'm so tired"—but now he just becomes angry. Often he goes off morose and alone to pray, and the only time he laughs is when he watches television.

Tonight, thank God, he was in a mood to forgo the prayers, and so after dinner we all watched a lot of offensively ignorant programs. I was disturbed to find myself laughing along with the canned laughter, but I have to admit the TV helps us get along better. Came back here after the news.

Not very tired, having slept so much of the afternoon, so began to read John Christopher's *The Possessors;* but good though it was, my mind began to wander to all the books I *haven't* yet read, and I got so depressed I turned on the radio. Find it takes my mind off things.

August 19

Slept long into the morning, then walked down to the brook, scratching groggily. Deborah was kneeling by the water, lost, it seemed, in daydream, and I was embarrassed because I'd come upon her talking to herself. We exchanged a few insincere words, and she went back toward the house.

Sat by some rocks, throwing blades of grass into the water. The sun on my head felt almost painful, as if my brain were growing too large for my skull. I turned and looked at the farmhouse. In the distance it looked like a picture at the other end of a large room, the grass for a carpet, the ceiling the sky. Deborah was stroking a cat, then seemed to grow angry when it struggled from her arms; I could hear the screen door slam as she went into the kitchen, but the sound reached me so long after the visual image that the whole scene struck me as somehow fake. I gazed up at the maples behind me and they seemed trees out of a cheap postcard, the kind in which thinly colored paint is dabbed over a black-and-white photograph; if you look closely you can see that the green in the trees is not merely in the leaves, but rather floats as a vapor over leaves, branches, parts of the sky. . . . The trees behind me seemed the productions of a poor painter, the color and shape not quite meshing. Parts of the sky were green, and pieces of the green seemed to float away from my vision. No matter how hard I tried, I couldn't follow them.

Far down the stream I could see something small and kicking, a black beetle, legs in the air, borne swiftly along in the current. Then it was gone.

Thumbed through the Bible while I ate my lunch—mostly cookies. By late afternoon I was playing word games while I lay on the grass near my room. The shrill twitter of the birds, I would say, the birds singing in the sun. . . . And inexorably I'd continue with the sun dying in the moonlight, the moonlight falling on the floor, the floor sagging to the cellar, the cellar filling with water, the water seeping into the ground, the ground twisting into smoke, the smoke staining the sky, the sky burning in the sun, the sun dying in the moonlight, the moonlight falling on the floor. . . . Melancholy progressions that held my mind like a whirlpool.

Sarr woke me for dinner; I had dozed off, and my clothes were damp from the grass. As we walked up to the house together he whispered that, an hour or so before, he'd come upon his wife bending over me, peering into my sleeping face. "Her eyes were wide," he said. "Like Bwada's." I said I didn't understand why he was telling me this.

"Because," he recited in a whisper, gripping my arm, "the heart is deceitful above all things, and desperately wicked: who can know it?"

I recognized that. Jeremiah XVII:9.

Dinner was especially uncomfortable; the two of them sat picking at their food, occasionally raising their eyes to one another like children in a staring contest. I longed for the conversations of our early days, inconsequential though they must have been, and wondered where things had first gone wrong.

The meal was dry and unappetizing, but the dessert looked delicious—chocolate mousse, made from an old family recipe. Deborah had served it earlier in the summer and knew both Sarr and I loved it. This time, however, she gave none to herself, explaining that she had to watch her weight.

"Then we'll not eat any!" Sarr shouted, and with that he snatched my dish from in front of me, grabbed his own, and hurled them both against the wall, where they splattered like mud balls.

Deborah was very still; she said nothing, just sat there watching us. She didn't look particularly afraid of this madman, I was happy to see—but *I* was. He may have read my thoughts, because as I got up from my seat he said much more gently, in the soft voice normal to him, "Sorry, Jeremy. I know you hate scenes. We'll pray for each other, all right?"

"Are you okay?" I asked Deborah. "I'm going out now, but I'll stay if you think you'll need me for anything." She stared at me with a slight smile and shook her head. I nodded toward her husband, and she shrugged.

"Things will work out," she said. I could hear Sarr laughing as I shut the door.

When I snapped on the light out here, I took off my shirt and stood in front of the little mirror. It had been nearly a week since I'd showered, and I'd become used to the smell of my body. My hair had wound itself into greasy brown curls, my beard was at least two weeks old, and my eyes . . . well, the eyes that stared back at me looked like those of an old man. The whites were turning yellow, like old teeth. I looked at my chest and arms, flabby at thirty, and I thought of the frightening alterations in my friend Sarr. I knew I'd have to get out of here.

Just glanced at my watch. It's now quite late: two-thirty. I've been packing my things.

August 20

I woke about an hour ago and continued packing. Lots of books to put away, but I'm just about done. It's not even nine A.M. yet, much earlier than I normally get up; but I guess the thought of leaving here fills me with energy.

The first thing I saw on rising was a garden spider whose body was as big as some of the mice the cats have killed. It was sitting on the ivy that grows over my windowsill—fortunately, on the other side of the screen. Apparently it had had good hunting all summer, preying on the insects that live in the leaves. Concluding that nothing so big and fearsome has a right to live, I held the spray can against the screen and doused the creature with poison. It struggled halfway up the screen, then stopped, arched its legs, and dropped backward into the ivy.

I plan to walk into town this morning and telephone the office in Flemington where I rented my car. If they can have one ready today, I'll hitch there to pick it up; otherwise I'll spend tonight here and pick it up tomorrow. I'll be leaving a little early in the season, but the Poroths already have my month's rent, so they shouldn't be too offended.

And anyway, how could I be expected to stick around here with all that nonsense going on, never knowing when my room might be ransacked, having to put up with Sarr's insane suspicions and Deborah's moodiness?

Before I go into town, though, I really must shave and shower for the good people of Gilead. I've been sitting inside here waiting for some sign the Poroths are up, but as yet—it's almost nine—I've heard nothing. I wouldn't care to barge in on them while they're still having breakfast or, worse, just getting up. . . . So I'll just wait here by the window till I see them.

. . . Ten o'clock now, and they still haven't come out. Perhaps they're having a talk. . . . I'll give them half an hour more, then I'm going in.

There my journal ends. Until today, almost a week later, I have not cared to set down any of the events that followed. But here in the temporary safety of this hotel room, protected by a heavy brass travel-lock I had sent up from the hardware store down the street, watched over by the good people of Flemington—and perhaps by something not good—I can continue my narrative.

The first thing I noticed as I approached the house was that the shades were drawn, even in the kitchen. Had they decided to sleep late this morning? I wondered. Throughout my thirty years I have come to associate drawn shades with a foul smell, the smell of a sickroom, of shamefaced poverty and food gone bad, of people lying too long beneath blankets; but I was not ready for the stench of decay that met me when I opened the kitchen door and stepped into the darkness. Something had died in that room—and not recently.

At the moment the smell first hit, four little shapes scrambled across the linoleum toward me and out into the daylight. The Poroths' cats.

By the other wall a lump of shadow moved; a pale face caught light penetrating the shades. Sarr's voice, its habitual softness exaggerated to a whisper: "Jeremy. I thought you were still asleep."

"Can I—"

"No. Don't turn on the light." He got to his feet, a black form towering against the window. Fiddling nervously with the kitchen door—the tin doorknob, the rubber bands stored around it, the fringe at the bottom of the drawn window shade—I opened it wider and let in more sunlight. It fell on the dark thing at his feet, over which he had been crouching: Deborah, the flesh at her throat torn and wrinkled like the skin of an old apple.

Her clothing lay in a heap beside her. She appeared long dead. The eyes were shriveled, sunken into sockets black as a skull's.

I think I may have staggered at that moment, because he came toward me. His steady, unblinking gaze looked so sincere—but why was he smiling? "I'll make you understand," he was saying, or something like that; even now I feel my face twisting into horror as I try to write of him. "I had to kill her. . . ."

"You—"

"She tried to kill me," he went on, silencing all questions. "The same thing that possessed Bwada . . . possessed her."

My hand played behind my back with the bottom of the window shade. "But her throat—"

"That happened a long time ago. Bwada did it. I had nothing to do with . . . that part." Suddenly his voice rose. "Don't you understand? She tried to stab me with the bread knife." He turned, stooped over, and clumsy in the darkness, began feeling about him on the floor. "Where is that thing?" he was mumbling. "I'll show you. . . ." As he crossed a beam of sunlight, something gleamed like a silver handle on the back of his shirt.

Thinking, perhaps, to help him search, I pulled gently on the window shade, then released it; it snapped upward like a gunshot, flooding the room with light. From deep within the center of his back protruded the dull wooden haft of the bread knife, buried almost completely but for an inch or two of gleaming steel.

He must have heard my intake of breath—that sight chills me even today, the grisly absurdity of the thing—he must have heard me because immediately he stood, his back to me, and reached up behind himself toward the knife, his arm stretching in vain, his fingers curling around nothing. The blade had been planted in a spot he couldn't reach.

He turned toward me and shrugged in embarrassment, a child caught in a foolish error. "Oh, yeah," he said, grinning at his own weakness. "I forgot it was there."

Suddenly he thrust his face into mine, fixing me in a gaze that never wavered, his eyes wide with candor. "It's easy for us to forget things," he explained—and then, still smiling, still watching, volunteered that last trivial piece of information, that final message whose words released me from inaction and left me free to dash from the room, to sprint in panic down the road to town, pursued by what had once been the farmer Sarr Poroth.

It serves no purpose here to dwell on my flight down that twisting dirt road, breathing in such deep gasps that I was soon moaning with every breath; how, with my enemy racing behind me, not even winded, his steps never flagging, I veered into the woods; how I finally lost him, perhaps from the inexperience of whatever thing now controlled his body, and was able to make my way back to the road, only to come upon him again as he rounded a bend; his laughter as he followed me, and how it continued long after I had evaded him a second time; and how, after hiding until nightfall in the old cement culvert, I ran the rest of the way in pitch-darkness, stumbling in the ruts, torn by vines, nearly blinding myself when I ran into a low branch, until I arrived in Gilead filthy, exhausted, and nearly incoherent.

Suffice it to say that my escape was largely a matter of luck, a physical wreck fleeing something oblivious to pain or fatigue; but that, beyond mere luck, I had been impelled by an almost ecstatic sense of dread produced by his last words to me, that last communication from an alien face smiling inches from my own, and which I chose to take as his final warning:

"Sometimes we forget to blink."

You can read the rest in the newspapers. The *Hunterdon County Democrat* covered most of the story, though its man wrote it up as merely another lunatic wife-slaying, the result of loneliness, religious mania, and a mysteriously tainted well. (Traces of insecticide were found, among other things, in the water.) The *Somerset Reporter* took a different slant, implying that I had been the third member of an erotic triangle and that Sarr had murdered his wife in a fit of jealousy.

Needless to say, I was by this time past caring what was written about me. I was too haunted by visions of that lonely, abandoned farmhouse, the wails of its hungry cats, and by the sight of Deborah's corpse, discovered by the police, protruding from that hastily dug grave beyond the cornfield.

Accompanied by state troopers, I returned to my ivy-covered outbuilding. A bread knife had been plunged deep into its door, splintering the wood on the other side. The blood on it was Sarr's.

My journal had been hidden under my mattress, and so was untouched, but (I look at them now, piled in cardboard boxes beside my suitcase) my precious books had been hurled about the room, their bindings slashed. My summer is over, and now I sit inside here all day listening to the radio, waiting for the next report. Sarr—or his corpse—has not been found.

I should think the evidence was clear enough to corroborate my story, but I suppose I should have expected the reception it received from the police. They didn't laugh at my theory of "possession"—not to my face, anyway—but they ignored it in obvious embarrassment. Some see a nice young bookworm gone slightly deranged after contact with a murderer; others believe my story to be the desperate fabrication of an adulterer trying to avoid the blame for Deborah's death.

I can understand their reluctance to accept my explanation of the events, for it's one that goes a little beyond the "natural," a little beyond the scientific considerations of motive, modus operandi, and fingerprints. But I find it quite unnerving that at least one official—an assistant district attorney, I think, though I'm afraid I'm rather ignorant of these matters—believes I am guilty of murder.

There has, of course, been no arrest. Still, I've been given the time-honored instructions against leaving town.

The theory proposing my own complicity in the events is, I must admit, rather ingenious—and so carefully worked out that it will surely gain more adherents than my own. This police official is going to try to prove that I killed poor Deborah in a fit of passion and, immediately afterward, disposed of Sarr. He points out that their marriage had been an observably happy one until I arrived, a disturbing influence from the city. My motive, he says, was simple lust—unrequited, to be sure—aggravated by boredom. The heat, the insects, and, most of all, the oppressive loneliness—all constituted an environment alien to any I'd been accustomed to, and all worked to unhinge my reason.

I have no cause for fear, however, because this affidavit should certainly establish my innocence. Surely no one can ignore the evidence of my journal (though I can imagine an antagonistic few maintaining that I wrote the journal not at the farm but here in the Union Hotel, this very week).

What galls me is not the suspicions of a few detectives, but the predicament their suspicions place me in. Quite simply, *I cannot run away.* I am compelled to remain locked up in this room, potential prey to whatever the thing that was Sarr Poroth has now become — the thing that was once a cat, and once a woman, and once . . . what? A large white moth? A serpent? A shrewlike thing with wicked teeth?

A police chief? A president? A boy with eyes of blood that sits beneath my window?

Lord, who will believe me?

It was that night that started it all, I'm convinced of it now. The night I made those strange signs in the tree. The night the crickets missed a beat.

I'm not a philosopher, and I can supply no ready explanation for why this new evil has been released into the world. I'm only a poor scholar, a bookworm, and I must content myself with mumbling a few phrases that keep running through my mind, phrases out of books read long ago when such abstractions meant, at most, a pleasant shudder. I am haunted by scraps from the myth of Pandora, and by a semantic discussion I once read comparing "unnatural" and "supernatural."

And something about "a tiny rent in the fabric of the universe. . . ."

Just large enough to let something in. Something not of nature, and hard to kill. Something with its own obscure purpose.

Ironically, the police may be right. Perhaps it was my visit to Gilead that brought about the deaths. Perhaps I had a hand in letting loose the force that, to date, has snuffed out the lives of four hens, three cats, and at least two human beings—but will hardly be content to stop there.

I've just checked. He hasn't moved from the steps of the courthouse; and even when I look out my window, the rose spectacles never waver. Who knows where the eyes beneath them point? Who knows if they remember to blink?

Lord, this heat is sweltering. My shirt is sticking to my skin, and droplets of sweat are rolling down my face and dripping onto this page, making the ink run.

My hand is tired from writing, and I think it's time to end this affidavit.

If, as I now believe possible, I inadvertently called down evil from the sky and began the events at Poroth Farm, my death will only be fitting. And after my death, many more. We are all, I'm afraid, in danger. Please, then, forgive this prophet of doom, old at thirty, his last jeremiad: "The harvest is past, the summer is ended, and we are not saved."

the ocean and all its devices

WILLIAM BROWNING SPENCER

Left to its own enormous devices the sea
in timeless reverie conceives of life,
being itself the world in pantomime.
—LLOYD FRANKENBERG,
THE SEA

The hotel's owner and manager, George Hume, sat on the edge of his bed and smoked a cigarette. "The Franklins arrived today," he said.

"Regular as clockwork," his wife said.

George nodded. "Eight years now. And why? Why ever do they come?"

George Hume's wife, an ample woman with soft motherly features, sighed. "They seem to get no pleasure from it, that's for certain. Might as well be a funeral they come for."

The Franklins always arrived in late fall when the beaches were cold and empty, and the ocean, under dark skies, reclaimed its terrible majesty. The hotel was almost deserted at this time of year, and George had suggested closing early for the winter. Mrs. Hume had said, "The Franklins will be coming, dear."

So what? George might have said. Let them find other accommodations this year. But he didn't say that. They were a sort of tradition, the Franklins, and in a world so fraught with change, one just naturally protected the rare, enduring pattern.

They were a reserved family who came to this quiet hotel in North Carolina like refugees seeking safe harbor. George couldn't close early and send the Franklins off to some inferior establishment. Lord, they might wind up at The Cove with its garish lagoon pool and gaudy tropical lounge. That wouldn't suit them at all.

The Franklins (husband, younger wife, and pale delicate-featured daughter) would dress rather formally and sit in the small opened section of the dining room—the rest of the room shrouded in dust covers while Jack, the hotel's aging waiter and handyman, would stand off to one side with a bleak, stoic expression.

Over the years, George had come to know many of his regular guests well. But the Franklins had always remained aloof and enigmatic. Mr. Greg Franklin was a man in his mid or late forties, a handsome man, tall—over six feet—with precise, slow gestures and an oddly uninflected voice, as though he were reading from some internal script that failed to interest him. His much younger wife was stunning, her hair massed in brown ringlets, her eyes large and luminous and containing something like fear in their depths. She spoke rarely, and then in a whisper, preferring to let her husband talk.

Their child, Melissa, was a dark-haired girl—twelve or thirteen now, George guessed—a girl as pale as the moon's reflection in a rain barrel. Always dressed impeccably, she was as quiet as her mother, and George had the distinct impression, although he could not remember being told this by anyone, that she was sickly, that some traumatic infant's illness had almost killed her and so accounted for her methodical, wounded economy of motion.

George ushered the Franklins from his mind. It was late. He extinguished his cigarette and walked over to the window. Rain blew against the glass, and lightning would occasionally illuminate the white-capped waves.

"Is Nancy still coming?" Nancy, their daughter and only child, was a senior at Duke University. She had called the week before, saying she might come and hang out for a week or two.

"As far as I know," Mrs. Hume said. "You know how she is. Everything on a whim. That's your side of the family, George."

George turned away from the window and grinned. "Well, I can't accuse your family of ever acting impulsively—although it would do them a world of good. Your family packs a suitcase to go to the grocery store."

"And your side steals a car and goes to California without a toothbrush or a prayer."

This was an old well-worked routine, of course, and they indulged it as they readied for bed. Then George turned off the light and the darkness brought silence.

It was still raining in the morning when George Hume woke. The violence of last night's thunderstorm had been replaced by a slow businesslike drizzle. Looking out the window, George saw the Franklins walking on the beach under black umbrellas. They were a cheerless sight. All three of them wore dark raincoats, and they might have been fugitives from some old Bergman film, inevitably tragic, moving slowly across a stark landscape.

When most families went to the beach, it was a more lively affair.

George turned away from the window and went into the bathroom to shave. As he lathered his face, he heard the boom of a radio, rock music blaring from the adjoining room, and he assumed, correctly, that his twenty-one-year-old daughter Nancy had arrived as planned.

Nancy had not come alone. "This is Steve," she said when her father sat down at the breakfast table.

Steve was a very young man—the young were getting younger—with a wide-eyed, waxy expression and a blond mustache that looked like it could be wiped off with a damp cloth.

Steve stood up and said how glad he was to meet Nancy's father. He shook George's hand enthusiastically, as though they had just struck a lucrative deal.

"Steve's in law school," Mrs. Hume said, with a proprietary delight that her husband found grating.

Nancy was complaining. She had, her father thought, always been a querulous girl, at odds with the way the world was.

"I can't believe it," she was saying. "The whole mall is closed. The only—and I mean *only*—thing around here that is open is that cheesy little drugstore and nobody actually buys anything in there. I know that, because I recognize stuff from when I was six. Is this some holiday I don't know about or what?"

"Honey, it's the off-season. You know everything closes when the tourists leave," her mother said.

"Not the for-Christ-sakes mall!" Nancy said. "I can't believe it." Nancy frowned. "This must be what Russia is like," she said, closing one eye as smoke from her cigarette slid up her cheek.

George Hume watched his daughter gulp coffee. She was not a person who needed stimulants. She wore an ancient gray sweater and sweatpants. Her blond hair was chopped short and ragged and kept in a state of disarray by the constant furrowing of nervous fingers. She was, her father thought, a pretty girl in disguise.

That night, George discovered that he could remember nothing of the spy novel he was reading, had forgotten, in fact, the hero's name. It was as though he had stumbled into a cocktail party in the wrong neighborhood, all strangers to him, the gossip meaningless.

He put the book on the nightstand, leaned back on the pillow, and said, "This is her senior year. Doesn't she have classes to attend?"

His wife said nothing.

He sighed. "I suppose they are staying in the same room."

"Dear, I don't know," Mrs. Hume said. "I expect it is none of our business."

"If it is not our business who stays in our hotel, then who in the name of hell's business is it?"

Mrs. Hume rubbed her husband's neck. "Don't excite yourself, dear. You know what I mean. Nancy is a grown-up, you know."

George did not respond to this, and Mrs. Hume, changing the subject, said, "I saw Mrs. Franklin and her daughter out walking on the beach again today. I don't know where Mr. Franklin was. It was pouring, and there they were, mother and daughter. You know . . ." Mrs. Hume paused. "It's like they were waiting for something to come out of the sea. Like a vigil they were keeping. I've thought it before, but the notion was particularly strong today. I looked out past them, and there seemed no separation between the sea and the sky, just a black wall of water." Mrs. Hume looked at herself in the dresser's mirror, as though her reflection might clarify matters. "I've lived by the ocean all my life, and I've just taken it for granted, George. Suddenly it gave me the shivers. Just for a moment. I thought, Lord, how big it is, lying there cold and black, like some creature that has slept at your feet so long you never expect it to wake, have forgotten that it might be brutal, even vicious."

"It's all this rain," her husband said, hugging her and drawing her to him. "It can make a person think some black thoughts."

George left off worrying about his daughter and her young man's living arrangements, and in the morning, when Nancy and Steve appeared for breakfast, George didn't broach the subject—not even to himself.

Later that morning, he watched them drive off in Steve's shiny sports car—rich parents, lawyers themselves?—bound for Wilmington and shopping malls that were open.

The rain had stopped, but dark, massed clouds over the ocean suggested that this was a momentary respite. As George studied the beach, the Franklins came into view. They marched directly toward him, up and over the dunes, moving in a soldierly, clipped fashion. Mrs. Franklin was holding her daughter's hand and moving at a brisk pace, almost a run, while her husband faltered behind, his gait hesitant, as though uncertain of the wisdom of catching up.

Mrs. Franklin reached the steps and marched up them, her child tottering in tow, her boot heels sounding hollowly on the wood planks. George nodded, and she passed without speaking, seemed not to see him. In any event, George Hume would have been unable to speak. He was accustomed to the passive, demure countenance of this self-possessed woman, and the expression on her face, a wild distorting emotion, shocked and confounded him. It was an unreadable emotion, but its intensity was extraordinary and unsettling.

George had not recovered from the almost physical assault of Mrs. Franklin's emotional state when her husband came up the stairs, nodded curtly, muttered something, and hastened after his wife.

George Hume looked after the retreating figures. Mr. Greg Franklin's face had been a mask of cold civility, none of his wife's passion written there, but the man's appearance was disturbing in its own way. Mr. Franklin had been soaking wet, his hair plastered to his skull, his overcoat dripping, the reek of salt water enfolding him like a shroud.

George walked on down the steps and out to the beach. The ocean was always some consolation, a quieting influence, but today it seemed hostile.

The sand was still wet from the recent rains, and the footprints of the Franklins were all that marred the smooth expanse. George saw that the Franklins had walked down the beach along the edge of the tide and returned at a greater distance from the water. He set out in the wake of their footprints, soon lost to his own thoughts. He thought about his daughter, his wild Nancy, who had always been boy-crazy. At least this one didn't have a safety pin through his ear or play in a rock band. *So lighten up,* George advised himself.

He stopped. The tracks had stopped. Here is where the Franklins turned and headed back to the hotel, walking higher up the beach, closer to the weedy debris-laden dunes.

But it was not the ending of the trail that stopped George's own progress down the beach. In fact, he had forgotten that he was absently following the Franklins' spore.

It was the litter of dead fish that stopped him. They were scattered at his feet in the tide. Small ghost crabs had already found the corpses and were laying their claims.

There might have been a hundred bodies. It was difficult to say, for not one of the bodies was whole. They had been hacked into many pieces, diced by some impossibly sharp blade that severed a head cleanly, flicked off a tail or dorsal fin. Here a scaled torso still danced in the sand, there a pale eye regarded the sky.

Crouching in the sand, George examined the bodies. He stood

up, finally, as the first large drops of rain plunged from the sky. No doubt some fishermen had called it a day, tossed their scissored bait, and gone home.

That this explanation did not satisfy George Hume was the result of a general sense of unease. *Too much rain.*

It rained sullenly and steadily for two days, during which time George saw little of his daughter and her boyfriend. Nancy apparently had the young man on a strict regimen of shopping, tourist attractions, and movies, and she was undaunted by the weather.

The Franklins kept inside, appearing briefly in the dining room for bodily sustenance and then retreating again to their rooms. And whatever did they do there? Did they play solitaire? Did they watch old reruns on TV?

On the third day, the sun came out, brazen, acting as though it had never been gone, but the air was colder. The Franklins, silhouetted like black crows on a barren field, resumed their shoreline treks.

Nancy and Steve rose early and were gone from the house before George arrived at the breakfast table.

George spent the day endeavoring to satisfy the IRS's notion of a small businessman's obligations, and he was in a foul mood by dinnertime.

After dinner, he tried to read, this time choosing a much-touted novel that proved to be about troubled youth. He was asleep within fifteen minutes of opening the book and awoke in an overstuffed armchair. The room was chilly, and his wife had tucked a quilt around his legs before abandoning him for bed. In the morning she would, he was certain, assure him that she had tried to rouse him before retiring, but he had no recollection of such an attempt.

"Half a bottle of wine might have something to do with that," she would say.

He would deny the charge.

The advantage of being married a long time was that one could argue without the necessity of the other's actual physical presence.

He smiled at this thought and pushed himself out of the chair, feeling groggy, head full of prickly flannel. He looked out the window. It was raining again—to the accompaniment of thunder and explosive strobelike lightning. The sports car was gone. The kids weren't home yet. Fine. Fine. None of my business.

Climbing the stairs, George paused. Something dark lay on the carpeted step, and as he bent over it, leaning forward, his mind sorted and discarded the possibilities: cat, wig, bird's nest, giant dust bunny. Touch and a strong olfactory cue identified the stuff: seaweed. Raising his head, he saw that two more clumps of the wet rubbery plant lay on ascending steps, and gathering them—with no sense of revulsion, for he was used to the ocean's disordered presence—he carried the seaweed up to his room and dumped it in the bathroom's wastebasket.

He scrubbed his hands in the sink, washing away the salty, stagnant reek, left the bathroom, and crawled into bed beside his sleeping wife. He fell asleep immediately and was awakened later in the night with a suffocating sense of dread, a sure knowledge that an intruder had entered the room.

The intruder proved to be an odor, a powerful stench of decomposing fish, rotting vegetation, and salt water. He climbed out of bed, coughing.

The source of this odor was instantly apparent, and he swept up the wastebasket, preparing to gather the seaweed and flush it down the toilet.

The seaweed had melted into a black liquid, bubbles forming on its surface, a dark gelatinous muck, simmering like heated tar. As George stared at the mess, a bubble burst, and the noxious gas it unleashed dazed him, sent him reeling backward with an inexplicable vision of some monstrous shadowy form, silhouetted against green, mottled water.

George pitched himself forward, gathered the wastebasket in his arms, and fled the room. In the hall he wrenched open a window and hurled the wastebasket and its contents into the rain.

He stood then, gasping, the rain savage and cold on his face, his undershirt soaked, and he stood that way, clutching the windowsill, until he was sure he would not faint.

Returning to bed, he found his wife still sleeping soundly and he knew, immediately, that he would say nothing in the morning, that the sense of suffocation, of fear, would seem unreal, its source irrational. Already the moment of panic was losing its reality, fading into the realm of nightmare.

The next day the rain stopped again, and this time the sun was not routed. The police arrived on the third day of clear weather.

Mrs. Hume had opened the door, and she shouted up to her husband, who stood on the landing, "It's about Mr. Franklin."

Mrs. Franklin came out of her room then, and George Hume thought he saw the child behind her, through the open door. The girl, Melissa, was lying on the bed behind her mother, and just for a moment it seemed that there was a spreading shadow under her, as though the bedclothes were soaked with dark water. Then the door closed as Mrs. Franklin came into the hall, and George identified the expression he had last seen in her eyes, for it was there again: fear, a racing engine of fear, gears stripped, the accelerator flat to the floor.

And Mrs. Franklin screamed, screamed and came falling to her knees and screamed again, prescient in her grief, and collapsed as George rushed toward her, and two police officers and a paramedic, a woman, came bounding up the stairs.

Mr. Franklin had drowned. A fisherman had discovered the body. Mr. Franklin had been fully dressed, lying on his back with his eyes open. His wallet—and seven hundred dollars in cash and a host of credit cards—was still in his back pocket, and a business card identified him as vice president of marketing for a software firm in Fairfax, Virginia. The police had telephoned Franklin's firm in Virginia and so learned that he was on vacation. The secretary had the hotel's number.

After the ambulance left with Mrs. Franklin, they sat in silence until the police officer cleared his throat and said, "She seemed to be expecting something like this."

The words dropped into a silence.

Nancy and Steve and Mrs. Hume were seated on one of the lobby's sofas. George Hume came out of the office in the wake of the other policeman, who paused at the door and spoke. "We'd appreciate it if you could come down and identify the body. Just a formality, but it's not a job for his wife, not in the state she's in." He coughed, shook his head. "Or the state he's in, for that matter. Body got tore up some in the water, and, well, I still find it hard to believe that he was alive just yesterday. I would have guessed he'd been in the water two weeks minimum—the deterioration, you know."

George Hume nodded his head as though he did know and agreed to accompany the officer back into town.

George took a long look, longer than he wanted to, but the body wouldn't let him go, made mute, undeniable demands.

Yes, this was Mr. Greg Franklin. Yes, this would make eight years that he and his wife and his child had come to the hotel. No, no, nothing out of the ordinary.

George interrupted himself. "The tattoos . . .," he said.

"You didn't know about the tattoos, I take it?" the officer said.

George shook his head. "No." The etched blue lines that laced the dead man's arms and chest were somehow more frightening than the damage the sea had done. Frightening because . . . because the reserved Mr. Franklin, businessman and stolid husband, did not look like someone who would illuminate his flesh with arcane symbols, pentagrams and ornate fish, their scales numbered according to some runic logic, and spidery incomprehensible glyphs.

"Guess Franklin wasn't inclined to wear a bathing suit."

"No."

"Well, we are interested in those tattoos. I guess his wife knew about them. Hell, maybe she has some of her own."

"Have you spoken to her?"

"Not yet. Called the hospital. They say she's sleeping. It can wait till morning."

An officer drove George back to the hotel, and his wife greeted him at the door.

"She's sleeping," Mrs. Hume said.

"Who?"

"Melissa."

For a moment, George drew a blank, and then he nodded. "What are we going to do with her?"

"Why, keep her," his wife said. "Until her mother is out of the hospital."

"Maybe there are relatives," George said, but he knew, saying it, that the Franklins were self-contained, a single unit, a closed universe.

His wife confirmed this. No one could be located, in any event.

"Melissa may not be aware that her father is dead," Mrs. Hume said. "The child is, I believe, a stranger girl than we ever realized. Here we were thinking she was just a quiet thing, well behaved. I think there is something wrong with her mind. I can't seem to talk to her, and what she says makes no sense. I've called Dr. Gowers, and he has agreed to see her. You remember Dr. Gowers, don't you? We sent Nancy to him when she was going through that bad time at thirteen."

George remembered child psychiatrist Gowers as a bearded man with a swollen nose and thousands of small wrinkles around his eyes. He had seemed a very kind but somehow sad man, a little like Santa Claus if Santa Claus had suffered some disillusioning experience, an unpleasant divorce or other personal setback, perhaps.

Nancy came into the room as her mother finished speaking. "Steve and I can take Melissa," Nancy said.

"Well, that's very good of you, dear," her mother said. "I've already made an appointment for tomorrow morning at ten. I'm sure Dr. Gowers will be delighted to see you again."

"I'll go too," George said. He couldn't explain it, but he was suddenly afraid.

The next morning when George came down to breakfast, Melissa was already seated at the table and Nancy was combing the child's hair.

"She isn't going to church," George said, surprised at the growl in his voice.

"This is what she wanted to wear," Nancy said. "And it looks very nice, I think."

Melissa was dressed in the sort of outfit a young girl might wear on Easter Sunday: a navy blue dress with white trim, white knee-socks, black shiny shoes. She had even donned pale blue gloves. Her black hair had been brushed to a satin sheen, and her pale face seemed just-scrubbed, with the scent of soap lingering over her. A shiny black purse sat next to her plate of eggs and toast.

"You look very pretty," George Hume said.

Melissa nodded, a sharp snap of the head, and said, "I am an angel."

Nancy laughed and hugged the child. George raised his eyebrows. "No false modesty here," he said. At least she could talk.

On the drive into town, Steve sat in the passenger seat while George drove. Nancy and Melissa sat in the backseat. Nancy spoke to the child in a slow, reassuring murmur.

Steve said nothing, sitting with his hands in his lap, looking out the window. *Might not be much in a crisis,* George thought. *A rich man's child.*

Steve stayed in the waiting room while the receptionist ushered Melissa and Nancy and George into Dr. Gowers's office. The psychiatrist seemed much as George remembered him, a silver-maned, benign old gent, exuding an air of competence. He asked them to sit on the sofa.

The child perched primly on the sofa, her little black purse cradled in her lap. She was flanked by George and Nancy.

Dr. Gowers knelt down in front of her. "Well, Melissa. Is it all right if I call you Melissa?"

"Yes, sir. That's what everyone calls me."

"Well, Melissa, I'm glad you could come and see me today. I'm Dr. Gowers."

"Yes, sir."

"I'm sorry about what happened to your father," he said, looking in her eyes.

"Yes, sir," Melissa said. She leaned forward and touched her shoe.

"Do you know what happened to your father?" Dr. Gowers asked.

Melissa nodded her head and continued to study her shoes.

"What happened to your father?" Dr. Gowers asked.

"The machines got him," Melissa said. She looked up at the doctor. "The real machines," she added. "The ocean ones."

"Your father drowned," Dr. Gowers said.

Melissa nodded. "Yes, sir." Slowly the little girl got up and began wandering around the room. She walked past a large saltwater aquarium next to a teak bookcase.

George thought the child must have bumped against the aquarium stand—although she hardly seemed close enough—because water spilled from the tank as she passed. She was humming. It was a bright, musical little tune, and he had heard it before, a children's song, perhaps? The words? Something like *by the sea, by the sea.*

The girl walked and gestured with a liquid motion that was oddly sophisticated, suggesting the calculated body language of an older and sexually self-assured woman.

"Melissa, would you come and sit down again so we can talk? I want to ask you some questions, and that is hard to do if you are walking around the room."

"Yes, sir," Melissa said, returning to the sofa and resettling between George and his daughter. Melissa retrieved her purse and placed it on her lap again.

She looked down at the purse and up again. She smiled with a child's cunning. Then, very slowly, she opened the purse and showed it to Dr. Gowers.

"Yes?" he said, raising an eyebrow.

"There's nothing in it," Melissa said. "It's empty." She giggled.

"Well, yes, it is empty," Dr. Gowers said, returning the child's smile. "Why is that?"

Melissa snapped the purse closed. "Because my real purse isn't here, of course. It's in the real place, where I keep my things."

"And where is that, Melissa?"

Melissa smiled and said, "You know, silly."

When the session ended, George phoned his wife.

"I don't know," he said. "I guess it went fine. I don't know. I've had no experience of this sort of thing. What about Mrs. Franklin?"

Mrs. Franklin was still in the hospital. She wanted to leave, but the hospital was reluctant to let her. She was still in shock, very disoriented. She seemed, indeed, to think that it was her daughter who had drowned.

"Did you talk to her?" George asked.

"Well, yes, just briefly, but as I say, she made very little sense, got very excited when it became clear I wasn't going to fetch her if her doctor wanted her to remain there."

"Can you remember anything she said?"

"Well, it was very jumbled, really. Something about a bad bargain. Something about, that Greek word, you know . . . *hubris.*"

"Hewbris?"

"Oh, back in school, you know, George. *Hubris.* A willful sort of pride that angers the gods. I'm sure you learned it in school yourself."

"You are not making sense," he said, suddenly exasperated—and frightened.

"Well," his wife said, "you don't have to shout. Of course I don't make any sense. I am trying to repeat what Mrs. Franklin said, and that poor woman made no sense at all. I tried to reassure her that Melissa was fine, and she screamed. She said Melissa was not fine at all and that I was a fool. Now you are shouting at me, too."

George apologized, said he had to be going, and hung up.

On the drive back from Dr. Gowers's office, Nancy sat in the backseat with Melissa. The child seemed unusually excited: her pale forehead was beaded with sweat, and she watched the ocean with great intensity.

"Did you like Dr. Gowers?" Nancy asked. "He liked you. He wants to see you again, you know."

Melissa nodded. "He is a nice one." She frowned. "But he doesn't understand the real words, either. No one here does."

George glanced over his shoulder at the girl. *You are an odd ducky,* he thought.

A large midday sun brightened the air and made the ocean glitter as though scaled. They were in a stretch of sand dunes and sea oats and high wind-driven waves, and except for an occasional lumbering trailer truck, they seemed alone in this world of sleek, eternal forms.

Then Melissa began to cough. The coughing increased in volume, developed a quick hysterical note.

"Pull over!" Nancy shouted, clutching the child.

George swung the car off the highway and hit the brakes. Gravel pinged against metal, the car fishtailed and lurched to a stop. George was out of the car instantly, in time to catch his daughter and the child in her arms as they came hurtling from the backseat. Melissa's face was red and her small chest heaved. Nancy had her arms around the girl's chest. "Melissa!" Nancy was shouting. "Melissa!"

Nancy jerked the child upward and back. Melissa's body convulsed. Her breathing was labored, a broken whistle fluttering in her throat.

George enfolded them both in his arms, and Melissa suddenly lurched forward. She shuddered and began to vomit. A hot, green odor, the smell of stagnant tidal pools, assaulted George. Nancy knelt beside Melissa, wiping the child's wet hair from her forehead. "It's gonna be okay, honey," she said. "You got something stuck in your throat. It's all right now. You're all right."

The child jumped up and ran down the beach.

"Melissa!" Nancy screamed, scrambling to her feet and pursuing the girl. George ran after them, fear hissing in him like some power line down in a storm, writhing and spewing sparks.

In her blue dress and kneesocks—shoes left behind on the beach now—Melissa splashed into the ocean, arms pumping.

Out of the corner of his eye, George saw Steve come into view. He raced past George, past Nancy, moving with a frenzied pinwheeling of arms. "I got her, I got her, I got her," he chanted.

Don't, George thought. *Please don't.*

The beach was littered with debris: old ocean-polished bottles, driftwood, seaweed, shattered conch shells. It was a rough ocean, still reverberating to the recent storm.

Steve had almost reached Melissa. George could see him reach out to clutch her shoulder.

Then something rose up in the water. It towered over man and child, and as the ocean fell away from it, it revealed smooth surfaces that glittered and writhed. The world was bathed with light, and George saw it plain. And yet, he could not later recall much detail. It was as though his mind refused entry to this monstrous thing, substituting other images—maggots winking from the eye sockets of some dead animal, flesh growing on a ruined structure of rusted metal—and while, in memory, those images were horrible enough and would not let him sleep, another part of his mind shrank from the knowledge that he had confronted something more hideous and ancient than his reason could acknowledge.

What happened next, happened in an instant. Steve staggered backward, and Melissa turned and ran sideways to the waves.

A greater wave, detached from the logic of the rolling ocean, sped over Steve, engulfing him, and he was gone, while Melissa continued to splash through the tide, now turning and running shoreward. The beast-thing was gone, and the old pattern of waves reasserted itself. Then Steve resurfaced, and with a lurch of understanding, as though the unnatural wave had struck at George's mind and left him dazed, he watched the head bob in the water, roll sickeningly, bounce on the crest of a second wave, and disappear.

Melissa lay facedown on the wet sand, and Nancy raced to her, grabbed her up in her arms, and turned to her father.

"Where's Steve?" she shouted over the crash of the surf.

You didn't see, then, George thought. *Thank God.*

George came up to his daughter and embraced her. His touch triggered racking sobs, and he held her tighter, the child Melissa between them.

And what if the boy's head rolls to our feet on the crest of the next wave? George thought, and the thought moved him to action. "Let's get Melissa back to the car," he said, taking the child from his daughter's arms.

It was a painful march back to the car, and George was convinced that at any moment either or both of his charges would bolt. He reached the car and helped his daughter into the backseat. She was shaking violently.

"Hold Melissa," he said, passing the child to her. "Don't let her go, Nancy."

George pulled away from them and closed the car door. He turned then, refusing to look at the ocean as he did so. He looked down, stared for a moment at what was undoubtedly a wet clump of matted seaweed, and knew, with irrational certainty, that Melissa had choked on this same seaweed, had knelt here on the ground and painfully coughed it up.

He told the police that Melissa had run into the waves and that Steve had pursued her and drowned. This was all he could tell them—someday he hoped he would truly believe that it was all there was to tell. Thank God his daughter had not seen. And he realized then, with shame, that it was not even his daughter's feelings that were foremost in his mind but rather the relief, the immense relief, of knowing that what he had seen was not going to be corroborated and that with time and effort, he might really believe it was an illusion, the moment's horror, the tricks light plays with water.

He took the police back to where it happened. But he would not go down to the tide. He waited in the police car while they walked along the beach.

If they returned with Steve's head, what would he say? *Oh yes, a big wave decapitated Steve. Didn't I mention that? Well, I meant to.*

But they found nothing.

Back at the hotel, George sat at the kitchen table and drank a beer. He was not a drinker, but it seemed to help. "Where's Nancy?" he asked.

"Upstairs," Mrs. Hume said. "She's sleeping with the child. She wouldn't let me take Melissa. I tried to take the child and I thought . . . I thought my own daughter was going to attack me, hit me. Did she think I would hurt Melissa? What did she think?"

George studied his beer, shook his head sadly to indicate the absence of all conjecture.

Mrs. Hume dried her hands on the dish towel and, ducking her head, removed her apron. "Romner Psychiatric called. A Dr. Melrose."

George looked up. "Is he releasing Mrs. Franklin?" *Please come and get your daughter,* George thought. *I have a daughter of my own.* Oh, how he wanted to see the last of them.

"Not just yet. No. But he wanted to know about the family's visits every year. Dr. Melrose thought there might have been something different about that first year. He feels there is some sort of trauma associated with it."

George Hume shrugged. "Nothing out of the ordinary, as I recall."

Mrs. Hume put a hand to her cheek. "Oh, but it was different. Don't you remember, George? They came earlier, with all the crowds, and they left abruptly. They had paid for two weeks, but they were gone on the third day. I remember being surprised when they returned the next year—and I thought then that it must have been the crowds they hated and that's why they came so late from then on."

"Well . . ." Her husband closed his eyes. "I can't say that I actually remember the first time."

His wife shook her head. "What can I expect from a man who can't remember his own wedding anniversary? That Melissa was just a tot back then, a little mite in a red bathing suit. Now that I think of it, she hasn't worn a bathing suit since."

Before going to bed, George stopped at the door to his daughter's room. He pushed the door open carefully and peered in. She slept as she always slept, sprawled on her back, mouth open. She had always fallen asleep abruptly, in disarray, gunned down by the sandman. Tonight she was aided by the doctor's sedatives. The child Melissa snuggled next to her, and for one brief moment the small form seemed sinister and parasitic, as though attached to his daughter, drawing sustenance there.

"Come to bed," his wife said, and George joined her under the covers.

"It's just that she wants to protect the girl," George said. "All she has, you know. She's just seen her boyfriend drown, and this . . . I think it gives her purpose, perhaps."

Mrs. Hume understood that this was in answer to the earlier question, and she nodded her head. "Yes, I know, dear. But is it healthy? I've a bad feeling about it."

"I know," George said.

The shrill ringing of the phone woke him. "Who is it?" his wife was asking as he fumbled in the dark for the receiver.

The night-ward clerk was calling from Romner Psychiatric. She apologized for calling at such a late hour, but there might be cause for concern. Better safe than sorry, etc. Mrs. Franklin had apparently —well, had definitely—left the hospital. Should she return to the hotel, the hospital should be notified immediately.

George Hume thanked her, hung up the phone, and got out of bed. He pulled on his trousers, tugged a sweatshirt over his head.

"Where are you going?" his wife called after him.

"I won't be but a minute," he said, closing the door behind him.

The floor was cold, the boards groaning under his bare feet. Slowly, with a certainty born of dread, expecting the empty bed, expecting the worst, he pushed open the door.

Nancy lay sleeping soundly.

The child was gone. Nancy lay as though still sheltering that small, mysterious form.

George pulled his head back and closed the door. He turned and hurried down the hall. He stopped on the stairs, willed his heart to silence, slowed his breathing. "Melissa," he whispered. No answer.

He ran down the stairs. The front doors were wide open. He ran out into the moonlight and down to the beach.

The beach itself was empty and chill; an unrelenting wind blew in from the ocean. The moon shone overhead as though carved from milky ice.

He saw them then, standing far out on the pier, mother and daughter, black shadows against the moon-gray clouds that bloomed on the horizon.

Dear God, George thought. *What does she intend to do?*

"Melissa!" George shouted, and began to run.

He was out of breath when he reached them. Mother and daughter regarded him coolly, having turned to watch his progress down the pier.

"Melissa," George gasped. "Are you all right?"

Melissa was wearing a pink nightgown and holding her mother's hand. It was her mother who spoke: "We are beyond your concern, Mr. Hume. My husband is dead, and without him the contract cannot be renewed."

Mrs. Franklin's eyes were lit with some extraordinary emotion, and the wind, rougher and threatening to unbalance them all, made her hair quiver like a dark flame.

"You have your own daughter, Mr. Hume. That is a fine and wonderful thing. You have never watched your daughter die, watched her fade to utter stillness, lying on her back in the sand, sand on her lips, her eyelids; children are so untidy, even dying. It is an unholy and terrible thing to witness."

The pier groaned, and a loud crack heralded a sudden tilting of the world. George fell to his knees. A long sliver of wood entered the palm of his hand, and he tried to keep from pitching forward.

Mrs. Franklin, still standing, shouted over the wind. "We came here every year to renew the bargain. Oh, it is not a good bargain. Our daughter is never with us entirely. But you would know, any parent would know, that love will take whatever it can scavenge, any small compromise. Anything less utter and awful than the grave."

There were tears running down Mrs. Franklin's face now, silver tracks. "This year I was greedy. I wanted Melissa back, all of her. And I thought, I am her mother. I have the first claim to her. So I demanded—*demanded*—that my husband set it all to rights. 'Tell them we have come here for the last year,' I said. And my husband allowed his love for me to override his reason. He did as I asked."

Melissa, who seemed oblivious to her mother's voice, turned away and spoke into the darkness of the waters. Her words were in no language George Hume had ever heard, and they were greeted with a loud rasping bellow that thrummed in the wood planks of the pier.

Then came the sound of wood splintering, and the pier abruptly tilted. George's hands gathered more spiky wooden needles as he slid forward. He heard himself scream, but the sound was torn away by the renewed force of the wind and a hideous roaring that accompanied the gale.

Looking up, George saw Melissa kneeling at the edge of the pier. Her mother was gone.

"Melissa!" George screamed, stumbling forward. "Don't move."

But the child was standing up, wobbling, her nightgown flapping behind her.

George leapt forward, caught the child, felt a momentary flare of hope, and then they both were hurtling forward and the pier was gone.

They plummeted toward the ocean, through a blackness defined by an inhuman sound, a sound that must have been the first sound God heard when He woke at the dawn of eternity.

And even as he fell, George felt the child wiggle in his arms. His arms encircled Melissa's waist, felt bare flesh. Had he looked skyward, he would have seen the nightgown, a pink ghost shape, sailing toward the moon.

But George Hume's eyes saw, instead, the waiting ocean and under it, a shape, a moving network of cold, uncanny machinery, and whether it was a living thing of immense size, or a city, or a machine, was irrelevant. He knew only that it was ancient beyond any land-born thing.

Still clutching the child, he collided with the hard, cold back of the sea.

George Hume had been raised in close proximity to the ocean. He had learned to swim almost as soon as he had learned to walk. The cold might kill him, would certainly kill him if he did not reach shore quickly—but that he did. During the swim toward shore he lost Melissa, and in that moment he understood not to turn back, not to seek the child.

He could not tell anyone how he knew a change had been irretrievably wrought and that there was no returning the girl to land. It was not something you could communicate—any more than you could communicate the dreadful ancient quality of the machinery under the sea.

Nonetheless, George knew the moment Melissa was lost to him. It was a precise and memorable moment. It was the moment the child had wriggled, with strange new sinewy strength, flicked her tail, and slid effortlessly from his grasp.

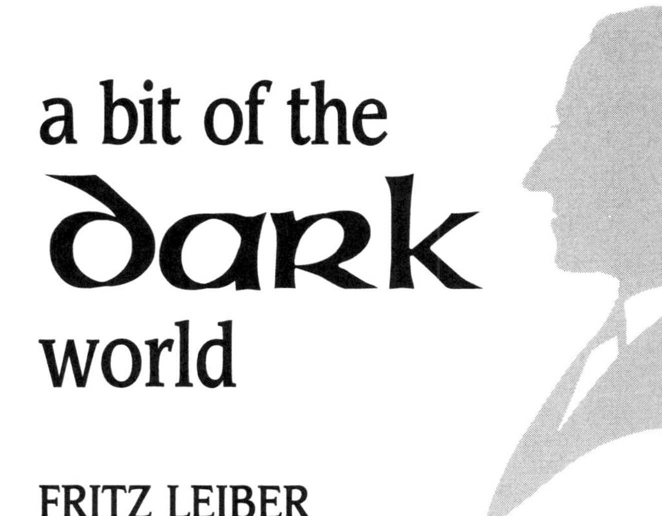

a bit of the dark world

FRITZ LEIBER

I

There was a crack in [his] head and a little bit of the Dark World came through and pressed him to death. —RUDYARD KIPLING, *THE PHANTOM 'RICKSHAW*

The antique-seeming dip-nosed black Volks touring car with its driver and two other passengers besides myself was buzzing up a saddle ridge of the Santa Monica Mountains, swinging close past the squat brush-choked peaks with their strange upjutting worn rocky pinnacles that looked like primeval monoliths or robed and hooded stone monsters.

We were moving with top down and slowly enough to glimpse sharply the occasional little pale lizard skitter or grasshopper whir up out of our way over the grey crushed stone. Once a shaggy grey cat—which Viki, clutching my arm in mock alarm, insisted was a wildcat—trotted across the narrow road ahead and disappeared in the dry aromatic underbrush. The whole area was a perfect fire hazard, and none of us needed to be reminded of the no-cigarette rule.

It was a brilliantly clear day with compact clouds that emphasized the dizzying inverted depth of the blue sky. Between clouds, the sun was dazzlingly bright. More than once, as we headed straight toward the low-trending distant incandescent orb along a switchback stretch, I was stung by its beams and suffered the penalty of black patches swimming in my vision for a minute or so. Next time we'd all remember sunglasses.

We had met only two cars and glimpsed only half a dozen houses and cabins since leaving the Pacific Coast Highway—a remarkable loneliness, considering that Los Angeles was a scant hour's drive behind us. It was a loneliness that had drawn Viki and myself apart with its silent intimations of mysteries and revelations, but not yet driven us together again by reason of its menace.

Franz Kinzman, sitting in front to the left, and his neighbor who had volunteered to do this stretch of the driving (a Mr. Morton or Morgan or Mortenson, I wasn't sure) seemed less affected by the landscape, as one would expect seeing they were both rather more familiar with it than Viki or I. Though it was hard to gauge reactions merely from the attitude of the back of Franz's close-cropped grey head or Mr. M.'s faded brown duck hat pulled low to shade his eyes.

We had just passed that point of the Little Sycamore Canyon road where all the Santa Barbara Islands—Anacapa, Santa Cruz, Santa Rosa, even distant San Miguel—are visible like an argosy of blue-grey, faintly granular clouds floating on the surface of the pale blue Pacific, when I suddenly remarked, for no profound major reason that I was aware of at the time, "I don't suppose it's any longer possible today to write a truly gripping story of supernatural horror—or for that matter to undergo a deeply disturbing experience of supernatural terror."

Oh, there were enough minor reasons for the topic of my remark. Viki and I had worked in a couple of cheap "monster" movies, Franz Kinzman was a distinguished science-fantasy writer as well as a research psychologist, and the three of us had often gabbed about the weird in life and art. Also, there had been the faintest hint of mystery in Franz's invitation to Viki and myself to spend with him the weekend of his return to Rim House after a month in L.A. Finally, the abrupt transition from a teeming city to a forbidding expanse of nature always has an eerie sting—as Franz immediately brought up without turning his head.

"I'll tell you the first condition for such an experience," he said as the Volks entered a cool band of shadow. "You've got to get away from the Hive."

"The Hive?" Viki questioned, understanding very well what he meant, I was sure, but wanting to hear him talk and have him turn his head.

Franz obliged. He has a singularly handsome, thoughtful, *noble* face, hardly of our times, though looking all of his fifty years and with eyes dark-circled ever since the death of his wife and two sons in a jet crash a year ago.

"I mean the City," he said as we buzzed into the sun again. "The human stamping ground, where we've policemen to guard us and psychiatrists to monitor our minds and neighbors to jabber at us and where our ears are so full of the clack of the mass media that it's practically impossible to think or sense or feel anything deeply, anything that's beyond humanity. Today the City, in its figurative sense, covers the whole world and the seas and by anticipation the spaceways. I think what you mean, Glenn, is that it's hard to get out of the City even in the wilderness."

Mr. M. honked twice at a blind hairpin turn and put in the next remark. "I don't know about that," he said, hunching determinedly over the wheel, "but I should think you could find all the horror and terror you wanted, Mr. Seabury, without going away from home, though it'd make pretty grim films. I mean the Nazi death camps, brainwashing, sex murders, race riots, stuff like that, not to mention Hiroshima."

"Right," I countered, "but I'm talking about supernatural horror, which is almost the antithesis of even the worst human violence and cruelty. Hauntings, the suspension of scientific law, the intrusion of the utterly alien, the sense of something listening at the rim of the cosmos or scratching faintly at the other side of the sky."

As I said that, Franz looked around at me sharply with what seemed an expression of sudden excitement and apprehension, but at that moment the sun blinded me again and Viki said, "Doesn't science fiction give you that, Glenn? I mean, horrors from other planets, the extraterrestrial monster?"

"No," I told her, blinking at a fuzzy black globe that crawled across the mountains, "because the monster from Mars or wherever has (at least as visualized by the author) so many extra feet, so many tentacles, so many purple eyes—as real as the cop on the beat. Or if he's a gas, he's a describable gas. The exact sort of goon that men will be meeting when the spaceships start traveling the starways. I'm thinking of something . . . well . . . ghostly, utterly weird."

"And it's that thing, Glenn—that ghostly, utterly weird thing—that you believe can't be written about effectively anymore, or experienced?" Franz asked me with an odd note of suppressed eagerness, eyeing me keenly, although the Volks was traveling a jouncy section. "Why?"

"You started to sketch the reasons yourself a moment ago," I said. My newest black globe was slipping sideways now, pulsing, starting to fade. "We've become too smart and shrewd and sophisticated to be scared by fantasies. Most especially we've got an army of experts to explain away the supernatural sort of thing the instant it starts to happen. The physicist boys have put matter and energy through the finest sieves—there's no room left in it for mysterious rays and influences, except for the ones they've described and cataloged. The astronomers are keeping tabs on the rim of the cosmos with their giant telescopes. The earth's been pretty thoroughly explored, enough to show there aren't any lost worlds in darkest Africa or Mountains of Madness near the South Pole."

"What about religion?" Viki suggested.

"Most religions," I replied, "steer away from the supernatural today—at least the religions that would attract an intellectual person. They concentrate on brotherhood, social service, moral leadership—or dictatorship!—and fine-drawn reconciliations of theology to the facts of science. They're not really interested in miracles or devils."

"Well, the occult then," Viki persisted. "Psionics."

"Nothing much there, either," I asserted. "If you *do* decide to go in for telepathy, ESP, hauntings—the supernatural sort of thing—you find that territory has all been staked out by Dr. Rhine, riffling his eternal Zener cards, and a bunch of other parapsychologists who tell you they've got the whole benign spirit world firmly in hand and who are as busy classifying and file-carding as the physicists.

"But worst of all," I went on as Mr. M. slowed the Volks for a potholed uphill stretch, "we've got seventy-seven breeds of certified psychiatrists and psychologists (excuse me, Franz!) all set to explain the least eerie feeling or sense of wonder we get in terms of the workings of our unconscious minds, our everyday human relationships, and our past emotional experiences."

Viki chuckled throatily and put in, "Supernatural dread almost always turns out to be nothing but childhood misconceptions and fears about sex. Mom's the witch with her breasts of mystery and her underground baby-factory, while the dark hot bristly demon dissolves to Dear Old Dad." At that moment the Volks, avoiding another dark spill of gravel, again aimed almost straight at the sun. I dodged it in part, but Viki got it full in the eyes, as I could tell from the odd way she was blinking sideways at the turreted hills a moment later.

"Exactly," I told her. "The point is, Franz, that these experts *are* experts, all joking aside, and they've divvied up the outer and inner worlds between them, and if we just start to notice something strange we turn to them at once (either actually or in our imaginations) and they have rational down-to-earth explanations all ready. And because each of the experts knows a *lot* more about his special field than we do, we have to accept their explanations—or else go off our own merry way, knowing in our heart of hearts that we're behaving like stubborn romantic adolescents or out-and-out crackpots.

"The result is," I finished as the Volks got past the potholes, "that there's no room left in the world for the weird—though plenty for crude, contemptuous, wisecracking, fun-poking imitations of it, as shown by the floods of corny 'monster' films and the stacks of monster and madness magazines with their fractionally educated hip cackling and beatnik jeers."

"Laughing in the dark," Franz said lightly, looking back where the thin dust the Volks raised was falling over the cliff toward the thorny dark ravines far below.

"Meaning?" Viki asked.

"People still are afraid," he stated simply, "and of the same things. They've just got more defenses against their fears. They've learned to talk louder and faster and smarter and funnier—*and* with more parroted expert-given authority—to shut their fears out. Why, I could tell you—" He checked himself. He really did seem intensely excited beneath the calm philosopher's mask. "I can make it clear," he said, "by an analogy."

"Do," Viki urged.

Half turned in his seat, Franz looked straight back at the two of us. A quarter of a mile ahead or so the road, climbing a little again, plunged into a stretch of heavy cloud-shadow, I noted with relief—I now had no less than three dark fuzzy globes crawling along the horizon and I yearned to be out of the sun. From the way Viki was squinting, I could tell she was in the same fix. Mr. M. with his pulled-down hat and Franz, faced around, seemed less affected.

Franz said, "Imagine that mankind is just one man—and his family—living in a house in a clearing in the midst of a dark dangerous forest, largely unknown, largely unexplored. While he works and while he rests, while he makes love to his wife or plays with his children, he's always keeping an eye on that forest.

"After a while he becomes prosperous enough to hire guards to watch the forest for him, men trained in scouting and woodcraft—your experts, Glenn. The man comes to depend on them for his safety, he defers to their judgment, he is perfectly willing to admit that each of them knows a little more about one small nearby sector of the forest than he does.

"But what if those guards should all come to him one day and say, 'Look, Master, there really is no forest out there at all, only some farmlands we're cultivating that stretch to the ends of the universe. In fact, there never was a forest out there at all, Master—you imagined all those black trees and choked aisles because you were scared of the witch doctor!'

"Would the man believe them? Would he have the faintest

justification for believing them? Or would he simply decide that his hired guards, vain of their little skills and scoutings, had developed delusions of omniscience?"

The cloud-shadow was very close now, just at the top of the slight climb we'd almost finished. Franz Kinzman leaned closer to us against the back of the front seat, and there was a hush in his voice as he said, "The dark dangerous forest is still there, my friends. Beyond the space of the astronauts and the astronomers, beyond the dark tangled regions of Freudian and Jungian psychiatry, beyond the dubious psi-realms of Dr. Rhine, beyond the areas policed by the commissars and priests and motivations-research men, far far beyond the mad half-hysterical laughter . . . the utterly unknown still *is* and the eerie and ghostly lurk, as much wrapped in mystery as ever."

With an exhilarating chilling and glooming, the Volks rolled into the sharply edged cloud-shadow. Switching around in his seat Franz began eagerly, intently, rapidly to search the landscape ahead, which seemed suddenly to expand, gain depth, and spring into sharper existence with the screening off of the blinding sun.

Almost at once his gaze fixed on a smoothly ridged grey stone pinnacle that had just come into view on the opposite rim of the canyon valley beside us. He slapped Mr. M. on the shoulder and pointed with his other hand at a small parking area, surfaced like the road, on the hillside bulge we were crossing.

Then, as Mr. M. swung the car to a grating stop in the indicated area just on the brink of the drop, Franz raised himself in his seat and, looking over the windshield, pointed commandingly at the grey pinnacle while lifting his other hand a little, fingers tautly spread, in a gesture enjoining silence.

I looked at the pinnacle. At first I saw nothing but the half-dozen rounded merging turrets of grey rock springing out of the brush-covered hilltop. Then it seemed that the last of my annoying after-images of the sun—dark, pulsing, fringe-edged—had found lodgement there.

I blinked and swung my eyes a little to make it go away or at least move off—after all, it was nothing but a fading disturbance in my retina that, purely by chance, momentarily coincided with the pinnacle.

It would not move away. It clung to the pinnacle, a dark translucent pulsing shape, as if held there by some incredible magnetic attraction.

I shivered, I felt all my muscles faintly chill and tighten at this unnatural linkage between the space inside my head and the space outside it, at this weird tie between the sort of figures that one sees in the real world and the kind that swim before the eyes when one closes them in the dark.

I blinked my eyes harder, swung my head from side to side. It was no use. The shaggy dark shape with the strange lines going out from it clung to the pinnacle like some giant clawed and crouching beast.

And instead of fading it now began to darken further, even to blacken, the faint lines got a black glitter, the whole thing began horridly to take on a definite appearance and expression, much as the figures we see swimming in the dark become faces or masks or muzzles or forms in response to our veering imagination—though now I felt no ability whatever to change the trend of the shaping of the thing on the pinnacle.

Viki's fingers dug into my arm with painful force. Without realizing it, we'd both stood up in the back of the car and were leaning forward, close to Franz. My own hands gripped the back of the front seat. Only Mr. M. hadn't raised up, though he was staring at the pinnacle, too.

Viki began, in a slow rasping strained voice, "Why, it looks like—"

With a sharp jerk of his spread-fingered hand, Franz commanded her to be silent. Then, without taking his eyes away from the crag, he dipped in the side pocket of his coat and was next reaching things back toward us.

I saw, without looking at them directly, that they were blank white cards and stub pencils. Viki and I took them—so did Mr. M.

Franz whispered hoarsely, "Don't say what you see. Write it down. Just your impressions. Now, quickly. The thing won't last long—I think."

For the next few seconds the four of us looked and scribbled and shivered—at least I know *I* was shuddering at one point, though not for an instant taking my eyes away.

Then, for me, the pinnacle was suddenly bare. I knew that it must have become so for the others too at almost the same instant, from the way their shoulders slumped and the strained sigh Viki gave.

We didn't say a word, just breathed hard for a moment or so, then passed the cards around and read them. Most of the writing or printing had the big sloppiness of something scribbled without looking at the paper, but beyond that there was a visible tremor or shakiness, especially in Viki's notes and my own.

Viki Quinn's:

Black tiger, burning bright. Blinding fur—or vines. Stickiness.

Franz Kinzman's:
Black Empress. Glittering cloak of threads.
Visual glue.
Mine (Glenn Seabury's):
Giant Spider. Black lighthouse. The web. The pull on the eyes.
Mr. M., whose writing was firmest:
I don't see anything. Except three people looking at a bare grey rock as if it were the door to Hell.

And it was Mr. M. who first looked up. We met his gaze. His lips sketched a tentative grin that seemed both sour and uneasy.

He said after a bit, "Well, you certainly had your young friends pretty well hypnotized, Mr. Kinzman."

Franz asked calmly, "Is that your explanation, Ed—hypnotic suggestion—for what happened, for what we thought happened?"

The other shrugged. "What else?" he asked more cheerfully. "Do you have another explanation, Franz—something that would account for it not working on me?"

Franz hesitated. I hung on his answer, wild to know if he'd known it was coming, as he'd seemed to, and how he'd known, and whether he'd had any comparable previous experiences. The hypnotism notion, though clever, was pure nonsense.

Finally, Franz shook his head and said firmly, "No."

Mr. M. shrugged and started the Volks.

None of us wanted to talk. The experience was still with us, pinning us down inside, and then the testimony of the cards was so complete in its way, the parallelisms so exact, the conviction of a shared experience so sure, that there was no great immediate urge to compare notes.

Viki did say to me, in the offhand way of a person checking a point of which he's almost certain, " 'Black lighthouse'—that means the light was black? Rays of darkness?"

"Of course," I told her and then asked in the same way, "Your 'vines,' Viki, your 'threads,' Franz—did they suggest those fine wire figures of curved planes and space you see in mathematical museums? Something linking a center to infinity?"

They both nodded. I said, "Like my web," and that was all the talk for a bit.

I took out a cigarette, remembered, and shoved it back in my top pocket.

Viki said, "Our descriptions . . . vaguely like descriptions of tarot cards . . . none of them actual tarots, though. . . ." Her remarks trailed off unanswered.

Mr. M. stopped at the top of a narrow drive that led down

sharply to a house of which the only visible part was the flat roof, topped by pale jagged gravel. He jumped out.

"Thanks for the lift, Franz," he said. "Remember to call on me—the phone's working again—if you people should need a lift in my car . . . or anything." He looked quickly toward the two of us in the backseat and grinned nervously. "Good-bye, Miss Quinn, Mr. Seabury. Don't—" he broke off, said simply, "So long," and walked rapidly down the drive.

Of course we guessed he'd been going to say, "Don't see any more black tigers with eight legs and lady's faces," or something like that.

Franz slid across into the driver's seat. As soon as the Volks got moving, I knew one reason the steady competent Mr. M. might have wanted to drive the mountainous stretch. Franz didn't exactly try to make the old Volks behave like a sports car, but his handling of it was in that direction—skittish, a bit dashing.

He mused aloud, "One thing keeps nagging me: Why didn't Ed Mortenson see it?—if 'see' is the right word."

So at last I was sure of Mr. M.'s name. It seemed a triumph. Viki said, "I can think of one possible reason, Mr. Kinzman. He isn't going where we're going."

II

> *Imagine one of the awful bird-catching spiders of South America translated into human form, and endowed with intelligence just less than human, and you will have some faint conception of the terror inspired by this appalling effigy.* —M. R. JAMES,
> *CANON ALBERIC'S SCRAP-BOOK*

Rim House was about two miles beyond Mr. Mortenson's place and likewise on the downhill (down-cliff, rather!) side of the road. It was reached by a decidedly one-lane drive. On the outside of the drive, edged by white-painted stones, was a near-vertical drop of over one hundred feet. On the inside was a forty-five-degree brush-dotted rocky slope between the drive and the road, which was climbing sharply along this stretch.

After about one hundred yards the drive widened to become the short, narrow, jutting plateau or terrace on which stood Rim House, occupying about half the available space. Franz, who had taken the first part of the drive with confident briskness, slowed the Volks to a crawl as soon as the house came in view, so we could scan the outside layout while still somewhat above it.

The house was built to the very edge of the drop, which here plunged down farther and even more sharply than it had along the drive. On the uphill side of the house, coming down to within two feet of it, was a dizzily expansive slope of raw earth with hardly a thing growing on it, as smoothly geometrical as a little section of the side of a vast brown cone. Along the very top of it a row of short white posts, so distant I couldn't see the cable joining them, marked the road we had left. The slope looked forty-five degrees to me—these things always look impossibly steep—but Franz said it was only thirty—a completely stabilized landslide. It had been burned over a year ago in a brush fire that had almost got the house, and still more recently there had been some minor slides started by repairs to the road above, accounting for the slope's unvegetated appearance.

The house was long, one-storey, its walls finished in grey asbestos shingles. The nearly flat roof, finished in grey asbestos sheets, sloped gently from the cliff side in. Midway the length of the house was a bend, allowing the house to conform to the curving top of the cliff and dividing it into two equal sections or angles, to call them that. An unroofed porch, lightly railed (Franz called it "the deck"), ran along the nearer angle of the house fronting north and thrusting several feet out over the drop, which at this point was three hundred feet.

On the side of the house toward the drive was a flagstone yard big enough to turn a car in and with a lightly roofed carport up against the house on the side away from the drop. As we drove down onto the yard, there was a slight *clank* as we crossed a heavy metal plate bridging a small neat ditch that ran along the foot of the raw earth slope, carrying off the water that would come down it—and also the water that would drain from the roof—during Southern California's infrequent but sometimes severe winter rains.

Franz backed the car around before we got out. It required four movements—swing to the corner of the house where the deck started, back with a sharp turn until the rear wheels were almost in the ditch, forward with a reverse turn until the front wheels were at the cliff edge by the metal bridgelet, then back into the carport until the rear of the car was almost up against a door that Franz told us led to the kitchen.

The three of us got out, and Franz led us to the center of the flagged yard for another look around before we went inside. I noticed that some of the grey flags were actually solid rock showing through the light soil cover, indicating that the plateau was not an earth terrace cut by men but a rocky flat-surfaced knob thrusting out of the hillside. It gave me a feeling of security that I especially welcomed because there were other impressions—sensations, rather—that were distinctly disturbing to me.

They were minor sensations, all of them, barely on the threshold of awareness. Ordinarily I don't think I'd have noticed them—I don't consider myself a sensitive person—but undoubtedly the strange experience of the thing on the pinnacle had keyed me up. To begin with, there was the hint of the nasty smell of burnt linen and with it an odd bitter brassy taste; I don't think I imagined these things, because I noticed Franz wrinkling his nostrils and working his tongue against his teeth. Then there was the feeling of being faintly brushed by threads, cobwebs, or the finest vines, although we were right out in the open and the nearest thing overhead was a cloud a half-mile up. And just as I felt that—the faintest feeling, mind you—I noticed Viki lightly and questingly run her hand across the top of her hair and down the back of her neck in the common gesture of "feeling for a spider."

All this time we were talking off and on—for one thing, Franz was telling us about buying Rim House on quite inexpensive terms five years back from the heir of a wealthy surfing and sports-car enthusiast who had run himself off a turn in Decker Canyon.

Finally, there were the sounds that were, I thought, breathing on the verge of audibility in the remarkably complete silence that flowed around us when the Volks's motor was cut off. I know that everyone who goes from the city to the country is troubled by sounds, but these were on the unusual side. There was an occasional whistling—too high-pitched for the ear's normal range—and a soft rumbling too low for it. But along with these perhaps fancied vibrations, three times I thought I heard the hissing rattle of fine gravel spilling down. Each time I looked quickly toward the slope, but never could catch the faintest sign of earth on the move, although there was admittedly a lot of slope to be scanned.

The third time I looked up the slope, some clouds had moved aside so that the upper rim of the sun peered back down at me. "Like a golden rifleman drawing a bead" was the grotesque figure of speech that sprang to my mind. I looked hurriedly away. I wanted no more black spots before my eyes for the present. Just then Franz led us up on the deck and into Rim House by the front door.

I was afraid that all the unpleasant sensations would intensify as we got inside—especially somehow the burnt-linen smell and the invisible cobwebs—so I was greatly cheered when instead they all vanished instantly, as though faced-down by the strong sense of Franz's genial, sympathetic, wide-ranging, highly civilized personality that the living room exuded.

It was a long room, narrow at first where it had to give space to the kitchen and utility room and a small bathroom at this end of the house, then broadening out to the full width of the building. There was no empty wall-space, it was completely lined with shelves—half of books, half of statuary, archaeological oddments, scientific instruments, tape recorder, hi-fi set, and the like. Near the inner wall, beyond the narrow section, were a big desk, some filing cabinets, and a stand with the phone.

There were no windows looking out on the deck. But just beyond the desk, where the bend in the house came, was a big view window looking out across the canyon at the craggy hills that completely cut off any sight of the Pacific. Facing the view window and close to it was a long couch backed by a long table.

At the end of the living room, a narrow hall led down the middle of the second angle of the house to a door that in turn let out into a most private grassy space that could be used for sunbathing and was just big enough for a badminton court—if anyone felt nervy enough to leap about, swatting at the bird on the edge of that great drop.

On the side of the hall toward the slope was a big bedroom—Franz's—and a large bathroom opening into the hall at the end of the house. On the other side were two only slightly smaller bedrooms, each with a view window that could be completely masked by heavy dark drapes. These rooms had been his boys', he remarked casually, but I noted with relief that there were no mementos or signs whatever left of youthful occupancy: my closet, in fact, had some women's clothes hanging in the back of it. These two bedrooms, which he assigned to Viki and myself, had a connecting door that could be bolted from both sides, but now stood unbolted but shut—a typical indication, albeit a minor one, of Franz's civilized tactfulness: he did not know, or at least did not presume to guess, the exact relationship between Viki and myself, and so left us to make our own arrangements as we saw fit—without any spoken suggestion that we should do so.

Also, each door to the hall had a serviceable bolt—Franz clearly believed in privacy for guests—and in each room was a little bowl of silver coins, no collector's items, just current American coinage. Viki asked about that and Franz explained deprecatingly, smiling at his own romanticism, that he'd copied the old Spanish California custom of the host providing guests with convenience money in that fashion.

Having been introduced to the house, we unloaded the Volks of our trifling luggage and the provisions Franz had picked up in L.A. He sighed faintly at the light film of dust that had accumulated everywhere during his month's absence, and Viki insisted that we pitch in with him and do a bit of housecleaning. Franz agreed without too much demurring. I think all of us were eager to work off the edge of this afternoon's experience and get feeling back in the real world again before we talked about it—I know I was.

Franz proved an easy man to help houseclean—thoughtful for his home but not at all fussy or finicky about it. And while wielding broom or mop Viki looked good in her sweater, toreador pants, and high-bound sandals—she wears the modern young-female's uniform with style rather than the customary effect of dreary intellectuality mated to a solemnly biologic femaleness.

When we'd done, we sat down in the kitchen with mugs of black coffee—somehow none of us wanted a drink—and listened to Franz's stew simmer.

"You'll want to know," he said without preface, "if I've had any previous eerie experiences up here, if I knew something was apt to happen when I invited you up for the weekend, whether the phenomena—pretentious term, isn't it?—seem to be connected with anything in the past of the region or the house or my own past—or with current activities here, including the scientific-military installations of the missile people—and finally whether I have any overall theory to account for them—such as Ed's suggestion about hypnotism."

Viki nodded. He'd adequately stated what was in our minds.

"About that last, Franz," I said abruptly. "When Mr. Mortenson first made that suggestion, I thought it was completely impossible, but now I'm not quite so sure. I don't mean you'd deliberately hypnotize us, but aren't there kinds of self-hypnosis that can be communicated to others? At any rate, the conditions were favorable for suggestion operating—we'd just been talking about the supernatural, there was the sun and its afterimages acting as an attention-capturer, then the sudden transition to shadow, and finally you pointing decisively at that pinnacle as if we all had to see something there."

"I don't believe that for one minute, Glenn," Viki said with conviction.

"Neither do I, really," I told her. "After all, the cards indicate we had remarkably similar visions—our descriptions were just different enough to make them convincing—and I don't see where that material could have been suggested to us during the trip out or at any earlier time when we were together. Still, the idea of some obscure sort of suggestion has crossed my mind. A blend of highway-hypnosis and sun-hypnosis, maybe? Franz, what were your earlier experiences? I take it there were some?"

He nodded but then looked at us both thoughtfully and said, "I don't think I should tell you about them in any detail, though. Not because I'm afraid of your being skeptical or anything like that, but simply because if I do, and then similar things happen to you, you'll be more likely to feel—and rightly—that the power of suggestion may have been at work.

"Still, I ought to answer your questions," he continued. "So here goes, briefly and in a general way. Yes, I had experiences while I was up here alone month before last—some of them like this afternoon's, some of them different. They didn't seem to link up with any particular folklore or occult theory or anything else, yet they frightened me so that I went down to L.A. and had my eyes checked by a very good oculist and had a psychiatrist and a couple of psychologists I trust give me a thorough checkup. They pronounced me fit and unwarped—likewise my eyes. After a month I had myself convinced that everything I'd seen or sensed had been hallucinatory, that I'd simply had a case of nerves, a fit of the horrors, from too much loneliness. I invited you two along partly to avoid restarting the cycle."

"You couldn't have been completely convinced, though," Viki pointed out. "You had those cards and pencils all ready in your pocket."

Franz grinned at the neatly scored point. "Right," he said, "I was still keeping in mind the off-trail chance and preparing for it. And then when I got in the hills, the set of my ideas changed. What had seemed completely inconceivable in L.A. became once more a borderline possibility. Queer. Come on, let's take a turn on the deck—it'll be cool by now."

We took our mugs along. It was moderately cool, all right, most of the canyon-valley had been in the shadow for at least two hours and a faint breeze flowed upward around our ankles. Once I'd got used to being on the edge of the terrific drop, I found it exhilarating. Viki must have too, for she leaned over with deliberately showy daring to peer.

The floor of the canyon was choked with dark trees and undergrowth. This thinned out going up the opposite face until just across from us there was a magnificent upthrusted and folded stratum of pale tan rock that the canyon wall cut in cross-section and showed us like a geology book. Above this fold was more undergrowth, then a series of tan and grey rocks with dark gullies and caves between them, leading by steps to a high grey summit-crag.

The slope behind the house completely cut off the sun from us, of course, but its yellow rays were still striking the tops of the wall across from us, traveling up them as the sun sank. The clouds had blown away east, where a couple were still visible, and none had come from the west to replace them.

In spite of being in a much cheerier "normal mood," I'd braced myself just a bit for the eerie little sensations as we'd come onto the deck, but they weren't there. Which somehow wasn't quite as reassuring as it ought to have been. I made myself admire the variegated rocky wall opposite.

"God, what a view to wake up to every morning!" Viki said enthusiastically. "You can feel the shape of the air and the height of the sky."

"Yes, it's quite a prospect," Franz agreed.

Then they came, the little ones, faint-footed as before, feather-treading the sensory thresholds—the burnt-linen odor, the bitter brassy tang, the brushing of skyey cobwebs, the vibrations not quite sound, the hissing rattling spill of ghost gravel . . . the minor sensations, as I'd named them to myself. . . .

I knew Viki and Franz were getting them too, simply because they said no more and I could sense them both holding very still . . . and then one of the last rays of the sun must have struck a mirror-surface in the summit-crag, perhaps an outcropping of quartz, for it struck back at me like a golden rapier, making me blink, and then for an instant the beam was glitteringly black and I thought I saw (though nothing like so clearly as I'd seen the black all-knowing spider-centipede on the pinnacle) a black shape—black with the queer churning blackness you see only at night with your eyes closed. The shape coiled rapidly down the crag, into the cavern gullies and around the rocks, and sank finally and utterly into the undergrowth above the fold and disappeared.

Along the way Viki had grabbed my arm at the elbow, and Franz had whipped round to look at us and then looked back.

It was strange. I felt frightened and at the same time eager, on the edge of marvels and mysteries about to be laid bare. And there had been something quite controlled about the behavior of all of us through it. One fantastically trivial point—none of us had spilled any coffee.

We studied the canyon wall above the fold for about two minutes.

Then Franz said, almost gaily, "Time for dinner. Talk afterwards."

I felt deeply grateful for the instant steadying, shielding, anti-hysterical, and yes, comforting effect of the house as we went back in. I knew it was an ally.

III

When the hard-boiled rationalist came to consult me for the first time, he was in such a state of panic that not only he himself, but I also felt the wind coming over the side of the lunatic asylum!

—CARL GUSTAV JUNG,
PSYCHE AND SYMBOL

We accompanied Franz's stew with chunks of dark pumpernickel and pale brick cheese and followed it with fruit and coffee, then took more coffee to the long couch facing the big view window in the living room. There was a spectral yellow glow in the sky, but it faded while we were settling ourselves. Soon the first star to the north glittered faintly—Dubhe, perhaps.

"Why is black a frightening color?" Viki put before us.

"Night," Franz said. "Though you'll get an argument as to whether it's a color or absence of color or simply basic sensory field. But is it intrinsically frightening?"

Viki nodded with pursed lips.

I said, "Somehow the phrase 'the black spaces between the stars' has always been an ultimate to me in terror. I can look at the stars without thinking of it, but the phrase gets me."

Viki said, "My ultimate horror is the idea of inky black cracks appearing in things, first in the sidewalk and the sides of houses, then in the furniture and floors and cars and things, finally in the pages of books and people's faces and the blue sky. The cracks are *inky* black—nothing ever shows."

"As if the universe were a gigantic jigsaw puzzle," I suggested.

"A little like that. Or a Byzantine mosaic. Glittering gold and glittering *black.*"

Franz said, "Your picture, Viki, suggests that sense of breaking-up we feel in the modern world. Families, nations, classes, other loyalty groups, falling apart. Things changing before you get to know them. Death on the installment plan—or decay by jumps. Instantaneous birth. Something out of nothing. Reality replacing science fiction so fast that you can't tell which is which. Constant sense of déjà vu—'I was here before—but when, how?' Even the possibility that there's no real continuity between events, just inexplicable gaps. And of course every gap—every crack—means a new perching place for horror."

"It also suggests the fragmentation of knowledge, as somebody called it," I said. "A world too big and complex to grasp in more than patches. Too much for one man. Takes teams of experts—and teams of teams. Each expert has his field, his patch, his piece of the jigsaw puzzle, but between any two pieces is a no-man's-land."

"Right, Glenn," Franz said sharply, "and today I think the three of us have plunged into one of the biggest of those no-man's-lands." He hesitated then and said with an odd diffidence, almost embarrassment, "You know, we're going to have to start talking sometime about what we saw—we can't let ourselves be gagged by this fear that anything we say will alter the picture of what the others saw and warp their testimony. Well, about the blackness of this thing or figure or manifestation I saw (I called it 'Black Empress,' but Sphinx might have been a better word—there was the suggestion of a long tigerish or serpentine body in the midst of the black fringy sunburst)—but about its blackness, now, that blackness was more than anything else like the glimmering dark the eyes see in the absence of light."

"Right," I said.

"Oh, yes," Viki chimed.

"There was a sense," Franz went on, "that the thing was in my eyes, in my head, but also out there on the horizon, on the pinnacle, I mean. That it was somehow both subjective—in my consciousness—and objective—in the material world—or"—he hesitated and lowered his voice—"or existing in some sort of space more fundamental, more primal and less organized than either of those.

"Why shouldn't there be other kinds of space than those we know?" he went on a shade defensively. "Other chambers in the great universal cave? Men have tried to imagine four, five, and more spatial dimensions. What's the space inside the atom or the nucleus *feel* like, or the space between the galaxies or beyond any galaxy? Oh, I know the questions I'm asking would be nonsense to most scientists—they're questions that don't make sense operationally or referentially, they'd say—but those same men can't give us the ghost of an answer to even the question of where and how the space of consciousness exists, how a jelly of nerve cells can support the huge flaming worlds of inner reality—they fob us off with the excuse (legitimate in its way) that science is about things that can be measured and pointed at, and who can measure or point at his thoughts? But consciousness *is*—it's the basis we all exist in and start from, it's the basis science starts from, whether or not science can get at it—so it's allowable for me to wonder whether there may not be a primal space that's a bridge between consciousness and matter . . . and whether the thing we saw may not exist in such a space."

"Maybe there *are* experts for this sort of thing and we're missing them," Viki said seriously. "Not scientists, but mystics and occultists, some of them at any rate—the genuine few among the crowd of fakers. You've got some of their books in your library. I recognized the titles."

Franz shrugged. "I've never found anything in occult literature that seemed to have a bearing. You know, the occult—very much like stories of supernatural horror—is a sort of game. Most religions too. Believe in the game and accept its rules—or the premises of the story—and you can have the thrills or whatever it is you're after. Accept the spirit world and you can see ghosts and talk to the dear departed. Accept Heaven and you can have the hope of eternal life and the reassurance of an all-powerful god working on your side.

Accept Hell and you can have devils and demons, if that's what you want. Accept—if only for story purposes—witchcraft, druidism, shamanism, magic, or some modern variant and you can have werewolves, vampires, elementals. Or believe in the influence and power of a grave, an ancient house or monument, a dead religion, or an old stone with an inscription on it—and you can have inner things of the same general sort. But I'm thinking of the kind of horror—and wonder too, perhaps—that lies beyond any game, that's bigger than any game, that's fettered by no rules, conforms to no man-made theology, bows to no charms or protective rituals, that strides the world unseen and strikes without warning where it will, much the same as (though it's of a different order of existence than all of these) lightning or the plague or the enemy atom bomb. The sort of horror that the whole fabric of civilization was designed to protect us from and make us forget. The horror about which all man's learning tells us nothing."

I stood up and moved close to the window. There seemed to be quite a few stars now. I tried to make out the big fold of rock in the hillside opposite, but the reflections on the glass got in the way.

"Maybe so," Viki said, "but there are a couple of those books I'd like to look at again. I think they're behind your desk."

"What titles?" Franz asked. "I'll help you find them."

"Meanwhile, I'll take a turn on the deck," I said as casually as I could, moving toward the other end of the room. They didn't call after me, but I had the feeling they watched me the whole way.

As soon as I'd pushed through the door—which took a definite effort of will—and shoved it to without quite shutting it behind me—which took another—I became aware of two things: that it was much darker than I'd anticipated—the big view window angled away from the deck and there was no other obvious light source except the stars—; two, that I found the darkness reassuring.

The reason for the latter seemed clear enough: the horror I'd glimpsed was associated with the sun, with blinding sunlight. Now I was safe from that—though if someone unseen should have struck a match in front of my face, the effect on me would have been extreme.

I moved forward by short steps, feeling in front of me with my hands at the level of the rail.

I knew why I'd come out here, I thought. I wanted to test my courage against the thing, whatever it was, illusory or real or something else, inside or outside our minds, or somehow as Franz had suggested, able to move in both regions. But beyond that, I realized now, there was the beginning of a fascination.

My hands touched the rail. I studied the black wall opposite, deliberately looking a little away and then back, as one does to make a faint star or a dim object come clear in the dark. After a bit I could make out a big pale fold and some of the rocks above it, but a couple of minutes' watching convinced me that it was possible endlessly to see dark shapes crossing it.

I looked up at the heavens. There was no Milky Way yet, but there would be soon, the stars were flashing on so brightly and thickly at this smog-free distance from L.A. I saw the Pole Star straight above the dark star-silhouetted summit-crag of the hillside across from me, and the Great Bear and Cassiopeia swinging from it. I felt the bigness of the atmosphere, I got a hint of the stupendous distance between me and the stars, and then—as if my vision could go out in all directions at will, piercing solidity as readily as the dark—I got a lasting, growing, wholly absorbing sense of the universe around me.

Lying behind me, a gently swelling, perfectly rounded section of the earth about a hundred miles high masked off the sun. Africa lay under my right foot through the earth's core, Australia under my left, and it was strange to think of the compressed incandescent stuff that lay between us under earth's cool mantle—blindingly glowing plastic metal or ore in a space where there were no eyes to see and no millionth of a free inch in which all that dazzling locked-up light could travel. I sensed the tortured ice of the frigid poles, the squeezed water in the deep seas, the fingers of mounting lava, the raw earth crawling and quivering with an infinitude of questing rootlets and burrowing worms.

Then for moments I felt I looked out glimmeringly through two billion pairs of human eyes, my consciousness running like fuse-fire from mind to mind. For moments more, I dimly shared the feelings, the blind pressures and pulls of a billion trillion motes of microscopic life in the air, in the earth, in the bloodstream of man.

Then my consciousness seemed to move swiftly outward from earth in all directions, like an expanding globe of sentient gas. I passed the dusty dry mote that was Mars, I glimpsed milkily banded Saturn with its great thin wheels of jumbled jagged ice. I passed frigid Pluto with its bitter nitrogen snows. I thought of how people are like plants—lonely little forts of mind with immense black distances barring them off from each other.

Then the speed of expansion of my consciousness became infinite and my mind was spread thin in the stars of the Milky Way and in the other gauzy star islands beyond it—above, below, to all sides, among the nadir stars as well as those of the zenith—and on the trillion trillion planets of those stars I sensed the infinite variety of self-conscious life—naked, clothed, furred, armor-shelled, and with cells floating free—clawed, handed, tentacled, pincered, ciliated, fingered by winds or magnetism—loving, hating, striving, despairing, imagining.

For a while it seemed to me that all these beings were joined in a dance that was fiercely joyous, poignantly sensuous, tenderly responsive.

Then the mood darkened and the beings fell apart into a trillion trillion trillion lonely motes locked off forever from each other, sensing only bleak meaninglessness in the cosmos around them, their eyes fixed forward only on universal death.

Simultaneously each dimensionless star seemed to become for me the vast sun it was, beating incandescently on the platform where my body stood and on the house behind it and the beings in it and on my body too, aging them with the glare of a billion desert moons, crumbling them all to dust in one coruscatingly blinding instant.

Hands gently grasped my shoulders, and at the same time Franz's voice said, "Steady, Glenn." I held still, though for a moment every nerve cell in me seemed on the verge of triggering, then I let out an uneven breath edged with laughter and turned and said in a voice that sounded to me quite dull, almost drugged, "I got lost in my imagination. For a minute there I seemed to be seeing everything. Where's Viki?"

"Inside leafing through *The Symbolism of the Tarot* and a couple of other books on the arcana of the fortune-telling cards, and grumbling that they don't have indexes. But what's this 'seeing everything,' Glenn?"

Haltingly I tried to tell him about my "vision," not conveying a hundredth of it, I felt. By the time I finished, I could see the blur of his face against the black wall of the house barely well enough to tell that he nodded.

"The universe fondling and devouring her children," his brooding comment came out of the dark. "I imagine you've run across in your reading, Glenn, the superficially sterile theory that the whole universe is in some sense alive or at least aware. There are lots of terms for it in the jargon of metaphysics: cosmotheism, theopantism, panpsychism, panpneumatism—but simply pantheism is the commonest. The idea that the universe is God, though for me God isn't the right term, it's been used to mean too many things. If you insist on a religious approach, perhaps what comes closest is the Greek idea of the Great God Pan, the mysterious nature deity, half animal, that frightened man and woman to panic in lonely places. Incidentally, panpneumatism is the most interesting to me of the obscurer concepts: old Karl von Hartmann's notion that the unconscious mind is the basic reality—it comes close to what we were saying inside about the possibility of a more fundamental space linking the inner and outer world and perhaps providing a bridge from anywhere to anywhere."

As he paused I heard a faint spill of gravel, then a second, though I got none of the other minor sensations.

"But whatever we call it," Franz went on, "there's something there, I feel—something less than God but more than the collective mind of man—a force, a power, an influence, a mood of things, a something more than subatomic particles, that is aware and that has grown with the universe and that helps to shape it." He had moved forward now, so that I saw his head silhouetted against the thick stars, and for a moment there was the grotesque illusion that it was the stars rather than his mouth that were speaking. "I think there are such influences, Glenn. Atomic particles alone can't sustain the flaming inner worlds of consciousness, there must be a pull from the future as well as a push from the past to keep us moving through time, there must be a ceiling of mind over life as well as a floor of matter beneath it."

Again, as his voice faded out, I heard the feathery hisses of gravel running—two close together, then two more. I thought uneasily of the slope behind the house.

"And if there are those influences," Franz continued, "I believe that man has grown enough in awareness today to be able to contact them without ritual or formula of belief, if they should chance to move or look his way. I think of them as sleepy tigers, Glenn, that mostly purr and dream and look at us through slitted eyes, but occasionally—perhaps when a man gets a hint of them—open their eyes to the full and stalk in his direction. When a man becomes ripe for them, when he's pondered the possibility of them, and then when he's closed his ears to the protective, mechanically augmented chatter of humanity, they make themselves known to him."

The spills of gravel, still faint as illusions, were coming now in a rapid rhythm like—it occurred to me at that instant—padding footsteps, each footstep dislodging a little earth. I sensed a faint brief glow overhead.

"For they're the same thing, Glenn, as the horror and wonder I talked about inside, the horror and wonder that lives beyond any game, that strides the world unseen and strikes without warning where it will."

At that instant the silence was ripped by a shrill scream of terror from the flagged yard between the house and the drive. For an instant my muscles were chilled and constricted and there was a gagging pressure in my chest. Then I lunged toward that end of the deck.

Franz darted into the house.

I plunged off the end of the deck, almost fell, twisted to my feet

—and stopped, suddenly at a loss for my next move.

Here I couldn't see a thing in the blackness. In stumbling, I'd lost my sense of direction—for the moment I didn't know which ways were the slope, the house, and the cliff edge.

I heard Viki—I thought it had to be Viki—gasping and sobbing strainingly, but the direction of *that* wouldn't come clear, except it seemed more ahead of me than behind me.

Then I saw, stretching up before me, a half-dozen or so thin close-placed stalks of what I can only describe as a more gleaming blackness—it differed from the background as dead black velvet does from dead black felt. They were barely distinguishable yet very real. I followed them up with my eyes as they mounted against the star-fields, almost invisible, like black wires, to where they ended—high up—in a bulb of darkness, defined only by the patch of stars it obscured, as tiny as the moon.

The black bulb swayed, and there was a corresponding rapid joggling in the crowded black stalks—though if they were free to move at the base, I ought to call them legs.

A door opened twenty feet from me, and a beam of white light struck across the yard, showing a streak of flagstones and the beginning of the drive.

Franz had come out of the kitchen door with a powerful flashlight. My surroundings jumped sideways into place.

The beam swept back along the slope, showing nothing else, then forward toward the cliff edge. When it got to the spot where I'd seen the ribbony black legs, it stopped.

There were no stalks, legs, or bands of any sort to be seen, but Viki was swaying and struggling there, her dark hair streaming across her face and half obscuring her agonized expression, her elbows tight to her sides, her hands near her shoulders and clawed outward—exactly as though she were gripping and struggling against the vertical bars of a tight cage.

The next instant the tension went out of her, as though whatever she'd been struggling against had vanished. She swayed and began to move in blind tottering steps toward the cliff edge.

That snapped my freeze and I ran toward her, grabbing her wrist as she stepped on the verge, and half-dragged, half-whirled her away from it. She didn't resist. Her movement toward the cliff had been accidental, not suicidal.

She looked at me, one side of her blanched face twitching, and said, "Glenn." My heart was thudding.

Franz yelled at us from the kitchen door, "Come on in!"

10

But the third Sister, who is also the youngest—! Hush! whisper whilst we talk of her! Her kingdom is not large, or else no flesh should live; but within that kingdom all power is hers. Her head, turreted like that of Cybele, rises almost beyond the reach of sight. She droops not; and her eyes, rising so high, might *be hidden by distance. But, being what they are, they cannot be hidden. . . . This youngest sister moves with incalculable motions, bounding, and with tiger's leaps. She carries no key; for, though coming rarely amongst men, she storms all doors at which she is permitted to enter at all. And her name is* Mater Tenebrarum*—our Lady of Darkness.*

—THOMAS DE QUINCEY,
SUSPIRIA DE PROFUNDIS

As soon as we got Viki inside, she recovered rapidly from her shock and at once insisted on telling us her story. Her manner was startlingly assured, interested, almost gay, as if some protective door in her mind were already closed against the absolute reality of what had happened.

At one point she even said, "It all still could have been a series of chance little sounds and sights, you know, combined with suggestion working powerfully—like the night I saw a burglar standing against the wall beyond the foot of my bed, saw him so clearly in the dark that I could have described him down to the cut of his moustache and the droop of his left eyelid . . . until the dawn coming on turned him into my roommate's black overcoat with a tan scarf thrown around the hanger and hook."

While she'd been reading, she said, she'd become aware of the ghost-spills of gravel, some of them seeming to rattle faintly against the back wall of the house, and she'd gone out at once through the kitchen to investigate.

Groping her way, moving a few steps beyond the Volks toward the center of the yard, she had looked toward the slope and at once seen moving across it an incredibly tall wispy shape that she described as "a giant harvestman, tall as ten trees. You know harvestmen, some people call them daddy longlegs, those utterly harmless pitifully fragile spiders that are nothing but a tiny brown inanimate-looking ball with eight bendy legs that are like lengths of stiffened brown thread."

She'd seen it quite clearly in spite of the darkness, because it was "black with a black shimmer." Once it had vanished completely when a car had turned the bend in the road above and its headlights had feebly swept the air high above the slope (that would have been the faint brief overhead glow I'd sensed)—but when the headlights swung away, the giant black glimmering harvestman had come back at once.

She hadn't been frightened (wonderstruck and terribly curious, rather) until the thing had come treading rapidly toward her, its shimmering black legs drawing closer and closer together until before she realized it they were a tight cage around her.

Then, as she discovered they weren't quite as thin and insubstantial as she'd imagined, and as she felt their feathery, almost bristly touch against her back and face and sides, she'd suddenly snapped and given that one terrific scream and started to struggle hysterically. "Spiders drive me wild," she finished lightly, "and there was the feeling I'd be sucked up the cage to the black brain in the stars—I thought of it as a black brain then, no reason why."

Franz didn't say anything for a bit. Then he began, in a rather heavy, halting way, "You know, I don't think I showed much foresight or consideration when I invited you two up here. Quite the opposite, in fact, even if I didn't then believe that. . . . Anyway, I don't feel right about it. Look here, you could take the Volks right now . . . or I could drive . . . and—"

"I think I know what you're getting at, Mr. Kinzman, and why," Viki said with a little laugh, standing up, "but I for one have had quite enough excitement for one night. I have no desire to top it off with watching for ghosts in the headlights for the next two hours." She yawned. "I want to hit that luxurious hay you've provided for me, right this minute. Night-night, Franz, Glenn." With no more word she walked down the hall and went into her bedroom, the far one, and closed the door.

Franz said, in a low voice, "I think you know I meant that very seriously, Glenn. It still might be the best thing."

I said, "Viki's got some kind of inner protection built up now. To get her to leave Rim House, we'd have to break it down. That would be rough."

Franz said, "Better rough, maybe, than what else might happen here tonight."

I said, "So far Rim House has been a protection for us. It's shut things out."

He said, "It didn't shut out the footsteps Viki heard."

I said, remembering my vision of the cosmos, "But Franz, if we're up against the sort of influence we think we are, then it seems to me pretty ridiculous to imagine a few miles of distance or a few bright lights making any more difference to its power than the walls of a house."

He shrugged. "We don't know," he said. "Did you see it, Glenn? Holding the light, I didn't see anything."

"Just like Viki described it," I assured him and went on to tell my own little tale. "If that was all suggestion," I said, "it was a pretty fancy variety." I squeezed my eyes and yawned; I was suddenly feeling very dull—reaction, I suppose. I finished, "While it was happening, and later while we were listening to Viki, there certainly were times when all I wanted was to be back in the old familiar world and the old familiar hydrogen bomb hanging over my head and all the rest of that stuff."

"But at the same time weren't you fascinated?" Franz demanded. "Didn't it make you crazy to know more?—the thought that you were seeing something utterly strange and that here was a chance really to understand the universe—at least to meet its unknown lords?"

"I don't know," I told him wearily. "I suppose so, in a way."

"What did the thing really seem like, Glenn?" Franz asked. "What kind of being?—if that's the right word."

"I'm not sure it is," I said. I found it difficult to summon the energy to answer his questions. "Not an animal. Not even an intelligence, as we understand it. More like the things we saw on the pinnacle and the crag." I tried to marshal my fatigue-drugged thoughts. "Halfway between reality and a symbol," I said. "If that means anything."

"But weren't you fascinated?" Franz repeated.

"I don't know," I said, pushing to my feet with an effort. "Look, Franz, I'm too beat to be able to do any more thinking now. It's just too hard to talk about these things. G'night."

"Good night, Glenn," he said as I walked to my bedroom. Nothing more.

Midway getting undressed, it occurred to me that my dazed sleepiness might be my mind's defense against having to cope with the unknown, but even that thought wasn't enough to rouse me.

I pulled on my pajamas and put out the light. Just then the door to Viki's bedroom opened and she stood there, wearing a light robe.

I had thought of looking in on her, but had decided that if she were sleeping it was the best thing for her and any attempt to check on her might break her inner protections.

But now I could tell from her expression, by the light from her room, that they were shattered.

At the same moment my own inner protection—the false sleepiness—was gone.

Viki closed the door behind her, and we moved together and put our arms around each other and stood there. After a while we lay down side by side on the bed under the view window that showed the stars.

Viki and I are lovers, but there wasn't an atom of passion in our embraces now. We were simply two, not so much frightened as completely overawed, people, seeking comfort and reassurance in each other's presence.

Not that we could hope to get any security, any protection, from each other—the thing looming above us was too powerful for that—but only a sense of not being alone, of sharing whatever might happen.

There wasn't the faintest impulse to seek temporary escape in lovemaking, as we might have done to shut out a more physical threat, the thing was too weird for that. For once Viki's body was beautiful to me in a completely cold abstract way that had no more to do with desire than the colors in an insect's wing-case or the curve of a tree or the glitter of a snowfield. Yet within this strange form, I knew, was a friend.

We didn't speak a word to each other. There were no easy words for most of our thoughts, sometimes no words at all. Besides, we shrank from making the slightest sound, as two mice would while a cat sniffs past the clump of grass in which they are hiding.

For the sense of a presence looming around and over Rim House was overpoweringly strong. Dipping *into* Rim House now too, for all the minor sensations came drifting down on us like near-impalpable snowflakes—the dark burnt taste and smell, the fluttering cobwebs, the bat-sounds and the wave-sounds and once again the feathery spills of gravel.

And above and behind them the sense of a black uprearing presence linked to the whole cosmos by the finest black filaments that in no way impeded it. . . .

I didn't think of Franz, I hardly thought of the things that had happened today, though now and then I would worry at the edge of a memory. . . .

We simply lay there and held still and looked at the stars. Minute after minute. Hour after hour.

At times we must have slept, I know I did, though blacked-out would be a better expression for it, for there was no rest and waking was a nightmarish business of slowly becoming aware of dark aches and chills.

After a long while I noticed that I could see the clock in the far corner of the room—because its dial was luminescent, I thought. The hands pointed to three o'clock. I gently turned Viki's face toward it, and she nodded that she could see it too.

The stars were what was keeping us sane, I told myself, in a world that might dissolve to dust at the faintest breath from the nearer presence.

It was just after I noticed the clock that the stars began to change color, all of them. First they had a violet tinge, which gradually shifted to blue, then green.

In an unimportant corner of my mind I wondered what sort of fine mist or dust drifting through the air could work that change.

The stars turned to dim yellow, to orange, to dark furnace-red, and then—like the last sparks crawling on a sooty chimney wall above a dead fire—winked out.

I thought crazily of the stars all springing away from earth, moving with such impossible swiftness that their light had shifted beneath the red into invisible ranges.

We should have been in utter darkness then, but instead we began to see each other and the things around us outlined by the faintest glimmer. I thought it was the first hint of morning, and I suppose Viki did too. We looked together at the clock. It was barely four-thirty. We watched the minute hand edge. Then we looked back at the window. It wasn't ghostly pale, as it would have been with dawn, but—and I could tell that Viki saw this too by the way she gripped my hand—it was a pitch-black square, framed by the white glimmer.

I could think of no explanation for the glimmer. It was a little like a whiter, paler version of the luminescence of the clock dial. But even more it was like the pictures one imagines in one's eyes in absolute darkness, when one wills the churning white sparks of the retinal field to coalesce into recognizable ghostly forms—it was as if that retinal dark had spilled out of our eyes into the room around us and we were seeing each other and our surroundings not by light but by the power of imagination—while each second increased the sense of miracle that the shimmering scene did not dissolve to churning chaos.

We watched the hand of the clock edge toward five. The thought that it must be getting light outside, and that something barred us from seeing that light, finally stirred me to move and speak, though the sense of an inhuman inanimate presence was as strong as ever.

"We've got to try and get out of here," I whispered.

Moving across the bedroom like a shimmering ghost, Viki opened the connecting door. The light had been on in her room, I remembered.

There wasn't the faintest glimmer visible through the door. Her bedroom was dead black.

I'd fix that, I thought. I switched on the lamp by the bed.

My room became solid black. I couldn't even see the face of the clock. *Light is darkness now,* I thought. *White is black.*

I switched off the light and the glimmer came back. I went to Viki where she was standing by the door and whispered to her to switch off the light in her room. Then I got dressed, mostly feeling around for my clothes, not trusting the ghostly light that was so much like a scene inside my head trembling on the verge of dissolution.

Viki came back. She was even carrying her little overnight bag. I inwardly approved the poise that action indicated, but I made no effort to take any of my own things. "My room was very cold," Viki said.

We stepped into the hall. I heard a familiar sound: the whir of a telephone dial. I saw a tall silver figure standing in the living room. It was a moment before I realized it was Franz, seen by the glimmer. I heard him say, "Hello, operator. Operator!" We walked to him.

He looked at us, holding the receiver to his ear. Then he put it down again and said, "Glenn. Viki. I've been trying to phone Ed Mortenson, see if the stars changed there, or anything else. But it doesn't work for me. You try your luck at getting the operator, Glenn."

He dialed once, then handed me the receiver. I heard no ringing, no buzz, but a sound like wind wailing softly. "Hello, operator," I said. There was no response or change, just that wind sound. "Wait," Franz said softly.

It must have been at least five seconds when my own voice came back to me out of the phone, very faintly, half drowned in the lonely wind, like an echo from the end of the universe. "Hello, operator."

My hand shook as I put down the phone. "The radio?" I asked.

"The wind sound," he told me, "all over the dial."

"Just the same, we've got to try to get out," I said.

"I suppose we should," he said with a faint ambiguous sigh. "I'm ready. Come on."

As I stepped onto the deck after Franz and Viki, I felt the intensified sense of a presence. The minor sensations were with us again, but far stronger now: the burnt taste made me gag almost, I wanted to claw at the cobwebs, the impalpable wind moaned and whistled loudly, the ghost-gravel hissed and splashed like the rapids of a river. All in near absolute darkness.

I wanted to run, but Franz stepped forward to the barely glimmering rail. I held on to myself.

The faintest glimmer showed a few lines of the rock wall opposite. But from the sky above it was beating a dead inkier blackness—*blacker than black,* I thought—that was eating up the glimmer everywhere, dimming it moment by moment. And with the inkier blackness came a chill that struck into me like needles.

"Look," Franz said. "It's the sunrise."

"Franz, we've got to get moving," I said.

"In a moment," he answered softly, reaching back his hand. "You go ahead. Start the car. Pull out to the center of the yard. I'll join you there."

Viki took the keys from him. She's driven a Volks. There was still enough glimmer to see by, though I trusted it less than ever. Viki started the car, then forgot and switched on the headlights. They obscured yard and drive with a fan of blackness. She switched them off and pulled to the center of the yard.

I looked back. Although the air was black with the icy sunlight, I could still see Franz clearly by the ghost light. He was standing where we'd left him, only leaning forward now, as though eagerly peering.

"Franz!" I called loudly against the weirdly wailing wind and the mounting gravel-roar. "Franz!"

There reared out of the canyon, facing Franz, towering above him, bending toward him a little, a filament-trailing form of shimmering velvet black—not the ghost light, but shimmering darkness itself—that looked like a gigantic hooded cobra, or a hooded madonna, or a vast centipede, or a giant figure of the cat-headed goddess Bast, or all or none of these.

I saw the silver of Franz's body begin to crumble and churn. In the same moment the dark form dipped down and enfolded him like the silk-gloved fingers of a colossal black hand or the petals of a vast black flower closing.

Feeling like someone who throws the first shovel of earth on the coffin of a friend, I croaked to Viki to go.

There was hardly any glimmer left—not enough to see the drive, I thought, as the Volks started up it.

Viki drove fast.

The sound of the spilling gravel grew louder and louder, drowning out the intangible wind, drowning out our motor. It rose to a thunder. Under the moving wheels, being transmitted up through them, the solid earth was shaking.

A bright pit opened ahead of us on the canyon side. For a moment it was as if we were driving through veils of thick smoke, then suddenly Viki was braking, we were turning into the road, and early daylight was almost blinding us.

But Viki didn't stop. She completed a near-full turn, so we were headed up the Little Sycamore Canyon road.

There was no trace of darkness at all, anywhere. The thunder that had shaken the ground was dying away.

She drove close to the edge where the road turned away at the head of the slope, and she stopped the car there.

Around us were the turreted hills. The sun hadn't yet climbed above them, but the sky was bright.

We looked down the slope. It was hollowed by the earth it had lost. No dust clouds obscured it anywhere, though there was dust rising now from the bottom of the canyon-valley.

The shrunken slope swept down straight from us to the cliff edge without a break, without a hummock, without one object thrusting up through. *Everything* had been carried away by the slide.

That was the end of Rim House and Franz Kinzman.

the perseids

ROBERT CHARLES WILSON

The divorce was finalized in the spring; I was alone that summer.

I took an apartment over a roti shop on Bathurst Street in Toronto. My landlords were a pair of ebullient Jamaican immigrants, husband and wife, who charged a reasonable rent and periodically offered to sell me grams of resinous, potent ganja. The shop closed at nine, but most summer nights the couple joined friends on a patio off the alley behind the store, and the sound of music and patois, cadences smooth as river pebbles, would drift up through my kitchen window. The apartment was a living room facing the street, a bedroom and kitchen at the rear; wooden floors and plaster ceilings with rusting metal caps where the gas fixtures had been removed. There was not much natural light, and the smell of goat curry from the kitchen downstairs was sometimes overwhelming. But taken all in all, it suited my means and needs.

I worked days at a secondhand bookshop, sorting and shelving stock, operating the antiquated cash register, and brewing cups of yerba maté for the owner, a myopic aesthete of some sixty years who subsisted on whatever dribble of profit he squeezed from the business. I was his only employee. It was not the work I had ever imagined myself doing, but such is the fortune of a blithe thirty-something who stumbles into the recession with a B.A. and negligible computer skills. I had inherited a little money from my parents, dead five years ago in a collision with a lumber truck on Vancouver Island; I hoarded the principal and supplemented my income with the interest.

I was alone and nearly friendless, and my free time seemed to stretch to the horizon, as daunting and inviting as a desert highway. One day in the bookshop I opened a copy of *Confessions of an English Opium-Eater* to the passage where De Quincey talks about his isolation from his fellow students at Manchester Grammar School: "For, whilst liking the society of some amongst them, I also had a deadly liking (perhaps a morbid liking) for solitude." Me, too, Thomas, I thought. Is it that the Devil finds work for idle hands, or that idle hands seek out the Devil's work? But I don't think the Devil had anything to do with it. (Other invisible entities, perhaps.) Alone, De Quincey discovered opium. I discovered Robin Slattery, and the stars.

We met prosaically enough: she sold me a telescope.

Amateur astronomy had been my teenage passion. When I lived with my parents on their country property north of Port Moody, I had fallen in love with the night sky. City people don't understand. The city sky is as gray and blank as slate, faintly luminous, like a smoldering trash fire. The few celestial bodies that glisten through the pollution are about as inspiring as beached fish. But travel far enough from the city and you can still see the sky the way our ancestors saw it, as a chasm beyond the end of the world in which the stars move as implacably and unapproachably as the souls of the ancient dead.

I found Robin working the show floor at a retail shop called Scopes & Lenses in the suburban flatlands north of the city. If you're like me, you often have a powerful reaction to people even before you speak to them: like or dislike, trust or fear. Robin was in the *like* column as soon as she spotted me and smiled. Her smile seemed genuine, though there was no earthly reason it should be: we were strangers, after all; I was a customer; we had these roles to play. She wore her hair short. Long, retro paisley skirt and two earrings in each ear. Sort of an art-school look. Her face was narrow, elfin, Mediterranean-dark. I guessed she was about twenty-five.

Of course the only thing to talk about was telescopes. I wanted to buy one, a good one, something substantial, not a toy. I lived frugally, but every couple of years I would squeeze a little money out of my investments and buy myself an expensive present. Last year, my van. This year, I had decided, a telescope. (The divorce had been expensive, but that was a necessity, not a luxury.)

There was plenty to talk about. 'Scopes had changed since I was a teenager. Bewilderingly. It was all Dobsonians, CCD imagers, object-acquisition software. . . . I took a handful of literature and told her I'd think about it. She smiled and said, "But you're serious, right? I mean, some people come in and look around and then do mail-order from the States. . . ." And then laughed at her own presumption, as if it were a joke, between us.

I said, "You'll get your commission. Promise."

"Oh, God, I wasn't *angling* . . . but here's my card . . . I'm in the store most afternoons."

That was how I learned her name.

Next week I put a 10-inch Meade Starfinder on my Visa card. I was back two days later for accessory eyepieces and a camera adapter. That was when I asked her out for coffee.

She didn't even blink. "Store closes in ten minutes," she said, "but I have to do some paperwork and make a deposit. I could meet you in an hour or so."

"Fine. I'll buy dinner."

"No, let me buy. You already paid for it. The commission—remember?"

She was like that.

Sometime during our dinner conversation she told me she had never looked through a telescope.

"You have to be kidding."

"Really!"

"But you know more about these things than I do, and I've looked through a lot of lenses."

She poked her fork at a plate of goat cheese torta as if wondering how much to say. "Well, I know *telescopes*. I don't know much astronomy. See, my father was into telescopes. He took photographs, 35mm long exposures, deep-sky stuff. I looked at the pictures; the pictures were great. But never, you know, through the eyepiece."

"Why not?" I imagined a jealous parent guarding his investment from curious fingers.

But Robin frowned as if I had asked a difficult question. "It's hard to explain. I just didn't want to. Refused to, really. Mmm . . . have you ever been alone somewhere on a windy night, maybe a dark night in winter? And you kind of get spooked? And you want to look out a window and see how bad the snow is, but you get this idea in your head that if you open the curtain something truly horrible is going to be out there staring right back at you? And you know it's childish, but you still don't open the curtain. Just can't bring yourself to do it. You know that feeling?"

I said I'd had similar experiences.

"I think it's a primate thing," Robin meditated. "Stay close to the fire or the leopard'll get you. Anyway, that's the way I feel about telescopes. Irrational, I know. But there it is. Here we are on this cozy planet, and out there are all kinds of things—vast blazing suns and frigid planets and the dust of dead stars and whole galaxies dying. I always had this feeling that if you looked too close, something might look back. Like, don't open the curtain. Don't look through the 'scope. Because something might look back."

Almost certainly someone or something was looking back. The arithmetic is plain: a hundred billion stars in the galaxy alone, many times that number of planets, and even if life is uncommon and intelligence an evolutionary trick shot, odds are that when you gaze at the stars, somewhere in that horizonless infinity another eye is turned back at you.

But that wasn't what Robin meant.

I knew what she meant. Set against the scale of even a single galaxy, a human life is brief and human beings less than microscopic. Small things survive because, taken singly, they're inconsequential. They escape notice. The ant is invisible in the shadow of a spruce bud or a clover leaf. Insects survive because, by and large, we only kill what we can see. The insect prayer: *Don't see me!*

Now consider those wide roads between the stars, where the only wind is a few dry grains of hydrogen and the dust of exploded suns. What if something walked there? Something unseen, invisible, immaterial—vaster than planets?

I think that's what Robin felt: her own frailty against the abysses of distance and time. *Don't look. Don't see me. Don't look.*

It was a friend of Robin's, a man who had been her lover, who first explained to me the concept of "domains."

By mid-September Robin and I were a couple. It was a relationship we walked into blindly, hypnotized by the sheer unlikeliness of it. I was ten years older, divorced, drifting like a swamped canoe toward the rapids of midlife; she was a tattooed Gen-Xer (the Worm Ouroboros circling her left ankle in blue repose) for whom the death of Kurt Cobain had been a meaningful event. I think we aroused each other's exogamous instincts. We liked to marvel at the chasm between us, that deep and defining gulf: Winona Ryder vs. Humbert Humbert.

She threw a party to introduce me to her friends. The prospect was daunting, but I knew this was one of those hurdles every relationship has to jump or kick the traces. So I came early and helped her clean and cook. Her apartment was the top of a subdivided house in Parkdale, off Queen Street. Not the fashionable end of Queen Street; the hooker and junkie turf east of Roncesvalles Avenue. Rent was cheap. She had decorated the rambling attic space with religious bric-a-brac from Goodwill thrift shops and the East Indian dollar store around the corner: ankhs, crosses, bleeding hearts, gaudy Hindu iconography. "Cultural stew," she said. "Artifacts from the new domain. You can ask Roger about that."

I thought: Roger?

Her friends arrived by ones and twos. Lots of students, a few musicians, the creatively unemployed. Many of them thought black was a party color. I wondered when the tonsure and the goatee had come back into style and felt set apart in jeans and sweatshirt, the wardrobe-for-all-occasions of another generation. But the people (beneath these appurtenances: people) were mostly friendly. Robin put on a CD of bhangra music and brought out a tall blue plastic water pipe, which circulated with that conspiratorial grace the cannabis culture inherits from its ancestors in Kennedy-era prehistory. This, at least, I recognized. Like Kennedy (they say), unlike Bill Clinton, I inhaled. But only a little. I wanted a clear head to get through the evening.

Robin covered a trestle table with bowls of kasha, rice cooked in miso (her own invention), a curry of beef, curry of eggplant, curry of chicken; chutneys from Kensington Market, loaves of sourdough and French bread and chapatis. Cheap red wine. There was a collective murmur of appreciation, and Robin gave me more credit than I deserved—all I had done was stir the pots.

For an hour after dinner I was cornered by a University of Toronto poli-sci student from Ethiopia who wanted me to understand how Mao had been betrayed by the revisionists who inherited his empire. He was, of course, the son of a well-to-do bureaucrat, and brutally earnest. I played vague until he gave up on me. Then, cut loose, I trawled through the room picking up fragments of conversation, names dropped: Alice in Chains, Kate Moss, Michelangelo Signorile. Robin took me by the elbow. "I'm making tea. Talk to Roger!"

Roger was tall and pale, with a shock of bleached hair threatening to obscure the vision in his right eye. He had the emaciated frame of a heroin addict, but it was willful, an aesthetic statement, and he dressed expensively.

Roger. "Domains." Fortunately I didn't have to ask; he was already explaining it to a pair of globe-eyed identical twins.

"It's McLuhanesque," one twin said; the other: "No, *ecological . . .*"

Roger smiled, a little condescendingly, I thought, but I was already wondering what he meant to Robin, or Robin to him. He put out his hand: "You must be Michael. Robin told me about you."

But not me about Roger. At least not much. I said, "She mentioned something about 'domains'—"

"Well, Robin just likes to hear me bullshit."

"No!" (The twins.) "Roger is *original.*"

It didn't take much coaxing. I can't reproduce his voice—cool, fluid, slightly nasal—but what he said, basically, was this:

Life, the biological phenomenon, colonizes domains and turns them into ecologies. In the domain of the ocean, the first ecologies evolved. The dry surface of the continents was a dead domain until the first plants (lichens or molds, I suppose) took root. The air was an empty domain until the evolution of the wing.

But domain theory, Roger said, wasn't just a matter of biology versus geology. A living system could *itself* become a domain. In fact, once the geological domains were fully colonized, living systems became the last terrestrial domain and a kind of intensive recomplication followed: treetops, colonizing the air, were colonized in turn by insects, by birds; animal life by bacteria, viruses, parasites, each new array creating its own new domain, and so ad infinitum.

What made Roger's notion original was that he believed human beings had—for the first time in millennia—begun to colonize a wholly new domain, which he called the *gnososphere:* the domain of culture, art, religion, language. Because we were the first aboard, the gnososphere felt more like geology than ecology: a body of artifacts, lifeless as a brick. But that appearance was already beginning to change. We had seen in the last decade the first glimmerings of competition, specifically from the kind of computer program called "artificial life," entities that live—and evolve—entirely in the logarithms of computers, the high alps of the gnososphere. Not competing for *our* ground, obviously, but that time might come (consider computer "viruses"), and—who knows?—the gnososphere might eventually evolve its own independent entities. Maybe already had. When the gnososphere was "made of" campfire stories and cave paintings, it was clearly not complex enough to support life. But the gnososphere at the end of the twentieth century had grown vast and intricate, a landscape both cerebral and electronic, born at the juncture of technology and human population, in which crude self-replicating structures (Nazism, say; Communism) had already proven their ability to grow, feed, reproduce, and die. Ideologies were like primitive DNA floating in a nutrient soup of radio waves, television images, words. Who could say what a more highly evolved creature—with protein coat, nucleus, mitochondria; with eyes and genitals—might be like? We might not be able to experience it at all, since no single human being could be its host; it would live through our collectivity, as immense as it was unknowable.

"Amazing," the twins said when Roger finished. *"Awesome."*

And suddenly Robin was beside me, handing out tea, taking my arm in a proprietary gesture meant, I hoped, for Roger, who smiled tolerantly. "He is amazing, isn't he? Or else completely insane."

"Not for me to say," Roger obliged. (The twins laughed.)

"Roger used to be a Fine Arts T.A. at the University," Robin said, "until he dropped out. Now he builds things."

"Sculpture?" I asked.

"Things. Maybe he'll show you sometime."

Roger nodded, but I doubted he'd extend the invitation. We were circling each other like wary animals. I read him as bright, smug, and subtly hostile. He obviously felt a powerful need to impress an audience. Probably he had once impressed Robin—she confirmed this later—and I imagined him abandoning her because, as audience, she had grown a little cynical. The twins (young, female) clearly delighted him. Just as clearly, I didn't.

But we were polite. We talked a little more. He knew the bookstore where I worked. "Been there often," he said. And it was easy to imagine him posed against the philosophy shelves, long fingers opening Kierkegaard, the critical frown fixed in place. After a while I left him to the twins, who waved me good-bye: "Nice meeting you!" *"Really!"*

When I was younger I read a lot of science fiction. Through my interest in astronomy I came to SF, and through both I happened across an astronomer's puzzle, a cosmological version of Pascal's wager. It goes like this: If life can spread through the galaxy, then, logically, it already has. Our neighbors should be here. Should have been here for millennia. Where are they?

I discussed it, while the party ran down, with the only guest older than I was, a graying science-fiction writer who had been hitting the pipe with a certain bleak determination. "The Oort cloud," he declared, *"that's* where they are. I mean, why bother with planets? For dedicated space technologies—and I assume they would send machines, not something as short-lived and finicky as a biological organism—a planet's not a really attractive place. Planets are heavy, corrosive, too hot for superconductors. Interesting places, maybe, because planets are where cultures grow, and why slog across all those light-years unless you're looking for something as complex and unpredictable as a sentient culture? But you don't, for God's sake, fill up their sky with spaceships. You stick around the Oort cloud, where it's nice and cold and there are cometary bodies to draw resources from. You hang out, you listen. If you want to talk, you pick your own time."

The Oort cloud is that nebulous ring around the solar system, well beyond the orbit of Pluto, composed of small bodies of dust and water ice. Gravitational perturbation periodically knocks a few of these bodies into elliptical orbits; traversing the inner solar system, they become comets. Our annual meteor showers—the Perseids, the Geminids, the Quadrantids—are the remnants of ancient, fractured comets. Oort cloud visitors, old beyond memory.

But in light of Roger's thesis I wondered if the question was too narrowly posed, the science-fiction writer's answer too pat. Maybe our neighbors had already arrived, not in silver ships but in metaphysics, informing the very construction and representation of our lives. The cave paintings at Lascaux, Chartres Cathedral, the Fox Broadcasting System—not their physicality (and they become less physical as our technology advances) but their intangible *grammar*—maybe this is the evidence they left us, a ruined archaeology of cognition, invisible because pervasive, inescapable: they are both here, in other words, and not here; they are us and not-us.

When the last guest was gone, the last dish stacked, Robin pulled off her shirt and walked through the apartment, coolly unself-conscious, turning off lights.

The heat of the party lingered. She opened the bedroom window to let in a breeze from the lakeshore. It was past two in the morning, and the city was relatively quiet. I paid attention to the sounds she made, the rustle as she stepped out of her skirt, the easing of springs in the thrift-shop bed. She wore a ring through each nipple, delicate turquoise rings that gave back glimmers of ambient light. I remembered how unfamiliar her piercings had seemed the first time I encountered them with my tongue, the polished circles, their chilly, perfect geometry set against the warmer and more complex terrain of breast and aureole.

We made love in that distracted after-a-party way while the room was still alive with the musk of the crowd, feeling like exhibitionists (I think she felt that way, too) even though we were alone.

It was afterward, in a round of sleepy pillow talk, that she told me Roger had been her lover. I put a finger gently through one of her rings, and she said Roger had piercings, too: one nipple and under the scrotum, penetrating the area between the testicles and the anus. Some men had the head of the penis pierced (a "Prince Albert"), but Roger hadn't gone for that.

I was jealous. Jealous, I suppose, of this extra dimension of intimacy from which I was excluded. I had no wounds to show her.

She said, "You never talk about your divorce."

"It's not much fun to talk about."

"You left Carolyn, or she left you?"

"It's not that simple. But, ultimately, I guess she left me."

"Lots of fighting?"

"No fighting."

"What, then?"

I thought about it. "Continental drift."

"What was her problem?"

"I'm not so sure it *was* her problem."

"She must have had a reason, though—or thought she did."

"She said I was never there." Robin waited patiently. I went on, "Even when I was with her, I was never *there*—or so she claimed. I'm not sure I know what she meant. I suppose, that I wasn't completely engaged. That I was apart. Held back. With her, with her friends, with her family—with anybody."

"Do you think that's true?"

It was a question I'd asked myself too often.

Sure, in a sense it *was* true. I'm one of those people who are often called loners. Crowds don't have much allure for me. I don't confide easily, and I don't have many friends.

That much I would admit to. The idea (which had come to obsess Carolyn during our divorce) that I was congenitally, hopelessly *set apart,* a kind of pariah dog, incapable of real intimacy . . . that was a whole 'nother thing.

We talked it around. Robin was solemn in the dark, propped on one elbow. Through the window, past the halo of her hair, I could see the setting moon. Far away down the dark street someone laughed.

Robin, who had studied a little anthropology, liked to see things in evolutionary terms. "You have a night watch personality," she decided, closing her eyes.

"Night watch?"

"Mm-hm. Primates . . . you know . . . protohominids . . . it's where all our personality styles come from. We're social animals, basically, but the group is more versatile if you have maybe a couple of hyperthymic types for cheerleaders, some dysthymics to sit home and mumble, and the one guy—you—who edges away from the crowd, who sits up when everybody else is asleep, who basically keeps the watches of the night. The one who sees the lions coming.

Good night vision and lousy social skills. Every tribe should have one."

"Is that what I am?"

"It's reassuring, actually." She patted my ass and said, "Keep watch for me, okay?"

I kept the watch a few minutes more.

In the morning, on the way to lunch, we visited one of those East Indian/West Indian shops, the kind with the impossibly gaudy portraits of Shiva and Ganesha in chrome-flash plastic frames, a cooler full of ginger beer and coconut pop, shelves of sandalwood incense and patchouli oil and bottles of magic potions (Robin pointed them out): St. John Conqueror Root, Ghost Away, Luck Finder, with labels claiming the contents were an Excellent Floor Polish, which I suppose made them legal to sell. Robin was delighted: "Flotsam from the gnososphere," she laughed, and it was easy to imagine one of Roger's gnostic creatures made manifest in this shop—for that matter, in this city, this English-speaking, Cantonese-speaking, Urdu-speaking, Farsi-speaking city—a slouching, ethereal beast of which one cell might be Ganesha, the Elephant-Headed Boy, and another Madonna, the Cone-Breasted Woman.

A city, for obvious reasons, is a lousy place to do astronomy. I worked the 'scope from the back deck of my apartment, shielded from streetlights, and Robin gave me a selection of broadband lens filters to cut the urban scatter. But I was interested in deep-sky observing, and I knew I wasn't getting everything I'd paid for.

In October I arranged to truck the 'scope up north for a weekend. I rented a van, and Robin reserved us a cabin at a private campground near Algonquin Park. It was way past tourist season, but Robin knew the woman who owned the property; we would have the place virtually to ourselves and we could cancel, no problem, if the weather didn't look right.

But the weather cooperated. It was the end of the month—coincidentally, the weekend of the Orionid meteor shower—and we were in the middle of a clean high-pressure cell that stretched from Alberta to Labrador. The air was brisk but cloudless, transparent as creek water. We arrived at the campsite Friday afternoon, and I spent a couple of hours setting up the 'scope, calibrating it, and running an extension cord out to the automatic guider. I attached a 35mm SLR camera loaded with hypersensitized Tech Pan film, and I did all this despite the accompaniment of the owner's five barking Yorkshire terrier pups. The ground under my feet was glacier-scarred Laurentian Shield rock; the meadow I set up in was broad and flat;

highway lights were pale and distant. Perfect. By the time I finished setting up, it was dusk. Robin had started a fire in the pit outside our cabin and was roasting chicken and bell peppers. The cabin overlooked a marshy lake thick with duckweed; the air was cool and moist, and I fretted about ground mist.

But the night was clear. After dinner Robin smoked marijuana in a tiny carved soapstone pipe (I didn't), and then we went out to the meadow, bundled in winter jackets.

I worked the 'scope. Robin wouldn't look through the eyepiece —her old phobia—but took a great, grinning pleasure in the Orionids, exclaiming at each brief etching of the cave-dark star-scattered sky. Her laughter was almost giddy.

After a time, though, she complained of the cold, and I sent her back to the cabin (we had borrowed a space heater from the owner) and told her to get some sleep. I was cold, too, but intoxicated by the sky. It was my first attempt at deep-sky photography and surprisingly successful: when the photos were developed later that week, I had a clean, hard shot of M100 in Coma Berenices, a spiral galaxy in full disk, arms sweeping toward the bright center; a city of stars beyond counting, alive, perhaps, with civilizations, so impossibly distant that the photons hoarded by the lens of the telescope were already millions of years old.

When I finally came to bed, Robin was asleep under two quilted blankets. She stirred at my pressure on the mattress and turned to me, opened her eyes briefly, then folded her cinnamon-scented warmth against my chest, and I lay awake smelling the hot coils of the space heater and the faint pungency of the marijuana she had smoked and the pine-resinous air that had swept in behind me, these night odors mysteriously familiar, intimate as memory.

We made love in the morning, lazy and a little tired, and I thought there was something new in the way she looked at me, a certain calculating distance, but I wasn't sure; it might just be the slant of light through the dusty window. In the afternoon we hiked out to a wild blueberry patch she knew about, but the season was over; frost had shriveled the last of the berries. (The Yorkshire terriers were at our heels, there and back.)

That night was much the same as the first except that Robin decided to stay back at the cabin reading an Anne Rice novel. I remembered that her father was an amateur astronomer and wondered if the parallel wasn't a little unsettling for her: there are limits to the pleasures of symbolic incest. I photographed M33 in Triangulum, another elliptical galaxy, its arms luminous with stars, and in the morning we packed up the telescope and began the long drive south.

She was moodier than usual. In the cabin of the van, huddled by the passenger door with her knees against her chest, she said, "We never talk about relationship things."

"Relationship things?"

"For instance, monogamy."

That hung in the air for a while.

Then she said, "Do you believe in it?"

I said it didn't really matter whether I "believed in" it; it just seemed to be something I did. I had never been unfaithful to Carolyn, unless you counted Robin; I had never been unfaithful to Robin.

But she was twenty-five years old and hadn't taken the measure of these things. "I think it's a sexual preference," she said. "Some people are, some people aren't."

I said—carefully neutral—"Where do you stand?"

"I don't know." She gazed out the window at October farms, brown fields, wind-canted barns. "I haven't decided."

We left it at that.

She threw a Halloween party, costumes optional—I wore street clothes, but most of her crowd welcomed the opportunity to dress up. Strange hair and body paint, mainly. Roger (I had learned his last name: Roger Russo) showed up wearing a feathered headdress, green dye, kohl circles around his eyes. He said he was Sacha Runa, the jungle spirit of the Peruvian *ayahuasqueros*. Robin said he had been investigating the idea of shamanic spirit creatures as the first entities cohabiting the gnososphere: she thought the costume was perfect for him. She hugged him carefully, pecked his green-dyed cheek, merely friendly, but he glanced reflexively at me and quickly away, as if to confirm that I had seen her touch him.

I had one of my photographs, the galaxy M33, enlarged and framed; I gave it to Robin as a gift.

She hung it in her bedroom. I remember—it might have been November, maybe as late as the Leonids, midmonth—a night when she stared at it while we made love: she on her knees on the bed, head upturned, raw-cut hair darkly stubbled on her scalp, and me behind her, gripping her thin, almost fragile hips, knowing she was looking at the stars.

Three optical illusions:

1) Retinal floaters. Those delicate crystalline motes, like rainbow-hued diatoms, that swim through the field of vision.

Some nights, when I've been too long at the 'scope, I see them drifting up from the horizon, a terrestrial commerce with the sky.

2) In 1877, Giovanni Schiaparelli mapped what he believed were the canals of Mars. Mars has no canals; it is an airless desert. But for decades the educated world believed in a decadent Martian civilization, doomed to extinction when its water evaporated to the frigid poles.

It was Schiaparelli who first suggested that meteor showers represent the remains of ancient shattered comets.

3) Computer-generated three-dimensional pictures—they were everywhere that summer, a fad. You know the kind? The picture looks like so much visual hash until you focus your eyes well beyond it; then the image lofts out, a hidden bas-relief—ether sculpture.

Robin believed TV worked the same way. "If you turn to a blank channel," she told me (December: first snow outside the window), "you can see pictures in the static, 3–D. And they move."

"What kind of pictures?"

"Strange." She was clearly uncomfortable talking about it. "Kind of like animals. Or bugs. Lots of arms. The eyes are very . . . strange." She gave me a shy look. "Am I crazy?"

"No." Everyone has a soft spot or two. "You look at these pictures often?"

"Hardly ever. Frankly, it's kind of scary. But it's also . . ."

"What?"

"Tempting."

I don't own a television set. One summer Carolyn and I had taken a trip to Mexico, and we had seen the famous murals at Teotihuacán. Disembodied eyes everywhere: plants with eyes for flowers, flowers exuding eyes, eyes floating through the convoluted images like lost balloons. Whenever people talk about television, I'm reminded of Teotihuacán.

Like Robin, I was afraid to look through certain lenses for fear of what might be looking back.

That winter, I learned more about Roger Russo.

He was wealthy. At least, his family was wealthy. The family owned Russo Precision Parts, an electronics distributor with a near-monopoly of the Canadian manufacturing market. Roger's older brother was the corporate heir-designate; Roger himself, I gather, was considered "creative" (that is, unemployable) and allowed a generous annual remittance to do with as he pleased.

Early in January (the Quadrantids, but they were disappointing that year), Robin took me to Roger's place. He lived in a house off Queen West—leased it from a cousin—a three-story brick Edwardian bastion in a Chinese neighborhood where the houses on each side had been painted cherry red. We trekked from the streetcar through fresh ankle-high snow; the snow was still falling, cold and granular. Robin had made the date: we were supposed to have lunch, the three of us. I think she liked bringing Roger and me together, liked those faint proprietary sparks that passed between us; I think it flattered her. Myself, I didn't enjoy it. I doubted Roger took much pleasure in it, either.

He answered the door wearing nothing but jogging pants. His solitary silver nipple ring dangled on his hairless chest; it reminded me—sorry—of a pull-tab on a soft drink can. He shooed us in and latched the door. Inside, the air was warm and moist.

The house was a shrine to his eccentricity: books everywhere, not only shelved but stacked in corners, an assortment too random to categorize, but I spotted early editions of William James (*Psychology,* the complete work) and Karl Jung; a ponderous hardcover *Phenomenology of the Mind,* Heidegger's *Being and Time*. We adjourned to a big wood-and-tile kitchen and made conversation while Roger chopped kohlrabi at a butcher-block counter. He had seen *Natural Born Killers* at a review theater and was impressed by it: "It's completely post-post—a deconstruction of *itself*—very image-intensive and, you know, florid, like early church iconography. . . ."

The talk went on like this. High-toned media gossip, basically. After lunch, I excused myself and hunted down the bathroom.

On the way back, I paused at the kitchen door when I heard Roger mention my name.

"Michael's not much of a watcher, is he?"

Robin: "Well, he is, actually—a certain kind of watcher."

"Oh—the astronomy . . ."

"Yes."

"That photograph you showed me."

"Yes, right."

That photograph, I thought. The one on her bedroom wall.

Later, in the winter-afternoon lull that softens outdoor sounds and amplifies the rumble of the furnace, Robin asked Roger to show me around the house. "The upstairs," she said, and to me: "It's so weird!"

"Thanks," Roger said.

"You know what I mean! Don't pretend to be insulted. *Weird* is your middle name."

I followed Roger's pale back up the narrow stairway, creaking risers lined with faded red carpet. Then, suddenly, we were in another world: a cavernous space—walls must have been knocked out—crowded with electronic kibble. Video screens, raw circuit boards, ribbon wire snaking through the clutter like eels through a gloomy reef. He threw a wall switch, and it all came to life.

"A dozen cathode-ray tubes," Roger said, "mostly yard-sale and electronic-jobber trash." Some were black and white, some crenellated with noise bars. "Each one cycles through every channel you can get from cable. I wired in my own decoder for the scrambled channels. The cycles are staggered, so mostly you get chaos, but every so often they fall into sync and for a split second the same image is all around you. I meant to install a satellite dish, feed in another hundred channels, but the mixer would have been . . . complex. Anyway, I lost interest."

"Not to sound like a Philistine," I said, "but what is it—a work of art?"

Roger smiled loftily. "In a way. Actually, it was meant to be a ghost trap."

"Ghost trap?"

"In the Hegelian sense. The *Weltgeist.*"

"Summoned from the gnososphere," Robin added.

I asked about the music. The music had commenced when he threw the switch: a strange nasal melody, sometimes hummed, sometimes chanted. It filled the air like incense. The words, when I could make them out, were foreign and punctuated with thick glottal stops. There were insect sounds in the background; I supposed it was a field recording, the kind of anthropological oddity a company called Nonesuch used to release on vinyl, years ago.

"It's called an *icaro,*" Roger said. "A supernatural melody. Certain Peruvian Indians drink *ayahuasca* and produce these songs. *Icaros*. They learn them from the spirit world."

Ayahuasca is a hallucinogenic potion made from a mixture of *Banisteriopsis caapi* vines and the leaves of *Psychotria viridis,* both rainforest plants. (I spent a day at the Robarts looking it up.) Apparently it can be made from a variety of more common plant sources, and *ayahuasca* churches like the Uniao do Vegetal have popularized its use in the urban centers of Brazil.

"And the third floor," Robin said, waving at the stairs dimly visible across the room, "that's amazing, too. Roger built an addition over what used to be the roof of the building. There's a greenhouse, an actual greenhouse! You can't see it from the street because the facade hides it, but it's huge. And there's a big open-air deck. Show him, Roger."

Roger shook his head: "I don't think it's necessary."

We were about to leave the room when three of the video screens suddenly radiated the same image: waterfall and ferns in soft focus, and a pale woman in a white skirt standing beside a Datsun that matched her blue-green eyes. It snagged Roger's attention. He stopped in his tracks.

"Rainha da Floresta," he murmured, looking from Robin to me and back again, his face obscure in the flickering light. "The lunar aspect."

The winter sky performed its long procession. One clear night in February, hungry for starlight, I zipped myself into my parka and drove a little distance west of the city—not with the telescope but with a pair of 10 x 50 Zeiss binoculars. Hardly Mount Palomar, but not far removed from the simple optics Galileo ground for himself some few centuries ago.

I parked off an access road along the ridge top of Rattlesnake Point, with a clear view to the frozen rim of Lake Ontario. Sirius hung above the dark water, a little obscured by rising mist. Capella was high overhead, and to the west I was able to distinguish the faint oval of the Andromeda galaxy, two-million-odd light-years away. East, the sky was vague with city glare and etched by the running lights of airliners orbiting Pearson International.

Alone in the van, breathing steam and balancing the binoculars on the rim of a half-open window, I found myself thinking about the E.T. paradox. They ought to be here . . . where are they?

The science-fiction writer at Robin's party had said they wouldn't come in person. Organic life is too brief and too fragile for the eons-long journeys between stars. They would send machines. Maybe self-replicating machines. Maybe sentient machines.

But, I thought, why machines at all? If the thing that travels most efficiently between stars is light (and all its avatars: X-rays, radio waves), then why not send *light itself?* Light *modulated,* of course; light alive with information. Light as medium. Sentient light.

Light as domain, perhaps put in place by organic civilizations, but inherited by—something else.

And if human beings are truly latecomers to the galaxy, then the network must already be ancient, a web of modulated signals stitching together the stars. A domain in which things—entities—creatures perhaps as diffuse and large as the galaxy itself, creatures made solely of information—live and compete and maybe even hunt.

An ecology of starlight, or better: a *jungle* of starlight.

The next day I called up Robin's SF-writer friend and tried out the idea on him. He said, "Well, it's interesting. . . ."

"But is it possible?"

"Sure, it's possible. Anything's possible. Possible is my line of work. But you have to keep in mind the difference between a possibility and a likelihood." He hesitated. "Are you thinking of becoming a writer, or just a career paranoid?"

I laughed. "Neither one." Though the laughter was a little forced.

"Well, then, since we're only playing, here's another notion for you. Living things—species capable of evolving—don't just live. They eat." (*Hunt,* I thought.) "They die. And most important of all: they reproduce."

You've probably heard of the hunting wasp. The hunting wasp paralyzes insects (the tarantula is a popular choice) and uses the still-living bodies to incubate and feed its young.

It's everybody's favorite Hymenoptera horror story. You can't help imagining how the tarantula must feel, immobilized but for its frantic heartbeat, the wasp larvae beginning to stir inside it . . . stir, and feed.

But maybe the tarantula isn't only paralyzed. Maybe it's entranced. Maybe wasp venom is a kind of insect ambrosia—*soma, amrta, kykeon*. Maybe the tarantula sees God, feels God turning in hungry spirals deep inside it.

I think that would be worse—don't you?

Was I in love with Robin Slattery? I think this narrative doesn't make that absolutely clear—too many second thoughts since—but yes, I was in love with Robin. In love with the way she looked at me (that mix of deference and pity), the way she moved, her strange blend of erudition and ignorance (the only Shakespeare she had read was *The Tempest,* but she had read it five times and attended a performance at Stratford), her skinny legs, her pyrotechnic fashion sense (one day black Goth, next day tartan miniskirt and kneesocks).

I paid her the close attention of a lover, and because I did, I knew by spring (the Eta Aquarids . . . early May) that things had changed.

She spent a night at my place, something she had been doing less often lately. We went into the bedroom with the sound of *soca* tapes pulsing like a heartbeat from the shop downstairs. I had covered one wall with astronomical photographs, stuck to the plaster with pushpins. She looked at the wall and said, "This is why men shouldn't be allowed to live alone—they do things like this."

"Is that a proposition?" I was feeling, I guess, reckless.

"No," she said, looking worried, "I only meant . . ."

"I know."

"I mean, it's not exactly *Good Housekeeping.*"

"Right."

We went to bed troubled. We made love, but tentatively, and

later, when she had turned on her side and her breathing was night-quiet, I left the bed and walked naked to the kitchen.

I didn't need to turn on lights. The moon cast a gray radiance through the rippled glass of the kitchen window. I only wanted to sit awhile in the cool of an empty room.

But I guess Robin hadn't been sleeping after all, because she came to the kitchen wrapped in my bathrobe, standing in the silver light like a quizzical barefoot monk.

"Keeping the night watch," I said.

She leaned against a wall. "It's lonely, isn't it?"

I just looked at her. Wished I could see her eyes.

"Lonely," she said, "out here on the African plains."

I wondered if her intuition was right, if there was a gene, a defective sequence of DNA, that marked me and set me apart from everyone else. The image of the watchman-hominid was a powerful one. I pictured that theoretical ancestor of mine. Our hominid ancestors were small, vulnerable, as much animal as human. The tribe sleeps. The watchman doesn't. I imagine him awake in the long exile of the night, rump against a rock in a sea of wild grasses, shivering when the wind blows, watching the horizon for danger. The horizon and the sky.

What does he see?

The stars in their silent migrations. The annual meteor showers. A comet, perhaps, falling sunward from the far reefs of the solar system.

What does he feel?

Yes: lonely.

And often afraid.

In the morning, Robin said, "As a relationship, I don't think we're working. There's this *distance* . . . I mean, it's lonely for me, too. . . ."

But she didn't really want to talk about it, and I didn't really want to press her. The dynamic was clear enough.

She was kinder than Carolyn had been, and for that I was grateful.

I won't chronicle the history of our breakup. You know how this goes. Phone calls less often, fewer visits; then times when the messages I left on her machine went unreturned, and a penultimate moment of drawing-room comedy when Roger picked up her phone and kindly summoned her from the shower for me. (I pictured her in a towel, hair dripping while she made her vague apologies—and Roger watching.)

No hostility, just drift; and finally silence.

Another spring, another summer—the Eta Aquarids, the Delta

Aquarids, at last the Perseids in the sweltering heat of a humid cicada-buzzing August, two and a half months since the last time we talked.

I was on the back deck of my apartment when the phone rang. It was still too hot to sleep, but *mirabile dictu,* the air was clear, and I kept the night watch in a lawn chair with my binoculars beside me. I heard the ring but ignored it—most of my phone calls lately had been sales pitches or marketing surveys, and the sky, even in the city (if you knew how to look), was alive with meteors, the best display in years. I thought about rock fragments old as the solar system, incinerated in the high atmosphere. The ash, I supposed, must eventually sift down through the air; we must breathe it, in some part; molecules of ancient carbon lodging in the soft tissue of the lung.

Two hours after midnight I went inside, brushed my teeth, thought about bed—then played the message on my answering machine.

It was from Robin.

"Mike? Are you there? If you can hear me, pick up . . . come on, *pick up!* [Pause.] Well, okay. I guess it's not really important. Shit. It's only that . . . there's something I'm not sure about. I just wanted to talk about it with someone. With you. [Pause.] You were always so *solid.* I thought it would be good to hear your voice again. Not tonight, huh? I guess not. Hey, don't worry about me. I'll be okay. But if you—"

The machine cut her off.

I tried calling back, but nobody answered the phone.

I knew her well enough to hear the anxiety in her voice. And she wouldn't have called me unless she was in some kind of trouble.

Robin, I thought, what lens did you look through? And what looked back?

I drove through the empty city to Parkdale, where there was no traffic but cabs and a few bad-tempered hookers; parked and pounded on Robin's door until her downstairs neighbors complained. She wasn't home, she'd gone out earlier, and I should fuck off and die.

I drove to Roger's.

The tall brick house was full of light.

When I knocked, the twins answered. They had shaved their heads since the last time I saw them. The effect was to make them even less distinguishable. Both were naked, their skin glistening with a light sheen of sweat and something else: spatters of green paint. Drops of it hung in their wiry, short pubic hair.

They blinked at me a moment before recognition set in. I couldn't recall their names (I thought of them as Alpha and Beta)—but they remembered mine.

"Michael!"

"Robin's friend!"

"What are *you* doing here?"

I told them I wanted to talk to Robin.

"She's real busy right now—"

"I'd like to come in."

They looked at each other as if in mute consultation. Then (one a fraction of a second after the other) they smiled and nodded.

Every downstairs light had been turned on, but the rooms I could see from the foyer were empty. One of Roger's *icaros* was playing somewhere; the chanting coiled through the air like the winding of a spring. I heard other voices, faintly, elsewhere in the house—upstairs.

Alpha and Beta looked alarmed when I headed for the stairs. "Maybe you shouldn't go up there, Michael."

"You weren't *invited.*"

I ignored them and took the steps two at a time. The twins hurried up behind me.

Roger's gnostic ghost trap was switched on, its video screens flashing faster than the last time I had seen it. No image lingered long enough to resolve, but the flickering light was more than random; I felt presences in it, the kind of motion that alerts the peripheral vision. The *icaro* was louder and more insinuating in this warehouse-like space, a sound that invaded the body through the pores.

But the room was empty.

The twins regarded me, smiling blandly, pupils big as half-dollars. "Of course, all this isn't *necessary*—"

"You don't have to *summon* something that's already *inside you*—"

"But it's *out there,* too—"

"In the images—"

"In the *gnososphere* . . ."

"Everywhere . . ."

The third floor: more stairs at the opposite end of the room. I moved that way with the maddening sensation that time itself had slowed, that I was embedded in some invisible congealed substance that made every footstep a labor. The twins were right behind me, still performing their mad Baedeker.

"The greenhouse!" (Alpha.)

"Yes, you should see it." (Beta.)

The stairs led to a door; the door opened into a jungle humidity lit by ranks of fluorescent bars. Plants were everywhere; I had to blink before I could make sense of it.

"*Psychotria viridis,*" Alpha said.

"And other plants—"

"Common grasses—"

"*Desmanthus illinoensis—*"

"*Phalaris arundinacea—*"

It was as Robin had described it, a greenhouse built over an expansion of the house, concealed from the street by an attic riser. The ceiling and the far walls were of glass, dripping with moisture. The air was thick and hard to breathe.

"Plants that contain DMT." (The twins, still babbling.)

"It's a drug—"

"And a *neurotransmitter.*"

"N,N-dimethyltryptamine . . ."

"It's what dreams are made of, Michael."

"Dreams and imagination."

"Culture."

"Religion!"

"It's the *opening—*"

I said, "Is she drugged? For Christ's sake, where is she?"

But the twins didn't answer.

I saw motion through the glass. The deck extended beyond the greenhouse, but there was no obvious door. I stumbled down a corridor of slim-leaved potted plants and put my hands against the dripping glass.

People out there.

"She's the *Rainha da Floresta—*"

"And Roger is *Santo Daime!*"

"All the archetypes, really . . ."

"Male and female, sun and moon . . ."

I swiped away the condensation with my sleeve. A group of maybe a dozen people had gathered on the wooden decking outside, night wind tugging at their hair. I recognized faces from Robin's parties, dimly illuminated by the emerald glow of the greenhouse. They formed a semicircle with Robin at the center of it—Robin and Roger.

She wore a white T-shirt but was naked below the waist. Roger was entirely naked and covered with glistening green dye. They held each other at arm's length, as if performing some elaborate dance, but they were motionless, eyes fixed on one another.

Sometime earlier the embrace must have been more intimate; his paint was smeared on Robin's shirt and thighs. She was thinner than I remembered, almost anorexic.

Alpha said, "It's sort of a wedding—"

"An *alchemical* wedding."

"And sort of a birth."

There had to be a door. I kicked over a brick and board platform, spilling plants and potting soil as I followed the wall. The door, when I found it, was glass in a metal frame, and there was a padlock across the clasp.

I rattled it, banged my palm against it. Where my hand had been, I could see through the smear of humidity. A few heads turned at the noise—including, I recognized, the science-fiction writer I had talked to long ago. But there was no curiosity in his gaze, only a desultory puzzlement. Roger and Robin remained locked in their peculiar trance, touching but apart, as if making room between them for . . . what?

No, something *had* changed: now their eyes were closed. Robin was breathing in short, stertorous gasps that made me think of a woman in labor. (A *birth,* the twins had said.)

I looked for something to break the glass—a brick, a pot.

Alpha stepped forward, shaking her head. "Too late for that, Michael."

And I knew—with a flood of grief that seemed to well up from some neglected swollen wound—that she was right.

I turned back. To watch.

Past understanding, there is only observation. All I know is what I saw. What I saw, with the glass between myself and Robin. With my cheek against the dripping glass.

Something came out of her.

Something came out of her.

Something came out of her and Roger, like ectoplasm; but especially from their eyes, flowing like hot blue smoke.

I thought their heads were on fire.

Then the smoke condensed between them, took on a solid form, suspended weightless in the space between their tensed bodies.

The shape it took was complex, barbed, hard-edged, luminous, with the infolded symmetries of a star coral and the thousand facets of a geode. Suddenly translucent, it seemed made of frozen light. Strange as it was, it looked almost obscenely organic. I thought of a seed, an achene, the dense nucleus of something potentially enormous: a fetal god.

I don't know how long it hovered between their two tensed bodies. I was distantly aware of my own breathing. Of the hot moisture of my skin against the greenhouse glass. The *icaro* had stopped. I thought the world itself had fallen silent.

Then the thing that had appeared between them, the bright

impossibility they had given birth to, began to rise, at first almost imperceptibly, then accelerating until it was suddenly gone, transiting the sky at, I guessed, the speed of light.

Commerce with the stars.

Then Robin collapsed.

I kicked at the door until, finally, the clasp gave way; then there were hands on me, restraining me, and I closed my eyes and let them carry me away.

She was alive.

I had seen her led down the stairs, groggy and emaciated but moving under her own volition. She needed sleep, the twins said. That was all.

They brought me to a room and left me alone with my friend the science-fiction writer.

He poured a drink.

"Do you know," he asked, "can you even begin to grasp what you saw here tonight?"

I shook my head.

"But you've thought about it," he said. "We talked. You've drawn some conclusions. And, as a matter of fact, in this territory, we're all ignorant. In the gnosphere, Michael, intuition counts for more than knowledge. My intuition is that what you've seen here won't be at all uncommon in the next few years. It may become a daily event—a part, maybe even the central part, of the human experience."

I stared at him.

He said, "Your best move, Michael, and I mean this quite sincerely, would be to just get over it and get on with your life."

"Or else?"

"No 'or else.' No threats. It doesn't matter what you do. One human being . . . we amount to nothing, you know. Maybe we dive into the future, like Roger, or we hang back, dig in our heels, but it doesn't matter. It really doesn't. In the end you'll do what you want."

"I want to leave."

"Then leave. I don't have an explanation to offer. Only a few ideas of my own, if you care to hear them."

I stayed awhile longer.

The Orionids, the Leonids: the stars go on falling with their serene implacability, but I confess, it's hard to look at them now. Bitter and hard.

Consider, he said, living things as large as the galaxy itself. Consider their slow ecology, their evolution across spans of time in which history counts for much less than a heartbeat.

Consider spores that lie dormant, perhaps for millennia, in the planetary clouds of newborn stars. Spores carried by cometary impact into the fresh biosphere (the *domain*) of a life-bearing world.

Consider our own evolution, human evolution, as one stage in a reproductive process in which *human culture itself* is the flower: literally, a flower, gaudy and fertile, from which fresh seed is generated and broadcast.

"Robin is a flower," he said, "but there's nothing special about that. Roger hastened the process with his drugs and paraphernalia and symbolic magic. So he could be among the first. The avant-garde. But the time is coming for all of us, Michael, and soon we won't need props. The thing that's haunted us as a species, the thing we painted on our cave walls and carved into our pillars and cornices and worshiped on our bloody altars and movie screens, it's almost here. We'll all be flowers, I think, before long."

Unless the flower is sterile—set apart, functionally alone, a genetic fluke.

But in another sense the flower is our culture itself, and I can't help wondering what happens to that flower after it broadcasts its seed. Maybe it wilts. Maybe it dies.

Maybe that's already happening. Have you looked at a newspaper lately?

Or maybe, like every other process in the slow ecology of the stars, it'll take a few centuries more.

I cashed in my investments and bought a house in rural British Columbia. Fled the city for reasons I preferred not to consider.

The night sky is dark here, the stars as close as the rooftop and the tall pines—but I seldom look at the sky.

When I do, I focus my telescope on the moon. It seems to me that sparks of light are gathering and moving in the Reiner Gamma area of Oceanus Procellarum. Faintly, almost furtively. Look for yourself. But there's been nothing in the journals about it. So it might be an optical illusion. Or my imagination.

The imagination is also a place where things live.

I'm alone.

It gets cold here in winter.

Robin called once. She said she'd tracked down my new number, that she wanted to talk. She had broken up with Roger. Whatever had happened that night in the city, she said, it was finished now. Life goes on.

Life goes on.

She said she got lonely these days and maybe she understood how it was for me, out there looking at the sky while everyone else sleeps.

(And maybe the watchman sees something coming, Robin, something large and terrible and indistinct in the darkness, but he knows he can't stop it and he can't wake anyone up. . . .)

She said we weren't finished. She said she wanted to see me. She had a little money, she said, and she wanted to fly out. Please, she said. Please, Michael. Please.

God help me, I hung up the phone.

Entropy

The failing sun grows dim as kalpas fly,
and Time grows weary of its endless flight
from nowhere into nothing—while the Night
expunges all the starlight from the sky.
The dust of worlds innebulates the stars,
and domineering Chaos claims its throne.
The last of men seek renascence on Mars,
alone among the zigguratic domes.

Two lovers join together with a lust
grown joyous in defiance of the Night;
they lose themselves on Mars, whose timeless dust
obscures their own, and disappear from sight.
But all the stars are blind; no eyes will see
our joyous end, our tragic destiny.

—KEITH ALLEN DANIELS